Previous volumes in The Essential Hal Clement:

I: *Trio for Slide Rule and Typewriter* - Three novels

Close to Critical
Iceworld
Needle

II: *Music of Many Spheres* -- short fiction

Introduction: Hal Clement *by Ben Bova*
Cold Front
Proof
Raindrop
Longline
Planetfall
Sun Spot
The Mechanic
Attitude
Halo
Impediment
Technical Error
Bulge
Probability Zero: Avenue of Escape
Status Symbol
The Logical Life
Stuck with It
Uncommon Sense

The Essential Hal Clement

Volume 3

Variations on a Theme by Sir Isaac Newton

The Meskin stories

Hal Clement

edited by Mark L. Olson and Anthony R. Lewis

The NESFA Press
Post Office Box 809
Framingham, MA 01701
2000

FIRST EDITION, September 2000
2nd Printing, September 2007

International Standard Book Number:
1-886778-08-6

Acknowledgments

The introduction by David Langford is original to this volume.

Mission of Gravity first published in *Astounding Science Fiction*, April–July 1953

"Lecture Demonstration" first published in *Astounding: John W. Campbell Memorial Anthology* edited by Harry Harrison, Random House, 1973

"Under" was written for this book and has appeared in *Analog*, January 2000

Star Light was first published in *Analog*, June–September 1970. At the author's request, this novel follows the Ballantine paperback text as modified by the author and should be considered the definitive text of this novel.

"Whirligig World" was first published in *Astounding Science Fiction*, June 1953

"I Discover Hal Clement" by Anthony R. Lewis is original to this volume

"The Perfect Hard SF Novel" by Mark L. Olson is original to this volume

All stories appear by permission of the author.

Note: We have been unable to trace the cover artist, Richard McKenna. The cover painting was given by the artist to Hal Clement as a gift in the 1950s. If the artist or the artist's estate contacts NESFA, it will be our pleasure to pay the usual fee for use of existing art.

Contents

The Essential Hal Clement
Volume 3

Variations on a Theme by Sir Isaac Newton

Introduction

by David Langford

There is a particular scene that plays itself out again and again at sf conventions, with all the doom-laden predictability of some Greek tragedy in which vengeful fate rewards hubris with banana skins. The Guest of Honour is waiting to speak. Dew glistens on this awesome being's wreath of laurel, small lightnings play about the majestic brow, and a practised flow of wit and wisdom impends. The audience leans forward in anticipation. First, though, the guest must be introduced by a red-faced, tongue-tied fan, overwhelmed by closeness to the Presence. "And now, er, it's time to welcome" (observers note the outward signs of a mind gone dreadfully blank) "someone who needs no introduction ...author of...of...many fine, er, books..."

More than once I have been that fan, and here I am doing it again while Hal Clement graciously waits in the wings. Certainly it's hard to stand back and say objective, reviewerly things about him, since his first novel *Needle* was very much one of my formative sf experiences. The book didn't make it into British paperback until 1963: when it reached me I was a shade over ten years old, just beginning to devour sf in bulk, and was captivated by this author who so lucidly brought scientific thinking to bear at every point. It wouldn't be wholly unreasonable to claim that Harry Clement Stubbs—Clement's full name, as every true fan knows—was my first really inspirational science teacher.

Later in my schooldays I was lucky enough to be led through physics by a patient and sympathetic teacher whose favourite catch-phrase, applied to a wide variety of phenomena, was: "There's a lot of good physics in that." Which was very true and always reminded me of Hal Clement.

It was Clement's deft dramatization of little and not-so-little aspects of physics that stuck in my memory: the pervading sense that science was an ever-present part of life rather than something that happened only in laboratories where white coats were being worn by the priesthood. One neat but unobtrusively made point in *Needle* was that an alien symbiont's best key to learning English was the exposition of universal principles in its boy host's school physics lessons—anticipating H. Beam Piper's "Omnilingual," with its famous use of the periodic table as a Rosetta Stone, by eight years. Even the dry bones of optics came alive when the location of the focal plane in a beached shark's eye (usefully forward of the retina) became an important practical issue for the alien lurker within.

Moving to the present volume, *Mission of Gravity*—that recognized classic of hard science fiction—made a lasting impression not only by showing that planetary gravity is full of rich possibilities going far beyond that rote-learned "thirty-two feet per second per second," but by presenting a sheaf of consequences in meticulous detail. The world Mesklin is not merely unusually massive and possessed of an unusually rapid spin, as another author might have typed out perfunctorily: its 18-minute day makes all the difference between a pull of 700 gravities at the poles and a barely human-survivable three at the equator. Naturally enough, since in polar gravity objects fall so fast and hard that they seem to teleport catastrophically to the ground, the denizens of Mesklin are terrified both of heights and of being under any structure.

Hal Clement's engaging brand of problem-solving sf assumes that despite all the strangeness the universe can throw at us, it remains in some underlying way reasonable and capable of being understood. As Einstein put it, "God is subtle, but He is not malicious." People, too. Even the bad guys in Clement novels are never quite irrationally evil, and it's one of the incidental charms of the Mesklin books *Mission of Gravity* and *Star Light* that there are literally no bad guys, but merely sensible, likeable people of differing shapes who have, or believe they have, somewhat conflicting goals.

Although Clement has been criticized for depicting aliens whose thought processes seem remarkably human, his certainty that there will be common ground is another facet—and rather an admirable one—of his staunch faith in universal principles and underlying reasonableness. Also, to be critically heretical for a moment, it makes for a more interesting variety of plots than Stanislaw Lem's eternal theme of non-communication: "There are nine-and-sixty ways to interpret Alien Grays / *And every single one of them is wrong!*"

In the Mesklin books, of course, it's the low-slung, centipede-like natives who keep stealing the show. Barlennan, captain of the ship *Bree,* is bright, brave, and experienced in sailing his world's liquid-methane seas. An admirable Competent Man in the Heinlein sense, he is slightly, subtly, almost unconsciously patronized as a "primitive" by the technologically advanced human visitors to Mesklin—who nevertheless need a big favour.

The immense journey to recover an Earth probe stranded in the high-g zone confronts Barlennan and his leggy crew with unexpected but ingeniously logical obstacles and menaces. Constantly in touch with humans by radio link, Barlennan is both grateful for the occasional scientific insights these visitors provide and increasingly suspicious about what—as a mere primitive—he's carefully not being told. As journey's end approaches, Barlennan makes some quiet plans to take matters into his own pincers...and we find ourselves cheering him on.

(Incidentally, I would love to think that Terry Pratchett was glancingly recalling the Mesklinites in his children's sf trilogy—*Truckers, Diggers* and *Wings*—featuring a colony of alien "nomes" stranded on Earth. Though humanoid these likeable beings are very small, surely indicating a high-gravity origin, and are eventually led to safety by a hero called Masklin. This fragment of literary intertextuality, if that's the correct jargon, is probably not worth an entire thesis.)

Star Light is a direct sequel to *Mission of Gravity,* also featuring human characters from Clement's exploration of another problem planet in *Close to Critical.* Incidentally, some of Clement's title puns may pass some readers by, though *Gravity* is obvious enough. *Close to Critical* deals with the planet Tenebra, whose temperature and pressure hover near the critical point for water, leading to bizarre ramifications of not-quite-weather. Complex processes of evaporation and condensation dominate the booby-trapped environment of *Still River.* And, returning to this volume, the massive world Dhrawn which is the setting of *Star Light* may well be a dead and rather lightweight star.

Since Dhrawn's surface gravity is a mere 40g or so, its exploration on behalf of humanity should be a mere romp for Barlennan and his trusty shipmates. The situation is complicated first by the fact that—as gradually emerges—Barlennan has been plotting again, without malice but more ambitiously and deviously than ever. Then, with one Mesklinite expedition ranging very far indeed from base, the unruly weather of Dhrawn begins to play up in unpredictable ways. A two-phase atmosphere combining water and ammonia at a wide variety of temperatures provides a series of unnerving shocks for both the ground crew and the human scientists confined to orbit. "I wish the human crowd had watched this world for a longer time before they sold us on the idea of exploring it for them," one of the centipedoid captains complains early in the narrative, as well he might.

I don't know whether Clement was familiar before 1970 (when *Star Light* was serialized in *Analog*) with Edward Lorenz's work on the deep frustrations of computerized weather prediction, leading to the 1963 paper "Deterministic Nonperiodic Flow"—later to become world-famous, with 100 or more citations a year, when chaos theory took off in the 1980s. *Star Light* captures the feel of atmospheric chaos nicely enough, though:

"Anyone who expects forecasting to be perfected in a couple of years for a world as big as Dhrawn, where we know an area the size of a large backyard and that with two phase-variables and a temperature range from fifty to over a thousand degrees Kelvin, must still believe in magic. He [the human expert Dr. Aucoin] said we were lucky the weather hadn't produced ice fields that turned into swamps when the temperature dropped and rain storms six feet deep with clear air underneath but icing up the cruiser bridges and forty other things his computer keeps coming up with every time he changes another variable."

What the *Encyclopedia of SF* entry on Clement calls "his sense that the Universe is wonderful" is rooted in the kind of insight that led to chaos theory: the full understanding that endlessly intricate wonders and marvels can arise from the interplay of a few simple equations, unremarkable-seeming properties and easily stated laws.

One can imagine Hal Clement's crowded desk as these novels took shape, covered in sheets of paper thick with orbital and gravitational calculations, a well-thumbed copy of the Rubber Bible to hand as the fearless author juggles with triple points or the properties of ammonia/ice eutectics. Younger readers will need to make a further supreme effort of imagination to visualize this scene's lack of any desktop computer. A great deal of old-fashioned skull sweat and slide-rule work went into the stories collected here; the 1953 essay "Whirligig World," long out of print until this omnibus, gives something of a peep behind the scenes.

Yet Clement's fiction is happily uncluttered by evidence of his teeming background calculations. The good old Latin tag *Ars est celare artem* can be translated as, "For God's sake take down all the scaffolding before you let the general public into the building." Our author is always careful to do precisely that. Like a teacher guiding pupils through tangled thickets of detail to some luminous general principle, he courteously works hard to make the path seem easy. And at the same time he tells us a taut, suspenseful story. What sf reader could ask for more?

...Somehow the fan introducer manages to stumble offstage; there are muffled crashes as he falls over unseen obstacles, but nobody is paying attention now. You, the audience, sigh your relief as Hal Clement rises at last to entertain and edify. Here is the man who in 1999 received the long overdue honour of SFWA Grand Master. He will earn your applause.

Mission of Gravity

1: Winter Storm

The wind came across the bay like something living. It tore the surface so thoroughly to shreds that it was hard to tell where liquid ended and atmosphere began; it tried to raise waves that would have swamped the *Bree* like a chip, and blew them into impalpable spray before they had risen a foot.

The spray alone reached Barlennan, crouched high on the *Bree*'s poop raft. His ship had long since been hauled safely ashore. That had been done the moment he had been sure that he would stay here for the winter; but he could not help feeling a little uneasy even so. Those waves were many times as high as any he had faced at sea, and somehow it was not completely reassuring to reflect that the lack of weight which permitted them to rise so high would also prevent their doing real damage if they did roll this far up the beach.

Barlennan was not particularly superstitious, but this close to the Rim of the World there was really no telling what could happen. Even his crew, an unimaginative lot by any reckoning, showed occasional signs of uneasiness. There was bad luck here, they muttered—whatever dwelt beyond the Rim and sent the fearful winter gales blasting thousands of miles into the world might resent being disturbed. At every accident the muttering broke out anew, and accidents were frequent. The fact that anyone is apt to make a misstep when he weighs about two and a quarter pounds instead of the five hundred and fifty or so to which he has been used all his life seemed obvious to the commander; but apparently an education, or at least the habit of logical thought, was needed to appreciate that.

Even Dondragmer, who should have known better... Barlennan's long body tensed and he almost roared an order before he really took in what was going on two rafts away. The mate had picked this moment, apparently, to check the stays of one of the masts, and had taken advantage of near-weightlessness to rear almost his full length upward from the deck. It was still a fantastic sight to see him towering, balanced precariously on his six rear-most legs, though most of the *Bree*'s crew had become fairly used to such tricks; but that was not what impressed Barlennan. At two pounds' weight, one held onto something or else was blown away by the first breeze; and no one could hold onto anything with six walking legs. When that gale struck—but already no order could be heard, even if the commander were to shriek his loudest. He had actually started to creep across the first buffer space separating him from the scene of action when he saw that the mate had fastened a set of lines to his harness and to the deck, and was almost as securely tied down as the mast he was working on.

Barlennan relaxed once more. He knew why Don had done it—it was a simple act of defiance to whatever was driving this particular storm, and he was deliberately impressing his attitude on the crew. Good fellow, thought Barlennan, and turned his attention once more to the bay.

No witness could have told precisely where the shore line now lay. A blinding whirl of white spray and nearly white sand hid everything more than a hundred yards from the *Bree* in every direction; and now even the ship was growing difficult to see as hard-driven droplets of methane struck bulletlike and smeared themselves over his eye shells. At least the deck under his many feet was still rock-steady; light as it now was, the vessel did not seem prepared to blow away. It shouldn't, the commander thought grimly, as he recalled the scores of cables now holding to deep-struck anchors and to the low trees that dotted the beach. It shouldn't—but his would not be the first ship to disappear while venturing this near the Rim. Maybe his crew's suspicion of the Flyer had some justice. After all, that strange being *had* persuaded him to remain for the winter, and had somehow done it without promising any protection to ship or crew. Still, if the Flyer wanted to destroy them, he could certainly do so more easily and certainly than by arguing them into this trick. If that huge structure he rode should get above the *Bree* even here where weight meant so little, there would be no more to be said. Barlennan turned his mind to other matters; he had in full measure the normal Mesklinite horror of letting himself get even temporarily under anything really solid.

The crew had long since taken shelter under the deck flaps—even the mate ceased work as the storm actually struck. They were all present; Barlennan had counted the humps under the protecting fabric while he could still see the whole ship. There were no hunters out, for no sailor had needed the Flyer's warning that a storm was approaching. None of them had been more than five miles from the security of the ship for the last ten days, and five miles was no distance to travel in this weight.

They had plenty of supplies, of course; Barlennan was no fool himself, and did his best to employ none. Still, fresh food was nice. He wondered how long this particular storm would keep them penned in; that was something the signs did not tell, clearly as they heralded the approach of the disturbance. Perhaps the Flyer knew that. In any case, there was nothing further to be done about the ship; he might as well talk to the strange creature. Barlennan still felt a faint thrill of unbelief whenever he looked at the device the Flyer had given him, and never tired of assuring himself once more of its powers.

It lay, under a small shelter flap of its own, on the poop raft beside him. It was an apparently solid block three inches long and about half as high and wide. A transparent spot in the otherwise blank surface of one end looked like an eye, and apparently functioned as one. The only other feature was a small, round hole in one of the long faces. The block was lying with this face upward, and the "eye" end projecting slightly from under the shelter flap. The flap itself opened downwind, of course, so that its fabric was now plastered tightly against the flat upper surface of the machine.

Barlennan worked an arm under the flap, groped around until he found the hole, and inserted his pincer. There was no moving part, such as a switch or button, inside, but that did not bother him—he had never encountered such devices any more than he had met thermal, photonic, or capacity-activated relays. He knew from experience that the fact of putting anything opaque into that hole was somehow made known to the Flyer, and he knew that there was no point whatever in his attempting to figure out how it was done. It would be, he sometimes reflected ruefully, something like teaching navigation to a ten-day-old child. The intelligence might be there—it was comforting to think so, anyway—but some years of background experience were lacking.

"Charles Lackland here." The machine spoke abruptly, cutting the train of thought. "That you, Barl?"

"This is Barlennan, Charles." The commander spoke the Flyer's language, in which he was gradually becoming proficient.

"Good to hear from you. Were we right about this little breeze?"

"It came at the time you predicted. Just a moment—yes, there is snow with it. I had not noticed. I see no dust as yet, however."

"It will come. That volcano must have fed ten cubic miles of it into the air, and it's been spreading for days."

Barlennan made no direct reply to this. The volcano in question was still a point of contention between them, since it was located in a part of Mesklin which, according to Barlennan's geographical background, did not exist.

"What I really wondered about, Charles, was how long this blow was going to last. I understand your people can see it from above, and should know how big it is."

"Are you in trouble already? The winter's just starting—you have thousands of days before you can get out of here."

"I realize that. We have plenty of food, as far as quantity goes. However, we'd like something fresh occasionally, and it would be nice to know in advance when we can send out a hunting party or two."

"I see. I'm afraid it will take some rather careful timing. I was not here last winter, but I understand that during that season the storms in this area are practically continuous. Have you ever been actually to the equator before?"

"To the what?"

"To the—I guess it's what you mean when you talk of the Rim."

"No, I have never been this close, and don't see how anyone could get much closer. It seems to me that if we went much farther out to sea we'd lose every last bit of our weight and go flying off into nowhere."

"If it's any comfort to you, you are wrong. If you kept going, your weight would start up again. You are on the equator right now—the place where weight is least. That is why I am here. I begin to see why you don't want to believe there is land very much farther north. I thought it might be language trouble when we talked of it before. Perhaps you have time enough to describe to me now your ideas concerning the nature of the world? Or perhaps you have maps?"

"We have a Bowl here on the poop raft, of course. I'm afraid you wouldn't be able to see it now, since the sun has just set and Esstes doesn't give light enough to help through these clouds. When the sun rises I'll show it to you. My flat maps wouldn't be much good, since none of them covers enough territory to give a really good picture."

"Good enough. While we're waiting for sunrise could you give me some sort of verbal idea, though?"

"I'm not sure I know your language well enough yet, but I'll try.

"I was taught in school that Mesklin is a big, hollow bowl. The part where most people live is near the bottom, where there is decent weight. The philosophers have an idea that weight is caused by the pull of a big, flat plate that Mesklin is sitting on; the farther out we go toward the Rim, the less we weigh, since we're farther from the plate. What the plate is sitting on no one knows; you hear a lot of queer beliefs on that subject from some of the less civilized races."

"I should think if your philosophers were right you'd be climbing uphill whenever you traveled away from the center, and all the oceans would run to the lowest point," interjected Lackland. "Have you ever asked one of your philosophers that?"

"When I was a youngster I saw a picture of the whole thing. The teacher's diagram showed a lot of lines coming up from the plate and bending in to meet right over the middle of Mesklin. They came through the bowl straight rather than slantwise because of the curve; and the teacher said weight operated along the lines instead of straight down toward the plate," returned the commander. "I didn't understand it fully, but it seemed to work. They said the theory was proved because the surveyed distances on maps agreed with what they ought to be according to the theory. That I *can* understand, and it seems a good point. If the shape weren't what they thought it was, the distances would certainly go haywire before you got very far from your standard point."

"Quite right. I see your philosophers are quite well into geometry. What I don't see is why they haven't realized that there are two shapes that would make the distances come out right. After all, can't you see that the surface of Mesklin curves *downward?* If your theory were true, the horizon would seem to be above you. How about that?"

"Oh, it is. That's why even the most primitive tribes know the world is bowl-shaped. It's just out here near the Rim that it looks different. I expect it's something to do with the light. After all, the sun rises and sets here even in summer, and it wouldn't be surprising if things looked a little queer. Why, it even looks as though the—horizon, you called it?—was closer to north and south than it is east and west. You can see a ship much farther away to the east or west. It's the light."

"Hmm. I find your point a little difficult to answer at the moment." Barlennan was not sufficiently familiar with the Flyer's speech to detect such a thing as a note of amusement in his voice. "I have never been on the surface far from the—er—Rim—and never can be, personally. I didn't realize that things looked as you describe, and I can't see why they should, at the moment. I hope to see it when you take that radio-vision set on our little errand."

"I shall be delighted to hear your explanation of why our philosophers are wrong," Barlennan answered politely. "When you are prepared to give it, of course. In the meantime, I am still somewhat curious as to whether you might be able to tell me when there will be a break in this storm."

"It will take a few minutes to get a report from the station on Toorey. Suppose I call you back about sunrise. I can give you the weather forecast, and there'll be light enough for you to show me your Bowl. All right?"

"That will be excellent. I will wait." Barlennan crouched where he was beside the radio while the storm shrieked on around him. The pellets of methane that splattered against his armored back failed to bother him—they hit a lot harder in the high latitudes. Occasionally he stirred to push away the fine drift of ammonia that kept accumulating on the raft, but even that was only a minor annoyance—at least, so far. Toward midwinter, in five or six thousand days, the stuff would be melting in full sunlight, and rather shortly thereafter would be freezing again. The main idea was to get the liquid away from the vessel or vice versa before the second freeze, or Barlennan's crew would be chipping a couple of hundred rafts clear of the beach. The *Bree* was no river boat, but a full-sized oceangoing ship.

It took the Flyer only the promised few minutes to get the required information, and his voice sounded once more from the tiny speaker as the clouds over the bay lightened with the rising sun.

"I'm afraid I was right, Barl. There is no letup in sight. Practically the whole northern hemisphere—which doesn't mean a thing to you—is boiling off its icecap. I understand the storms in general last all winter. The fact that they come separately in the higher southern latitudes is because they get broken up into very small cells by Coriolis deflection as they get away from the equator."

"By what?"

"By the same force that makes any projectile you throw swerve so noticeably to the left—at least, while I've never seen it under your conditions, it would practically have to on this planet."

"What is 'throw'?"

"My gosh, we haven't used that word, have we? Well, I've seen you jump—no, by gosh, I haven't either!—when you were up visiting at my shelter. Do you remember that word?"

"No."

"Well, 'throw' is when you take some other object—pick it up—and push it hard away from you so that it travels some distance before striking the ground!"

"We don't do that up in reasonable countries. There are lots of things we can do here which are either impossible or very dangerous there. If I were to 'throw' something at home, it might very well land on someone—probably me."

"Come to think of it, that might be bad. Three G's here at the equator is bad enough; you have nearly seven hundred at the poles. Still, if you could find something small enough so that your muscles could throw it, why couldn't you catch it again, or at least resist its impact?"

"I find the situation hard to picture, but I think I know the answer. There isn't time. If something is let go—thrown or not—it hits the ground before anything can be done about it. Picking up and carrying is one thing; crawling is one thing; throwing and—jumping?—are entirely different matters."

"I see—I guess. We sort of took for granted that you'd have a reaction time commensurate with your gravity, but I can see that's just man-centered thinking. I guess I get it."

"What I could understand of your talk sounded reasonable. It is certainly evident that we are different; we will probably never fully realize just how different. At least we are enough alike to talk together—and make what I hope will be a mutually profitable agreement."

"I am sure it will be. Incidentally, in furtherance of it you will have to give me an idea of the places you want to go, and I will have to point out on your maps the place where I want you to go. Could we look at that Bowl of yours now? There is light enough for this vision set."

"Certainly. The Bowl is set in the deck and cannot be moved; I will have to move the machine so that you can see it. Wait a moment."

Barlennan inched across the raft to a spot that was covered by a smaller flap, clinging to deck cleats as he went. He pulled back and stowed the flap, exposing a clear spot on the deck; then he returned, made four lines fast about the radio, secured them to strategically placed cleats, removed the radio's cover, and began to work it across the deck. It weighed more than he did by quite a margin, though its linear dimensions were smaller, but he was taking no chances of having it blown away. The storm had not eased in the least, and the deck itself was quivering occasionally. With the eye end of the set almost to the Bowl, he propped the other end up with spars so that the Flyer could look downward. Then he himself moved to the other side of the Bowl and began his exposition.

Lackland had to admit that the map which the Bowl contained was logically constructed and, as far as it went, accurate. Its curvature matched that of the planet quite closely, as he had expected—the major error being that it was concave, in conformity with the natives' ideas about the shape of their world. It was about six inches across and roughly one and a quarter deep at the center. The whole map was protected by a transparent cover—probably of ice, Lackland guessed—set flush with the deck. This interfered somewhat with Barlennan's attempts to point out details, but could not have been removed without letting the Bowl fill with ammonia snow in moments. The stuff was piling up wherever it found shelter from the wind. The beach was staying relatively clear, but both Lackland and Barlennan could imagine what was happening on the other side of the hills that paralleled it on the south. The latter was secretly glad he was a sailor. Land travel in this region would not be fun for some thousands of days.

"I have tried to keep my charts up to date," he said as he settled down opposite the Flyer's proxy. "I haven't attempted to make any changes in the Bowl, though, because the new regions we mapped on the way up were not extensive enough to show. There is actually little I can show you in detail, but you wanted a general idea of where I planned to go when we could get out of here.

"Well, actually I don't care greatly. I can buy and sell anywhere, and at the moment I have little aboard but food. I won't have much of that by the time winter is over, either; so I had planned, since our talk, to cruise for a time around the low-weight areas and pick up plant products which can be obtained here—materials that are valued by the people farther south because of their effect on the taste of food."

"Spices?"

"If that is the word for such products, yes. I have carried them before, and rather like them—you can get good profit from a single shipload, as with most commodities whose value depends less on their actual usefulness than on their rarity."

"I take it, then, that once you have loaded here you don't particularly care where you go?"

"That is right. I understand that your errand will carry us close to the Center, which is fine—the farther south we go, the higher the prices I can get; and the extra length of the journey should not be much more dangerous, since you will be helping us as you agreed."

"Right. That is excellent—though I wish we had been able to find something we could give you in actual payment, so that you would not feel the need to take time in spice-gathering."

"Well, we have to eat. You say your bodies, and hence your foods, are made of very different substances from ours, so we can't use your foodstuffs. Frankly, I can't think of any desirable raw metal or similar material that I couldn't get far more easily in any quantity I wanted. My favorite idea is still that we get some of your machines, but you say that they would have to be built anew to function under our conditions. It seems that the agreement we reached is the best that is possible, under those circumstances."

"True enough. Even this radio was built specifically for this job, and you could not repair it—your people, unless I am greatly mistaken, don't have the tools. However, during the journey we can talk of this again; perhaps the things we learn of each other will open up other and better possibilities."

"I am sure they will," Barlennan answered politely.

He did not, of course, mention the possibility that his own plans might succeed. The Flyer would hardly have approved.

2: The Flyer

The Flyer's forecast was sound; some four hundred days passed before the storm let up noticeably. Five times during that period the Flyer spoke to Barlennan on the radio, always opening with a brief weather forecast and continuing a more general conversation for a day or two each time. Barlennan had noticed earlier, when he had been learning the strange creature's language and paying personal visits to its outpost in the "Hill" near the bay, that it seemed to have a strangely regular life cycle; he found he could count on finding the Flyer sleeping or eating at quite predictable times, which seemed to have a cycle of about eighty days. Barlennan was no philosopher—he had at least his share of the common tendency to regard them as impractical dreamers—and he simply shrugged this fact off as something pertaining to a weird but admittedly interesting creature. There was nothing in the Mesklinite background that would enable him to deduce the existence of a world that took some eighty times as long as his own to rotate on its axis.

Lackland's fifth call was different from the others, and more welcome for several reasons. The difference was due partly to the fact that it was off schedule; its pleasant nature to the fact that at last there was a favorable weather forecast.

"Barl!" The Flyer did not bother with preliminaries—he knew that the Mesklinite was always within sound of the radio. "The station on Toorey called a few minutes ago. There is a relatively clear area moving toward us. He was not sure just what the winds would be, but he can see the ground through it, so visibility ought to be fair. If your hunters want to go out I should say that they wouldn't be blown away, provided they wait until the clouds have been gone for twenty or thirty days. For a hundred days or so after that we should have very good weather indeed. They'll tell me in plenty of time to get your people back to the ship."

"But how will they get your warning? If I send this radio with them I won't be able to talk to you about our regular business, and if I don't, I don't see—"

"I've been thinking of that," interrupted Lackland. "I think you'd better come up here as soon as the wind drops sufficiently. I can give you another set—perhaps it would be better if you had several. I gather that the journey you will be taking for us will be dangerous, and I know for myself it will be long enough. Thirty-odd thousand miles as the crow flies, and I can't yet guess how far by ship and overland."

Lackland's simile occasioned a delay; Barlennan wanted to know what a crow was, and also flying. The first was the easier to get across. Flying for a living creature, under its own power, was harder for him to imagine than throwing—and the thought was more terrifying. He had regarded Lackland's proven ability to travel through the air as something so alien that it did not really strike home to *him.* Lackland saw this, partly.

"There's another point I want to take up with you," he said. "As soon as it's clear enough to land safely, they're bringing down a crawler. Maybe watching the rocket land will get you a little more used to the whole flying idea."

"Perhaps," Barlennan answered hesitantly. "I'm not sure I want to see your rocket land. I did once before, you know, and—well, I'd not want one of the crew to be there at the time."

"Why not? Do you think they'd be scared too much to be useful?"

"No." The Mesklinite answered quite frankly. "I don't want one of them to see me as scared as I'm likely to be."

"You surprise me, Commander." Lackland tried to give his words in a jocular tone. "However, I understand your feelings, and I assure you that the rocket will not pass above you. If you will wait right next to the wall of my dome I will direct its pilot by radio to make sure of that."

"But how close to overhead will it come?"

"A good distance sideways, I promise. That's for my own safety as well as your comfort. To land on this world, even here at the equator, it will be necessary for him to be using a pretty potent blast. I don't want it hitting my dome, I can assure you."

"All right. I will come. As you say, it would be nice to have more radios. What is this 'crawler' of which you speak?"

"It is a machine which will carry me about on land as your ship does at sea. You will see in a few days, or in a few hours at most."

Barlennan let the new word pass without question, since the remark was clear enough anyway. "I will come, and will see," he agreed.

The Flyer's friends on Mesklin's inner moon had prophesied correctly. The commander, crouched on his poop, counted only ten sunrises before a lightening of the murk and lessening of the wind gave their usual warning of the approaching eye of the storm. From his own experience he was willing to believe, as the Flyer had said, that the calm period would last one or two hundred days.

With a whistle that would have torn Lackland's eardrums had he been able to hear such a high frequency the commander summoned the attention of his crew and began to issue orders.

"There will be two hunting parties made up at once. Dondragmer will head one, Merkoos the other; each will take nine men of his own choosing. I will remain on the ship to co-ordinate, for the Flyer is going to give us more of his talking machines. I will go to the Flyer's Hill as soon as the sky is clear to get them; they, as well as other things he wants, are being brought down from Above by his friends, therefore all crew members will remain near the ship until I return. Plan for departure thirty days after I leave."

"Sir, is it wise for you to leave the ship so early? The wind will still be high." The mate was too good a friend for the question to be impertinent, though some commanders would have resented any such reflection on their judgment. Barlennan waved his pincers in a manner denoting a smile.

"You are quite right. However, I want to save the time, and the Flyer's Hill is only a mile away."

"But—"

"Furthermore it is downwind. We have many miles of line in the lockers; I will have two bent to my harness, and two of the men—Terblannen and Hars, I think, under your supervision, Don—will pay those lines out through the bitts as I go. I may—probably will—lose my footing, but if the wind were able to get such a grip on me as to break good sea cord, the *Bree* would be miles inland by now."

"But even losing your footing—suppose you were to be lifted into the air—" Dondragmer was still deeply troubled, and the thought he had uttered gave even his commander pause for an instant.

"Falling—yes—but remember that we are near the Edge—at it, the Flyer says, and I can believe him when I look north from the top of his Hill. As some of you have found, a fall means nothing here."

"But you ordered that we should act as though we had normal weight, so that no habits might be formed that would be dangerous when we returned to a livable land."

"Quite true. This will be no habit, since in any reasonable place no wind could pick me up. Anyway, that is what we do. Let Terblannen and Hars check the lines—no, check them yourself. It will take long enough.

"That is all for the present. The watch under shelter may rest. The watch on deck will check anchors and lashings." Dondragmer, who had the latter watch, took the order as a dismissal and proceeded to carry it out in his usual efficient manner. He also set men to work cleaning snow from the spaces between rafts, having seen as clearly as his captain the possible consequences of a thaw followed by a freeze. Barlennan himself relaxed, wondering sadly just which ancestor was responsible for his habit of talking himself into situations that were both unpleasant to face and impossible to back out of gracefully.

For the rope idea was strictly spur-of-the-moment, and it took most of the several days before the clouds vanished for the arguments he had used on his mate to appeal to their inventor. He was not really happy even when he lowered himself onto the snow that had drifted against the lee rafts, cast a last look backward at his two most powerful crew members and the lines they were managing, and set off across the wind-swept beach.

Actually, it was not too bad. There was a slight upward force from the ropes, since the deck was several inches above ground level when he started; but the slope of the beach quickly remedied that. Also, the trees which were serving so nobly as mooring points for the *Bree* grew more and more thickly as he went inland. They were low, flat growths with wide-spreading tentacular limbs and very short, thick trunks, generally similar to those of the lands he knew deep in the southern hemisphere of Mesklin. Here, however, their branches arched sometimes entirely clear of the ground, left relatively free by an effective gravity less than one two-hundredth that of the polar regions. Eventually they grew close enough together to permit the branches to intertwine, a tangle of brown and black cables which furnished excellent hold. Barlennan found it possible, after a time, practically to climb toward the Hill, getting a grip with his front pincers, releasing the hold of his rear ones, and twisting his caterpillar-like body forward so that he progressed almost in inchworm fashion. The cables gave him some trouble, but since both they and the tree limbs were relatively smooth no serious fouling occurred.

The beach was fairly steep after the first two hundred yards; and at half the distance he expected to go, Barlennan was some six feet above the *Bree*'s deck level. From this point the Flyer's Hill could be seen, even by an individual whose eyes were as close to the ground as those of a Mesklinite; and the commander paused to take in the scene as he had many times before

The remaining half mile was a white, brown, and black tangle, much like that he had just traversed. The vegetation was even denser, and had trapped a good deal more snow, so that there was little or no bare ground visible.

Looming above the tangled plain was the Flyer's Hill. The Mesklinite found it almost impossible to think of it as an artificial structure, partly because of its monstrous size and partly because a roof of any description other than a flap of fabric was completely foreign to his ideas of architecture. It was a glittering metal dome some twenty feet in height and forty in diameter, nearly a perfect hemisphere. It was dotted with large, transparent areas and had two cylindrical extensions containing doors. The Flyer had said that these doors were so constructed that one could pass through them without letting air get from one side to the other. The portals were certainly big enough for the strange creature, gigantic as he was. One of the lower windows had an improvised ramp leading up to it which would permit a creature of Barlennan's size and build to crawl up to the pane and see inside. The commander had spent much time on that ramp while he was first learning to speak and understand the Flyer's language; he had seen much of the strange apparatus and furniture which filled the structure, though he had no idea of the use to which most of it was put. The Flyer himself appeared to be an amphibious creature—at least, he spent much of the time floating in a tank of liquid. This was reasonable enough, considering his size. Barlennan himself knew of no creature native to Mesklin larger than his own race which was not strictly an ocean or lake dweller—though he realized that, as far as weight alone was considered, such things might exist in these vast, nearly unexplored regions near the Rim. He trusted that he would meet none, at least while he himself was ashore. Size meant weight, and a lifetime of conditioning prevented his completely ignoring weight as a menace.

There was nothing near the dome except the ever present vegetation. Evidently the rocket had not yet arrived, and for a moment Barlennan toyed with the idea of waiting where he was until it did. Surely when it came it would descend on the farther side of the Hill—the Flyer would see to that, if Barlennan himself had not arrived. Still, there was nothing to prevent the descending vessel from passing *over* his present position; Lackland could do nothing about that, since he would not know exactly where the Mesklinite was. Few Earthmen can locate a body fifteen inches long and two in diameter crawling horizontally through tangled vegetation at a distance of half a mile. No, he had better go right up to the dome, as the Flyer had advised. The commander resumed his progress, still dragging the ropes behind him.

He made it in good time, though delayed slightly by occasional periods of darkness. As a matter of fact it was night when he reached his goal, though the last part of his journey had been adequately illuminated by light from the windows ahead of him. However, by the time he had made his ropes fast and crawled up to a comfortable station outside the window the sun had lifted above the horizon on his left. The clouds were almost completely gone now, though the wind was still strong, and he could have seen in through the window even had the inside lights been turned out.

Lackland was not in the room from which this window looked, and the Mesklinite pressed the tiny call button which had been mounted on the ramp. Immediately the Flyer's voice sounded from a speaker beside the button.

"Glad you're here, Barl. I've been having Mack hold up until you came. I'll start him down right away, and he should be here by next sunrise."

"Where is he now? On Toorey?"

"No; he's drifting at the inner edge of the ring, only six hundred miles up. He's been there since well before the storm ended, so don't worry about having kept him waiting yourself. While we're waiting for him, I'll bring out the other radios I promised."

"Since I am alone, it might be well to bring only one radio this time. They are rather awkward things to carry, though light enough, of course."

"Maybe we should wait for the crawler before I bring them out at all. Then I can ride you back to your ship—the crawler is well enough insulated so that riding outside it wouldn't hurt you, I'm sure. How would that be?"

"It sounds excellent. Shall we have more language while we wait, or can you show me more pictures of the place you come from?"

"I have some pictures. It will take a few minutes to load the projector, so it should be dark enough when we're ready. Just a moment—I'll come to the lounge."

The speaker fell silent, and Barlennan kept his eyes on the door which he could see at one side of the room. In a few moments the Flyer appeared, walking upright as usual with the aid of the artificial limbs he called crutches. He approached the window, nodded his massive head at the tiny watcher, and turned to the movie projector. The screen at which the machine was pointed was on the wall directly facing the window; and Barlennan, keeping a couple of eyes on the human being's actions, squatted down more comfortably in a position from which he could watch it in comfort. He waited silently while the sun arched lazily overhead. It was warm in the full sunlight, pleasantly so, though not warm enough to start a thaw; the perpetual wind from the northern icecap prevented that. He was half dozing while Lackland finished threading the machine, stumped over to his relaxation tank, and lowered himself into it. Barlennan had never noticed the elastic membrane over the surface of the liquid which kept the man's clothes dry; if he had, it might have modified his ideas about the amphibious nature of human beings. From his floating position Lackland reached up to a small panel and snapped two switches.

The room lights went out and the projector started to operate. It was a fifteen-minute reel, and had not quite finished when Lackland had to haul himself once more to his feet and crutches with the information that the rocket was landing.

"Do you want to watch Mack, or would you rather see the end of the reel?" he asked. "He'll probably be on the ground by the time it's done."

Barlennan tore his attention from the screen with some reluctance. "I'd rather watch the picture, but it would probably be better for me to get used to the sight of flying things," he said. "From which side will it come?"

"The east, I should expect. I have given Mack a careful description of the layout here, and he already had photographs; and I know an approach from that direction will be somewhat easier, as he is now set. I'm afraid the sun is interfering at the moment with your line of vision, but he's still about forty miles up—look well above the sun."

Barlennan followed these instructions and waited. For perhaps a minute he saw nothing; then his eye was caught by a glint of metal some twenty degrees above the rising sun.

"Altitude ten—horizontal distance about the same," Lackland reported at the same moment. "I have him on the scope here."

The glint grew brighter, holding its direction almost perfectly—the rocket was on a nearly exact course toward the dome. In another minute it was close enough for details to be visible—or would have been, except that everything was now hidden in the glare of the rising sun. Mack hung poised for a moment a mile above the station and as far to the east; and as Belne moved out of line Barlennan could see the windows and exhaust ports in the cylindrical hull. The storm wind had dropped almost completely, but now a warm breeze laden with a taint of melting ammonia began to blow from the point where the exhaust struck the ground. The drops of semiliquid spattered on Barlennan's eye shells, but he continued to stare at the slowly settling mass of metal. Every muscle in his long body was at maximum tension, his arms held close to his sides, pincers clamped tightly enough to have shorn through steel wire, the hearts in each of his body segments pumping furiously. He would have been holding his breath had he possessed breathing apparatus at all similar to that of a human being. Intellectually he knew that the thing would not fall—he kept telling himself that it could not; but having grown to maturity in an environment where a fall of six inches was usually fatally destructive even to the incredibly tough Mesklinite organism, his emotions were not easy to control. Subconsciously he kept expecting the metal shell to vanish from sight, to reappear on the ground below flattened out of recognizable shape. After all, it was still *hundreds of feet* up...

On the ground below the rocket, now swept clear of snow, the black vegetation abruptly burst into flame. Black ash blew from the landing point, and the ground itself glowed briefly. For just an instant this lasted before the glittering cylinder settled lightly into the center of the bare patch. Seconds later the thunder which had mounted to a roar louder than Mesklin's hurricanes died abruptly. Almost painfully, Barlennan relaxed, opening and shutting his pincers to relieve the cramps.

"If you'll stand by a moment, I'll be out with the radios," Lackland said. The commander had not noticed his departure, but the Flyer was no longer in the room. "Mack will drive the crawler over here—you can watch it come while I'm getting into armor."

Actually Barlennan was able to watch only a portion of the drive. He saw the rocket's cargo lock swing open and the vehicle emerge; he got a sufficiently good look at the crawler to understand everything about it—he thought—except what made its caterpillar treads move. It was big, easily big enough to hold several of the Flyer's race unless too much of its interior was full of machinery. Like the dome, it had numerous and large windows; through one of these in the front the commander could see the armored figure of another Flyer, who was apparently controlling it. Whatever drove the machine did not make enough noise to be audible across the mile of space that still separated it from the dome.

It covered very little of that distance before the sun set, and details ceased to be visible. Esstes, the smaller sun, was still in the sky and brighter than the full moon of Earth, but Barlennan's eyes had their limitations. An intense beam of light projected from the crawler itself along its path, and consequently straight toward the dome, did not help either. Barlennan simply waited. After all, it was still too far for really good examination even by daylight, and would undoubtedly be at the Hill by sunrise.

Even then he might have to wait, of course; the Flyers might object to the sort of examination he really wanted to give their machinery.

3: Off the Ground

The tank's arrival, Lackland's emergence from the dome's main air lock, and the rising of Belne all took place at substantially the same moment. The vehicle stopped only a couple of yards from the platform on which Barlennan was crouched. Its driver also emerged; and the two men stood and talked briefly beside the Mesklinite. The latter rather wondered that they did not return to the inside of the dome to lie down, since both were rather obviously laboring under Mesklin's gravity; but the newcomer refused Lackland's invitation.

"I'd like to be sociable," he said in answer to it, "but honestly, Charlie, would you stay on this ghastly mudball a moment longer than you had to?"

"Well, I could do pretty much the same work from Toorey, or from a ship in a free orbit for that matter," retorted Lackland. "I think personal contact means a good deal. I still want to find out more about Barlennan's people—it seems to me that we're hardly giving him as much as we expect to get, and it would be nice to find out if there were anything more we could do. Furthermore, he's in a rather dangerous situation himself, and having one of us here might make quite a difference—to both of us."

"I don't follow you."

"Barlennan is a tramp captain—a sort of free-lance explorer-trader. He's completely out of the normal areas inhabited and traveled through by his people. He is remaining here during the southern winter, when the evaporating north polar cap makes storms which have to be seen to be believed here in the equatorial regions—storms which are almost as much out of his experience as ours. If anything happens to him, stop and think of our chances of meeting another contact!

"Remember, he normally lives in a gravity field from two hundred to nearly seven hundred times as strong as Earth's. We certainly won't follow him home to meet his relatives! Furthermore, there probably aren't a hundred of his race who are not only in the same business but courageous enough to go so far from their natural homes. Of those hundred, what are our chances of meeting another? Granting that this ocean is the one they frequent most, this little arm of it, from which this bay is an offshoot, is six thousand miles long and a third as wide—with a very crooked shore line. As for spotting one, at sea or ashore, from above—well, Barlennan's *Bree* is about forty feet long and a third as wide, and is one of their biggest oceangoing ships. Scarcely any of it is more than three inches above the water, besides.

"No, Mack, our meeting Barlennan was the wildest of coincidences; and I'm not counting on another. Staying under three gravities for five months or so, until the southern spring, will certainly be worth it. Of course, if you want to gamble our chances of recovering nearly two billion dollars' worth of apparatus on the results of a search over a strip of planet a thousand miles wide and something over a hundred and fifty thousand long—"

"You've made your point," the other human being admitted, "but I'm still glad it's you and not me. Of course, maybe if I knew Barlennan better—" Both men turned to the tiny, caterpillarlike form crouched on the waist-high platform.

"Barl, I trust you will forgive my rudeness in not introducing Wade McLellan," Lackland said. "Wade, this is Barlennan, captain of the *Bree,* and a master shipman of his world—he has not told me that, but the fact that he is here is sufficient evidence."

"I am glad to meet you, Flyer McLellan," the Mesklinite responded. "No apology is necessary, and I assumed that your conversation was meant for my ears as well." He performed the standard pincer-opening gesture of greeting. "I had already appreciated the good fortune for both of us which our meeting represents, and only hope that I can fulfill my part of the bargain as well as I am sure you will yours."

"You speak English remarkably well," commented McLellan. "Have you really been learning it for less than six weeks?"

"I am not sure how long your 'week' is, but it is less than thirty-five hundred days since I met your friend," returned the commander. "I am a good linguist, of course—it is necessary in my business; and the films that Charles showed helped very much."

"It is rather lucky that your voice could make all the sounds of our language. We sometimes have trouble that way."

"That, or something like it, is why I learned your English rather than the other way around. Many of the sounds we use are much too shrill for your vocal cords, I understand." Barlennan carefully refrained from mentioning that much of his normal conversation was also too high-pitched for human ears. After all, Lackland might not have noticed it yet, and the most honest of traders thinks at least twice before revealing all his advantages. "I imagine that Charles has learned some of our language, nevertheless, by watching and listening to us through the radio now on the *Bree.*"

"Very little," confessed Lackland. "You seem, from what little I have seen, to have an extremely well-trained crew. A great deal of your regular activity is done without orders, and I can make nothing of the conversations you sometimes have with some of your men, which are not accompanied by any action."

"You mean when I am talking to Dondragmer or Merkoos? They are my first and second officers, and the ones I talk to most."

"I hope you will not feel insulted at this, but I am quite unable to tell one of your people from another. I simply am not familiar enough with your distinguishing characteristics."

Barlennan almost laughed.

"In my case, it is even worse. I am not entirely sure whether I have seen you without artificial covering or not."

"Well, that is carrying us a long way from business—we've used up a lot of daylight as it is. Mack, I assume you want to get back to the rocket and out where weight means nothing and men are balloons. When you get there, be sure that the receiver-transmitters for each of these four sets are placed close enough together so that one will register on another. I don't suppose it's worth the trouble of tying them in electrically, but these folks are going to use them for a while as contact between separate parties, and the sets are on different frequencies. Barl, I've left the radios by the air lock. Apparently the sensible program would be for me to put you and the radios on top of the crawler, take Mack over to the rocket, and then drive you and the apparatus over to the *Bree.*"

Lackland acted on this suggestion, so obviously the right course, before anyone could answer; and Barlennan almost went mad as a result.

The man's armored hand swept out and *picked up* the tiny body of the Mesklinite. For one soul-shaking instant Barlennan felt and saw himself suspended long feet away from the ground; then he was deposited on the flat top of the tank. His pincers scraped desperately and vainly at the smooth metal to supplement the instinctive grips which his dozens of suckerlike feet had taken on the plates; his eyes glared in undiluted horror at the emptiness around the edge of the roof, only a few body lengths away in every direction. For long seconds—perhaps a full minute—he could not find his voice; and when he did speak, he could no longer be heard. He was too far away from the pickup on the platform for intelligible words to carry—he knew that from earlier experience; and even at this extremity of terror he remembered that the sirenlike howl of agonized fear that he wanted to emit would have been heard with equal clarity by everyone on the *Bree,* since there was another radio there.

And the *Bree* would have had a new captain. Respect for his courage was the only thing that had driven that crew into the storm-breeding regions of the Rim. If that went, he would have no crew and no ship—and, for all practical purpose, no life. A coward was not tolerated on any ocean-going ship in any capacity; and while his homeland was on this same continental mass, the idea of traversing forty thousand miles of coast line on foot was not to be considered.

These thoughts did not cross his conscious mind in detail, but his instinctive knowledge of the facts effectually silenced him while Lackland picked up the radios and, with McLellan, entered the tank below the Mesklinite. The metal under him quivered slightly as the door was closed, and an instant later the vehicle started to move. As it did so, a peculiar thing happened to its non-human passenger.

The fear might have—perhaps should have—driven him mad. His situation can only be dimly approximated by comparing it with that of a human being hanging by one hand from a window ledge forty stories above a paved street.

And yet he did not go mad. At least, he did not go mad in the accepted sense; he continued to reason as well as ever, and none of his friends could have detected a change in his personality. For just a little while, perhaps, an Earthman more familiar with Mesklinites than Lackland had yet become might have suspected that the commander was a little drunk; but even that passed.

And the fear passed with it. Nearly six body lengths above the ground, he found himself crouched almost calmly. He was holding tightly, of course; he even remembered, later, reflecting how lucky it was that the wind had continued to drop, even though the smooth metal offered an unusually good grip for his sucker-feet. It was amazing, the viewpoint that could be enjoyed—yes, he enjoyed it—from such a position. Looking down on things really helped; you could get a remarkably complete picture of so much ground at once. It was like a map; and Barlennan had never before regarded a map as a picture of country seen from above.

An almost intoxicating sense of triumph filled him as the crawler approached the rocket and stopped. The Mesklinite waved his pincers almost gaily at the emerging McLellan visible in the reflected glare of the tank's lights, and was disproportionately pleased when the man waved back. The tank immediately turned to the left and headed for the beach where the *Bree* lay; Mack, remembering that Barlennan was unprotected, thoughtfully waited until it was nearly a mile away before lifting his own machine into the air. The sight of it, drifting slowly upward apparently without support, threatened for just an instant to revive the old fear; but Barlennan fought the sensation grimly down and deliberately watched the rocket until it faded from view in the light of the lowering sun.

Lackland had been watching too; but when the last glint of metal had disappeared, he lost no further time in driving the tank the short remaining distance to where the *Bree* lay. He stopped a hundred yards from the vessel, but he was quite close enough for the shocked creatures on the decks to see their commander perched on the vehicle's roof. It would have been less disconcerting had Lackland approached bearing Barlennan's head on a pole.

Even Dondragmer, the most intelligent and levelheaded of the *Bree*'s complement—not excepting his captain—was paralyzed for long moments; and his first motion was with eyes only, taking the form of a wistful glance toward the flame-dust tanks and "shakers" on the outer rafts. Fortunately for Barlennan, the crawler was not downwind; for the temperature was, as usual, below the melting point of the chlorine in the tanks. Had the wind permitted, the mate would have sent a cloud of fire about the vehicle without ever thinking that his captain might be alive.

A faint rumble of anger began to arise from the assembled crew as the door of the crawler opened and Lackland's armored figure emerged. Their half-trading, half-piratical way of life had left among them only those most willing to fight without hesitation at the slightest hint of menace to one of their number; the cowards had dropped away long since, and the individualists had died. The only thing that saved Lackland's life as he emerged into their view was habit—the conditioning that prevented their making the hundred-yard leap that would have cost the weakest of them the barest flick of his body muscles. Crawling as they had done all their lives, they flowed from the rafts like a red and black waterfall and spread over the beach toward the alien machine. Lackland saw them coming, of course, but so completely misunderstood their motivation that he did not even hurry as he reached up to the crawler's roof, picked up Bar-lennan, and set him on the ground. Then he reached back into the vehicle and brought out the radios he had promised, setting them on the sand beside the commander; and by then it had dawned on the crew that their captain was alive and apparently unharmed. The avalanche stopped in confusion, milling in undecided fashion midway between ship and tank; and a cacophony of voices ranging from deep bass to the highest notes the radio speaker could reproduce gabbled in Lackland's suit phones. Though he had, as Barlennan had intimated, done his best to attach meaning to some of the native conversation he had previously heard, the man understood not a single word from the crew. It was just as well for his peace of mind; he had long been aware that even armor able to withstand Mesklin's eight-atmosphere surface pressure would mean little or nothing to Mesklinite pincers.

Barlennan stopped the babble with a hoot that Lackland could probably have heard directly through the armor, if its reproduction by the radio had not partially deafened him first. The commander knew perfectly well what was going on in the minds of his men, and had no desire to see frozen shreds of Lackland scattered over the beach.

"Calm down!" Actually Barlennan felt a very human warmth at his crew's reaction to his apparent danger, but this was no time to encourage them. "Enough of you have played the fool here at no-weight so that you all should know I was in no danger!"

"But you forbade—"

"We thought—"

"You were *high*—" A chorus of objections answered the captain, who cut them short.

"I know I forbade such actions, and I told you why. When we return to high-weight and decent living we must have no habits that might result in our thoughtlessly doing dangerous things like that—" He waved a pincer-tipped arm upward toward the tank's roof. "You all know what proper weight can do; the Flyer doesn't. He put me up there, as you saw him take me down, without even thinking about it. He comes from a place where there is practically no weight at all; where, I believe, he could fall many times *his* body length without being hurt. You can see that for yourselves: if he felt properly about high places, how could he *fly?*"

Most of Barlennan's listeners had dug their stumpy feet into the sand as though trying to get a better grip on it during this speech. Whether they fully digested, or even fully believed, their commander's words may be doubted; but at least their minds were distracted from the action they had intended toward Lackland. A faint buzz of conversation arose once more among them, but its chief overtones seemed to be of amazement rather than anger. Dondragmer alone, a little apart from the others, was silent; and the captain realized that his mate would have to be given a much more careful and complete story of what had happened. Dondragmer's imagination was heavily backed by intelligence, and he must already be wondering about the effect on Barlennan's nerves of his recent experience. Well, that could be handled in good time; the crew presented a more immediate problem.

"Are the hunting parties ready?" Barlennan's question silenced the babble once more.

"We have not yet eaten," Merkoos replied a little uneasily, "but everything else—nets and weapons—is in readiness."

"Is the food ready?"

"Within a day, sir." Karondrasee, the cook, turned back toward the ship without further orders.

"Don, Merkoos. You will each take one of these *radios.* You have seen me use the one on the ship—all you have to do is talk anywhere near it. You can run a really efficient pincer movement with these, since you won't have to keep it small enough for both leaders to see each other.

"Don, I am not certain that I will direct from the ship, as I originally planned. I have discovered that one can see over remarkable distances from the top of the flyer's traveling machine; and if he agrees I shall ride with him in the vicinity of your operations."

"But, sir!" Dondragmer was aghast. "Won't—won't that thing scare all the game within sight? You can hear it coming a hundred yards away, and see it for I don't know how far in the open. And besides—" He broke off, not quite sure how to state his main objection. Barlennan did it for him.

"Besides, no one could concentrate on hunting with me in sight so far off the ground—is that it?" The mate's pincers silently gestured agreement, and the movement was emulated by most of the waiting crew.

For a moment the commander was tempted to reason with them, but he realized in time the futility of such an attempt. He could not actually recapture the viewpoint he had shared with them until so recently, but he did realize that before that time he would not have listened to what he now considered "reason" either.

"All right, Don. I'll drop that idea—you're probably right. I'll be in radio touch with you, but will stay out of sight."

"But you'll be riding on that thing? Sir, what has happened to you? I know I can *tell* myself that a fall of a few feet really means little here at the Rim, but I could never bring myself to invite such a fall deliberately; and I don't see how anyone else could. I couldn't even picture myself up on top of that thing."

"You were most of a body length up a mast not too long ago, if I remember aright," returned Barlennan dryly, "or was it someone else I saw checking upper lashings without unshipping the stick?"

"That was different—I had one end on the deck," Dondragmer replied a trifle uncomfortably.

"Your head still had a long way to fall. I've seen others of you doing that sort of thing too. If you remember, I had something to say about it when we first sailed into this region."

"Yes, sir, you did. Are those orders still in force, considering—" The mate paused again, but what he wanted to say was even plainer than before. Barlennan thought quickly and hard.

"We'll forget the order," he said slowly. "The reasons I gave for such things being dangerous are sound enough, but if any of you get in trouble for forgetting when we're back in high-weight it's your own fault. Use your own judgment on such matters from now on. Does anyone want to come with me now?"

Words and gestures combined in a chorus of emphatic negatives, with Dondragmer just a shade slower than the rest. Barlennan would have grinned had he possessed the physical equipment.

"Get ready for that hunt—I'll be listening to you," he dismissed his audience. They streamed obediently back toward the *Bree,* and their captain turned to give a suitably censored account of the conversation to Lackland. He was a little preoccupied, for the conversation just completed had given rise to several brand-new ideas in his mind; but they could be worked out when he had more leisure. Just now he wanted another ride on the tank roof.

4: Breakdown

The bay on the southern shore of which the *Bree* was beached was a tiny estuary some twenty miles long and two in width at its mouth. It opened from the southern shore of a larger gulf of generally similar shape some two hundred fifty miles long, which in turn was an offshoot of a broad sea which extended an indefinite distance into the northern hemisphere—it merged indistinguishably with the permanently frozen polar cap. All three bodies of liquid extended roughly east and west, the smaller ones being separated from the larger on their northern sides by relatively narrow peninsulas. The ship's position was better chosen than Barlennan had known, being protected from the northern storms by both peninsulas. Eighteen miles to the west, however, the protection of the nearer and lower of these points ceased; and Barlennan and Lackland could appreciate what even that narrow neck had saved them. The captain was once more ensconced on the tank, this time with a radio clamped beside him.

To their right was the sea, spreading to the distant horizon beyond the point that guarded the bay. Behind them the beach was similar to that on which the ship lay, a gently sloping strip of sand dotted with the black, rope-branched vegetation that covered so much of Mesklin. Ahead of them, however, the growths vanished almost completely. Here the slope was even flatter and the belt of sand grew ever broader as the eye traveled along it. It was not completely bare, though even the deep-rooted plants were lacking; but scattered here and there on the wave-channeled expanse were dark, motionless relies of the recent storm.

Some were vast, tangled masses of seaweed, or of growths which could claim that name with little strain on the imagination; others were the bodies of marine animals, and some of these were even vaster. Lackland was a trifle startled—not at the size of the creatures, since they presumably were supported in life by the liquid in which they floated, but at the distance they lay from the shore. One monstrous hulk was sprawled over half a mile inland; and the Earthman began to realize just what the winds of Mesklin could do even in this gravity when they had a sixty-mile sweep of open sea in which to build up waves. He would have liked to go to the point where the shore lacked even the protection of the outer peninsula, but that would have involved a further journey of over a hundred miles.

"What would have happened to your ship, Barlennan, if the waves that reached here had struck it?"

"That depends somewhat on the type of wave, and where we were. On the open sea, we would ride over it without trouble; beached as the *Bree* now is, there would have been nothing left. I did not realize just how high waves could get this close to the Rim, of course—now that I think of it, maybe even the biggest would be relatively harmless, because of its lack of weight."

"I'm afraid it's not the weight that counts most; your first impression was probably right."

"I had some such idea in mind when I sheltered behind that point for the winter, of course. I admit I did not have any idea of the actual size the waves could reach here at the Rim. It is not too surprising that explorers tend to disappear with some frequency in these latitudes."

"This is by no means the worst, either. You have that second point, which is rather mountainous if I recall the photos correctly, protecting this whole stretch."

"Second point? I did not know about that. Do you mean that what I can see beyond the peninsula there is merely another bay?"

"That's right. I forgot you usually stayed in sight of land. You coasted along to this point from the west, then, didn't you?"

"Yes. These seas are almost completely unknown. This particular shore line extends about three thousand miles in a generally westerly direction, as you probably know—I'm just beginning to appreciate what looking at things from above can do for you—and then gradually bends south. It's not too regular; there's one place where you go east again for a couple of thousand miles, but I suppose the actual straight-line distance that would bring you opposite my home port is about sixteen thousand miles to the south—a good deal farther coasting, of course. Then about twelve hundred miles across open sea to the west would bring me home. The waters about there are very well known, of course, and any sailor can cross them without more than the usual risks of the sea."

While they had been talking, the tank had crawled away from the sea, toward the monstrous hulk that lay stranded by the recent storm. Lackland, of course, wanted to examine it in detail, since he had so far seen practically none of Mesklin's animal life; Barlennan, too, was willing. He had seen many of the monsters that thronged the seas he had traveled all his life, but he was not sure of this one.

Its shape was not too surprising for either of them. It might have been an unusually streamlined whale or a remarkably stout sea snake; the Earthman was reminded of the Zeuglodon that had haunted the seas of his own world thirty million years before. However, nothing that had ever lived on Earth and left fossils for men to study had approached the size of this thing. For six hundred feet it lay along the still sandy soil; in life its body had apparently been cylindrical, and over eighty feet in diameter. Now, deprived of the support of the liquid in which it had lived, it bore some resemblance to a wax model that had been left too long in the hot sun. Though its flesh was presumably only about half as dense as that of Earthly life, its tonnage was still something to stagger Lackland when he tried to estimate it; and the three-times-Earth-normal gravity had done its share.

"Just what do you do when you meet something like this at sea?" he asked Barlennan.

"I haven't the faintest idea," the Mesklinite replied dryly. "I have seen things like this before, but only rarely. They usually stay in the deeper, permanent seas; I have seen one once only on the surface, and about four cast up as is this one. I do not know what they eat, but apparently they find it far below the surface. I have never heard of a ship's being attacked by one."

"You probably wouldn't," Lackland replied pointedly. "I find it hard to imagine any survivors in such a case. If this thing feeds like some of the whales on my own world, it would inhale one of your ships and probably fail to notice it. Let's have a look at its mouth and find out." He started the tank once more, and drove it along to what appeared to be the head end of the vast body.

The thing had a mouth, and a skull of sorts, but the latter was badly crushed by its own weight. There was enough left, however, to permit the correction of Lackland's guess concerning its eating habits; with those teeth, it could only be carnivorous. At first the man did not recognize them as teeth; only the fact that they were located in a peculiar place for ribs finally led him to the truth.

"You'd be safe enough, Barl," he said at last. "That thing wouldn't dream of attacking you. One of your ships would not be worth the effort, as far as its appetite is concerned—I doubt that it would notice anything less than a hundred times the *Bree*'s size."

"There must be a lot of meat swimming around in the deeper seas," replied the Mesklinite thoughtfully. "I don't see that it's doing anyone much good, though."

"True enough. Say, what did you mean a little while ago by that remark about permanent seas? What other kind do you have?"

"I referred to the areas which are still ocean just before the winter storms begin," was the reply. "The ocean level is at its highest in early spring, at the end of the storms, which have filled the ocean beds during the winter. All the rest of the year they shrink again. Here at the Rim, where shore lines are so steep, it doesn't make much difference; but up where weight is decent the shore line may move anywhere from two hundred to two thousand miles between spring and fall." Lackland emitted a low whistle.

"In other words," he said, half to himself, "your oceans evaporate steadily for over four of my years, precipitating frozen methane on the north polar cap, and then get it all back in the five months or so that the northern hemisphere spends going from its spring to autumn. If I was ever surprised at those storms, that ends it." He returned to more immediate matters.

"Barl, I'm going to get out of this tin box. I've been wanting samples of the tissue of Mesklin's animal life ever since we found it existed, and I couldn't very well take a paring from you. Will the flesh of this thing be very badly changed in the length of time it has probably been dead? I suppose you'd have some idea."

"It should still be perfectly edible for us, though from what you have said you could never digest it. Meat usually becomes poisonous after a few hundred days unless it is dried or otherwise preserved, and during all that time its taste gradually changes. I'll sample a bit of this, if you'd like." Without waiting for an answer and without even a guilty glance around to make sure that none of his crew had wandered in this direction, Barlennan launched himself from the roof of the tank toward the vast bulk beside it. He misjudged badly, sailing entirely over the huge body, and for just an instant felt a twinge of normal panic; but he was in full control of himself before he landed on the farther side. He leaped back again, judging his distance better this time, and waited while Lackland opened the door of his vehicle and emerged. There was no air lock on the tank; the man was still wearing pressure armor, and had simply permitted Mesklin's atmosphere to enter after closing his helmet. A faint swirl of white crystals followed him out—ice and carbon dioxide, frozen out of the Earth-type air inside as it cooled to Mesklin's bitter temperature. Barlennan had no sense of smell, but he felt a burning sensation in his breathing pores as a faint whiff of oxygen reached him, and jumped hastily backward. Lackland guessed correctly at the cause of his action and apologized profusely for not giving proper warning.

"It is nothing," the captain replied. "I should have foreseen it—I got the same sensation once before when you left the Hill where you live, and you certainly told me often enough how the oxygen you breathe differs from our hydrogen—you remember, when I was learning your language."

"I suppose that's true. Still, I could hardly expect a person who hasn't grown up accustomed to the idea of different worlds and different atmospheres to remember the possibility all the time. It was still my fault. However, it seems to have done you no harm; I don't yet know enough about the life chemistry of Mesklin even to guess just what it might do to you. That's why I want samples of this creature's flesh."

Lackland had a number of instruments in a mesh pouch on the outside of his armor, and while he was fumbling among them with his pressure gauntlets Barlennan proceeded to take the first sample. Four sets of pincers shredded a portion of skin and underlying tissue and passed it along to his mouth; for a few moments he chewed reflectively.

"Not at all bad," he remarked at last. "If you don't need all of this thing for your tests, it might be a good idea to call the hunting parties over here. They'd have time to make it before the storm gets going again, I should think, and there'll certainly be more meat than they could reasonably expect to get any other way."

"Good idea," Lackland grunted. He was giving only part of his attention to his companion; most of it was being taken up by the problem of getting the point of a scalpel into the mass before him. Even the suggestion that he might be able to use the entire monstrous body in a laboratory investigation—the Mesklinite did possess a sense of humor—failed to distract him.

He had known, of course, that living tissue on this planet must be extremely tough. Small as Barlennan and his people were, they would have been flattened into senseless pulp under Mesklin's polar gravity had their flesh been of mere Earthly consistency. He had expected some difficulty in getting an instrument through the monster's skin; but he had more or less unthinkingly assumed that, once through, his troubles would be over in that respect. He was now discovering his error; the meat inside seemed to have the consistency of teak. The scalpel was of a superhard alloy which would have been difficult to dull against anything as long as mere muscular strength was employed, but he could not drive it through that mass and finally had to resort to scraping. This produced a few shreds which he sealed in a collecting bottle.

"Is any part of this thing likely to be softer?" he asked the interested Mesklinite as he looked up from this task. "I'm going to need power tools to get enough out of this body to satisfy the boys on Toorey."

"Some parts inside the mouth might be a little more tractable," Barlennan replied. "However, it would be easier for me to nip off pieces for you, if you'll tell me the sizes and parts you want. Will that be all right, or do your scientific procedures demand that the samples be removed with metal instruments for some reason?"

"Not that I know of—thanks a lot; if the bio boys don't like it they can come down and do their own carving," returned Lackland. "Go right ahead. Let's follow your other suggestion, too, and get something from the mouth; I'm not really sure I'm through skin here." He waddled painfully around the head of the stranded behemoth to a point where gravity-distorted lips had exposed teeth, gums, and what was presumably a tongue. "Just get bits small enough to go in these bottles without crowding." The Earthman tentatively tried the scalpel once more, finding the tongue somewhat less obdurate than the earlier sample, while Barlennan obediently nipped off fragments of the desired size. An occasional piece found its way to his mouth—he was not really hungry, but this was fresh meat—but in spite of this drain the bottles were soon filled.

Lackland straightened up, stowing the last of the containers as he did so, and cast a covetous glance at the pillarlike teeth. "I suppose it would take blasting gelatine to get one of those out," he remarked rather sadly.

"What is that?" asked Barlennan.

"An explosive—a substance that changes into gas very suddenly, producing loud noise and shock. We use such material for digging, removing undesirable buildings or pieces of landscape, and sometimes in fighting."

"Was that sound an explosive?" Barlennan asked.

For an instant Lackland made no answer. A *boom!* of very respectable intensity, heard on a planet whose natives are ignorant of explosives and where no other member of the human race is present, can be rather disconcerting, especially when it picks such an incredibly apt time to happen; and to say that Lackland was startled would be putting it mildly. He could not judge accurately the distance or size of the explosion, having heard it through Barlennan's radio and his own sound discs at the same time; but a distinctly unpleasant suspicion entered his mind after a second or two.

"It sounded very much like one," he answered the Mesklinite's question somewhat belatedly, even as he started to waddle back around the head of the dead sea monster to where he had left the tank. He rather dreaded what he would find. Barlennan, more curious than ever, followed by his more natural method of travel, crawling.

For an instant, as the tank came in sight, Lackland felt an overwhelming relief; but this changed to an equally profound shock as he reached the door of the vehicle.

What remained of the floor consisted of upcurled scraps of thin metal, some still attached at the bases of the walls and others tangled among the controls and other interior fittings. The driving machinery, which had been under the floor, was almost completely exposed, and a single glance was enough to tell the dismayed Earthman that it was hopelessly wrecked. Barlennan was intensely interested in the whole phenomenon.

"I take it you were carrying some explosive in your tank," he remarked. "Why did you not use it to get the material you wanted from this animal? And what made it act while it was still in the tank?"

"You have a genius for asking difficult questions," Lackland replied. "The answer to your first one is that I was not carrying any; and to the second, your guess is as good as mine at this point."

"But it must have been something you were carrying," Barlennan pointed out. "Even I can see that whatever it was happened under the floor of your tank, and wanted to get out; and we don't have things that act like that on Mesklin."

"Admitting your logic, there was nothing under that floor that I can imagine blowing up," replied the man. "Electric motors and their accumulators just aren't explosive. A close examination will undoubtedly show traces of whatever it was if it was in any sort of container, since practically none of the fragments seem to have gone outside the tank—but I have a rather worse problem to solve first, Barl."

"What is that?"

"I am eighteen miles from food supplies, other than what is carried in my armor. The tank is ruined; and if there was ever an Earthman born who could walk eighteen miles in eight-atmosphere heated armor under three gravities, I'm certainly not the one. My air will last indefinitely with these algae gills and enough sunlight, but I'd starve to death before I made the station."

"Can't you call your friends on the faster moon, and have them send a rocket to carry you back?"

"I could; probably they already know, if anyone is in the radio room to hear this conversation. The trouble is if I have to get that sort of help Doc Rosten will certainly make me go back to Toorey for the winter; I had trouble enough as it was persuading him to let me stay. He'll have to hear about the tank, but I want to tell him from the station—after getting back there without his help. There just isn't energy around here to get me back, though; and even if I could get more food into the containers in this armor without letting your air in, you couldn't get into the station to get the food."

"Let's call my crew, anyway," Barlennan remarked. "They can use the food that's here—or as much of it as they can carry. I have another idea too, I think."

"We are coming, Captain." Dondragmer's voice came from the radio, startling Lackland, who had forgotten his arrangement to let each radio hear the others, and startling the commander himself, who had not realized that his mate had learned so much English. "We will be with you in a few days at most; we took the same general direction as the Flyer's machine when we started." He gave this information in his native language; Barlennan translated for Lackland's benefit.

"I can see that *you* won't be hungry for quite a while," the man replied, glancing somewhat ruefully at the mountain of meat beside them, "but what was this other idea of yours? Will it help with my problem?"

"A little, I think." The Mesklinite would have smiled had his mouth been sufficiently flexible. "Will you please step on me?"

For several seconds Lackland stood rigid with astonishment at the request; after all, Barlennan looked more like a caterpillar than anything else, and when a man steps on a caterpillar—then he relaxed, and even grinned.

"All right, Barl. For a moment I'd forgotten the circumstances." The Mesklinite had crawled over to his feet during the pause; and without further hesitation Lackland took the requested step. There proved to be only one difficulty.

Lackland had a mass of about one hundred sixty pounds. His armor, an engineering miracle in its own way, was about as much more. On Mesklin's equator, then, man and armor *weighed* approximately nine hundred fifty pounds—he could not have moved a step without an ingenious servo device in the legs—and this weight was only about a quarter greater than that of Barlennan in the polar regions of his planet. There was no difficulty for the Mesklinite in supporting that much weight; what defeated the attempt was simple geometry. Barlennan was, in general, a cylinder a foot and a half long and two inches in diameter; and it proved a physical impossibility for the armored Earthman to balance on him.

The Mesklinite was stumped; this time it was Lackland who thought of a solution. Some of the side plates on the lower part of the tank had been sprung by the blast inside; and under Lackland's direction Barlennan, with considerable effort, was able to wrench one completely free. It was about two feet wide and six long, and with one end bent up slightly by the native's powerful nippers, it made an admirable sledge; but Barlennan, on this part of his planet, weighed about three pounds. He simply did not have the necessary traction to tow the device—and the nearest plant which might have served as an anchor was a quarter of a mile away. Lackland was glad that a red face had no particular meaning to the natives of this world, for the sun happened to be in the sky when this particular fiasco occurred. They had been working both day and night, since the smaller sun and the two moons had furnished ample light in the absence of the storm clouds.

5: Mapping Job

The crew's arrival, days later, solved Lackland's problem almost at once.

The mere number of natives, of course, was of little help; twenty-one Mesklinites still did not have traction enough to move the loaded sledge. Barlennan thought of having them carry it, placing a crew member under each corner; and he went to considerable trouble to overcome the normal Mesklinite conditioning against getting under a massive object. When he finally succeeded in this, however, the effort proved futile; the metal plate was not thick enough for that sort of treatment, and buckled under the armored man's weight so that all but the supported corner was still in contact with the ground.

Dondragmer, with no particular comment, spent the time that this test consumed in paying out and attaching together the lines which were normally used with the hunting nets. They proved, in series, more than long enough to reach the nearest plants; and the roots of these growths, normally able to hold against the worst that Mesklin's winds could offer, furnished all the support needed. Four days later a train of sledges, made from all the accessible plates of the tank, started back toward the *Bree* with Lackland and a tremendous load of meat aboard; and at a fairly steady rate of a mile an hour, reached the ship in sixty-one days. Two more days of work, with more crew members assisting, got Lackland's armor through the vegetation growing between the ship and his dome, and delivered him safely at the air lock. It was none too soon; the wind had already picked up to a point where the assisting crew had to use ground lines in getting back to the *Bree,* and clouds were once again whipping across the sky.

Lackland ate, before bothering to report officially what had happened to the tank. He wished he could make the report more complete; he felt somehow that he should know what had actually happened to the vehicle. It was going to be very difficult to accuse someone on Toorey of inadvertently leaving a cake of gelatine under the tank's floor.

He had actually pressed the call button on the station-to-satellite set when the answer struck him; and when Dr. Rosten's lined face appeared on the screen he knew just what to say.

"Doc, there's a spot of trouble with the tank."

"So I understand. Is it electrical or mechanical? Serious?"

"Basically mechanical, though the electrical system had a share. I'm afraid it's a total loss; what's left of it is stranded about eighteen miles from here, west, near the beach."

"Very nice. This planet is costing a good deal of money one way and another. Just what happened—and how did you get back? I don't think you could walk eighteen miles in armor under that gravity."

"I didn't—Barlennan and his crew towed me back. As nearly as I can figure out about the tank, the floor partition between cockpit and engine compartment wasn't airtight. When I got out to do some investigating, Mesklin's atmosphere—high-pressure hydrogen—began leaking in and mixing with the normal air under the floor. It did the same in the cockpit, too, of course, but practically all the oxygen was swept out through the door from there and diluted below danger point before anything happened. Underneath—well, there was a spark before the oxygen went."

"I see. What caused the spark? Did you leave motors running when you went out?"

"Certainly—the steering servos, dynamotors, and so on. I'm glad of it, too; if I hadn't, the blast would probably have occurred after I got back in and turned them on."

"Hmph." The director of the Recovery Force looked a trifle disgruntled. "Did you have to get out at all?" Lackland thanked his stars that Rosten was a biochemist.

"I didn't exactly have to, I suppose. I was getting tissue samples from a six-hundred-foot whale stranded on the beach out there. I thought someone might—"

"Did you bring them back?" snapped Rosten without letting Lackland finish.

"I did. Come down for them when you like—and have we another tank you could bring along?"

"We have. I'll consider letting you have it when winter is over; I think you'll be safer inside the dome until then. What did you preserve the specimens with?"

"Nothing special—hydrogen—the local air. I supposed that any of our regular preservatives would ruin them from your point of view. You'd better come for them fairly soon; Barlennan says that meat turns poisonous after a few hundred days, so I take it they have micro-organisms here."

"Be funny if they hadn't. Stand by; I'll be down there in a couple of hours." Rosten broke the connection without further comment about the wrecked tank, for which Lackland felt reasonably thankful. He went to bed, not having slept for nearly twenty-four hours.

He was awakened—partially—by the arrival of the rocket. Rosten had come down in person, which was not surprising. He did not even get out of his armor; he took the bottles, which Lackland had left in the air lock to minimize the chance of oxygen contamination, took a look at Lackland, realized his condition, and brusquely ordered him back to bed.

"This stuff was probably worth the tank," he said briefly. "Now get some sleep. You have some more problems to solve—I'll talk to you again when there's a chance you'll remember what I say. See you later." The air-lock door closed behind him.

Lackland did not, actually, remember Rosten's parting remarks; but he was reminded, many hours later, when he had slept and eaten once more.

"This winter, when Barlennan can't hope to travel, will last only another three and a half months," the assistant director started almost without preamble. "We have several reams of telephotos up here which are not actually fitted into a map, although they've been collated as far as general location is concerned. We couldn't make a real map because of interpretation difficulties. Your job for the rest of this winter will be to get in a huddle with those photos and your friend Barlennan, turn them into a usable map, and decide on a route which will take him most quickly to the material we want to salvage."

"But Barlennan doesn't want to get there quickly. This is an exploring-trading voyage as far as he's concerned, and we're just an incident. All we've been able to offer him in return for that much help is a running sequence of weather reports, to help in his normal business."

"I realize that. That's why you're down there, if you remember; you're supposed to be a diplomat. I don't expect miracles—none of us do—and we certainly want Barlennan to stay on good terms with us; but there's two billion dollars' worth of special equipment on that rocket that couldn't leave the pole, and recordings that are literally priceless—"

"I know, and I'll do my best," Lackland cut in, "but I could never make the importance of it clear to a native—and I don't mean to belittle Barlennan's intelligence; he just hasn't the background. You keep an eye out for breaks in these winter storms, so he can come up here and study the pictures whenever possible."

"Couldn't you rig some sort of outside shelter next to a window, so he could stay up even during bad weather?"

"I suggested that once, and he won't leave his ship and crew at such times. I see his point."

"I suppose I do too. Well, do the best that you can—you know what it means. We should be able to learn more about gravity from that stuff than anyone since Einstein." Rosten signed off, and the winter's work began.

The grounded research rocket, which had landed under remote control near Mesklin's south pole and had failed to take off after presumably recording its data, had long since been located by its telemetering transmitters. Choosing a sea and/or land route to it from the vicinity of the *Bree*'s winter quarters, however, was another matter. The ocean travel was not too bad; some forty or forty-five thousand miles of coastal travel, nearly half of it in waters already known to Barlennan's people, would bring the salvage crew as close to the helpless machine as this particular chain of oceans ever got. That, unfortunately, was some four thousand miles; and there simply were no large rivers near that section of coast which would shorten the overland distance significantly.

There was such a stream, easily navigable by a vessel like the *Bree,* passing within fifty miles of the desired spot; but it emptied into an ocean which had no visible connection with that which Barlennan's people sailed. The latter was a long, narrow, highly irregular chain of seas extending from somewhat north of the equator in the general neighborhood of Lackland's station almost to the equator on the opposite side of the planet, passing fairly close to the south pole on the way—fairly close, that is, as distances on Mesklin went. The other sea, into which the river near the rocket emptied, was broader and more regular in outline; the river mouth in question was at about its southernmost point, and it also extended to and past the equator, merging at last with the northern icecap. It lay to the east of the first ocean chain, and appeared to be separated from it by a narrow isthmus extending from pole to equator—narrow, again by Mesklinite standards. As the photographs were gradually pieced together, Lackland decided that the isthmus varied from about two to nearly seven thousand miles in width.

"What we could use, Barl, is a passage from one of these seas into the other," remarked Lackland one day. The Mesklinite, sprawled comfortably on his ledge outside the window, gestured agreement silently. It was past midwinter now, and the greater sun was becoming perceptibly dimmer as it arched on its swift path across the sky to the north. "Are you sure that your people know of none? After all, most of these pictures were taken in the fall, and you say that the ocean level is much higher in the spring."

"We know of none, at any season," replied the captain. "We know something, but not much, of the ocean you speak of; there are too many different nations on the land between for very much contact to take place. A single caravan would be a couple of years on the journey, and as a rule they don't travel that far. Goods pass through many hands on such a trip, and it's a little hard to learn much about their origin by the time our traders see them in the western seaports of the isthmus. If any passage such as we would like exists at all, it must be here near the Rim where the lands are almost completely unexplored. Our map—the one you and I are making—does not go far enough yet. In any case, there is no such passage south of here during the autumn; I have been along the entire coast line as it was then, remember. Perhaps, however, this very coast reaches over to the other sea; we have followed it eastward for several thousand miles, and simply do not know how much farther it goes."

"As I remember, it curves north again a couple of thousand miles past the outer cape, Barl—but of course that was in the autumn, too, when I saw it. It's going to be quite troublesome, this business of making a usable map of your world. It changes too much. I'd be tempted to wait until next autumn so that at least we could use the map we made, but that's four of my years away. I can't stay here that long."

"You could go back to your own world and rest until the time came though I would be sorry to see you go."

"I'm afraid that would be a rather long journey, Barlennan."

"How far?"

"Well—your units of distance wouldn't help much. Let's see. A ray of light could travel around Mesklin's 'rim' in—ah—four fifths of a second." He demonstrated this time interval with his watch, while the native looked on with interest. "The same ray would take a little over eleven of my years; that's—about two and a quarter of yours, to get from here to my home."

"Then your world is too far to see? You never explained these things to me before."

"I was not sure we had covered the language problem well enough. No, my world cannot be seen, but I will show you my sun when winter is over and we have moved to the right side of yours." The last phrase passed completely over Barlennan's head, but he let it go. The only suns he knew were the bright Belne whose coming and going made day and night, and the fainter Esstes, which was visible in the night sky at this moment. In a little less than half a year, at midsummer, the two would be close together in the sky, and the fainter one hard to see; but Barlennan had never bothered his head about the reason for these motions.

Lackland had put down the photograph he was holding, and seemed immersed in thought. Much of the floor of the room was already covered with loosely fitted pictures; the region best known to Barlennan was already mapped fairly well. However, there was yet a long, long way to go before the area occupied by the human outpost would be included; and the man was already being troubled by the refusal of the photographs to fit together. Had they been of a spherical or nearly spherical world like Earth or Mars, he could have applied the proper projection correction almost automatically on the smaller map which he was constructing, and which covered a table at one side of the chamber; but Mesklin was not even approximately spherical. As Lackland had long ago recognized, the proportions of the Bowl on the *Bree*—Barlennan's equivalent of a terrestrial globe—were approximately right. It was six inches across and one and a quarter deep, and its curvature was smooth but far from uniform.

To add to the difficulty of matching photographs, much of the planet's surface was relatively smooth, without really distinctive topographic feature; and even where mountains and valleys existed, the different shadowing of adjacent photographs made comparison a hard job. The habit of the brighter sun of crossing from horizon to horizon in less than nine minutes had seriously disarranged normal photographic procedure; successive pictures in the same series were often illuminated from almost opposite directions.

"We're not getting anywhere with this, Barl," Lackland said wearily. "It was worth a try as long as there might be short cuts, but you say there are none. You're a sailor, not a caravan master; that four thousand miles overland right where gravity is greatest is going to stump us."

"The knowledge that enables you to fly, then, cannot change weight?"

"It cannot." Lackland smiled. "The instruments which are on that rocket grounded at your south pole should have readings which might teach us just that, in time. That is why the rocket was sent, Barlennan; the poles of your world have the most terrific surface gravity of any spot in the Universe so far accessible to us. There are a number of other worlds even more massive than yours, and closer to home, but they don't spin the way Mesklin does; they're too nearly spherical. We wanted measures in that tremendous gravity field—all sorts of measures. The value of the instruments that were designed and sent on that trip cannot be expressed in numbers we both know; when the rocket failed to respond to its takeoff signal, it rocked the governments of ten planets. We *must* have that data, even if we have to dig a canal to get the *Bree* into the other ocean."

"But what sort of devices were on board this rocket?" Barlennan asked. He regretted the question almost in the same instant; the Flyer might wonder at such specific curiosity, and come to suspect the captain's true intentions. However, Lackland appeared to take the query as natural.

"I'm afraid I can't tell you, Barl. You simply have no background which would give words like 'electron' and 'neutrino' and 'magnetism' and 'quantum' any meaning at all. The drive mechanism of the rocket might mean a little more to you, but I doubt it." In spite of Lackland's apparent freedom from suspicion, Barlennan decided not to pursue the subject.

"Would it not be well," he said, "to seek the pictures that show the shore and inland regions east of here?"

Lackland replied, "There is still some chance, I suppose, that they do meet; I don't pretend to have memorized the whole area. Maybe down next to the icecap—how much cold can you people stand?"

"We are uncomfortable when the sea freezes, but we can stand it—if it does not get too much colder. Why?"

"It's just possible you may have to crowd the northern icecap pretty closely. We'll see, though." The Flyer riffled through the stack of prints, still taller than Barlennan was long, and eventually extracted a thin sheaf. "One of these..." His voice trailed off for a few moments. "Here we are. This was taken from the inner edge of the ring, Barl, over six hundred miles up, with a narrow-angle telephoto lens. You can see the main shore line, and the big bay, and here, on the south side of the big one, the little bay where the *Bree* is beached. This was taken before this station was built—though it wouldn't show anyway.

"Now let's start assembling again. The sheet east of this..." He trailed off again, and the Mesklinite watched in fascination as a readable map of the lands he had not yet reached took form below him. For a time it seemed they were to be disappointed, for the shore line gradually curved northward as Lackland had thought; indeed, some twelve hundred miles to the west and four or five hundred north, the ocean seemed to come to an end—the coast curved westward again. A vast river emptied into it at this point, and with some hope at first that this might be a strait leading to the eastern sea, Lackland began fitting the pictures that covered the upper reaches of the mighty stream. He was quickly disabused of this idea, by the discovery of an extensive series of rapids some two hundred and fifty miles upstream; east of these, the great river dwindled rapidly. Numerous smaller streams emptied into it; apparently it was the main artery for the drainage system of a vast area of the planet. Interested by the speed with which it broke up into smaller rivers, Lackland continued building the map eastward, watched with interest by Barlennan.

The main stream, as far as it could be distinguished, had shifted direction slightly, flowing from a more southerly direction. Carrying the mosaic of pictures in this direction, they found a range of very fair-sized mountains, and the Earthman looked up with a rueful shake of his head. Barlennan had come to understand the meaning of this gesture.

"Do not stop yet!" the captain expostulated. "There is a similar range along the center of my country, which is a fairly narrow peninsula. At least build the picture far enough to determine how the streams flow on the other side of the mountains." Lackland, though not optimistic—he recalled the South American continent on his own planet too clearly to assume any symmetry of the sort the Mesklinite seemed to expect—complied with the native's suggestion. The range proved to be fairly narrow, extending roughly east-northeast by west-southwest; and rather to the man's surprise the numerous "water" courses on the opposite side began very quickly to show a tendency to come together in one vast river. This ran roughly parallel with the range for mile after mile, broadening as it went, and hope began to grow once more. It reached a climax five hundred miles downstream, when what was now a vast estuary merged indistinguishably with the "waters" of the eastern ocean. Working feverishly, scarcely stopping for food or even the rest he so badly needed in Mesklin's savage gravity, Lackland worked on; and eventually the floor of the room was covered by a new map—a rectangle representing some two thousand miles in an east-west line and half as far in the other dimension. The great bay and tiny cove where the *Bree* was beached showed clearly at its western end; much of the other was occupied by the featureless surface of the eastern sea. Between lay the land barrier.

It was narrow; at its narrowest, some five hundred miles north of the equator, it was a scant eight hundred miles from coast to coast, and this distance was lessened considerably if one measured from the highest usable points of the principal rivers. Perhaps three hundred miles, part of it over a mountain range, was all that lay between the *Bree* and a relatively easy path to the distant goal of the Earthmen's efforts. Three hundred miles; a mere step, as distances on Mesklin went.

Unfortunately, it was decidedly more than a step to a Mesklinite sailor. The *Bree* was still in the wrong ocean; Lackland, after staring silently for many minutes at the mosaic about him, said as much to his tiny companion. He expected no answer, or at most a dispirited agreement; his statement was self-evidently true—but the native fooled him.

"Not if you have more of the metal on which we brought you and the meat back!" was Barlennan's instantaneous reply.

6: The Sled

For another long moment Lackland stared out the window into the sailor's eyes, while the implications of the little creature's remark sank into his mind; then he stiffened into something as closely approaching an alert attitude as the gravity permitted.

"You mean you would be willing to tow the *Bree* overland on a sledge, as you did me?"

"Not exactly. The ship outweighs us very much, and we would have the same trouble with traction that we did before. What I had in mind was *your* towing, with another tank."

"I see. I—see. It would certainly be possible, unless we hit terrain that the tank couldn't pass. But would you and your crew be willing to make such a journey? Would the extra trouble and distance from your home be repaid by the little we could do for you?"

Barlennan extended his pincers in a smile.

"It would be much better than what we originally planned. There are trading goods that come from the shores of the eastern ocean to our country, by the long caravan routes overland; by the time they reach the ports on our own sea, they are already fabulously expensive, and an honest trader cannot make a decent profit from them. This way, if I picked them up directly—well, it would be certainly very worth while indeed, for me. Of course, you would have to promise to bring us back across the isthmus when we returned."

"That would certainly be fair enough, Barl; I'm sure my people will gladly agree to it. But how about the land travel itself? This is country you know nothing about, as you have said; might not your crew be afraid of unknown land, and high hills over them, and maybe animals larger than can possibly grow in your part of the world?"

"We have faced dangers before," the Mesklinite replied. "I was able to get used to high places—even the top of your tank. As for animals, the

Bree is armed with fire, and none that walk on land could be as large as some that swim the oceans."

"That's true enough, Barl. Very well. I was not trying to discourage you, goodness knows; but I wanted to be sure you had thought the matter over before you embarked on such a project. It's hardly one that can be backed out of in the middle."

"That I can readily understand, but you need not fear, Charles. I must return to the ship now; the clouds are gathering again. I will tell the crew what we are going to do; and lest the thoughts of fear should come to any of them, I will remind them that the profits of the voyage will be shared according to rank. There is no member of that crew who would put fear in the way of wealth."

"And you?" Lackland chuckled as he asked the question.

"Oh, I'm not afraid." The Mesklinite vanished into the night as he spoke the words, and Lackland was never sure just how he meant them.

Rosten, when he heard the new plan, made a number of caustic remarks to the effect that Lackland could certainly be counted on for ideas that would give him use of a tank.

"It seems as though it should work, though," he admitted grudgingly. "Just what sort of sled are we supposed to build for this ocean liner of your friend's? How big is it, again?"

"The *Bree* is about forty feet long and fifteen across; I suppose it draws five or six inches. It's made of a lot of rafts about three feet long and half as wide, roped together so they can move fairly freely—I can guess why, on this world."

"Hmph. So can I. If a ship that long had its two ends supported by waves while the middle hung free, up near the pole, it would be in pieces before long whether it started that way or not. How is it driven?"

"Sails; there are masts on twenty or thirty of the rafts. I suspect there may be centerboards on some of them too, retractable so the ship can be beached; but I never asked Barlennan. I don't really know how far advanced the art of sailing is on this world, but from the casual way in which he speaks of crossing long stretches of open ocean, I assume they know about beating into a wind."

"Seems reasonable. Well, we'll build something out of light metal here on the moon, and cart it down to you when we finish."

"You'd better not bring it down until winter's over. If you leave it inland it'll get lost under the snow, and if you drop it at the seashore someone may have to dive for it, if the water line goes up the way Barlennan expects."

"If it's going to, why is it waiting so long? The winter is more than half over, and there's been a fantastic amount of precipitation in the parts of the southern hemisphere that we can see."

"Why ask me things like that? There are meteorologists on the staff, I believe, unless they've gone crazy trying to study this planet. I have my own worries. When do I get another tank?"

"'When you can use it; after winter is over, as I said. And if you blow that one up it'll be no use howling for another, because there isn't one closer than Earth."

Barlennan, hearing the gist of this conversation at his next visit some hundreds of days later, was perfectly satisfied. His crew was enthusiastic about the proposed trip; they might, as he had implied, be lured by the prospective gain, but there was liberally distributed among them a share of the plain love of adventure which had carried Barlennan so far into unknown territory.

"We will go as soon as the storms break," he said to Lackland. "There will still be much snow on the ground; that will help where the course lies over land different from the loose sand of the beach."

"I don't think it will make much difference to the tank," replied Lackland.

"It will to us," pointed out Barlennan. "I admit it would not be dangerous to be shaken off the deck, but it would be annoying in the middle of a meal. Have you decided what would be the best course to follow across the land?"

"I've been working on it." The man brought out the map that was the result of his efforts. "The shortest route, that we discovered together, has the disadvantage of requiring that I tow you over a mountain range. It might be possible, but I don't like to think of the effects on your crew. I don't know how high those mountains are, but any altitude is too much on this world.

"I've worked out this route, which I've shown by a red line. It follows up the river that empties into the big bay on this side of the point, for about twelve hundred miles—not counting the small curves in the river, which we probably won't have to follow. Then it goes straight across country for another four hundred or so, and reaches the head of another river. You could probably sail down that if you wanted, or have me keep on towing—whichever would be faster or more comfortable for you. Its worst feature is that so much of it runs three or four hundred miles south of the equator—another half gravity or more for me to take. I can handle it, though."

"If you are sure of that, I would say that this is indeed the best way." Barlennan gave his statement after careful study of the map. "Your towing will probably be faster than sailing, at least in the river where there will probably be no room to tack." He had to use his own language for the last word; Lackland received the explanation of its meaning with satisfaction. He had guessed correctly about the extent of nautical progress among Barlennan's people, it seemed.

With the route agreed on, there was little more for Lackland to do while Mesklin drifted along its orbit toward the next equinox. That would not be too long, of course; with the southern hemisphere's midwinter occurring almost exactly at the time the giant world was closest to its sun, orbital motion during fall and winter was extremely rapid. Each of those seasons was a shade over two Earthly months in length—spring and summer, on the other hand, each occupied some eight hundred and thirty Earth days, roughly twenty-six months. There should be plenty of time for the voyage itself.

Lackland's enforced idleness was not shared aboard the *Bree.* Preparations for the overland journey were numerous and complicated by the fact that no member of the crew knew exactly what the ship would have to face. They might have to make the entire journey on stored food; there might be animal life along the way sufficient not only to feed them but to provide trading material if its skins and bones were of the right sort. The trip might be as safe as the sailors avowedly believed all land journeys to be, or they might face dangers from both the terrain and the creatures inhabiting it. About the first they could do little; that was the Flyer's responsibility. Concerning the second, weapons were brought to a high degree of readiness. Bigger clubs than even Hars or Terblannen could swing up in the higher latitudes were manufactured; some of the plants which stored crystals of chlorine in their stems were found, and the flame tanks replenished from them. There were, of course, no projectile weapons; the idea had never developed on a world where none of the inhabitants had ever seen a solid, unsupported object because it fell too fast to be visible. A .50-caliber bullet fired horizontally at Mesklin's pole would drop over one hundred feet in its first hundred yards of travel. Barlennan, since meeting Lackland, had come to have some idea of the "throw" concept and had even considered asking the Flyer about the possibility of weapons based on the principle; but he had decided to stick to more familiar arms. Lackland, on his part, had done a little wondering about the possible results of meeting a race, on their trip across the isthmus, which had developed the bow and arrow. He did a little more than Barlennan with the thought; he outlined the situation to Rosten and asked that the towing tank be equipped with a 40-millimeter gun with thermite and explosive shells. After the usual grumbling Rosten had acquiesced.

The sled was finished easily and quickly; large amounts of sheet metal were available, and the structure was certainly not complicated. Following Lackland's advice, it was not brought to the surface of Mesklin immediately, since the storms were still depositing their loads of ammonia-tainted methane snow. The ocean level had still not risen appreciably near the equator, and the meteorologists had been making unkind remarks at first about Barlennan's truthfulness and linguistic ability; but as sunlight reached farther and farther into the southern hemisphere with the approach of spring, and new photographs were secured and compared with those of the preceding fall, the weather men grew silent and were observed wandering around the station muttering distractedly to themselves. The sea level in the higher latitudes had already risen several hundreds of feet, as the native had predicted, and was still rising visibly as the days went by. The phenomenon of widely differing sea levels at the same time on the same planet was a little outside the experience of Earth-trained meteorologists, and none of the non-human scientists with the expedition could throw any light on the matter, either. The weather men were still racking their brains when the sun's diurnal arc eased southward past the equator and spring officially began in Mesklin's southern hemisphere.

The storms had decreased tremendously in both frequency and intensity long before this time, partly because the planet's extreme flattening had cut down the radiation on the north polar cap very rapidly after midwinter and partly because Mesklin's distance from the sun had increased more than fifty per cent during the same time; Barlennan, when consulted on the matter, proved perfectly willing to start the journey with the astronomical advent of spring, and showed no apparent anxiety about equinoctial gales.

Lackland reported the natives' readiness to the station on the inner moon, and the operation of transferring tank and sled to the surface was started at once; everything had been in readiness for weeks.

Two trips of the cargo rocket were necessary, though the sledge was light and the thrust developed by the hydrogen-iron slugs fantastically high. The sled was brought down first, with the intention of letting the crew of the *Bree* haul it onto the structure while the rocket went back for the tank; but Lackland warned against landing close to the ship, so that the clumsy-looking vehicle was left beside the dome until the tractor arrived to tow it over to the shore. Lackland himself drove the tractor, although the crew of the rocket stood by to satisfy their curiosity and, if needed, lend assistance with the loading procedure.

No human help was needed. The Mesklinites, under a mere three Earth gravities, were perfectly capable physically of lifting their ship and walking off with it; and the insuperable mental conditioning that prevented their getting any part of their bodies underneath such a mass did not prevent their towing it easily across the beach with ropes—each crewman, of course, anchored firmly to a tree with one or both sets of rear pincers. The *Bree*, sails furled and centerboards retracted, slid easily across the sand and onto the gleaming platform of metal. Barlennan's winter-long vigilance to keep her from freezing to the beach had proved adequate; also, in the last couple of weeks, the ocean level had started to rise as it had already done farther south. The advancing liquid, which had already necessitated moving the vessel two hundred yards inland, would certainly have melted her free had that been necessary.

The builders of the sledge, on distant Toorey, had provided eyes and cleats in sufficient numbers to allow the sailors to lash the *Bree* firmly in place. The cordage used appeared remarkably thin to Lackland, but the natives showed full confidence in it. They had some justice, the Earthman reflected; it had held their ship on the beach during storms when he himself would not have cared to walk abroad in full armor. It might, he reflected, be worth while to find out if the cordage and fabric the Mesklinites used could stand terrestrial temperatures.

This train of thought was interrupted by Barlennan's approach with the report that all was ready on the ship and sledge. The latter was already attached to the tank by its tow cable; the tank itself was stocked with sufficient food to last its one-man crew for several days. The plan was to re-supply Lackland by rocket whenever necessary, landing far enough ahead so that the flying rocket would not cause too much perturbation to the natives on the ship. This was not to be done oftener than strictly necessary; after the first accident, Lackland did not intend to open the tank to the outer air oftener than he could possibly help.

"I guess we're ready to go, then, little friend," he said in response to Barlennan's statement. "I won't need sleep for a good many hours yet, and we can get quite a distance upstream in that time. I wish your days were of a decent length; I'm not too happy about driving over a snow field in the dark. I don't think even your crew could pull the tank out of a hole, even if they could find the traction."

"I rather doubt it myself, though my ability to judge weight is very uncertain here at the Rim," the captain replied. "I doubt that the risk is very great, however; the snow isn't sticky enough to do a good job of covering a large hole."

"Unless it drifted in to fill it completely. Well, I'll worry about that if and when it happens. All aboard!" He entered the tank, sealed the door, pumped out the Mesklinite atmosphere, and released the Earthly air that had been compressed into tanks before opening the door earlier. The small tank that held the algae whose job was to keep the air fresh glimmered as the circulators began driving bubbles through it. A tiny spectrometric "sniffer" reported the hydrogen content of the air to be negligible; once assured of this, Lackland started his main motors without further hesitation, and headed the tank and its unwieldy trailer into the east.

The near flatness of the country around the cove changed gradually. In the forty days or so before Lackland had to stop for sleep, they had covered some fifty miles, and were in an area of rolling hills which reached heights of three or four hundred feet. No trouble had been encountered, either in pulling the sledge or in riding it. Barlennan reported on his radio that the crew were enjoying the experience, and that the unusual idleness had not bothered anyone yet. The speed of the tank and its tow was about five miles an hour, which was a good deal faster than the usual Mesklinite crawl; but in the negligible—to them—gravity, some of the crew were going overside and experimenting with other methods of travel. None had actually jumped as yet, but it looked as though Barlennan might have companions before long who shared his newly acquired indifference to falls.

No animal life had been seen so far, but there had been occasional tiny tracks in the snow which apparently belonged to creatures similar to those the *Bree*'s crew had hunted for food during the winter. The plant life was distinctly different; in some places the snow was almost hidden by grasslike vegetation that had grown up through it, and on one occasion the crew was held spellbound at the sight of a growth which to Lackland resembled a rather stumpy tree. The Mesklinites had never seen anything grow so far from the ground.

While Lackland slept as comfortably as he could in his cramped quarters, the crew spread out over the surrounding country. They were at least partly motivated by a desire for fresh food, but salable cargo was the goal that really moved them. All were familiar with a wide variety of the plants which produced what Lackland had called spices, but none of these grew anywhere in the neighborhood. There were numerous growths bearing seeds, and nearly all had leaflike appendages of one sort or another and roots; the trouble was there seemed no way of telling whether these were even safe to eat, to say nothing of being palatable. None of Barlennan's sailors was rash or naive enough to take even a taste of a plant he had never seen; too much of Mesklin's vegetable life protected itself with fearsome efficiency with poisons. The usual means of testing in such cases involved trusting to the senses of any of several small animals commonly used by the Mesklinites as pets; what a *parsk* or a *ternee* would eat was safe. Unfortunately, the only such animal aboard the *Bree* had not survived the winter—or rather, the equator; it had blown away in the advance gust of one of the winter storms when its owner failed to lash it down in time.

The sailors did, indeed, bring numerous hopeful-looking specimens back to the ship; but none of them could offer a practical suggestion as to what to do with his find. Dondragmer alone made what might be termed a successful trip; more imaginative than his fellows, he had thought to look *under* objects, and had indeed turned over a great many stones. He had been a little uneasy at first, but his nervousness had finally worn off completely; and a genuine enthusiasm for the new sport had possessed him. There were lots of things to be found under even quite heavy stones, he discovered; and he presently returned to the ship carrying a number of objects which everyone agreed must be eggs. Karondrasee took them in charge—no one was afraid of eating any sort of animal food—and presently the opinion was confirmed. They *were* eggs—very good, too. Only after they had been consumed did anyone think of hatching some of them to learn what sort of animal they might belong to; and with that thought voiced, Dondragmer carried it a step further by suggesting that perhaps they might hatch an animal which could serve in the place of the missing *ternee.* This idea was enthusiastically accepted, and parties sallied forth once more to look for eggs. The *Bree* had become practically an incubator by the time Lackland woke up.

Making sure that all the *Bree*'s crew had returned aboard, he restarted the tank and resumed the eastward journey. The hills grew higher in the next few days, and twice they crossed streams of methane, fortunately so narrow that the sled could actually bridge them. It was well that the rise in the hills was gradual, for there was a little uneasiness among the sailors whenever they had to look down any distance; but that, Barlennan reported, was gradually decreasing.

And then, some twenty days after the start of the second lap of the journey, their minds were taken completely off the terrors of height by something which seized and froze the attention of every living being on both vehicles.

7: Stone Defense

Up to this time, most of the hills had been gentle, smooth slopes, their irregularities long since worn off by weather. There had been no sign of the holes and crevasses which Lackland somewhat feared before starting. The hilltops had been smoothly rounded, so that even had their speed been much higher the crossing of one would hardly have been noticed. Now, however, as they topped such an acclivity and the landscape ahead came into view, a difference in the next hill caught every eye at once.

It was longer than most they had crossed, more a ridge across their path than a mound; but the great difference was in the top. Instead of the smooth, wind-worn curve presented by its fellows, it seemed at first glance actually jagged; a closer look showed that it was crowned with a row of boulders spaced with regularity that could only mean intelligent arrangement. The rocks ranged from monstrous things as big as Lackland's tank down to fragments of basketball size; and all, while rough in detail, were generally spherical in shape. Lackland brought his vehicle to an instant halt and seized his glasses—he was in partial armor, but was not wearing the helmet. Barlennan, forgetting the presence of his crew, made a leap over the twenty yards separating the *Bree* from the tank and settled firmly on top of the latter. A radio had been fastened there for his convenience long before, and he was talking almost before he had landed.

"What is it, Charles? Is that a city, such as you were telling me about on your own world? It doesn't look very much like your pictures."

"I was hoping you could tell me," was the answer. "It certainly is not a city, and the stones are too far apart for the most part to be any sort of wall or fort that I could imagine. Can you see anything moving around them? I can't with these glasses, but I don't know how keen your eyesight is."

"I can just see that the hilltop is irregular; if the things on top are loose stones, I'll have to take your word for it until we're closer. Certainly I can see nothing moving. Anything my size would be impossible to see at that distance anyway, I should think."

"I could see you at that range without these glasses, but I couldn't count your eyes or arms. With them I can say pretty certainly that that hilltop is deserted. Just the same, I'll practically guarantee that those stones didn't get there by accident; we'd better keep eyes open for whoever set them up. Better warn your crew." Lackland mentally noted the fact of Barlennan's poorer eyesight; he was not physicist enough to have predicted it from the size of the native's eyes.

For two or three minutes, while the sun moved far enough to reveal most of the areas previously in shadow, they waited and watched; but nothing except the shadows moved, and finally Lackland started the tank once more. The sun set while they were descending the slope. The tank had only one searchlight, which Lackland kept aiming at the ground in his path; so they could not see what, if anything, went on among the stones above. Sunrise found them just crossing another brook, and tension mounted as they headed uphill once more. For a minute or two nothing was visible, as the sun was directly ahead of the travelers; then it rose far enough to permit clear forward vision. None of the eyes fastened on the hilltop could detect any change from its appearance of the night before. There was a vague impression, which Lackland found was shared by the Mesklinites, that there were now more stones; but since no one had attempted to make a count of them before, this could not be proved. There was still no visible motion.

It took five or six minutes to climb the hill at the tank's five-mile speed, so the sun was definitely behind them when they reached the top. Lackland found that several of the gaps between the larger stones were wide enough for the tank and sled, and he angled toward one of these as he approached the crest of the ridge. He crunched over some of the smaller boulders, and for a moment Dondragmer, on the ship behind, thought one of them must have damaged the tank; for the machine came to an abrupt halt. Barlennan could be seen still on top of the vehicle, all his eyes fixed on the scene below him; the Flyer was not visible, of course, but after a moment the *Bree*'s mate decided that he, too, must be so interested in the valley beyond as to have forgotten about driving.

"Captain! What is it?" Dondragmer hurled the question even as he gestured the weapons crew to the flame tanks. The rest of the crew distributed themselves along the outer rafts, clubs, knives, and spears in readiness, without orders. For a long moment Barlennan gave no answer, and the mate was on the point of ordering a party overboard to cover the tank—he knew nothing of the nature of the jury-rigged quick-firer at Lackland's disposal—when his captain turned, saw what was going on, and gave a reassuring gesture.

"It's all right, I guess," he said. "We can see no one moving, but it looks a little like a town. Just a moment and the Flyer will pull you forward so that you can see without going overboard." He shifted back to English and made this request to Lackland, who promptly complied. This action produced an abrupt change in the situation.

What Lackland had seen at first—and Barlennan less clearly—was a broad, shallow, bowllike valley entirely surrounded by hills of the type they were on. There should, Lackland felt, have been a lake at the bottom; there was no visible means of escape for rain or melted snow. Then he noticed that there was no snow on the inner slopes of the hills; their topography was bare. And strange topography it was.

It could not possibly have been natural. Starting a short distance below the ridges were broad, shallow channels. They were remarkably regular in arrangement; a cross section of the hills taken just below where they started would have suggested a very pretty series of ocean waves. As the channels led on downhill toward the center of the valley they grew narrower and deeper, as though designed to lead rain water toward a central reservoir. Unfortunately for this hypothesis, they did not all meet in the center—they did not even all reach it, though all got as far as the relatively level, small floor of the valley. More interesting than the channels themselves were the elevations separating them. These, naturally, also grew more pronounced as the channels grew deeper; on the upper half of the slopes they were smoothly rounded ridges, but as the eye followed them down their sides grew steeper until they attained a perpendicular junction with the channel floors. A few of these little walls extended almost to the center of the valley. They did not all point toward the same spot; there were gentle curves in their courses that gave them the appearance of the flanges of a centrifugal pump rather than the spokes of a wheel. Their tops were too narrow for a man to walk on.

Lackland judged that channels and separating walls alike were some fifteen or twenty feet wide where they broke off. The walls themselves, therefore, were quite thick enough to be lived in, especially for Mesklinites; and the existence of numerous openings scattered over their lower surfaces lent strength to the idea that they actually were dwellings. The glasses showed that those openings not directly at the bottoms of the walls had ramps leading up to them; and before he saw a single living thing, Lackland was sure he was examining a city. Apparently the inhabitants lived in the separating walls, and had developed the entire structure in order to dispose of rain. Why they did not live on the outer slopes of the hills, if they wanted to avoid the liquid, was a question that did not occur to him.

He had reached this point in his thoughts when Barlennan asked him to pull the *Bree* over the brow of the hill before the sun made good seeing impossible. The moment the tank began to move, a score of dark figures appeared in the openings that he had suspected were doorways; no details were visible at that distance, but the objects, whatever they were, were living creatures. Lackland heroically refrained from stopping the tank and snatching up the glasses once more until he had pulled the *Bree* into a good viewing position.

As it turned out, there was no need for him to have hurried. The things remained motionless, apparently watching the newcomers, while the towing maneuver was completed; he was able to spend the remaining minutes before sunset in a careful examination of the beings. Even with the glasses some details were indistinguishable—for one reason, they seemed not to have emerged entirely from their dwellings; but what could be seen suggested strongly that they belonged to the same race as Barlennan's people. The bodies were long and caterpillarlike; several eyes—they were hard to count at that distance—were on the foremost body segment, and limbs very similar to if not identical with Barlennan's pincer-equipped arms were in evidence. The coloration was a mixture of red and black, the latter predominating as in the *Bree*'s complement.

Barlennan could not see all this, but Lackland relayed the description to him tensely until the city below faded from sight in the dusk. When he stopped talking the captain issued a boiled-down version in his own language to the tensely waiting crew When that was done Lackland asked:

"Have you ever heard of people living this close to the Rim, Barl? Would they be at all likely to be known to you, or even speak the same language?"

"I doubt it very much. My people become very uncomfortable, as you know, north of what you once called the 'hundred-G line.' I know several languages, but I can't see any likelihood of finding one of them spoken here."

"Then what shall we do? Sneak around this town, or go through it on the chance its people are not belligerent? I'd like to see it more closely, I admit, but we have an important job to do and I don't want to risk its chances of success. You at least know your race better than I possibly can; how do you think they'll react to us?"

"There's no one rule, there. They may be frightened out of their wits at your tank, or my riding on it—though they might not have normal instincts about height, here at the Rim. We've met lots of strange people in our wanderings, and sometimes we've been able to trade and sometimes we've had to fight. In general, I'd say if we kept weapons out of sight and trade goods in evidence, they would at least investigate before getting violent. I'd like to go down. Will the sled fit through the bottom of those channels, do you think?"

Lackland paused. "I hadn't thought of that," he admitted after a moment "I'd want to measure them more carefully first. Maybe it would be best if the tank went down alone first, with you and anyone else who cared for the ride traveling on top. That way we might look more peaceful, too—they must have seen the weapons your men were carrying, and if we leave them behind—"

"They didn't see any weapons unless their eyes are a great deal better than ours," pointed out Barlennan. "However, I agree that we'd better go down first and measure—or better yet, tow the ship around the valley first and go down afterward as a side trip; I see no need to risk her in those narrow channels."

"That's a thought Yes, I guess it would be the best idea, at that. Will you tell your crew what we've decided, and ask if any of to come down with us afterward?"

Barlennan agreed, and returned to the *Bree* for the purpose—he could speak in a lower tone there, although he did not feel that there was any real danger of being overheard and understood.

The crew in general accepted the advisability of taking the ship around rather than through the city, but from that point on there was a little difficulty. All of them wanted to see the town, but none would even consider riding on the tank, often as they had seen their captain do so without harm. Dondragmer broke the deadlock by suggesting that the crew, except for those left to guard the *Bree,* follow the tank into the town; there was no need to ride, since all could now keep up the speed the vehicle had been using up to this time.

The few minutes this discussion consumed brought the sun once more above the horizon; and at Barlennan's signal the Earthman swung the tank ninety degrees and started around the rim of the valley just below its coping of boulders. He had taken a look at the city before starting, and saw no sign of life; but as the tank and its tow swung into motion heads appeared once more at the small doors—many more of them, this time. Lackland was able to concentrate on his driving, sure now that their owners would still be there when he was free to examine them more closely. He attended to his job for the few days required to get the sled around to the far side of the valley; then the tow cable was cast off, and the nose of the tank pointed downhill.

Practically no steering was required; the vehicle tended to follow the course of the first channel it met, and went by itself toward the space which Lackland had come to regard—wholly without justification—as the market place of the town. Approximately half of the *Bree's* crew followed; the rest, under the second mate, remained as guards on the ship. Barlennan, as usual, rode on the tank's roof, with most of the small supply of trade goods piled behind him.

The rising sun was behind them as they approached from this side of the valley, so the seeing was good. There was much to see; some of the town's inhabitants emerged entirely from their dwellings as the strangers approached. Neither Lackland nor Barlennan attached any significance to the fact that all who did this were on the far side of the open space; those closer to the approaching travelers remained well under cover.

As the distance narrowed, one fact became evident; the creatures were not, in spite of initial appearances, of the same race as Barlennan. Similar they were, indeed; body shape, proportions, number of eyes and limbs—all matched; but the city dwellers were over three times the length of the travelers from the far south. Five feet in length they stretched over the stone floors of the channels, with body breadth and thickness to match.

Some of the things had reared the front third of their long bodies high into the air, in an evident effort to see better as the tank approached—an act that separated them from Barlennan's people as effectively as their size. These swayed a trifle from side to side as they watched, somewhat like the snakes Lackland had seen in museums on Earth. Except for this barely perceptible motion they did not stir as the strange metal monster crawled steadily down the channel it had chosen, almost disappeared as the walls which formed the homes of the city dwellers rose gradually to its roof on either side, and finally nosed its way out into the open central space of the town through what had become an alley barely wide enough for its bulk. If they spoke, it was too quietly for either Lackland or Barlennan to hear; even the gestures of pincer-bearing arms that took the place of so much verbal conversation with the Mesklinites Lackland knew was missing. The creatures simply waited and watched.

The sailors edged around the tank through the narrow space left—Lackland had just barely completed emerging from the alley—and stared almost as silently as the natives. Dwellings, to them, consisted of three-inch-high walls with fabric roofs for weather protection; the idea of a covering of solid material was utterly strange. If they had not been seeing with their own eyes the giant city dwellers actually inside the weird structures, Barlennan's men would have taken the latter for some new sort of natural formation.

Lackland simply sat at his controls, looked, and speculated. This was a waste of time, really, since he did not have enough data for constructive imagination; but he had the sort of mind that could not remain completely idle. He looked about the city and tried to picture the regular life of its inhabitants, until Barlennan's actions attracted his attention.

The captain did not believe in wasting time; he was going to trade with these people, and, if they wouldn't trade, he would move on. His action, which focused Lackland's attention on him, was to start tossing the packaged trade goods from the roof beside him, and calling to his men to get busy. This they did, once the packages had stopped falling. Barlennan himself leaped to the ground after the last bundle—an act which did not seem to bother in the least the silently watching giants—and joined in the task of preparing the goods for display. The Earthman watched with interest.

There were bolts of what looked like cloth of various colors, bundles that might have been dried roots or pieces of rope, tiny covered jars and larger empty ones—a good, varied display of objects whose purpose, for the most part, he could only guess at.

With the unveiling of this material the natives began to crowd forward, whether in curiosity or menace Lackland could not tell. None of the sailors showed visible apprehension—he had come to have some ability at recognizing this emotion in their kind. By the time their preparations seemed to be complete an almost solid ring of natives surrounded the tank. The way it had come was the only direction unblocked by their long bodies. The silence among the strange beings persisted, and was beginning to bother Lackland; but Barlennan was either indifferent to it or able to conceal his feelings. He picked an individual out of the crowd, using no particular method of choice that the Earthman could see, and began his selling program.

How he went about it Lackland was utterly unable to understand. The captain had said he did not expect these people to understand his language, yet he spoke; his gestures were meaningless to Lackland, though he used them freely. How any understanding could be transmitted was a complete mystery to the alien watcher; yet apparently Barlennan was having some degree of success. The trouble was, of course, that Lackland in his few months' acquaintance with the strange creatures had not gained more than the tiniest bit of insight into their psychology. He can hardly be blamed; professionals years later were still being puzzled by it. So much of the Mesklinite action and gesticulation is tied in directly with the physical functioning of their bodies that its meaning, seen by another member of the same race, is automatically clear; these giant city dwellers, though not of Barlennan's precise species, were similar enough in make-up so that communication was not the problem Lackland naturally assumed it would be.

In a fairly short time, numbers of the creatures were emerging from their homes with various articles which they apparently wished to trade, and other members of the *Bree*'s crew took active part in the bargaining. This continued as the sun swept across the sky and through the period of darkness—Barlennan asked Lackland to furnish illumination from the tank. If the artificial light bothered or surprised the giants at all, even Barlennan was unable to detect any signs of the fact. They paid perfect attention to the business at hand, and when one had gotten rid of what he had or acquired what he seemed to want, he would retire to his home and leave room for another. The natural result was that very few days passed before Barlennan's remaining trade goods had changed hands, and the articles freshly acquired were being transferred to the roof of the tank.

Most of these things were as strange to Lackland as the original trade materials had been; but two attracted his attention particularly. Both were apparently living animals, though he could not make out their details too well because of their small size. Both appeared to be domesticated; each stayed crouched at the side of the sailor who had purchased it, and evinced no desire to move away. Lackland guessed—correctly, as it turned out—that these were creatures of the sort the sailors had been hoping to raise in order to test possible plant foods.

"Is that all the trading you're going to do?" he called, as the last of the local inhabitants drifted away from the neighborhood of the tank.

"It's all we can do," replied Barlennan. "We have nothing more to trade. Have you any suggestions, or do you want to continue our journey now?"

"I'd like very much to find out what the interiors of those houses are like; but I couldn't possibly get through the doors, even if I could discard my armor. Would you or any of your people be willing to try to get a look inside?" Barlennan was a trifle hesitant.

"I'm not sure whether it would be wise. These people traded peacefully enough, but there's something about them that bothers me, though I can't exactly put a nipper on it. Maybe it's because they didn't argue enough over prices."

"You mean you don't trust them—you think they'll try to get back what they've given, now that you're out of trade goods?"

"I wouldn't say precisely that; as I said, I don't have actual reason for my feeling. I'll put it this way; if the tank gets back to the valley rim and hooked up to the ship so that we're all ready to go, and we've had no trouble from these things in the meantime, I'll come back down and take that look myself. Fair enough?"

Neither Barlennan nor Lackland had paid any attention to the natives during this conversation; but for the first time the city dwellers did not share this indifference. The nearer giants turned and eyed, with every indication of curiosity, the small box from which Lackland's voice was coming. As the talk went on, more and more of them drew near and listened; the spectacle of someone talking to a box too small, they knew, to contain any intelligent creature seemed, for the first time, to break down a wall of reserve that not even the tank had been able to affect. As Lackland's final agreement to Barlennan's suggestion came booming from the tiny speaker, and it became evident that the conversation was over, several of the listeners disappeared hastily into their homes and emerged almost at once with more objects. These they presented, with gestures which the sailors now understood quite well. The giants wanted the radio, and were willing to pay handsomely for it.

Barlennan's refusal seemed to puzzle them. Each in turn offered a higher price than his predecessor. At last Barlennan made an ultimate refusal in the only way he could; he tossed the set onto the roof of the tank, leaped after it, and ordered his men to resume throwing the newly acquired property up to him. For several seconds the giants seemed nonplused; then, as though by signal, they turned away and disappeared into their narrow doorways.

Barlennan felt more uneasy than ever, and kept watch on as many portals as his eyes could cover while he stowed the newly bought goods; but it was not from the dwellings that the danger came. It was the great Hars who saw it, as he half reared himself over his fellows in imitation of the natives to toss a particularly bulky package up to his captain. His eye chanced to rove back up the channel they had descended; and as it did so he gave one of the incredibly loud hoots which never failed to amaze—and startle—Lackland. He followed the shriek with a burst of speech which meant nothing to the Earthman; but Barlennan understood, looked, and said enough in English to get the important part across.

"Charles! Look back uphill! *Move!*"

Lackland looked, and in the instant of looking understood completely the reason for the weird layout of the city. One of the giant boulders, fully half the size of the tank, had become dislodged from its position on the valley rim. It had been located just above the wide mouth of the channel down which the tank had come; the slowly rising walls were guiding it squarely along the path the vehicle had followed. It was still half a mile away and far above; but its downward speed was building up each instant as its tons of mass yielded to the tug of a gravity three times as strong as that of the Earth!

8: Cure for Acrophobia

Flesh and blood have their limits as far as speed is concerned, but Lackland came very close to setting new ones. He did not stop to solve any differential equations which would tell him the rock's time of arrival; he threw power into the motors, turned the tank ninety degrees in a distance that threatened to twist off one of its treads, and got out from the mouth of the channel which was guiding the huge projectile toward him. Only then did he really come to appreciate the architecture of the city. The channels did not come straight into the open space, as he had noticed; instead, they were so arranged that at least two could guide a rock across any portion of the plaza. His action was sufficient to dodge the first, but it had been foreseen; and more rocks were already on their way. For a moment he looked around in all directions, in a futile search for a position which was not about to be traversed by one of the terrible projectiles; then he deliberately swung the nose of the tank into one of the channels and started uphill. There was a boulder descending this one too; a boulder which to Barlennan seemed the biggest of the lot—and to be growing bigger each second. The Mesklinite gathered himself for a leap, wondering if the Flyer had lost his senses; then a roar that outdid anything his own vocal apparatus could produce sounded beside him. If his nervous system had reacted like that of most Earthly animals he would have landed halfway up the hill. The startle reaction of his race, however, was to freeze motionless, so for the next few seconds it would have taken heavy machinery to get him off the tank roof. Four hundred yards away, fifty yards ahead of the plunging rock, a section of the channel erupted into flame and dust—the fuses on Lackland's shells were sensitive enough to react instantly even to such grazing impact. An instant later the rock hurtled into the dust cloud, and the quick-firer roared again, this time emitting half a dozen barks that blended almost indistinguishably with each other. A fair half of the boulder emerged from the dust cloud, no longer even roughly spherical. The energy of the shells had stopped it almost completely; friction took care of the rest long before it reached the tank. It now had too many flat and concave surfaces to roll very well.

There were other boulders in position to roll down this channel, but they did not come. Apparently the giants were able to analyze a new situation with fair speed, and realized that this method was not going to destroy the tank. Lackland had no means of knowing what else they might do, but the most obvious possibility was a direct personal attack. They could certainly, or almost certainly, get to the top of the tank as easily as Barlennan and repossess everything they had sold as well as the radio; it was hard to see how the sailors were to stop them. He put this thought to Barlennan.

"They may try that, indeed," was the answer. "However, if they try to climb up we can strike down at them; if they jump we have our clubs, and I do not see how anyone can dodge a blow while sailing through the air."

"But how can you hold off alone an attack from several directions at once?"

"I am not alone." Once again came the pincer gesture that was the Mesklinite equivalent of a smile.

Lackland could see the roof of his tank only by sticking his head up into a tiny, transparent view dome, and he could not do this with the helmet of his armor on. Consequently he had not seen the results of the brief "battle" as they applied to the sailors who had accompanied him into the city.

These unfortunates had been faced with a situation as shocking as had their captain when he first found himself on the roof of the tank. They had seen objects—heavy objects—actually *falling* on them, while they themselves were trapped in an area surrounded by vertical walls. To climb was unthinkable, though the sucker-feet which served them so well in Mesklin's hurricanes would have served as adequately in this task; to jump as they had now seen their captain do several times was almost as bad—perhaps worse. It was not, however, physically impossible; and when minds fail, bodies are apt to take over. Every sailor but two jumped; one of the two exceptions climbed—rapidly and well—up the wall of a "house." The other was Hars, who had first seen the danger. Perhaps his superior physical strength made him slower than the others to panic; perhaps he had more than the normal horror of height. Whatever the reason, he was still on the ground when a rock the size of a basketball and almost as perfectly round passed over the spot he was occupying. For practical purposes, it might as well be considered to have struck an equivalent volume of live rubber; the protective "shell" of the Mesklinites was of a material chemically and physically analogous to the chitin of Earthly insects, and had a toughness and elasticity commensurate with the general qualities of Mesklinite life. The rock bounded twenty-five feet into the air against three gravities, hurtling entirely over the wall which would normally have brought it to a stop, struck at an angle the wall of the channel on the other side, rebounded, and went clattering from wall to wall up the new channel until its energy was expended. By the time it had returned, in more leisurely fashion, to the open space the main action was over; Hars was the only sailor still in the plaza. The rest had brought some degree of control into their originally frantic jumps and had either already reached the top of the tank beside their captain or were rapidly getting there; even the climber had changed his method of travel to the more rapid leaping.

Hars, unbelievably tough as he was by terrestrial standards, could not take the sort of punishment he had just received completely without injury. He did not have his breath knocked out, since he lacked lungs, but he was scraped, bruised, and dazed by the impact. Fully a minute passed before he could control his motions sufficiently to make a co-ordinated attempt to follow the tank; why he was not attacked during that minute neither Lackland, Barlennan, nor Hars himself was ever able to explain satisfactorily. The Earthman thought that the fact that he was able to move at all after such a blow had frightened any such thoughts out of the minds of the city dwellers; Barlennan, with a more accurate idea of Mesklinite physique, thought that they were more interested in stealing than in killing and simply saw no advantage in attacking the lone sailor. Whatever the reason, Hars was permitted to regain his senses in his own time and, eventually, to regain the company of his fellows. Lackland, finally brought up to date on just what had happened, waited for him; when he finally reached the vehicle two of the crew had to descend and practically throw him to the roof, where the rest promptly undertook first-aid measures.

With all his passengers safely aboard, some of them crowded so close to the edge of the roof that their new-found indifference to height was a trifle strained, Lackland headed uphill once more. He had warned the sailors to keep clear of the gun muzzle, and kept the weapon trained ahead of him; but there was no motion on the ridge, and no more rocks fell. Apparently the natives who had launched them had retreated to the tunnels which evidently led up from their city. This, however, was no assurance that they would not come out again; and everyone on and in the tank kept a sharp lookout for any sort of motion.

The channel they were climbing was not the same as the one they had descended, and consequently did not lead directly to the sled; but the *Bree* became visible some distance before they reached the top, owing to the tank's height. The crew members who had been left behind were still there, all looking with evident anxiety down into the city. Dondragmer muttered something in his own language concerning the stupidity of not keeping an all-around watch, which Barlennan repeated in amplified form in English. However, the worry proved fruitless; the tank reached the stranded sled, turned, and was hitched up to its load without further interference. Lackland, once more under way, decided that the giants had overestimated the effectiveness of the gun; an attack from close quarters—emerging, for example, from the concealed tunnel mouths which must shelter the individuals who started the rocks downhill—would leave the weapon completely helpless, since neither high explosive nor thermite shells could be used close to the *Bree* or her crew.

With great reluctance he decided that there could be no more exploration until the *Bree* had reached the waters of the eastern ocean. Barlennan, when this conclusion was offered for his consideration, agreed, though he made some reservations in his own mind. Certainly while the Flyer slept his own crew was going to keep working.

With the expedition once more under way and the tangible results of the interruption rapidly being transferred from tank roof to ship by leaping Mesklinites, Lackland made a call to Toorey, listened humbly to the expected blast when Rosten learned what he had been doing, and silenced him as before with the report that much plant tissue was now available if Rosten would send down containers for it.

By the time the rocket had landed far enough ahead of them to preserve the Mesklinite nervous systems, had waited for their arrival, picked up the new specimens, and waited once more until the tank had traveled safely out of range of its takeoff blast, many more days had passed. These, except for the rocket's visit, were relatively uneventful. Every few miles a boulder-rimmed hilltop was sighted, but they carefully avoided these, and none of the giant natives were seen outside their cities. This fact rather worried Lackland, who could not imagine where or how they obtained food. With nothing but the relatively boring job of driving to occupy his mind, he naturally formed many hypotheses about the strange creatures. These he occasionally outlined to Barlennan, but that worthy was not much help in deciding among them, and Lackland got little of value from their conversations.

One of his own ideas, however, bothered him. He had been wondering just why the giants built their cities in such a fashion. They could hardly have been expecting either the tank or the *Bree*. It seemed a rather impractical way to repel invasion by others of their own kind, who evidently, from the commonness of the custom, could hardly be taken by surprise.

Still, there was a possible reason. It was just a hypothesis; but it would account for the city design, and for the lack of natives in the country outside, and for the absence of anything resembling farm lands in the neighborhood of the cities. It involved a lot of "iffing" on Lackland's part even to think of such an idea in the first place, and he did not mention it to Barlennan. For one thing, it left unexplained the fact that they had come this far unmolested—if the idea were sound, they should by now have used up a great deal more of the quick-firer's ammunition. He said nothing, therefore, and merely kept his own eyes open; but he was not too surprised, one sunrise when they had come perhaps two hundred miles from the city where Hars received his injuries, to see a small hillock ahead of the cavalcade suddenly rear up on a score of stubby, elephantine legs, lift as far as possible a head mounted on a twenty-foot neck, stare for a long moment out of a battery of eyes, and then come lumbering to meet the oncoming tank.

Barlennan for once was not riding in his usual station on the roof, but he responded at once to Lackland's call. The Earthman had stopped the tank, and there were several minutes to decide on a course of action before the beast would reach them at its present rate of speed.

"Barl, I'm willing to bet you've never seen anything like that. Even with tissue as tough as your planet produces, it could never carry its own weight very far from the equator."

"You are quite right; I haven't. I have never heard of it, either, and don't know whether or not it's likely to be dangerous. I'm not sure I want to find out, either. Still, it's meat; maybe..."

"If you mean you don't know whether it eats meat or vegetables, I'll bet on the former," replied Lackland. "It would be a very unusual plant-eater that would come toward something even larger than itself immediately upon sighting it—unless it's stupid enough to think the tank is a female of its own species, which I very much doubt. Also, I was thinking that a large flesh-eater was the easiest way to explain why the giants never seem to come out of their cities, and have them built into such efficient traps. They probably lure any of these things that come to their hilltop by showing themselves at the bottom, as they did with us, and then kill them with rocks as they tried on the tank. It's one way of having meat delivered to your front door."

"All that may be true, but is not of present concern," Barlennan replied with some impatience. "Just what should we do with this one? That weapon of yours that broke up the rock would probably kill it, but might not leave enough meat worth collecting; while if we go out with the nets we'll be too close for you to use it safely should we get in trouble."

"You mean you'd consider using your nets on a thing that size?"

"Certainly. They would hold it, I'm sure, if only we could get it into them. The trouble is that its feet are too big to go through the meshes, and our usual method of maneuvering them into its path wouldn't do much good. We'd have to get the nets around its body and limbs somehow, and then pull them tight."

"Have you a method in mind?"

"No—and we wouldn't have time to do much of the sort anyway; he'll be here in a moment."

"Jump down and unhitch the sled. I'll take the tank forward and keep him occupied for a while, if you want. If you decide to take him on, and get in trouble later, you all should be able to jump clear before I use the gun."

Barlennan followed the first part of the suggestion without hesitation or argument, slipping off the rear of the deck and undoing with a single deft motion the hitch which held the tow cable to the tank. Giving a hoot to let Lackland know the job was done, he sprang aboard the *Bree* and quickly gave his crew the details of the new situation. They could see for themselves by the time he had finished, for the Flyer had moved the tank forward and to one side, clearing their line of sight to the great animal. For a short time they watched with much interest, some astonishment, but no fear to speak of as the tank maneuvered with its living counterpart.

The creature stopped as the machine resumed its forward motion. Its head dropped down to a yard or so from the ground, and the long neck swung as far as possible first to one side and then the other, while the multiple eyes took in the situation from all possible angles. It paid no attention to the *Bree;* either it failed to notice the small movements of the crew, or regarded the tank as a more pressing problem. As Lackland moved toward one flank, it slewed its gigantic body around to keep facing it squarely. For a moment the Earthman thought of driving it into a full hundred-and-eighty-degree turn, so that it would be facing directly away from the ship; then he remembered that this would put the *Bree* in his line of fire should he have to use the gun, and stopped the circling maneuver when the stranded sled was at the monster's right. With that eye arrangement, it would be as likely to see the sailors moving behind it as in front, anyway, he reflected.

Once more he moved toward the animal. It had settled down, belly to the ground, when he stopped circling; now it rose once more to its many legs and drew its head back almost into its great trunk, in what was apparently a protective gesture. Lackland stopped once more, seized a camera, and took several photographs of the creature; then, since it seemed in no mood to press an attack, he simply looked it over for a minute or two.

Its body was a trifle larger than that of an Earthly elephant; on Earth, it might have weighed eight or ten tons. The weight was distributed about evenly among the ten pairs of legs, which were short and enormously thick. Lackland doubted that the creature could move much faster than it had already.

After a minute or two of waiting, the creature began to grow restless; its head protruded a little and began to swing back and forth as though looking for other enemies. Lackland, fearing that its attention would become focused on the now helpless *Bree* and her crew, moved the tank forward another couple of feet; his adversary promptly resumed its defensive attitude. This was repeated several times, at intervals which grew progressively shorter. The feinting lasted until the sun sank behind the hill to the west; as the sky grew dark Lackland, not knowing whether the beast would be willing or able to carry on a battle at night, modified the situation by turning on all the tank's lights. This, at least, would presumably prevent the creature from seeing anything in the darkness beyond, even if it were willing to face what to it must be a new and strange situation.

Quite plainly, it did not like the lights. It blinked several times as the main spotlight burned into its eyes, and Lackland could see the great pupils contract; then, with a wailing hiss that was picked up by the roof speaker and clearly transmitted to the man inside, it lumbered a few feet forward and struck.

Lackland had not realized that he was so close—or, more correctly, that the thing could reach so far. The neck, even longer than he had at first estimated, snapped to full length, carrying the massive head forward and a trifle to one side. As it reached full travel, the head tipped a trifle and came slashing sideways. One of the great tusks clanged resoundingly against the tank's armor, and the main light went out in the same instant. Another, shriller hiss suggested to Lackland that the current feeding the light had grounded into the armor through some portion of the monster's head; but he was not taking time out to analyze the possibility. He backed away hastily, cutting the cabin lights as he did so. He did not want one of those tusks striking a cabin port with the force it had just expended on the upper armor. Now only the running lights, mounted low in the front of the vehicle and set well into the armor, were illuminating the scene. The animal, encouraged by Lackland's retreat, lurched forward again and struck at one of these. The Earthman did not dare extinguish it, since it would have left him effectively blind; but he sent a frantic call on the radio.

"Barl! Are you doing anything about your nets? If you're not about ready for action, I'm going to have to use the gun on this thing, meat or no meat. You'll have to stay away if I do; he's so close that high explosive would endanger the tank, and I'll have to use thermite."

"The nets are not ready, but if you'll lead him back a few more yards he'll be downwind of the ship, and we can take care of him another way."

"All right." Lackland did not know what the other way could be, and was more than a little doubtful of its effectiveness, whatever it was; but as long as retreat would suit the captain he was prepared to co-operate. It did not for an instant occur to him that Barlennan's weapon might endanger the tank; and, in all fairness, it probably did not occur to Barlennan either. The Earthman, by dint of repeated and hasty withdrawals, kept the tusks from his plating most of the time; the monster did not seem to have the intelligence to anticipate motion on his part. Two or three minutes of this dodging satisfied Barlennan.

He, too, had been busy in those minutes. On the leeward rafts, toward the dueling monster and machine, were four devices closely resembling bellows, with hoppers mounted above their nozzles. Two sailors were now at each bellows, and at their captain's signal began pumping for all they were worth. At the same time a third operator manipulated the hopper and sent a stream of fine dust flowing into the current from the nozzle. This was picked up by the wind and carried toward the combatants. The darkness made it difficult to estimate its progress; but Barlennan was a good judge of wind, and after a few moments of pumping suddenly snapped out another order.

The hopper crews promptly did something at the nozzle of the bellows each was tending; and as they did so, a roaring sheet of flame spread downwind from the *Bree* to envelop both of the fighters. The ship's crew were already sheltered behind their tarpaulins, even the "gunners" being protected by flaps of fabric that formed part of their weapons; but the vegetation that sprouted through the snow was neither tall nor dense enough to shelter the fighters. Lackland, using words that he had never taught Barlennan, hurled the tank backward out of the flame cloud with a prayer for the quartz in his portholes. His adversary, though evidently as anxious to dodge, seemed to lack the necessary control. It lurched first one way, then the other, seeking escape. The flame died out in seconds, leaving a cloud of dense white smoke which gleamed in the tank's running lights; but either the brief fire had been sufficient or the smoke was equally deadly, for the monster's disorganization grew steadily worse. Its aimless steps grew shorter and feebler as the legs gradually lost the power to support its vast bulk, and presently it stumbled and rolled on one side. The legs kicked frantically for a time, while the long neck alternately retracted and stretched to full length, lashing the fanged head frantically through the air and against the ground. By sunrise the only remaining motion was an occasional twitch of head or leg; within a minute or two thereafter all activity of the giant creature ceased. The crew of the *Bree* had already swarmed overboard and across the dark patch where the snow had boiled from the ground, bent on acquiring meat. The deadly white cloud was farther downwind now, and gradually settling. Lackland was surprised to note traces of *black* dust on the snow where the cloud had passed.

"Barl, what on Earth—or rather, on Mesklin—was the stuff you used for that fire cloud? And didn't it occur to you that it might crack the windows in this tank?" The captain, who had remained on the ship and was near one of his radios, answered promptly.

"I'm sorry, Charles; I didn't know what your windows are made of, and never thought of our flame cloud as a danger to your great machine. I will be more careful next time. The fuel is simply a dust which we obtain from certain plants—it is found as fairly large crystals, which we have to pulverize very carefully and away from all light." Lackland nodded slowly, digesting this information. His chemical knowledge was slight, but it was sufficient to make a good guess at the fuel's nature. Ignited by light—burned in hydrogen with a white cloud—black specks on the snow—it could, as far as he knew, be only one thing. Chlorine is solid at Mesklin's temperature; it combines violently with hydrogen, and hydrogen chloride is white when in fine powder form; methane snow boiled from the ground would also give up its hydrogen to the voracious element and leave carbon. Interesting plant life this world sported! He must make another report to Toorey—or perhaps he had better save this tidbit in case he annoyed Rosten again.

"I am very sorry I endangered your tank." Barlennan still seemed to feel apologetic. "Perhaps we had better let you deal with such creatures with your gun; or perhaps you could teach us to use it. Is it, like the radios, especially built to work on Mesklin?" The captain wondered if he had gone too far with this suggestion, but decided it had been worth it. He could neither see nor interpret Lackland's answering smile.

"No, the gun was not remade or changed for this world, Barl. It works fairly well here, but I'm afraid it would be pretty useless in your country." he picked up a slide rule, and added one more sentence after employing it for a moment. "The farthest this thing could possibly shoot at your pole would be just about one hundred fifty feet."

Barlennan, disappointed, said nothing further. Several days were spent in butchering the dead monster. Lackland salvaged the skull as a further protection from Rosten's ire, and the cavalcade resumed its journey.

Mile after mile, day after day, the tank and its tow inched onward. Still they sighted occasional cities of the rock-rollers; two or three tines they picked up food for Lackland which had been left in their path by the rocket; quite frequently they encountered large animals, some like the one Barlennan's fire had slain, others very different in size and build. Twice specimens of giant herbivores were netted and killed by the crew to furnish meat, much to Lackland's admiration. The discrepancy in size was far greater than that existing between Earthly elephants and the African pygmies who sometimes hunted them.

The country grew hillier as they progressed, and with the rising ground the river, which they had followed intermittently for hundreds of miles, shrank and split into numerous smaller streams. Two of these tributaries had been rather difficult to cross, requiring that the *Bree* be unlashed from the sled and floated across at the end of a towrope while tank and sled drove below the surface on the river bed. Now, however, the streams had become so narrow that the sled actually bridged them and no such delays occurred.

At long last, fully twelve hundred miles from where the *Bree* had wintered and some three hundred south of the equator, with Lackland bowing under an additional half gravity, the streams began to bear definitely in the general direction of their travel. Both Lackland and Barlennan let several days pass before mentioning it, wishing to be sure, but at last there was no more doubt that they were in the watershed leading to the eastern ocean. Morale, which had never been low, nevertheless improved noticeably; and several sailors could now always be found on the tank's roof hoping for the first glimpse of the sea as they reached each hilltop. Even Lackland, tired sometimes to the point of nausea, brightened up; and as his relief was the greater, so proportionately greater was his shock and dismay when they came, with practically no warning, to the edge of an escarpment; an almost sheer drop of over sixty feet, stretching as far as the eye could see at right angles to their course.

9: Over the Edge

For long moments nothing was said. Both Lackland and Barlennan, who had worked so carefully over the photographs from which the map of their journey had been prepared, were far too astonished to speak. The crew, though by no means devoid of initiative, decided collectively and at the first glance to leave this problem to their captain and his alien friend.

"How could it have been there?" Barlennan was first to speak. "I can see it's not high, compared to the vessel from which your pictures were taken, but should it not have cast a shadow far across the country below, in the minutes before sunset?"

"It should, Barl, and I can think of only one reason it escaped us. Each picture, you recall, covered many square miles; one alone would include all the land we can see from here, and much more. The picture that does cover this area must have been made between sunrise and noon, when there would have been no shadow."

"Then this cliff does not extend past the boundary of that one picture?"

"Possibly; or, just as possibly, it chanced that two or three adjacent shots were all made in the morning—I don't know just what course the photo rocket flew. If, as I should imagine, it went east and west, it wouldn't be too great a coincidence for it to pass the cliff several times running at about the same time of day.

"Still, there's little point in going through that question. The real problem, since the cliff obviously *does* exist, is how to continue our journey." That question produced another silence, which lasted for some time. It was broken, to the surprise of at least two people, by the first mate.

"Would it not be advisable to have the Flyer's friends far above learn for us just how far this cliff extends to either side? It may be possible to descend an easier slope without too great a detour. It should not be hard for them to make new maps, if this cliff was missed on the first." Barlennan translated this remark, which was made in the mate's own language. Lackland raised his eyebrows.

"Your friend may as well speak English himself, Barl—he appears to know enough to understand our last conversation. Or do you have some means of communicating it to him that I don't know about?"

Barlennan whirled on his mate, startled and, after a moment, confused. He had not reported the conversation to Dondragmer; evidently the Flyer was right—his mate had learned some English. Unfortunately, however, the second guess had also some truth; Barlennan had long been sure that many of the sounds his vocal apparatus could produce were not audible to the Earthman, though he could not guess at the reason. For several seconds he was confused, trying to decide whether it would be better to reveal Dondragmer's ability, the secret of their communication, both together, or, if he could talk fast enough, neither. Barlennan did the best he could.

"Apparently Dondragmer is sharper than I realized. Is it true that you have learned some of the Flyer's language, Don?" This he asked in English, and in a pitch that Lackland could hear. In the shriller tones that his own language employed so much he added, "Tell the truth—I want to cover up as long as possible the fact that we can talk without his hearing. Answer in his own language, if you can." The mate obeyed, though not even his captain could have guessed at his thoughts.

"I have learned much of your language, Charles Lackland. I did not realize you would object."

"I don't mind at all, Don; I am very pleased and, I admit, surprised. I would gladly have taught you as well as Barl if you had come to my station. Since you have learned on your own—I suppose from comparing our conversations and your captain's resultant activities—please enter our discussion. The suggestion you made a moment ago was sound; I will call the Toorey station at once."

The operator on the moon answered immediately, since a constant guard was now being maintained on the tank's main transmitter frequency through several relay stations drifting in Mesklin's outer ring. He indicated understanding of the problem, and promised that a survey would be made as quickly as possible.

"As quickly as possible," however, meant quite a number of Mesklin's days; and while waiting the trio endeavored to formulate other plans in case the cliff could not be rounded within a reasonable distance.

One or two of the sailors expressed a willingness to jump down the cliff, to Barlennan's anxiety—he felt that the natural fear of height should not be replaced with *complete* contempt, even though the entire crew now shared his willingness to climb and jump. Lackland was called upon to help dissuade these foolhardy individuals, which he managed to do by computing that the sixty-foot drop of the cliff was about equal to a one-foot fall at the latitude of their home country. This revived enough memory of childhood experience to put a stop to the idea. The captain, thinking over this event afterward, realized that by his own lifelong standards he had a crew composed entirely of lunatics, with himself well to the front in degree of aberration; but he was fairly sure that this particular form of insanity was going to be useful.

Ideas more practical than these were not forthcoming for some time; and Lackland took the opportunity to catch up on his sleep, which he badly needed. He had had two long sessions in his bunk, interrupted by a hearty meal, when the report of the surveying rocket came in. It was brief and discouraging. The cliff ran into the sea some six hundred miles northeast of their present location, almost exactly on the equator. In the opposite direction it ran for some twelve hundred miles, growing very gradually lower, and disappearing completely at about the five-gravity latitude. It was not perfectly straight, showing a deep bend away from the ocean at one point; the tank had struck it at this point. Two rivers fell over its edge within the limits of the bay, and the tank was neatly caught between them, since in the interests of common sanity the *Bree* could never be towed across either without first going many miles upstream from the tremendous cataracts. One of the falls was about thirty miles away, almost due south; the other approximately a hundred miles distant to the north and east around the curve of the cliff. The rocket had not, of course, been able to examine the entire stretch of escarpment in complete detail from the altitude it had had to maintain, but the interpreter was very doubtful that the tank could scale it at any point. The best bet, however, would be near one of the falls, where erosion was visible and might conceivably have created negotiable paths.

"How in blazes can a cliff like this form?" Lackland asked resentfully when he had heard all this. "Eighteen hundred miles of ridge just high enough to be a nuisance, and we have to run right into it. I bet it's the only thing of its kind on the planet."

"Don't bet too much," the surveyor retorted. "The physiography boys just nodded in pleasure when I told them about it. One of them said he was surprised you hadn't hit one earlier; then another piped up and said actually you'd expect most of them farther from the equator, so it wasn't surprising at all. They were still at it when I left them. I guess you're lucky that your small friend is going to do most of the traveling for you."

"That's a thought." Lackland paused as another idea struck him. "If these faults are so common, you might tell me whether there are any more between here and the sea. Will you have to run another survey?"

"No. I saw the geologists before I started on this one, and looked. If you can get down this step, you're all right—in fact, you could launch your friend's ship in the river at the foot and he could make it alone. Your only remaining problem is to get that sailboat hoisted over the edge."

"To get—hmm. I know you meant that figuratively, Hank, but you may have something there. Thanks for everything; I may want to talk to you later." Lackland turned away from the set and lay back on his bunk, thinking furiously. He had never seen the *Bree* afloat; she had been beached before he encountered Barlennan, and on the recent occasions when he had towed her across rivers he had himself been below the surface most of the time in the tank. Therefore he did not know how high the vessel floated. Still, to float at all on an ocean of liquid methane she must be extremely light, since methane is less than half as dense as water. Also she was not hollow—did not float, that is, by virtue of a large central air space which lowered her average density, as does a steel ship on Earth. The "wood" of which the *Bree* was made was light enough to float on methane and support the ship's crew and a substantial cargo as well.

An individual raft, therefore, could not weigh more than a few ounces—perhaps a couple of pounds, on this world at this point. At that rate, Lackland himself could stand on the edge of the cliff and let down several rafts at a time; any two sailors could probably lift the ship bodily, if they could be persuaded to get under it. Lackland himself had no rope or cable other than what he was using to tow the sled; but that was one commodity of which the *Bree* herself had an ample supply. The sailors should certainly he able to rig hoisting gear that would take care of the situation—or could they? On Earth it would be elementary seamanship; on Mesklin, with these startling but understandable prejudices against lifting and jumping and throwing and everything else involving any height, the situation might be different. Well, Barlennan's sailors could at least tie knots, and the idea of towing should not be too strange to them now; so undoubtedly the matter could be straightened out. The real, final problem was whether or not the sailors would object to being lowered over the cliff along with their ship. Some men might have laid that question aside as strictly a problem for the ship's captain, but Lackland more than suspected that he would have to contribute to its solution.

Barlennan's opinion, however, was certainly needed at this point; and reaching out a heavy arm, Lackland energized his smaller transmitter and called his tiny friend.

"Barl, I've been wondering. Why couldn't your people lower the ship over the cliff on cables, one raft at a time, and reassemble it at the bottom?"

"How would you get down?"

"I wouldn't. There is a large river about thirty miles south of here that should be navigable all the way to the sea, if Hank Stearman's report is accurate. What I'm suggesting is that I tow you over to the fall, help you any way I can in getting the *Bree* over the edge, watch you launch her in the river, and wish you the best of luck—all we can do for you from then on is give weather and navigation information, as we agreed. You have ropes, do you not, which will hold the weight of a raft?"

"Of course; ordinary cordage would take the weight of the entire ship in this neighborhood. We'd have to snub the lines against trees or your tank or something like that; the whole crew together couldn't furnish traction enough for the job. Still, that's no problem. I'd say you had the answer, Charles."

"How about the personnel? Will they like the idea of being lowered down that way?" Barlennan thought for a moment.

"I think it will be all right. I'll send them down on the rafts, with a job to do like fending off from the cliff. That will keep them from looking straight down, and sufficiently occupied so they shouldn't be thinking of the height. Anyway, with this light feeling everyone has"—Lackland groaned silently—"no one's much afraid of a fall anyway; not even as much as they should be. We'll make that part, all right. Had we better start for that cataract right away?"

"All right." Lackland hauled himself to his controls, suddenly very weary. His part of the job was nearly over, sooner than he had expected, and his body shrieked for relief from the endless weight it had dragged around for the last seven months. Perhaps he shouldn't have stayed through the winter, but tired as he was, he could not regret it.

The tank swung to the right and started moving once more, parallel to the cliff edge two hundred yards away. The Mesklinites might be getting over their horror of heights, but Lackland was developing one. Besides, he had never attempted to repair the main spotlight since their first battle with Mesklin's animal life, and he had no intention of driving close to that edge at night with only the running lights to guide him.

They made the cataract in a single lap of about twenty days. Both natives and Earthman heard it long before they arrived, at first a vague trembling in the air that gradually rose through a muted thunder to a roar that put even the Mesklinite vocal equipment to shame. It was day when they came in sight of it, and Lackland stopped involuntarily as they did so. The river was half a mile wide where it reached the brink, and smooth as glass—no rocks or other irregularities appeared to exist in its bed. It simply curled over the edge and spilled downward. The fall had eroded its way for a full mile back from the cliff line; and they had a splendid view of the gorge. The ripple marks gave no clue to the liquid's speed of fall, but the violence with which the spray erupted from the bottom did. Even in this gravity and atmosphere a permanent cloud of mist hid the lower half of the curved sheet, thinning gradually away from its foot to reveal the roiled, eddied surface of the lower river. There was no wind except that created by the fall itself, and the stream grew rapidly calmer as it moved smoothly away toward the ocean.

The crew of the *Bree* had gone overboard the moment the tank stopped; and the way they were strung out along the rim of the gorge indicated that there would not be much morale difficulty during the descent. Now Barlennan called them back to the ship, and work commenced at once. Lackland relaxed once more while cordage was dragged forth and a plumb line dropped over the edge to secure a more precise measure of the cliff's height. Some of the sailors began securing all loose gear about the rafts, though preparations for the original journey had left little to do in this respect; others reached down between the rafts and began unfastening the lashings which held them together and checking at the same time the buffers that held them safely apart. They were fast workers, and raft after raft was dragged away from the main body of the ship.

Barlennan and his first mate, once this work was well under way, went over to the edge to determine the best place for the lowering operation. The gorge itself was rejected at once; the river within its walls was too rough, even if they had wanted to do their reassembling while afloat. It turned out, however, that almost any point on the cliff face would be suitable, so the officers quickly chose one as close as possible to the mouth of the gorge. The reassembled ship or its separate parts would have to be dragged to the river without the tank's help, and there was no point in making the journey any longer than necessary.

A scaffold of masts was arranged at the edge to give a point of suspension far enough out to prevent rope friction, though the masts were not long enough to hold a raft completely away from the cliff face; a block and tackle, which Lackland observed with interest, was attached to the scaffold, and the first raft dragged into position. It was adjusted in a rope sling that would carry it horizontally, the main cable attached to the sling and hitched around a tree, several sailors seized the cable, and the raft was pushed over the edge.

Everything held up, but Dondragmer and his captain inspected each part very, very carefully before the mate and one of the crew crawled aboard the platform that hung somewhat slanted against the rock an inch or so below the edge. For a moment after they had gone aboard everyone watched expectantly; but again nothing happened, and Dondragmer finally gave the signal to lower away. All the crew members who were not on the cable rushed to the edge to watch the descent. Lackland would have liked to watch it himself, but had no intention of venturing either the tank or his armored person close enough to do so. Beside his own uneasiness at the height, the sight of the cordage the Mesklinites were using made him unhappy; it looked as though an Earthly clerk would scorn it for tying a two-pound bag of sugar.

An excited hooting and general withdrawal from the edge indicated the safe arrival of the first raft, and Lackland blinked as the sailors proceeded to stack several more on top of each other while the cable was being drawn up. Apparently no more time than could be helped was to be wasted. Confident as he was in Barlennan's judgment, the Earthman suddenly decided he wanted to watch the stack of rafts make the descent. He was on the point of donning his armor when he remembered that it was not necessary; he relaxed again, called Barlennan, and asked him to arrange one or more of the little communicators so that their "eyes" could cover the desired activity. The captain complied immediately, having a sailor lash one of the sets to the scaffold so that it looked almost straight down and placing another on top of the pile of rafts which had just been secured in their rope sling. Lackland switched from one to the other as the operation proceeded. The first was a trifle more disconcerting than he had expected, since the supporting cable was visible for only a few feet from the pickup lens and the load seemed to be floating down without support; the other gave him a view of the cliff face that would undoubtedly have been highly interesting to a geologist. With the descent half completed, it occurred to him to call Toorey to invite the interested parties to watch. The geology department responded and commented freely during the rest of the process.

Load after load went down, with little variety to make the operation more interesting. Toward the end a longer cable was installed and the lowering was done from below, since the greater part of the crew had now descended; and Lackland had a suspicion of the reason when Barlennan finally turned away from the scene of action and leaped toward the tank. The radio which had been used from that position was permanently mounted, and had not been taken down with the others.

"We have only about two more loads, Charles," the captain opened. "There will be a slight problem in connection with the last one. We'd like to keep all our gear if possible, which means dismantling and sending down the masts used for our lowering tackle. We don't want to throw them down because we're not sure they'd take it—the soil below is very rocky. Would you be willing to get into your armor and lower the final load by hand? I will arrange for it to consist of one raft, those few masts and the associated tackle, and myself." Lackland was startled by the last item.

"You mean you would trust yourself to my strength, knowing that I'm already under three and a half times my normal gravity and will have the weight of my armor as well?"

"Certainly. The armor will easily be heavy enough to serve as anchor, and if you take a turn of the rope about your own body you can pay it out gradually. I don't see any difficulty; the load will be only a few of your pounds."

"Not that way, perhaps, but there's another point. Your rope is very thin indeed, and the handling clamps of my armor are somewhat clumsy when it comes to managing small objects. What if the cord slips out of my grip?" That silenced Barlennan for a moment.

"What is the smallest object you could handle with reasonable security?"

"Oh—one of your masts, I should say."

"There is no trouble, then. We will wind the rope about a mast, and you can use that as a windlass. You can toss mast and rope over afterward; if the stick is broken the loss will not be too great."

Lackland shrugged. "It's your health and property, Barl. I don't have to say I'll be careful; I wouldn't want anything to happen to you, especially through my negligence. I'll be out shortly." The Mesklinite, satisfied, leaped back to the ground and began to give the necessary orders to the few remaining sailors. The second last load went down with all of these; and a few moments later the Earthman emerged from his conveyance.

Barlennan was waiting for him. A single raft now lay at the cliff edge, tied in its sling and ready to go. A radio and the bundled remains of the scaffolding lay upon it, and the captain was dragging the mast which had the line wrapped about it toward Lackland. The man's approach was slow, for the terrible fatigue seemed to grow with every instant; but he finally reached a point about ten feet from the edge, reached over as far as his clumsy garment would permit, and took the mast from the tiny being who had reared up to meet him. Without a word of caution or any other suggestion of doubt in his big friend, Barlennan turned back to the raft, made sure its cargo was lashed securely, pushed it until it was teetering on the edge of the cliff, and climbed aboard.

He turned for a last look at Lackland, and the man could have sworn that he winked. Then, "Hang on, Charles," came the voice over the radio; and the captain stepped deliberately to the outer edge of the precariously balanced raft. His pincers were securely caught in the lashings, which was all that kept him aboard as the platform teetered once and slipped over the rim.

There was enough slack in the line Lackland was holding to permit a couple of feet of fall; and raft and passenger vanished instantly. A sharp jerk told the man that at least the line was still holding, and an instant later Barlennan's voice cheerfully conveyed the same information. "Lower away!" was the concluding phrase; and Lackland obeyed.

It was rather like handling a kite, at least in the form of windlass he was using—simply a cord wound on a stick. It revived childhood memories; but if he lost this kite he would, he knew, be much longer in getting over it. He did not have the best possible grip on the mast, and he slowly pivoted so as to wind the cord about his body before he tried to change holds. Then, satisfied, he paid out slowly.

Barlennan's voice came at intervals, always with something encouraging; it was as though the midget had an idea of the anxiety in Lackland's mind. "Halfway now." "Smooth going." "You know, I don't mind looking down even this far, now." "Almost there—just a little more—that's it; I'm down. Hold onto the tackle for a little, please; I'll tell you when the area is clear and it's all right to throw it down."

Lackland continued to obey. For a keepsake, he tried to break off a foot or two from the end of the cable, but found it impossible even with armored hands. However, the edge of one of the locking snaps on his armor proved sharp enough to cut the stuff, and he wound the souvenir around his arm before starting to carry out the remaining requests of his ally.

"We have things out from underneath, Charles; you can let go your end of the rope and toss the mast over whenever you want." The fine cord slithered instantly out of sight, and the ten-inch twig that was one of the *Bree*'s main booms followed. *Seeing* things fall free in triple gravity, Lackland found, was even worse than thinking about it. Maybe it would be better at the poles—then you couldn't see them at all. Not where an object falls some two miles in the first second! But perhaps the abrupt vanishing would be just as hard on the nerves. Lackland shrugged off these thoughts and turned back to the tank.

For the couple of hours the process took he watched the *Bree*'s reassembly through the vision sets. With just the traces of a wish that he might go along, he saw the cluster of rafts pushed out into the broad stream, and listened to the farewells of Barlennan, Dondragmer, and the crew—he could guess at the meaning of the sounds uttered even by the sailors who spoke no English. Presently the current bore the vessel far enough from the cliff to be seen from the tank's position. Lackland raised a hand silently in farewell, and watched her as she shrank slowly and finally vanished toward the distant sea.

For long minutes he sat silently; then roused himself to call the Toorey base.

"You may as well come and pick me up. I've done all I can on the surface."

10: Hollow Boats

The river, once away from the vicinity of the great fall, was broad and slow. At first the air trapped by the descending "water" furnished a breeze toward the sea, and Barlennan ordered the sails set to take advantage of it; but this presently died out and left the ship at the mercy of the current. This was going in the right direction, however, and no one complained. The land adventure had been interesting and profitable, for several of the plant products collected could certainly be sold at high prices once they reached home; but no one was sorry to be afloat again. Some looked back at the waterfall as long as it could be seen, and once everyone stared into the west to catch a glimpse of the rocket as the muted thunder of its approach reached them; but in general the feeling was one of anticipation.

The banks on either side began to draw more and more attention as they proceeded. During their overland journey they had become accustomed to the sight of an occasional upright growth of the sort that the Flyer had called a "tree," usually seeing one every few days. They had been fascinating objects at first, and had, indeed, proved a source of one of the foods they planned to sell at home. Now the trees were becoming more and more numerous, threatening to replace the more familiar sprawling, rope-branched plants entirely, and Barlennan began to wonder if even a colony planted here might not be able to support itself by trade in what the Flyer had called fir cones.

For a long time, fully fifty miles, no intelligent life was sighted, though animals in fair numbers were seen along the banks. The river itself teemed with fish, though none appeared large enough to constitute a danger to the *Bree*. Eventually the river on either side became lined with trees, which extended no one could tell how far inland; and Barlennan, spurred by curiosity, ordered the ship steered closer to shore to see what a forest—he had no such word for it, of course—looked like.

It was fairly bright even in the depths of the wood, since the trees did not spread out at the top nearly as much as is common on Earth, but it was strange enough. Drifting along almost in the shadow of the weird plants, many of the crew felt a resurgence of their old terror of having solid objects overhead; and there was a general feeling of relief when the captain silently gestured the helmsman to steer away from the bank once more.

If anyone lived there they were welcome to it. Dondragmer expressed this opinion aloud, and was answered by a general mutter of approval. Unfortunately, his words were either not heard or not understood by listeners on the bank. Perhaps they were not actually afraid that the *Bree*'s crew meant to take their forest away from them, but they decided to take no chances; and once more the visitors from high-weight suffered an experience with projectile weapons.

The armory this time consisted entirely of spears. Six of them flew silently from the top of the bank and stuck quivering in the *Bree*'s deck; two more glanced from the protective shells of sailors and clattered about on the rafts before coming to rest. The sailors who had been hit leaped convulsively from pure reflex, and both landed yards away in the river. They swam back and clambered aboard without assistance, for all eyes were directed toward the source of the mysterious attack. Without orders the helmsman angled more sharply toward the center of the river.

"I wonder who sent those—and if they used a machine like the Flyer's. There wasn't the same noise." Barlennan spoke half aloud, not caring whether he were answered. Terblannen wrenched one of the spears out of the deck and examined its hardwood point; then, experimentally, he threw it back at the receding shore. Since throwing was a completely new art to him, except for experiments such as he had made in getting objects to the top of the tank in the stone-rollers' city, he threw it as a child throws a stick, and it went spinning end over end back to the woods. Barlennan's question was partly answered; short as his crewman's arms were, the weapon reached the bank easily. The invisible attackers at least didn't *need* anything like Lackland's gun, if they were anything like ordinary people physically. There seemed no way to tell what the present attackers were, and the captain had no intention of finding out by direct examination. The *Bree* kept on downstream, while an account of the affair went winging up to Lackland on distant Toorey.

For fully a hundred miles the forest continued while the river widened gradually. The *Bree* kept out in midstream for a time after her single encounter with the forest dwellers, but even that did not keep her completely out of trouble. Only a few days after the arrival of the spears, a small clearing was sighted on the left bank. His viewpoint only a few inches off the surface prevented Barlennan from seeing as well as he would have liked, but there were certainly objects in that clearing worthy of examination. After some hesitation he ordered the ship closer to that bank. The objects looked a little like trees, but were shorter and thicker. Had he been higher he would have seen small openings in them just above ground level which might have been informative; Lackland, watching through one of the vision sets, compared the things at once to pictures he had seen of the huts of African natives, but he said nothing yet. Actually he was more interested in a number of other items lying partly in and partly out of the river in front of what he already assumed to be a village. They might have been logs or crocodiles, for they were not too clearly visible at this distance, but he rather suspected they were canoes. It would be interesting to see how Barlennan reacted to a boat so radically different from his own.

It was quite a while, however, before anyone on the *Bree* realized that the "logs" were canoes or the other mysterious objects dwellings. For a time, in fact, Lackland feared that they would drift on downstream without ever finding out; their recent experience had made Barlennan very cautious indeed. However, there were others besides Lackland who did not want the ship to drift by without stopping, and as she approached the point on her course opposite the village a red and black flood of bodies poured over the bank and proved that the Earthman's conjecture had been correct. The loglike objects were pushed into the stream, each carrying fully a dozen creatures who apparently belonged to the identical species as the *Bree*'s crew. They were certainly alike in shape, size, and coloring; and as they approached the ship they uttered earsplitting hoots precisely like those Lackland had heard on occasion from his small friends.

The canoes were apparently dugouts, hollowed out sufficiently so that only the head end of each crew member could be seen; from their distribution, Lackland suspected that they lay herringbone fashion inside, with the paddles operated by the foremost sets of pincer-equipped arms.

The *Bree*'s leeward flame throwers were manned, though Barlennan doubted that they would be useful under these conditions. Krendoranic, the munitions officer, was working furiously at one of his storage bins, but no one knew what he was up to; there was no standard procedure for his department in such a situation. Actually, the entire defense routine of the ship was being upset by the lack of wind, something that almost never occurred on the open sea.

Any chance there might have been to make effective use of the flame dust vanished as the fleet of canoes opened out to surround the *Bree.* Two or three yards from her on all sides, they glided to a stop, and for a minute or two there was silence. To Lackland's intense annoyance, the sun set at this point and he was no longer able to see what went on. The next eight minutes he had to spend trying to attach meaning to the weird sounds that came over the set, which was not a very profitable effort since none of them formed words in any language he knew. There was nothing that denoted any violent activity; apparently the two crews were simply speaking to each other in experimental fashion. He judged, however, that they could find no common language, since there appeared to be nothing like a sustained conversation.

With sunrise, however, he discovered that the night had not been wholly uneventful. By rights, the *Bree* should have drifted some distance downstream during the darkness; actually, she was still opposite the village. Furthermore she was no longer far out in the river, but only a few yards from the bank. Lackland was about to ask Barlennan what he meant by taking such a risk, and also how he had managed to maneuver the *Bree,* when it became evident that the captain was just as surprised as he at this turn of events.

Wearing a slightly annoyed expression, Lackland turned to one of the men sitting beside him, with the remark:

"Barl has let himself get into trouble already. I know he's a smart fellow, but with over thirty thousand miles to go I don't like to see him getting held up in the first hundred."

"Aren't you going to help him? There's a couple of billion dollars, not to mention a lot of reputations, riding with him."

"What can I do? All I could give would be advice, and he can size up the situation better than I can. He can see it better, and is dealing with his own sort of people."

"From what I can see, they're about as much his sort as the South Sea Islanders were Captain Cook's. I grant they appear to be the same species, but if they're, say, cannibals your friend may really be in hot water."

"I still couldn't help him, could I? How do you talk a cannibal out of a square meal when you don't know his language and aren't even facing him in person? What attention would he pay to a little square box that talked to him in a strange language?" The other raised his eyebrows a trifle.

"While I'm not mind reader enough to predict that one in detail, I would suggest that in such a case he might just possibly be scared enough to do almost anything. As an ethnologist I can assure you that there are primitive races on a lot of planets, including our own Earth, who would bow down, hold square dances, and even make sacrifices to a box that talked to them."

Lackland digested that remark in silence for a few moments, nodded thoughtfully, and turned back to the screens.

A number of sailors had seized spare masts and were trying to pole back toward the center of the river, but were having no success. Dondragmer, after a brief investigation around the outer rafts, reported that they were in a cage formed of piles driven into the river bed; only the upstream side was open. It might or might not be coincidence that the cage was just large enough to accommodate the *Bree.* As this report was made, the canoes drifted away from the three closed sides of the cage and congregated on the fourth; and the sailors, who had heard the mate's report and prepared to pole in the upstream direction, looked to Barlennan for instructions. After a moment's thought, he motioned the crew to the far end of the ship and crawled alone to the end facing the assembled canoes. He had long since figured out how his ship had been moved; with the coming of darkness some of the paddlers must have gone quietly overboard, swum beneath the *Bree,* and pushed her where they wanted. There was nothing too surprising in that; he himself could exist for some time beneath the surface of river or ocean, which normally carried a good deal of dissolved hydrogen. What bothered him was just why these people wanted the ship.

As he passed one of the provision lockers he pulled back its cover and extracted a piece of meat. This he carried to the edge of the ship and held out toward the crowd of now silent captors. Presently some unintelligible gabbling sounded among them; then this ceased, as one of the canoes eased slowly forward and a native in the bow reared up and forward toward the offering. Barlennan let him take it. It was tested and commented upon; then the chief, if that was his position, tore off a generous fragment, passed the rest back to his companions, and thoughtfully consumed what he had kept. Barlennan was encouraged; the fact that he hadn't kept it all suggested that these people had some degree of social development. Obtaining another piece, the captain held it out as before; but this time, when the other reached for it, it was withheld. Barlennan put it firmly behind him, crawled to the nearest of the piles that were imprisoning his ship, indicated it, gestured to the *Bree,* and pointed out into the river. He was sure his meaning was plain, as undoubtedly it was; certainly the human watchers far above understood him, though no word of their language had been used. The chief, however, made no move. Barlennan repeated the gestures, and finished by holding out the meat once more.

Any social consciousness the chief possessed must have been strictly in connection with his own society; for as the captain held out the meat a second time a spear licked out like the tongue of a chameleon, impaled the food, jerked it out of Barlennan's grasp, and was withdrawn before any one of the startled sailors could move. An instant later the chief gave a single barking order; and as he did so half the crew of each of the canoes behind him leaped forward.

The sailors were completely unused to aerial assault, and had also relaxed a trifle when their captain began his negotiation; in consequence, there was nothing resembling a fight. The *Bree* was captured in something less than five seconds. A committee headed by the chief began at once to investigate the food lockers, and their satisfaction was evident even through the language barrier. Barlennan watched with dismay as the meat was dragged out on deck in obvious preparation for transferral to a canoe, and for the first time it occurred to him that there was a possible source of advice which he had not yet used.

"Charles!" he called, speaking English for the first time since the incident had begun. "Have you been watching?" Lackland, with mixed anxiety and amusement, answered at once.

"Yes, Barl; I know what's been going on." He watched the *Bree*'s captors for reaction as he spoke, and had no reason to feel disappointed. The chief, who had been facing away from the point where the radios were lashed, switched ends like a startled rattlesnake and then began looking around for the source of the voice with an unbelievably human air of bewilderment. One of his men who had been facing the radios indicated to him the one whose speaker Lackland had used, but after poking around the impenetrable box with knife and lance the chief obviously rejected this suggestion. This was the moment the Earthman chose for speaking again.

"Do you think there's any chance of getting them scared of the radios, Barl?"

The chief's head was about two inches from the speaker this time, and Lackland had made no effort to reduce the volume. Consequently there was no question where the sound had come from; and the chief began backing away from the noisy box. He was evidently trying to go slowly enough to satisfy his self-respect and fast enough to suit his other emotions, and once again Lackland had trouble in not laughing aloud.

Before Barlennan had a chance to reply Dondragmer moved over to the pile of meat, selected a choice piece, and laid it in front of the radio set with every indication of humility. He had taken a chance on having a pair of knives meet in his body, and knew it; but his guards were too absorbed by the new situation to take offense at his motion. Lackland, understanding how the mate had interpreted his own lead, followed on; he reduced the volume in the hope that his next utterance would seem less like anger to the canoeists, and heartily approved the mate's action.

"Good work, Don. Every time one of you does something like that I'll try to show approval; and I'll bark like nobody's business at anything

I don't want our new acquaintances to be doing. You know the appropriate actions better than I, so just do everything in your power to make 'em think these radio boxes are high-powered beings who'll deliver lightning if properly annoyed."

"I understand; we can hold our end," replied the mate. "I thought that was what you had in mind."

The chief, gathering his courage once more, suddenly lunged at the nearest radio with his spear. Lackland remained silent, feeling that the natural result on the wooden point would be impressive enough; the sailors entered with a will into the game outlined by the Flyer. With what Lackland supposed were the equivalent of gasps of pious horror, they turned away from the scene and covered their eyes with their pincers. After a moment, seeing that nothing further was happening, Barlennan offered another piece of meat, at the same time gesturing in a way meant to convey the impression that he was begging for the life of the ignorant stranger. The river people were quite evidently impressed, and the chief drew back a little, gathered his committee, and began to discuss the whole situation with them. Finally one of the chief's counselors, in what was evidently an experiment, picked up a piece of meat and gave it to the nearest radio. Lackland was about to express gentle thanks when Dondragmer's voice came, "Refuse it!" Not knowing why but willing to trust the mate's judgment, Lackland turned up the volume and emitted a lionlike roar. The donor leaped back in genuine and unmistakable terror; then, at a sharp order from the chief, he crawled forward, retrieved the offending bit of food, selected another from the pile on the deck, and presented that.

"All right." It was the mate's voice again, and the Earthman lowered the volume of the speaker.

"What was wrong the other time?" he asked quietly.

"I wouldn't have given that piece to a *ternee* belonging to my worst enemy," replied Dondragmer.

"I keep finding resemblances between your people and mine in the darnedest situations," Lackland remarked. "I hope this business is suspended for the night; I can't see what's going on in the dark. If anything happens that I should react to, for heaven's sake tell me." This remark was prompted by the arrival of sunset once more, and Barlennan assured him that he would be kept informed. The captain had recovered his poise, and was once again more or less in control of the situation—as far as a prisoner could be.

The night was spent by the chief in discussion; his voice, interrupted occasionally by others which must belong to his counselors, came clearly to the Earthmen far above. By dawn he had apparently reached a decision. He had drawn a little apart from his counselors and laid down his weapons; now, as sunlight slanted once more across the deck, he advanced toward Barlennan, waving the latter's guards away as he approached. The captain, already fairly sure in his mind what the other wanted, waited calmly. The chief halted with his head a few inches from Barlennan's, paused impressively for a moment, and began to speak.

His words were still unintelligible to the sailors, naturally enough; but the gestures accompanying them were clear enough to give the speech meaning even to the distant human watchers.

Quite plainly, he wanted a radio. Lackland found himself speculating idly on just what supernatural powers the chief supposed the device to possess. Perhaps he wanted it to protect the village from enemies, or to bring luck to his hunters. That was not really an important question, however; what mattered would be his attitude when the request was refused. That might possibly be rather anti-social, and Lackland was still worrying a trifle.

Barlennan, showing what his human friend felt was rather more courage than sense, answered the speech briefly; a single word and a gesture which Lackland had long since come to recognize comprised the reply. "No" was the first Mesklinite word which Lackland learned beyond doubt, and he learned it for the first time now. Barlennan was very definite.

The chief, to the relief of at least one watcher, did not take a belligerent attitude. Instead, he gave a brief order to his men. Several of these at once laid aside their weapons and began restoring the looted food to the lockers from which it had been taken. If freedom were not enough for one of the magic boxes, he was willing to pay more. Both Barlennan and Lackland more than suspected that the fellow was now afraid to use force, badly as his possessive instincts were aroused.

With half the food returned, the chief repeated his request; when it was refused as before, he gave an amazingly human gesture of resignation and ordered his men to restore the rest. Lackland was getting uneasy.

"What do you think he'll do when you refuse him now, Barl?" he asked softly. The chief looked at the box hopefully; perhaps it was arguing with its owner, ordering him to give his captor what he wanted.

"I'm not sure enough to venture a prediction," the Mesklinite replied. "With luck, he'll bring us more stuff from the village to add to the price; but I'm not sure luck goes that far. If the radio were less important, I'd give it to him now."

"For heaven's sake!" The ethnologist sitting beside Lackland practically exploded at this point. "Have you been going through all this rigmarole and risking your life and those of your men just to hang onto a cheap vision set?"

"Hardly cheap," muttered Lackland. "They were designed to hold up at Mesklin's poles, under Mesklinite atmosphere, and through the handling of Mesklinite natives."

"Don't quibble!" snapped the student of cultures. "What are those sets down there for if not to get information? Give one to that savage! Where could it be better placed? And how could we observe the everyday life of a completely strange race better than through that eye? Charles, sometimes I wonder at you!"

"That will leave three in Barlennan's possession, of which one absolutely *must* get to the south pole. I see your point, but I think we'd better get Rosten's approval before we actually leave one this early on the way."

"Why? What does he have to do with it? He's not risking anything like Barlennan, and doesn't care about watching that society like some of the rest of us. I say leave it; I'm sure Barlennan wants to leave it; and it seems to me that Barlennan has the final say in any case."

The captain, who had of course overheard this, cut in.

"You forget, friend of Charles, that the radios are not my property. Charles let me take them, at my suggestion to be sure, as a safety measure, so that at least one would reach its goal even though unavoidable incidents deprived me of the others. It seems to me that he, not I, is the one whose word should be final." Lackland answered instantly.

"Do as you think best, Barl. You are on the spot; you know your world and its people better than any of us can hope to; and if you do decide to leave one with these people, even that will do some good to my friends, as you have heard."

"Thank you, Charles." The captain's mind was made up in the instant the Flyer finished speaking. Fortunately the chief had listened enthralled to the conversation, making no attempt to further his own interests while it was going on; now Barlennan, keeping up the play to the end, called some of his crew and gave swift orders.

Moving very circumspectly and never touching a radio at any time, the sailors prepared a rope sling. Then they pried the set up from a "safe" distance with spars, and poked and pushed until the sling was in position under and around it. This accomplished, one of the sling handles was given very respectfully to Barlennan. He in turn gestured the chief closer, and with an air of handling something precious and fragile, handed the loop of rope to him. Then he gestured toward the counselors, and indicated that they should take the other handles. Several of them moved forward, rather gingerly; the chief hastily designated three for the honor, and the others fell back.

Very slowly and carefully the bearers moved the radio to the edge of the *Bree*'s outermost raft. The chief's canoe glided up—a long, narrow vessel evidently hollowed to a paper-thin shell from the trunk of one of the forest trees. Barlennan viewed it with distrust. He himself had never sailed anything but a raft; hollow vessels of any kind were strange to him. He felt certain that the canoe was too small to carry the weight of the radio; and when the chief ordered the greater part of the crew out of it he barely suppressed the equivalent of a negative headshake. He felt that the lightening thus obtained would be insufficient. He was more than startled when the canoe, upon receiving its new freight, merely settled a trifle. For a few seconds he watched, expecting vessel and cargo to pop suddenly below the surface; but nothing of the sort happened, and it became evident that nothing would.

Barlennan was an opportunist, as had been proved months ago by his unhesitating decision to associate with the visitor from Earth and learn his language. This was something new, and obviously worth learning about; if ships could be made that would carry so much more weight for their size, the knowledge was obviously vastly important to a maritime nation. The logical thing to do was to acquire one of the canoes.

As the chief and his three co-workers entered the craft, Barlennan followed. They delayed shoving off as they saw his approach, wondering what he might want. Barlennan himself knew what he wanted, but was not sure he could get away with what he planned to try. His people, however, had a proverb substantially identical in meaning with Earth's "Nothing venture, nothing gain," and he was no coward.

Very carefully and respectfully he touched the radio, leaning across the half inch of open river surface between ship and canoe to do so. Then he spoke.

"Charles, I'm going to get this little ship if I have to come back and steal it. When I finish talking, please answer—it doesn't matter what you say. I'm going to give these people the idea that the boat which carried the radio is too changed for ordinary use, and must take the radio's place on my deck. All right?"

"I was brought up to disapprove of racketeers—I'll translate that word for you sometime—but I admire your nerve. Get away with it if you can, Barl, but please don't stick the neck you don't have out too far." He fell silent and watched the Mesklinite turn his few sentences to good account.

As before, he employed practically no spoken language; but his actions were reasonably intelligible even to the human beings, and clear as crystal to his erstwhile captors. First he inspected the canoe thoroughly, and plainly if reluctantly found it worthy. Then he waved away another canoe which had drifted close, and gestured several members of the river tribe who were still on the *Bree*'s deck away to a safe distance. He picked up a spear which one of the counselors had discarded to take up his new position, and made it clear that no one was to come within its length of the canoe.

Then he measured the canoe itself in spear lengths, took the weapon over to where the radio had been, and ostentatiously cleared away a spot large enough to take the craft; at his order, several of his own crew gently rearranged the remaining radios to make room for their new property. More persuasion might have been attempted, but sunset cut the activity short. The river dwellers did not wait out the night; when the sun returned, the canoe with the radio was yards away, already drawn up on shore.

Barlennan watched it with anxiety. Many of the other canoes had also landed, and only a few still drifted near the *Bree*. Many more natives had come to the edge of the bank and were looking over; but to Barlennan's intense satisfaction, none came any closer to the loaded canoe. He had apparently made some impression.

The chief and his helpers carefully unloaded their prize, the tribe maintaining its original distance. This was, incidentally, several times the spear's length demanded by Barlennan. Up the bank the radio went, the crowd opening wide to let it through and disappearing after it; and for long minutes there was no more activity. The *Bree* could easily have pushed out of her cage at this time, the crews of the few canoes remaining on the river showing little interest in what she did, but her captain did not give up that easily. He waited, eyes on the shore; and at long last a number of long black and red bodies appeared over the bank. One of these proceeded toward the canoe; but Barlennan realized it was not the chief, and uttered a warning hoot. The native paused, and a brief discussion ensued, which terminated in a series of modulated calls fully as loud as any that Lackland had heard Barlennan utter. Moments later the chief appeared and went straight to the canoe; it was pushed off by two of the counselors who had helped carry the radio, and started at once toward the *Bree*. Another followed it at a respectful distance.

The chief brought up against the outer rafts at the point where the radio had been loaded, and immediately disembarked. Barlennan had given his orders as soon as the canoe left the bank, and now the little vessel was hauled aboard and dragged to the space reserved for it, still with every evidence of respect. The chief did not wait for this operation to be finished; he embarked on the other canoe and returned to shore, looking back from time to time. Darkness swallowed up the scene as he climbed the bank.

"You win, Barl. I wish I had some of your ability; I'd be a good deal richer than I am now, if I were still alive by some odd chance. Are you going to wait around to get more out of them tomorrow?"

"We are leaving now!" the captain replied without hesitation.

Lackland left his dark screen and went to his quarters for his first sleep in many hours. Sixty-five minutes—rather less than four of Mesklin's days—had passed since the village was sighted.

11: Eye of the Storm

The *Bree* sailed into the eastern ocean so gradually that no one could say exactly when the change was made. The wind had picked up day by day until she had normal open-sea use of her sails; the river widened rod by rod and at last mile by mile until the banks were no longer visible from the deck. It was still "fresh water"—that is, it still lacked the swarming life that stained practically all of the ocean areas in varying tints and helped give the world such a startling appearance from space—but the taste was coming, as sailor after sailor verified to his own great satisfaction.

Their course was still east, for a long peninsula barred their way to the south, according to the Flyers. Weather was good, and there would be plenty of warning of any change from the strange beings that watched them so carefully. There was plenty of food still aboard, enough to last easily until they reached the rich areas of the deep seas. The crew was happy.

Their captain was satisfied as well. He had learned, partly from his own examination and experiment and partly from Lackland's casual explanations, how it was that a hollow vessel like the canoe could carry so much more weight for its size than could a raft. He was already deep in plans for the building of a large ship—as big or bigger than the *Bree*—built on the same principle and able to carry the profits of ten voyages in one. Dondragmer's pessimism failed to shake his rosy dream; the mate felt that there must be some reason such vessels were not used by their own people, though he could not say what the reason might be.

"It's too simple," he kept pointing out. "Someone would have thought of it long ago if that's all there was to it." Barlennan would simply point astern, where the canoe now followed gaily at the end of a rope, laden with a good half of their food. The mate could not shake his head after the fashion of an old family coachman looking over the new horseless carriage, but he would certainly have done so if he had possessed a neck.

He brightened up when they finally swung southward, and a new thought struck him.

"Watch it sink as soon as we start to get a little decent weight!" he exclaimed. "It may be all right for the creatures of the Rim, but you need a good solid raft where things are normal."

"The Flyer says not," replied Barlennan. "You know as well as I do that the *Bree* doesn't float any higher here at the Rim than she does at home. The Flyer says it's because the methane weighs less too, which sounds as though it might be reasonable." Dondragmer did not answer; he simply glanced, with an expression equivalent to a complacent smile, at the tough wood spring balance and weight that formed one of the ship's principal navigating instruments. As that weight began to droop, he was sure, something that neither his captain nor the distant Flyer had counted on would happen. He did not know what it would be, but he was certain of the fact.

The canoe, however, continued to float as the weight slowly mounted. It did not, of course, float as high as it would have on Earth, since liquid methane is less than half as dense as water; its "water" line, loaded as it was, ran approximately halfway up from keel to gunwale, so that fully four inches was invisible below the surface. The remaining four inches of free-board did not diminish as the days went by, and the mate seemed almost disappointed. Perhaps Barlennan and the Flyer were correct after all.

The spring balance was starting to show a barely visible sag from the zero position—it had been made, of course, for use where weight was scores or hundreds of times Earth-normal—when the monotony was broken. Actual weight was about seven Earths. The usual call from Toorey was a little late, and both the captain and mate were beginning to wonder whether all the remaining radios had failed for some reason when it finally arrived. The caller was not Lackland but a meteorologist the Mesklinites had come to know quite well.

"Barl," the weather man opened without preamble, "I don't know just what sort of storm you consider too bad to be out in—I suppose your standards are pretty high—but there seems to be one coming that I certainly wouldn't want to ride out on a forty-foot raft. It's a tight cyclone, of what I would consider hurricane force even for Mesklin, and on the thousand-mile course I've been observing so far it has been violent enough to stir up material from below and leave a track of contrasting color on the sea."

"That's enough for me," Barlennan replied. "How do I dodge it?"

"That's the catch; I'm not sure. It's still a long way from your position, and I'm not absolutely sure it will cross your course just when you're at the wrong point. There arc a couple of ordinary cyclones yet to pass you, and they will change your course some and possibly even that of the storm. I'm telling you now because there is a group of fairly large islands about five hundred miles to the southeast, and I thought you might like to head for them. The storm will certainly strike them, but there seem to be a number of good harbors where you could shelter the *Bree* until it was over."

"Can I get there in time? If there's serious doubt about it I'd prefer to ride it out in the open sea rather than be caught near land of any sort."

"At the rate you've been going, there should be plenty of time to get there and scout around for a good harbor."

"All right. What's my noon bearing?"

The men were keeping close track of the *Bree*'s position by means of the radiation from the vision sets, although it was quite impossible to see the ship from beyond the atmosphere with any telescope, and the meteorologist had no trouble in giving the captain the bearing he wanted. The sails were adjusted accordingly and the *Bree* moved off on the new course.

The weather was still clear, though the wind was strong. The sun arced across the sky time after time without much change in either of these factors; but gradually a high haze began to appear and thicken, so that the sun changed from a golden disc to a rapidly moving patch of pearly light. Shadows became less definite, and finally vanished altogether as the sky became a single, almost uniformly luminous dome. This change occurred slowly, over a period of many days, and while it was going on the miles kept slipping beneath the *Bree*'s rafts.

They were less than a hundred miles from the islands when the minds of the crew were taken off the matter of the approaching storm by a new matter. The color of the sea had shifted again, but that bothered no one; they were as used to seeing it blue as red. No one expected signs of land at this distance, since the currents set generally across their course and the birds which warned Columbus did not exist on Mesklin. Perhaps a tall cumulus cloud, of the sort which so frequently forms over islands, would be visible for a hundred miles or more; but it would hardly show against the haze that covered the sky. Barlennan was sailing by dead reckoning and hope, for the islands were no longer visible to the Earthmen overhead.

Nevertheless, it was in the sky that the strange event occurred.

From far ahead of the *Bree,* moving with a swooping, dipping motion that was utterly strange to the Mesklinites and would have been perfectly familiar to the human beings, there appeared a tiny dark speck. No one saw it at first, and by the time they did it was too near and too high to be in the field of view of the vision sets. The first sailor to notice it gave vent to the usual hoot of surprise, which startled the human watchers on Toorey but was not particularly helpful to them. All they could see as their wandering attentions snapped back to the screens was the crew of the *Bree,* with the front end of every caterpillarlike body curled upward as its owner watched the sky.

"What is it, Barl?" Lackland called instantly.

"I don't know," the captain replied. "I thought for an instant it might be your rocket down looking for the islands to guide us better, but it's smaller and very different in shape."

"But it's something *flying?*"

"Yes. It does not make any noise like your rocket, however. I'd say it was being blown by the wind, except that it's moving too smoothly and regularly and in the wrong direction. I don't know how to describe it; it's wider than it is long, and a little bit like a mast set crosswise on a spar. I can't get closer than that."

"Could you angle one of the vision sets upward so we could get a look at it?"

"We'll try." Lackland immediately put through a call on the station telephone for one of the biologists.

"Lance, it looks as though Barlennan had run into a flying animal of some sort. We're trying to arrange a look at it. Want to come down to the screen room to tell us what we're looking at?"

"I'll be right with you." The biologist's voice faded toward the end of the sentence; he was evidently already on his way out of the room. He arrived before the sailors had the vision set propped up, but dropped into a chair without asking questions. Barlennan was speaking again.

"It's passing back and forth over the ship, sometimes in straight lines and sometimes in circles. Whenever it turns it tips, but nothing else about it changes. It seems to have a little body where the two sticks meet..." He went on with his description, but the object was evidently too far outside his normal experience for him to find adequate similes in a strange language.

"If it does come into view, be prepared to squint," the voice of one of the technicians cut in. "I'm covering that screen with a high-speed camera, and will have to jump the brightness a good deal in order to get a decent exposure."

"...there are smaller sticks set across the long one, and what looks like a very thin sail stretched between them. It's swinging back toward us again, very low now—I think it may come in front of your eye this time..."

The watchers stiffened, and the hand of the photographer tightened on a double-pole switch whose closing would activate his camera and step up the gain on the screen. Ready as he was, the object was well into the field before he reacted, and everyone in the room got a good glimpse before the suddenly bright light made their eyes close involuntarily. They all saw enough.

No one spoke while the cameraman energized the developing-frequency generator, rewound his film through its poles, swung the mounted camera toward the blank wall of the room, and snapped over the projection switch. Everyone had thoughts enough to occupy him for the fifteen seconds the operation required.

The projection was slowed down by a factor of fifty, and everyone could look as long as he pleased. There was no reason for surprise that Barlennan had been unable to describe the thing; he had never dreamed that such a thing as flying was possible until after his meeting with Lackland a few months before, and had no words in his own language for anything connected with the art. Among the few English words of that group he had learned, "fuselage" and "wing" and "empennage" were not included.

The object was not an animal. It had a body—fuselage, as the men thought of it—some three feet long, half the length of the canoe Barlennan had acquired. A slender rod extending several feet rearward held control surfaces at its extremity. The wings spanned a full twenty feet, and their structure of single main spar and numerous ribs was easily seen through the nearly transparent fabric that covered them. Within his natural limitations, Barlennan had done an excellent job of description.

"What drives it?" asked one of the watchers suddenly. "There's no propeller or visible jet, and Barlennan said it was silent."

"It's a sailplane." One of the meteorological staff spoke up. "A glider, operated by someone who has all the skill of a terrestrial sea gull at making use of the updrafts from the front side of a wave. It could easily hold a couple of people Barlennan's size, and could stay aloft until they had to come down for food or sleep."

The *Bree*'s crew were becoming a trifle nervous. The complete silence of the flying machine, their inability to see who or what was in it, bothered them; no one likes to be watched constantly by someone he can't see. The glider made no hostile move, but their experience of aerial assault was still fresh enough to leave them uneasy about its presence. One or two had expressed a desire to practice their newly acquired art of throwing, using any hard objects they could find about the deck, but Barlennan had sternly forbidden this. They simply sailed on, wondering, until the hazy dome of the sky darkened with another sunset. No one knew whether to be relieved or worried when the new day revealed no trace of the flying machine. The wind was now stronger, and almost directly across the *Bree*'s course from the northeast; the waves had not yet followed it and were decidedly choppy in consequence. For the first time Barlennan perceived a disadvantage in the canoe; methane that blew or washed inboard stayed there. He found it necessary before the day was over to haul the little vessel up to the outer rafts and place two men aboard to bail—an act for which he had neither a word nor proper equipment.

The days passed without reappearance of the glider, and eventually only the official lookouts kept their eyes turned upward in expectation of its return. The high haze thickened and darkened, however, and presently turned to clouds which lowered until they hung a scant fifty feet above the sea. Barlennan was informed by the Earthmen that this was not good flying weather, and eliminated the watch. Neither he nor the human beings stopped to wonder how the first glider had found its way on a night too hazy for the stars to provide guidance.

The first of the islands to come into view was fairly high, its ground rising quickly from sea level to disappear into the clouds. It lay downwind from the point where they first sighted it; and Barlennan, after consulting the sketch map of the archipelago he had made from the Earthmen's descriptions, kept on course. As he had expected, another island appeared dead ahead before the first had faded from sight, and he altered course to pass to leeward of it. This side, according to observation from above, was quite irregular and should have usable harbors; also, Barlennan had no intention of coasting the windward shore during the several nights which would undoubtedly be required for his search.

This island appeared to be high also; not only did its hilltops reach the clouds, but the wind was in large measure cut off as the *Bree* passed into its lee. The shore line was cut by frequent fiords; Barlennan was intending simply to sail across the mouth of each in the hunt, but Dondragmer insisted that it would be worth while to penetrate to a point well away from the open sea. He claimed that almost any beach far enough up would be adequate shelter. Barlennan was convinced only to the point of wanting to show the mate how wrong he was. Unfortunately for this project, the first fiord examined made a sharp hook-turn half a mile from the ocean and opened into what amounted to a lake, almost perfectly circular and about a hundred yards in diameter. Its walls rose into the mist except at the mouth where the *Bree* had entered and a smaller opening only a few yards from the first where a stream from the interior fed into the lake. The only beach was between the two openings.

There was plenty of time to secure both vessel and contents, as it happened; the clouds belonged to the second of the two "normal" cyclones the meteorologist had mentioned, rather than to the major storm. Within a few days of the *Bree*'s arrival in the harbor the weather cleared once more, though the wind continued high. Barlennan was able to see that the harbor was actually the bottom of a bowl-shaped valley whose walls were less than a hundred feet in height, and not particularly steep. It was possible to see far inland through the cleft cut by the small river, provided one climbed a short distance up the walls. In doing this, shortly after the weather cleared, Barlennan made a disconcerting discovery: sea shells, seaweeds, and bones of fairly large sea animals were thickly scattered among the land-type vegetation clothing the hillside. This continued, he discovered upon further investigation, quite uniformly around the valley up to a height fully thirty feet above the present sea level. Many of the remains were old, decayed almost to nothing, and partly buried; these might be accounted for by seasonal changes in the ocean level. Others, however, were relatively fresh. The implication was clear—on certain occasions the sea rose far above its present level; and it was possible that the *Bree* was not in as safe a position as her crew believed.

One factor alone limited Mesklin's storms to the point where sea travel was possible: methane vapor is far denser than hydrogen. On Earth, water vapor is lighter than air, and contributes enormously to the development of a hurricane once it starts; on Mesklin, the methane picked up from the ocean by such a storm tends, in a relatively short time, to put a stop to the rising currents which are responsible for its origin. Also the heat it gives up in condensing to form the storm clouds is only about a quarter as great as would be given by a comparable amount of water—and that heat is the fuel for a hurricane, once the sun has given the initial push.

In spite of all this, a Mesklinite hurricane is no joke. Barlennan, Mesklinite though he was, learned this very suddenly. He was seriously considering towing the *Bree* as far upstream as time would permit when the decision was taken out of his hands; the water in the lake receded with appalling suddenness, leaving the ship stranded fully twenty yards from its edge. Moments later the wind shifted ninety degrees and increased to a speed that made the sailors cling for dear life to deck cleats, if they happened to be on board, and to the handiest vegetation if they did not. The captain's shrill hoot ordering those off the ship to return went completely unheard, sheltered as they were in the almost complete circle of the valley walls; but no one needed any order. They picked their way, bush by bush, never holding with less than two sets of pincers, back to where their comrades had already lashed themselves as best they could to the vessel that was threatening every moment to lift into the wind's embrace. Rain—or, more properly, driven spray that had come completely across the island—lashed at them for long minutes; then both it and the wind ceased as though by magic. No one dared release his lashings, but the slowest sailors now made a final dash for the ship. They were none too soon.

The storm cell at sea level was probably three miles or so in diameter; it was traveling at about sixty or seventy miles per hour. The ending of the wind was only temporary; it meant that the center of the cyclone had reached the valley. This was also the low-pressure zone; and as it reached the sea at the mouth of the fiord, the flood came. It rose, gathering speed as it came, and spurted into the valley like the stream from a hose. Around the walls it swirled, picking up the *Bree* on the first circle; higher and higher, as the ship sought the center of the whirlpool—fifteen, then twenty, then twenty-five feet before the wind struck again.

Tough as the wood of the masts was, they had snapped long since. Two crewmen had vanished, their lashing perhaps a little too hastily completed. The new wind seized the ship, bare of masts as she was, and flung her toward the side of the whirlpool; like a chip, both for helplessness and magnitude, she shot along the stream of liquid now pouring up the little river toward the island's interior. Still the wind urged her, now toward the side of the stream; and as the pressure rose once more, the flood receded as rapidly as it had risen—no, not quite; the portion now floating the *Bree* had nowhere to go except back out through the little river-course, and that took time. Had daylight lasted, Barlennan might even in his ship's present condition have guided her back along that stream while she still floated; but the sun chose this moment to set, and in the darkness he ran aground. The few seconds delay was enough; the liquid continued to recede, and when the sun returned it looked upon a helpless collection of rafts some twenty yards from a stream that was too narrow and too shallow to float any one of them.

The sea was completely out of sight beyond the hills; the limp form of a twenty-foot-long sea monster stranded on the other side of the brook gave a graphic picture of the helplessness of the Gravity Expedition.

12: Wind Riders

Much of what had happened had been seen from Toorey; the radio sets, like most of the less prominent articles about the *Bree*'s deck, had remained lashed in position. Not much had been distinguishable, of course, while the vessel had been whirling in the brief maelstrom; but her present situation was painfully clear. None of the people in the screen room could find anything helpful to say.

The Mesklinites could say little, either. They were used to ships on dry land, since that happened fairly often during late summer and fall as the seas receded in their own latitudes; but they were not accustomed to having it happen so suddenly, and to have so much high ground between them and the ocean. Barlennan and the mate, taking stock of the situation, found little to be thankful for.

They still had plenty of food, though that in the canoe had vanished. Dondragmer took occasion to point out the superiority of rafts, neglecting to mention that the supplies in the canoe had been tied down carelessly or not at all owing to a misplaced confidence in the high sides of the boat. The little vessel itself was still at the end of its towline, and still undamaged. The wood of which it had been made shared the springiness of the low-growing plants of the higher latitudes. The *Bree* herself, constructed of similar materials though in much less yielding form, was also intact, though the story might have been different had there been many rocks in the wall of the round valley. She was and had remained right side up, owing to her construction—Barlennan admitted that point without waiting for the mate to bring it up. The complaints were not in any way connected with lack of ship or supplies, but with lack of an ocean to float them on.

"The surest way would be to take her apart, as we did before, and carry her over the hills. They're not very steep, and there still isn't enough weight to matter." Barlennan made this suggestion after long thought.

"You're probably right, Captain; but wouldn't it save time to separate the rafts only lengthwise, so that we have rows the full length of the ship? We could carry or drag those over to the stream, and surely they'd float before we went down very far." Hars, now his former self after his encounter with the rock, made this suggestion.

"That sounds promising. Hars, why don't you find out just how far down that would be? The rest can start unlashing as Hars suggested, and unloading where we have to. Some of the cargo will be in the way of the lashings, I'm afraid."

"I wonder if the weather is still too bad for those flying machines?" Dondragmer asked, of no one in particular. Barlennan glanced upward.

"The clouds are still low and the wind high," he said. "If the Flyers are right—and they ought to know, I should think—the weather is still too bad. However, it won't hurt to look up occasionally. I rather hope we see one again."

"One I wouldn't much mind myself," replied the mate dryly. "I suppose you want a glider to add to the canoe. I'll tell you right now that I might, in extremity, get into the canoe, but the day I climb onto one of those flying machines will be a calm winter morning with both suns in the sky." Barlennan did not answer; he had not consciously considered adding a glider to his collection, but the idea rather struck his fancy. As for flying in it—well, changed as he was, there were limits.

The Flyers reported clearing weather, and the clouds obediently thinned over the next few days. Greatly improved though the flying weather was, few crew members thought to watch the sky. All were too busy. Hars's plan had proved feasible, the stream being deep enough for the rafts only a few hundred yards toward the sea and wide enough for a single raft very little farther down. Barlennan's statement that the additional weight would mean little proved wrong; every component was twice as heavy as it had been where they last saw Lackland, and they were not accustomed to lifting *anything*. Powerful as they were, the new gravity taxed their hoisting abilities to the point where it was necessary to unload the rafts before the rows of little platforms could be partly carried and dragged to the stream. Once they were partly immersed, the going was much simpler; and after a digging squad had widened the banks up to the point nearest the *Bree*'s resting place the job became almost easy. Not too many hundred days passed before the long, narrow string of rafts, reloaded, was being towed once more toward the sea.

The flying machines appeared just after the ship had entered that portion of the stream where its walls were steepest, shortly before it emptied into the lake. Karondrasee saw them first; he was on board at the time, preparing food while the others pulled, and his attention was freer than theirs. His hoot of alarm roused Earthmen and Mesklinites alike, but the former as usual could not see the approaching visitors since the vision sets were not aimed high enough.

Barlennan saw all too clearly, however. There were eight of the gliders, traveling fairly close together but by no means in tight formation. They came straight on, riding the updraft on the leeward side of the little valley until they were almost over the ship; then they changed course to pass in front of her. As each swooped overhead, it released an object, turned, and swung back to the lee side to recover its altitude.

The falling objects were distinct enough; every sailor could see that they were spears, very much like those the river dwellers had used but with much heavier tips. For a moment the old terror of falling objects threatened to send the crew into hysteria; then they saw that the missiles would not strike them, but fall some distance in front. A few seconds later the gliders swooped again, and the sailors cowered in expectation of an improved aim; but the spears fell in about the same place. With the third pass it became evident that their aim was deliberate; and presently their purpose became apparent. Every projectile had fallen in the still narrow stream, and penetrated more than half its length into the firm clay bottom; by the end of the third run, two dozen stakes formed by the spear handles were effectually blocking the ship's passage downstream.

As the *Bree* approached the barricade, the bombardment stopped. Barlennan had thought it might be continued to prevent their approaching and clearing the obstacle away, but when they reached it they found this to be superfluous. The spears were there to stay; they had been dropped from nearly a hundred feet with superlative aim in a field of seven gravities, and nothing short of power machinery was going to extract them. Terblannen and Hars proved that in five minutes of fruitless upward tugging.

"Can't you cut them?" Lackland asked from his distant observation point. "Those pincers of yours are pretty powerful, as I know."

"These are wood, not metal," Barlennan replied. "We would need one of your hard metal saws, which you claimed would attack even our wood—unless you have some machine for pulling them out."

"You must have tools which will cut it; how do you do repair work on your ship? The rafts certainly didn't grow in that shape."

"Our cutting tools are made of animal teeth set in strong frames, and most of them are not very portable. What we have we will use, but I doubt that we'll be given time to do much."

"I should think you could keep attackers away by fire."

"We can, if they come from downwind. I find it hard to imagine their being that stupid." Lackland fell silent, while the crew fell to work on the stakes with such edged tools as they could find. Their personal knives were of hardwood and would make no impression on the spears, but as Barlennan had intimated, there were a few bone and ivory cutters, and these began to chip away at the incredibly tough wood. Digging was also attempted by some of the crew who lacked tools; they took turns in sinking to the bottom of the inches-deep brook, working the clay loose, and letting its particles wash away in the sluggish current. Dondragmer watched these workers for a time, then pointed out that it would probably be easier to dig a canal around the obstruction than to grub out two dozen sticks from a depth of some four feet. This suggestion was eagerly adopted by the members of the crew who had nothing to cut with, and work progressed at a remarkable rate.

The gliders kept circling while all this was going on; apparently they either remained overnight or were replaced by others during the minutes of darkness—no one could tell which. Barlennan kept a sharp watch on the hills to either side of the stream, expecting ground forces to appear at any moment; but for a long time his own crew and the gliders formed the only moving parts of the scenery. The crews of the gliders themselves remained invisible; no one could even tell how many or what sort of creatures rode in the machines, though both human beings and Mesklinites had come to take more or less for granted that they belonged to Barlennan's race. They showed no evident anxiety about the sailors' digging activities, but it became apparent finally that the excavation had not gone unnoticed. The job was about three quarters finished when they took action; another series of bombing runs left the path of the new waterway as completely staked off as the original. As before, pains were apparently taken to avoid transfixing any of the crew. The action, however, was about as discouraging as if it had been a personal assault; quite evidently the digging process was useless, since the work of days could be nullified in a matter of minutes. Some other line of procedure must be devised.

At the Earthmen's advice, Barlennan had long since ordered his men not to gather in large groups; but now he drew them in toward the ship, establishing a loose cordon parallel to the string of rafts on each side of the creek. The men were far enough apart so there was no really tempting target from above, and close enough to support each other in case an attack actually developed. There they stayed; Barlennan wished it made evident that the next move was up to the personnel of the gliders. They failed to make it, however, for several more days.

Then a dozen more of the flimsy craft appeared in the distance, swooped overhead, split into two groups, and landed on the hilltops to either side of the imprisoned ship. The landings were made as the Flyers had foretold, into the wind; the machines skidded to a stop in a few feet from their point of touchdown. Four beings emerged from each, leaped to the wings, and hastily tied the gliders down, using the local bushes as anchors. What had been assumed all along now proved to be a fact; they were identical in form, size, and coloring with the sailors of the *Bree.*

Once the gliders were secured, their crews proceeded to set up a collapsible structure upwind from them, and attach cords equipped with hooks to this. They appeared to be measuring quite carefully the distance from this device to the nearest glider. Only when this task was completed did they pay any attention to the *Bree* or her crew. A single prolonged wail that sounded from one hilltop to the other apparently served as a signal that the work was complete.

Then the glider crews on the leeward hill began to descend the slope. They did not leap, as they had during the action subsequent to landing, but crawled in the caterpillarlike fashion which was the only means of locomotion Barlennan's people had known prior to his exploration of the Rim. In spite of this they made good speed and were within reasonable throwing distance—as several of the more pessimistic sailors regarded it—by sundown. They stopped at that point and waited for the night to pass; there was just enough light from the moons for each party to see that the other did nothing suspicious. With the coming of sunlight the advance was resumed, and eventually terminated with one of the newcomers only a yard or so from the nearest sailor, while his companions hung a few feet farther back. None of the party seemed to be armed, and Barlennan went to meet them, first ordering two sailors to swing one of the vision sets so that it pointed directly at the place of meeting.

The glider pilot wasted no time, but began speaking as soon as Barlennan stopped in front of him. The captain failed to understand a word. After a few sentences the speaker appeared to realize this; he paused and after a moment continued at somewhat slower speed in what Barlennan judged to be a different language. To save the time that a random search through the tongues known to the other would consume, Barlennan this time indicated his lack of comprehension verbally. The other shifted languages once more, and rather to his surprise Barlennan heard his own speech, uttered slowly and badly pronounced, but quite comprehensible.

"It is long since I have heard your tongue spoken," the other said. "I trust I can still be understood when I use it. Do you follow me?"

"I can understand you perfectly well," replied Barlennan.

"Good. I am Reejaaren, linguist for Marreni, who is Officer of the Outer Ports. I am ordered to find out who you are and where you are from, and your purpose in sailing the seas about these islands."

"We are on a trading journey, with no particular destination." Barlennan had no intention of talking about his connection with the creatures of another world. "We did not know of the existence of these islands; we simply were heading away from the Rim, of which we had had enough. If you wish to trade with us we are willing to do business; if not, we ask only to be allowed to continue our journey."

"Our ships and gliders trade on these seas—we have never seen others," replied Reejaaren. "I fail to understand one point. The trader far to the south from whom I learned your language said that he came from a country that lay on the farther side of a sea across the western continent. We know that there is no sea passage from that ocean to this between here and the ice; yet you were sailing from the north when we first sighted you. That would suggest that you were quartering back and forth through these seas in deliberate search of land. How does that square with your story? We do not like spies."

"We came from the north, after crossing the land between this ocean and ours." Barlennan had no time to think up a convincing lie, though he realized that the truth was likely to be unbelievable. Reejaaren's expression showed that he was right.

"Your ship was obviously built with large tools, which you do not have. That means a shipyard, and there is none to the north on this ocean. Do you want me to believe you took her apart and dragged her across that much land?"

"Yes." Barlennan felt that he saw his way out.

"How?"

"How do you fly? Some would find that much harder to believe." The question was not quite as good a one as Barlennan had hoped, judging by the interpreter's reaction.

"I am sure you do not expect me to tell you that. Mere trespassers we may tolerate; but spies receive much harder treatment."

The captain covered up as well as he could. "I did not expect you to tell me. I was simply pointing out as tactfully as possible that perhaps you should not have asked me how we crossed the land barrier."

"Oh, but I should—and must. You do not yet seem to realize your position, stranger. What you think of me is unimportant; but what I think of you counts a great deal. To put it simply, to leave here as you desire you will have to convince me that you are harmless."

"But what harm could we do you—the crew of a single ship? Why should you fear us so?"

"We do not fear you!" The answer was sharp and emphatic. "The damage you could do is obvious—one person, let alone a ship-load, could take away information which we do not wish to give. We realize, of course, that the barbarians could not learn the secret of flight unless it were very carefully explained to them; that is why I laughed at your question. Still, you should be more careful."

Barlennan had not heard any laughter, and began to suspect a good deal about the interpreter and his people. A half-truth that seemed like yielding on Barlennan's part would probably be the best move.

"We had much help pulling the ship across the land," he said, putting a little sullenness in his tone.

"From the rock-rollers and river-dwellers? You must have a remarkably persuasive tongue. We have never received anything but missiles from them." To Barlennan's relief, Reejaaren did not pursue the subject any farther. He returned to more immediate matters.

"So you desire to trade with us, now that you are here. What have you to trade? And I suppose you wish to go to one of our cities?" Barlennan sensed the trap, and answered accordingly.

"We will trade here, or anywhere else you desire, though we would rather not go any farther from the sea. All we have to trade at the moment is a load of foods from the isthmus, which you doubtless have in great quantity already because of your flying machines."

"Food can usually be sold," the interpreter replied noncommittally. "Would you be willing to do your trading before you got any closer to the sea?"

"If necessary, as I said, though I don't see why it should be necessary. Your flying machines could catch us before we got very far, if we tried to leave the coast before you wanted, couldn't they?" Reejaaren might have been losing his suspicions up to this point, but the last question restored them in full force.

"Perhaps we could, but that is not for me to say. Marreni will decide, of course, but I suspect you might as well plan on lightening your ship here. There will be port fees, of course, in any case."

"Port fees? This is no port, and I didn't land here; I was washed up."

"Nevertheless, foreign ships must pay port fees. I might point out that the amount is determined by the Officer of the Outer Ports, and he will get much of his impression of you through me. A little more courtesy might be in order." Barlennan restrained his temper with difficulty, but agreed aloud that the interpreter spoke the clearest truth. He said it at some length, and apparently mollified that individual to some extent. At any rate he departed without further threats, overt or implied.

Two of his fellows accompanied him; the other remained behind. Men from the other gliders hastily seized the two ropes attached to the collapsible framework and pulled. The cords stretched unbelievably, until their hooks were finally fastened to an attachment in the glider's nose. The aircraft was then released and the ropes contracted to their original length, hurling the glider into the air. Barlennan instantly formed a heartfelt desire for some of that stretching rope. He said so, and Dondragmer sympathized. He had heard the entire conversation, and sympathized also with his captain's feelings toward the linguist for the Officer of the Outer Ports.

"You know, Barl, I think we could put that lad in his place. Want to try it?"

"I'd love to, but I don't think we can afford to let him get mad at us until we're good and far away. I don't want him and his friends dropping their spears on the *Bree* now or any other time."

"I don't mean to make him angry, but afraid of us. 'Barbarians'—he'll eat that word if I have to cook it personally for him. It all depends on certain things: do the Flyers know how these gliders work, and will they tell us?"

"They probably know, unless they've had better ones for so long they've forgotten—"

"So much the better, for what I have in mind."

"—but I'm not sure whether they'll tell. I think you know by now what I'm really hoping to get out of this trip; I want to learn everything I possibly can of the Flyers' science. That's why I want to get to that rocket of theirs near the Center; Charles himself said that it contained much of the most advanced scientific equipment they have. When we have that, there won't be a pirate afloat or ashore who'll be able to touch the *Bree,* and we'll have paid our last port dues—we'll be able to write our own menus from then on."

"I guessed as much."

"That's why I wonder whether they'll tell what you want; they may suspect what I'm after."

"I think you're too suspicious yourself. Have you ever *asked* for any of this scientific information you want to steal?"

"Yes; Charles always said it was too difficult to explain."

"Maybe he was right; maybe he doesn't know it himself. I want to ask one of his people about these gliders, anyway; I want to watch that Reejaaren grovel."

"Just what is this idea of yours, anyway?"

Dondragmer told him, at length. The captain was dubious at first, but gradually grew more enthusiastic; and finally they went over to the radios together.

13: Slip of the Tongue

Fortunately Reejaaren did not return for a good many days. His people remained; four to six gliders were always drifting overhead, and several more squatted on the hilltops beside their catapults. The number of aircraft did not change noticeably, but the population of the hilltops increased day by day. The Earthmen above had entered into Dondragmer's plan with enthusiasm and, Barlennan suspected, some little amusement. A few of the sailors were unable to pick up what was needed with sufficient speed, and had to be left out of the main plan in one sense; but even they understood the situation and would, Barlennan was sure, be able to contribute to the desired effect. In the meantime he put them to work repairing the shattered masts, whose rigging had at least kept them with the ship.

The plan was matured and well rehearsed long before the interpreter's return, and the officers found themselves impatient to try it out though Dondragmer had been spending time at the radio meanwhile on yet another project. In fact, after controlling themselves for a few days, the captain and mate strolled one morning up the hill toward the parked gliders with a full determination to make a test of the idea, though neither had said a word to the other about his intention. The weather had completely cleared long since, and there was only the perpetual wind of Mesklin's seas to help or hinder flying. Apparently it wanted to help; the gliders were tugging at their tie-down cables like living creatures, and crewmen were standing by the wings with a secure grip on the surrounding bushes, evidently ready to add their strength if necessary to that of the restraining lines.

Barlennan and Dondragmer approached the machines until they were ordered sharply to halt. They had no idea of the rank or authority of the individual giving the order, since he wore no insignia; but it was not part of their plan to argue such matters. They halted, and looked over the machines casually from a distance of thirty or forty yards, while the crewmen looked back rather belligerently. Apparently Reejaaren's superciliousness was not a rare trait with his nation.

"You look astonished, barbarians," one of them remarked after a brief silence. "If I thought you could learn anything by looking at our machines, I would have to force you to stop. As it is, I can only assure you that you look rather childish." He spoke Barlennan's tongue with an accent not much worse than that of the chief linguist.

"There seems little to learn from your machines. You could save much trouble with the wind in your present situation by warping the front of your wings down; why do you keep so many people busy instead?" He used the English word for "wings," not having one in his own language. The other requested an explanation; receiving it, he was startled out of his superiority for a moment.

"You have seen gliders before? Where?"

"I have never seen *your* type of flying machine in my life," Barlennan answered. His words were truthful, though their emphasis was decidedly misleading. "I have not been this close to the Rim before, and I should imagine that these flimsy structures would collapse from their added weight if you flew them much farther south."

"How—" The guard stopped, realizing that his attitude was not that of a civilized being toward a barbarian. He was silent for a moment, trying to decide just what his attitude should be in this case; then he decided to pass the problem higher in the chain of command. "When Reejaaren returns, he will no doubt be interested in any minor improvements you may be able to suggest. He might even reduce your port fee, if he deems them of sufficient value. Until then, I think you had better stay entirely away from our gliders; you might notice some of their more valuable features, and then we would regretfully have to consider you a spy." Barlennan and his mate retired to the *Bree* without argument, highly satisfied with the effect they had produced, and reported the conversation in its entirety to the Earthmen.

"How do you think he reacted to the implication that you had gliders capable of flying up in the two-hundred-gravity latitudes?" asked Lackland. "Do you think he believed you?"

"I couldn't say; he decided about then either that he was saying too much or hearing too much, and put us in storage until his chief returns. I think we started the right attitude developing, though."

Barlennan may have been right, but the interpreter gave no particular evidence of it when he returned. There was some delay between his actual landing and his descent of the hill to the *Bree,* and it seemed likely that the guard had reported the conversation; but he made no reference to it at first.

"The Officer of the Outer Ports has decided to assume for the moment that your intentions are harmless," he began. "You have of course violated our rules in coming ashore without permission; but he recognized that you were in difficulties at the time, and is inclined to be lenient. He authorizes me to inspect your cargo and evaluate the amount of the necessary port fee and fine."

"The Officer would not care to see our cargo for himself and perhaps accept some token of our gratitude for his kindness?" Barlennan managed to keep sarcasm out of his voice. Reejaaren gave the equivalent of a smile.

"Your attitude is commendable, and I am sure we will get along very well with each other. Unfortunately, he is occupied on one of the other islands, and will be for many days to come. Should you still be here at the end of that time, I am sure he will be delighted to take advantage of your offer. In the meantime we might proceed to business."

Reejaaren lost little if any of his superiority during his examination of the *Bree*'s cargo, but he managed to give Barlennan some information during the process which he would probably have died rather than give consciously. His words, of course, tended to belittle the value of everything he saw; he harped endlessly on the "mercy" of his so far unseen chief Marreni. However, he appropriated as fine a respectable number of the "fir cones" that had been acquired during the journey across the isthmus. Now these should have been fairly easy to obtain here, since the distance could not be too great for the gliders—in fact, the interpreter had made remarks indicating acquaintance with the natives of those regions. If, then, Reejaaren held the fruit as being of value, it meant that the "barbarians" of the isthmus were a little too much for the interpreter's highly cultured people, and the latter were not so close to being the lords of creation as they wanted people to think. That suggested that the mate's plan had a very good chance of success, since the interpreter would probably do almost anything rather than appear inferior to the "barbarian" crew of the *Bree*. Barlennan, reflecting on this, felt his morale rise like the Earthmen's rocket; he was going to be able to lead this Reejaaren around like a pet *ternee*. He bent all his considerable skill to the task, and the crew seconded nobly.

Once the fine was paid, the spectators on the hills descended in swarms; and the conclusion about the value of the fir-cone-like fruit was amply confirmed. Barlennan at first had a slight reluctance to sell all of it, since he had hoped to get really high prices at home; but then he reflected that he would have to go back through the source of supply before reaching his home in any case.

Many of the buyers were evidently professional merchants themselves, and had plentiful supplies of trade goods with them. Some of these were also edibles, but on their captain's orders the crew paid these little attention. This was accepted as natural enough by the merchants; after all, such goods would be of little value to an overseas trader, who could supply his own food from the ocean but could hardly expect to preserve most types of comestibles for a long enough time to sell at home. The "spices" which kept more or less permanently were the principal exception to this rule, and none of these were offered by the local tradesmen.

Some of the merchants, however, did have interesting materials. Both the cord and the fabric in which Barlennan had been interested were offered, rather to his surprise. He personally dealt with one of the salesmen who had a supply of the latter. The captain felt its unbelievably sheer and even more incredibly tough texture for a long time before satisfying himself that it was really the same material as that used in the glider wings. Reejaaren was close beside him, which made a little care necessary. He learned from the merchant that it was a woven fabric in spite of appearances, the fiber being of vegetable origin—the canny salesman refused to be more specific—the cloth being treated after weaving with a liquid which partly dissolved the threads and filled the holes with the material thus obtained.

"Then the cloth is windproof? I think I could sell this easily at home. It is hardly strong enough for practical uses like roofing, but it is certainly ornamental, particularly the colored versions. I will admit, though it is hardly good buying procedure, that this is the most salable material I have yet seen on this island."

"Not strong enough?" It was Reejaaren rather than the merchant who expressed indignation. "This material is made nowhere else, and is the only substance at once strong and light enough to form the wings of our gliders. If you buy it, we will have to give it to you in bolts too small for such a purpose—no one but a fool, of course, would trust a sewn seam in a wing."

"Of course," Barlennan agreed easily. "I suppose such stuff could be used in wings here, where the weight is so small. I assure you that it would be quite useless for the purpose in high latitudes; a wing large enough to lift anyone would tear to pieces at once in any wind strong enough to furnish the lift." This was almost a direct quote from one of his human friends, who had been suggesting why the gliders had never been seen in countries farther south.

"Of course, there is very little load on a glider in these latitudes," Reejaaren agreed. "Naturally there is no point in building them stronger than necessary here; it adds to the weight." Barlennan decided that his tactical adversary was not too bright.

"Naturally," he agreed. "I suppose with the storms you have here your surface ships must be stronger. Do they ever get flung inland the way mine was? I never saw the sea rise in that fashion before."

"We naturally take precautions when a storm is coming. The rising of the sea occurs only in these latitudes of little weight, as far as I have been able to observe. Actually our ships are very much like yours, though we have different armament, I notice. Yours is unfamiliar to me—doubtless our philosophers of war found it inadequate for the storms of these latitudes. Did it suffer seriously in the hurricane that brought you here?"

"Rather badly," Barlennan lied. "How are your own ships armed?" He did not for a second expect the interpreter to answer the question in any way, except perhaps a resumption of his former haughtiness, but Reejaaren for once was both affable and cooperative. He hooted a signal up the hill to some of his party who had remained above, and one of these obediently came down to the scene of bargaining with a peculiar object in his pincers.

Barlennan had never seen a crossbow, of course, or any other missile weapon. He was suitably impressed when Reejaaren sent three quartz-tipped bolts in a row thudding for over half their six-inch length into the hard trunk of a plant some forty yards away. He also lost most of his surprise at the interpreter's helpfulness; such a weapon would be so much dead weight before the *Bree* was a quarter of the way to her home latitudes. More as a test than anything else, Barlennan offered to buy one of the crossbows; the interpreter pressed it on him as a gift, together with a bundle of bolts. That was good enough for the captain; as a trader, he naturally enjoyed being taken for a fool. It was usually profitable.

He secured an incredible quantity of the wing fabric—Reejaaren either forgot to make sure it was in small bolts, or no longer considered it necessary—much of the elastic rope, and enough of the local artifacts to fill the *Bree*'s decks, except for the normal requirements of working space and the area devoted to a reasonable food reserve. He was rid of everything salable that he had brought to the island, with the possible exception of the flame throwers. Reejaaren had not mentioned these since he had been told they were damaged, though he had obviously recognized them as armament of some sort. Barlennan actually thought of giving him one, minus chlorine ammunition, but realized he would have to explain its operation and even demonstrate. This he had no intention of doing; if these people were not familiar with the weapons he did not want them to know the truth of their nature, and if they were he did not want to be caught in a lie. It was much nicer to have Reejaaren in a good humor.

With the selling completed, the crowd of local people gradually melted away; and at last there remained only the gliders and their crews, some of the latter down near the ship and others on the hilltops by their machines. Barlennan found the interpreter among the former group, as usual; he had spent much time talking casually to the sailors. They had reported that he was, as expected, pumping them gently about the flying ability of their people. They had filled their part of the game with noncommittal replies that nevertheless "accidentally" revealed a considerable knowledge of aerodynamics. Naturally, they carefully gave no hint as to how recently the knowledge had been acquired—or its source. Barlennan at this point was reasonably sure that the islanders, or at least their official representative, believed his people capable of flight.

"That seems to be all I can give or take," he said as he secured Reejaaren's attention. "We have, I think, paid all necessary fees. Is there any objection to our departing?"

"Where do you plan to go now?"

"Southward, toward decent weight. We do not know this ocean at all, except by vague reports from some of our merchants who have made the overland journey. I should like to see more of it."

"Very well. You are free to go. Doubtless you will see some of us on your travels—I occasionally go south myself. Watch out for more storms."

The interpreter, apparently the picture of cordiality, turned up the hill. "We may see you at the coast," he added, looking back. "The fiord where you first landed has been suggested as possibly improvable to harbor status, and I want to inspect it." He resumed his journey to the waiting gliders.

Barlennan turned back to the ship, and was about to give orders for immediate resumption of the downstream journey—the goods had been loaded as fast as they were purchased—when he realized that the stakes dropped by the gliders still barred the way. For an instant he thought of calling the islander back and requesting their removal; then he thought better of it. He was in no position to make a demand, and Reejaaren would undoubtedly grow supercilious again if he put it as a request. The *Bree*'s crew would dig out of their own troubles.

On board, he issued an order to this effect, and the cutters were once more picked up; but Dondragmner interrupted.

"I'm glad to see that this work wasn't wasted time," he said.

"What?" asked the captain. "I knew you were at some stunt of your own for the last forty or fifty days, but was too busy to find out what it was. We were able to handle the trading without you. What have you been doing?"

"It was an idea that struck me just after we were first caught here; something you said to the Flyers about a machine to pull out the stakes gave it to me. I asked them later if there was such a machine that was *not* too complicated for us to understand, and after some thinking one of them said there was. He told me how to make it, and that's what I've been doing. If we rig a tripod by one of the stakes, I'll see how it works."

"But what is the machine? I thought all the Flyers' machines were made of metal, which we couldn't fashion because the kinds that are hard enough need too much heat."

"This." The mate displayed two objects on which he had been working. One was simply a pulley of the most elementary design, quite broad, with a hook attached. The other was rather similar but double, with peg-like teeth projecting from the circumference of both wheels. The wheels themselves were carved from a solid block of hardwood, and turned together. Like the first pulley. this was equipped with a hook; in addition there was a strap of leather threaded through the guards of both wheels, with holes punched in it to match the peg teeth, and the ends buckled together so that it formed a continuous double loop. The whole arrangement seemed pointless to the Mesklinites— Dondragmer, who did not yet understand why the device worked, or even whether it actually would. He took it over in front of one of the radios and spread it out on the deck.

"Is this now assembled correctly?" he asked.

"Yes, it should work if your strap is strong enough," came the answer. "You must attach the hook of the single pulley to the stake you want to extract; I am sure you have methods of doing that with rope. The other pulley must be fastened to the top of the tripod. I've told you what to do from then on."

"Yes, I know. It occurred to me that instead of taking much time to reverse the machine after it was wound up tightly, however, I could unfasten the buckle and rethread it."

"That would work, provided you were not lifting a load that had to be supported in the meantime," replied the Earthman, "Good for you, Don."

The crew immediately headed for the original group of stakes, but Barlennan called to them to wait.

"There aren't so many blocking the canal we were digging. Don, did the Flyer say how long it would take to pull them out with that contraption?"

"He wasn't sure, since he didn't know how deeply they were buried or how fast we could operate it; but he guessed at a day or so each—faster than we could cut through them."

"But not so fast that we wouldn't gain time by having some of us finish that canal while you take however many men you need to pull the stakes in it. Incidentally, did he have any name for the thing?"

"He called it a differential hoist. The second word is plain enough, but I don't see how to translate the first—it's just a noise to me."

"Me too. Differential it is. Let's get to work; your watch to the hoist, and mine to the canal." The crew buckled down with a will.

The canal was finished first, since it quickly became evident that most of the crew would be free to dig; two sailors, taking turns on the hoist at intervals of a few minutes, proved enough to start the spear shafts sliding very slowly out of the hard ground. To Barlennan's satisfaction the heads came with them, so that he had eight very effective-looking spears when the operation was completed. His people did little work in stone, and the quartz heads were extremely valuable in his estimation.

Once through the barrier, the distance to the lake was relatively short; and there they stopped to reassemble the *Bree* in her natural form. This was quickly accomplished—indeed, the crew might now be considered expert at the task—and once more the ship floated in relatively deep water. The Earthmen above heaved a collective sigh of relief. This proved to be premature.

The gliders had been passing back and forth throughout the journey from the trading site. If their crews had been at all surprised at the method used to extract the spears, no evidence had appeared of the fact. Barlennan, of course, hoped they had seen and added the information to the list of his own people's superior accomplishments. He was not too surprised to see a dozen gliders on the beach near the mouth of the fiord, and ordered the helmsman to turn the ship ashore at that point. Perhaps at least the islanders would notice that he had recovered the spears intact.

Reejaaren was the first to greet them as the *Bree* anchored a few yards offshore. "So your ship is seaworthy again, eh? I'd try to meet any more storms a long way from land, if I were you."

"Right," Barlennan agreed. "The difficulty in a sea you don't know is being sure where you stand in that respect. Perhaps you would tell us the disposition of lands in this sea? Or would you, perhaps, have charts you could provide us with? I should have thought to ask before."

"Our charts of these islands, of course, are secret," the interpreter replied. "You should be out of the group in forty or fifty days, however, and then there is no land for some thousands of days' sail to the south. I do not know your ship's speed, so I cannot guess just when you are likely to make it. Such lands as there are are mostly islands at first; then the coast of the land you crossed turns east, and if you keep straight south you will encounter it at about—" He gave an expression which referred to a spring-balance reading, and corresponded to about forty-five Earth gravities of latitude. "I could tell you about many of the countries along that coast, but it would take a long time. I can sum it up by saying that they will probably trade rather than fight—though some will undoubtedly do their best not to pay for what they get."

"Will any of them assume we are spies?" Barlennan asked pleasantly.

"There is that risk, naturally, though few have secrets worth stealing. Actually they will probably try to steal yours, if they know you have any. I should not advise your discussing the matter of flying while there."

"We did not plan to," Barlennan assured him, with glee that he managed to conceal. "We thank you for the advice and information." He gave the order to hoist the anchor, and for the first time Reejaaren noticed the canoe, now trailing once more at the end of its towrope and loaded with food.

"I should have noticed that before," the interpreter said. "I would never have doubted your story of coming from the south. How did you get that from the natives?" In the answer to this question Barlennan made his first serious mistake in dealing with the islander.

"Oh, we brought that with us; we frequently use them for carrying extra supplies. You will notice that its shape makes it easy to tow." He had picked up his elementary notions of streamlining from Lackland not too long after acquiring the canoe.

"Oh, you developed that craft in your country too?" the interpreter asked curiously. "That is interesting; I had never seen one in the south. May I examine it, or do you not have time? We have never bothered to use them ourselves." Barlennan hesitated, suspecting this last statement to be a maneuver of the precise sort he himself had been employing; but he saw no harm in complying, since Reejaaren could learn nothing more from a close examination than he could from where he was. After all, it was the canoe's shape that was important, and anyone could see that. He allowed the *Bree* to drift closer inshore, pulled the canoe to him with the towrope, and gave it a push toward the waiting islander. Reejaaren plunged into the bay and swam out to the little vessel when it ran aground, in a few inches of liquid. The front part of his body arched upward to look into the canoe; powerful pincer-tipped arms poked at the sides. These were of ordinary wood, and yielded springily to the pressure; and as they did so the islander gave a hoot of alarm that brought the four gliders in the air swinging toward the *Bree* and the shore forces up to full alertness.

"Spies!" he shrieked. "Bring your ship aground at once, Barlennan—if that is your real name. You are a good liar, but you have lied yourself into prison this time!"

14: The Trouble with Hollow Boats

Barlennan had been told at various times during his formative years that he was someday pretty sure to talk himself into more trouble than he could talk himself out of. At various later times during his career this prediction had come alarmingly close to fulfillment, and each time he had resolved to be more careful in the future with his tongue. He felt the same way now, together with an injured feeling arising from the fact that he did not yet know just what he had said that had betrayed his mendacity to the islander. He did not have time to theorize over it, either; something in the line of action was called for, the quicker the better. Reejaaren had already howled orders to the glider crews to pin the *Bree* to the bottom if she made a move towards the open sea, and the catapults on shore were launching more of the machines to reinforce those already aloft. The wind was coming from the sea at a sufficient angle to be lifted as it struck the far wall of the fiord, so the flyers could remain aloft as long as necessary. Barlennan had learned from the Earthmen that they probably could not climb very high—high enough for effective missile dropping—under the thrust of the updrafts from ocean waves; but he was a long way from the open sea where they would have to depend on such currents. He had already had a chance to observe their accuracy, and dismissed at once any idea of trusting to his dodging ability to save his ship.

As so frequently happened, the action was performed by a crew member while he was debating the best course. Dondragmer snatched up the crossbow that had been given them by Reejaaren, nocked a bolt, and cocked the weapon with a speed that showed he could not have been completely absorbed in his hoist project at all times. Swinging the weapon shoreward, he rested it on its single support leg and covered the interpreter with the point.

"Hold on, Reejaaren; you're moving in the wrong direction." The islander stopped on his way out of the bay, liquid dripping from his long body, and doubled his front half back toward the ship to see what the mate meant. He saw clearly enough, but seemed for a moment undecided about the proper course of action.

"If you want to assume I'll probably miss because I've never handled one of these things, go right ahead. I'd like to find out myself. If you don't start coming this way in an awfully short time, though, it will be just as though you had tried to escape. Move!" The last word was issued in a barking roar that removed much of the interpreter's indecision. He apparently was not quite sure of the mate's incompetence; he continued the doubling movement, re-entered the bay, and swam out to the *Bree.* If he thought of concealing himself by submerging during the process, he evidently lacked the courage to try it. As he well knew, the methane was only a few inches deep even at the ship's location, and would hardly protect him from a bolt hurled with force enough to penetrate three inches of wood after a forty-yard trajectory under seven gravities. He did not think of it in those terms, of course, but he knew very well what those projectiles could do.

He clambered aboard, shaking with rage and fear together.

"Do you think this will save you?" he asked. "You have simply made things worse for yourselves. The gliders will drop in any event if you try to move, whether I am aboard or not."

"You will order them not to."

"They will obey no order I give while I am obviously in your power; you should know that if you have any sort of fighting force."

"I've never had much to do with soldiers," Barlennan replied. He had recovered the initiative, as he usually did once things had started in a definite direction. "However, I'll believe you for the time being. We'll just have to hold you here until some understanding is reached concerning this nonsense about our going ashore—unless we can take care of those gliders of yours in the meantime. It's a pity we didn't bring some more modern armament into this backward area."

"You can stop that nonsense now," returned the captive. "You have nothing more than the rest of the savages of the south. I'll admit you fooled us for a time, but you betrayed yourself a moment ago."

"And what did I say that made you think I'd been lying?

"I see no reason to tell you. The fact that you don't yet know just proves my point. It would have been better for you if you hadn't fooled us so completely; then we'd have been more careful with secret information, and you wouldn't have learned enough to make your disposal necessary."

"And if you hadn't made that last remark, you might have talked us into surrendering," cut in Dondragmer, "though I admit it's not likely. Captain, I'll bet that what you slipped up on was what I've been telling you all along. It's too late to do anything about that now, though. The question is how to get rid of these pesky gliders; I don't see any surface craft to worry about, and the folks on shore have only the crossbows from the gliders that were on the ground. I imagine they'll leave things to the aircraft for the time being." He shifted to English. "Do you remember anything we heard from the Flyers that would help us get rid of these pesky machines?" Barlennan mentioned their probable altitude limitations over open sea, but neither could see how that helped at the moment.

"We might use the crossbow on them." Barlennan made the suggestion in his own language, and Reejaaren sneered openly. Krendoranic, the munitions officer of the *Bree,* who like the rest of the crew had been listening eagerly, was less contemptuous.

"Let's do that," he cut in sharply. "There's been something I've wanted to try ever since we were at that river village."

"What?"

"I don't think you'd want me to talk about it with our friend listening. We'll show him instead, if you are willing." Barlennan hesitated a moment, then gave consent.

Barlennan looked a trifle worried as Krendoranic opened one of the flame lockers, but the officer knew what he was doing. He removed a small bundle already wrapped in lightproof material, thus giving evidence of at least some of his occupation during the nights since they had left the village of the river-dwellers.

The bundle was roughly spherical, and evidently designed to be thrown by arm-power; like everyone else, Krendoranic had been greatly impressed by the possibilities of this new art of throwing. Now he was extending his idea even further, however.

He took the bundle and lashed it firmly to one of the crossbow bolts, wrapping a layer of fabric around bundle and shaft and tying it at either end as securely as possible. Then he placed the bolt in the weapon. He had, as a matter of duty, familiarized himself with the weapon during the brief trip downstream and the reassembly of the *Bree,* and had no doubt about his ability to hit a sitting target at a reasonable distance; he was somewhat less sure about moving objects, but at least the gliders could only turn rapidly if they banked sharply, and that would give him warning.

At his order, one of the sailors who formed part of his flamethrower crew moved up beside him with the igniting device, and waited. Then to the intense annoyance of the watching Earthmen, he crawled to the nearest of the radios and set the leg of the bow on top of it to steady himself and the weapon in an upward position. This effectively prevented the human beings from seeing what went on, since the radios were set to look outward from a central point and neither of the others commanded a view of the first.

As it happened, the gliders were still making relatively low passes, some fifty feet above the bay, and coming directly over the *Bree* on what could on an instant's notice become bomb runs; so a much less experienced marksman than the munitions officer could hardly have missed. He barked a command to his assistant as one of the machines approached, and began to lead it carefully. The moment he was sure of his aim, he gave a command of execution and the assistant touched the igniter to the bundle on the slowly rising arrow point. As it caught, Krendoranic's pincer tightened on the trigger and a line of smoke marked the trail of the missile from the bow.

Krendoranic and his assistant ducked wildly back to deck level and rolled upwind to get away from the smoke released at the start; sailors to leeward of the release point leaped to other side. By the time they felt safe, the air action was almost over.

The bolt had come as close as possible to missing entirely; the marksman had underestimated his target's speed. It had struck about as far aft on the main fuselage as it could, and the bundle of chlorine powder was blazing furiously. The cloud of flame was spreading to the rear of the glider and leaving a trail of smoke that the following machines made no effort to avoid. The crew of the target ship escaped the effects of the vapor, but in a matter of seconds their tail controls burned away. The glider's nose dropped and it fluttered down to the beach, pilot and crew leaping free just before it touched. The two aircraft which had flown into the smoke also went out of control as the hydrogen chloride fumes incapacitated their personnel, and both settled into the bay. All in all, it was one of the great anti-aircraft shots in history.

Barlennan did not wait for the last of the victims to crash, but ordered the sails set. The wind was very much against him, but there was depth enough for the centerboards, and he began to tack out of the fiord. For a moment it looked as though the shore personnel were about to turn their own crossbows on the ship, but Krendoranic had loaded another of his frightful missiles and aimed it toward the beach, and the mere threat sent them scampering for safety—upwind; they were sensible beings for the most part.

Reejaaren had watched in silence, while his bodily attitude betrayed blank dismay. Gliders were still in the air, and some were climbing as though they might attempt runs from a higher altitude; but he knew perfectly well that the *Bree* was relatively safe from any such attempt, excellent though his aimers were. One of the gliders did make a run at about three hundred feet, but another trail of smoke whizzing past spoiled his aim badly and no further attempts were made. The machines drifted in wide circles well out of range while the *Bree* slipped on down the fiord to the sea.

"What in blazes has been happening, Barl?" Lackland, unable to restrain himself longer, decided it was safe to speak as the crowd on shore dwindled with distance. "I haven't been butting in for fear the radios might spoil some of your plans, but please let us know what you've been doing."

Barlennan gave a brief résumé of the events of the last few hundred days, filling in for the most part the conversations his watchers had been unable to follow. The account lasted through the minutes of darkness, and sunrise found the ship almost at the mouth of the fiord. The interpreter had listened with shocked dismay to the conversation between captain and radio; he assumed, with much justice, that the former was reporting the results of his spying to his superiors, though he could not imagine how it was being done. With the coming of sunrise he asked to be put ashore in a tone completely different from any he had used before; and Barlennan, taking pity on a creature who had probably never asked for a favor in his life from a member of another nation, let him go overboard from the moving vessel fifty yards from the beach. Lackland saw the islander dive into the sea with some relief; he knew Barlennan quite well, but had not been sure just what course of action he would consider proper under the circumstances.

"Barl," he said after a few moments' silence, "do you suppose you could keep out of trouble for a few weeks, until we get our nerves and digestions back up here? Every time the *Bree* is held up, everyone on this moon ages about ten years."

"Just who got me into this trouble?" retorted the Mesklinite. "If I hadn't been advised to seek shelter from a certain storm—which it turned out I could have weathered better on the open sea—I'd certainly never have met these glider makers. I can't say that I'm very sorry I did, myself; I learned a lot, and I know at least some of your friends wouldn't have missed the show for anything. From my point of view this trip has been rather dull so far; the few encounters we have had have all terminated very tamely, and with a surprising amount of profit."

"Just which do you like best, anyway: adventure or cash?"

"Well—I'm not sure. Every now and then I let myself in for something just because it looks interesting; but I'm much happier in the end if I make something out of it."

"Then please concentrate on what you're making out of this trip. If it will help you any to do that, we'll collect a hundred or a thousand shiploads of those spices you just got rid of and store them for you where the *Bree* wintered; it would still pay us, if you'll get that information we need."

"Thanks, I expect to make profit enough. You'd take all the fun out of life."

"I was afraid you'd feel that way. All right, I can't order you around, but please remember what this means to us."

Barlennan agreed, more or less sincerely, and swung his ship once more southward. For some days the island they had left was visible behind them, and often they had to change course to avoid others. Several times they saw gliders skimming the waves on the way from one island to another, but these always gave the ship a wide berth. Evidently news spread rapidly among these people. Eventually the last visible bit of land slipped below the horizon, and the human beings said that there was no more ahead—good fixes could once more be obtained with the weather in its present clear state.

At about forty-gravity latitude they directed the ship on a more southeasterly course to avoid the land mass which, as Reejaaren had said, swung far to the east ahead of her. Actually the ship was following a relatively narrow passage between two major seas, but the strait was far too wide for that fact to be noticeable from shipboard.

One minor accident occurred some distance into the new sea. At around sixty gravities the canoe, still following faithfully at the end of its towrope, began to settle visibly in the sea. While Dondragmer put on his best "I told you so" expression and remained silent, the little vessel was pulled up to the ship's stern and examined. There was quite a bit of methane in the bottom, but when she was unloaded and pulled aboard for examination no leak was visible. Barlennan concluded that spray was responsible, though the liquid was much clearer than the ocean itself. He put the canoe back in the sea and replaced its load, but detailed a sailor to inspect every few days and bail when necessary. This proved adequate for many days; the canoe floated as high as ever when freshly emptied, but the rate of leakage grew constantly greater. Twice more she was pulled aboard for inspection without result; Lackland, consulted by radio, could offer no explanation. He suggested that the wood might be porous, but in that case the leaking should have been present from the beginning.

The situation reached a climax at about two hundred gravities, with more than a third of the sea journey behind them. The minutes of daylight were longer now as spring progressed and the *Bree* moved ever farther from her sun, and the sailors were relaxing accordingly. The individual who had the bailing job was not, therefore, very attentive as he pulled the canoe up the stern rafts and climbed over its gunwale. He was aroused immediately thereafter. The canoe, of course, settled a trifle as he entered; and as it did so, the springy wood of the sides gave a little. As the sides collapsed, it sank a little farther—and the sides yielded more—and it sank yet farther—

Like any feedback reaction, this one went to completion in a remarkably short time. The sailor barely had time to feel the side of the canoe pressing inward when the whole vessel went under and the outside pressure was relieved. Enough of the cargo was denser than methane to keep the canoe sinking, and the sailor found himself swimming where he had expected to be riding. The canoe itself settled to the end of its towrope, slowing the *Bree* with a jerk that brought the entire crew to full alertness.

The sailor climbed back into the *Bree,* explaining what had happened as he did so. All the crew whose duties did not keep them elsewhere rushed to the stern, and presently the rope was hauled in with the swamped canoe at the end of it. With some effort, the canoe and such of its load as had been adequately lashed down were hauled aboard, and one of the sets turned to view it. The object was not very informative; the tremendous resilience of the wood had resulted in its recovering completely even from this flattening, and the canoe had resumed its original shape, still without leaks. This last fact was established after it had once more been unloaded. Lackland, looking it over, shook his head and offered no explanation. "Tell me just what happened—what everyone who saw anything at all did see."

The Mesklinites complied, Barlennan translating the stories of the crewman who had been involved and the few others who had seen the event in any detail. It was the first, of course, that provided the important bit of information.

"Good Earth!" Lackland muttered, half aloud. "What's the use of a high school education if you can't recall it when needed later on? Pressure in a liquid corresponds to the weight of liquid above the point in question—and even methane under a couple of hundred gravities weighs a good deal per vertical inch. That wood's not much thicker than paper, either; a wonder it held so long." Barlennan interrupted this rather uninformative monologue with a request for information.

"I gather you now know what happened," he said. "Could you please make it clear to us?"

Lackland made an honest effort, but was only partly successful. The concept of pressure, in a quantitative sense, defeats a certain number of students in every high school class.

Barlennan did get the idea that the deeper one went into the sea the greater was the crushing force, and that the rate of increase with depth went up along with gravity; but he did not connect this force with others such as wind, or even the distress he himself had experienced when he submerged too rapidly in swimming.

The main point, of course, was that any floating object had to have some part of itself under the surface, and that sooner or later that part was going to be crushed if it was hollow. He avoided Dondragmer's eye as this conclusion was reached in his conversation with Lackland, and was not comforted when the mate pointed out that this was undoubtedly where he had betrayed his falsehood when talking to Reejaaren. Hollow ships used by his own people, indeed! The islanders must have learned the futility of that in the far south long since.

The gear that had been in the canoe was stowed on deck, and the voyage continued. Barlennan could not bring himself to part with the now useless little vessel, though it took up a good deal of space. He disguised its uselessness thinly by packing it with food supplies which could not have been heaped so high without the sides of the canoe to retain them. Dondragmer pointed out that it was reducing the ship's flexibility by extending the length of two rafts, but the captain did not let this fact worry him.

Time passed as it had before, first hundreds and then thousands of days. To the Mesklinites, long-lived by nature, its passage meant little; to the Earthmen the voyage gradually became a thing of boredom, part of the regular routine of life. They watched and talked to the captain as the line on the globe slowly lengthened; measured and computed to determine his position and best course when he asked them to; taught English to or tried to learn a Mesklinite language from sailors who sometimes also grew bored; in short, waited, worked where possible, and killed time as four Earthly months—nine thousand four hundred and some odd Mesklinite days—passed. Gravity increased from the hundred and ninety or so at the latitude where the canoe had sunk to four hundred, and then to six, and then further, as indicated by the wooden spring balance that was the *Bree*'s latitude gauge. The days grew longer and the nights shorter until at last the sun rode completely around the sky without touching the horizon, though it dipped toward it in the south. The sun itself seemed shrunken to the men who had grown used to it during the brief time of Mesklin's perihelion passage. The horizon, seen from the *Bree*'s deck through the vision sets, was *above* the ship all around, as Barlennan had so patiently explained to Lackland months before; and he listened tolerantly when the men assured him it was an optical illusion. The land that finally appeared ahead was obviously above them too; how could an illusion turn out to be correct? The land was really there. This was proved when they reached it; for reach it they did, at the mouth of a vast bay that stretched on to the south for some two thousand miles, half the remaining distance to the grounded rocket. Up the bay they sailed, more slowly as it finally narrowed to the dimensions of a regular estuary and they had to tack instead of seeking favorable winds with the Flyers' help, and finally to the river at its head. Up this they went too, no longer sailing except at rare, favorable intervals; for the current against the blunt faces of the rafts was more than the sails could usually overcome, broad as the river still was. They towed instead, a watch at a time going ashore with ropes and pulling; for in this gravity even a single Mesklinite had a respectable amount of traction. More weeks, while the Earthmen lost their boredom and tension mounted in the Toorey station. The goal was almost in sight, and hopes ran high.

And they were dashed, as they had been for a moment months before when Lackland's tank reached the end of its journey. The reason was much the same; but this time the *Bree* and its crew were at the bottom of a cliff, not the top. The cliff itself was three hundred feet high, not sixty; and in nearly seven hundred gravities climbing, jumping and other rapid means of travel which had been so freely indulged at the distant Rim were utter impossibilities for the powerful little monsters who manned the ship.

The rocket was fifty miles away in horizontal distance; in vertical, it was the equivalent, for a human being, of a climb of nearly thirty-five— up a sheer rock wall.

15: High Ground

The change of mind that had so affected the *Bree*'s crew was not temporary; the unreasoning, conditioned fear of height that had grown with them from birth was gone. They still, however. had normal reasoning power; and in this part of their planet a fall of as much as half a body's length was nearly certain to be fatal even to their tough organisms. Changed as they were, most of them felt uneasy as they moored the *Bree* to the riverbank only a few rods from the towering cliff that barred them from the grounded rocket.

The Earthmen, watching in silence, tried futilely to think of a way up the barrier. No rocket that the expedition possessed could have lifted itself against even a fraction of Mesklin's gravity; the only one that had ever been built able to do so was already aground on the planet. Even had the craft been capable, no human or qualified non-human pilot could have lived in the neighborhood; the only beings able to do that could no more be taught to fly a rocket than a Bushman snatched straight from the jungle.

"The journey simply isn't as nearly over as we thought." Rosten, called to the screen room, analyzed the situation rapidly. "There should be some way to the plateau or farther slope—whichever is present—of that cliff. I'll admit there seems to be no way Barlennan and his people can get *up;* but there seems to be nothing preventing their going around." Lackland relayed this suggestion to the captain.

"That is true," the Mesklinite replied. "There are, however, a number of difficulties. It is already getting harder to procure food from the river; we are very far from the sea. Also, we have no longer any idea of how far we may have to travel, and that makes planning for food and all other considerations nearly impossible. Have you prepared, or can you prepare, maps with sufficient detail to let us plan our course intelligently?"

"Good point. I'll see what can be done." Lackland turned from the microphone to encounter several worried frowns. "What's the matter? Can't we make a photographic map as we did of the equatorial regions?"

"Certainly," Rosten replied. "A map can be made, possibly with a lot of detail; but it's going to be difficult. At the equator a rocket could hold above a given point, at circular velocity, only six hundred miles from the surface—right at the inner edge of the ring. Here circular velocity won't be enough, even if we could use it conveniently. We'd have to use a hyperbolic orbit of some sort to get short-range pictures without impossible fuel consumption; and that would mean speeds relative to the surface of several hundred miles a second. You can see what sort of pictures that would mean. It looks as though the shots will have to be taken with long-focus lenses, at extremely long range; and we can only hope that the detail will suffice for Barlennan's needs."

"I hadn't thought of that," admitted Lackland. "We can do it, though; and I don't see any alternative in any case. I suppose Barlennan could explore blind, but it would be asking a lot of him."

"Right. We'll launch one of the rockets and get to work." Lackland gave the substance of this conversation to Barlennan, who replied that he would stay where he was until the information he needed was obtained.

"I could either go on upstream, following the cliff around to the right, or leave the ship and the river and follow to the left. Since I don't know which is best from the point of view of distance, we'll wait. I'd rather go upstream, of course; carrying food and radios will be no joke otherwise."

"All right. How is your food situation? You said something about its being hard to get that far from the ocean."

"It's scarcer, but the place is no desert. We'll get along for a time at least. If we ever have to go overland we may miss you and your gun, though. This crossbow has been nothing but a museum piece for nine tenths of the trip."

"Why do you keep the bow?"

"For just that reason—it's a good museum piece, and museums pay good prices. No one at home has ever seen, or as far as I know even dreamed of, a weapon that works by throwing things. You couldn't spare one of your guns, could you? It needn't work, for that purpose."

Lackland laughed. "I'm afraid not; we have only one. We don't expect to need it, but I don't see how we could explain giving it away." Barlennan gave the equivalent of an understanding nod, and turned back to his own duties. He had much to bring up to date on the bowl that was his equivalent of a globe; the Earthmen, throughout the trip, had been giving him bearing and distance to land in all directions, so he was able to get most of the shores of the two seas he had crossed onto the concave map.

It was also necessary to see to the food question; it was not, as he had told Lackland, really pressing, but more work with the nets was going to be necessary from now on. The river itself, now about two hundred yards wide, appeared to contain fish enough for their present needs, but the land was much less promising. Stony and bare, it ran a few yards from one bank of the stream to end abruptly against the foot of the cliff; from the other, a series of low hills succeeded each other for mile after mile, presumably far beyond the distant horizon. The rock of the escarpment's face was polished glass-smooth, as sometimes happens even on Earth to the rocks at the sliding edges of a fault. Climbing it, even on Earth, would have required the equipment and body weight of a fly (on Mesklin, the fly would have weighed too much). Vegetation was present, but not in any great amount, and in the first fifty days of their stay no member of the *Bree*'s crew saw any trace of land animal life. Occasionally someone thought he saw motion, but each time it turned out to be shadows cast by the whirling sun, now hidden from them only by its periodic trips beyond the cliff. They were so near the south pole that there was no visible change in the sun's altitude during the day.

For the Earthmen, the time was a little more active. Four of the expedition, including Lackland, manned the rocket and dropped planetward from the rapidly moving moon. From their takeoff point the world looked rather like a pie plate with a slight bulge in the center; the ring was simply a line of light, but it stood out against the background of star-studded blackness and exaggerated the flattening of the giant world.

As power was applied both to kill the moon's orbital velocity and bring them out of Mesklin's equatorial plane the picture changed. The ring showed for what it was, but even the fact that it also had two divisions did not make the system resemble that of Saturn. Mesklin's flattening was far too great for it to resemble anything but itself—a polar diameter of less than twenty thousand miles compared to an equatorial one of some forty-eight thousand has to be seen to be appreciated. All the expedition members had seen it often enough now, but they still found it fascinating.

The fall from the satellite's orbit gave the rocket a very high velocity, but, as Rosten had said, it was not high enough. Power had to be used in addition; and although the actual pass across the pole was made some thousands of miles above the surface, it was still necessary for the photographer to work rapidly. Three runs were actually made, each taking between two and three minutes for the photography and many more for the whipping journey around the planet. They made reasonably sure that the world was presenting a different face to the sun each time, so that the height of the cliff could be checked by shadow measurements on all sides; then, with the photographs already fixed and on one of the chart tables, the rocket spent more fuel swinging its hyperbola into a wide arc that intercepted Toorey, and killing speed so that too much acceleration would not be needed when they got there. They could afford the extra time consumed by such a maneuver; the mapping could proceed during the journey.

Results, as usual with things Mesklinite, were interesting if somewhat surprising. In this case, the surprising fact was the size of the fragment of planetary crust that seemed to have been thrust upward en bloc. It was shaped rather like Greenland, some thirty-five hundred miles in length, with the point aimed almost at the sea from which the *Bree* had come. The river leading to it, however, looped widely around and actually contacted its edge at almost the opposite end, in the middle of the broad end of the wedge. Its height at the edges was incredibly uniform; shadow measurements suggested that it might be a trifle higher at the point end than at the *Bree*'s present position, but only slightly. There were no sawtooth shadows to indicate gaps in the wall.

Except at one point. One picture, and one only, showed a blurring of the shadow that might be a gentler slope. It was also in the broad end of the wedge, perhaps eight hundred miles from where the ship now was. Still better, it was upstream—and the river continued to hug the base of the cliff. It looped outward at the point where the shadow break existed as though detouring around the rubble pile of a collapsed slope, which was very promising indeed. It meant that Barlennan had sixteen or seventeen hundred miles to go instead of fifty, with half of it overland; but even the overland part should not be overwhelmingly difficult. Lackland said so, and was answered with the suggestion that he make a more careful analysis of the surface over which his small friend would have to travel. This, however, he put off until after the landing, since there were better facilities at the base.

Once there, microscopes and densitometers in the hands of professional cartographers were a little less encouraging, for the plateau itself seemed rather rough. There was no evidence of rivers or any other specific cause for the break in the wall that Lackland had detected; but the break itself was amply confirmed. The densitometer indicated that the center of the region was lower than the rim, so that it was actually a gigantic shallow bowl; but its depth could not be determined accurately, since there were no distinct shadows across the inner portion. The analysts were quite sure, however, that its deepest part was still well above the terrain beyond the cliffs.

Rosten looked over the final results of the work, and sniffed.

"I'm afraid that's the best we can do for him," he said at last. "Personally, I wouldn't have that country on a bet even if I could live in it. Charlie, you may have to figure out some way to give moral support; I don't see how anyone can give physical."

"I've been doing my best all along. It's a nuisance having this crop up when we were so close to home plate. I just hope he doesn't give us up as a bad job this close to the end; he still doesn't believe everything we say, you know. I wish someone could explain that high-horizon illusion to his—and my—satisfaction; that might shake him out of the notion that his world is a bowl, and our claim to come from another is at least fifty per cent superstition on our part."

"You mean you don't understand why it looks higher?" one of the meteorologists exclaimed in a shocked tone.

"Not in detail, though I realize the air density has something to do with it."

"But it's simple enough—"

"Not for me."

"It's simple for anyone. You know how the layer of hot air just above a road on a sunny day bends sky light back upward at a slight angle, since the hot air is less dense and the light travels faster in it; you see the sky reflection and tend to interpret it as water. You get more extensive mirages sometimes even on Earth, but they're all based on the same thing—a 'lens' or 'prism' of colder or hotter air refracts the light. It's the same here, except the gravity is responsible; even hydrogen decreases rapidly in density as you go up from Mesklin's surface. The low temperature helps, of course."

"All right if you say so; I'm not a—" Lackland got no chance to finish his remark; Rosten cut in abruptly and grimly.

"Just how fast does this density drop off with altitude?" The meteorologist drew a slide rule from his pocket and manipulated it silently for a moment.

"Very roughly, assuming a mean temperature of minus one-sixty, it would drop to about one per cent of its surface density at around fifteen or sixteen hundred feet." A general stunned silence followed his words.

"And—how far would it have dropped at—say—*three hundred feet?*" Rosten finally managed to get the question out. The answer came after a moment of silent lip movement.

"Again very roughly, seventy or eighty percent—probably rather more."

Rosten drummed his fingers on the table for a minute or two, his eyes following their motions; then he looked around at the other faces.

All were looking back at him silently.

"I suppose no one can suggest a bright way out of this one; or does someone really hope that Barlennan's people can live and work under an air pressure that compares to their normal one about as that at forty or fifty thousand feet does to ours?"

"I'm not sure." Lackland frowned in concentration, and Rosten brightened a trifle. "There was some reference a long time ago to his staying under water—excuse me, under methane—for quite a while, and swimming considerable distances. You remember those river-dwellers must have moved the *Bree* by doing just that. If it's the equivalent of holding breath or a storage system such as our whales use, it won't do us any good; but if he can actually get a fair part of the hydrogen he needs from what's in solution in Mesklin's rivers and seas, there might be some hope." Rosten thought for a moment longer.

"All right. Get your little friend on the radio and find out all he knows himself about this ability of his. Rick, look up or find out somehow the solubility of hydrogen in methane at eight atmospheres pressure and temperatures between minus one forty-five and one eighty-five Centigrade. Dave, put that slide rule back in your pocket and get to a calculator; get as precise a value of the hydrogen density on that cliff top as physics, chemistry, math, and the gods of good weather men will let you. Incidentally, didn't you say there was a drop of as much as three atmospheres in the center of some of those tropical hurricanes? Charlie, find out from Barlennan whether and how much he and his men felt that. Let's go." The conference broke up, its members scattering to their various tasks. Rosten remained in the screen room with Lackland, listening to his conversation with the Mesklinite far below.

Barlennan agreed that he could swim below the surface for long periods without trouble; but he had no idea how he did it. He did not breathe anyway, and did not experience any feeling comparable to the human sense of strangulation when he submerged. If he stayed too long and was too active the effect was rather similar to sleepiness, as nearly as he could describe it; if he actually lost consciousness, however, it stopped there; he could be pulled out and revived as much later as anyone cared as long as he didn't starve in the meantime. Evidently there was enough hydrogen in solution in Mesklin's seas to keep him alive, but not for normal activity. Rosten brightened visibly.

"There is no discomfort of the sort you suggest in the middle of the worst storms I have ever experienced," the captain went on. "Certainly no one was too weak to hold on during that one which cast us on the island of the gliders—though we were in its center for only two or three minutes, of course. What is your trouble? I do not understand what all these questions are leading to." Lackland looked to his chief for permission, and received a silent nod of affirmation.

"We have found that the air on top of this cliff, where our rocket is standing, is very much thinner than at the bottom. We doubt seriously that it will be dense enough to keep you and your people going."

"But that is only three hundred feet; why should it change that much in such a short distance?"

"It's that gravity of yours; I'm afraid it would take too long to explain why, but on any world the air gets thinner as you go higher, and the more the gravity the faster that change. On your world the conditions are a trifle extreme."

"But where is the air at what you would call normal for this world?"

"We assume at sea level; all our measures are usually made from that reference."

Barlennan was thoughtful for a little while. "That seems silly; I should think you'd want a level that stayed put to measure from. Our seas go up and down hundreds of feet each year—and I've never noticed any particular change in the air."

"I don't suppose you would, for several reasons; the principal one is that you would be at sea level as long as you were aboard the *Bree,* and therefore at the bottom of the atmosphere in any case. Perhaps it would help you to think of this as a question of what weight of air is above you and what weight below."

"Then there is still a catch," the captain replied. "Our cities do not follow the seas down; they are usually on the seacoast in spring and anywhere from two hundred miles to two thousand inland by fall. The slope of the land is very gentle, of course, but I am sure they are fully three hundred feet above sea level at that time." Lackland and Rosten stared silently at each other for a moment; then the latter spoke.

"But you're a lot farther from the pole in your country—but no, that's quibbling. Even if gravity were only a third as great you'd be experiencing tremendous pressure changes. Maybe we've been taking nova precautions for a red dwarf." He paused for a moment, but the Mesklinite made no answer. "Would you be willing, then, Barlennan, to make at least an attempt to get up to the plateau? We certainly will not insist on your going on if it proves too hard on your physical make-up, but you already know its importance to us."

"Of course I will; we've come this far, and have no real reason to suppose what's coming will be any worse than what's past. Also, I want..." He paused briefly, and went on in another vein. "Have you yet found any way of getting up there, or is your question still hypothetical?" Lackland resumed the human end of the conversation.

"We have found what looks like a way, about eight hundred miles upstream from your present position. We can't be sure you can climb it; it resembles a rock fall of very moderate slope, but we can't tell from our distance how big the rocks may be. If you can't get up there, though, I'm afraid you just can't get up at all. The cliff seems to be vertical all around the plateau except for that one point."

"Very well, we will head upstream. I don't like the idea of climbing even small rocks here, but we'll do our best. Perhaps you will be able to give suggestions when you can see the way through the vision sets."

"It will take you a long time to get there, I'm afraid."

"Not too long; for some reason there is a wind along the cliff in the direction we wish to go. It has not changed in direction or strength since we arrived several score days ago. It is not as strong as the usual sea wind, but it will certainly pull the *Bree* against the current—if the river does not grow too much swifter."

"This one does not grow too much narrower, at any rate, as far as you will be going. If it speeds up, it must be because it grows shallower All we can say to that is that there was no sign of rapids on any of the pictures."

"Very well, Charles. We will start when the hunting parties are all in."

One by one the parties came back to the ship, all with some food but none with anything interesting to report. The rolling country extended as far in all directions as anyone had gone; animals were small, streams scarce, and vegetation sparse except around the few springs. Morale was a trifle low, but it improved with the news that the *Bree* was about to travel again. The few articles of equipment that had been disembarked were quickly reloaded on the rafts, and the ship pushed out into the stream. For a moment she drifted seaward, while the sails were being set; then they filled with the strangely steady wind and she bore up against the current, forging slowly but steadily into unknown areas of the hugest planet man had yet attempted to explore.

16: Valley of Wind

Barlennan rather expected the riverbanks to become more barren as his ship ascended the stream, but if anything, the reverse was the case. Clumps of sprawling, octopuslike growths hugged the ground at either bank, except where the cliff on his left crowded the river too closely to leave them room. After the first hundred miles from the point where they had waited, several streams were seen emptying into the main course; and a number of the crewmen swore they saw animals slinking among the plants. The captain was tempted to land a hunting party and await its return, but two considerations decided him against it. One was the wind, which still blew steadily the way he wanted to go; the other was his desire to reach the end of the journey and examine the miraculous machine the Flyers had set down and lost on the polar wastes of his world.

As the journey progressed, the captain grew more and more astonished at the wind; he had never before known it to blow steadily for more than a couple of hundred days in any direction. Now it was not merely maintaining direction but was turning to follow the curve of the cliff, so that it was always practically dead astern. He did not actually let the watch on deck relax completely, but he did not object when a man turned his attention away from his section of rigging for a day or so. He himself had lost count of the number of days since it had been necessary to trim sails.

The river retained its width, as the Flyers had foretold; as they had also intimated was possible, it grew shallower and swifter. This should have slowed the *Bree* down, and actually did so; but not as much as it might have, for the wind began also to increase. Mile after mile went by, and day after day; and the meteorologists became frantic. Imperceptibly the sun crept higher in its circles about the sky, but much too slowly to convince those scientists that it was responsible for the increased wind force. It became evident to human beings and Mesklinites alike that something about the local physiography must be responsible; and at long last Barlennan became confident enough to stop briefly and land an exploring and hunting party, sure that the wind would still be there when he re-embarked.

It was, and the miles flowed once more under the *Bree*'s rafts. Eight hundred miles, the Flyers had said. The current of the river made the log indication much more than that, but at last the break that had been foretold appeared in the wall of rock, far ahead of them.

For a time the river flowed straight away from it, and they could see it in profile—a nearly straight slope, angling up at about twenty degrees, projecting from the bottom fifty feet of the cliff. As they approached, the course of the stream bent out away from the wall at last, and they could see that the slope was actually a fan-shaped spill radiating from a cleft less than fifty yards wide. The slope grew steeper within the cut, but might still be climbable; no one could tell until they were close enough to see what sort of debris composed the spill itself. The first near view was encouraging; where the river touched the foot of the slope, it could be seen to be composed of pebbles small even by the personal standards of the crew members. If they were not too loose, climbing should be easy.

Now they were swinging around to a point directly in front of the opening, and as they did so the wind at last began to change. It angled *outward* from the cliff, and its speed increased unbelievably. A roar that had sounded as a faint murmur for the last several days in the ears of crewmen and Earthmen alike now began to swell sharply, and as the *Bree* came directly opposite the opening in the rock the source of the sound became apparent.

A blast of wind struck the vessel, threatening to split the tough fabric of her sails and sending her angling across the stream away from the wall of rock. At the same instant the roar increased to almost explosive violence, and in the space of less than a minute the ship was struggling in a storm that vied with any she had encountered since leaving the equator. It lasted only moments; the sails had already been set to catch a quartering wind, and they put enough upstream motion into the ship's path to carry her across the worst of the wind before she could run aground. Once out of it, Barlennan hastily turned his vessel to starboard and ran her across the short remaining distance to shore while he collected his wits. This accomplished, he did what was becoming a habit in unfamiliar situations; he called the Earthmen and asked for an explanation. They did not disappoint him; the voice of one of the weather men answered promptly, vibrant with the overtones the captain had learned to associate with human pleasure.

"That accounts for it, Barl! It's the bowl shape of that plateau! I should say that you'd find it easier to get along up there than we had believed. I can't see why we didn't think of it before!"

"Think of what?" The Mesklinite did not actually snarl, but his puzzlement showed clearly to the crew members who heard him.

"Think what a place like that could do in your gravity, climate, and atmosphere. Look: winter in the part of Mesklin you know—the southern hemisphere—coincides with the world's passage of its closest point to the sun. That's summer in the north, and the icecap boils off—that's why you have such terrific and continual storms at that season. We already knew that. The condensing moisture—methane—whatever you want to call it—gives up its heat and warms the air in your hemisphere, even though you don't see the sun for three or four months. The temperature probably goes up nearly to the boiling point of methane—around minus one forty-five at your surface pressure. Isn't that so? Don't you get a good deal warmer in winter?"

"Yes," admitted Barlennan.

"Very well, then. The higher temperature means that your air *doesn't* get thin so rapidly with altitude—you might say the whole atmosphere expands. It expands, and pours over the edge into that bowl you're beside like water into a sinking soup plate. Then you pass the vernal equinox, the storms die out, and Mesklin starts moving away from the sun. You cool off—right?—and the atmosphere shrinks again; but the bowl has a lot caught inside, with its surface pressure now higher than at the corresponding level outside the bowl. A lot of it spills over, of course, and tends to flow away from the cliff at the bottom—but gets deflected to the left by the planet's spin. That's most of the wind that helped you along. The rest is this blast you just crossed, pouring out of the bowl at the only place it can, creating a partial vacuum on either side of the cleft, so that the wind tends to rush toward it from the sides. It's simple!"

"Did you think of all that while I was crossing the wind belt?" asked Barlennan dryly.

"Sure—came to me in a flash. That's why I'm sure the air up there must be denser than we expected. See?"

"Frankly, no. However, if you are satisfied I'll accept it for now. I'm gradually corning to trust the knowledge of you Flyers. However, theory or no theory, what does this mean to us practically? Climbing the slope in the teeth of that wind is not going to be any joke."

"I'm afraid you'll have to. It will probably die down eventually, but I imagine it will be some months before the bowl empties—perhaps a couple of Earthly years. I think, if it's at all possible for you, Barl, it would be worth attempting the climb without waiting."

Barlennan thought. At the Rim, of course, such a hurricane would pick up a Mesklinite bodily and drive him out of sight in seconds; but at the Rim such a wind could never form, since the air caught in the bowl would have only a tiny fraction of its present weight. That much even Barlennan now had clear.

"We'll go now," he said abruptly to the radio, and turned to give orders to the crew.

The *Bree* was guided across the stream—Barlennan had landed her on the side away from the plateau. There she was dragged well out of the river and her tie lines secured to stakes—there were no plants capable of taking the desired load growing this close to the landslide. Five sailors were selected to remain with the ship; the rest harnessed themselves, secured the draglines of their packs to the harness, and started at once for the slope.

For some time they were not bothered by the wind; Barlennan had made the obvious approach, coming up the side of the fan of rubble. Its farthest parts, as they had already seen, were composed of relatively fine particles—sand and very small pebbles; as they climbed, the rock fragments grew constantly larger. All could understand the reason for this; the wind could carry the smallest pieces farthest, and all began to worry a trifle about the size of the rocks they would have to climb over in the cut itself.

Only a few days were consumed in reaching the side of the wall's opening. The wind was a little fresher here; a few yards on, it issued from behind the corner with a roar that made conversation ever harder as they approached. Occasional eddies struck them, giving a tiny taste of what was to come; but Barlennan halted for only a moment. Then, making sure that his pack was close behind him and securely attached to his harness, he gathered himself together and crawled into the full blast of the wind. The others followed without hesitation.

Their worst fears failed to materialize; climbing individual boulders was not necessary. Such huge fragments were present, indeed, but the downhill side of each was nearly covered by a ramp of finer material that had been swept into the relatively sheltered area by the everlasting wind. The ramps overlapped to a great extent, and where they did not it was always possible to travel across the wind from one to another. Their way was tortuous, but they slowly climbed.

They had to modify the original idea that the wind was not really dangerous. One sailor became hungry, paused in what he thought was shelter, and attempted to take a piece of food from his pack; an eddy around his sheltering rock, caused probably by his very presence which disturbed the equilibrium attained after months and years of steady wind, caught in the open container. It acted like a parachute, snatched its unfortunate owner out of his shelter and down the slope. He was gone from sight in a cloud of freshly disturbed sand in moments, and his fellows looked away. A six-inch fall under this gravity could kill; there would be many such falls before their comrade reached the bottom. If by chance there were not, his own hundreds of pounds of weight would be scraped against the rocks hard enough and fast enough to accomplish the same end. The survivors dug their feet in a little farther, and gave up all thought of eating before they reached the top.

Time after time the sun crossed ahead of them, shining down the cleft. Time after time it appeared behind, blazing into the opening from the opposite direction. Each time the rocks about them lighted up under its direct impact they were a little farther up the long hill; each time, they began at last to feel, the wind was just a little less furious as it roared past their long bodies. The cleft was visibly wider, and the slope gentler. Now they could see the cliff opening out forward and to each side; at last the way ahead of them became practically horizontal and they could see the broad regions of the upper plateau ahead. The wind was still strong, but no longer deadly; and as Barlennan led the way to the left it decreased still further. It was not sharply defined here as it was below; it fed into the cleft from all directions, but from that very fact its strength decreased rapidly as they left the cut behind them. At long last they felt safe in stopping, and all immediately opened their packs and enjoyed a meal for the first time in some three hundred days—a long fast even for Mesklinites.

With hunger attended to, Barlennan began to look over the country ahead. He had stopped his group to one side of the cut, almost at the edge of the plateau, and the ground sloped down away from him around nearly half the compass. It was discouraging ground. The rocks were larger, and would have to be traveled around—climbing any of them was unthinkable. Even keeping to one direction among them would be impossible; no one could see more than a few yards in any direction once the rocks surrounded him, and the sun was utterly useless as a means of guidance. It would be necessary to keep close to the edge (but not too close; Barlennan repressed an inward shudder). The problem of finding the rocket when they reached its neighborhood would have to be solved on the spot; the Flyers would surely be able to help there.

The next problem was food. There was enough in the packs for a long time—probably for the eight hundred miles back to the point above the *Bree*'s old halting place; but there would have to be some means of replenishing the supply, for it would never last the round trip or maintain them at the rocket for any length of time. For a moment Barlennan could not see his way through this problem; then a solution slowly grew on him. He thought it over from every angle and finally decided it was the best that could be managed. Once settled on details, he called Dondragmer.

The mate had brought up the rear on the arduous climb, taking without complaint the bits of sand loosened by the others which had been hurled cruelly against him by the wind. He seemed none the worse for the experience, however; he could have matched the great Hars for endurance, if not for strength. He listened now to the captain's orders without any show of emotion, though they must have disappointed him deeply in at least one way. With his duties clear, he called together the members of his watch who were present, and added to them half the sailors of the captain's watch. Packs were redistributed; all the food was given to the relatively small group remaining with Barlennan, and all the rope except for a single piece long enough to loop through the harnesses of Dondragmer's entire company. They had learned from experience—experience they had no intention of repeating.

These preliminaries attended to, the mate wasted no time; he turned and led his group toward the slope they had just ascended with such effort, and presently the tail of the roped-together procession vanished into the dip that led to the cleft. Barlennan turned to the others.

"We will have to ration food strictly from now on. We will not attempt to travel rapidly; it would do us no good. The *Bree* should get back to the old stopping place well before us, but they will have some preparations to make before they can help us. You two who have radios, don't let anything happen to them; they're the only things that will let us find out when we're near the ship—unless someone wants to volunteer to look over the edge every so often. Incidentally, that may be necessary anyway; but I'll do it if it is."

"Shall we start right away, Captain?"

"No. We will wait here until we know that Dondragmer is back to the ship. If he runs into trouble we will have to use some other plan, which would probably require us to go back down ourselves; in that case it would be a waste of time and effort to have traveled any distance, and would cost time that might be valuable in getting back."

Meanwhile, Dondragmer and his group reached the slope without difficulty. They stopped just long enough for the mate to make sure that all harnesses were securely fastened at regular intervals along the rope he had brought; then he attached his own at the rear, and gave the order to start down.

The rope proved a good idea; it was harder even for the many feet of the Mesklinites to keep their traction while heading downward than it had been on the way up. The wind showed no tendency to pick anyone up this time, since they had no packs on which it could get a grip, but the going was still awkward. As before, everyone lost all track of time, and all were correspondingly relieved when the way opened ahead and they were able to swing to the left out of the wind's path. They still found themselves looking *down,* of course, which was extremely hard on Mesklinite nerves; but the worst of the descent was over. Only three or four days were consumed in getting down the rest of the way and aboard the still waiting *Bree.* The sailors with the ship had seen them coming long enough in advance to develop a number of theories, mostly tragic in tone, concerning the fate of the rest of the party. They were quickly reassured, and the mate reported his arrival to the men on Toorey so that they could relay the information to Barlennan on the plateau. Then the ship was dragged back to the river—a real task, with a quarter of the crew missing and the full power of polar gravity to plaster the rafts to the beach, but it was finally accomplished. Twice the vessel hung up on small pebbles that had not quite stopped her going the other way; the differential hoist was put to effective use. With the *Bree* once more afloat, Dondragmer spent much of the time on the downstream trip examining the hoist. He already knew its principles of construction well enough to have made one without help; but he could not quite figure out just *why* it worked. Several Earthmen watched him with amusement, but none was discourteous enough to show the fact—and none dreamed of spoiling the Mesklinite's chance of solving the problem by himself. Even Lackland, fond as he was of Barlennan, had long since come to the conclusion that the mate was considerably his captain's superior in general intelligence, and rather expected that he would be regaling them with a sound mechanical explanation before the *Bree* reached her former stopping place; but he was wrong.

The position of the grounded rocket was known with great accuracy; the uncertainty was less than half a dozen miles. Its telemetering transmitters—not all the instruments had been of permanent-record type—had continued to operate for more than an Earth year after the failure to answer takeoff signals; in that time an astronomical number of fixes had been taken on the location of the transmitters. Mesklin's atmosphere did not interfere appreciably with radio.

The *Bree* could also be located by radio, as could Barlennan's party; it would be the job of the Earthmen to guide the two groups together and, eventually, lead them to the grounded research projectile. The difficulty was in obtaining fixes from Toorey; all three targets were on the "edge" of the disc as seen from the moon. Still worse, the shape of the planet meant that a tiny error in the determination of signal direction could mean a discrepancy of some thousands of miles on the world's surface; the line of the antenna just about grazed the flattest part of the planet. To remedy this, the rocket that had photographed the planet so much was launched once more, and set into a circular orbit that crossed the poles at regular intervals.

From this orbit, once it was accurately set up, fixes could be taken with sufficient precision on the tiny transmitters that the Mesklinites were carrying with them.

The problem became even simpler when Dondragmer finally brought the *Bree* to its former halting place and established a camp. There was now a fixed transmitter on the planet, and this made it possible to tell Barlennan how much farther he had to go within a minute or two of any time he chose to ask. The trip settled down to routine once more—from above.

17: Elevator

For Barlennan himself it was hardly routine. The upper plateau was as it had seemed from the beginning: arid, stony, lifeless, and confusing. He did not dare go far from the edge; once among those boulders, direction would quickly vanish. There were no hills of any size to serve as land marks, or at least none which could be seen from the ground. The thickly scattered rocks hid everything more than a few yards away, towering into the line of sight in every direction except toward the edge of the cliff.

Travel itself was not too difficult. The ground was level, except for the stones; these merely had to be avoided. Eight hundred miles is a long walk for a man, and a longer one for a creature only fifteen inches long who has to "walk" by rippling forward caterpillar style; and the endless detours made the actual distance covered much more than eight hundred miles. True, Barlennan's people could travel with considerable speed, all things considered; but much had to be considered.

The captain actually began to worry somewhat about the food supply before the trip was over. He had felt that he was allowing a generous safety margin when he first conceived the project; this idea had to be sharply modified. Time and again he anxiously asked the human beings far above how much farther he had to go; sometimes he received an answer—always discouraging—and sometimes the rocket was on the other side of the planet and his answer came from Toorey, telling him to wait a short time for a fix. The relay stations were still functioning, but they could not be used to take a directional reading on his radio.

It did not occur to him until the long walk was nearly over that he could have cut across among the stones after all. The sun by itself, of course, could not have served him as a directional guide; it circled the horizon completely in less than eighteen minutes, and a very accurate clock would be necessary to calculate the actual desired course from its apparent direction. However, the observers in the rocket could have told him at any time whether the sun was in front of him, behind him, or to a particular side with respect to his desired direction of travel. By the time this occurred to anyone, the remaining distance could be covered about as easily by keeping the edge in sight; the cliff was nearly straight between where Barlennan then was and the rendezvous point.

There was still a little food, but not too much, when they finally reached a position where the Earthmen could find no significant difference in the positions of the radios. Theoretically, the first thing to do should have been to proceed with the next phase of Barlennan's plan in order to replenish the supply of eatables; but actually there was a serious step to be taken first. Barlennan had mentioned it before the march began, but no one had really considered the matter with any care. Now it stared them in the eye.

The Earthmen had said they were about as close to the *Bree* as they could get. There should be, then, food only a hundred yards below them; but before they could take any steps toward getting it, someone—and probably several people—must *look over the edge.* They must *see* just where they were in relation to the ship; they must rig up lifting tackle to bring the food up; in short, they must look fully three hundred feet straight down—and they had excellent depth perception.

Still, it had to be done; and eventually it was done. Barlennan, as befitted his position, set the example.

He went—not too rapidly, it must be admitted—to the three-foot limit and fixed his eyes on the low hills and other terrain features visible between him and the distant horizon. Slowly he let his gaze wander downward to closer and closer objects, until it was blocked by the lip of rock directly ahead of him. Without haste, he looked back and forth, getting used to seeing things that he could tell already were below him. Then, almost imperceptibly, he inched forward to take in more and more of the landscape near the foot of the cliff. For a long time it looked generally the same, but he managed to keep his attention principally on the new details he could see rather than on the fearful thing he was doing. At last, however, the river became visible, and he moved forward almost rapidly. The far bank was there, the spot where most of the hunting parties had landed after swimming across; from above, even the branching and rebranching trails they had left—he had never realized that such things showed so plainly from overhead.

Now the near bank could be seen, and the mark where the *Bree* had been drawn up before; a little farther—and the *Bree* herself was there, not a bit changed, sailors sprawled on her rafts or moving slowly about the bank in the neighborhood. For just an instant Barlennan forgot all about height and moved forward another body loop to call out to them. That loop put his head over the edge.

And he looked straight down the cliff.

He had thought that being lifted to the roof of the tank was the most hideous experience—at first—that he had ever undergone. He was never sure, after this, whether or not the cliff was worse. Barlennan did not know just how he got back from the cliff face, and he never asked his men whether he had needed help. When he fully realized his surroundings once more he was a good, safe two yards from the edge, still shaking and uncertain of himself. It took days for his normal personality and thinking ability to resume course.

He finally decided what could—and must—be done. He had been all right merely looking at the ship; the trouble had occurred when his eyes actually had a line to follow between his own position and that remote lower level. The Earthmen suggested this point, and after thought Barlennan agreed. That meant it was possible to do all that was necessary; they could signal the sailors below, and do any rope-pulling needed, as long as they did not actually look down the cliff face itself. Keeping heads a safe couple of inches back from the rim was the key to sanity—and life.

Dondragmer had not seen his captain's head on its brief appearance, but he knew that the other party had arrived at the cliff top. He, too, had been kept informed of its progress by the Flyers. Now he and his crew began examining the edge of the rock wall above them with extreme care while those above pushed a pack to the extreme verge and moved it back and forth. It was finally seen from below, almost exactly above the ship; Barlennan had noticed before giddiness overwhelmed him that they were not exactly in the right spot, and the error had been corrected in showing the signal.

"All right, we have you." Dondragmer made the call in English, and it was relayed by one of the men in the rocket.

The sailor above thankfully stopped waving the empty pack, set it down projecting slightly over the edge so it could still be seen, and moved back to a safe distance from the verge. Meanwhile the rope that had been brought along was broken out. One end was bent firmly around a small boulder, Barlennan taking extreme pains with this operation; if the rope were lost, everyone on the plateau would almost certainly starve to death.

Satisfied at last on this matter, he had the rest of the cable carried close to the edge; and two sailors began carefully paying it over. Dondragmer was informed of their state of progress, but did not station anyone underneath to take the end as it came down. If anyone slipped above and the whole coil went over, the point immediately below could be rather uncomfortable, light as the cable was. He waited until Barlennan reported the line as completely paid out; then he and the rest of the crew went over to the foot of the cliff to find it.

The extra rope had fallen into a tight bundle on the hard ground. Dondragmer's first act was to cut off the excess, straighten it out, and measure it. He had a very accurate idea now of the height of the cliff, for during the long wait he had had time to do much careful checking of shadow lengths.

The excess rope proved to be insufficiently long to reach again the full height of the cliff; so the mate obtained another length from the *Bree,* made sure it was long enough, attached it to the section hanging from the cliff top, and informed the Earthmen that Barlennan could start pulling up.

It was a hard job, but not too hard for the powerful beings at the upper end; and in a relatively short time the second rope was at the top of the cliff and the worst fears of the captain were eased. Now if a cable were dropped they at least had a spare.

The second load was very different from the first, as far as ease of hoisting went. It was a pack loaded with food, weighing about as much as one of the sailors. Normally a single Mesklinite could not lift such a weight anywhere near this part of the planet, and the relatively small crew with Barlennan had their work cut out for them. Only by snagging the rope around a convenient boulder and taking frequent rests did they finally manage to get the load up to and over the edge, and when it was done the rope showed distinct signs of wear all along its length from contact with the boulder as well as the cliff edge itself. Something obviously had to be done, and while he and his group were celebrating the end of the strict food rationing Barlennan decided what it would have to be. He gave the appropriate orders to the mate after the feast.

The next several loads, in accordance with Barlennan's instructions, consisted of several masts and spars, more rope, and a number of pulleys of the sort they had used previously in lowering the *Bree* over the cliff at the distant equator. These were used to construct a tripod and hoist arrangement similar to what they had used before—very gingerly, since the pieces had to be lifted into position for lashing and the old prejudice against having solid objects overhead was present in full force. Since the Mesklinites could not reach far from the ground now anyway, most of the lashing was done with the pieces involved lying flat; the assembly was then pried up into position with other spars as levers and boulders which had been laboriously rolled to convenient locations as fulcrums. A similar team of men, working under their natural conditions, could have done a corresponding job in an hour; it took the Mesklinites many times as long—and none of the watching Earthmen could blame them.

The tripod was assembled and erected well back from the edge, then inched laboriously into position as close to that point as could be managed and its legs propped in place with small boulders which the watching men classed mentally as pebbles. The heaviest of the pulleys was attached to the end of a mast as firmly as possible, the rope threaded through it, and the mast levered into position so that about a quarter of its length projected over the abyss past the supporting tripod. Its inner end was also weighted in place with the small stones. Much time was consumed in this work, but it proved worth while. Only a single pulley was used at first, so the hoisting crew still had their load's full weight to handle; but the friction was largely eliminated, and a cleat attached to the inner end of the mast simplified the holding problem while the crew rested.

Load after load of supplies came up, while the crew below hunted and fished endlessly to keep the stream flowing. The area around the hoisting tackle began to take on a settled appearance; indeed, most of the sailors found time between spells at the rope to erect inch-high walls of pebbles around selected areas of their own so that the neighborhood came gradually to resemble more than slightly one of the cities of their own land. No fabric was available for roofs—or rather, Barlennan wasted no effort bringing any up from below—but in other respects the enclosures were almost homelike.

The supplies on hand were already more than one person could conveniently carry; Barlennan planned to establish caches along the route to the rocket. The journey was not expected to be as long as from the cleft they had climbed, but their stay at the site of the crippled machine would be long, and every provision to make it safe was to be taken. Actually, Barlennan would have liked a few more men on the plateau, so that he could leave some at the hoist and take others with him; but there were certain practical difficulties connected with that. For another group to travel up to the cleft, climb it, and come back to their present station seemed too lengthy a job; nobody liked to think of the alternative. Barlennan, of course, did; but an experiment on the part of one of the crew made it a difficult subject to broach.

That individual, after getting his captain's approval—Barlennan regretted giving it later—and having the crewmen below warned away, had rolled a bullet-sized pebble to the edge of the cliff and given it a final shove. The results had been interesting, to both Mesklinites and Earthmen. The latter could see nothing, since the only view set at the foot of the cliff was still aboard the *Bree* and too distant from the point of impact to get a distinct view; but they heard as well as the natives. As a matter of fact, they saw almost as well; for even to Mesklinite vision the pebble simply vanished. There was a short note like a breaking violin string as it clove the air, followed a split second later by a sharp report as it struck the ground below.

Fortunately it landed on hard, slightly moist ground rather than on another stone; in the latter case, there would have been a distinct chance of someone's being killed by flying splinters. The impact, at a speed of approximately a mile a second, sent the ground splashing outward in a wave too fast for any eye to see while it was in motion, but which froze after a fraction of a second, leaving a rimmed crater surrounding the deeper hole the missile had drilled in the soil. Slowly the sailors gathered around, eying the gently steaming ground; then with one accord they moved a few yards away from the foot of the cliff. It took some time to shake off the mood that experiment engendered.

Nevertheless, Barlennan wanted more men at the top; and he was not the individual to give up a project for fear it might not work. He came out with the proposal of an elevator one day, met the expected flat silence, but continued to revert to the subject at regular intervals as the work went on. As Lackland had long since noted, the captain was a persuasive individual. It was a pity that the present job of persuasion was done in the native language, for the men would greatly have enjoyed hearing Barlennan's remarkably varied and original approaches and seeing his listeners go from utter refusal to consideration, through unsympathetic listening, to grudging consent. They never became enthusiastic partisans of the idea, but Barlennan did not expect miracles anyway. Actually, it is very likely that his success was not entirely due to his own efforts. Dondragmer badly wanted to be among those present when the rocket was reached; he had been extremely unhappy at being ordered back down with the group that returned to the ship, though his ingrained dislike of people who argued against orders had prevented his allowing his feelings to show. Now that there seemed to he a chance to get back to the active group, as he looked on it, he found it much easier than might otherwise have been the case to persuade himself that being pulled up a cliff on the end of a rope really wasn't so bad. In any case, he reflected, if the rope broke he'd never know it. He therefore became a disciple of the captain's views among the sailors at the bottom of the cliff; and as they realized that their senior officer intended to go first, and actually seemed to *want* to go, much of their natural sales resistance disappeared. The automatic relays had now been completed, and Barlennan could talk directly to the other group, so his full strength of personality could also come into play.

The upshot was that a small wooden platform was constructed with a low, solid railing—Dondragmer's invention—that would prevent anyone from seeing down once he was inside. The whole arrangement was supported in a rope sling that would hold it in a horizontal position; this was a relic of the previous hoisting experience at the equator.

The platform, all ropes and knots carefully tested by a tug of war that greatly interested the human spectators, was dragged over beneath the hoist and attached to the main rope. At the request of the mate, some slack was given from above and the last knot tested in the same fashion as the others; satisfied that all was secure, Dondragmer promptly climbed onto the platform, put the last section of railing in place, and gave the signal to hoist. The radio had been dragged over from the ship; Barlennan heard the mate directly. He joined his crew at the rope.

There was practically no swinging, anyway; Dondragmer remembered how uncomfortable that had been the last time he had been on such a device. Here the wind, though still blowing steadily along the cliff, was unable to budge perceptibly the pendulum of which he was a part; its cord was too narrow to furnish a grip for air currents, and the weight of its bob too enormous to be easily shifted by them. This was fortunate not merely from the point of view of comfort; if a swing had started from any cause, its period would have been around half a second at the start, decreasing as he ascended to a value that would have amounted to nearly sonic vibration and almost certainly pulled the structure at the top from its foundations.

Dondragmer was a being of straightforward, practical intelligence, and he made no attempt to do any sightseeing as he ascended. On the contrary, he kept his eyes carefully closed, and was not ashamed to do so. The trip seemed endless, of course; in actual fact, it took about six days. Barlennan periodically stopped proceedings while he inspected the hoist and its anchorage, but these were always sound.

At long last the platform appeared above the edge of the cliff and its supporting sling reached the pulley, preventing any further elevation. The edge of the elevator was only an inch or so from the cliff; it was long and narrow, to accommodate the Mesklinite form, and a push on one end with a spar sent the other swinging over solid ground. Dondragmer, who had opened his eyes at the sound of voices, crawled thankfully off and away from the edge.

The watching Lackland announced his safety even before Barlennan could do so to the waiting sailors below, and his words were at once translated by one who knew some English. They were relieved, to put it mildly; they had seen the platform arrive, but could not tell the condition of its passenger. Barlennan took advantage of their feelings, sending the lift down as fast as possible and starting another passenger up.

The whole operation was completed without accident; ten times in all the elevator made its trip before Barlennan decided that there could be no more taken from below without making the supply job of those who remained too difficult.

The tension was over now, however, and once again a feeling that they were in the final stages of the mission spread through Earthmen and natives alike.

"If you'll wait about two minutes, Barl," Lackland relayed the information given him by one of the computers, "the sun will be exactly on the direction line you should follow. We've warned you that we can't pin the rocket down closer than about six miles; we'll guide you into the middle of the area that we're sure contains it, and you'll have to work out your own search from there. If the terrain is at all similar to what you have where you are now, that will be rather difficult, I fear."

"You are probably right, Charles; we have had no experience with such matters. Still, I am sure we will solve that problem; we have solved all others—frequently with your help, I confess. Is the sun in line yet?"

"Just a moment—there! Is there any landmark even reasonably distant which you can use to hold your line until the sun comes around again?"

"None, I fear. We will have to do the best we can, and take your corrections each day."

"That's a bit like dead reckoning where you don't know the winds or currents, but it will have to do. We'll correct our own figures every time we can get a fix on you. Good luck!"

18: Mound Builders

Direction was a problem, as all concerned found out at once. It was physically impossible to maintain a straight line of travel; every few yards the party had to detour around a boulder that was too high to see or climb over. The physical structure of the Mesklinites aggravated the situation, since their eyes were so close to the ground. Barlennan tried to make his detours in alternate directions, but he had no means of checking accurately the amount of each one. It was a rare day when the direction check from the rocket did not show them to be twenty or thirty degrees off.

About every fifty days a check was made on the position of the transmitter—there was only one moving now; another had been left with the group at the hoist—and a new direction computed. High-precision work was required, and occasionally some doubt was felt about the accuracy of a given fix. When this happened Barlennan was always warned, and left to his own discretion. Sometimes, if the Earthmen did not sound too doubtful of their own work, he would go on; at others, he would wait for a few days to give them a chance for a better fix. While waiting he would consolidate his position, redistributing pack loads and modifying the food rations when it seemed necessary. He had hit upon the idea of trail blazing almost before starting, and a solid line of pebbles marked their path from the edge. He had the idea of eventually clearing all the stones from a path and heaping them on each side, thus making a regular road; but this would be later, when trips back and forth between the grounded rocket and the supply base became regular.

The fifty miles passed slowly under their many feet, but pass it finally did. The men, as Lackland said, had done all they could; to the best of their ability to measure, Barlennan should now be standing beside the stranded machine. Both the vision set and the captain's voice clearly informed him that no such state of affairs existed, which did not surprise him at all.

"That's the best we can do, Barl. I'll swear, knowing our math boys, that you're within six miles of that gadget, and probably a good deal less. You can organize your men better than I for a search. Anything we can do we certainly will, but I can't imagine what it might be at this point. How do you plan to arrange matters?"

Barlennan paused before answering. A six-mile circle is an appalling area to search when visibility averages three or four yards. He could cover territory most rapidly, of course, by spreading out his men; but that raised to the point of near certainty the chance of losing some of them. He put this point up to Lackland.

"The rocket itself is about twenty feet tall," the man pointed out. "For practical purposes your vision circle is therefore larger than you say. If you could only get up on one of those larger boulders you'd probably see the ship from where you are—that's what's so annoying about the whole situation."

"Of course; but we can't do that. The large rocks are six or eight of your feet in height; even if we could climb their nearly vertical sides, I would certainly never again look down a straight wall, and will not risk having my men do so."

"Yet you climbed that cleft up to the plateau."

"That was different. We were never beside an abrupt drop."

"Then if a similar slope led up to one of these boulders, you wouldn't mind getting that far from the ground?"

"No, but—hmmm. I think I see what you're driving at. Just a moment." The captain looked at his surroundings more carefully. Several of the great rocks were nearby; the highest, as he had said, protruded some six feet from the hard ground. Around and between them were the ever-present pebbles that seemed to floor the whole plateau. Possibly if Barlennan had ever been exposed to solid geometry he would not have made the decision he did; but having no real idea of the volume of building material he was undertaking to handle, he decided that Lackland's idea was sound.

"We'll do it, Charles. There's enough small rock and dirt here to build anything we want." He turned from the radio and outlined the plan to the sailors. If Dondragmer had any doubts about its feasibility he kept them to himself; and presently the entire group was rolling stones. Those closest to the selected rock were moved close against it, and others against these, until a circle of bare ground began to spread outward from the scene of operations. Periodically a quantity of the hard soil was loosened by harder pincers and spread onto the layer of small rocks; it was easier to carry and filled more space—until the next layer of stone tamped it down.

Progress was slow but steady. Some indication of the time it took may be gained from the fact that at one point part of the group had to be sent back along the blazed trail for further food supplies—a thing which had been unnecessary in the eight-hundred-mile walk from the cleft; but at last the relatively flat top of the boulder felt the tread of feet, probably for the first time since the inner energies of Mesklin had pushed the plateau to its present elevation. The ramp spread down and to each side from the point of access; no one approached the other side of the boulder, where the drop was still sheer.

From the new vantage point Lackland's prediction was fulfilled—after months of travel and danger, the goal of the expedition was in sight. Barlennan actually had the vision set hauled up the ramp so the Earthmen could see it too; and for the first time in over an Earth year, Rosten's face lost its habitual grim expression. It was not much to see; perhaps one of the Egyptian pyramids, plated with metal and placed far enough away, would have looked somewhat like the blunt cone that lifted above the intervening stones. It did not resemble the rocket Barlennan had seen before—in fact, it did not greatly resemble any rocket previously built within twenty light-years of Earth; but it was obviously something that did not belong to Mesklin's normal landscape, and even the expedition members who had not spent months on the monstrous planet's surface seemed to feel weight roll from their shoulders.

Barlennan, though pleased, did not share the abandon that was approaching party intensity on Toorey. He was better able than those whose view depended on television to judge just what lay between his present position and the rocket. This appeared no worse than what they had already crossed, but it was certainly no better. There would no longer be the Earthmen's guidance, either; and even with the present vantage point, he could not quite see how the party was to maintain its line of march for the mile and a half that they would have to travel. The men did not actually know the direction now, so their method would not work—or would it? He could *tell them* when the sun lay in the right direction; after that they could call him each time it passed through the same bearing. For that matter, one man could stay here and give the same information without bothering the Flyers—but wait; he had only one radio now. It could not be in both places at once. For the first time Barlennan really missed the set that had been left with the river-dwellers.

Then it occurred to him that he might not need a radio. True, the air did not carry sound so well here—it was the only aspect of the thinner atmosphere of the plateau that the sailors had noticed at all—but the Mesklinite voice, as Lackland had remarked, was something that had to be heard to be believed. The captain decided to try it; he would leave one man here on the lookout platform, whose duty would consist of hooting with all the energy the muscles around his swimming-siphon could muster each time the sun passed straight above the gleaming cone that was their goal. The trail would be blazed as before so that he could follow when the others arrived.

Barlennan outlined this idea to the group. Dondragmer pointed out that on the basis of past experience they might even so go too far to one side, since there would be no way of making fixes as the Earthmen had done to correct cumulative errors; the fact that the watcher's voice did not sound from directly opposite the sun at any time would mean nothing in this echo-rich neighborhood. He admitted, however, that it was the best idea so far, and did stand a good chance of bringing them within sight of the rocket. A sailor was chosen, therefore, to man the observation post, and the trip was resumed in the new direction.

For a short distance the post itself remained in sight, and it was possible to judge the error that had crept into their course each time the sailor's voice was heard. Presently, however, the rock on which he was standing was lost behind others of equal size, and navigation settled down to the task of making sure they were heading as closely as possible toward the sun each time the echoing hoot sounded in their ears. The sound grew weaker as the days passed, but with no other sounds on the lifeless plateau to cover it there was never any doubt of what they heard.

None of them even yet considered themselves experienced enough in land travel to estimate accurately the distance covered, and all were used to arriving much later than original hopes called for; so the group was pleasantly surprised when finally the monotony of the desert of stone was broken by a change in the landscape. It was not exactly the change that had been expected, but it attracted attention for all that.

It was almost directly ahead of them, and for a moment several of the group wondered whether they had in some incomprehensible way traveled in a circle. A long slope of mixed dirt and pebbles showed between the boulders. It was about as high as the one they had built to the observation station; but as they approached they saw it extended much farther to each side—as far, in fact, as anyone could see. It lapped around large boulders like an ocean wave frozen in mid-motion; even the Mesklinites, totally unused to explosion or meteor craters, could see that the material had been hurled outward from some point beyond the slope. Barlennan, who had seen rockets from Toorey land more than once, had a pretty good idea of the cause and of what he was going to see even before the party topped the rise. He was right in general, if not in detail.

The rocket stood in the center of the bowl-shaped indentation that had been blasted by the fierce wash of her supporting jets. Barlennan could remember the way snow had swirled out of the way when the cargo rocket landed near Lackland's "Hill." He could appreciate the fact that the lifting power used here must have been far mightier in order to ease the bulk of this machine down, smaller though it was. There were no large boulders near it, though a few reared up near the sides of the bowl. The ground inside was bare of pebbles; the soil itself had been scooped out so that only four or five of the projectile's twenty feet of height rose above the general run of rocks covering the plain.

Its base diameter was almost as great as its height, and remained so for perhaps a third of the way upward. This, Lackland explained when the vision set had been brought to bear on the interior of the blast crater, was the part housing the driving power.

The upper part of the machine narrowed rapidly to a blunt point, and this housed the apparatus which represented such a tremendous investment in time, intellectual effort, and money on the part of so many worlds. A number of openings existed in this part, as no effort had been made to render the compartments airtight. Such apparatus as required either vacuum or special atmosphere in which to function was individually sealed.

"You said once, after the explosion in your tank that wrecked it so completely, that something of the sort must have happened here," Barlennan said. "I see no signs of it; and if the holes I see were open when you landed it, how could enough of your oxygen still be there to cause an explosion? You told me that beyond and between worlds there was no air, and what you had would leak out through any opening."

Rosten cut in before Lackland could answer. He and the rest of the group had been examining the rocket on their own screen.

"Barl is quite right. Whatever caused the trouble was not an oxygen blast. I don't know what it was. We'll just have to keep our eyes open when we go inside, in the hope of finding the trouble—not that it will matter much by then, except to people who want to build another of these things. I'd say we might as well get to work; I have a horde of physicists on my neck simply quivering for information. It's lucky they put a biologist in charge of this expedition; from now on there won't be a physicist fit to approach."

"Your scientists will have to contain themselves a little longer," Barlennan interjected. "You seem to have overlooked something."

"What?"

"Not one of the instruments you want me to put before the lens of your vision set is within seven feet of the ground; and all are inside metal walls which I suspect would be rather hard for us to remove by brute force, soft as your metals seem to be."

"Blast it, you're right, of course. The second part is easy; most of the surface skin is composed of quick-remove access plates that we can show you how to handle without much trouble. For the rest—hmm. You have nothing like ladders, and couldn't use them if you had. Your elevator has the slight disadvantage of needing at least an installation crew at the top of its travel before you can use it. Offhand, I'm afraid I'm stuck for the moment. We'll think of something, though; we've come too far to be stumped now."

"I would suggest that you spend from now until my sailor gets here from the lookout in thought. If by that time you have no better idea, we will use mine."

"What? You have an idea?"

"Certainly. We got to the top of that boulder from which we saw your rocket; what is wrong with using the same method here?" Rosten was silent for fully half a minute; Lackland suspected he was kicking himself mentally.

"I can only see one point," he said at last. "You will have a much larger job of rock-piling than you did before. The rocket is more than three times as high as the boulder where you built the ramp, and you'll have to build up all around it instead of on one side, I suspect."

"Why can we not simply make a ramp on one side up to the lowest level containing the machines you are interested in? It should then be possible to get up the rest of the way inside, as you do in the other rockets."

"For two principal reasons. The more important one is that you won't be able to climb around inside; the rocket was not built to carry living crews, and has no communication between decks. All the machinery was built to be reached from outside the hull, at the appropriate level. The other point is that you cannot start at the lower levels; granted that you could get the access covers off, I seriously doubt that you could lift them back in place when you finished with a particular section. That would mean that you'd have the covers off all around the hull before you built up to the next level; and I'm rather afraid that such a situation would not leave enough metal in place below to support the sections above. The top of the cone would—or at least might—collapse. Those access ports occupy the greater part of the skin, and are thick enough to take a lot of vertical load. Maybe it was bad design, but remember we expected to open them only in space, with no weight at all.

"What you will have to do, I fear, is bury the rocket completely to the *highest* level containing apparatus and then dig your way down, level by level. It may even be advisable to remove the machinery from each section as you finish with it; that will bring the load to an absolute minimum. After all, there'll only be a rather frail-looking skeleton when you have all those plates off, and I don't like to picture what would happen to it with a full equipment load times seven hundred, nearly."

"I see." Barlennan took his turn at a spell of silent thought. "You yourself can think of no alternative to this plan? It involves, as you rightly point out, much labor."

"None so far. We will follow your recommendation, and think until your other man comes from the observation point. I suspect we work under a grave disadvantage, though—we are unlikely to think of any solution which does not involve machinery we couldn't get to you."

"That I had long since noticed."

The sun continued to circle the sky at a shade better than twenty degrees a minute. A call had long since gone echoing out to the observation platform to let the guide know his work was done; he was presumably on the way in. The sailors did nothing except rest and amuse themselves; all, at one time or another, descended the easy slope of the pit the blasts had dug to examine the rocket at close quarters. All of them were too intelligent to put its operation down to magic, but it awed them nonetheless. They understood nothing of its principle of operation, though that could easily have been made clear if Lackland had stopped to wonder how a race that did not breathe could nevertheless speak aloud. The Mesklinites possessed in well-developed form the siphon arrangement, similar to that of Earthly cephalopods, which their amphibious ancestors had used for high-speed swimming; they used it as the bellows for a very Earthly set of vocal cords, but were still able to put it to its original function. They were well suited by nature to understand the rocket principle.

Their lack of understanding was not all that aroused the sailors' respect. Their race built cities, and they had regarded themselves as good engineers; but the highest walls they ever constructed reached perhaps three inches from the ground. Multi-storied buildings, even roofs other than a flap of fabric, conflicted too violently with their almost instinctive fear of solid material overhead. The experiences of this group had done something to change the attitude from one of unreasoning fear to one of intelligent respect for weight, but the habit clung nevertheless. The rocket was some eighty times the height of any artificial structure their race had ever produced; awe at the sight of such a thing was inevitable.

The arrival of the lookout sent Barlennan back to the radio, but there was no better idea than his own to be had. This did not surprise him at all. He brushed Rosten's apologies aside, and set to work along with his crew. Not even then did any of the watchers above think of the possibility of their agent's having ideas of his own about the rocket. Curiously enough, such a suspicion by then would have come much too late—too late to have any foundation.

Strangely, the work was not as hard or long as everyone had expected. The reason was simple; the rock and earth blown out by the jets was relatively loose, since there was no weather in the thin air of the plateau to pack it down as it had been before. A human being, of course, wearing the gravity nullifier the scientists hoped to develop from the knowledge concealed in the rocket, could not have pushed a shovel into it, for the gravity was a pretty good packing agent; it was loose only by Mesklinite standards. Loads of it were being pushed down the gentle inner slope of the pit to the growing pile around the tubes; pebbles were being worked clear of the soil and set rolling the same way, with a hooted warning beforehand. The warning was needed; once free and started, they moved too fast for the human eye to follow, and usually buried themselves completely in the pile of freshly moved earth.

Even the most pessimistic of the watchers began to feel that no more setbacks could possibly occur, in spite of the number of times they had started to unpack shelved apparatus and then had to put it away again. They watched now with mounting glee as the shining metal of the research projectile sank lower and lower in the heap of rock and earth, and finally vanished entirely except for a foot-high cone that marked the highest level in which machinery had been installed.

At this point the Mesklinites ceased work, and most of them retreated from the mound. The vision set had been brought up and was now facing the projecting tip of metal, where part of the thin line marking an access port could be seen. Barlennan sprawled alone in front of the entrance, apparently waiting for instructions on the method of opening it; and Rosten, watching as tensely as everyone else, explained to him. There were four quick-disconnect fasteners, one on each corner of the trapezoidal plate. The upper two were about on a level with Barlennan's eyes; the others some six inches below the present level of the mound. Normally they were released by pushing in and making a quarter turn with a broad-bladed screwdriver; it seemed likely that Mesklinite pincers could perform the same function. Barlennan, turning to the plate, found that they could. The broad, slotted heads turned with little effort and popped outward, but the plate did not move otherwise.

"You had better fasten ropes to one or both of those heads, so you can pull the plate outward from a safe distance when you've dug down to the others and unfastened them," Rosten pointed out. "You don't want that piece of hardware falling on top of anyone; it's a quarter of an inch thick. The lower ones are a darned sight thicker, I might add."

The suggestion was followed, and the earth scraped rapidly away until the lower edge of the plate was uncovered. The fasteners here proved no more troublesome than their fellows, and moments later a hard pull on the ropes unseated the plate from its place in the rocket's skin. For the first fraction of an inch of its outward motion it could be seen; then it vanished abruptly, and reappeared lying horizontally while an almost rifle-like report reached the ears of the watchers. The sun, shining into the newly opened hull, showed clearly the single piece of apparatus inside; and a cheer went up from the men in the screen room and the observing rocket.

"That did it, Barl! We owe you more than we can say. If you'll stand back and let us photograph that as it is, we'll start giving you directions for taking out the record and getting it to the lens." Barlennan did not answer at once; his actions spoke some time before he did.

He did not get out of the way of the eye. Instead he crawled toward it and pushed the entire set around until it no longer covered the nose of the rocket.

"There are some matters we must discuss first," he said quietly.

19: New Bargain

Dead silence reigned in the screen room. The head of the tiny Mesklinite filled the screen, but no one could interpret the expression on the completely unhuman "face." No one could think of anything to say; asking Barlennan what he meant would be a waste of words, since he obviously planned to tell anyway. He waited for long moments before resuming his speech; and when he did, he used better English than even Lackland realized he had acquired.

"Dr. Rosten, a few moments ago you said that you owed us more than you could hope to repay. I realize that your words were perfectly sincere in one way—I do not doubt the actuality of your gratitude for a moment—but in another they were merely rhetorical. You had no intention of giving us any more than you had already agreed to supply—weather information, guidance across new seas, possibly the material aid Charles mentioned some time ago in the matter of spice collecting. I realize fully that by your moral code I am entitled to no more; I made an agreement and should adhere to it, particularly since your side of the bargain has largely been fulfilled already.

"However, I want more; and since I have come to value the opinions of some, at least, of your people I want to explain why I am doing this—I want to justify myself, if possible. I tell you now, though, that whether I succeed in gaining your sympathy or not, I will do exactly as I planned.

"I am a merchant, as you well know, primarily interested in exchanging goods for what profit I can get. You recognized that fact, offering me every material you could think of in return for my help; it was not your fault that none of it was of use to me. Your machines, you said, would not function in the gravity and pressure of my world; your metals I cannot use—and would not need if I could; they lie free on the surface in many parts of Mesklin. Some people use them for ornaments; but I know from talk with Charles that they cannot be fashioned into really intricate forms without great machines, or at least more heat than we can easily produce. We do know the thing you call fire, by the way, in ways more manageable than the flame cloud; I am sorry to have deceived Charles in that matter, but it seemed best to me at the time.

"To return to the original subject, I refused all but the guidance and weather information of the things you were willing to give. I thought some of you might be suspicious of that, but I have heard no sign of it in your words. Nevertheless, I agreed to make a voyage longer than any that has been made in recorded history to help solve your problem. You had told me how badly you needed the knowledge; none of you appeared to think that I might want the same thing, though I asked time and again for just that when I saw one or another of your machines. You refused answers to those questions, making the same excuse every time. I felt, therefore, that any way in which I could pick up some of the knowledge you people possess was legitimate. You have said, at one time or another, much about the value of what you call 'science,' and always implied was the fact that my people did not have it. I cannot see why, if it is good and valuable to your people, it would not be equally so to mine.

"You can see what I am leading up to. I came on this voyage with exactly the same objective in my mind that was in yours when you sent me; I came to learn. I want to know the things by which you perform such remarkable acts. You, Charles, lived all winter in a place that should have killed you at once, by the aid of that science; it could make as much difference in the lives of my people, I am sure you will agree.

"Therefore I offer you a new bargain. I realize that my failure to live up to the letter of the old one may make you reluctant to conclude another with me. That will be simply too bad; I make no bones about pointing out that you can do nothing else. You are not here; you cannot come here; granting that you might drop some of your explosives down here in anger, you will not do so as long as I am near this machine of yours. The agreement is simple: knowledge for knowledge. You teach me, or Dondragmer, or anyone else in my crew who has the time and ability to learn the material, all the time we are working to take this machine apart for you and transmit the knowledge it contains."

"Just a—"

"Wait, Chief." Lackland cut short Rosten's expostulation. "I know Barl better than you do. Let me talk." He and Rosten could see each other in their respective screens, and for a moment the expedition's leader simply glared. Then he realized the situation and subsided.

"Right, Charlie. Tell him."

"Barl, you seemed to have some contempt in your tone when you referred to our excuse for not explaining our machines to you. Believe me, we were not trying to fool you. They are complicated; so complicated that the men who design and build them spend nearly half their lives first learning the laws that make them operate and the arts of their actual manufacture. We did not mean to belittle the knowledge of your people, either; it is true that we know more, but it is only because we have had longer in which to learn.

"Now, as I understand it, you want to learn about the machines in this rocket as you take it apart. Please, Barl, take my word as the sincerest truth when I tell you first that I for one could not do it, since I do not understand a single one of them; and second, that not one would do you the least good if you did comprehend it. The best I can say right now is that they are machines for measuring things that cannot be seen or heard or felt or tasted—things you would have to see in operation in other ways for a long time before you could even begin to understand. That is not meant as insult; what I say is almost as true for me, and I have grown up from childhood surrounded by and even using those forces. I do not understand them. I do not expect to understand them before I die; the science we have covers so much knowledge that no one man can even begin to learn all of it, and I must be satisfied with the field I do know—and perhaps add to it what little one man may in a lifetime.

"We cannot accept your bargain, Barl, because it is physically impossible to carry out our side of it."

Barlennan could not smile in the human sense, and he carefully refrained from giving his own version of one. He answered as gravely as Lackland had spoken.

"You can do your part, Charles, though you do not know it.

"When I first started this trip, all the things you have just said were true, and more. I fully intended to find this rocket with your help, and then place the radios where you could see nothing and proceed to dismantle the machine itself, learning all your science in the process.

"Slowly I came to realize that all you have said is true. I learned that you were *not* keeping knowledge from me deliberately when you taught us so quickly and carefully about the laws and techniques used by the glidermakers on that island. I learned it still more surely when you helped Dondragmer make the differential pulley. I was expecting you to bring up those points in your speech just now; why didn't you? They were good ones.

"It was actually when you were teaching us about the gliders that I began to have a slight understanding of what was meant by your term 'science.' I realized, before the end of that episode, that a device so simple you people had long since ceased to use it actually called for an understanding of more of the universe's laws than any of my people realized existed. You said specifically at one point, while apologizing for a lack of exact information, that gliders of that sort had been used by your people more than two hundred years ago. I can guess how much more you know now—guess just enough to let me realize what I can't know.

"But you can still do what I want. You have done a little already, in showing us the differential hoist. I do not understand it, and neither does Dondragmer, who spent much more time with it; but we are both sure it is some sort of relative to the levers we have been using all our lives. We want to start *at the beginning,* knowing fully that we cannot learn all you know in our lifetimes. We do hope to learn enough to understand how you have found these things out. Even I can see it is not just guesswork, or even philosophizing like the learned ones who tell us that Mesklin is a bowl. I am willing at this point to admit you are right; but I would like to know how you found out the same fact for your own world. I am sure you knew before you left its surface and could see it all at once. I want to know why the *Bree* floats, and why the canoe did the same, for a while. I want to know what crushed the canoe. I want to know why the wind blows down the cleft all the time—no, I didn't understand your explanation. I want to know why we are warmest in winter when we can't see the sun for the longest time. I want to know why a fire glows, and why flame dust kills. I want my children or theirs, if I ever have any, to know what makes this radio work, and your tank, and someday this rocket. I want to know much—more than I can learn, no doubt; but if I can start my people learning for themselves, the way you must have—well, I'd be willing to stop selling at a profit." Neither Lackland nor Rosten found anything to say for a long moment. Rosten broke the silence.

"Barlennan, if you learned what you want, and began to teach your people, would you tell them where the knowledge came from? Do you think it would be good for them to know?"

"For some, yes; they would want to know about other worlds, and people who had used the same way to knowledge they were starting on. Others—well, we have a lot of people who let the rest pull the load for them. If they knew, they wouldn't bother to do any learning themselves; they'd just ask for anything particular they wanted to know—as I did at first; and they'd never realize you weren't telling them because you couldn't. They'd think you were trying to cheat them. I suppose if I told anyone, that sort would find out sooner or later, and—well, I guess it would be better to let them think I'm the genius. Or Don; they'd be more likely to believe it of him."

Rosten's answer was brief and to the point.

"You've made a deal."

20: Flight of the *Bree*

A gleaming skeleton of metal rose eight feet above a flat-topped mound of rock and earth. Mesklinites were busily attacking another row of plates whose upper fastenings had just been laid bare. Others were pushing the freshly removed dirt and pebbles to the edge of the mound. Still others moved back and forth along a well-marked road that led off into the desert, those who approached dragging flat, wheeled carts loaded with supplies, those departing usually hauling similar carts empty. The scene was one of activity; practically everyone seemed to have a definite purpose. There were two radio sets in evidence now, one on the mound where an Earthman was directing the dismantling from his distant vantage point and the other some distance away.

Dondragmer was in front of the second set, engaged in animated conversation with the distant being he could not see. The sun still circled endlessly, but was very gradually descending now and swelling very, very slowly.

"I am afraid," the mate said, "that we will have serious trouble checking on what you tell us about the bending of light. Reflection I can understand; the mirrors I made from metal plates of your rocket made that very clear. It is too bad that the device from which you let us take the lens was dropped in the process; we have nothing like your glass, I am afraid."

"Even a reasonably large piece of the lens will do, Don," the voice came from the speaker. It was not Lackland's voice; he was an expert teacher, he had found, but sometimes yielded the microphone to a specialist. "Any piece will bend the light, and even make an image—but wait; that comes later. "Try to find what's left of that hunk of glass, Don, if your gravity didn't powder it when the set landed." Dondragmer turned from the set with a word of agreement; then turned back as he thought of another point.

"Perhaps you could tell what this 'glass' is made of, and whether it takes very much heat? We have good hot fires, you know. Also there is the material set over the Bowl—ice, I think Charles called it. Would that do?"

"Yes, I know about your fires, though I'm darned if I see how you do burn plants in a hydrogen atmosphere, even with a little meat thrown in. For the rest, ice should certainly do, if you can find any. I don't know what the sand of your river is made of, but you can try melting it in one of your hottest fires and see what comes out. I certainly don't guarantee anything, though; I simply say that on Earth and the rest of the worlds I know ordinary sand will make a sort of glass, which is greatly improved with other ingredients. I'm darned if I can see either how to describe those ingredients to you or suggest where they might be found, though."

"Thank you; I will have someone try the fire. In the meantime, I will search for a piece of lens, though I fear the blow when it struck left little usable. We should not have tried to take the device apart near the edge of the mound; the thing you called a 'barrel' rolled much too easily."

Once more the mate left the radio, and immediately encountered Barlennan.

"It's about time for your watch to get on the plates," the captain said. "I'm going down to the river. Is there anything your work needs?"

Dondragmer mentioned the suggestion about sand.

"You can carry up the little bit I'll need, I should think, without getting the fire too hot; or did you plan on a full load of other things?"

"No plans; I'm taking the trip mainly for fun. Now that the spring wind has died out and we get breezes in every old direction, a little navigation practice might be useful. What good is a captain who can't steer his ship?"

"Fair enough. Did the Flyers tell you what this deck of machines was for?"

"They did pretty well, but if I were really convinced about this space-bending business I'd have swallowed it more easily. They finished up with the old line about words not really being enough to describe it. What else beside words can you use, in the name of the Suns?"

"I've been wondering myself; I think it's another aspect of this quantity-code they call mathematics. I like mechanics best myself; you can do something with it from the very beginning." He waved an arm toward one of the carts and another toward the place where the differential pulley was lying.

"It would certainly seem so. We'll have a lot to take home—and some, I guess, we'd better not be too hasty in spreading about." He gestured at what he meant, and the mate agreed soberly. "Nothing to keep us from playing with it now, though." The captain went his way, and Dondragmer looked after him with a mixture of seriousness and amusement, he rather wished that Reejaaren were around; he had never liked the islander, and perhaps now he would be a little less convinced that the *Bree*'s crew was composed exclusively of liars.

That sort of reflection was a waste of time, however. He had work to do. Pulling plates off the metal monster was less fun than being told how to do experiments, but his half of the bargain had to be fulfilled. He started up the mound, calling his watch after him.

Barlennan went on to the *Bree.* She was already prepared for the trip, two sailors aboard and her fire hot. The great expanse of shimmering, nearly transparent fabric amused him; like the mate, he was thinking of Reejaaren, though in this case it was of what the interpreter's reaction would be if he saw the use to which his material was being put. Not possible to trust sewn seams, indeed! Barlennan's own people knew a thing or two, even without friendly Flyers to tell them. He had patched sails with the stuff before they were ten thousand miles from the island where it had been obtained, and his seams had held even in front of the valley of wind.

He slipped through the opening in the rail, made sure it was secured behind him, and glanced into the fire pit, which was lined with metal foil from a condenser the Flyers had donated. All the cordage seemed sound and taut; he nodded to the crewmen. One heaped another few sticks on the glowing, flameless fire in the pit; the other released the moorings.

Gently, her forty-foot sphere of fabric bulging with hot air, the new *Bree* lifted from the plateau and drifted riverward on the light breeze.

Under

"That looks all right. Come aboard, Cookie. *Then* reach out and light it. Hars, lift—NOW!"

Neither crewman acknowledged the orders verbally; they acted. Karondrasee whipped aboard in normal centipede fashion, scooped a coal from the lifting fire into the long spoon waiting for the purpose beside the furnace, reached through the handiest crenellation in the *Bree*'s mostly solid gunwale, and steadied the burning fragment over the frayed-out end of rope fuse beside the basket. He wasn't bothered by the form of address; there was need for haste, "Cookie" was shorter than "Flight Engineer," the duties overlapped heavily, and he was filling both of them. He was, however, annoyed and uneasy for other reasons; he had had to spend many days treating the three lengths of cord with meat juice and, as he saw it, wasting two of them. As cook of the old *Bree*'s crew he was used to seeing the results of his labors vanish, but he disliked seeing them burn up. That was the annoying part.

He was uneasy as well, because things might not work this time as they had on the two test burns. The first had not been dangerous, of course; it had simply served to show whether his juice treatment would really turn rope into a useful fuse. That sample was short enough to need only a day or so to make.

The second test should either not have worked at all or produced a simple, harmless fire fountain. By doing the latter it had encouraged everyone. Now the third and potentially most dangerous trial was under way.

The captain seemed unsure, too. He was watching the fuse as closely as Karondrasee was. So was Sherrer.

Hars was not. He was tending his lifting fire and eyeing the tensely swollen bag of the third *Bree*. He knew enough about the present test to want the ship to lift quickly, but if it rose *too* quickly, that would of course be the Captain's fault. Hars was obeying orders.

That last thought was also in Barlennan's mind, and he was watching the delivery of the bit of fire tensely. If he *had* given Hars his order too soon—

Strictly speaking, he had. He felt the basket's deck stir under him, and saw the figures on the Flyers' instrument change. He would have stopped breathing for a moment if he had been a breather. Karondrasee, however, also knew the plan, knew what would have to be done if the fuse failed to light, and certainly didn't want to get out and push the coal to the right place while the balloon rose without him. As he saw his spoon rising slowly from its target, he tipped it over without waiting for an order.

No one actually saw the coal drop; falling, here, was much too fast for even Mesklinite vision. Cook and captain did see, as the air below it was compressed enough to speed its combustion rate by perhaps an order of magnitude, a sudden flash on the ground half an inch to one side of the fuse end. Before either could comment or even curse, the rope ignited—apparently from radiation, but conceivably from a flying spark, though neither witness could vouch for the latter. They didn't really care; the wadded rope-end was starting to glow, and that was all that mattered.

"Lighted all right?"

"Yes." Barlennan didn't bother to look at the block of polymer from which the question had emerged. "Hars, up as fast as you can. Never mind checking wind. I'd like to keep on this side of the rock to see what happens, but getting to the other may be safer and staying out of reach will be safest of all. I wish someone knew what 'out of reach' was, but if we do blow that way *up* will mean a lot more than *sideways*."

"Right, Captain. Up it is."

Up it was. Not rapidly; it took a lot of lift to start an upward motion near Mesklin's south pole, even though once started acceleration tended to be high. That was why more than a thousand feet of fuse had been laid out, and the original test of its burn rate had been made.

"Please keep this eye aimed at the rock, wherever we go." The block spoke again.

"Right. Sherrer will see to it," the captain responded, still without looking at the communicator. "We have you blocked up far enough to look over the rail already, and he'll wedge the back up more it it's needed."

"Are you set to turn it too, or will it be easier to rotate the whole balloon?"

"Much easier, though it'll cost a little lift. It will also make it unnecessary for you to look across the fire. Don't worry yet, it should take half a day to burn down."

"I never worry. I just wonder." Jeanette Parkos, who had taken up Charles Lackland's communication duties when health had forced him to return to Earth, was rich in comments like that. She had greatly improved Barlennan's Spacelang in the last few thousand days, and to his surprise and in spite of her alien hearing and vocal limitations she already spoke Stennish much more fluently and clearly than her predecessor ever had.

"I'd appreciate a bit of down tilt whenever Sherrer can provide it," she now suggested. "I can't see up to the horizon, but I can't see down enough for anything within a couple of miles, either. You're a lot closer to the rock than that, according to the tracker readout, and I hope you're closer still when it goes. I sometimes wish this thing had a wider field of view. Of course, I sometimes wish it could zoom closer, too."

Barlennan was not entirely sure that he shared the hope, though he wanted a good view himself. The Flyer was on Toorey, Mesklin's inner moon. Her communicator would let her see what went on. The closer to the rock the better for her, but nothing could, presumably, happen to her at that distance. Barlennan lacked both the distance and the seeing equipment, and wasn't sure which he missed more. The Flyers had assured him that there couldn't possibly be enough energy in the propellant cell now being tested to lift the rock above it any significant distance, but the Flyers had been wrong before. He remembered vividly the Foucault pendulum fiasco; they had been certain it would give a convincing demonstration, this close to the pole, that Mesklin rather than the sky was doing the spinning. Unfortunately no one, native or alien, had been able to observe the six-inch pendulum's plane of motion; its period was too short, and like any tuning fork its vibration had been damped out by the air a few seconds after it had been started.

They had all *heard* it, of course.

None of the Flyers seemed to remember that now. Barlennan had not seen an explosive in action since Lackland had used his tank's gun so many thousands of days before, since the previous cell test had produced only the hoped-for fire fountain; but he had been told in detail how such substances were used elsewhere in the universe. These accounts, and a vivid memory of the effect of the shells Lackland had used, left him wondering why no one seemed to worry about the behavior of *pieces* of the rock.

Unlike Jeanette, Barlennan was a rather efficient worrier; he had not raised the question with her because he knew the aliens were extremely knowledgeable in spite of their occasional slips, and he still didn't like to look ignorant. Answers beginning with "Of course" bothered him, especially in front of his crew, most of whom were now fairly fluent in the alien common language.

"Can you tell if it's still burning, and how far it has to go?" the Flyer queried.

"'Fraid not. The fire doesn't give any light to speak of by daylight. Too bad there's no night now—though if there were, we'd have to plan pretty tightly so the fire would reach the cell by daylight and we could see what happens to the rock."

"It might have helped, but since we couldn't be sure just when the fuse would run out—well, it's academic anyway. Even if you could control your landing point well enough you'd probably not have time to get there now, get out, cut the fuse, and start over. We'll just wait and hope. Good work, Sher; I think I see the rock now, though I can't be sure it's the right one. It *looks* like the pictures we got before, but there are such a lot of them—rocks, I mean—this close to the edge of the plateau that I could be wrong. Too bad that fuse doesn't smoke."

Since cooking fires on Mesklin don't normally smoke either and other kinds of fire are extremely rare, some minutes were used in explaining the last word; but someone remembered the Stennish for "fog" eventually, and there remained an unknowable length of suspense time when interpretation was managed. The earlier tests had given the Flyers some idea of the fuse burning rate, but the two had disagreed by over ten percent. Tension mounted, therefore, as the minutes passed.

Especially for the captain, as *Bree Three* was drifting toward the rock, keeping Sherrer busy and Barlennan worried. Their height *should* be great enough now to be pretty safe provided the aliens hadn't overlooked anything important, but there was no way to be sure they hadn't.

And, in fact, they had.

There was no flash; the cell salvaged from the rocket's liftoff equipment had been worked as far under the giant boulder as the latter's shape, the hardness of the packed ground, and Mesklinite psychology had allowed. A solid object several body lengths high and wide was not something a sane native wanted close to him, much less extending overhead, though the crew had gotten more or less used in the last hundred thousand days or so to the three-hundred-foot cliff edging the plateau. They were no longer, perhaps, wholly sane by their species' standards.

This cell held a directional charge like the other, its individual macromolecules oriented to send all the exhaust in one direction, and had been aimed slightly downward and away from the rock this time. It therefore started by digging up an enormous cloud of dust. None of the aliens on Toorey was an explosives expert, and none had considered all the likely results of blocking what should have been a free stream of hot gas with several tons of dirt, dirt very solidly packed by Mesklin's polar gravity.

Essentially, all the unit's directional qualities were lost as its reaction products hit ground and were scattered randomly. It might as well have been a half-ton-mass chemical bomb. The big rock did shatter. Being correct on this point did not please the captain as much as it might have; he watched tensely, knowing that if anything did go wrong there would be no time to give Hars a meaningful order.

None of the large fragments got far, and none could be seen in flight except near the tops of their trajectories, where they produced a hazy, discontinuous roof a foot or more thick and very little farther from the ground for a brief moment. Some of the much smaller stuff reached terminal velocity at other points, both upward and downward, and was visible very briefly to both Flyers and Mesklinites before hitting the surface again. Everything except for really fine dust had settled out before the sound wave reached the balloon.

This was least surprising to the natives. The quick-firing gun which had been used during the near-equatorial part of their earlier odyssey had accustomed them to the sound of explosions, but had given them no clue to the speed of pressure waves in air. Their own voices had a volume astonishing to the Flyers, and they were aware in principle that there was a delay between hooting and hearing, but they had never considered the fact quantitatively.

The real trouble was that the crew of the balloon had, at the recent briefing, been assured that nothing of this sort should happen with a directional charge; it was supposed to take several seconds to burn out, waste much less of its energy in sound, and eject its gases in essentially all one direction as the earlier one had done. That one had been aimed straight up; this had been supposed to dig.

Barlennan added another item to his mental file of Flyer fallibilities. It wasn't really needed; the creatures had, carefully and often, made it clear that tested scientific beliefs were always tentative though usually more reliable than speculation. One could never, obviously, be sure that all the relevant data had been secured or properly considered.

"Hey! Look at that ripple!"

The alien voice was not that of Jeanette, but the captain understood it well enough. Ripples he knew about. Near the equator they could be watched quite easily, though close to the poles they moved much too quickly to be visible.

He also did not expect them on solid ground, here or anywhere. The word "solid" was a concept which to him did not include waves, large or small. The phenomenon was very brief; it was lucky he had been looking in the right direction. It *was* a ripple, flickering across the ground from where much of the smashed rock still lay, in all directions. The quivering of each boulder it passed was quite visible, rapid as the passage was. He realized that the wave had started and gone under the balloon before he heard anything, but only later realized—when it was pointed out to him—that the disturbance must have traveled faster than sound. He didn't bother to ask why even then.

The alien watchers on the satellite realized that the ripple must be a seismic wave, but none had a really good look at it just at first; it was out of the viewer field, close to the horizon as much of that was, in much less than a second. High-speed cameras had recorded it all, of course, but time was needed to play these records back, and there had not yet been time.

One of the Mesklinites, favored by a far wider field of vision, called attention to the real results of the blast.

"LOOK!" The word was a bellow in Stennish, which Jeanette didn't bother to translate to her fellows.

"Show us! Let us look too!" she cried. "Where? What? Turn the lens!"

Sherrer was a little slow in responding, his attention being focused toward a spot at the edge of the cliff, half a mile from the balloon and from where the rock had been, and at right angles to the line of sight between these. Barlennan reached for the rotation valve lines, but the balloon was as usual slow in responding.

Starting at the point nearest the blast, the edge of the precipice was starting to crumble away and, of course, to disappear. Cracks nearly parallel to the cliff face and up to a meter from it were appearing. Others nearly perpendicular to them were also showing briefly; then the outer sides of the prisms they outlined were leaning slightly farther out and promptly vanishing. New cracks closer to the balloon than the new edge appeared immediately, outlining sections which were vanishing in turn. The disturbance was spreading in both directions from the point where it had started—the point where, Barlennan realized, the "ripple" must first have reached the cliff face.

His memory flashed to the rockfall, hundreds of miles away, where he and some of his crew had first climbed to the plateau tens of thousands of days before. That had not stretched very far along the cliff. Right now his people and vessel, the original *Bree,* were ten miles along the edge from this new point of collapse and should be safe—

If this one spread no farther than the other. Neither he nor any of the Flyers had been able to explain what had caused that other fall. A vertical cliff three hundred feet high and of any length at all near a Mesklin pole was unbelievable enough; the now well determined fact that it completely rimmed a continent-sized area of the giant planet was worse.

The general layered appearance, which the Flyers claimed to mean sedimentary rock, was hard even for them to reconcile with an unbroken vertical cliff. There should be rock fragments—more reasonably rock powder—at the bottom. All along the bottom. Barlennan had often heard them arguing about whether the perfectly vertical joints in the cliff face implied that the plateau had been lifted or the surroundings lowered, but it had been another of the inconclusive debates which seldom held his attention for long.

No guess at what might have caused that local fall had ever come close to explaining why it had stayed local; it was easy to imagine something like a careless footfall's (whose?) starting the break—but what could possibly have kept it from dominoing both ways the whole ten- or twelve-thousand-mile circumference of the continent? And for that matter, what had studded so many thousands of square miles of the plateau's outer edge with boulders up to truck size, most of them lying *on* the surface rather than even partially buried? No one on Toorey was in the least surprised that Mesklin showed tectonic activity, and no one was too surprised that this differed in detail from anything familiar to Human, Drommian, and the other researchers' experience.

The edges of the plateau which had been seen, only a small fraction of its total circumference, did appear to be sedimentary rock, but this did nothing to make theorizing simpler.

Would the same unknown cause, or any other, operate to stop the spread of this fall? *Were* his crew members safe? The original *Bree* was ashore on the far side of the river, a little farther from the base of the cliff than the scarp itself was high. Many of those below would be away from the ship, farther still from the cliff, hunting, and presumably safe. Others, though, might well be fishing, since the river was a major source of food.

There was nothing Barlennan could do. The Flyers were still calling for attention. There was nothing they could possibly do either, but they deserved to watch. Barlennan was a responsible and reasonably fair-minded adult, and never thought of blaming them for what was happening.

The slow swiveling of the balloon finally brought the lens to face the cliff edge, not at the nearest point but well to the right, where the unaffected edge itself could still be seen. The captain stopped the rotation there. The new edge was now much closer to the balloon and—

And its growth was slowing? Surely it was slowing?

Barlennan's people, after many thousands of days piling dirt and rocks around the alien rocket in the course of business, had a very clear concept of angle of repose. The collapse couldn't possibly extend much farther back from the original edge than it was now getting, the captain told himself.

The whole plateau would never crumble to fragments, obviously. At least, it hadn't the other time.

But that was not the immediate problem. How far *along* would the disintegration extend? How safe were his other men? And how would he get his people and the stuff the Flyers wanted to recover physically, such as the inertial tracker, back to the equator if his original ship were lost? Taking the balloon across thousands of miles of ocean was ridiculous; it could carry fuel to heat its air for only a few days, in spite of Karondrasee's endless research into different juices with maybe more effective enzymes. It could not carry the whole crew, even if the stuff wanted by the Flyers were all left behind.

"We've warned Dondragmer." Jeanette's voice caught the captains's attention at this point in his thoughts. "No one is on the cliff side of the river. A dozen are away hunting. The ones still at the ship are getting as far from the river and the cliff as quickly as they can carry the radio."

"Can they carry it while keeping it pointed so you can see what happens to the cliff, and tell me?" asked Barlennan.

"Don said he'd try." That was enough for anyone who knew the mate.

"Can you see from it right now?"

"Yes. It's pointed along the cliff in the direction the fall will come from, but the view isn't too steady."

"North" and "South" were not useful words this close to the pole, though the latter had been located very exactly long before.

"I'd suggest there can't be any danger farther than, say, three times the river's width away from the cliff foot. When they get that far, maybe they could put the set down occasionally to give us a steadier look and better pictures."

"Maybe. But leave that decision to Dondragmer."

"Of course. But you still have two cameras besides that one; maybe he could leave it—"

"We've been using all three. Dondragmer decides. I know what I'd do with my present knowledge, but he's *there*."

"All right." There were beings, most of them non-human, on Toorey who might have argued further, but Jeanette Parkos was not one of them. She was very conscious of who was in charge on the surface, and as chief communicator realized clearly who would be blamed if any major disagreement should develop with the Mesklinites. "We'll report to you as well as we can when the collapse gets in sight from where Dondragmer is, if it does."

"Good. I'm still hoping it won't. That other one we climbed to get up here—"

"The other one is much narrower than this one is already. Whatever caused it can't have been as energetic."

Another alien voice cut in. "That's silly! Practically all the energy involved now is coming from falling rock. You have a chain reaction."

"But that must have been true for the other fall, too!"

Barlennan turned his attention back to the still spreading collapse. He had learned long ago the futility of listening to Flyers arguing theoretical points when anything was actually going on. They got too far behind real time much too quickly. No doubt it was because they were too far away to feel personally involved. The captain was not; he turned his eyes back to the explosion site.

At least, nothing more was flying through the air. Their own climb had ceased, according to the tracker and his own eyes; the balloon had reached its ceiling, which was low because of the rapid decrease of air density with altitude. Hars' efforts were now focussed on keeping its height constant; altitude control was highly unstable. Even a slight dip caused a decrease in balloon volume, and hence a decrease in lift, which tended to make the dip deeper. It was like the hollow boat's behavior, so many gravities to the north. Hars had developed a high skill at handling this problem; it had been he who had conceived the deflectors which gave quick control over how much hot air was actually entering the bag, and eliminated much of the control lag involved in merely feeding fuel or sprinkling meat juice on the fire.

"It's coming." The human voice sounded less excited than the captain felt was appropriate, but Jeanette was not, of course, in danger herself. One should make allowances.

"How close?"

"It's just come around the point about three miles upstream."

"How far is the debris spreading out into the river?"

"I can't tell very well yet. The set is on the ground, or as near as no matter. The edge view I get for the bend seems to show repose at about forty degrees for the stuff near the top, and maybe twenty near the bottom. That would mean anything that's more than about one cliff height away from the original bottom should be safe."

"That does not quite include the ship," Barlennan pointed out.

Dondragmer cut in. "There wouldn't be time to get back to the ship, much less to tow it overland any distance, before the fall gets here."

"All right. Make sure the crew is safe. Head for the site where this balloon was built; that has to be safe, and a lot of our stuff is there anyway."

"Yes, Captain. We'll start searching for ship building materials at once, when we get there. Have you further orders?"

"None for now, except when you think you're far enough out to be safe you should set the Flyers' eye where they can see what happens. Remember they can see things over again, and could be able to tell us how best to find and recover anything that gets buried."

Dondragmer was probably the least susceptible of the *Bree*'s crew to being startled, and had spent many thousands of days burying and then digging out the alien rocket, but the thought of excavating a rockfall jolted him. Several of the crew could tell this. None, however, said anything, and the communicator was set down and pointed as the captain had ordered. The natives stayed where they were afterward, and nervously watched the collapse region as it neared them.

They could see that the falling material was pretty certain not to reach them, but Mesklinites in general are not calm about *anything*'s falling. Not even Mesklinites with the background of Barlennan's crew.

The roar of the rocks was loud enough now to drown out even their voices, and there was no conversation as the wave thundered past in front of them.

From Toorey, the view through the lens involved less emotion, though several of the watchers were already, and everyone hoped prematurely, wondering what the loss of the original *Bree* would do to their plans. More were observing, in as much detail as the optics allowed, the way new vertical joints appeared closer and closer to the watchers, delimiting sections of rock which began to tilt slowly outward—a slow fall was a phenomenon on Mesklin—and then develop horizontal cracks which shot back toward the areas already bared by the downward disappearance of previously loosened material. The rock above each crack tilted slightly outward and vanished in its turn, reappearing as it shattered on the growing slope below. Lower segments of the falling prisms were just as invisible during their falls, but didn't fragment as completely before coming to rest. The repose angle grew steeper as the eye traveled upward and encountered less and less fine material and more and more large slabs and columns.

On any other world the details would have been mostly hidden by dust—with or without an atmosphere to suspend it.

Not on this one.

The collapse wave thundered past. Dondragmer retained enough presence of mind to turn the vision set to the left, so the Flyers could keep watching its progress. This was just as well, because it let them see its sudden halt.

The wave was fully two miles past by this time; whatever stopped its progress could not have helped the ship still on the river bank. But it did stop.

Within seconds, the debris seemed to have reached equilibrium. The observers, local and offworld, found themselves looking at a new straight-up cliff far to their left extending *inward* from the former face, roughly toward the grounded rocket. Its lower section was partly hidden by the scree slope so suddenly formed, but what could be seen was as nearly vertical as the original had been.

Several of the Mesklinites, rendered more nearly insane than their fellows by the events of the last thousands of days, promptly started back toward the cliff, slanting downstream to get a look at the end of the fall. Dondragmer was equally curious but ordered them back. Jeanette interrupted his commands.

"It's probably safe enough, Don. The stuff must have reached repose angle right away."

"No doubt you are right, Flyer Jeanette, but we will first bring the captain up to date with events. He could not have seen this, unless the balloon has moved remarkably fast in the right direction. You would know better, but I can't see it from here. Also, you do not mention that the repose angle, if it really is that, is much steeper for the higher, larger fragments than for the much finer material near the bottom."

"You know," cut in another alien voice, "this will be the first chance we've ever had to get a close look at the rock making up that cliff. We could see it was sedimentary, if horizontal layering means anything, but all we could tell was that the bottom fifty feet or so was light gray in color, the next layer up was a lot darker, and for the rest of the way up there were variously light and dark bands up to the nearly black one at the top. That one's silicate—mostly amphibole, the gear on the rocket told us years ago right after the landing, but this will be the first time we'll be able to tell anything about the other layers."

"*What* will we be able to tell?" snapped another. "Just what will color tell us, and what else will we be able to see?"

Dondragmer, like the captain, tuned out the argument. He had more important problems to face.

There was no more visible rock motion anywhere along the fall; the stuff must, indeed, have reached some sort of equilibrium. There was no more sound even from the left, where falling material must presumably have taken a little longer to fill space around the new corner.

But something—the "smoke" described a little while before? well, maybe ordinary fog—was *rising* from the far side of the river, over the newly fallen material. Even after watching balloons, the sight of something flowing upward was startling. Explanation would have to wait, though.

There were fragments of all shades and several colors at the bottom of the fall, but the mate was more concerned with what might be *under* it. What had happened to the *Bree?* And for that matter, what might have happened to the river? He didn't worry about the captain, who had presumably been almost as much out of danger as the Flyers. After a few moments' thought, he headed toward where the ship had been, ordering a few of the crew to come with him carrying the communicator, and sending off others to examine the edge of the fall both up and down stream.

Almost immediately he had a question to ask the aliens above.

"It's getting a lot warmer as we get near the fallen stuff. Can you suggest why?"

Even Jeanette could, but one of the scientists undertook the explanation. Not even Dondragmer had really grasped much thermodynamics yet, but many of the natives had a fairly clear idea of energy. Every falling pebble had lost a lot of potential—

Quite a lot. More than enough, for the stuff originally near the top, to bring its temperature above the melting point of water, one of the aliens figured. Not that any of the natives knew what water was, or that there was any reason to believe there was any around.

"Better stay away for a little while," the alien concluded his or her remarks. "It shouldn't take long to cool again; your air is a very good conductor of heat. Actually, it must be radiation you're feeling; there ought to be a pretty strong wind from where you are *toward* the cliff."

"There is. It's still uncomfortable, but we can stand more if we have to."

"Just wait a while."

The mate saw nothing else to do.

Barlennan would have done the same, if the choice had been offered. Hars had worked the balloon rather jerkily downward from its ceiling until the basket was only a few yards above the tallest boulders, but at every level the wind was now toward the cliff edge. It was carrying them far too rapidly for a safe landing; hooking the car on a boulder and tipping the crew out was not acceptable. They could easily have fallen several body lengths. The cliff edge—or rather, the nearest point of the new slope—was less than half a mile away; much less, now. It seemed safest as well as unavoidable to go out beyond it and drop below the level of the plateau, a maneuver which should at least provide a wider choice of wind directions.

It didn't. There still was only one choice, it turned out. A little later, after his quick physics lesson, Dondragmer could have told his captain what the choice would be, but the information would have been of little help.

As *Bree Three* neared the top of the slope, the temperature rose abruptly, the balloon started upward, and the surroundings faded from sight.

Neither the need nor the possibility of instrument flying had ever occurred to Barlennan or any of his crew. They had felt the upward surge, tiny as the acceleration was compared to the local gravity, and the captain could tell from the tracker readings that the climb was continuing. The instrument had been the first one salvaged from the very top of the rocket; its main purposes had been to help guide the original landing, with the additional hope that if the south pole were not found exactly its distance from the rocket could be determined and, possibly, seismic measurements be secured later.

To Barlennan, the temperature rise plus the upward acceleration suggested an upward air current heated from below and outside the balloon; Hars judged the same and reacted at once, slanting the vanes to waste hot air to the sides. The captain's first thought was that this was the proper reaction; then he realized that the climb couldn't possibly last long, but might very well take them above the balloon's normal ceiling. If the upward impulse ceased at some point, which it could hardly help doing, even full fire might not be enough to keep a catastrophic descent from following.

"Keep it hot! Hot as you can!" he hooted. The fireman reversed the slope of the guides without question, though perhaps not without uneasiness. For several seconds the crew remained without reference points, though the figures on the instrument showed they were still climbing; then the surrounding fog began to thin, and sun and sky could once again be seen.

The ground directly below could not, nor that along the former line of the cliff edge; they were still in fog. Toward the plateau, however, boulders were visible once more. In the opposite direction the less rugged area of the lowland showed fuzzily at first, but quickly cleared. Evidently they were still traveling in the same direction. A glance at the inertial reading confirmed this.

The readout was reliable to fourteen places, even here; it had been made visible on the surface of the baseball-sized sphere to permit initial calibration, and Barlennan was not the only member of his crew to have learned to interpret the characters. Hexadecimal readings weren't too difficult for people who normally used base eight. The tracker was completely solid, with no moving parts larger than electrons, and the gravity had produced no readable change in its behavior, the Flyers had reported. It had, after all, been designed for such a field.

It quickly became just as evident that the expected descent had started, and Hars, without further orders, heaped more fuel on the fires. Karondrasee sprinkled a contribution from his juice tank. Barlennan looked upward rather than at the approaching ground; wrinkling of the balloon fabric from rising pressure would mean more than the narrowing of the space still below them, however read. It occurred fleetingly to him that a small sealed balloon at regular temperature might serve as an even quicker method of determining rate of descent. One could watch it swell toward full or crumple toward flatness.

It would also be something they should be able to make themselves. There would be no other inertial instruments until they got back to the equator, where Flyers could land.

But that could be thought out later, if he were alive to think about it. They were descending fast now, as even vision could tell when he glanced downward, but at least the skin was still smooth. The balloon was maintaining its volume in spite of the rising outside pressure; Hars was doing his job.

The possibility of the bag's bursting during a climb had bothered the crews during the earliest flights, but the Flyers had assured them that the opening through which hot air entered it would never let the pressure get too high inside.

Again fleetingly, Barlennan wondered whether they might be wrong again.

They weren't, this time. The descent slowed and stopped, though it was fortunate they were no longer over the plateau. The cliff now was hidden by the same fog which had concealed the rest of the world on the upward surge, and the numbers said they were over a hundred feet lower than the rocket. At this point the voice of Jeanette, which had been surprisingly silent for the last few minutes, sounded again.

"Captain, what's happened? Where are you? We can't see anything but the sort of ground across the river from the cliff, and it doesn't have enough features for any of us to recognize. We can read the tracker, but can't match figures with landscape yet. Can you turn the eye so we can see the cliff and the boulder country?"

"Turning," Barlennan replied, gesturing Karondrasee toward the rotation lines. "I'm not sure, but I think we're pretty close to where the test was made, only we've passed the cliff. If it still is a cliff. Can your eye see through fog? If it can, you'll know better than I where we are when you look back. Where's Dondragmer? I should be able to—"

"I can hear you, Captain. I can't make a very good report. The falling of the cliff stopped a couple of miles after it passed us, but we can't get back to where the ship was yet. It's too hot. The Flyers say that's to be expected, and at least the lower part of the fall is producing fog too dense to see through. Luckily the wind's now blowing toward the rockfall and keeping fog and heat away from us, but we can't get really near the ship yet."

"Can you see enough to guess whether it escaped?"

"No, sir. And if it's still uncovered it may not stay that way long. If you and the balloon were here you could tell better than we can, but it looks to us as though the very bottom of the fall were still moving this way. More like flowing than falling."

"I see the wind near the ground where we are is also moving toward the rocks, and now that you mention it, I think we can see that outward flow, too. We'll see it better when we get closer; we've let down pretty far—more honestly, we were pretty low when Hars killed our drop—and yes, we're blowing back toward the cliff now."

The conversation had been in Stennish. but Parkos had been able to follow it.

"Then you'd better climb again, Captainl" she cried. "If you're carried too close to the slope—well, I don't know how much heat you can stand, but you'll be cycling though that updraft again. You'll be starting from lower down, where it should be a lot hotter!"

Hars spoke as he manipulated the guides, without waiting for orders. "Worse than that, Captain. I don't think we have enough fuel to manage another descent like this one. We'd better get up into the flow away from the plateau, get some more distance, and then land before we're carried back in again. The fog up there is blowing out past us the way we need to go, so there's a good wind not too far up."

Barlennan gestured assent to the fireman.

"Don, you must have heard that. Unless something serious happens, we won't call you again until we're on the ground. You can tell me anything you think worth while. Jeanette, you must have had a good look at the fog yourself by now. Can you see through it?"

"Probably no better than you. We can see the stuff lifting from the rocks at the edge of the slope; they must be pretty hot. Did you smell anything, familiar or otherwise, while you were in it? We're trying to guess what could be boiling."

"There was some ammonia. Nothing else I could tell, but ordinary methane seems likely, too. How about the rest of you?" The others gestured negatively.

"That's interesting just the same. Have you smelled any ammonia since you left the equatorial regions?"

"No. Not that I can remember." Once more the others agreed with him.

"It's hard to see how that stuff could be so far from the equator at this season," remarked another human voice. "I'd expect most of the planet's supply to be frozen in the other hemisphere right now."

Once more the captain focussed his attention on his more immediate problems. Hars had found the wind they needed and was holding altitude with his usual skill, and the line of fog was once more receding; but the fuel was getting very low indeed. It would not be good to let down into the other wind too early, of course; but if it took them too long to reach a safe distance, there might not be enough fire to make the descent and landing safely.

"Your judgment, Hars," the captain said. "Get as far as you think will let us down without flattening us. Don't wait for my orders."

The fireman gestured understanding without taking his attention from his levers. Barlennan had never learned to like situations where he wasn't in personal control, but he had long ago learned to be a captain. There were situations which didn't leave time for orders.

In Barlennan's opinion, his pilot started the letdown too soon, but he said nothing. Hars almost certainly had a better idea of how much fuel the descent would take, and if the pilot were actually allowing a greater safety margin than the captain thought necessary, there was an excellent chance that he was right. Watching the balloon's still wrinkle-free skin seemed wiser than interfering. At least, any dents would appear near the bottom first.

It had occurred long ago to one of the alien watchers that if the lower half of the balloon were to cave in sufficiently, the bag might serve as a fair parachute. She had then calculated the terminal velocity of the resulting system in the polar regions and decided not to mention the idea to anyone. The resulting ignorance spared the captain some worry.

Barlennan was partly right; the descent had started too soon, from one point of view. They were in the grip of the cliffward wind well before they reached the ground. It might, however, be too late as well; the fuel was going rapidly. The natives were unfamiliar with alien literature and would probably never have thought of using part of their basket for the fuel. This was probably just as well, since anything which distracted Hars from his piloting would very probably have killed the four of them. As it was, they were saved almost certainly by the fact that something else was approaching from the direction of the cliff.

It was not methane. At least, it certainly was not ocean-pure methane; it could barely be called a liquid. Slush or mud would be better words. It lay under them as the supporting heat dwindled below the ability of the guiding deflectors to keep the balloon contents hot enough.

The first wrinkles appeared in the bag; Karondrasee's bellow of alarm just barely preceded contact between the basket and the semi-fluid. The car stopped almost at once, after a fall violent enough to make the stuff splash and jolt the occupants severely; the bag took rather longer to touch. The cordage tried to pull the basket toward the cliff as the wind still dragged at the balloon. For just a moment Barlennan thought the car would be tipped over and dump its fire, and had enough time to wonder what would happen when the latter met the whatever-it-was; then it appeared that there was enough weight stuck—frozen?—under their feet to hold them nearly level.

They were more or less safe, it appeared, for the moment, but like Dondragmer they were uncomfortably warm.

There seemed no practical way out of the basket for the moment; the stuff surrounding them appeared dangerously hot, and there was no way to tell yet whether this would get worse, or better, or remain unchanged, not that the last would be much help.

The captain didn't bother to ask the Flyers anything.

"Dondragmer, can you hear me?"

"Yes, Captain."

"Have you been able to get back near the ship?"

"We're closer."

"How's the heat? We're down, but are stuck in some sort of goo. There's a lot of ammonia smell, but it doesn't look much like ammonia."

"That's happened here, too. It's what's keeping us from getting any closer to where the ship was. It looks and smells to me like the methane-ammonia slush we saw a good deal of where we wintered and met the Flyers, but that may be just a guess. If it's right, the ammonia should freeze after a while and sink and leave ordinary methane on top, which should soon be cool enough to swim in. The Flyers won't commit themselves either, but agree we should watch for clear liquid to show on top of the stuff."

"I hadn't thought of that, but here we'll have to wait anyway. I hope we don't cook while we're still waiting."

"Is your fire out? Or is there any chance of flying the *Bree* again?"

"None, I'd say, unless we can get rid of whatever is stuck all over the bottom of the basket and must have kept us from tipping over when we hit. Maybe we should take a chance on putting the heater out. I've been a little uneasy about letting fire get near the stuff around us, or vice versa, because I thought that might burn too; but if you're right there won't be any trouble."

"*If* I'm right. Pardon me for sounding like a Flyer, but I said I was guessing."

"Now that you've reminded me, I'm guessing right along with you. In any case, it's getting warmer all the time here, and something has got to be done."

"How about just going over the side, and seeing if being farther from your fire will be enough?"

Barlennan did not answer at once. If such an experiment were to be tried, there was just one person who would have to go over first. He temporized briefly.

"There's no sign of the stuff settling, where you are? No liquid on top?"

"No. If it's going to happen, it should be upstream where you are, first, I'd guess."

"Is there any stream? There doesn't seem to be any flow here."

"No. I suppose the fall blocked it."

"But the methane from upriver should flow around, and even if the original bed were filled with rock the river should just be pushed out farther from the cliff than before."

"Maybe it was," the mate answered thoughtfully. "Maybe that's the liquid part of this stuff. But if it is, I wonder where the ammonia came from?"

"We're arguing like Flyers," the captain cut off the debate. "I'll reach over and find out how hot this stuff is."

The caterpillarlike Mesklinite anatomy was not constructed for toe-dipping; Barlennan had to reach over the side with one end or the other of his body, and lower a set of pincers into the stuff. He chose to use his head end, for whatever help his eyes might give him.

"Barlennan?" It was Jeanette's voice.

"I hear you."

"Are you all right, and is the tracker still working?"

"We're uncomfortable but still alive. I haven't looked at the machine since we stopped. I don't suppose heat will hurt it, considering who made it. I'll shade it so I can see the figures and get a reading."

"Whenever you can, please. There are people here who will have trouble breathing until they learn its condition, now that we know you're all right. Its reading here hasn't changed for some minutes now."

Jeanette was not actually a skilled liar, but had some natural diplomatic ability. It seemed unlikely that the captain, just now, would be able to sympathize very well with people worrying more about the instrument's condition than his own.

"That's reasonable," Barlennan concurred. "We've been stranded for some time now. Here's what I read." He pronounced the symbols carefully.

"Good. That's what we have here. If it should change its reading, please let me know."

Another thought struck the captain. "Can you tell us whether the fall is still going on, upstream? Dondragmer says it stopped just below his location."

"It did. We can see clearly with his communicator. I can't answer your question. You're practically at the pole, we're over the equator. The only reason we can see your area at all from here is atmospheric refraction, which doesn't help the image. Otherwise you'd be below our horizon. We'd have to send out another mapping rocket."

"Do your people think that's worth doing? I'd be glad of any information I could get from that direction."

"I'll ask." The Flyer's voice fell silent, and there seemed no more excuse for delay in testing the slush, if that's what it was.

Gingerly, his head and a few inches of his body over the basket's gunwale, Barlennan reached a chela toward the nearly white stuff. The sun was low as always at this latitude and season. At the moment it was beyond cliff and fog, but there was plenty of light. He could feel some warmth from the surface of whatever-it-was, but it didn't seem as bad as before.

About like the inside of the balloon bag, which had been found to be bearable much earlier when control lines had tangled in flight.

The stuff was soft, though it resisted a little when poked. Whether it would be firm enough to support his weight, and what would happen if it weren't, were still open questions. There was only one way to get answers that the captain could see. At least, only one which could preserve his self-respect; he *could* order one of the others to climb over. He didn't.

The stuff did resemble the slush they had encountered near the equator, as the mate had said. It was uncomfortably but not dangerously warm. It did not support him until he had sunk perhaps a third of his body volume. His report, when he finally got back in the basket with the assistance of the others and a length of rope, paraphrased history for some of the human listeners.

"Too soft to walk on, too hard to swim in. We're here for a while, but we can stand the heat. Have you tried it, Dondragmer?"

"Yes, Captain. You describe it well. We think we can see the ship, but whatever it is is almost entirely immersed in the slush, and we can't be sure. If it is, it's well to this side of the fallen rocks."

"Good. Find out for sure as quickly as possible."

The mate acknowledged the order which both knew to be superfluous.

Half a day later, with the sun on their own side of the former cliff, nothing had been accomplished except testing the inertial tracker. This had been carried from one side of the basket to the other, and the change in readings on its surface and at the receivers on Toorey had remained in agreement. Barlennan was not surprised; from his point of view nothing at all violent had happened during the wrecking of *Bree Three*.

The slush was still slush. This surprised the Flyers, who seemed to feel that if anything were going to settle at all it should do it pretty quickly on Mesklin; Barlennan had no basis for an opinion, though he certainly wished that something would happen.

Fog was still rising from the slope a few hundred feet away. The Flyer prediction that the wind should cool the fallen rock fairly quickly seemed to have been another mistake. Barlennan didn't raise the subject; he was quite sure that the beings would point out that they hadn't actually specified a time numerically. This was quite true, and qualified as an excuse even by the captain's standards.

There had been, twice, sounds from inside the fog suggesting that rocks had moved, and the four people in the basket were alert for anything more of the sort. Dondragmer's people had heard nothing like it, the mate reported; but they, too, were listening. Anything like that should happen upstream first, each told himself. This was not mentioned aloud.

The fire had not been extinguished after the captain's experiment, but was now dead for lack of fuel. There were plenty of Mesklin's scraggy plants in sight in various directions on the shore beyond the slush, but there was no way to reach them; and there seemed not to be enough of them to get *Bree Three* into the air again in any case. Karondrasee had plenty of meat juice in his tank, but there seemed no way to use it.

It was two whole days before anything noteworthy happened, and its development then was gradual.

There were more of the falling-rock sounds. Nothing could be seen; the fog, if anything, was thicker, and the *Breeze* toward the rubble slope somewhat faster.

Then another quite familiar sound made itself heard.

"Captain! A current! Flowing—" Hars uttered the words very softly for a Mesklinite, though Jeanette had no trouble hearing him. She heard the trickling of liquid, too, since the pilot had been doing his best not to drown it out with his own voice.

"Which way? Can any of you tell?" she asked. Barlennan couldn't decide himself; the sound had seemed to come first from the direction of the rocks, then from what had been upstream, then from many directions at once. The most convincing came from the fog.

Flowing liquid? Methane? Was the ammonia, if that's what it was, finally starting to settle?

Methane, yes. Settling ammonia, apparently not. Motion caught the eyes of the four crewmen in several directions almost at once. Most of it was from cliffward and upstream, but Barlennan caught sight of a trickle which seemed to rise from almost under the basket, a rivulet which spread, and grew, and flowed downriver as he watched. Others appeared and behaved the same way, more and more, minute after minute; then quite suddenly, they vanished in a single spreading sheet of liquid which they now realized covered much of the landscape in the upstream direction. It was as though the river had resumed flowing, and was coming up *through* the slush, and making a new bed for itself beyond the tumbled rocks which had filled the old one.

It was methane, as taste promptly proved—it was not a laboratory situation to the Mesklinites, who were by now pretty thirsty anyway. The river was being reborn.

Yes, reborn. There was plenty of liquid coming from upstream, but there was nearly as much—perhaps more—welling up from under the slush and from the direction of the rocks.

The basket began to move, as Jeanette promptly reported.

"We know," the captain replied tersely.

"Will you float?" asked the Flyer.

"We should. The basket's made of wood—real wood, not that funny stuff from the ammonia flats. What we need to know is whether it'll float *level.* We didn't worry that much about weight distribution when we made it."

"How about the bag?"

"That's another question. We may have to cut it free. Depends whether it acts more like a sea anchor or a sail. Dondragmer, we must be heading your way. I can't guess how long we'll be getting there."

"We're watching, Captain. If you have to free the bag, we'll try to capture it, and you of course. The slush is still slush down here, but we're watching for liquid, too. If the thing we think is the ship starts to move, I'll take swimmers to do what we can."

"Good. We're going to be busy here, but one of us will keep in touch. If you don't hear from us for more than a few seconds, you'll know something we didn't expect has happened. In that case, send some people up this way to give any help they can. We're going faster, I think. The bag is dragging behind us, whether it's touching bottom or feeling wind I don't know. Probably wind, I think; there's an upstream component to that now, and the bag itself is pulling a little toward the fog. It's pulling us that way too."

"Hadn't you better cut loose, then, Captain?"

"Not until we can see whether moving in toward the rock is good or bad. We're standing by to cut if we have to. There doesn't seem to be anything yet for us to hit."

Barlennan kept a running comment going, as he had promised, while basket and bag headed downstream. The nearest motionless objects were now either too distant—features on the land away from the cliff—or too vague, like the fog, to allow a trustworthy estimate of speed. It was one of the Flyers who pointed out that the tracker was moving downstream surprisingly fast. He didn't seem really sure that it was surprising; all earlier estimates of the river current had come from direction measurements of the communicator outputs, which were not very reliable with the line of sight to the moon practically horizontal. This was not the tracker's first trip to the lower ground, but was its first ride on what had become a surface vehicle.

One of the watchers remarked audibly that he has surprised the vehicle wasn't in white water; another, not bothering to correct the name of the liquid, suggested that the first speaker think gravity. Just what would "white" imply about the current's speed on Mesklin?

The twelve-plus kilometers an hour was several times any earlier estimate, however unreliable that might have been. It implied a source of liquid unrelated to what had been seen of the upstream areas from earlier balloon flights. This was not merely methane which had found its way, after some delay, around the recent rock fall.

The people on the basket finally observed this, too. The drag toward the rocks had been maintained as wind kept its grip on the now rapidly flattening bag. The sharp rocks were suddenly passing uncomfortably close to a structure which had been designed for lightness. Contact could be awkward even if the pieces continued to float, as they no doubt would. Barlennan heard himself commenting on this as part of his running report, and interrupted the monologue with a sudden, sharp order.

"All of you! Cut it free!"

Simultaneously the bag caught on a sharp, solid rock corner, jerking the basket to a halt; anywhere near the equator the crew would have been hurled overboard. Karondrasee, in fact, did get jerked over the side.

For just a moment the cook could be seen borne away from the suddenly anchored car; then, as the others finished cutting the dozen cords which had held basket and bag together, the former resumed its downstream rush even more rapidly than before. It was now relatively motionless with respect to the swimmer, and he had no trouble wriggling back to what might or might not be safety. He needed no help getting aboard through one of the gunwale crenellations, and the fact that he brought a good deal of methane with him made no real difference. In spite of the total absence of spray, the footing on board was already extremely wet. During the brief halt, the river had spilled over the upstream gunwale and nearly washed several more objects into the river.

The communicator was high enough above the deck to stay clear, but the inertial tracker was not. Neither were the three remaining natives. It was Hars, perhaps more concerned with all things connected with flying, who curled his long body about the sphere, gripping it with every leg which could be brought to the task. Sailor and instrument washed rapidly across the deck in the direction from which Karondrasee was swimming, but they did not go overboard.

Hars' own display of personal strength surprised no one, but his fellows and the watching Flyers were all rather startled that the gunwale seized by one of his chelae did not tear loose from the rest of the basket. He uncoiled partly, still retaining his grip on the tracker, and spread the load on the gunwale with more pincers; by the time the cook was safely aboard, the sloshing of liquid across the deck had ceased and the tension had eased.

"It would have been easy enough to find," Barlennan remarked. "I know it would have sunk, but the river's pretty clear."

"Is the bottom solid?" a Flyer voice—again, not Jeanette's—asked pointedly.

"I don't know, but it looks—" the captain paused, then went on, "Just a moment." He vanished over the rail. His crew watched with interest but no great concern; the aliens were highly concerned but couldn't watch. The long body reappeared and moved in front of the lens.

"It might have been serious at that. It's the same slushy stuff, and it's travelling—not as fast as the river, but if the tracker had sunk we'd never have found it. Good work, Hars." The exhaled breaths were audible through the communicator, but carried no meaning to the natives.

Dondragmer could not see anything nor hear everything, but had been able to infer what was happening.

"Is anyone watching ahead, Captain? You must be travelling pretty fast. We're getting ourselves and the radio back from the river; it seems from what you said it's a lot wider arid faster where you are now, and that it became so very suddenly. All of us are staying with the radio as we move it; I'm sure the Flyers know that faster-moving methane carries things more easily."

"Sixth-power law," a barely audible alien voice muttered. The words were not in Stennish, but the mate understood both them and their mathematical implications. Barlennan got the former only, but no order was needed to drive the mate to greater haste. The captain had heard the question about looking ahead, and without acknowledging the words was doing so.

Actually, looking aside was more worrisome; the basket was still closer than he liked to the edge of the rock fall.

Worse—*much* worse—it could be seen that much of the finer waste from the cliff was being washed away by the current, leaving widening spaces between the larger fragments.

Well, the Flyers weren't *always* wrong, of course.

He could not see what was happening to the loosened stuff. The surface was too turbulent to offer a clear view below it.

He remembered his earlier promise and began describing the new phenomenon to Dondragmer. Sherrer, his flexible body partly overside, rotated the basket to let the communicator eye look ahead. His chelae were poorly shaped for the work, but his paddling did have results.

"You seem to be approaching a bend to the right, in both fog and river," Jeanette remarked. "I'd guess it's that kink—that point—in what used to be the cliff, a couple of miles or so upstream from where Don is."

Barlennan saw no reason to disagree, and the possibilities which a quick change in flow might offer were enough to focus his attention. "Dondragmer, is your part of the river widening at all rapidly? It should be if the Flyer's right. How well are you moving the radio? Can you keep it moving and also let it look upstream?"

"We are moving. I'm not sure about change in width, since we re away from the river itself now. We're keeping the lens pointed more or less upstream, but I'm afraid they're not getting a very steady view."

"Don't worry about that, Don. We can take pix when it's steady and look at them. You're right about keeping the viewer as safe as possible."

"Thank you, Flyer Jeanette."

It was indeed a turn to the right, the captain saw as they approached it. The current was visibly swifter; they were still close enough to the shattered, pulverized, and steaming rocks for this to be very obvious.

He suddenly realized that *everything* at the foot of the pile was much larger now; the fragments resembled the gigantic—to him—slabs and prisms which had earlier shown only on the higher and steeper part of the fall.

It was hard to tell from this close, but the general slope seemed to be steeper, too, as though the whole fallen mass were still gently sinking.

Maybe it was. The fine stuff below was certainly vanishing.

There was a fan of standing ripples angling out across their course ahead; the mate would almost certainly have been curious about this, but Barlennan was just uneasy. The river was still liquid. He felt it again to make sure. He did not, however, wonder what made these little ridges in it—only what would happen to the basket and its passengers when they reached them.

Which they would do in seconds. Would they be hitting liquid, or something solid enough to support those humps which lay a little *above* the general river level, or something slippery which would bend the raft's structure into its own shape?

It was liquid, both its high and its low parts, they found. Motionless waves were something new to Barlennan, and he reported as well as he could to his mate and the aliens. The basket was still intact, though everyone aboard had felt the deck under his feet follow the up-and-down displacement of the surface as they passed the still ripples. The Flyers seemed unsurprised, but Barlennan was not asking for explanations just yet.

The foursome ceased thinking about the ripples at once. The next event was prompt, less unfamiliar, and more frightening.

There was an eddy on the downstream side of the point, where the liquid swept around, They had all seen such things before, but never in gravity this high. If there had been time to think, they might have foreseen this one, though not in full detail. They had never, after all, *felt* one in gravity this high either.

Barlennan tried to keep reporting.

"We're around the corner. We can't see you, though—"

"I haven't seen you, either."

"Not surprising. There's a hollow in the methane, we're quite a bit below the river level, and can't see much but the rocks—when we're looking that way."

"Captain! What's happening? The eye and the tracker both say you're—you're moving in a tight circle. How can?—"

It was often nice to have the Flyers tell him what was going on and advise him what to do about it. It was sometimes nice to have them unable to tell him what was going on, thus providing a little salting to the flavor of omniscience they claimed not to want. It was not nice when he didn't know what to do about it himself. He described what was happening in as much detail as he could observe, and as he did so realized what was probably going to happen next.

The broad swirl of liquid cut in toward the edge of the rock slope and divided there, some swerving back upstream and some resuming its original journey down. At the point where the division occurred, the biggest rocks were visibly *settling* still. Not fast, but visibly. The finer stuff had washed out from between and among them, and the higher and larger items were crowding vertically closer to each other as the material originally separating them vanished.

The pieces were big. They were very big, and as the seconds brought the basket closer the face of the slope began to change. It grew still steeper, and the spaces between the huge boulders seemed to open like mouths, leading into the face of the bank—with throats leading *under* it.

All four sailors were familiar with the hazard of *striking* rocks. They had even, occasionally, been swept between rocks.

But they were Mesklinites, and if any of their colleagues had ever been carried *under* rocks no one had ever heard about it. The four paddled frantically but without much result, even after the captain got them all paddling in the same direction. The basket flung itself toward the bank, swerving only at the last moment, with some of the huge fragments close enough for even the Mesklinites to touch.

The swerve was upstream, back toward the point, which meant that they would be going through it all again. And perhaps again, and again...

The rocks were still quite hot, though the wind toward the rocky bank made things a little better. Methane striking the fragments didn't actually splash, though it did rise a short distance above its regular level before boiling into invisibility and reappearing as fog. Spray was extremely rare this far from the equator.

They reached the upstream side of the eddy, swept out into the main current once more, but were not yet free. It was going to be *again*.

But only once. They were carried back toward the fallen cliff somewhat farther downstream this time. The settling was still going on, but less rapidly; could one hope it was actually stopping? that the mud was nearly all gone, and the big fragments resting directly on each other? Well, yes, one could hope. There were no sounds of falling and grinding, after all.

The lowest part of the rock pile was now definitely much steeper and formed of really huge fragments, with open spaces between sometimes wide enough for one of the old *Bree*'s rafts; and the current was not dividing at the very edge any more. Methane was flowing *into* the interstices, flowing almost as rapidly as in the farther-out parts of the eddy. There was no way to paddle the basket fast enough and far enough either up- or downstream to get it carried in either direction. It was going to travel *into* the wreckage of the cliff.

Not even the Flyers could find words. They could see it coming; their lens at the moment was pointing in the basket's direction of motion. None of them ever admitted whether the fate of the natives or the loss of the communicator and tracker concerned them more.

There were other communicators, of course, and Dondragmer might prove to be a better agent than his captain; but there was only the one tracker, and great things had been planned for it once it had been found to be still functional. If it could be carried over land and sea all the way back to the equator, while being followed from above by communicator waves so that gravity and inertial effects could be distinguished, what *couldn't* be learned of Mesklin's interior?

No one had yet discussed this project with Barlennan, and in any case it would not have been the captain's primary concern just now. He and his men were being washed underground, on what amounted to a patch of driftwood. It was much, much later before any of them realized how lucky it was that the sun was ahead of them, on the high side of the cliff, just then.

It grew relatively dark the moment they had rock nearly surrounding them, with only a modest illumination from the sunlit ground across the river. Their heads and eyes turned back toward the light, and stayed there as the view narrowed; and before they really saw and could respond to the unimaginable tonnage of material suddenly *above* them, the darkness was complete except for the faint glow of the tracker's numbers.

The Flyers, Barlennan thought after a moment, should have commented on the darkness or the fact that the tracker was still indicating motion or *something,* but the communicator was silent. It remained so after several hopeful calls by the captain.

It had never occurred to him that whatever carried the messages to and from Toorey might be blocked by intervening rock. The concept of a completely surrounding bed of intervening anything had never crossed his mind.

For a moment he managed to concentrate on all he could see. The digits on the tracker screen agreed with his own sensations; they were speeding up, slowing down, jerking from side to side—the basket was in fact still being carried by a current, which was weaving its way around things. He should have been able to tell which way and how far, from the tracker readings; should, indeed, have been able to retrace their path if he had had any *control* of their motion. The general direction was indeed obvious; they were heading deeper under the former cliff. How far under was another matter; he didn't remember the position reading when they had gone into the dark, and the succession of numbers which had followed that moment had been too complex to memorize.

It was never clear to any of them later how they were able to keep thinking—why the four of them didn't succumb at once to total panic. The Flyers commented later how fortunate it was that all four had had balloon experience, but it was not clear to Barlennan why that should help them with the concept of heavy material *overhead.* He tended to credit his own retention of sanity to his profession. He was a captain, he was responsible, he was used to doing whatever he could that was called for at the moment, and leaving what he couldn't control to luck. This may have corresponded to an almost human personal arrogance. Even so, every little while—he had no way of telling how often—the thought of what he was *under* threatened to crowd his attention away from everything else.

Anything to take that awareness away from him would have helped. He would even have welcomed a theoretical argument from the Flyers. Why all this open space under the cliff, or where the cliff had been? How much mud had there been to wash away, and how had it vanished this quickly so far from the actual river? Or had it? How far did the open space extend? Up and down, probably not very; they were still floating, and it was hard to imagine how the methane surface could have gotten either above the river outside or very far below it. That inspiration caused him to focus on the vertical readings of the tracker for a while; he found that their height was indeed almost constant.

But liquid flows downhill, and this was flowing, so there must be at least a small drop. There might be a big one farther ahead; this didn't seem very good to think of either.

How deep was it? What were their chances of grounding—and staying there in the dark with too much of the world overhead? He thought of trying to find out by swimming, but could imagine no way for a swimmer to find the basket again. He realized later what his failure to think of safety ropes must have implied about his state of mind.

They could call to each other, of course; he tried that.

Multiple echoes responded to his hoots and made sound direction meaningless. In a way this was comforting; Mesklin's stratosphere started only a few hundred meters above the general surface at this latitude. The air, after cooling for a very short distance upward, began to rise in temperature with increasing altitude, so that sounds originating at one spot refracted downward again before going too far. Complex echo patterns from sounds of distant origin were standard, and these gave a slight—very slight—suggestion of clear air above. They actually fooled Karondrasee, who asked, "Captain! It's got to be open above after all! Why is it so dark?"

The captain was quick enough to reply that he didn't know, and almost as quickly inspired to ask, "See if you can think of an answer before the Flyers tell us." That should provide something to distract all the others.

Hars, though, seemed somehow able to think coherently, at least for the moment.

"Captain, shouldn't we do something to secure the instruments? We could run aground any time, though we do seem to be getting carried around things so far, and we don't know how hard we'd strike. The radio isn't any good to us right now, but the tracker might make a lot of difference. If it went overboard I don't see how we'd ever get back out."

"Right. I don't see how we can manage that anyway until the current lets us go, but secure them just the same. The radio will be easy enough; it

Name: james mccauley
Email: jade916476673@aol.com
Phone: 7322403068
Address: 37 woodridge avenue
toms river, NJ 08755
US

Name: james mccauley
Email: jade916476673@aol.com
Phone: 7322403068
Address: 37 woodridge avenue
toms river, NJ 08755
US

Code	Product	Quantity
1-886778-06-X	Trio for Slide Rule and Typewriter: The Essential Hal Clement, Volume 1	1
1-886778-07-8	Music of Many Spheres: The Essential Hal Clement, Volume 2	1
1-886778-08-6	Variations on a Theme by Sir Isaac Newton: The Essential Hal Clement, Volume 3	1
0-915368-60-9	His Share of Glory: The Complete Short Science Fiction of C. M. Kornbluth	1

was made to be fastened to things. The tracker wasn't, though. All of you try to think of a hitch or something to holds it fast."

"Why did they make it ball-shaped?" Even Sherrer sounded more annoyed than afraid. "Didn't they ever think of having to keep it from falling overboard?"

Barlennan could think of no useful answer. He had a fairly clear idea of where the rocket had traveled, but no real notion of ballistics. "Salvage all the cordage you can find," was all he said. "Coil it up and stow it around your bodies. Hars, stay with the tracker and hold onto it as well as you can until we solve the tie-down problem. Think of this as a doldrum situation. We do what we can to make use of wind, or current, or an animal we can harpoon to tow us, and hope that one or another of them will happen. Only this time we have a whole new list of things we need to be ready for, and don't know anything on the list."

"Shouldn't we perhaps moor to something, Cptain?" asked Sherrer. "The tracker says we're getting farther from the river all the time. The farther we travel, the farther we'll have to go to get back."

"If you can find a way to moor us, I'll agree. Personally I can't see what we're passing."

"Of course we can't see, but we can reach out to feel. Surely some of the broken cliff must be rough enough for a grip!"

"For a grip, maybe. For a rope? Well, reach out and learn what you can." The sailor presumably obeyed, but made no report for a long time.

Nothing particular happened during that time—whether a day or an hour none of them could tell. Cordage was found and secured. Hars contrived a spherical, close-meshed net of some of the finer lines, and enclosed the tracker in this. Without commenting to the captain, he secured it to his own body. Like the rest, he had a strong feeling that this device, if anything, was most likely to get them back to daylight.

Again, Barlennan began wishing for Flyer theories and arguments. He found himself even thinking along Flyer lines. *Why* was there liquid so far under what had been a layer of solid rock hundreds of feet thick? The fact that the rock was no longer solid did not explain where the liquid filling the new space could be coming from. *Why* was there any place away from the original river for it to flow *to*? (Item not to think of: liquid flows downhill; where were they being carried?) *Why* had the finer material been washed, or carried somehow, away from the really large fragments of rock, even in here, apparently turning the whole fallen area into a random stack of slabs and columns long enough and wide enough, as it had seemed from their last glimpses outside, to enclose more empty space than rock? *Where* had the fine stuff gone? (Well, downstream, obviously.) Where had the medium-sized stuff gone? (No obvious answer.)

Why did they all seem to be sane in a situation which should have driven any normal person out of his mind? (Or were they? No, Captain, keep away from that thought, too.) They were, after all, experienced and competent members of a dangerous profession, and knew that quite often a dangerous situation offered a good chance of getting something worth while out of it. (And of course a better one of not living to enjoy the profit.) *That* last thought had been banished from all their minds years before, of course. They were still alive; therefore they were lucky.

Where had the underpinnings of the plateau gone, actually? That was a real Flyer question. And the Flyers were in no position to answer it.

They would want to know the answer, though. And Barlennan and his people were the only ones likely ever to be able to provide one.

That was a thought to bolster sanity. The Flyers always wanted information.

Sherrer was having more trouble. His sounds, when he made any at all, were less and less understandable words and more and more short howls of terror. When words could be made out, they were ones that only magnified the fear.

"The world is up there... it's heavy... it can flatten us... what can keep it from falling? We're..."

"Quiet!" snapped the captain. "Why should it fall? It hasn't yet, and..." his voice trailed off. The stuff above, after all, hadn't had that much time to finish the settling it seemed to have started. It could quite easily be getting ready to fall farther. And it was indeed heavy. There was no way of convincing themselves they were back near the equator, where a healthy person could lift rocks like that. No way, even if they couldn't see. Stop catching Sherrer's fears, Captain...

Even if they couldn't see...

He jerked out another order; his own mind was recovering, it seemed. "Sherrer, bend a good line around yourself, at least twenty body lengths, and make sure its other end is secure to the basket—to some really strong part of the basket. Then go overboard carefully and try to find how deep it is, and whether there *is* anything we could moor to. Don't leave too much slack; keep most of it coiled against you and stay close to us at first."

"Yes, sir." Barlennan listened anxiously; giving the fellow something to occupy his mind was one thing, putting him where he wouldn't *expect* to see upward might be even better. The information would be useful, of course, but the action *might* keep the fellow from complete panic.

The liquid was quiet; they were moving with it, not through it, and the sound as it slid around the rocks which must be there was hardly audible. The other three could hear as Sherrer measured his line, secured it at both ends, and slipped overboard. Without order, Hars gripped the inboard end of the cord with a holding nipper.

"He's pulling away a bit, Captain; I don't suppose he can see to keep near us. I'll give him a tug or two to let him know." Barlennan didn't bother to answer. "There's some slack, now. What pull there is is smooth; he can't have met anything solid."

Sherrer's voice abruptly sounded, muffled by the methane-air interface but quite audible. The Mesklinite vocal apparatus, a modified part of their ancestors' swimming siphons, worked impressively well in both media. "We're going a little better than walking speed, Captain. I'm on the bottom. It seems to be that slush rather than rock most of the time, though I hit something solid every little while. Shall I try to slow the basket, if I can get a good grip on anything?" The sailor seemed perfectly calm now.

"Try, but not too hard; if you get pulled free by the basket, don't fight it," replied Barlennan.

"Yes, sir. The liquid's getting shallower, I think."

There was no more after that to be said; the sailor had been right about decreasing depth. Moments later, everyone still in the basket recognized the sensation as their craft ran aground on an oozy surface. Instantly the captain snapped further orders.

"You two—lines on yourselves and go overside. Get away from here in different directions. Use voice softly to keep yourselves apart—no echoes if you can help it. Find out everything there is around here, out as far as your lines will allow. If there *is* anything we can moor to, report at once and then start doing it."

He was obeyed promptly, and submerged hoots and howls began to echo around the basket. There were, it turned out, plenty of rocks projecting from the ammonia-smelling ooze; some of them barely broke the surface of the methane, many extended upward farther than the sailors could reach. In less than half a day, as well as anyone could guess, they were moored solidly to five different bases, two of them too high to flip a noose over. At least they shouldn't get any farther from the outside.

Getting back to it might be rather different.

All three of the sailors who had been overboard sounded easier in their minds. The captain wasn't sure whether this could be attributed to lack of upward vision, or just to being occupied; but there was a way to test.

He groped his way to the now cold fire box—cold only in comparison to its working state; the surroundings still felt like the inside of the balloon bag in flight—and felt for the control baffles which had directed the lifting air. These were made of the same fabric as the bag itself, stretched on light wooden frames. Carefully he nipped out a section of the material and deliberately spread it over his head and eyes.

The only obvious difference was that he could no longer see the tracker's characters. He felt no easier about what lay overhead.

But then, that hadn't bothered him, the captain, as much before as he thought it should have. A better subject was needed, though Barlennan had never heard of guinea pigs.

"Sherrer! Come aboard."

"Yes, Captain." If the sailor were uneasy, his voice failed to betray the fact. He came over the side in a few seconds, presumably coiling his safety line as he came.

"Here, sir."

"Can you think of any way back?"

"No, sir. We're—we're underneath—" The voice trembled.

"Don't be ashamed of being scared. It would probably mean something worse if you weren't. Did you feel better while you were working just now?"

"Yes, Captain."

"Feel the piece of sail cloth I'm holding here."

"I have it, sir."

"Put it over your head and eyes, like this." Barlennan helped. "Find some thin line and tie it there. Then go back overboard, and check the bottom all around us for small rocks. I think we can use some—as many as you can find."

Sherrer was neither stupid nor unimaginative, but was not the sort to ask anything like "How?" to an order. He simply obeyed. Barlennan was satisfied. He didn't want rocks, he wanted information, and would have had a hard time in answering a "how" or a "why" just then. The Flyers had not taught him any psychology, but his profession had; and he had grasped certain principles of research—not as well as his mate, but better than vaguely. Sherrer obviously shouldn't know in advance what was expected—or rather, hoped. Let him look for rocks for half a day or so, and then come aboard with them, and give him something else to do with the hood still over his eyes. Something not *too* demanding of his attention—

But how about Barlennan's own attention? Captain or not, there were moments when the tonnage above seemed to fill his mind. There was *nothing* else to think of. Nothing else in the world. Maybe he'd better make another hood for himself.

No. He was the captain, and he knew what was up there. If anyone could ignore it without special help, he should be the one.

Of course, it would be nice if something else were to get his attention away from the World Above.

It was, indeed, a relief when something did.

Jeanette had spent several minutes calling Barlennan after his communicator had gone silent and dark. She had his verbal reports up to that time, and wasn't very hopeful after it; the fadeout hadn't been quite instantaneous. The drifters hadn't hit anything hard and suddenly, up to the time sound and picture had faded. The waves the communicators used were long enough to reach their goal by diffraction even when Toorey was on the far side of the cliff from the *Bree*'s crew, so the basket must have been pretty well *surrounded* by some obstacle within a second or two after that. Barlennan had reported that the methane was flowing into openings in the rock fall; she had seen this, as well.

And Jeanette had as clear an idea as any human being possibly could of what being inside a cave or a tunnel at "normal" gravity must mean to a Mesklinite.

She switched to Dondragmer's set at once. He also had heard his captain's messages, delayed barely a second by the round trip to Toorey, and had as clear an idea as the Flyer of what had happened. Some of his sailors had already been ordered downstream to investigate the end of the rock fall; after a moment's thought, he let them go on. He split the remainder into two groups, sending one up toward the point where the eddy had presumably caused all the trouble and keeping the rest with him to get as close as possible as quickly as possible to where he was now pretty sure the original *Bree* was stranded.

The stream had started to widen now as the captain had reported earlier from his upstream position, but the methane at the edge away from the plateau was not uncomfortably warm. Maybe they could reach the ship, or what they hoped was the ship, without getting scalded. The mate told the Flyers what he was doing, and led the way. The river was widening, its edge coming to meet them. The radio remained behind; swimming with it was not an option, and walking on the bottom with it seemed inadvisable. Whoever carried it would be able to talk to the others and report to Toorey, but its viewing equipment would be useless unless it could be held above the surface. It seemed better to learn what could be found out, and then come back for the communicator. No one on the moon was pleased, but no one argued.

The bottom was ordinary ground at first. It had been dry land since long before the *Bree*'s arrival, presumably; the liquid methane was spreading wider and wider past its former bank, and there had been little change in the volume of flow in the thousands of days since their first arrival.

There was presumably little change now; the overflow represented liquid displaced from its former bed by rock.

The crew waded for a while, then had to swim, watching where they were headed part of the time but checking below the surface frequently. They were something like half way to where the ship seemed to be when the bottom began to show lighter in color, and closer examination showed that it was now the same ammonia slush reported earlier by the captain's quartet. It was being washed downstream, they could see at first; then it covered the bottom with a uniform sheet of white, and its motion couldn't be seen. Physical contact indicated that it *was* still moving.

The methane was getting deeper, and Dondragmer kept a close eye on what he was now almost certain was the *Bree*. It had been hauled well ashore, but was now out in the stream—or rather, the stream had spread well past it. It would have to be floating soon. Perhaps it was floating now, the mate realized; they were all swimming, and would be carried downstream at the same rate, and the slope across the river was completely hidden by fog, so it was not easy to tell who or what was moving.

It *was* the ship. It *was* afloat. It was easy to reach, fortunately; but it was not merely drifting along with the swimmers. The wind was toward the rock fall here, too, and the *Bree* was being carried very slowly toward the slope as the balloon basket had done.

For just a moment the mate thought of making sail; then he realized that the wind was toward the rocks and the depth too shallow to lower centerboards and sail effectively across it. With only ten men aboard, rowing would be futile.

Almost futile. Maybe they could keep her away from the rocks long enough to get the radio back aboard—no, they were already leaving that equipment upstream. Dondragmer ordered four of his crew back overboard.

"Get the radio, and start taking it downstream. We're not very far from the end of the rock fall, now; maybe when we get there the heat will ease off and the wind change. If it doesn't, well, the ship's a lot bigger than the balloon basket, and we may be able to paddle it so the rafts catch in a space too narrow to let us through."

The crewmen obeyed. One of those remaining behind raised another point.

"Will the rafts hold together if we catch her across a passage that way?"

"I don't know. Do any extra lashing you can between the outboard rafts before we hit. There aren't enough of us to keep her off, we'll soon be in the fog, and it can't be far from there to the rocks—it seems to be formed by methane hitting them and boiling. I'm surprised the wind doesn't let us see the edge of the fall; the captain could, further up."

The ship had enough cordage to keep them all busy for the next few minutes. The mate saw his swimming party reach shore and head back upstream to where he could still see the communicator. The downstream party was still in sight as well. The river seemed to be growing even wider there, but its members were staying ashore for faster travel.

The mate had time to think as he lashed. His thoughts rather paralleled the captain's; where did all this methane come from? Unlike Barlennan, he came up with a plausible explanation.

The original river had been fairly deep. If it had been well filled with fallen rock, it would *have* to spread over more ground, or travel faster, or both. But this idea, as the Flyers had often warned was likely to be the case, gave rise to more questions.

If the methane were being displaced by the rocks, why was it flowing *toward* them? There was at the moment no way to ask the customers and, of course, no certainty that they would be able to answer. He would have to do more thinking himself.

And just now there was no time to do that. They were into the fog.

Dondragmer silently berated himself for leaving to chance something he might have controlled. Even the few men now on board could have paddled to turn the cluster of rafts so that its longer side was toward the rocks, and thus improve its chance of catching rather than being swept between rocks and out of daylight and under—

He hadn't been thinking of *under*. Deliberately.

Luck had been with them, as it turned out, but the mate still felt stupid. They didn't touch sidewise, but the starboard bow raft of the cluster hit first on a rock barely above the surface. The after portion swung counterclockwise as the current kept pushing inward. The aft starboard raft struck, harder than anyone liked, on a huge slab which tilted up out of sight in the fog. The midships section continued to push shoreward briefly, but one aspect of the ship's basic design proved its salvation. Ropes stretched, rafts along the starboard side heaved, and the *Bree* came to rest with bow and stern pressed firmly against equally firm rocks and with another fragment of the fall *under* her just forward of amidships. While the rocks stayed there, so would the *Bree*. At the moment, with the darkness farther in easily visible even with the fog, this was a relief.

Dondragmer gave no one time to think. He ordered one of the men overboard with the longest light line aboard.

"Bend this around you. We'll fasten the other end to the ship. Get to the bottom and start shoreward, taking the line with you. Try not to get washed downstream. If you run out of line before you reach shore—you probably will—surface and try to spot landmarks which will let you know where you are and how far downstream we've traveled. Then do your best to keep there and yell for the others. We should still be in hearing for them. If you make contact, tell them to bring the radio as close to this place as they can."

"All right," the sailor affirmed, "but couldn't someone start calling from where we are? Then they could be looking for me and have the spot marked a lot better when they see me."

"Good. Right. We'll do that. Over with you; they'll still have to see you; they certainly won't see us."

The crewman vanished with no more words.

The line paid out slowly, occasionally going slack for a moment. Dondragmer suspected that the sailor was occasionally losing contact with the bottom, a forgivable offense since the Mesklinite body averaged just barely denser than liquid methane and there was certainly a current. He didn't want to ask, since one of his other men was, in response to orders, hooting as loudly as he could to get the attention of the downstream party. The mate concentrated on keeping track of the length of line paid out.

This eventually reached its end. Rather than have it jerked from his grip and possibly even from the rail to which it had been secured, the mate tightened his own grip and began gently tugging as the end approached. An answering set of tugs came almost at once, and the sailor's voice was audible between the bellows from the *Bree*'s deck.

"Located, sir. I'm only about a hundred lengths or a little more from shore. I'm off the slush, and there's plant stuff here I could tie the line to, but I want to make sure it's solid first."

"Right. Carry on. I'm sure you can hear Felmethes calling. Can you see the others? Can you tell whether they hear him?"

"Can't see them, sir, but I think I can hear them. Can't you?" Dondragmer gestured to Felmethes to be silent for a moment. The fellow had, of course, been pausing to listen for answers at regular intervals, but was glad enough to wait a little longer.

After a few seconds a long roar that seemed like a Mesklinite voice was audible, but no words could be distinguished. The sound ended eventually, and Dondragmer called to Kentherrer at the other end of the line.

"Could you hear that? Could you understand them?"

"Yes, sir. They keep asking if it's you, and say they can't understand you. There must be something about echoes along the rock faces."

"Could be. See if you can make them understand *you*. If so, tell them what's happened, and have them come back here."

A perfectly comprehensible pattern of hoots in Kentherrer's voice was the response; evidently he was more or less in touch with the other party but having trouble with clear communication. Dondragmer was patient. He was not exactly worried about the captain; there was very little hope that he and his fellows were alive, and rather less that they were sane. It was better not to rush into anything until there was at least a vague idea of where to rush.

Besides, it was not likely that anything at all could be done about the missing balloonists until the *Bree* could be brought ashore and rigged again. Even then, it was far from clear just *what* could be done. The most obvious technique, searching among and under the fallen rocks, was unpromising even if there were some way of telling where to start the search.

Come to think of it, there was a way for that. Barlennan had described in a good deal of detail the area downstream from the point where the eddy started. The point should still be there, and maybe even the eddy. If necessary, they could leave the ship where she was and search as a climbing or a swimming party.

Under the rocks? Well, maybe.

Kentherrer's voice had faded, but could still just barely be heard. The party must be coming back. It seemed to the mate better to wait until they arrived, rather than attempt a three-cornered conversation through the echoes.

He felt just a little foolish when Felmethes went overboard and began talking in an ordinary voice, submerged, first to Kentherrer and then, only a little louder, to the downstream party. He hadn't heard, or at least distinguished, the message from the latter saying that they were going to submerge; but that, by his standards, was no excuse for not remembering that words could be made out much farther in methane than in air.

He had had no experience with complex echoes under the surface, and it would be a long time before he knew about the speed/wavelength relation and such phenomena as diffraction, but Dondragmer went overboard anyway, and listened to the conversation for a moment. The downstream party was indeed on the way back. He joined in loudly.

The group had made out and acknowledged his order to get the communicator. Then another pattern of hoots, as blurred and devoid of meaning as the first sounds in air along the rocks, interfered with the conversation.

Words were indistinguishable. So were individual voice patterns. But the one other party under Dondragmer's orders *should* be on land, and a quick flow to the *Bree*'s deck and back into the methane—Mesklinite hearing was not confined to any one part of the body surface—made it obvious that this noise too was originating in liquid. The same body of liquid which was flowing along the face of the rock fall.

And into it. The sound must be coming from the captain's group. At least one of them was alive.

Barlennan could make out neither words nor individual voices either, but the leading fringe of the noise pattern, before the echoes ruined its structure, left him no doubt that it was a *voice*. He didn't have to think. Words or no words, if he could hear the speakers, they should be able to hear him. If they heard him, they would know he was still alive. If they knew he was alive, they wouldn't give up on him and his party. He and his men were as good as rescued.

Except, of course, for minor factors such as how anyone could find them in this lightless maze where sounds came from all possible directions at once, that they had practically no food with them, and were in about the last place on Mesklin where anything edible could be expected to turn up unless it were washed in from outside.

Come to think of it, why shouldn't food wash in from outside? There were plenty of fish in the river, and the current was coning from that direction. Why were they lying here hungry instead of fishing? Well, they couldn't see, of course, and you can't hear fish—but it was something to think about. Hard. He ordered his men to think about it, and went back to the basic problem.

Barlennan's group knew, in a sense, where they were; the inertial tracker was readable. But there was no way to get its readings to anyone else; if the radio was blocked as it seemed to be, the tracker's signals to Toorey must be equally unreadable to the Flyers. The echoes in the maze ruined any high-volume talking even if Dondragmer knew he was alive, and what else could lead rescuers close enough for quiet, echo-free talk? The captain could think of nothing. Could the mate, or the Flyers?

Jeanette didn't need to relay Dondragmer's report to the other Flyers; enough people were already with her in the com room. The relief that the captain might still be alive and sane—however garbled, the sound had been brief and seemingly better then raving—was tempered by the same doubts that Barlennan himself felt. Could that noise source be found? Could Mesklinites deliberately search, personally or otherwise, the maze under the rock fall? How long could the captain and his people live and remain sane to be rescued? On a more cold-blooded level, could the tracker be salvaged if he didn't?

The Drommian who voiced this question had the grace to show embarrassment, but even the human and other beings present couldn't dismiss the thought completely from their minds. There were still Mesklinites at work salvaging the rocket contents, but there were no more trackers.

Dondragmer thought of that aspect very fleetingly, and only to wonder about and dismiss at once the chance of using the tracker somehow to find its holders. It seemed far more practical to examine the area where the basket had disappeared. There might be meaningful clues among the rocks.

He left a watch of four men on the *Bree,* and with everyone else not at the rocket set out upstream, carrying the radio. Some of the group had been sent that way earlier, and the rest did not catch up with them until reaching the point level with the eddy, days later. From this position they could see much farther up-stream, and the balloon bag which had been caught and separated from the basket was easily visible. The mate sent half a dozen sailors to salvage it, and with the rest took to the river, swimming across below the eddy and spreading along the foot of the tumbled fragments to look for other traces.

There didn't seem to be any. If the basket had brushed against anything on the way inside, either nothing had scraped off or, if it had, had vanished down river. The loudest possible hoot in air brought no response from the rocks, but when it was repeated from below the surface it was answered at once, more loudly than before. Several of the sailors muttered satisfaction; but all fell silent when they saw the mate looking thoughtfully into the widest of the gaps where methane was still flowing in.

The eddy seemed as strong as the captain had reported. He had said nothing about the speed of flow into the rocks, but all could see that it was faster than anyone could be expected to paddle anything. It didn't seem faster than a person could swim, but if one were too far inside to see daylight there would be no way of knowing which way to swim.

"They're in there somewhere," the mate said slowly. No one disagreed; no one said anything.

"Kentherrer, use a safety line and check how deep it is here. *Don't* go inside. Three of you, hold his line." He paused until Kentherrer was submerged. "Tell me if you have any trouble holding on," he added. He did not specify whether this meant to the rope or to the rock, and the sailors didn't ask.

The line was paid out for about four body lengths before it went slack. It was not pointing straight down; the swimmer had been carried a short distance into the cleft by the current, but seemed calm enough when he reappeared.

"The bottom hasn't any of that slush," he reported. "It seems to be sort of gravel. I suppose really fine stuff would be carried inside."

"Could you get good footing on it?" Dondragmer asked.

"Not—not very good, sir."

The mate and the crew knew each other's thoughts perfectly well. The former made some allowances for the objectivity of Kentherrer's report.

"We'd probably be safe enough, if we roped together. If anyone lost grip on the bottom, the others could hold him until he got it back. I don't—

see—anything to do but—go in and search."

"Under all that?" one of the men asked before he could control himself. Dondragmer was silent for perhaps a minute. He was reasonably sure they would follow him if he went first, but wasn't quite sure he could lead. Not there.

"You may have something," he said at last. "*Under* it, in the dark, there'd be no way to tell where we were going or where we'd searched already. But *over* it—"

By ordinary Mesklinite standards, *over* was little better than under. One could fall, of course, with a couple of hundred times Rim weight. But this was the *Bree*'s crew, who had been getting used to *up* and *over* in various ways for something like a hundred thousand days now. *Over* just wasn't as bad.

One of the sailors was sent back to the radio to tell the Flyers what the mate had in mind, and to relay any later messages. In a couple of days the mate and his remaining men were linked in a network of cordage, no one closer than eight body lengths to any other, and no one connected to others by less than four separate safety lines. The climbing was clearly not going to be easy or quick, but it would be as safe as the mate could arrange.

Mesklinite legs are extremely short and their feet are not adapted for climbing, but they grip well on any reasonably rough surface. They have evolved for low as well as high gravity, and in the low-gravity latitudes there is always the risk of being blown away.

These rocks were rough, in most places. The joints along which they had separated in the recent fall were not, for the most part, slickensides. Travel over them was fairly easy, except for the distraction of looking down so much of the time. Not even the sailors were totally immune to that fear.

The rope spiderweb began to flow up and over the fallen slabs. Once all were away from the methane, Dondragmer ordered them to clamber horizontally upstream to the point where the eddy current went straightest into the maze. This served two purposes; it made it likely that they were upstream from wherever the captain might be, and could search downstream with reasonable certainty of passing him—whether they knew it or not. Also, it gave some practice in climbing before getting too far *up*.

It even gave some practice in falling. Twice one of the sailors lost his grip and found himself hanging from a set of ropes. Both times a hoot of alarm was cut off sharply as the faller realized he was being supported, and managed to control his emotion with his intelligence. Most encouraging of all, neither time did anyone on the other end of the ropes lose his grip.

So they started uphill. The rocks were noticeably cooler now. Even with the fog, there was little trouble keeping direction. Each time the web had moved about twice its own width the climbers paused and called loudly. After some days, they reached the top of the slope and were against vertical rock again; they moved a couple of web diameters downstream, and started down again.

Every few days they called across the river to report their lack of result to the Flyers. They could make out the voice of the sailor on watch there clearly enough, but he had trouble untangling their words from the echoes. The messages, however, were simple enough—"Nothing yet" as a rule—and there was no real confusion.

Back at the bottom, still fastened together, they swam back across to the radio, reported in more detail, then rested and went hunting and fishing. Fed as well, they returned to the up-and-down coverage of the fall.

Every so often, an undermethane call was made; it was always answered by a sailor at the methane's edge. Dondragmer wondered more and more seriously as the days went on what the lost group was doing for food. He was even slower than the captain in thinking of possible fish, but when he did, was much faster in realizing the problems of fishing in the dark. There had been very little food on the balloon, and it had been many days, now.

It was the food question which decided Barlennan to take some action of his own. Fish either weren't around or were able to sense groping chelae, and there had been no fishhooks aboard the balloon. He realized that any information the others might have about his location would be invalidated if they left it, but being found dead of starvation seemed a more serious risk. Besides, he could see no way of the crew's having any such information. He had also realized that there should be no trouble in deciding which way to go, if they went; not only did the tracker provide a clue, but the current was still flowing past them, apparently unchanged. If they could travel against it, they should sooner or later reach the river.

Unfortunately, while it was not flowing nearly as fast as any of them could swim, it was just in the wrong direction, and their own personal strength was failing—not seriously yet, because they'd been simply lying in the basket and occasionally answering what were presumably the mate's calls, but swimming against a current...

Even *crawling* against a current...

Crawling would be better, if they could keep hold of the bottom. Better still, if they could anchor themselves to the bottom. The radio and the tracker would help with that, and should be brought along in any case. A few rocks would hold the basket down; but they couldn't drag the whole basket against the current, whether it were ballasted or not.

So they'd salvage material from the basket and, as well as they could in the dark, make a container to carry a few rocks. It might not work out;

basket-weaving in the dark did not promise well; but it was better than starving passively.

He told the others what they were going to do.

A deafening roar, accompanied by a trembling of the rock on which the basket lay, suggested that he had the right idea.

The same roar was heard by the others, even those at the rocket over a dozen miles away. The search web was headed downward on its fourth round trip. Each of its members felt the same quivering under his feet, and froze in position, looking wildly in every direction. The Flyers heard, but of course felt nothing.

The sailor at the radio came closest to seeing; he could tell by the sound direction that the disturbance was somewhere upriver, even with the rumbling echoes that followed it, but there was still fog in that direction.

No one, even Barlennan with the most restricted sight, had the least doubt that rocks were settling still. The Flyers wondered why; the Mesklinites, where. Neither could even guess at an answer, but the natives could, and did, hope. The operative fact was that if anyone could do anything whatever, it needed to be soon.

There was no way that Dondragmer's efforts could be speeded significantly; trying to climb around faster, it quickly became obvious, simply increased the time lost retrieving dangling climbers. The Flyers had already launched an observation craft to get better pictures and maps of the locale, but days would be needed to obtain those, probably more days to get any pattern for the continuing settling of the rock fall, and no obvious reason to believe that the information would really be useful to anyone but abstract researchers.

But Barlennan could do *something*. Motion in the right direction, however slow, was better than staying where they were, and they did know the right direction. Upcurrent.

But they were already somewhat weakened by hunger. In a sense, they had some food; Karondrasee's juice tank was perhaps half full. Unfortunately, the juice had been selected for its catalytic properties, as observed by the cook, on the plant tissue used for lifting fires, not for its caloric content. It was also most repulsive to taste—the cook knew that; he had distinguished his various trial samples by that sense, since he had no other laboratory facilities. Even the Flyers had admitted that there was little choice, though the alien chemists had expressed the very lowest opinions of that analytical technique.

The tank, however, would be enough denser than methane to help hold them on the bottom, provided they replaced the air now partly filling it with liquid. There seemed at the moment nothing to be lost by diluting the juice and bringing the load along.

Discussion was brief. All three of the crewmen could see the situation as clearly as their captain, and it was not just a matter of obeying orders.

All four of them were now wearing the improvised hoods; even Barlennan had decided that it made things a *little* easier not to expect to see, and as long as the current flowed there was no real need to consult the tracker. There was no way of knowing just when the four of them submerged with radio, tracker, small basket of rocks, and juice tank with its top valve open, but it was long enough for one more roar of settling rock. Barlennan was actually delayed by this; he was slightly afraid that his men would be tempted into unwise haste, and insisted on a final recheck of every knot, both in the lines holding the equipment and those linking the travelers together. This delay did put a slight strain on discipline.

Progress was slow. Even with the extra weight, traction was poor. The tank proved to be the least effective ballast and Karondrasee, who was carrying it, was frequently lifted from the bottom, and whenever this happened his next in line, Hars—cook and tank were last—had to find something to hold onto himself. Sometimes there was nothing in reach, and they would lose in a few seconds several times as much distance as they had gained in the preceding few.

And they were getting hungrier, and more tired. None knew how much time passed. Every little while they would bellow to let others know they were still alive. They always heard answers, but there was no way of being sure whether these were coming more quickly or not. It would have been very encouraging if they had been.

Travel did get easier after a dozen or more reports, but for a slightly discouraging reason.

The current was losing its force. There was a perfectly plausible explanation: the space behind them, whatever it was, where the methane had been going was at last being filled up. Barlennan had been learning, however; he told himself firmly that there *might* be other explanations. He put the question before the others, more as a distraction than in hope of alternatives. He got none, but distractions were still useful even with the hoods; there was still a lot, no one could guess how much, of Mesklin overhead.

It was also getting somewhat cooler, they could feel, though the slush underfoot was still slush and still provided very poor traction.

And they were getting hungrier all the time. That in itself made travel more and more difficult. Chemically, evolution in an energy-demanding environment had given them the equivalent of a very large human glycogen reservoir for their size, but even that had its limits. They were nearing those limits.

The juice tank was now very dilute; they had not bothered to close the valve. This made the taste more bearable when they finally gave up and tried it. However, there is little to be gained by adding more catalyst, even just the right catalyst which this was not, when the supply of reactant is nearly gone. No one felt any less hungry than before, and the cook/flight engineer, whose digestive equipment might have been affected by his earlier experiments, was extremely uncomfortable for a time. He was quite unable to crawl or swim, and the party had to wait where it was.

Another roar and shudder of settling rocks enabled him to find some strength, and they moved on. The current was nearly gone, and they were guided now by the tracker, much more slowly even than before. The captain made the next report hoot by himself, hoping that its relative weakness would give the listeners a suggestion of their plight.

It didn't work; the sailor on watch below the surface who had been doing the answering didn't notice the difference. There was a good reason for this, it was realized later. The captain was now much closer to the searchers. However, the rumbling echoes of his voice still lasted about as long as ever and hid the volume difference. He himself failed to notice any change in the answer; he blamed it later on the distraction caused by hunger.

Hars, more than any of the others, hated to feel his energy going. He also hated to fail, and he still felt responsible for the tracker he was carrying. He probably had the least idea of any of the four why the echo problem should be less in air than in methane, but he had reached a point where anything seemed worth trying.

They had done all their calling under methane, for obvious reasons; sound traveled better there, as everyone knew. On the other hand, one grew tired more quickly there, though Hars didn't know why. One was lighter below the surface, obviously, but for some reason had more endurance above. "Hydrogen concentration" was not even words to him. But if there were anything to climb out on, he knew he would feel better.

He began to mutter aloud. Just mutter. He would have done something else if he had been leading, but the captain was in front. The others could hear, of course, and Barlennan began to worry. Sherrer's lack of balance had been serious enough; Hars was by far the most powerful of the group, even now. If he were to panic, it might make the final difference. Especially with them roped together. After a little thought, he spoke to the sailor.

"Hars, what's the matter?"

The pilot was actually embarrassed. "Well, Captain, I was wondering whether we could find a slope and get up in air for a little while. We could do with some rest, and it would be better than under methane. I didn't realize I was thinking out loud."

Bartlennan thought quickly. Shortage of air—hydrogen—at this point was not actually as serious as shortage of food, but it was certainly much more uncomfortable. It didn't much matter where they were if one of the rock settlings took place near them. They were as likely to be found in one place as another, after all; and if they really couldn't get out from under—

"All right. Change the setup. Hars and I will travel side by side, a rope length apart. Sherrer will be at my right, Karondrasee at Hars' left. It will be harder to keep the line straight, but we'll be more likely to find an upslope."

It took some time to rearrange the safety lines, but they were slightly rested when it was done and they were advancing in the new formation. It was harder to travel, however, since they could not be as much help to each other. Even the captain was ready to call a halt where they were when the rope connecting Karondrasee and Hars dragged on the bottom.

There was some sort of bulge. Hope of a sort began to rise as they examined and found a continuing slope. A solid one, of rock. The hope was mostly for comfort, not rescue, but the comfort was that of fresh air. They crowded together and began to creep upward. The slope was very shallow, and not difficult to climb even in their conditions; and for a while all feared that it might not reach the surface.

Fortunately. All but Hars had to stop for rest before they reached surface. With the four huddled together to rest, there was enough slack to let the pilot crawl a little ahead of the others, and in less than five body lengths he broke the surface.

With his encouragement and help, the other three also emerged into air, and relaxed gratefully.

Nearly starved, they were really in no state for rest to do them much good, but they could still enjoy the sensation. Even Barlennan waited much longer than he should have before issuing the order to go on. His mind and conscience argued against giving up, but he knew that more time in air would not really help. Another rock shudder emphasized this, but still he hesitated. Lying still felt so good—

So he had not yet spoken, and not yet decided to, when airborne sounds reached them.

Voices. Not really understandable yet, but obviously broken up into words this time. The four hooted in unison, reflexively. Shorter wave lengths don't diffract so badly, and sound waves are *much* shorter in air.

The only real question then was whether Dondragmer's people would climb down or Barlennan's climb up, and that was easy to settle.

The distance wasn't great; the mate's party could see how close they were to river level, but the captain's group lacked the needed strength. The members of the net above were out in daylight, able to look down at the spaces below, where they would descend into unknowable *depths*. Well, not really unknowable; the captain and the others obviously weren't *very* far down, but the word was *down.* But they could climb down.

The mate, still attached to four safety lines, descended with food, and after half a dozen false turns managed to deliver it. Then, one at a time, rested and fed, each with three lines firmly attached to him, the balloonists were partly hauled and partly climbed up to the web. A sailor brought the lines back down for the next rescue, and another one for the next, and when one descended for the last time, he and Barlennan used two ropes apiece to get back to daylight.

There had been some debate about the communicator and the tracker.

The former had been hauled up ahead of the captain on a pair of carefully fastened lines, but the inertial equipment had gone up even earlier, still fastened to Hars. It remained attached to him until everyone had crossed the river to the other communicator; he refused to abandon the duty until the whole group, except the ones still at the rocket, was together.

The Flyers understood, they thought. They certainly didn't complain. All Barlennan could overhear and understand was another of their theoretical arguments.

"Look, there's only one explanation. We know that rock is sedimentary—"

"Know?"

"Well, it's pretty obvious. One of the layers of the plateau, just below the foot of the cliff, has to be ammonia. That's mineral there. A lot of it was melted by the falling rock, and the Mesklinites smelled it—"

"Smelled something like it."

"What else could that be?"

"How do I know? I'm not a Mesklinite."

A third voice cut in. "The two of you are just gabbling. We haven't seen a layer that looked like ammonia—it'd be white, like ice."

"It *would* be ice."

"All right, but we haven't seen any."

"It's underground at river level."

"But how could—?"

"That's what I'm saying! We've got to check—I mean, Barlennan's people have to check—"

"How? They don't have drills, or shovels, or picks, and you can't expect a Mesklinite to go tunneling, do you?"

The captain had never heard this verb, but context suggested its meaning, rather too clearly.

"Why not? Barlennan's had lots of time underground now, and he's still all right."

"How do you know he is?"

The captain started to tune out, as usual. Just another of the theory-based wrangles among Flyers, which of course *might* lead to something later.

Then he saw what the something probably would be. The Flyers were very persuasive beings—

Any being with muscles and a nervous system complex enough to consider alternatives consciously can shudder. Dondragmer was obviously listening, too.

Introduction to "Lecture Demonstration"

From *Astounding: John W. Campbell Memorial Anthology*,
edited by Harry Harrison, Random House, 1973

I have been a high-school teacher for a quarter of a century, a student for nearly twice as long. "Lecture Demonstration" may show me as the former to people who did not know John Campbell, but not to those who did.

He bought my first story over thirty years ago when I was a college sophomore. Since then we have exchanged thousands of words of correspondence and spent many, many hours in conversation. We sometimes agreed, sometimes did not. I was trained in theory—astronomy and chemistry—and still tend to center my extrapolation on one factor alone, like a politician. John's education was in engineering, and he tended to remember better than I that all the rules are working at once: when he focused on one, it was to start an argument.

We were alike in one way. The phrase "of course" set either of us going. It's such fun to take apart a remark where those words appear! To show why, or how, or under what circumstances it isn't true at all! That attitude was the seed of Mission of Gravity, *the story on which I am content (so far) to let my reputation rest, and how much of that story was John is for future Ph.D. candidates to work out. He provided none of the specific scientific points, for once, but the general attitude underlying it was so obviously Campbellian that I have been flattered more than once to hear that "of course" Hal Clement was a Campbell pseudonym.*

He would certainly have had as much fun writing Mission of Gravity *as I did. Low-gravity planets and high-gravity planets were old hat to science-fiction fans, but Of Course no one planet can vary greatly in its gravity. So, naturally, Mesklin was born, thousands of times the mass of Earth, but whirling so rapidly on its axis that its equatorial diameter is more than twice the polar value, less than eighteen minutes pass from noon to noon, and a man massing a hundred and eighty pounds weighs five hundred and forty at Mesklin's equator and nearly sixty tons at its poles.*

Its people were fun to make up too. Little, many-legged types afraid of flying away with the wind at their low-gravity equator; about at the cultural level of Marco Polo—and one of them at least was a much sharper trader. He followed along very co-operatively when the strange beings from the sky hired him, until he had them where he wanted them. Then he held out—for scientific knowledge.

Of Course one doesn't interfere with the development of a primitive tribe by teaching it modem technology.

"Lecture Demonstration" takes place during the formative years of the College on Mesklin, when the teachers are still learning too, and Mesklinites are finding that human beings are quite human.

Whatever that may mean.

Lecture Demonstration

The wind wasn't really strong enough to blow him away, but Estnerdole felt uneasy on his feet just the same. The ground was nearly bare rock, a gray-speckled, wind-polished reddish mass which the voice from the tank had been calling a "sediment." It was dotted every few yards with low, wide-spreading, rubbery bushes whose roots had somehow eaten their way into a surface which the students' own claws could barely scratch.

Of course the plants themselves could provide anchorage if necessary. The ex-sailor's nippers were tensed, ready to seize any branch that might come in handy if he did slip. While the gusts of hydrogen sweeping up from the sea at his right wouldn't have provided much thrust for a sail, the feeble gravity of Mesklin's equator—less than two percent of what he was used to in the higher latitudes—made Estnerdole feel as though anything at all could send him flying. It took a long time, as he had been warned, to get used to conditions at the World's Rim; even the bulky metal tank crawling beside him seemed somehow unsteady.

He was beginning to wonder whether he had been right to sign on for the College—the weird establishment where beings from the sky taught things that only the most imaginative Mesklinites had ever dreamed of. It would be fine to be able to perform miracles, of course, but the preliminaries—or what the aliens insisted were necessary preliminaries—got very dreary at times.

This walk out on the peninsula, for example. How could the aliens know what the rocks below the surface were like, or what kind would appear at the surface at a given place, and how they had been folded up to make this long arm of dry land? And, most of all, why was any of this worth knowing? True, he had seen some of the holes drilled near the school and had even examined the cylinders of stone extracted from them; but how could anyone feel even moderately sure that things were the same a few cables away? It seemed like expecting the wind to blow from the north on one hilltop merely because it was doing the same on the next one.

Well, the alien teachers said that questions should be asked when things weren't clear. Maybe one would help here—if only Destigmet wouldn't cut in with his own version of the answer. That was the worst of asking questions. You couldn't be sure that everyone else didn't already know the correct answer...

But Estnerdole had learned a way around that.

"Des!" he called, loudly enough to be sure that the other students would also hear. "I'm still not straight on one thing. The human said that this exercise was to tell whether the peninsula is a cuesta or a hogback. I still don't see the difference. It seems to me that they could be pretty much the same thing. How do you know that anything you call a cuesta isn't a small part of a hogback, or wouldn't be if you looked over enough ground?"

Destigmet started to answer in a self-assured tone, "It's simply a matter of curvature. A cuesta is a flat layer of rock which has a softer layer under it which has eroded away, while a hogback—" He paused, and Estnerdole's self-esteem took an upward turn. Perhaps this know-it-all was going to run aground on the same problem. If Des just had to give up and ask the instructor, everything would be solved. If he didn't, at least there would be the fun of hearing him struggle through the explanation; and if it didn't come easily, there would be nothing embarrassing about checking with the tank driver.

The voice which came suddenly from the vehicle was therefore an annoyance and a disappointment. Estnerdole did not blame a malicious power for interfering with his hopes, since Mesklinites have little tendency toward superstition in the mystical sense, but he was not pleased.

"We will turn south now," the alien voice said in perfectly comprehensible, though accented, Stennish. "I haven't said much yet, because the ground we've been covering is similar to that near the College. I hope you have a clear idea of what lies underneath there. You remember that the cores show about twelve meters of quartz sandstone and then over twenty of water ice, followed by several more layers of other silicate sediments. It shouldn't have changed much out here. However, you will recall that along the center of this peninsula the surface looks white from space—you have been shown pictures. I am guessing, therefore, that erosion has removed the sandstone and uncovered the ice at the top of a long fold. This is of course extrapolation, and is therefore a risky conclusion. If I'm right, you will get some idea of what can be inferred from local measurements, and if I am wrong we will spend as much time as we can to find out why.

"It will take us only a few minutes to reach the edge of the white strip. Any of you who don't mind the climb may ride on the tank. Now, I want each of you to think out in as much detail as your knowledge and imagination permit just what the contact area should be like—thickness of sandstone near it, smoothness of the two surfaces, straightness of the junction, anything else which occurs to you. I know you may feel some uncertainty about making predictions on strictly dry-land matters, but remember I'm taking an even worse chance. You're sailors, but at least you're Mesklinites. I'm from a completely different world. There, I'm stopping; any of you who wish, climb on. Then we'll head south."

Estnerdole decided to ride. The top of the tank was seven or eight body lengths above the ground and acrophobia is a normal, healthy state of mind for a Mesklinite; but College students were expected to practice overriding instinct with intelligence wherever possible. There would obviously be a better view of the landscape from the top of the vehicle. Estnerdole, Destigmet, and four of the remaining ten class members made their way up the sides of the machine by way of the ladderlike grips provided to suit their pincers. The other six elected to remain afoot. They took up positions beside and ahead of the tank as it resumed motion, the flickering legs which rimmed their eighteen-inch wormlike bodies barely visible to the giant alien inside as they kept pace with him.

Visibility dropped as night fell, and for nearly nine minutes the tank's floodlights guided the party. Then the sun reappeared on their left. By this time the edge of the dark rock they were traversing was visible from the tank roof, only a few hundred yards ahead. The teacher slowed, and as the ground party began to draw ahead, he called its members back. "Hold on. We're almost close enough to check predictions, and I'd like to get a few of them on record first. Has anyone seen details yet which surprised him?"

Estnerdole remained silent; he had made no predictions he would trust, and did not expect to be surprised by anything. Destigmet also said nothing, but his friend suspected that it was for a different reason. None of the others had anything to say either, and the teacher sighed inaudibly inside his machine. It was the same old story, and he knew better than to let the silence last too long. "There's something *I* didn't guess," he finally said. "The edge of the dark rock isn't as straight as I had expected—it looks almost wavy. Can anyone suggest why?"

Destigmet spoke up after a brief pause. "How about the bushes? I see them growing along the edge. Could they have interfered with the erosion?"

"Possibly. How could you check on that possibility?"

"See whether the rock where they're growing is any higher or lower than where they aren't."

"All right. Let's see."

And that was why the group was all together when the shell of sandstone gave way under the tank.

The human teacher observed less of the event than his pupils. The yielding ledge freed his vehicle for a fall of some fifty feet under three times his normal gravity, and one second was not long enough for him to appreciate the situation. His safety clamps, padded and reinforced though they were, had not been designed for any such shock, though it was just as well they were there. Neither was the shell of the tank, and even the students least familiar with the alien machinery could tell that something was wrong with it. The evidence was not visual; a stink of oxygen permeated the neighborhood and for a moment sent the Mesklinites scurrying as far as they could. Even a creature which doesn't actually breathe because it is small enough for high-pressure hydrogen to reach all its tissues by direct diffusion may have evolved a sense of smell.

The space into which they had dropped was windy, and the oxygen quickly became imperceptible. Estnerdole crept back to the side of the motionless tank; like his fellows, he was of course uninjured. The fall had meant no more to them physically than a similar one on Phobos would have to a human being, though any fall can be expected to provide an emotional jolt to a Mesklinite.

"Teacher! Dr. LaVerne! Can you answer us?"

There was no response, and after a moment the sailor began to examine the machine in detail, looking for visible damage. The process was hampered by the fact that it was three quarters buried in white powder—the ammonia snow which had been blowing from the north for weeks as winter for Mesklin's habitable hemisphere drew on. The snow formed a slope of about thirty degrees, extending into a hollow which reached east and west as far as Estnerdole could see. The cavern's north face was walled by a nearly vertical cliff of clear, glassy material. The roof, now pierced by the hole through which the party had fallen, was rock. Sunlight slanting through the hole was reflected by the ammonia which formed the south side and illuminated the immediate area for the moment, though the light changed constantly as the beam scanned along the slope.

The exposed portion of the tank showed no visible cracks; the oxygen must have leaked from some place below. Light was shining from the exposed windows, and Estnerdole made his way to the nearest of these by means of the climbing grips which studded the shell. Destigmet was close behind.

Neither was really familiar with the vehicle's interior, so neither could be sure whether the apparent chaos of objects within was normal or not. The form of the teacher was visible, motionless in the control seat. His armor, which they had seen often enough to know well, appeared intact; but the transparent front of the headpiece seemed to have colored liquid over part of its inner surface. The human being's head could not be discerned in detail. Neither sailor was familiar with the appearance of human blood, but both had good imaginations—even though they lacked real circulatory systems of their own.

"We'll have to get in somehow and get him out of there," Destigmet said. "He'll have to get back to the College somehow, and we certainly can't carry the tank."

"But if we break in or open the door, our air will get in too, and he can't stand that. Shouldn't we, or some of us, go back ourselves and bring human help?"

"Our air is already inside—at least, his came out, and ours has much higher pressure. Either his armor saved him, or it's too late already. Certainly if any of us *can* get out, one should go for help; but the rest must get to him and at least do our best to see that—well, to see whether we can do anything. Come on, everyone—dig out the door and try to get it open while we can still see. One of you climb the hill."

The snow was loose and powdery, defeating any attempt to dig a narrow hole. The door of the tank was on the downhill side, which helped some. The bulk of the vehicle kept the entire mass of white dust from sliding down. Legs working at near-invisible speed hurled the stuff away from the metal in clouds, and as the minutes passed, the lower part of the vehicle grew more and more visible. The five minutes or so of daylight left when they started was not nearly enough to let them shift all those cubic yards of material, but enough light came from the windows to let the Mesklinites work through the night; and within two days the door was uncovered. There would have been no difficulty in opening it, but even Destigmet was a little uneasy about doing so in spite of his earlier logic. "Let's check the window once more," he said. "Maybe—" He left the sentence unfinished and began the climb to the nearest window.

He had scarcely started, however, when the hull of the tank shifted slightly, tilting toward the cluster of watching Mesklinites. Destigmet had never jumped in his life—the concept was alien to a being reared in nearly three hundred Earth gravities—but his reflexes did something. Suddenly he found himself over twenty yards away from the tank, close to the glassy cliff which formed the other wall of their prison.

His fellows had also scattered, but not quite so abruptly. They were delayed mostly by bad traction, the fluffy material under their claws doing most of the initial moving. Destigmet had been on the tank.

The latter did not complete its threatened fall, for the moment. It was resting entirely on the loose, white dust which had saved it from flattening like an egg under an elephant's foot, and most of this had been removed from the downhill side; but it did not yet fall. The Mesklinites approached again with caution. Even they, in a place where everything's weight seemed negligible to them, had no wish to be underneath that mass if it really did topple.

"I thought your weight must have shifted it, but something else must be moving inside," remarked Estnerdole. "Maybe the teacher is in better shape than we thought."

"A person's weight doesn't mean a thing here," returned Destigmet. "It must be him moving. Let's get to that window."

"If he is moving around, the climb will be pretty risky. Nothing but luck is keeping that thing from rolling the rest of the way down the slope now."

"No matter. We have to find out. Come on." Destigmet led the way up the loose material, but before any of the Mesklinites had reached the tank, it became evident that its occupant was once more active. Its outer lights suddenly flashed on.

Estnerdole gave a hoot of relief, and followed it with words. "Dr. LaVerne! How can we help you?"

For several seconds there was no answer, but the tank wavered even more alarmingly. Then the door opened, and the giant figure of the armored alien appeared in the opening. It tottered a moment, then fell outward into the snow. The tank rocked away as the man's weight left it, swung forward again in a way which would have brought Estnerdole's heart to his mouth if he had possessed a heart, and then stopped once more.

The Mesklinites swarmed forward with the common intent of dragging the human being away from the dangerous neighborhood, but before they reached him he started crawling under his own power. His voice came haltingly from his helmet speaker. "Stay back—all of you—I can make it—you couldn't move me in this stuff anyway."

Estnerdole and two of the others kept coming; with Mesklinites as with other intelligent races, some customs override selfish caution. The three tiny figures swarmed around the struggling monster, trying to speed its faltering trip away from the danger zone, but they promptly found that the teacher had been right; they couldn't help. It was not that the five hundred kilograms of weight were too much for them—any one of them could have lifted that. The trouble was the footing. A Mesklinite's legs end in insectlike claws, except for the nippers on the fore and aft pairs; the claws provide excellent traction on the wooden deck of a ship or the hard-packed soil which covers much of Mesklin. But a sand dune or a heap of ammonia snow is a different matter. The students' efforts to push the huge bulk of their teacher simply drove their own bodies into the loose fluff.

LaVerne was only partly aware of their presence. He had more or less recovered from the shock of his fall, and had seen enough to evaluate the situation fairly well; but he was not really in full possession of his faculties. He knew he was on a sloping surface of loose material, and that the tank was rather likely to roll over on him at any moment; his whole attention was focused on getting out of the way. The warning to the students had been little more than reflexive, like their own move to help him, and he did not follow up the order. He simply crawled as well as the situation permitted. A human observer might have had trouble deciding whether his mode of progress should have been called crawling or swimming, but he did make progress. He never was sure whether it took him five seconds or a whole minute, but presently he found himself on smooth, solid rock with the white slope safely behind him. He relaxed with a sigh, and only slowly became aware of the dozen caterpillarlike figures around him.

With an effort he managed to lever himself to a sitting position. His students waited silently. He took in the nearly buried tank, the cliff in the opposite direction, the rock roof above with sunlight slanting through the jagged hole, and the darkness which swallowed the seemingly endless cavern to east and west. The Mesklinites were reasonably familiar with human facial expression and tried to read his, but they could make out little in the poor light through the face plate, which was partly obscured by blood from his nose. They waited for him to speak, and were not surprised when his first words formed pertinent questions. "How long did it take you to do that digging job? How long has that fellow been trying to climb the hill?"

Destigmet answered, "Only a few days; we didn't keep close count."

"Hmph. He hasn't gotten very far. I'm reminded of an animal on my own world which traps its prey in pits rather like this—loose stuff at its angle of repose. Climbing such a surface is nearly impossible. What will he do if he gets to the top? That hole is twenty of your body lengths away from the bank."

"But, Doctor!" pointed out Estnerdole, "the stone itself is not very thick. If we *can* reach the top, we know the stone comes to an end only a short distance to the south. We can dig our way out from under the edge easily enough."

"True enough. All right, the rest of you might as well try climbing too. So, for that matter, might I; if I get out on the surface I can call for help instead of having to send a runner."

"Rest first," advised Destigmet. "You can't be in very good condition yet. You must have been hurt some, if the state of your face plate means anything."

"All right. I want to think, anyway."

Near-silence fell while the rest of the students began to climb. Two or three, starting just below the stranded tank, had little trouble getting as far as the vehicle; but from there on it was a different matter. The creatures were tiny, some eighteen inches long with split-cylinder bodies an inch and a half in diameter. They were light; their half-pound masses weighed less than a kilogram at Mesklin's equator. Even that weight, however, sank their tiny legs full-length into the snow. The motion of the short limbs could be inferred from the clouds of white dust which sprayed backward from the small bodies. A hollow formed around each slender form, with material sifting down into it from the front and sides. Behind, it built up into something approaching a level surface, and slowly—very slowly—the Mesklinites followed their fellow uphill. Sometimes one would speed up briefly as he encountered a slightly more firmly packed area; almost as often he would slide back a body length or two, spraying frantic clouds of white dust, before resuming forward motion. Every few seconds a pile of snow behind one of them would collapse and slide downhill, spreading its material out until a new approach to the angle of repose was attained.

Minutes—long minutes—passed. Those who had used the tank as a starting point were four or five yards up the slope, not too far behind the one who had started so long before. The rest, whose slipping had started at a lower level, had made little visible progress. The little fans and rivulets of sliding snow, first behind one and then another of the dozen red-and-black figures, were as hypnotic as the patterns in a bonfire; LaVerne had to wrench his attention away from them, suddenly realizing that he had more serious jobs than being a spectator.

Slowly and painfully he hoisted himself to his feet. He could manage this at all only with the aid of ingenious lever-and-ratchet systems in the joints of his armor which let him concentrate on one part of the job at a time, and rest frequently without losing what he had gained. Once up, he turned slowly around, clarifying the mental picture he had already developed of the space they had fallen into. It was not too hard to infer how the cavern must have formed.

As he had guessed, the layer of water ice under the sandstone had been bared by erosion at the top of the fold which formed the peninsula.

The stone must have worn virtually to a knife edge; no wonder it had failed to support the tank's weight once the underlying ice had gone. Ice was hard enough at Mesklin temperatures to stand mechanical erosion reasonably well, of course, but there was another factor operating here. Each year, as the giant world swung past periastron and the northern hemisphere began its summer, storms started sweeping ammonia snow from the virtually world-wide northern "ice" cap across the equator. This naturally buffered the local temperature near the freezing point of ammonia, which the Mesklinite student scientists had selected as the arbitrary control point for temperature in the scales they were developing.

Once the protecting silica had eroded away, the solid ammonia encountered the equally solid water, and liquid resulted. Not only was some heat generated, but the solutions of the two had considerably lower freezing points than either compound alone—a fact which the present crop of students had all faced in their most elementary courses. The ice layer had melted, or dissolved, if one preferred to think of it that way, for fifty or sixty yards back from the edge of the protecting stone. Later in the season when the ammonia had evaporated, this would show a beautiful overhanging ledge extending probably for miles east and west. With luck, LaVerne would be able to see it; since the College had been set up less than half a Mesklin year before, no one had had the chance yet.

LaVerne was not so much a scientist as a teacher. Still, he knew enough physical chemistry to wonder about the age of the peninsula—how long it would take the weight of overlying rock to squeeze the ice to the top of the fold and empty the filling from the sandwich. Maybe it had been going on for years already, and if they stayed in the cavern they could measure the creep of the south wall toward them. Maybe—

A hoot that was almost deafening even through his helmet jerked his wandering mind back to the current realities. He knew about Mesklinite voices, of course, but no human being ever got used to their more extreme volumes. He turned as quickly as he could from the ice cliff to the slope which his students had been trying to climb. By the time he really got his eyes focused on the scene, the key events had happened; but it was obvious enough what they had been.

The snow being kicked downhill by the climbers had been piling up against the tank. The earlier digging had left the vehicle almost without support on its downhill side, and what any thoughtful witness would have predicted had finally occurred. By the time LaVerne completed his turn, the machine was well into a full roll downhill toward him, and almost completely hidden inside a developing avalanche. The hoot, coming from several Mesklinites at once, had been stimulated by their discovery that they were involved in the slide; its upper edge was propagating rapidly toward the top of the slope and was already above the highest of the climbers.

The man had little thought for his students just then. The rolling tank was heading straight toward him, and he could not possibly move fast enough to get out of its way. He was several yards from the bottom of the slope, but that might not be far enough. It all depended on whether the tank would reach the stone with enough energy to roll those few yards—*let's see; it looks as though it would land right side up; then onto its right side, then the top, then the left—that should bring it right to my feet. If there's one more quarter-turn left in it, I'm flat.* LaVerne wondered later how he was able to analyze the matter so calmly as the mass of metal came whispering down on him in its envelope of dusty snow.

Actually it scarcely rolled at all, coming to rest with an ear-shattering clang on its right side. The man had a good heart—he would never have been allowed to serve on Mesklin otherwise—and was able to switch his attention back to his students almost at once; but the switch did his heart little more good than the juggernauting tank had. The Mesklinites were invisible.

For a moment, real fear struck him—intelligent fear based on foresight, not just panic. If those people were gone, he would most certainly not get back to the college. Then little white fountains of dust began to erupt from various points near the bottom of the slope, and one after another the Mesklinites emerged. None of them had been buried deeply enough to matter. All was well.

Except that there seemed no way to get out of the cave.

Ideas flowed from all directions, since the Meslinites were an imaginative lot; but none of these seemed very practical. Estnerdole suggested that the cave be explored in the east-west directions, on the chance that there might be a more usable way out. The objection to this was that not even the Mesklinites could see in the total darkness which obtained away from the area sunlit from their entry hole. Destigmet proposed cutting climbing notches in the cliff of water ice and reaching the top that way; unfortunately, ice met stone many yards from the hole, and there was no reason to hope that even the natives, insectlike as they appeared to human beings, could possibly crawl inverted along the stone ceiling. LaVerne, conditioned by a childhood on Earth, thought briefly of packing the snow to make a more reliable support and with it actually constructing steps up the slope. Fortunately for his reputation with the Mesklinites, he remembered in time that ammonia, unlike water, is denser in the solid than in the liquid phase. It does not, therefore, tend to melt under pressure; trying to make even a snowball out of the powdery stuff which had trapped them would be like trying to do it with a handful of sand.

"All I can suggest," he said at last, "is for some or all of you to start climbing again—maybe farther apart this time, so one person's avalanche doesn't involve everyone else. At least the tank won't be a problem any more. It will be slow, but if even one of you can get to the top, he can go back to the College and get help. I can last here for days, with the air supplies in the tank, so there's no emergency."

"I'm afraid there is, Doctor," pointed out Estnerdole. "You can't get into the tank. It's lying on its right side, with the door underneath. Unless there is some outside connection you can reach to replenish the oxygen in your armor, you are rather limited in your supply."

The man was silent for several seconds, except for a brief muttering which the students could not make out clearly. "You're right, Es," he said at last. "It is an emergency after all, for me. Do you suppose you people are strong enough to turn the tank right side up?"

The Mesklinites were somewhat doubtful, but clustered around to try. LaVerne, who shared the exaggerated idea of Mesklinite physical strength which was so common among human beings, was not surprised when the vehicle stirred under their efforts; indeed, he was disappointed when it lofted only a few millimeters. After some seconds it settled back where it had been, and one of the students reappeared from the narrow space underneath. "We can move it, but that's all. We'd have to get this side up several body lengths before it would rock over the right way, and there's nothing to stand on."

Destigmet wriggled into view behind the speaker. "I can think of only two things to do, and you've already suggested one of them," he said. "The first is for someone to start climbing again. The other is for us to lift the tank once more, while you pack snow under it to hold it up and let us get a fresh purchase. Maybe we can work it up that way before you run out of air."

"All right," agreed LaVerne. "It would be better if I had something to serve as a shovel, but let's get at it. I'm using oxygen just standing here worrying."

For a while it looked possible, if not really hopeful. Carrying the dusty snow in his armored hands proved impractical, but he found that he could do fairly well pushing a mass of it ahead of him as he crawled—and crawling was far easier than trying to walk. Essentially, he was sweeping rather than carrying. He managed to get what would have been several shovelfuls, if he had had a shovel, against the space at the edge of the tank where the Mesklinites had disappeared once more. At his call they strained upward again, and as quickly as he could he pushed the material into the widening space. "That's all," he reported when he had done his best, and the students relaxed again. So did the pile of snow. LaVerne, optimistic by nature, felt sure that the tank had not settled quite back to its original position, and kept trying; but after an hour which left him more exhausted than he had ever felt in his three Earth years on Mesklin, he had to admit that the idea was qualitatively sound but quantitatively inadequate.

During those days, the student who was trying to climb the slope had made little progress. Once he had gotten nearly a third of the way before sliding most of the way back in a smother of white dust; four or five times he had lost the fight in the first yard or two. The rest of his attempts came between those limits.

But it finally became evident that the man's air was not going to be the real limiting factor. Destigmet pointed out another one to him. "Some time ago, Doctor, one of your fellows taught us about a fact he claimed was very basic—the Law of Conservation of Energy. If I have the terminology right, we can apply very large forces by your standards, but as that law should tell you, there is a limit to the amount of work we can do without food. None of us expected to need food in this class, and we brought none with us."

One of the others cut in. "Won't people from the College start looking for us anyway? This class should have been over days ago."

LaVerne frowned invisibly behind the blood-stained face plate, which he had no means of cleaning. "They'll be looking, but finding us will be another story," he said. "They'd expect to see the tank miles away on the smooth surface of the peninsula. When they don't, they'll think we got swept into the sea, or went off to the forest country for some reason. They won't look over this area closely enough to find the hole we left, I suspect. It's possible we'll get out of this with their help, but don't count on it."

Estnerdole suddenly became excited. "Why not build a tower we can climb, with the water ice from the cliff? We can chip it out easily enough without tools, or even melt it out with the snow—no, that wouldn't leave us any to work with, but—" His voice trailed off as more difficulties became apparent to him.

LaVerne was pessimistic, too, after the just-completed practical demonstration of how much material would be needed even to prop up the tank. Then he brightened. "We could use the ice to get this machine upright—big chunks of it would be more practical and easier to move than the snow. Of course, even that doesn't get us any closer to getting out of here; the tank certainly isn't going to climb this sandhill even if I get into it. If only—" He paused, and the ensuing silence stretched out for long seconds. Even with the man hidden in his armor, the listeners got the impression that something had happened. Then he spoke again, and his tone confirmed the suspicion. "Thanks, Es. That does it. Start digging ice, gentlemen. We'll be out of here in a couple of hours!"

Actually, it took less than three days.

"You look bothered," remarked Thomasian, LaVerne's department head. "Delayed shock from your narrow escape, or what?"

"It wasn't that narrow," replied the teacher. "I had hours of air still in the suit when the spinner picked us up, and we could have worked the tank upright to get at more if I had needed it. You'd have searched the area closely enough to find that hole sooner or later."

"Later would probably have been too late—and the really narrow squeak I was thinking of was the fall. Fifteen meters under three gees—sooner you than me. If it hadn't been for that snow bank, we'd have had to cut you out of the flattened remains of that tank—not that it would have been worth doing. Of course any of your students should have been able to think of tossing pieces of water ice over the slope, especially after you'd discussed with them why the cuesta was so deeply undercut. So should you, for that matter—"

"Hogback," LaVerne responded almost automatically. "Sure, all sorts of ideas are obvious afterward. At the time, I wasn't quite sure that this one would work, even if I did sound as enthusiastic as I could and even though I did have experience to go by. Still, I was afraid it would simply melt holes in the slope; but it went fine. The liquid formed where the two ices met just soaked into the surrounding snow, spreading out and diluting the water ice until the mixture's melting point came up to the local temperature again—and froze into a continuous mass. It was hard enough for Estnerdole to climb out and go for help in less than an hour, I'd guess; I didn't actually time it."

"What was the experience you could go by? And if it was so easy and safe, what's bothering you?"

"The same thing. A teaching problem. They claim that Mesklinite psychology is enough like ours for teaching techniques to be about the same, effectively. They expect us to—er—'relate' new facts to known experience."

"Of course. So?"

"So the experience in question should obviously be one familiar to the students, not just the teacher. What sparked this idea for me was the memory of sugar getting lumpy in the bowl when it gets damp. You know, I'm just a little shaky on the local biochemistry, chief—tell me: what do Mesklinites use for coffee, and what do they put in it?"

Star Light

1: Pit Stop

Beetchermarlf felt the vibrations die out as his vehicle came to a halt, but instinctively looked outside before releasing the *Kwembly*'s helm. It was wasted effort, of course. The sun, or rather, the body he was trying to think of as *the* sun, had set nearly twenty hours before. The sky was still too bright for stars to be seen, but not bright enough to show details on the almost featureless dusty snow field around him. Behind, which was the only direction he could not see from the center of the bridge, the *Kwembly*'s trail might have provided some visual reference; but from his post at the helm there was no clue to his speed.

The captain, stretched out on his platform above and behind the helmsman, interpreted correctly the latter's raised head. If he was amused, he concealed the fact. With nearly two human lifetimes spent on Mesklin's unpredictable oceans he had never learned to like uncertainty, merely to live with it. Commanding a "vessel" he did not fully understand, travelling on land instead of sea and knowing that his home world was over three parsecs away did nothing to bolster his own self-confidence, and he sympathized fully with the youngster's lack of it.

"We're stopped, helmsman. Secure, and start your hundred-hour maintenance check. We'll stay here for ten hours."

"Yes, sir." Beetchermarlf slipped the helm into its locking notch. A glance at the clock told him that over an hour of his watch remained, so he began checking the cables which connected the steering bar with the *Kwembly*'s forward trucks.

The lines were visible enough, since no effort had been made to conceal essential machinery behind walls. The builders of the huge vehicle and her eleven sister "ships" had not been concerned with appearance. It took only a few seconds to make sure that the few inches of cable above the bridge deck were still free of wear. The helmsman gestured an "all's well" to the captain, rapped on the deck for clearance, waited for acknowledgment from below, opened the starboard trap and vanished down the ramp to continue his inspection.

Dondragmer watched him go with no great concern. His worries were elsewhere, and the helmsman was a dependable sailor. He put the steering problem from his mind for the moment, and reared the front portion of his eighteen-inch body upward until his head was level with the speaking tubes. A sirenlike wail which could have been heard over one of Mesklin's typhoons and was almost ridiculous in the silence of Dhrawn's snow field secured the attention of the rest of the crew.

"This is the captain. Ten hours halt for maintenance check; watch on duty get started. Research personnel follow your usual routine, being sure to check with the bridge before going outside. No flying until the scouts have been overhauled. Power distribution, acknowledge!"

"Power checking." The voice from the speaking tube was a little deeper than Dondragmer's.

"Life support, acknowledge!"

"Life support checking."

"Communication, acknowledge!"

"Checking."

"Kervenser to the bridge for standby! I'm going outside. Research, give me outside conditions!"

"One moment. Captain." The pause was brief before the voice resumed, "Temperature 77; pressure 26.1; wind from 21, steady at 200 cables per hour; oxygen fraction standard at 0.0122."

"Thanks. That doesn't seem too bad."

"No. With your permission, I'll come out with you to get surface samples. May we set up the drill? We can get cores to a fair depth in less than ten hours."

"That will be all right. I may be outside before you get to the lock, if you take time to collect the drill gear, but you are cleared outside when ready. Tell Kervenser the number of your party, for the log."

"Thank you, Captain. We'll be there right away."

Dondragmer relaxed at his station; he would not, of course, leave the bridge until his relief appeared, even with the engines stopped. Kervenser would be some minutes in arriving, since he would have to turn his current duties over to a relief of his own. The wait was not bothersome, however, since there was plenty to think about. Dondragmer was not the worrying type (the Mesklinite nervous system does not react to uncertainty in that way) but he did like to think situations out before he lived them.

The fact that he was some ten or twelve thousand miles from help if the *Kwembly* were ever crippled was merely background, not a special problem. It did not differ essentially from the situation he had faced for most of his life on Mesklin's vast seas. The principal ripple on his normally placid self-confidence was stirred up by the machine he commanded. It resembled in no way the flexible assemblage of rafts which was his idea of a ship. He had been assured that it would float if occasion arose; it actually had floated during tests on distant Mesklin where it had been built. Since then, however, it had been disassembled, loaded into shuttle craft and lifted into orbit around its world of origin, transferred in space to an interstellar flier, shifted back to another and very different shuttle after the three-parsec jump, and brought to Dhrawn's surface before being reassembled. Dondragmer had personally supervised the disassembly and reconstruction of the *Kwembly* and her sister machines, but the intervening steps had not been carried out under his own eye. This formed the principal reason for his wanting to go outside now; high as was his opinion of Beetchermarlf and the rest of his picked crew, he liked first-hand knowledge.

He did not, of course, mention this to Kervenser when the latter reached the bridge. It was something which went without saying. Anyway, the first officer presumably felt the same himself.

"Maintenance checks are under way. The researchers are going out to sink a well, and I'm going out to look things over," was all Dondragmer said as he resigned his station. "You can signal me with outside lights if necessary. It's all yours."

Kervenser snapped two of his nippers light-heartedly. "I'll ride it, Don. Enjoy yourself." The captain left by way of the still open hatch which had admitted his relief, telling himself as he went that Kervenser wasn't as casual as he sounded.

Four decks down and sixty feet aft of the bridge was the main air lock. Dondragmer paused several times on the way to talk to members of his crew as they worked among the cords, beams, and piping of the *Kwembly*'s interior. By the time he reached the lock four scientists were already there with their drilling gear, and had started to don their air suits. The captain watched critically as they wriggled their long bodies and numerous legs into the transparent envelopes, made the tests for tightness, and checked their hydrogen and argon supplies. Satisfied, he gestured them into the lock and began suiting up himself. By the time he was outside the others were well on with setting up their apparatus.

He glanced at them only briefly as he paused at the top of the ramp leading from lock to ground. He knew what they were doing and could take it for granted, but he could never be that casual about the weather. Even as he latched the outer lock portal behind him, he was looking at as much of the sky as the towering hull of his command permitted.

The darkness was deepening very, very slowly as Dhrawn's two-month rotation carried the feeble sun farther below the horizon. As at home, the horizon itself seemed to be somewhat above his level of sight all around. The gravity-squeezed atmosphere responsible for this effect would also set the stars twinkling violently when they became visible. Dondragmer glanced toward the bow, but the twin stars which guarded the south celestial pole, Fomalhaut and Sol, were still invisible.

A few cirrus clouds showed above, drifting rapidly toward the west. Evidently the winds a thousand or two feet above were opposed to the surface ones, as was usual during the daytime. This might change shortly, Dondragmer knew; only a few thousand miles to the west was country in which the setting of the sun would make a greater temperature change than it did here, and there might be weather changes in the next dozen hours. Exactly what sort of changes, was more than his Mesklinite sailor background, even fortified with alien meteorology and physics, enabled him to guess.

For the moment, though, all seemed well. He made his way down the ramp to the snow and a hundred yards to the east, partly to make sure of the rest of the sky and partly to get an overall view of his command before commencing a detailed inspection.

The western sky was no more threatening than the rest, and he favored it with only a brief glance.

The *Kwembly* looked just as usual. To a human being it would probably have suggested a cigar made of dough and allowed to settle on a flat table for a time. It was slightly over a hundred feet in length, between twenty and twenty-five in breadth, and its highest point was nearly twenty feet above the snow. Actually there were two such points; the upper curve of the hull, about a third of the way back, and the bridge itself. The latter was a twenty-foot crosspiece whose nearly square outlines somewhat spoiled the smooth curves of the main body. It was almost at the bow, permitting helmsman, commander, and conning personnel to watch the ground as they traveled almost to the point where the forward trucks covered it.

The flat bottom of the vehicle was nearly a yard off the snow, supported on an almost continuous set of tread-bearing trucks. These were individually castered and connected by a bewildering rigging of fine cables, allowing the *Kwembly* to turn in a fairly short radius with reasonably complete control of her traction. The trucks were separated from the hull proper by what amounted to a pneumatic mattress, which distributed traction and adapted to minor ground irregularities.

A caterpillarlike figure was making its way slowly along the near side of the land-cruiser, presumably Beetchermarlf continuing his inspection of the rigging. Twenty yards closer to the captain the short tower of the core drill had been erected. Above, clinging to the holdfasts which studded the hull but could hardly be seen at the captain's distance, other crew members were climbing about as they inspected the seams for tightness. This, to a Mesklinite, was a nerve-stretching job. Acrophobia was a normal and healthy state of mind to a being reared on a world where polar gravity was more than six hundred times that of Earth, and even "home" gravity a third of that. Dhrawn's comparatively feeble pull, scarcely thirteen hundred feet per second squared, took some of the curse off climbing, but hull inspection was still the least popular of duties. Dondragmer crawled back across the hard-packed mixture of white crystals and brown dust, interrupted by occasional sprawling bushes, and made his way up the side to help out with the job.

The great, curved plates were of boron fiber bonded with oxygen- and fluorine-loaded polymers. They had been fabricated on a world none of the Mesklinites had ever seen, though most of the crew had had dealings with its natives. The human chemical engineers had designed those hull members to withstand every corrosive agent they could foresee. They fully realized that Dhrawn was one of the few places in the universe likely to be even worse in this respect than their own oxygen-and-water world. They were quite aware of its gravity. They had all these factors in mind when they synthesized the hull members and the adhesives which held them together: both the temporary cements used during the testing on Mesklin and the supposedly permanent ones employed in reassembling the vehicles on Dhrawn. Dondragmer had every confidence in the skill of those men, but he could not forget that they had not faced and never expected to face the conditions their products were fighting. These particular parachute packers would never be asked to jump, though that analogy would have been lost on a Mesklinite.

Much as the captain respected theory, he very well knew the gap between it and practice, so he devoted full attention to examining the joints between the great hull sections.

By the time he had satisfied himself that they were still sound and tight, the sky had become noticeably darker. Kervenser, in response to a rap on the outside of the bridge and a few gestures, had turned on some of the outside lights. By their aid the climbers finished their work and made their way back onto the snow.

Beetchermarlf appeared from under the great hull and reported his tiller lines in perfect shape. The workers at the drill had recovered several feet of core, and were taking this into the laboratory as soon as each segment was obtained, in view of the ambient temperature. Actually the local "snow" seemed to be nearly all water at the surface, and therefore safely below its melting point, but no one could be sure how true this would be deeper down.

The artificial light made the sky less noticeable. The first warning of changing weather was a sudden gust of wind. The *Kwembly* rocked slightly on her treads, the tiller lines singing as the dense air swept past them. The Mesklinites were not inconvenienced. In Dhrawn's gravity blowing them away would have been a job for a respectable tornado. They weighed about as much as a life-sized gold statue would have on Earth. Dondragmer, digging his claws reflexively into the dusty snow, was not bothered by the wind; but he was much annoyed at his own failure to notice earlier the clouds which accompanied it. These had changed from the fleecy cirrus perhaps a thousand feet above to broken stratus-type scud at half that height. There was no precipitation yet, but none of the sailors doubted that it would come soon. They could not guess, however, what form it would take or how violent it might be. They had been a year and a half on Dhrawn, by human measure, but this was not nearly long enough to learn all the moods of a world far larger than their own. Even had that world completed one of its own revolutions, instead of less than a quarter of one, it would not have been time enough and Dondragmer's crew knew it.

The captain's voice rose above the song of the wind.

"Inside, everyone. Berjendee, Reffel, and Stakendee to me to help with the drilling gear. First man inside tell Kervenser to stand by on engines and be ready to swing bow to wind when the last of us is aboard." Dondragmer knew as he gave the command that it might be impossible to obey it. It was quite likely that the maintenance check might be at a stage which would prevent engine start. Having issued the order, however, he thought about it no further. It would be carried out if possible, and his attention was needed elsewhere. The drilling equipment was top priority; it was research apparatus, which was the entire reason for the Mesklinites' presence on Dhrawn. Even Dondragmer, comparatively free of that suspicion of human intentions and motives which affected many Mesklinites, suspected that the average human scientist would value the drilling equipment more highly than the lives of one or two of the crew.

The researchers had already withdrawn the bit and started inside with it when he reached them. The crank and gear box of the muscle-powered device followed, leaving only the supporting frame and guide towers. These were less critical, since they could be replaced without human assistance, but since the wind was growing no worse, the captain and his helpers stayed to salvage them also. By the time this had been done, the others had vanished inside and Kervenser was clearly impatient on the bridge above.

Thankfully Dondragmer shepherded his group up the ramp and through the lock door, which he latched behind them. They were now standing on a yard-wide shelf running the length of the lock, facing an equally wide pool of liquid ammonia which formed the inboard half of the compartment. The most heavily burdened of the group climbed into the liquid grasping holds similar to those on the outer hull; others, like the captain, simply dived in. The inner wall of the lock extended four feet below the surface, and had a three-foot clearance between its lower edge and the bottom of the tank. Passing under this and climbing the far side, they emerged on a ledge similar to that at the entrance. Another door gave them ingress to the midsection of the *Kwembly.*

There was a slight stink of oxygen about them—a few bubbles of outside air usually accompanied anything which went through the lock—but the ubiquitous ammonia vapor and the catalyst surfaces exposed at many sites within the hull had long ago proven capable of keeping this nuisance under control. Most of the Mesklinites had learned not to mind the odor too much especially since, as far as anyone knew, really small traces of the gas were harmless.

The researchers doffed their suits and made off with their apparatus and the cases which had protected their cores from the liquid ammonia. Dondragmer dismissed the others to their regular duties, and headed for the bridge. Kervenser started to leave the command station as the captain came through the hatch, but the latter waved him back and went to the starboard end of the superstructure. Portions of its floor were transparent. The human designers had originally intended it all to be so, but they had failed to allow for Mesklinite psychology. Crawling about on the hull was bad enough, but standing on a transparent floor over fifteen feet or so of empty air was beyond all reason. The captain stopped at the edge of one of the floor panes and looked down gingerly.

The grayish surface about the huge vehicle was unchanged; the wind which shook the hull was making no apparent impression on the snow which had been packed by two-score Earth gravities for no one knew how much time. Even the eddies around the *Kwembly* showed no signs of their presence, though Dondragmer had rather expected them to be digging holes at the edges of his treads. Farther out, to the limit reached by the lights, nothing could be seen on the expanse except holes where the cores had been dug and the whipping branches of an occasional bush. He watched these closely for several minutes, expecting the wind to make some impression there if anywhere, but finally shifted his attention to the sky.

A few bright stars were beginning to show between the patches of scud, but the Guardians of the Pole could not be seen. They were only a few degrees above the southern horizon—much of that due to refraction—and the clouds further blocked the slanting view. There was still no sign of rain or snow, and no way of telling which, if either, to expect. The temperature outside was still just below the melting point of pure ammonia and far below that of water, but mixed precipitation was more than likely. What these would do to the nearly pure water-ice under him was more than Dondragmer cared to guess; he knew about the mutual solubility of water and ammonia, but had never attempted to memorize phase diagrams or freezing-point tables of the various possible mixtures. If the snow did dissolve, the *Kwembly* might get a chance to show her floating ability. He was not eager to make the test.

Kervenser interrupted his thoughts.

"Captain, we will be ready to move in four or five minutes. Do you want driving power?"

"Not yet. I was afraid that the wind would cut the snow out from under us and tip us over, like backwash on a beached ship, and I wanted to be bow-on if that happened; but there seems to be no danger of it so far. Have the maintenance checks continue except for items which would interfere with a five-minute warning for drive power."

"That's what we're doing, Captain. I set it up when your order came in a few minutes ago."

"Good. Then we'll keep outside lights on and watch the ground around us until we're ready to go again, or until the blow ends."

"It's a nuisance not being able to guess when that will be."

"It is. At home a storm seldom lasts more than a day, and never more than an hour or so. This world turns so slowly that storm cells can be as big as a continent, and could take hundreds of hours to pass. We'll just have to wait this one out."

"You mean we can't travel until the wind goes down?"

"I'm not sure. Air scouting would be risky, and we couldn't go fast enough without it for scouting to be worth the trouble, as far as the human crowd is concerned."

"I don't like going so fast anyway. You can't really look over a place unless you stop for a while. We must be missing a lot that even the human funnies would find interesting."

"They seem to know what they want—something about being able to decide whether Dhrawn is a planet or a star—and they pay the bills. I admit it gets boring for people with nothing to occupy them but routine."

Kervenser let that remark pass without comment, if not without notice. He knew his commander would not have been deliberately insulting, even after the mate's slighting remark about human beings. This was a point on which Dondragmer differed rather sharply from many of his fellows, who took for granted that the aliens were out for what they could get, like any good traders. The commander had spent more time in close communication with human, Paneshk, and Drommian scientists than had almost any other Mesklinite and, having a rather tolerant and accommodating personality to start with, had become what many of the other Mesklinites regarded as soft with respect to the aliens.

Discussion of the matter was rare, and Beetchermarlf's arrival forestalled it this time. He reported completion of checkout. Dondragmer relieved him, ordered him to send the new helmsman to the bridge, and fell silent until the latter arrived. Takoorch, however, was not the sort to live with silence; and when he reached the bridge lost little time in starting what he doubtless considered a conversation. Kervenser, amused as usual by the fellow's imagination and gall, kept him going; however, Dondragmer ignored all but occasional snatches of the conversation. He was more interested in what was going on outside, little as that seemed to be at the moment.

He cut off the bridge lights and all the outside ones but the lowest floods, giving himself a better view of the sky without completely losing touch with the surface. The clouds were fewer and smaller, but they seemed to be moving past quite as rapidly as before. The sound of the wind remained about the same. More stars were slowly appearing. Once he glimpsed one of the Guardians, as the Mesklinite sailors had so quickly named them, low to the south. He could not tell which it was; Sol and Fomalhaut were about equally bright from Dhrawn, and their violent twinkling through the huge world's atmosphere made color judgment unreliable. The glimpse was brief anyway, since the clouds were not completely gone.

"—the whole starboard group of rafts peeled off, with everyone but me on the main body—"

Still no rain or snow, and the clearing skies made them seem less likely now, to the captain's relief. A check with the laboratory through one of the speaking tubes informed him that the temperature was dropping; it was now 75, three degrees below ammonia melting point. Still close enough for trouble with mixtures, but heading in the right direction.

"—of the islands south and west of Dingbar. We'd been ridden ashore by a storm bulge, and were high and dry with half the drift boards broken. I—"

The stars overhead were almost uninterrupted now; the scud had nearly vanished. The constellations were familiar, of course. Most of the brighter stars in the neighborhood were little affected by a three-parsec change in viewpoint. Dondragmer had had plenty of time to get used to the minor changes, anyway, and no longer noticed them. He tried to find the Guardians once more, but still had no luck. Maybe there were still clouds to the south. It was too dark now to be sure. Even cutting the rest of the floods for a moment didn't help. It did, however, attract the attention of the other two, and the flow of anecdote ceased for a moment.

"Anything changing, Captain?" Kervenser's jocular attitude vanished at the possibility of action.

"Possibly. Stars are showing above, but not to the south. Not anywhere near the horizon, in fact. Try a spot."

The first officer obeyed, and a spear of light flicked upward from a point behind the bridge as he touched one of the few electrical controls. Dondragmer manipulated a pair of pull cables, and the beam swung toward the western horizon. A wail, the rough equivalent of a human grunt of surprise, came from Kervenser as the descending beam became more visible parallel to the ground.

"Fog!" exclaimed the helmsman. "Thin, but that's what's blocking the horizon." Dondragmer gave a gesture of agreement as he reared to a speaking tube.

"Research!" he hooted. "Possible precipitation. Check what it is, and what it could do to this water-ice under us."

"It will take a while to get a sample, sir," came the answer. "We'll be as quick as we can. Are we cleared outside, or will we have to work through the hull?"

The captain paused for a moment, listening to the wind and remembering how it had felt.

"You're cleared out. Be as quick as you can."

"On the way, Captain."

At Dondragmer's gesture, the first officer cut off the spot, and the three went to the starboard end of the bridge to watch the outside party.

They moved quickly but the haze was becoming more noticeable by the time the lock opened. Two caterpillarlike forms emerged carrying a cylindrical package between them. They made their way forward to a point almost under the watchers, and set up their equipment—essentially a funnel facing into the wind and feeding into a filter. It took several minutes to convince them that they had a big enough sample, but eventually they dismantled the equipment, sealed the filter into a container to preserve it from the lock fluid and made their way back to the entrance.

"I suppose it will take them a day to decide what it is, now," grumbled Kervenser.

"I doubt it," replied the captain. "They've been playing with quick tests for water-ammonia solutions. I think Borndender said something about density being enough, given a decent-sized sample."

"In that case, why are they taking so long?"

"They could hardly be out of their air suits yet," the captain pointed out patiently.

"Why should they get out of them before making delivery to the lab? Why couldn't—"

A hoot from a speaking tube interrupted him. Dondragmer acknowledged.

"Just about pure ammonia, sir. I think it was supercooled liquid droplets; it froze into a froth in the filter, and let quite a bit of outside air loose when it melted in here. If you should smell oxygen for the next few minutes, that's it. It may start icing up the hull, and if it coats the bridge, as it did the filter, it will interfere with your seeing, but that's all I can guess at right now in the way of trouble."

It was not all Dondragmer could imagine, but he acknowledged the information without further comment.

"This sort of thing hasn't happened since we've been here," he remarked. "I wonder whether it's some sort of seasonal change coming on. We are getting closer to this body's sun. I wish the human crowd had watched this world for a longer time before they sold us on the idea of exploring it for them. It would be so nice to know what comes next. Kervenser, start engines. When ready, turn bow into wind and proceed ahead dead slow, if you can still see out. If not, circle as sharply as possible to port, to stay on surface we know. Keep an eye on the treads—figuratively, of course; we can't see them without going out—and let me know if there's evidence that anything is sticking to them. Post a man at the stern port; our trail might show something. Understand?"

"The orders, yes, sir. What you're expecting, no."

"I may be wrong, and if I'm right there's probably nothing to do anyway. I don't like the idea of going outside to clear the treads manually. Just hope."

"Yes, sir." Kervenser turned to his task, and as the fusion engines in the *Kwembly*'s trucks came to life, the captain turned to a block of plastic about four inches high and wide and a foot long, which lay beside his station. He inserted one of his nippers in a small hole in the side of the block, manipulated a control, and began to talk.

2: Grandstand

His voice traveled fast, but it was a long time on the way. The radio waves carrying it sped through Dhrawn's heavy but quickly thinning atmosphere and through the space beyond for second after second. They weakened as they traveled, but half a minute after they had been radiated their energy was still concentrated enough to affect a ten-foot dish antenna. The one they encountered was projecting from a cylinder some three hundred feet in diameter and half as long: it formed one end of a structure resembling a barbell, spinning slowly about an axis perpendicular to its bar and midway between its weights.

The current induced by the waves in the antenna flicked, in a much shorter time, into a pinhead-size crystal which rectified it, enveloped it, used the envelope to modulate an electron stream provided by a finger-sized generator beside it and thus manipulated an amazingly old-fashioned dynamic cone in a thirty-foot-square room near the center of the cylinder. Just thirty-two seconds after Dondragmer uttered his words they were reproduced for the ears of three of the fifteen human beings seated in the room. He did not know who would be there at the time, and therefore spoke the human tongue he had learned rather than his own language; so all three understood him.

"This is an interim report from the *Kwembly.* We stopped two and a half hours ago for routine maintenance and investigation. Wind was about 200 cables at the time, from the west, sky partly cloudy. Shortly after we got to work the wind picked up to over 3,000 cables—"

One of the human listeners was wearing a puzzled expression, and after a moment managed to catch the eye of another.

"A Mesklinite cable is about 206 feet, Boyd," the latter said softly. "The wind jumped from about five miles an hour to over sixty."

"Thanks, Easy." Their attention returned to the speaker.

"Fog has now closed us in completely, and is getting ever thicker. I don't dare move as I had planned; just in circles to keep the treads from icing. The fog is supercooled ammonia according to my scientists, and the local surface is water snow. It doesn't seem to have occurred to my research people, but with the temperature in the seventies it seems to me there's a chance of the fog's dissolving some of the water-ice to make a liquid. I realize this machine is supposed to float, and I don't suppose the surface would melt very deeply anyway, but I'm wondering whether anyone has thought much about what will happen if a liquid freezes around our treads. I have to admit I never have, but the thought of chipping the ship loose by muscle power isn't inviting. I know there's no special equipment on board to handle such a situation, because I assembled and loaded this machine myself. I'm simply calling to report that we might possibly be here a good deal longer than planned. I'll keep you informed, and if we do get immobilized we'll be glad of projects to keep our scientists busy. They've already done most of the things you set up for an ordinary stop."

"Thanks, Don," replied Easy. "We'll stand by. I'll ask our observers and aerologists whether they can make a guess about the size of your fog bank, and how long it's likely to stay around you. They may have some useful material already, since you've been on the night side for a day or so. For that matter, they may even have current pictures; I don't know all the limits of their instruments. Anyway, I'll check and let you know."

The woman opened her microphone switch and turned to the others as her words sped toward Dhrawn.

"I wish I could tell from Don's voice whether he's really worried or not," she remarked. "Every time those people run into something new on that horrible world, I wonder how we ever had the gall to send them there or how they had the courage to go."

'They certainly weren't forced or tricked into it, Easy," pointed out one of her companions. "A Mesklinite who has spent most of his life as a sailor, and covered his home planet from equator to south pole, certainly isn't naive about any of the aspects of exploring or pioneering. We couldn't have kidded them if we'd wanted to."

"I know that in my head, Boyd, but my stomach doesn't always believe it. When the *Kwembly* was bogged in sand only five hundred miles from the settlement, I was grinding enamel off my teeth until they worked her loose. When Densigeref's *Smof* was trapped in a cleft by a mud flow that formed under it and let it down, I was almost the only one who backed up Barlennan's decision to send another of the big land-rovers to the rescue. When the *Esket*'s crew disappeared with a couple of very good friends of mine, I fought both Alan and Barlennan on the decision *not* to send a rescue crew. And I still think they were wrong. I know there's a job to be done and that the Mesklinites agreed to do it with a clear understanding of its risks, but when one of those crews gets into trouble I just can't help imagining myself down there with them and I tend to take their side when there's an argument about rescue action. I suppose I'll be fired from this place eventually because of that, but it's the way I'm made."

Boyd Mersereau chuckled.

"Don't worry, Easy. You have that job just because you do react that way. Please remember that if we do disagree strongly with Barlennan or any of his people, we're six million miles and forty g's of potential away and he's probably going to do what he wants anyway. Whenever it gets to that point, it's very much to our advantage to have someone up here whom he can regard as being on his side. Don't change a bit, please."

"Humph." If Elise Hoffman was either pleased or relieved, she failed to show it. "That's what Ib is always saying, but I've been writing him off as prejudiced."

"I'm sure he is, but that doesn't necessarily disqualify him from forming a sound opinion. You must believe some things he says."

"Thanks, Easy," Dondragmer's answer interrupted the discussion. He was using his own language this time, which neither of the men understood very well. "I'll be glad of any word your observers can supply. You needn't report to Barlennan unless you particularly want to. We aren't actually in trouble yet and he has enough on his mind without being bothered by maybes. The research suggestions you can send down straight to the lab on set two; I'd probably mix them up if I relayed. I'll sign off now, but we'll keep all four sets manned."

The speaker fell silent, and Aucoin, the third human listener, got to his feet, looking at Easy for a translation. She obliged.

"That means work," he said. "We had a number of longer programs planned for later in the *Kwembly*'s trip, but if Dondragmer may be delayed long where he is, I'd better see which of them would fit now. I got enough of that other speech to suggest that he doesn't really expect to move soon. I'll go to Computation first and have them reproduce a really precise set of position bearings for him from the shadow satellites, then I'll go to Atmospherics for their opinion and then I'll be in the planning lab."

"I may see you in Atmospherics," replied Easy. "I'm going now to get the information Dondragmer wanted, if you'll stand watch here, Boyd."

"All right, for a while. I have some other work to do myself, but I'll make sure the *Kwembly*'s screens are covered. You'd better tell Don who's here, though, so he won't send up an emergency message in Stennish or whatever he calls his native language. Come to think of it, though, I suppose sixty seconds extra delay wouldn't matter much, considering what little we could do for him from here."

The woman shrugged, spoke a few words of the little sailor's language into the transmitter, waved to Mersereau, and was gone before Dondragmer received her last phrase. Alan Aucoin had already left.

The meteorology lab was on the "highest" level of the cylinder, enough closer to the spin axis of the station to make a person about ten percent lighter than in the communication room. Facilities for exercise being as limited as they were, powered elevators had been omitted from the station's design, and intercoms were regarded as strictly emergency equipment. Easy Hoffman had the choice of a spiral stairway at the axis of symmetry of the cylinder or any of several ladders. Since she wasn't carrying anything, she didn't bother with the stairs. Her destination was almost directly "above" Communications, and she reached it in less than a minute.

The most prominent features in this room were two twenty-foot-diameter hemispherical maps of Dhrawn. Each was a live-vision screen carrying displays of temperature, reference-altitude pressure, wind velocity, where it was obtainable, and such other data as could be obtained either from the low-orbiting shadow satellites or the Mesklinite exploring crews. A spot of green light marked the Settlement just north of the equator, and nine fainter yellow sparks scattered closely around it indicated the exploring land-cruisers. Against the background of the gigantic planet their spread made an embarrassingly small display, scattered over a range of some eight thousand miles east and west and twenty or twenty-five thousand north and south, on the western side of what the meteorologists called Low Alpha. The yellow lights, except for two well out in the colder regions to the west, formed a rough arc framing the Low. Eventually it was to be ringed with sensing stations, but little more than a quarter of its eighty-thousand-mile perimeter had so far been covered.

The cost had been high—not merely in money, which Easy tended to regard as merely a measure of effort expended, but in life. Her eyes sought the red-ringed yellow light just inside the Low which marked the position of the *Esket.* Seven months—three and a half of Dhrawn's days—had passed since any human being had seen a sign of her crew, though her transmitters still sent pictures of her interior. Easy thought grimly, now and again, of her friends Kabremm and Destigmet; and occasionally she bothered Dondragmer's conscience, though she had no way of knowing this, by talking about them to the *Kwembly*'s commander.

"H'lo, Easy," and "Hi, Mom," cut into her gloomy thoughts.

"Hello, weather men," she responded. "I have a friend who'd like a forecast. Can you help?"

"If it's for here in the station, sure," answered Benj.

"Don't be cynical, son. You're old enough to understand the difference between knowing nothing and not knowing everything. It's for

Dondragmer of the *Kwembly.*" She indicated the yellow light on the map, and outlined the situation. "Alan is bringing an exact position, if that will help."

"Probably not much," Seumas McDevitt admitted. "If you don't like cynicism I'll have to pick my words carefully; but the light on the screen there should be right within a few hundred miles, and I doubt that we can compute a precise enough forecast for that to make a significant difference."

"I wasn't sure you'd have enough material for any predictions at all," Easy countered. "I understand that weather comes from the west even on this world, and the area to the west has been out of sunlight for days now. Can you see such places well enough to get useful data?"

"Oh, sure." Benj's sarcasm had vanished and the enthusiasm which had caused him to put down atmospheric physics as his post-primary tentative was taking over. "We don't get much of our measurement from reflected sunlight anyway; nearly all is direct radiation from the planet. There's a lot more emitted than it receives from the sun anyway; you've heard the old argument as to whether Dhrawn ought to be called a star or a planet. We can tell ground temperature, a good deal about ground cover, lapse rates, and clouds. Winds are harder—" he hesitated, seeing McDevitt's eye on him and unable to read the meteorologist's poker face. The man read the trouble in time and nodded him on before the rush of self-confidence had lost momentum. McDevitt had never been a teacher, but he had the touch.

"Winds are harder because of the slight uncertainty in cloud heights and the fact that adiabatic temperature changes often have more to say about the location of clouds than air mass identities do. In that gravity, the air density drops by half about every hundred yards of climb, and that makes for terrific PV changes in temperature—" he paused again, this time eying his mother. "Do you know about that sort of thing, or should I slow down?"

"I'd hate to have to solve quantitative problems on what you've just been saying," Easy replied, "but I think I have a fair qualitative picture. I get the impression that you're a little doubtful about telling Don to the nearest minute when his fog is going to clear. Would a report from him on surface pressures and winds be any help? The *Kwembly* has instruments, you know."

"It might," McDevitt admitted as Benj nodded silently. "Can I talk to the *Kwembly* directly? And will any of them understand me? My Stennish doesn't exist yet."

"I'll translate if I can keep your technical terms straight," replied Easy. "If you plan to do more than a one-month tour here, though, it would be a good idea to try to pick up the language of our little friends. Many of them know some of ours, but they appreciate it."

"I know. I plan to. I'd be glad if you'd help me."

"When I can, certainly; but you'll see a lot more of Benj."

"Benj? He came here three weeks ago with me, and hasn't had any better chance to learn languages than I have. We've both been checking out on the local observation and computer nets, and filling in on the project background." Easy grinned at her son.

"That's as may be. He's a language bug like his mother, and I think you'll find him useful, though I admit he got his Stennish from me rather than the Mesklinites. He insisted on my teaching him something that his sisters wouldn't be able to listen in on. Write as much of that off to parental pride as you like, but give him a try. Later, that is; I'd like that information for Dondragmer as soon as we can get it. He said the wind was from the west at about sixty miles an hour, if that helps at all."

The meteorologist pondered a moment.

"I'll run what we have through integration, with that bit added," he said finally. "Then we can give him something when we call, and if the numerical details he gives us then are too different we can make another run easily enough. Wait a moment."

He and the boy turned to their equipment, and for several minutes their activities meant little to the woman. She knew, of course, that they were feeding numerical data and weighting values into computing devices which were presumably already programmed to handle the data appropriately. She was pleased to see Benj apparently handling his share of the work without supervision. She and her husband had been given to understand that the boy's mathematical powers might not prove up to the need of his field of interest. Of course, what he was doing now was routine which could be handled by anyone with a little training whether he really understood it or not, but Easy chose to interpret the display as encouraging.

"Of course," McDevitt remarked as the machine was digesting its input, "there'll be room for doubt anyway. This sun doesn't do very much to the surface temperature of Dhrawn, but its effect is not completely negligible. The planet has been getting closer to the sun almost ever since we really got going here three years ago. We didn't have any surface reports except from half a dozen robots until the Mesklinite settlement was set up a year and a half later, and even their measurements still cover only a tiny fraction of the planet. Our prediction work is almost entirely empirical, no matter how much we want to believe in the laws of physics, and we really don't have enough data for empirical rules yet."

Easy nodded. "I realize that, and so does Dondragmer," she said. "Still, you have more information than he does, and I guess anything is welcome to him at this point. I know if I were down there thousands of miles from any sort of help, in a machine which is really in the test stage, and not even able to see what was around me—well, I can tell you from experience that it helps to be in touch with the outside. Not just in the way of conversation, though that helps, but so they could more or less see me and know what I was going through."

"We'd have an awful time seeing him," put in Benj. "Even when the air at the other end is clear, six million miles is a long way for telescope work."

"You're right, of course, but I think you know what I mean," his mother said quietly. Benj shrugged and said no more; in fact, a rather tense silence ensued for perhaps half a minute.

It was interrupted by the computer, which ejected a sheet of cryptic symbols in front of McDevitt. The other two leaned over his shoulders to see it, though this did Easy little good. The boy spent about five seconds glancing over the lines of information, and emitted a sound halfway between a snort of contempt and a laugh. The meteorologist glanced up at him.

"Go ahead, Benj. You can be as sarcastic as you like on this one. I'd advise against letting Dondragmer have these results uncensored."

"Why? What's wrong with them?" asked the woman.

"Well, most of the data, of course, was from shadow satellite readings. I did plug in your wind report, with a bit of uncertainty. I don't know what sort of instruments the caterpillars have down there, or how precisely the figures were transmitted to you; and you did say *about* sixty for the wind speed. I didn't mention the fog, since you didn't tell me any more than the fact that it was there, and I had no numbers. The first line of this computer run says that visibility in normal light—normal to human eyes, that is, and about the same to Mesklinite ones, I gather—is twenty-two miles for a one-degree blur."

Easy raised her eyebrows. "Just how do you account for something like that? I thought all the old jokes about weather men had gone pretty well out of date?"

"Actually, they just got stale. I account for it by the simple fact that we don't and can't have complete information for the machine. The most obvious lack is a detailed topographic chart of the planet, especially the couple of million square miles west of the *Kwembly.* A wind coming up or down a slope of six inches per mile at any respectable speed would change its air mass temperature rapidly just from PV change, as Benj pointed out a few minutes ago. Actually, the best maps we have of the topography were worked out from just that effect, but they're pretty sketchy. I'll have to get more detailed measurements from Dondragmer's people and give them another run. Did you say Aucoin was getting a more exact position for the *Kwembly?*"

Easy had no time to answer; Aucoin himself appeared in the room. He did not bother with greetings, and took for granted that the meteorologists would have the background information from Easy.

"Eight point four five five degrees south of the equator, seven point nine two three east of the Settlement meridian. That's as close as they'll swear to. Is a thousand yards or so too much uncertainty for what you need?"

"Everybody's being sarcastic today," muttered McDevitt. "Thanks, that'll be fine. Easy, can we go down to Comm and have that talk with Dondragmer?"

"All right. Do you mind if Benj comes along, or is there work he should be doing here? I'd like him to meet Dondragmer, too."

"And incidentally display his linguistic powers. All right, he may come. You, too, Alan?"

"No. There's other work to do. I'd like to know the details on any forecast you consider trustworthy, though, and anything Dondragmer reports which might conceivably affect Planning. I'll be in PL."

The weather man nodded. Aucoin took himself off in one direction, and the other three made their way down ladders to the communication room. Mersereau had disappeared, as he had intimated he might, but one of the other watchers had shifted his position to keep an eye on the *Kwembly*'s screens. He waved and returned to his place as Easy entered. The others paid the party little attention. They had been aware of Easy's and Mersereau's departures simply because of the standing rule that there were never to be fewer than ten observers in the room at once. The stations were not assigned on a rigid schedule; this had been found to lead to the equivalent of road hypnosis.

The four communication sets tied to the *Kwembly* had their speakers centered in front of a group of six seats. The corresponding vision screens were set higher, so that they could also be seen from the general seats further back. Each of the six "station" seats was equipped with a microphone and a selector switch permitting contact with any one or all four of the *Kwembly*'s radios.

Easy settled herself in a comfortably central chair and switched its microphone to the set on Dondragmer's bridge. There was little to be seen on the corresponding screen, since the transmitter's eye was pointed forward toward the bridge windows and the Mesklinites' report of fog was perfectly correct. The helmsman's station and its occupant could be partly seen in the lower left-hand corner of the screen; the rest was gray blankness marked off into rectangles by the window braces. The bridge lights were subdued, but the fog beyond the windows was illuminated by the *Kwembly*'s outside floods, Easy judged.

"Don!" she called. "Easy here. Are you on the bridge?" She snapped on a timer and shifted her selector switch to the set in the laboratory. "Borndender, or whoever is there," she called, still in Stennish, "we can't get a reliable weather prediction with the information we have. We're talking to the bridge, but we'd be glad if you could give us as exactly as possible your present temperature, wind velocity, outside pressure, anything quantitative you have on the fog, and—" she hesitated.

"And the same information for the past few hours, with times given as closely as possible," Benj cut in in the same language.

"We'll be ready to receive as soon as the bridge finishes talking," continued the woman.

"We could also use whatever you have on air, fog, and snow composition," added her son.

"If there is any other material you think might be of help, it will also be welcome," finished Easy. "You're there and we aren't, and there must be some ideas about Dhrawn's weather you've formed on your own." The timer sounded a bell note. "The bridge is coming in now. We'll be waiting for your words when the captain finishes."

The speaker's first words overlapped her closing phrase. The timer had been set for the light-speed lag of a round-trip message between Dhrawn and the station, and the bridge had answered promptly.

"Kervenser here, Mrs. Hoffman. The captain is below in the life-support room. I'll call him here if you like, or you can switch to the set down there, but if you have any advice for us we'd like it as quickly as possible. We can't see a body-length from the bridge and don't dare move, except in circles. The fliers gave us an idea of the neighborhood before we stopped and it seems solid enough, but we certainly can't take a chance on going forward. We're going dead slow, in a circle about twenty-five cables in diameter. Except when we're bow or stern to the wind, the ship feels as though it were going to capsize every few seconds. The fog has been freezing as it hits the windows, which is why we can't see out. The tracks still seem to be clear, I suppose because they're moving and ice gets cracked off before it can hurt, but I expect the tiller lines to freeze up any time, and getting the ice off them will be a glorious job. I suppose it will be possible to work outside, but I'd hate to do it myself until the wind stops. Having an air suit ice up sounds unpleasant. Any thoughts?"

Easy waited patiently for Kervenser to finish. The sixty-four-second message delay had had a general effect on everyone who did much talking between station and planet; they developed a strong tendency to say as much as possible at one time, guessing at what the other party wanted to hear. When she knew that Kervenser had finished and was waiting for an answer, she quickly summarized the message which had been given the scientists. As with them, she omitted all mention of the computer result which had insisted that the weather must be clear. The Mesklinites knew that human science was not infallible—most of them had, in fact, a much more realistic and healthy idea of its limitations than many human beings—but there was no point in making one's self look too silly if it could be helped. She was not, of course, a meteorologist, but she was human and Kervenser would probably lump her in with the others.

The group waited almost silently for the first officer's answer when she finished. Benj's muttered translation for the benefit of McDevitt took only a few seconds longer than the message itself. When the response finally came it was merely an acknowledgment and a polite hope that the human beings could furnish useful information soon; the *Kwembly* scientists were sending up the requested material at once.

Easy and her son readied themselves for the data. She started a recorder to check any technical terms before attempting translation, but the message came through in the human language. Evidently Borndender was sending. McDevitt recovered promptly from his surprise and began taking notes, while the boy kept his eyes on the pencil point and his ears on the speaker.

It was just as well that Easy was not needed for translation. Well as she knew Stennish, there were many words strange to her in both languages; she couldn't have interpreted either way. She knew that she should not be embarrassed by the fact, but she couldn't help it. She could not help thinking of the Mesklinites as representing a culture like that of Robin Hood or Haroun al Raschid, though she knew perfectly well that several hundred of them had received very comprehensive scientific and technical educations in the last half century. The fact had not been widely published, since there was a widespread notion that it was bad to release much advanced knowledge to "backward" peoples. It was likely to give them an inferiority complex and prevent further progress.

The weather men didn't care. When the final "over" came through, McDevitt and his assistant uttered a hasty "Thank You" into the nearest microphone and hurried off toward the laboratory. Easy, noting that the selector switch had been set for the bridge radio, corrected it and returned a more careful acknowledgment before signing off. Then, deciding that she would be useless in the meteorology lab, she settled back on the chair which gave her the best view of the *Kwembly*'s four screens, and waited for something to happen.

Mersereau returned a few minutes after the others had left, and had to be brought up to date. Otherwise, nothing of note occurred. There was an occasional glimpse of a long, many-legged form on one of the screens, but the Mesklinites were going about their own affairs with no particular regard for the watchers.

Easy thought of starting another conversation with Kervenser; she knew and liked this officer almost as well as she did his captain. However, the thought of the lag between remark and answer discouraged her, as it often did when there was nothing of importance to be said.

Even with no lag, conversation languished. There was little for Easy and Mersereau to say to each other which had not already been said; a year away from Earth could be counted on to exhaust most subjects of conversation except professional shop talk and matters of private, personal interest. She had little of the latter in common with Mersereau, though she liked him well enough, and their professions overlapped only in connection with talking to Mesklinites.

In consequence there was little sound in the communication room. Every few minutes one or another of the exploring land-cruisers would send in a report, which would be duly relayed to the Settlement; but most of the human beings on watch had no more occasion for small talk than Easy and Boyd Mersereau. Easy found herself trying to guess when the weather men would be back with their forecast and how reliable the new one would be. Say, two minutes to the lab, or one, if they hurried; one more to feed the new material into the computer; two for the run; five minutes of arguing, since she knew her son, over whether this prediction was really any better than the last; a repeat run with modified weights on the variables; two minutes back down to the comm room, since they certainly wouldn't hurry this time. They'd still be arguing. They should be here soon.

But before they made it, things changed. Quite suddenly, the bridge screen demanded attention. It had been quiet, with gray windows masked by frozen ammonia dominating the foreshortened image of part of the helmsman. The latter had been almost motionless, his tiller bar well over to one side as the *Kwembly* pursued the circular path described by Kervenser.

Then the windows were suddenly clear, though little could be seen beyond them; the communicator's angle of view was not depressed enough to reach ground within range of the lights. Two more Mesklinites appeared and flowed over to the windows, looking out and gesturing with obvious excitement. Mersereau pointed to another screen; there was excitement in the lab, too. So far, none of the little explorers had seen fit to report what was going on. Easy judged they were too occupied with immediate problems; furthermore it was customary for them to keep their sound volume down, or off completely, unless they specifically wanted to speak to the human beings.

At this point the weather men returned. Easy saw her son out of the corner of her eye, and asked without looking around, "Do you have anything useful this time?"

McDevitt answered briefly, "Yes. Shall I have Benj translate it to them?"

"No. They're in some sort of trouble, it seems. Give them the word yourself. Dondragmer would certainly be on the bridge, or will be by the time your words get there, when anything like this is going on. Here, use this seat and mike."

The meteorologist obeyed without question. It would be the last time for many months that he would pay Easy that compliment. He began talking as he settled into the seat.

"Dondragmer, you should have about nineteen hours of reduced visibility. The freezing fog should last for less than another hour; the temperature is going down, and the fog will change to ammonia crystals which shouldn't stick to your windows. If you can get rid of the ice already there, you should at least see through them into the snow. The wind will decrease gradually for about five more hours. By that time, the temperature should be low enough so you needn't worry about eutectic melting. There will be higher clouds for another forty-five hours—" He went on, but Easy had stopped listening.

Near the end of McDevitt's second sentence, long before the beginning of his message could have reached Dhrawn, a Mesklinite had approached the bridge pickup so closely that his grotesque face nearly filled the screen. One of his nipper-equipped arms reached out of sight to one side, and Easy knew he was activating the voice transmitter. She was not surprised to hear the captain speaking in a much calmer tone than she could have managed under the circumstances.

"Easy, or whoever is on watch, please get a special report to Barlennan. The temperature has gone up six degrees, to one hundred three, in the last few minutes, the ice has melted from the windows, and we are afloat."

3: Nerve Center

Perhaps it was unkind for Dondragmer to have given his report in the human language. The time taken for translation might have eased the shock a trifle for McDevitt. The worst part, as the meteorologist said later, was realizing that his own prediction was on its way to Dhrawn and nothing could stop it. For a moment he had a wild notion of getting a ship and racing the radio waves to the planet so as to shadow them from the *Kwembly's* receivers. The thought was only a flicker; only so much can be done in thirty-two seconds. Besides, none of the tenders then at the station was capable of faster-than-light flight. Most of them were used in servicing the shadow satellites.

Easy, in the next seat, didn't seem to have noticed the discrepancy between the prediction and Dondragmer's report; at least, she hadn't glanced at him with the expression which nine out of ten of his friends would have used. Well, she wouldn't, he thought. That's why she's on this job.

The woman was manipulating her selector switch again, with her attention focused on a smaller screen above the *Kwembly's* four. At first an indicator beside it glowed red; as she worked her switches it turned green and the image of an office-like room with fully a dozen Mesklinites in view appeared on the screen. Easy began her report instantly.

She was brief. All she could give was a repetition of Dondragmer's few sentences. She had finished long before there was any evidence on the screen that her words were being received.

When the response came, however, it was satisfying. Every caterpillarlike body in sight looped toward the pickup. While Easy had never learned to read expression on the Mesklinite "face," there was no misunderstanding the wildly waving arms and snapping pincers. One of the creatures raced toward a semicircular doorway at the far side of the room and disappeared through it. In spite of the creature's red and black coloration, Easy found herself reminded of the sight, a few years before, of one of her daughters inhaling a strand of spaghetti. A Mesklinite in a hurry under forty Earth gravities appears legless to human eyes.

The sound was not on yet from the Dhrawn end, but there was a rising buzz of conversation in the human communication room. It was not unusual for exploring land-cruisers to run into difficulties. In general the working Mesklinites took such difficulties more calmly than the human beings who were watching helplessly. In spite of the lack of intercom in the station, people began entering the room and filling the general seats. Screen after screen in the front monitoring areas was tuned to the "headquarters" unit in the Settlement. Meanwhile Easy and Mersereau were dividing their attention among the four sets reporting from the *Kwembly,* with only an occasional glance at the other picture.

It was not obvious on the screens that the vehicle was afloat because the transmitters shared any motion it might have, and there was little loose equipment whose motion might have betrayed a pitch or a roll. The bulk of the crew were sailors by training. Lifelong habit prevented them from leaving things unsecured. Easy kept closest watch on the bridge screen hoping to spot something outside which could give a clue to what was occurring, but nothing recognizable could be seen through the windows.

Then the panes were blotted out once more as Dondragmer came back into the foreground and expanded his report.

"There seems to be no immediate danger. The wind is pulling us along fairly rapidly, judging by our wake. Our magnetic course is 66. We are floating level, submerged to about deck two. Our scientists are trying to compute the density of this liquid, but no one has ever bothered to work out displacement tables for this hull as far as I know. If you human beings happen to have that information, my people would be glad to get it. Unless we run into something solid, and I can't guess at the chances of that, we'll be safe. All machinery is functioning properly, except that the treads have nothing to bite on. They race if we give them power. That's all for now. If your shadow satellites can keep track of our location, we'll be glad of that information as often as you can manage. Tell Barlennan everything is all right so far."

Easy shifted microphone connections and repeated the captain's report as nearly verbatim as she could. She saw, in due course, that it was being taken down in writing at the other end. She rather hoped that the writer would have some question to ask: not that she was likely to be able to answer it, but she was beginning to get a helpless, useless feeling again. The Mesklinite, however, merely acknowledged the information and headed for the door with his notes. Easy was left wondering how far he had to go to get them to the commander. No human being had a very good idea of the layout of the Mesklinite base.

As a matter of fact, the trip was brief. Most of it appeared to be outdoors because of the settlers' attitude toward massive objects overhead: an attitude hard to overcome even on a world where gravity was only a fraction of its normal Mesklin value. The roofs of the Settlement were almost all of transparent film brought from their home world. The only departure from a common, city-wide floor level was dictated by terrain. The thought of either a basement or a second story would never have occurred to a Mesklinite. The many-decked *Kwembly* and her sister vehicles were of basically human and Paneshk design.

The messenger wove through a maze of corridors for some two hundred yards before reaching the commander's office. This was at the northern edge of the cluster of foot-high structures which formed the greater part of the Settlement. The Settlement itself was close to the edge of a six-foot cliff extending almost a mile east and west, broken by a dozen or so artificial ramps. On the ground below the cliff, but still with their bridges looming above the transparent coverings of the "city," were two of the huge land-cruisers. The wall of Barlennan's room was also transparent and looked directly out on the nearer of these vehicles; the other was parked some thousand feet to the east. A few air suited Mesklinites were also visible outside, dwarfed by the monstrous vehicles they were tending.

Barlennan was watching this group of mechanics critically when the runner entered. The latter used no formality, but burst into Easy's relayed report as he entered the compartment. By the time the commander had swerved around to receive the written version, he had heard it all orally.

It was not satisfactory, of course. Barlennan had had time to think up a number of questions since the first messenger had arrived, and this message answered none of them. The commander controlled his impatience.

"I take it there hasn't been anything useful from the human weather experts yet."

"Nothing at all, sir, to us. They may have been talking to the *Kwembly* without our hearing, of course."

"True enough. Has word gone to our own weather people?"

"Not as far as I know, sir. There's been nothing very useful to tell them, but Guzmeen may have sent a message there, too."

"All right. I want to talk to them myself anyway. I'll be at their complex for the next half hour or more. Tell Guz."

The messenger made the affirmative nipper gesture and vanished through the door he had entered by. Barlennan took another, making his way slowly westward through building after building and over the enclosed connecting ramps which made the Settlement a single unit. Most of the ramps on his course sloped upward, so that by the time he turned south away from the cliff he was some five feet higher than his office, though not yet on a level with the bridges of the land-cruisers behind him. The roof fabric bulged a little more tautly above him, since the nearly pure hydrogen in the station did not drop as rapidly in pressure with increasing altitude as did Dhrawn's much denser gas mixture. The Settlement had been built at an elevation which was quite high for Dhrawn. The total outside pressure was about the same as that at Mesklin's sea level. It was only when the land-cruisers descended to lower elevations that they carried extra argon to keep their internal pressure balanced.

Since Dhrawn's air carried about two per cent oxygen, the Mesklinites were careful about leaks. Barlennan still remembered the awkward results of an oxygen-hydrogen explosion shortly after he had first encountered human beings.

The research complex was the westernmost and highest side of the colony. It was fairly well separated from most of the other structures and differed from them in having a solid, though still transparent, roof. It also came closer than any other part of the Settlement to having a second story, since a number of instruments were mounted on the roof where they could be reached by ramps and liquid-trap air locks. By no means all the instruments had been furnished by the alien sponsors of the Settlement; the Mesklinites had been using their own imaginations and ingenuity for fifty years, although they had not really felt free about doing so until reaching Dhrawn.

Like the exploring vehicles, the laboratory complex was a mixture of crudeness and sophistication. Energy was supplied by hydrogen-fusion units; chemical glassware was home-made. Communication with the orbiting station was by solid-state electromagnetic beam transmitter; but messages were carried physically about the complex by runners. Steps were being taken to change this, unknown to the human beings. The Mesklinites understood the telegraph and were on the verge of making telephones able to transmit their own voice range. However, neither telephone nor telegraph was being installed in the Settlement because most of Barlennan's administrative effort was being concentrated on the project which had provoked Easy's sympathy for the *Esket*'s crew. It takes a lot of work to lay cross-country telegraph lines.

Barlennan was saying nothing about this to his sponsors. He liked human beings, though he did not go as far in that direction as Dondragmer: he was always aware of their amazingly short life span, which prevented him from getting to really know the people he worked with before they were replaced by others. He was rather concerned about the possibility of human, Drommian, and Paneshk finding out just how ephemeral they all were, for fear it might depress them. It had, in fact, become Mesklinite policy to evade discussion on the matter of age with aliens. It was also policy not to depend more heavily than could be avoided on them. You never knew whether the next ones to take over would have the same attitudes. They were intrinsically undependable, most Mesklinites felt; Dondragmer's confidence in them was a glaring exception.

All this was known to the Mesklinite scientists who saw the commander arrive. Their first concern was with the immediate situation. "Is someone in trouble, or are you just visiting?"

"Trouble, I'm afraid," replied Barlennan. He briefly outlined Dondragmer's situation. "Collect anyone you think may be useful and come to the map." He made way to the forty-foot-square chamber whose floor was the "map" of Low Alpha, and waited. Very little of the area had been "mapped," so far. He felt, as he had so often before, that there was a long, long job ahead. Still, the map was more encouraging to him than its human counterpart some millions of miles above was to its human viewers. Both showed the arc covered by the land cruisers and something of the landscape. The Mesklinites had indicated this in spidery black lines suggesting a sketch of human nerve cells, complete with cell bodies.

The specific Mesklinite data centered mostly around the spot where the *Esket* lay. This information, marked in red, had been obtained without direct human assistance. This was one place in the Settlement where there would be no vision transmitter as long as Barlennan was running things.

Now, however, he focused his attention several feet to the south of the *Esket,* where there was discouragingly little data in either red or black. The line representing the track of the *Kwembly* looked lonesome. Barlennan had raised his front end as high as was comfortable, bringing his eyes six or seven inches from the floor, and was looking at the map gloomily when the scientists began to arrive. Bendivence was either very optimistic or very pessimistic. The commander couldn't decide which was the more likely reason for his having called nearly twenty people to the conference. They gathered a few feet from him, reared up and waited politely for his information and questions. He started without preamble.

"The *Kwembly* was here at her last report," he indicated. "It had been crossing a field of snow, water snow, nearly clear of dissolved material but quite dirty according to Don's science people."

"Borndender?" queried someone. Barlennan gestured affirmatively and went on.

"The snow field started here." He crawled to a spot nearly four feet northwest of the position marker. "It lies between a couple of mountain ridges, which we have indicated only roughly. Destigmet's balloons haven't gotten this far south yet, or at least word hasn't reached us and Don's fliers haven't seen much. Just now, while the *Kwembly* was stopped for a routine maintenance check, a heavy wind came up, and then a dense fog of pure or nearly pure ammonia. Then, quite suddenly, the temperature rose several degrees and they found themselves afloat, being blown roughly eastward by the wind. We would like explanations and we badly need constructive advice. Why did the temperature go up, and why did the snow melt? Is there any connection between the two? Remember that the highest temperature they mentioned was only about a hundred and three, twenty-six or -seven degrees below the melting point of water. Why the wind? How long is it likely to last? It's carrying the *Kwembly* toward the hot regions inside Low Alpha south of the *Esket* site." He gestured toward a heavily red-marked section of the floor. "Can we tell how far they'll be carried? I didn't want Dondragmer to go out on this trip, and I certainly don't want to lose him even if we don't agree completely.

"We'll call for what help we can get from the men, but you'll have to use your brains, too. I know some of you have been trying to make sense out of Dhrawn's climatology; do you have any worthwhile ideas which might apply here?"

Several minutes of silence followed. Even those in the group most given to uttering rhetorical speeches had been working with Barlennan too long to risk them now. For some time no really constructive ideas came up. Then one of the scientists scuttled toward the door and vanished, with "Just a moment, I have to check a table" floating behind him. He was back within thirty seconds.

"I can account for the temperature and melting," he said firmly. "The ground surface was water ice, the fog ammonia. The heat of solution as they met and mixed would have caused the temperature rise. Ammonia-water solutions form eutectics which can melt as low as seventy-one."

Mild hoots of appreciation and approving gestures of nipper-equipped arms greeted this suggestion. Barlennan went with the crowd, though words had been used which were not entirely familiar to him. But he was not through with his questions.

"Does that give us any idea how far the *Kwembly* will be carried?"

"Not in itself. We need information about the extent of the original snow field," was the answer. "Since only the *Kwembly* has been in the area, about the only hope is the photo maps made by the humans. You know how little we can get from those. Half the time you can't differentiate between ice and clouds. Besides they were all made before we landed here."

"Give it a try, anyway," ordered Barlennan. "With luck, you can at least tell whether those mountain ranges to the east are blocking the

Kwembly's present path. If they are, it's hard to see how the craft could be carried more than a few hundred thousand cables."

"Right," answered one of the investigators. "We'll check. Ben, Dees, come along; you're more used to the photos than I am." The three vanished through the door. The others broke up into small groups, muttering arguments to each other and waving excitedly, now at the map underfoot, now at items presumably in the nearby laboratories. Barlennan endured this for several minutes before deciding that a little more guidance was needed.

"If that plateau Don was crossing was such pure water, there couldn't have been any ammonia precipitation there for a long, long time. Why should things have changed so suddenly?"

"It almost has to be a seasonal effect," answered one of the men. "I can only guess, but I'd say it had something to do with some consistent change in the wind pattern. Air currents from different parts of the planet will be saturated with water or ammonia according to the nature of the surface they pass over, mostly its temperature, I suppose. The planet is nearly twice as far from its sun at one time as at another and its axis is much more inclined than Mesklin's. It's easy to believe that at one time of year only water is precipitated on that plateau and at another it gets supplied with ammonia. Actually, the vapor pressure of water is so low that it's hard to see what situation would get water into the atmosphere without supplying even more ammonia, but I'm sure it's possible. We'll work on it, but it's another of those times when we'd be a lot better off with world-wide, year-round information. These human beings seem to be in an awful hurry; they could have waited a few more years to land us here, I should think."

Barlennan made the gesture whose human equivalent would have been a noncommittal grunt. "The field data *would* be convenient. Just think of yourself as being here to get it instead of having it given to you."

"Of course. Are you going to send the *Kalliff* or the *Hoorsh* out to help Dondragmer? This is certainly different from the *Esket* situation."

"From our point of view, yes. It might look funny to the humans, though, if I insisted on sending out a rescue cruiser this time after letting them talk me out of it before. I'll think it over. There's more than one way of sailing upwind. You do that theoretical work you've just been talking about, but be thinking about what you'd want to take on a field trip up toward the *Kwembly*."

"Right, Commander." The scientist started to turn away, but Barlennan added a few more words.

"And Jemblakee. No doubt you'll be strolling over to Communications to talk to your human colleagues. Please don't mention this, what was it, heat of solution and eutectic business. Let them mention it first, if they're going to, and be properly impressed when and if they do. You understand?"

"Perfectly." The scientist would have shared a grin of understanding with his commander if their faces had been capable of that sort of distortion. Jemblakee left, and after a moment's thought Barlennan did the same. The remaining researchers and technicians might possibly be the better for his presence to keep their centerboards down but he had other things to do. If they couldn't hold course without his pincers on their helms, they'd just have to drift for a while.

He should talk to the human station soon; but if there was going to be an argument, as seemed rather likely, he had better do a little course-plotting himself. Some of the two-legged giants, Aucoin, for example, who seemed to have a great deal to say about their policy, were reluctant to expend or even risk any sort of reserve equipment, no matter how important the action seemed from the Mesklinite viewpoint. Since the aliens had paid for it, this was perfectly understandable, even laudable. Still there was nothing immoral about talking them around to a more convenient attitude if it could be done. If he could arrange it, the best plan would be to work through that particularly sympathetic female named Hoffman. It was too bad the human beings kept such irregular hours; if they had set up decent, regular watches in their communication section Barlennan would long since have worked out their schedule and been able to pick his party. He wondered, not for the first time, whether the irregular schedule might not be deliberately set up to block that very action, but there seemed no way to find out. He could hardly ask.

The Settlement's comm center was far enough from the laboratories to give him thinking time en route. It was also close enough to his office to encourage a pause for making a few notes before actually opening the verbal fencing match.

The central theme would have to be the question of rescue, if Dondragmer's trouble wound up crippling his cruiser. If the previous situation involving the *Esket* months before were any indication, the tightwads up above would be basically against sending the *Kalliff.* Of course, there was nothing they could do if Barlennan chose to go his own way in that matter, or in any other, but the commander was hoping to keep that fact cushioned in the decencies of polite conversation. He would be happiest if that aspect of the situation never came up at all. This was one reason he hoped to work Easy Hoffman into the other end of the discussion. For some reason, she seemed prone to take the Mesklinite side when disagreements arose. She was certainly one reason that there had been no open argument during the *Esket* incident, though a more important reason was that Barlennan had never had the slightest intention of sending a rescue cruiser before and had therefore actually been siding with Aucoin.

Well, he could at least go as far as the comm room door and find out who was on duty above. With the rippling equivalent of a shrug, he lifted his sprawled eighteen inches from the office floor and made his way into the corridor. It was at that moment that the wind reached the Settlement.

There was no fog at first or for some minutes thereafter. Barlennan, promptly changing his plans as the roof began rippling, got all the way back to the laboratories; but before he had a chance to get any constructive information from his scientists the stars began to fade. Within a few minutes the lights showed a solid gray ceiling a body-length above the Mesklinites. The ceilings here were rigid and did not vibrate in the wind as those in the corridor had, but the sound outside was loud enough to make more than one of the scientists wonder how stable the buildings actually were. They didn't express the thought aloud in the commander's presence but he could interpret the occasional upward glances when the whine of the heavy outside air increased in pitch.

It occurred to him that his present location was about the most useless possible one for a commander who was not a scientist, since the people around him were about the only ones in the Settlement to whom he could not reasonably give orders. He asked just one question, was informed in reply that the wind speed was about half that Dondragmer had reported some ten thousand miles away, then headed for the communication room.

He thought briefly of going back to the office on the way, but knew that anyone wanting him would find him almost as quickly at Guzmeen's station. Meanwhile a question had crossed his mind which could probably be answered by relay from the human station faster than any other way, and that question seemed more and more important as the seconds passed. Forgetting that he wanted to make sure that Easy Hoffman was on duty above, he shot into the radio room and politely nudged aside the staff member in front of the transmitter. He began to speak almost before he was in position and the sight of Hoffman's features when the screen lit up was a pleasant surprise rather than a major relief.

"The wind and fog are here, too," he began abruptly. "Some people were outdoors. There's nothing I can do about them at the moment; but some were working in the cruisers parked outside. You could check through their communicators as to whether everything is all right there. I'm not too worried, since the wind speed is now much less than Don reported. Besides, the air is much less dense at this height; but we can't see at all through this fog, so I'd be relieved to know about the men in the cruisers."

Easy's image had started to speak part way through the commander's request, obviously not in answer, since there had not been time enough for the speed-of-light round-trip. Presumably the human beings had something of their own to say. Barlennan concentrated on his own message until it was done, knowing that Guzmeen or one of his crew would be writing down whatever came in. Message crossing under these circumstances was a frequent event and was handled by established routine.

With his own words on the way, the commander turned to ask what the humans had wanted but the question was interrupted. An officer shot into the room and began reporting as soon as he saw Barlennan.

"Sir, all groups but the two who checked out at the north gates are accounted for. One of these was working in the *Hoorsh,* the other was leveling ground for the new complex twenty cables north, on the other side of the parking valley. There were eight people in the first group, twenty in the second."

Barlennan made the gesture of understanding, all four nippers clicking shut simultaneously. "We may have radio reports from the space station shortly on the *Hoorsh* group," he replied. "How many who were actually outside after the wind and fog arrived have come in? What do they report on living and traveling conditions? Was anyone hurt?"

"No one hurt, sir. The wind was only a minor inconvenience; they came in because they couldn't see to work. Some of them had trouble finding their way. My guess is that the ground-levelling crew is still groping its way back, unless they just decided to wait it out where they were. The ones on the *Hoorsh* may not even have noticed anything, inside. If the first bunch stays out of contact too long, I'll send out a messenger."

"How will you keep *him* from getting lost?"

"Compass, plus picking someone who works outside a lot and knows the ground well."

"I'm not—" Barlennan's objection was interrupted by the radio.

"Barlennan," came Easy's voice, "the communicators in the *Hoorsh* and the *Kalliff* are all working. As far as we can see, there is no one in the *Kalliff* and it's just sitting there; nothing is moving. There are at least three, and possibly five, men in the life-support section of the *Hoorsh.* The man covering those screens has seen as many as three at once in the last few minutes but isn't too confident of recognizing individual Mesklinites. The cruiser doesn't seem to be affected. The people aboard are going about their business and paying no attention to us. Certainly they weren't trying to send an emergency message up. Jack Bravermann is trying to get their attention on that set now but I don't think there's anything to worry about. As you say, slower wind and thinner air should mean that your settlement is in no danger if the *Kwembly* wasn't hurt."

"I'm not worried, at least not much. If you'll wait a moment, I'll find out what your last message but one was and try to answer it," returned

Barlennan. He turned to the duty officer whose place at the set he had taken. "I assume you got what she said."

"Yes, Sir. It wasn't urgent, just interesting. Another interim report has come up from Dondragmer. The *Kwembly* is still afloat, still drifting, though he thinks it has dragged bottom once or twice and the wind is still blowing there. Because of their own motion, his scientists won't commit themselves to an opinion on whether the wind velocity has changed or not."

The commander gestured acceptance, turned back to the communicator, and said, "Thanks, Mrs. Hoffman. I appreciate your sending even 'no change' reports so quickly. I will stay here for a while, so if anything really does happen I will know as soon as possible. Have your atmospheric scientists come up with predictions they trust? Or explanations of what happened?"

To the other Mesklinites in the room it was obvious that Barlennan was doing his best to keep his expression unreadable as he asked this question. His arms and legs were carefully relaxed, chelae neither too tightly closed nor gaping open, his head neither too high nor too close to the floor, his eyes fixed steadily on the screen. The watchers did not know in detail what was in his mind, but could tell that he attached more than face value to the question. Some of them wondered why he bothered to control himself so, since it was most unlikely that any human being could interpret his body expression anyway; but those who knew him best realized that he would never take a chance on a matter like that. After all, there were some human beings, of whom Elise Rich Hoffman was emphatically one, who seemed to think very easily from the Mesklinite viewpoint, besides speaking Stennish as well as human vocal equipment would permit.

All watched the screen with interest, wondering whether the human being on it would show signs of having noticed the commander's attitude when her answer came back. All communication room personnel were reasonably familiar with human facial expressions; most of them could recognize at least a dozen different human beings by face or voice alone, the commander having long ago expressed a strong desire that such abilities be cultivated. Barlennan, his glance leaving the screen for a moment and roving around the circle of intent listeners, was amused at their expressions even while he was annoyed at his own obviousness. He wondered how they would react to whatever answer Easy returned, but he never found out.

The human female had evidently received the question and was starting to form a sentence in reply, when her attention was distracted. For several seconds she was obviously listening to something and her eyes shifted away from the pickup of the Settlement communicator. Then her attention came back to Barlennan.

"Commander. Dondragmer has reported again. The *Kwembly* has stopped, or almost stopped, aground. They are still being dragged a little, however; the flow of liquid has not slowed. They have been tipped so that the trucks are out of contact with whatever surface is below them. If they aren't dragged free by the river, they're there to stay; and Dondragmer thinks the level is going down."

4: Small Talk

It was a curious, helpless sensation for Beetchermarlf. The *Kwembly*'s helm was connected to the trucks by simple pulley-and-cord rigging; even Mesklinite muscles could not turn the trucks when the vehicle was at rest, and, while forward motion made steering possible, it certainly did not make it easy. Now, as the vehicle floated with the driving units clear of the bottom, the helm flopped limply in response to a casual nudge or even to a slight roll of the hull. In theory, the cruiser was maneuverable at sea, but this required installing driving paddles on the treads, something most easily done on land. Dondragmer had thought fleetingly, as he realized they were adrift, of sending out air suited men to attempt the task, then decided it wasn't worth the risk even if everyone were attached solidly to the hull by life-lines. It was likely enough, as far as anyone could tell, that they might reach the end or the edge of the river or lake or whatever they were floating on before any such job could be completed, anyway. If men were outside when that happened, life-lines would be of little use.

The same thoughts had crossed the helmsman's mind as he lay at his station, but he did not voice them. Beetchermarlf was young, but not so young as to assume that no one else could recognize the obvious. He was quite prepared to grant his captain's professional competence.

As the minutes slipped by, however, he began to worry at Dondragmer's failure to issue any orders. Something should be possible; they couldn't just drift eastward. He glanced at the compass; yes, eastward, indefinitely. There had been hills that way according to the last flight reports, the same hills which had bordered the snow field on their left, sometimes showing slightly above the distant horizon, for the last three or four thousand miles. Judging by their color they were rock, not ice. If the surface the *Kwembly* was floating on was simply melted snow field, they almost had to hit something soon. Beetchermarlf had no more idea than anyone else how fast they were going but his confidence in the strength of the hull matched that of the captain. He had no more wish to strike a reef on Dhrawn than he had ever had on Mesklin.

Anyhow, the wind should not move them too fast, given the air density. The top of the hull was smoothly curved except for the bridge, and the trucks on the bottom should give plenty of drag. As far as the air scouts had been able to tell, the snow field had been level, so the liquid itself shouldn't be moving. Come to think of it, the outside pressure should give a check on that. The helmsman stirred at the thought, glanced up at the captain, hesitated, and then spoke.

"Sir, how about checking hull-squeeze watch? If there is any current where we're floating, we'd have to be going downhill, and that should show—" Dondragmer interrupted.

"But the surface was level—no, you're right. We should check." He reared up to the bank of speaking tubes and called the laboratory. "Born, how is the pressure? You're keeping track, of course."

"Of course, Captain. Both bow and stern safety bladders have been expanding ever since we began to float. We've descended about six body lengths in twice that many minutes. I'm about ready to tap more argon."

Dondragmer acknowledged, and looked back at his helmsman.

"Good for you. I should have thought of that. That means we are being carried by current as well as wind and all bets on speed, distance, and where we stop are off. There couldn't be a current unless the air scouts missed a slope, and if there's a slope this plateau must drain somewhere."

"We're secure for rough travel, Sir. I don't see what else we can do."

"There's one thing," Dondragmer said grimly. He reared to the tubes again, and emitted the sirenlike general quarters call. Reasonably sure that all were listening, he pulled his head back so as to be equally distant from all the tubes, and spoke loudly enough to get through them all.

"All hands into air suits as quickly as possible. You are relieved from stations for that purpose, but get back as soon as you can." He lowered himself to his command bench and addressed Beetchermarlf. "Get your suit and mine, and bring them back here. Quickly!"

The helmsman was back with the garments in ninety seconds. He started to assist the captain with his, but was dismissed by an emphatic gesture and went to work on his own. In two minutes both, protected except for head covering, were back at their stations.

The haste, as it turned out, was unnecessary. More minutes passed while Beetchermarlf toyed with the useless helm, and Dondragmer wondered whether the human scientists were ever going to come through with any information and what use it was likely to be if they did. He hoped that satellite fixes could give him some idea of the *Kwembly*'s speed; it would, he thought rather cynically, be nice to know how hard they were likely to hit whatever finally stopped them. Such fixes were, he knew, hard to get on order; there were over thirty of the "shadow satellites" in orbit but they were less than three thousand miles above the surface. No attempt had been made to arrange their orbits so that their limited fields of visual and microwave coverage would be either uniform or complete; communication was not their primary purpose. The main human base, in synchronous orbit over six million miles above the Settlement meridian, was supposed to need no help with that task. Also, the ninety-plus mile per second orbital speed of the lower satellites, helpful though the human observers claimed it to be for moving-baseline location checking, still seemed to Dondragmer an inevitable cause of difficulty. He was not at all hopeful about getting his speed from this source. That was just as well, because he never did.

Once, about half an hour after they had gone adrift, a brief shudder ran through the *Kwembly* and the captain duly reported to the station that they had probably touched bottom. Everyone else on board made the same assumption and tension began to mount.

There was a little warning just before the end. A hoot from the laboratory speaking tube was followed by a report that pressure had started to rise more rapidly, and that an additional release of argon into the ship's atmosphere had been necessary to keep the safety bladders from rupturing. There was no sensation of increasing speed, but the implication of the report was plain enough. They were descending more rapidly. How fast were they going horizontally? The captain and helmsman looked at each other, not asking the question aloud but reading it in each other's expressions. More minutes passed; the tension mounted, chelae gripping stanchions and holdfasts ever more tightly.

Then there was a thunderous clang, and the hull swerved abruptly; another, and it tilted sharply to starboard. For several seconds it pitched violently, and those near bow and stern could feel it yawing as well, though the fog still blocked any outside view which might have explained the sensation. Then there was another, much louder clang and the *Kwembly* rolled some sixty degrees to starboard; but this time she did not recover. Scraping, grinding sounds suggested that she was moving slightly, but no real change of attitude accompanied them. For the first time, the sound of liquid rushing past the hull became noticeable.

Dondragmer and his companion were unhurt. To beings who regarded two hundred Earth gravities as normal and six hundred as a most minor inconvenience, that sort of acceleration meant nothing. They had not even lost their grips, and were still at their posts. The captain was not worried about direct injuries to his crew. His first words showed that he was considering matters much further ahead.

"By stations, report!" he bellowed into the speaking tubes. "Check hull soundness at all points, and report all cracks, open breaks, dents, and other evidence for leaks. Lab personnel to emergency stations, and check for oxygen. Life-support, cut tank circulation until the oxygen check is done. Now!"

Apparently the speaking tubes were intact, at least. Hoots of response began to return immediately. As the reports accumulated, Beetchermarlf began to relax. He had not really expected the shell which protected him from Dhrawn's poisonous air to withstand anything like such a shock and his respect for alien engineering went up several grades. He had regarded artificial structures of any sort as normally inferior in strength and durability to any living body. He had, of course, excellent reason for such an attitude. Nevertheless, it appeared when all the reports were finally in, that there were no major structural failures or even visible cracks. Whether the normal leaks, unavoidable in a structure which had to have entrances for personnel and equipment, not to mention hull openings for instruments and control lines, were any worse than they had been, would not be known for a while. Pressure monitoring and oxygen checking would of course continue as normal routine.

Power was still on, which surprised no one. The twenty-five independent hydrogen converters, identical modules which could be moved from any energy-using site in the *Kwembly* to any other, were solid-state devices with no moving parts larger than the molecules of gaseous fuel which were fed into them. They could have been placed under the hammer of a power forge without damage.

Most of the outside lights were gone, or at least inoperative, though these could be replaced. Some were still working, however, and from the submerged end of the bridge it was possible to see out. Fog still blocked the view from the upper end. Dondragmer made his way very gingerly to the low end and took a brief look at the conglomeration of rounded rocks with diameters from half his own length to twenty times that, into which his craft had managed to wedge itself. Then he climbed carefully back to his station, energized the sound system of his radio and transmitted the report which Barlennan was to hear a little over a minute later. Without waiting for an answer, he began issuing orders to the helmsman.

"Beetch, stand by here in case the men have anything to say. I'm going to make a complete check myself, especially of the air locks. With all there is to be said for our design, we didn't have this much of a roll in mind when we settled on it. We may only be able to use the small emergency locks, since the main one seems to be underneath us at the moment. It may be blocked on the outside even if we can open the inner door and find the septum still submerged. Chatter with the human beings if you want. The more of us who can use their language and the more of them who can use ours, the better. You have the bridge."

Dondragmer made the habitual, but now rather futile, gesture of rapping on the hatch for clearance; then he opened it and disappeared, leaving Beetchermarlf alone.

The helmsman had no urge at the moment for idle talk with the station above. His captain had left him with too much to think about.

He was not exactly delighted at being left in charge of the bridge, under the circumstances. He was not even too concerned about the main air lock's being blocked; the smaller ones were adequate, though not for life-support equipment, he suddenly remembered. Well, at the moment the desirability of going out seemed very small but if the *Kwembly* were permanently disabled that need would have to be faced.

The real question, in that event, was just what good going outside would do. The twelve thousand miles or so, which Beetchermarlf thought of as nearly fourteen million cables, was a long, long walk, especially with a load of life-support equipment. Without that apparatus it was not to be thought of. Mesklinites were amazingly tough organisms mechanically and had a temperature tolerance range which was still disbelieved by many human biologists, but oxygen was another matter. Its partial pressure outside at the moment was presumably about fifty pounds per square inch, quite enough to kill any member of the *Kwembly*'s crew in seconds.

The most desirable thing at the moment was to get the big machine back on her treads. How, and whether, this could be done would depend largely on the stream of liquid flowing past the stranded hull. Working outside in that current might not be impossible, but it was going to be difficult and dangerous. The air suited Mesklinites would have to be heavily ballasted to stay put at any task and life-lines would complicate the details.

The stream might not, of course, be permanent. It had apparently just come into existence with the change in weather and it might cease flowing as suddenly. However, as Beetchermarlf well knew, there is a difference between weather and climate. If the river were seasonal, its "temporary" nature might still turn out to be too long for the Mesklinites; Dhrawn's year was some eight times as long as that of Earth and over one and a half times that of Mesklin.

This was an area where human information might be useful. The aliens had been observing Dhrawn carefully for nearly half of one of its years and casually for much longer. They should have *some* idea of its seasons. The helmsman wondered whether it would be out of order for him to put such a question to someone in the orbiting station, since the captain had not. Of course, the captain *had* said he could use the radio for chatter and had made no mention of what might or might not be said.

The idea that there was anything except the *Esket* incident which should not be discussed with the human sponsors of the Dhrawn expedition had not gone down the chain of command as far as Beetchermarlf. The young helmsman had almost made up his mind to initiate a call to the station when the radio beside him spoke. It spoke, furthermore, in his own language, though the accent was not above reproach.

"Dondragmer. I know you must be busy but if you can't talk now I'd be glad if someone else could. I am Benjamin Hoffman, an assistant in the aerology lab here at the station, and I'd like two kinds of help if anyone can find time to give it.

"For myself, I'd like practice in language; it must be obvious that I need it. For the lab, we're in a very embarrassing position. Twice in a row we've worked out weather predictions for your part of the planet which have been way, way off. We just don't have enough detailed information to do the job properly. The observations we can make from here don't resolve enough and there aren't anywhere near enough reporting stations down there. You and the others have planted a lot of automatics on your trips, but they still don't cover much of the planet, as you know. Since good predictions will be as useful to you as they will be to us, I thought maybe I could talk things out in real detail with some of your scientists and maybe work out the weather patterns where you know enough to supplement the background calculations and really get good forecasts, at least right in your neighborhood."

The helmsman replied eagerly.

"The captain is not on the bridge, Benjaminhoffman. I am Beetchermarlf, one of the helmsmen, now on watch. Speaking for myself, I should be very glad to exchange language practice when duties permit, as now. I am afraid the scientists will be pretty busy for a while; I may be myself, most of the time. We are having some trouble, though you may not know all the details. The captain did not have time for the full story in the report I heard him send up a few minutes ago. I will give you as complete a picture as I can of the situation and some thoughts which have occurred to me since the captain left the bridge. You might record the information for your people and comment on my ideas if you wish. If you don't think they're worth mentioning to the captain, I won't. He'll be busy enough without them anyway. I'll wait until you tell me you're ready to record, or that you don't want to, before I start." Beetchermarlf paused, not entirely for the reason he had just given. He suddenly wondered whether he should bother one of these alien beings with his own ideas which began to seem crude and poorly worked out to him.

Still, the factual reports had to be useful. There was much detailed information about the *Kwembly*'s present situation which the men could not possibly know yet. By the time Benj's approval came from the speaker, the helmsman had recovered some of his self-confidence.

"That will be fine, Beetchermarlf. I'm ready to tape your report. I was going to anyway, for language practice. I'll pass on whatever you want. Even if your weather men are busy, maybe the two of us could try to do what I suggested with the weather information. You can probably get their measurements, and you're on the spot and can see everything and if you're one of the sailors Barlennan recruited on Mesklin you certainly know something about weather. For all I know, you may have spent a couple of my lifetimes in that place on Mesklin learning engineering and research methods. Come ahead; I'm ready here."

This speech completed the restoration of Beetchermarlf's morale. It had been only ten of Mesklin's years since alien education had started for a selected few of its natives. This human being must be five years old or younger. Of course, there was no telling what that might mean in the way of maturity for his species, and one could not very well ask; but in spite of the aura of supernormality which tended to surround all the aliens, one just did not think of a five-year-old as a superior being.

As relaxed as anyone could well be on a floor with a sixty-degree tilt, the sailor began his description of the *Kwembly*'s situation. He gave a detailed account of the trip down what now had to be recognized as a river, and of its conclusion. He described minutely what could now be seen from the bridge. He explained how they were now stranded off their tracks, and emphasized the situation which faced the crew if this could not be corrected. He even detailed the structure of the air-locks, and explained why the main one was probably unusable and the others possibly so.

"It will help a great deal in the captain's planning," he concluded, "if we can have some trustworthy estimate of what will happen to this river, and especially whether and when it will run dry. If the whole snow field melts at this season and runs off the plateau through this one drain, I suppose we're here for the best part of a year and will have to plan accordingly. If you can give any hope that we can work on dry land without having to wait too long, though, it would be very good to know."

Benj was rather longer than sixty-four seconds in answering this; he, too, had been given material for thought.

"I have your details on tape, and have sent it up to Planning," his words came through at last. "They'll distribute copies to the labs. Even I can see that figuring out the life story of your river is going to be a nasty job; maybe an impossible one without a lot more knowledge. As you say, the whole snow field might be starting a seasonal melt. If the waters of

North America had to drain out through one river you'd be there for a long time. I don't know how much of the place your aerial scout reports cover, and I don't know how ambiguous the photos from up here may be, but I'll bet when it's all down on maps there'll still be room for argument. Even if everyone agrees on a conclusion, well, we still don't know much about that planet."

"But you've had so much experience with other planets, many of them!" returned Beetchermarlf. "I should think that would be of some help."

Again the answer was longer in coming back than light-lag alone would explain.

"Men and their friends have had experience on a lot of planets, that's true, and I've read a good deal of it. The trouble is, practically none of it helps here. There are three kinds of planet, basically. One we call Terrestrial, like my own home; it is small, dense, and practically without hydrogen. The second is the Jovian, or Type Two, which tends to be much larger and much less dense because they have kept most of their hydrogen from the time they originally formed, we think. Those two were the only kinds we knew about before we left our own star's neighborhood, because they are the only kinds in our system.

"Type Three is very large, very dense, and very hard to account for. Theories which had the Type Ones losing their hydrogen because of their initially small mass, and the Twos keeping theirs because of their greater mass, were fine as long as we'd never heard of the Threes. Our ideas were perfectly satisfactory and convincing as long as we didn't know too much, if you'll forgive my sounding like my basic science teacher.

"Type Three is the sort you're on. There are none of them around any sun with a Type One planet. I suppose there must be a reason for that, but I don't know what it is. Well, nothing was known about them among the Community races until we learned to travel between stars and began to do it on a large scale, large enough so the principal interest of wandering ships wasn't just new habitable planets. Even then we couldn't study them first hand, any more than we could the Jovian worlds. We could send down a few special, very expensive and usually very unreliable robots, but that was all. Your species is the first we've ever encountered able to stand the gravity of a Type Three or the pressure of a Type Two, for that matter."

"But isn't Mesklin a Type Three, by your description? You must know a lot about it by now; you've been in touch with our people for something like ten years, and some of you have even landed at the Rim, I mean the equator."

"More like fifty of our years. The trouble is that Mesklin isn't a Type Three. It's a peculiar Two. It would have had all the hydrogen of any Jovian world if it hadn't been for its rotation, that terrific spin which gives your world an eighteen-minute day and a shape like a fried egg. There aren't any others like it which we've found yet, and no intermediate cases that anyone's recognized, or at least that I've heard of. That's why the Community races were willing to go to so much trouble and effort and spend so much time building up contact with your world and setting up this expedition to Dhrawn. We'll find out a good deal in thirty years or so about that world's makeup from the neutrino counters in the shadow satellites but the seismic equipment you people have been planting will add a lot of detail and remove a lot of ambiguity. So will your chemical work. In five or six of your years we may know enough about that rock ball to make a sensible guess why it's there or at least, whether it ought to be called a star or a planet."

"You mean you only made contact with the people of Mesklin so you could learn more about Dhrawn?"

"No, I didn't mean that at all. People are people and worth getting to know for their own sake—at least, both my parents feel that way, though I've met folks who certainly don't. I don't think the idea for the Dhrawn project got started until long after your College was under way. My mother or Dr. Aucoin could tell you when. It was long before I was born. Of course, when it dawned on someone that you folks *could* make first-hand investigation of a place like Dhrawn, everyone jumped at the chance."

This, of course, forced Beetchermarlf to ask a question which he would ordinarily have regarded as a strictly human affair and none of his business, like the matter of how mature a five-year-old should be. It slipped out before he caught himself; for over an hour thereafter he and Benj were arguing over the reasons for such activities as the Dhrawn project and why such a vast amount of effort should be devoted to an activity with no obvious material return in prospect. Benj did not defend his side too well. He was able to give the usual answers about the force of curiosity, which Beetchermarlf could see up to a point; he knew enough history to have heard how close man and several other species had come to extinction from energy starvation before they had developed the hydrogen fusion converter; but he was too young to be really eloquent. He lacked the experience to be able to point out convincingly, even to himself, the complete dependence of any culture on its understanding of the laws of the universe. The conversation never became heated, which would have been difficult in any argument where there is a built-in cooling-down period between any remark and its answer. The only really satisfactory progress made was in Benj's mastery of Stennish.

The discussion was interrupted by Beetchermarlf's suddenly becoming aware of a change in his surroundings. For the last hour his entire attention had been on Benj's words and his own replies. The canted bridge and gurgling liquid had receded to the far background of his mind. He was quite surprised to realize abruptly that the pattern of lights twinkling above him was Orion. The fog had gone.

Alert once more to his surroundings, he noticed that the water line around the bridge seemed just a trifle lower. Ten minutes' careful watching convinced him that this was so. The river *war* falling.

Part way through the ten minutes he had, of course, been queried about his sudden silence by Benj, and had given the reason. The boy had immediately notified McDevitt, so that by the time Beetchermarlf was sure about the changing water level there were several interested human beings on hand above to hear about it. The helmsman reported briefly to them on the radio and only then did he call through the speaking tubes for Dondragmer.

The captain was far aft, behind the laboratory section and just forward of the compartment containing the pressure bladder, when the call came. There was a pause after the helmsman finished speaking, and Beetchermarlf expected the captain to come bursting through the bridge hatchway after a few seconds; but Dondragmer did not yield to the temptation. The ports in the rest of the hull, including the compartment where he was, were much too small to permit a clear estimate of the water level, so he had to accept his helmsman's judgment. Dondragmer was willing to do this, rather to the young sailor's surprise.

"Keep track as exactly as you can of the rate of fall, until you are relieved," was his order. "Let me and the human beings know the rate as soon as you can guess it reliably; tell us thereafter whenever you change your estimate."

Beetchermarlf acknowledged the order and clambered across the bridge to a point where he could mark the water line with a scratch on one of the window stanchions. Reporting the action to the captain and the human listeners, he returned to his station keeping his eyes fixed on the mark. The ripples in the liquid were several inches high, settling down only at rare intervals, hence it was some time before he could be at all sure of the change in depth. There were two or three impatient queries from above, which he answered politely in the best he could muster of his limited human language, before Benj reported that he was once more alone except for nonentities watching other cruisers. Most of the time thereafter until Takoorch arrived as bridge relief was spent by the two in describing their home worlds, correcting each other's misconceptions about Earth and Mesklin by way of language practice and, though neither was fully aware of it, developing a warm personal friendship.

Beetchermarlf returned six hours later to let Takoorch go (actually the interval was twenty-four days by Mesklinite reckoning, a standard watch length) and found that the water was down nearly a foot from his reference mark. Takoorch informed him that the human Benj had just returned from a rest period. The younger helmsman wondered privately just how soon after Tak's arrival the other had found it was time to take a rest. Naturally he could not ask such a question, but as he settled back into his station he sent a call radiating upward.

"I'm back on, Benj. I don't know how recently Tak made a report to you, but the water is down over half a body length and the current seems much slower. The wind is nearly calm. Have your scientists anything to report?"

He had time during the answer delay to realize that the last question had been rather pointless, since the principal news wanted from the human scientists was the probable duration of the river, but there was nothing to be done about it now. Besides, maybe they *did* have something of value.

"Your friend Takoorch did tell us about the water and wind, among a good many other things," Benj's voice announced. "It's good to have you back, Beetch. I haven't heard anything from the labs, but it seems to me from what you've said about the way you're tipped and the rate the water's been dropping, and from what I can judge from the cruiser model I have here, that another sixty or seventy hours should leave you dry. That's if the water keeps dropping at the same rate, of course. It might do that if it's flowing away through a nice smooth channel but I wouldn't count on that. I hate to sound pessimistic but my guess is that it will slow down before all the liquid is gone."

"You may be right," agreed Beetchermarlf. "On the other hand, with the current easing off we can probably work outside safely enough before it's all gone." This was a prophetic remark. It was still on its way to the station when a speaking tube hooted for attention.

"Beetchermarlf! Inform the human beings that you will be relieved immediately by Kervenser, and report at once to the starboard after emergency lock in your air suit. I want a check of the trucks and tiller lines. Two others will go with you for safety. I am more interested in accuracy than speed. If there is any damage which would be easier to fix while we are still tilted than it would be after we are level, I want to know about it. After you make that check, take a general look around. I want a rough idea of how solidly we are wedged into this position and how much work it will take to level us and get us loose. I will be outside myself making a similar check, but I want another opinion."

"Yes, sir," the helmsman responded. He almost forgot to notify Benj, for this time the order was a distinct surprise, not the fact that he was to go outside, but that the captain had chosen him to check his own judgment.

The air suits had been removed when Dondragmer was convinced that the hull was sound, but Beetchermarlf was back into his in half a minute and at the designated lock moments later. The captain and four sailors, all suited, were waiting. The crewmen held coils of rope.

"All right, Beetch," greeted the captain. "Stakendee will go out first and attach his line to the handiest climbing grip. You will follow, then Praffen. Each of you will attach his line to a different grip. Then go about your assignments. Wait—fasten these to your suit harness; you'll float without ballast." He handed four weights equipped with quick-release clips for harness attachment to the helmsman.

Egress was made in silence through the tiny lock. It was essentially a U-shaped liquid trap, fundamentally similar in operation to the main one and deep enough so that the *Kwembly*'s tilt did not quite spoil its operation. The fact that the outer end was in liquid anyway may have made the difference. Beetchermarlf, emerging directly into the current, was glad of Stak's steadying grip as he sought anchorage for his own safety line.

A minute later the third member of their group had joined them, and together they clambered the short distance that separated them from the river bottom. This was composed of the rounded rocks which had been visible from the bridge, arranged in an oddly wavelike pattern whose crests extended across the direction of the current. At first glance, Beetchermarlf got the impression that the cruiser had stranded in the trough between two of these waves. Enough of the outside lights were still working to make seeing possible, if not quite ideal.

The trio made their way around the stern to get a look at their vehicle's underside. While this was much less well lighted, it was obvious at once that there would be a great deal to report to Dondragmer.

The *Kwembly* had been supported by a set of sixty trucks, each some three feet wide and twice as long, arranged in five longitudinal rows of twelve. All swiveled on casters and were interconnected by a maze of tiller ropes which were Beetchermarlf's main responsibility. Each of the trucks had a place to install a power unit, and had its own motor consisting of a six-inch-thick shaft whose micro-structure gave it a direct grip on the rotating magnetic field which was one of the forms in which the fusion units could deliver their energy. If no power box was installed, the truck rolled free. At the time of the accident, ten of the *Kwembly*'s twenty-five converters had been on trucks, arranged in point-forward V patterns fore and aft.

Eighteen trucks from the rear of the cruiser, including all five of the powered ones at that end, were missing.

5: Fryer to Freezer

Strictly speaking, all of them weren't missing. Several could be seen lying on the boulders, evidently dislodged at the time of the final impact. Whether any had gone with the earlier bumps, presumably miles upstream, Beetchermarlf could not guess and was rather afraid to find out. That could be checked later. Inspecting what was left would have to come first. The helmsman set to it.

The front end seemed to have sustained no damage at all; the trucks were still present and their maze of tiller lines in proper condition. Amidships, many of the lines had snapped in spite of the enormous strength of the Mesklinite fiber used in them. Some of the trucks were twisted out of alignment; several, indeed, swung freely to the touch. The pattern of missing parts aft was regular and rather encouraging. Numbering from the port side, Row 1 had lost its last five trucks; Rows 2 and 3 their last four; Row 4 the last three; Row 5, on the starboard side, its last two. This suggested that they had all yielded to the same impact, which had wiped diagonally across the bottom of the hull; and since some of the detached units were in the neighborhood, there seemed a good chance that they all would be.

The inspectors were surprised at how little damage had been done by the trucks tearing away. Beetchermarlf and his companions had had nothing to do with the design of the *Kwembly* and her sister machines. None of them had more than the roughest idea of the sort of thinking which had been involved. They had never considered the problems inherent in building a machine powered by the most sophisticated energy sources ever developed, but operated by beings from a culture still in the muscle-and-wind stage; beings who would be cut off from *any* repair and replacement facilities once they were on Dhrawn. This was the reason the steering was done by tiller and rope rather than by powered selsyns or similar devices; why the air locks were so simple, and not completely foolproof; why the life-support system was not only manually operated (except for the lights which kept the plants alive) but had even been designed and built by Mesklinite scientists and technicians.

A few hundred of the beings had received an extensive body of "alien" education, though no attempt had been made to spread the new knowledge through the Mesklinite culture. Nearly all of the "college graduates" were now on Dhrawn, together with recruits like Beetchermarlf; mostly young, reasonably intelligent volunteers from among the sailors of Barlennan's maritime nation. These were the people who would have to perform any repairs and all regular maintenance on the land-cruisers, and this fact had to be kept constantly in the foreground of the designers' minds. Designing vehicles capable of covering thousands of miles of Dhrawn's environment in a reasonable length of time, and at the same time reasonably safely under Mesklinite handling, had inevitably resulted in equipment with startling qualities. Beetchermarlf should not have been surprised either that the pieces of his cruiser went back together so readily, or that the cruisers had suffered so little damage.

Of course, the intelligence of the Mesklinites had been taken into account. It was the main reason for not depending on robots: these had proved unsatisfactory in the early days of space exploration. Mesklinite intelligence was obviously comparable to that of human beings, Drommians, or Paneshks: a fact surprising in itself, since all four planets appeared to have evolved their life forms over widely different lengths of geological time. It was also fairly certain that Mesklinites were much longer-lived, on the average, than human beings, though Mesklinites were oddly reluctant to discuss this; indeed, what this would mean in terms of their general competence was as problematic as Dhrawn itself. It had been a risky project from all angles, with most of the risk being taken by the Mesklinites. The giant barge drifting in orbit near the human station, which was supposed to be able to evacuate the entire Settlement in emergency, was little more than a gesture, especially for the beings afield in the land-cruisers.

None of this was in the minds of the three sailors inspecting the *Kwembly*'s damage. They were simply surprised and delighted to find that the lost trucks had merely popped out of the sockets in which they normally swivelled and into which they could apparently be replaced with little trouble, provided they could be found. With this problem settled to his satisfaction, Beetchermarlf made a brief cast over the river bottom to the limits imposed by the safety lines and found twelve of the trucks within that radius. Some of these were damaged: tracks broken or with missing links; bearing wheels cracked; a few axles bent. The three gathered all the material they could reach and transport and brought it back to the *Kwembly*'s stern. The helmsman considered doubling up on the safety lines and increasing their search radius but decided to report to Dondragmer and get his approval first. Indeed, the helmsman was a bit surprised that the captain had not appeared earlier, in view of his announced intention of checking outside.

He found the reason when he and his companions went back around the stern to the lock. Dondragmer, his two companions of the original sortie and six more crewmen, who had evidently been summoned in the meantime, were near the middle of the *Kwembly* laboring to remove boulders from the region of the main air lock.

The breathing suits had no special communication equipment, and the transmissive matching between their hydrogen-argon filling and the surrounding liquid was extremely poor; but the Mesklinite voice, built around a swimming siphon rather than a set of lungs (the hydrogen-using midgets lacked lungs) was another thing which had bothered human biologists. The helmsman caught his captain's attention with a deep hoot and gestured him to follow around the stern of the cruiser. Dondragmer assumed that the matter was important and came along after directing the others to continue their work. One look and a few sentences from Beetchermarlf brought him abreast of the situation.

After a few seconds' thought he rejected the idea of looking immediately for the missing trucks. The water was still going down; it would be safer and easier to conduct the search when it was gone, if this did not take too long. In the meantime repairs could be started on the ones which had already been found. Beetchermarlf acknowledged the order and began to sort the damaged equipment in order to plan the work.

Care was necessary; some parts were light enough to be borne away by the current when detached from the rest of the assemblies. Some such items were already missing, and had presumably gone in just that fashion. The helmsman had a portable light brought to the scene and stationed one of his helpers a few yards downstream to catch anything which got away from him. He thought how helpful a net would be but there was no such item aboard the *Kwembly*. It would be possible to make one from the miles of cordage she carried, but it hardly seemed worth the time.

Eight hours of labor, interrupted by occasional rests spent chatting with Benj, saw three of the damaged trucks again serviceable. Some of their parts were not of the original quality, Beetchermarlf and the others having improvised freely. They had used Mesklinite fabric and cord as well as alien polymers and alloys which were on hand. Their tools were their own; their culture had high standards of craftsmanship and such things as saws, hammers, and the usual spectrum of edged tools were familiar to the sailors. The fact that they were made of the Mesklinite equivalents of bone, horn, and shell was no disparagement to them, considering the general nature of Mesklinite tissue.

Replacing the repaired units in their swivels took muscle even by Mesklinite standards. It also took more tool work, as metal in the mountings had been bent out of shape when the trucks were torn free. The first three had to be placed in Row 4, since Row 5 was pressed against the boulders of the river bottom and the other three were too high to be reached conveniently. Beetchermarlf bowed to necessity, attached the trucks where he could, and went back to fixing more.

The river continued to fall and the current continued to decrease. Dondragmer ordered the helmsman and his helpers to move their work area from beneath the hull, anticipating what would happen as the buoyant force on the *Kwembly* decreased. His caution was justified when, with a grinding of boulders, the vehicle slipped from its sixty-degree tilt to about thirty, bringing two more rows of trucks within reach of the bottom and forcing two workmen to duck between stones to avoid being crushed.

At this point it became obvious that even if the water fell further, the cruiser would not. A point on its port underside about a third of the way back from the bow and between Rows 1 and 2 was now resting on a single rock some eighteen feet in diameter and half buried in the river bottom: a hopeless object to dislodge even without the *Kwembly*'s weight on it. Beetchermarlf kept on with his assigned job but couldn't help wondering how the captain proposed to lift his craft off that eminence. He was also curious about what would happen when and if he succeeded. The rocky surface which formed the river bed was the last sort of thing the cruiser's designers had had in mind as a substrate and the helmsman doubted seriously that she could run on such a base. High-gravity planets tend to be fairly level, judging by Mesklin (the only available example), and even if an area were encountered where traction seemed unpromising, the designers must have supposed that the crew need merely refrain from venturing onto it. This was another good example of the reason manned exploration was generally better than the automated kind.

Beetchermarlf, in a temporarily philosophical mood, concluded that foresight was likely to depend heavily on the amount of hindsight available.

Dondragmer, pondering the same problem, getting his vehicle free, was no nearer a solution than his helmsman some fifty hours after going aground. The first officer and the scientists were equally baffled. They were not worried, except for the captain, and even his feeling did not exactly parallel human "worry." He had kept to himself and Beetchermarlf (who had been on the bridge at the time) a conversation he had had with the human watchers a few hours before.

It had begun as a regular progress report, on an optimistic tone. Dondragmer was willing to admit that he hadn't thought of a workable plan yet but not that he was unlikely to think of one. Unfortunately, he had included in the remark the phrase "we have plenty of time to work it out."

Easy, at the other end, had been forced to disagree.

"You may not have as much as you think. Some of the people here have been considering those boulders. They are round, or nearly so, according to your report and what we can see on the bridge set. The most likely cause of that shape, according to our experience, is washing around in a stream bed or on a beach. Moving rocks that big would require a tremendous current. We're afraid that the stream which carried you there is just a preliminary trickle, the first thaw of the season, and if you don't get away soon you'll face a lot more water coming down."

Dondragmer had considered briefly.

"All right, but we're already doing all we can. Either we get away in time, or we don't; we can't do better than our best. If your scientists can give any sort of specific forecast of this super-flood we'll be glad of it, of course; otherwise we'll have to go on as we are. I'll leave a man on the radio here, of course, unless I have too much for them to do; in that case, try the lab. Thanks for the information, I guess."

The captain had gone back to work and to thought. He was not one to panic; in emergencies he seemed calmer than in a personal argument. Basically, his philosophy was the one he had just expressed: to do all one could in the time available, with the full knowledge that time would run out some day. At the moment, he only wished he knew what all he could do was.

The big rock was the main problem. It was keeping the drivers from traction, and until they not only touched bottom but bore heavily on it there was no moving the *Kwembly* with her own power. She might conceivably have been shifted by muscle power at Mesklin's Rim, or on Earth, but not under Dhrawn's gravity. Even a two-foot boulder was hard to move in that field.

There was rigging inside which could be set up as lifting tackle but none of it could begin to support the vehicle's weight as a static load even if its mechanical advantage were adequate.

Some trucks, four, to be exact, were in contact with the troublesome rock itself. Several more in Row 5 were touching bottom. None of these was powered at the moment but converters could be transferred to them.

If the four on the rock, and the ones forward from them, and some of the Row 5 trucks, were all to be powered why couldn't the cruiser simply be backed off?

She could. No reason at all to doubt it. On level ground with reasonable traction any four well-spaced power units could drive her. With her weight concentrated on only a few trucks, traction should be better than normal and a backward move would be mainly downhill.

It was not lack of self-confidence which caused Dondragmer to outline this plan to the human being on communication watch; he was announcing his intentions, not asking for advice. The man who heard him was not an engineer and gave casual approval to the move. As a matter of routine he reported the situation to Planning so that the information could be distributed. Consequently it reached an engineer within an hour or so, long before Dondragmer was ready to execute his plan.

It caused a raising of eyebrows, a quick examination of a scale model of the *Kwembly,* and two minutes of rapid slide-rule work.

The engineer was a poor linguist, but this was not the only reason he went looking for Easy Hoffman. He did not know Dondragmer very well, had no idea how the Mesklinite would react to criticism; he had worked with Drommians, since there were some connected with the Dhrawn project and he felt it safest to have his point presented by the official oil-spreader. Easy, when found, promptly assured him that she had never known Dondragmer to resent reasonable advice, but agreed that her better knowledge of Stennish would probably help even though the captain was fluent in the human tongue. They went together to the communication room.

Benj was there, as was usual when he was not on duty. He had by now made friends with several more of the Mesklinites, though he still liked Beetchermarlf best. The latter's long work hours resulting from the accident had not entirely prevented them from conversing and Benj's Stennish had improved greatly; he was now almost as good as his mother believed.

When Easy and the engineer arrived, he was listening to Takoorch and was not too sorry to interrupt the exchange with the news that there was an important message for the captain.

It took several minutes to get Dondragmer to the bridge; like the rest of the crew he had been working almost constantly, though by luck he happened to be inside when the call came.

"I'm here, Easy," his voice finally came through. "Tak said you had a business call. Go ahead."

"It's about this way you plan to back off the rock, Don," she began. "We don't have the whole picture here, of course, but there are two things bothering our engineers. One is the fact that your forward truck will run off the stone while you still have ten feet or more of hull, including some of your bridge, over it. Have you measured to see whether there's any risk of bare hull slamming down on the stone as the truck rolls off? Also, toward the end of the maneuver, you'll have your hull supported almost entirely at the ends. The pneumatic undercarriage may distribute the load but my friend here isn't sure it will; further, if you get the bare hull instead of the mattress taking half the *Kwembly*'s weight, Dhrawn's gravity is going to make a very respectable effort to break your land-ship in half. Have you checked those points?"

Dondragmer had to admit to himself that he had not and that he had better do so before the project went much farther. He conceded this on the radio, thanked Easy and her friend, and headed for the main lock, long since cleared for use.

Outside, the current had dropped to the point where life-lines were no longer necessary. Water depth was down to about seven feet, measured from the average level of the smallest boulders. The water line was, indeed, at about the most inconvenient possible level for seeing the whole picture. He had to climb part way up the rock, a difficult task in itself, though helped by the fact that he had some buoyancy; from there he had to follow the forward trucks to a point where he could compare the curvature of the big boulder and that of the *Kwembly*'s lower bow. He could not be completely sure, since moving the hull backward would change its pitch, but he did not like what he saw. The human engineer was probably right. Not only was there risk of hull damage, but the steering bar came through the hull just ahead of the mattress by means of a nearly air-tight mechanical seal backed by a liquid trap and made its key connections with the maze of tiller-ropes. Serious damage to the bar would not actually cripple the vehicle, since there was a duplicate aft, but it was not a risk to be taken casually.

The answer to the whole situation was staring him in the face by that time but he was another hour or more in seeing it. A human psychologist, when he heard about this later, was very annoyed. He had been looking for significant differences between human and Mesklinite minds, and was finding what he considered an undue number of points of similarity.

The solution involved work, of course. Even the smallest boulders were heavy. Still, they were numerous, and it was not necessary to go far for a plentiful supply. With the entire crew of the *Kwembly* at the job except for Beetchermarlf and those still helping him with the trucks, a ramp of piled stones grew with fair speed from the stern of the trapped vehicle toward the key rock.

It was a help to Beetchermarlf. As fast as he readied a damaged bearing unit for service, he found himself able to get at new installation sites which had been out of reach before. He and the stone-carriers finished almost together, allowing for four trucks which he had been unable to repair because of missing parts. He had made thrifty use of these, cannibalizing them for the needs of some of the others, and had spotted the unavoidable gaps in traction widely enough to keep the cruiser's weight reasonably well distributed. To work on Row 5, practically buried in the river bottom, he had had to deflate that part of the mattress. Pumping it up again when the two trucks were replaced caused the hull to shift slightly, to the alarm of Dondragmer and several workers underneath; fortunately the motion was insignificant.

The captain had spent most of the time shuttling between the radio, where he kept hoping for a reliable prediction of the next flood, and the work site, where he divided his attention between the progress of the ramp and the view upstream. By the time the ramp was complete the water was less than a yard deep, and the current had ceased entirely; they were in a pool rather than a stream.

It was now full night; the sun had been gone for nearly a hundred hours. The weather had cleared completely, and workers outside could see the violently twinkling stars. Their own sun was not visible; it was barely so at the best of times this deep in Dhrawn's heavy atmosphere, and at the moment was too close to the horizon. Not even Dondragmer knew offhand whether it was slightly above or slightly below. Sol and Fomalhaut, which even the least informed of the crew knew to be indicators of south, glowed and wavered over a low eminence a few miles in that direction. The imaginary line connecting the two had tilted less than twenty degrees, human scale, since dark; the Mesklinite navigators would have said less than four.

Outside the range of the *Kwembly*'s own lights it was almost totally black. Dhrawn is moonless; the stars provide no more illumination than they do on Earth or Mesklin.

Temperature was nearly the same. Dondragmer's scientists had been measuring the environment as completely as their knowledge and equipment allowed, then sending the results to the station above. The captain had been quietly hoping for some useful information in return, though he realized that the human beings didn't owe him any. The reports, after all, were simply part of the job the Mesklinites had engaged to do in the first place.

He had also suggested to his own men that they try some independent thinking. Borndender's answer to what he regarded as sarcasm had been to the effect that if the human beings would supply him with reports from other parts of Dhrawn and with computer time with which to correlate them, he would be glad to try. The captain had not intended sarcasm;

he knew perfectly well the vast difference between explaining why a ship floats on water or ammonia and explaining why 2.3 millicables of 60-20 rain fell at the Settlement between Hour 40 and Hour 100 of Day 2. He suspected that his researcher's misinterpretation had been deliberate; Mesklinites were often quite human when in search of excuses and Borndender was currently feeling annoyed with his own lack of usefulness. Without bringing this aspect of the matter into the open, the captain merely repeated that useful ideas would be welcome, and left the lab.

Even the scientists were ordered outside when the time finally came to use the ramp. Borndender was irritated at this and muttered something as he went about the academic nature of the difference between being inside the *Kwembly* and outside her if anything drastic happened. Dondragmer, however, had not made a suggestion; he had issued an order, and not even the scientists denied either his right or his competence to do so. Only the captain himself, Beetchermarlf and a technician named Kensnee in the life-support compartment were to be aboard when the start was made. Dondragmer had considered acting as his own helmsman and taking a chance on the life equipment but reflected that Beetchermarlf knew the tiller cable layout better and was more likely to sense anything going wrong in that department. Inside power was not directly concerned with motion, but if any slip or collapse of the ramp caused trouble with the life-support system it was better to have someone on hand. This support system was even more important than the cruiser: in an emergency the crew could conceivably walk back to the Settlement carrying their air equipment even if the cruiser were ruined.

The reasoning behind the evacuation order should have left Beetchermarlf and Kensnee as the only ones aboard, with even the captain watching from outside. Dondragmer was not prepared to be so reasonable. He had stayed aboard.

Tension in the crowd of caterpillar like beings gathered outside the monster hull mounted as the drivers took up the slack in their treads. Because Dondragmer could not see the tense crowd from the bridge, he was calm; Beetchermarlf could feel their mood and was perturbed. The human watchers, observing by way of a set which had been taken from the life-support room and secured on a rock projecting from the water a hundred yards from the land-cruiser, could see nothing until the cruiser actually started to move. They were all calm except Easy and Benj.

The boy was paying little attention to the outside view, instead he was watching the bridge screen on which part of Beetchermarlf was visible. He had one set of chelae on the tiller, holding it fast; the other three sets were darting with almost invisible speed among the grips of the engine control lines, trying to equalize the pull of the different trucks. He had made no attempt to power more than the usual ten; the cords which normally cross-connected them, so that a single line would work them all, had been realigned for individual control. Beetchermarlf was very, very busy.

As the *Kwembly* began to inch backward, one of the human beings commented explosively.

"Why in blazes didn't they put remote controls, or at least torque and thrust indicators, on that bridge? That poor bug is going crazy. I don't see how he can tell when a particular set of tracks is even gripping, let alone how it responds to his handling."

"If he had fancy indicators he probably couldn't," replied Mersereau. "Barlennan wanted no more sophisticated gear on those vehicles than his people could repair on the spot, except where there was really no choice. I agreed with him, and so did the rest of the planning board. Look—she's sliding off, smooth as ice."

A chorus of expressive hoots came from the speaker, muffled by the fact that most of the beings emitting them were under water. For a long moment, a score or so of the 'midship trucks were hanging free as the stern of the *Kwembly* came off the ramp and moved back over the river bed. The engineer who had been afraid of the bridge effect crossed his fingers and rolled his eyes upward. Then the bow dipped as the forward trucks came down onto the ramp in their turn, and weight was once more decently distributed. The twisting stress, which no one had considered seriously, lessened as the cruiser eased onto the relatively level cobbling of the river bed and came to a halt. The crew divided and poured around bow and stern to get to the main lock, no one thinking to pick up the communicator. Easy thought of reminding the captain, but decided that it would be more tactful to wait.

Dondragmer had not forgotten the instrument. As the first members of the crew emerged from the inner surface of the lock pool, his voice echoed through the speaking tubes.

"Kervenser! Reffel! Take the scout fliers out at once. Reffel, pick up the communicator outside; make sure the shutter is in the flier before you start; then make a ten-minute sweep north to east and back. Kervenser, sweep west and around to south for the same time. Borndender, report when all your measuring equipment is aboard. Beetchermarlf and Takoorch, outside and realign the engine control cords to normal."

His communicator at the bridge had the sound on, so Easy heard and translated these orders, though the reference to a shutter meant nothing to any of them. She and her colleagues watched the screen of the outside set with interest as the two tiny helicopters rose from the upper lock, one of them sweeping toward the pickup and presumably settling outside its field of view. The other was still climbing as it left the screen, heading west. The picture rocked as the set was picked up by Reffel and wrestled into its space aboard the flier. Easy flicked a switch absent-mindedly to record the scenes for future map work as the viewpoint lifted from the ground.

Dondragmer would have appreciated being able to watch the same screen but could only wait for a relayed verbal report from Reffel or a delayed but direct one from Kervenser. Actually, Reffel did not bother to relay. The ten-minute flights produced no information demanding speedy delivery. What it amounted to, as Dondragmer reported to the human audience, was that the *Kwembly* was in a valley some fifteen miles wide, with walls of bare rock quite steep by Dhrawn's standards. The pilots estimated the slope at twenty to thirty degrees. They were also remarkably high, fully forty feet. To the west there had been no sign of a new flood as far as Kervenser had flown. He noted that the boulders strewing the valley floor gave way to bare rock within a mile or two and there were numerous pools like the one in which the *Kwembly* was now standing. To the east, the stones and pools continued as far as Reffel had gone. Dondragmer pondered these data for a while after relaying this information to the satellite, then ordered one of the fliers back to work.

"Kerv, get back aloft. The helmsmen won't be done for hours yet. Go as far west along the valley as you can in an hour and check as closely as your lights will allow for any sign of more water starting down. Make that three hours, unless you have a positive finding, of course, or have to turn back because of bad visibility. I'm going off watch. Tell Stakendee to take the bridge before you leave."

Even Mesklinites get tired but Dondragmer's thought that this was the right time to get some rest was unfortunate, as Barlennan pointed out to him later. When the captain insisted that there would have been nothing for him to do even if he had been fully alert, his superior gave the Mesklinite equivalent of a snort of contempt.

"You'd have managed to find something. You did later."

Dondragmer refrained from pointing out that this proved that his omission was not a serious error; but he had to admit to himself that it had appeared so at the time.

It was almost eight hours after Kervenser's departure that a crewman hooted outside the door of the captain's quarters. When Dondragmer responded, the other squeezed the situation into a single sentence.

"Sir, Kervenser and the helmsmen are still outside, and the pool of water we're in has frozen."

6: POLICY

Impatience and irritation were noticeable in the Planning Laboratory but so far no tempers had actually been lost. Ib Hoffman, back for less than two hours from a month-long errand to Earth and Dromm, had said practically nothing except to ask for information. Easy, sitting beside him, had said nothing at all so far but she could see that something would have to be done shortly to turn the conversation into constructive channels. Changing the Project's basic policy might be a good idea, it often was. But right now, it was futile for the people at this end of the table to spend time blaming each other for the present one. Still less useful was the scientists' bickering at the other end. They were still wondering why a lake should freeze when the temperature had been rising. A useful answer might lead to some useful action but to Easy it seemed a question for the laboratory rather than for a conference room.

If her husband didn't take a hand in the other discussion soon, she would have to do something herself, she decided.

"I've heard all about that side of it before, and I still don't buy it!" snapped Mersereau. "Up to a point it's good common sense, but I think we're way past that point. I realize that the more complex the equipment, the fewer people you need to run it; but you also need more specialized apparatus and specially trained personnel to maintain and repair it. If the land-cruisers had been as fully automated as some people wanted, we could have gotten along with a hundred Mesklinites on Dhrawn instead of a couple of thousand *at first;* but the chances are that every one of these machines would be out by now because we couldn't possibly have landed all the backup equipment and personnel they'd need. There aren't enough technically trained Mesklinites in existence yet, for one thing. I agreed with that, Barlennan agreed with it; it was common sense, as I said.

"But you, and for some reason Barlennan, went even farther. He was against including helicopters. I know there were some characters in the

Project who assumed you could never teach a Mesklinite to fly, and maybe it was racial acrophobia that was motivating Barlennan; but at least he was able to realize that without air scouting the land-cruisers wouldn't dare travel more than a few miles an hour over new ground, and it would take roughly forever to cover even Low Alpha at that rate. We did convince him on that basis.

"But there was a lot of stuff we'd have been glad to provide, which would have been useful and have paid its way, which *he* talked *us* out of using. No weapons; I agree they'd probably have been futile. But no short-range radio equipment? No intercoms in the Settlement? It's dithering nonsense for Dondragmer to have to call us, six million miles away, and ask us to relay his reports to Barlennan at the Settlement. It's usually not critical, since Barl couldn't help him physically and the time delay doesn't mean much, but it's silly at the best of times. It *is* critical now, though, when Don's first mate has disappeared, presumably within a hundred miles of the *Kwembly* and possibly less than ten, and there's no way in the galaxy to get in touch with him either from here or from the cruiser. Why was Barl against radios, Alan? And why are you?"

"The same reason you've just given," Aucoin answered with just a trace of acerbity. "The maintenance problem."

"You're dithering. There isn't any maintenance problem on a simple voice, or even a vision, communicator. There were four of them, as I understand it, being carried around on Mesklin with Barlennan's first outside-sponsored trip fifty years or so ago, and not one of them gave the slightest trouble. There are sixty on Dhrawn right now, with not a blip of a problem from any of them in the year and a half they've been there. Barlennan must know that, and you certainly do. Furthermore, why do we relay what messages they do send by voice? We could do it automatically instead of having a batch of interpreters hashing things up (sorry, Easy) and you can't tell me there'd be a maintenance problem for a relay unit in this station. Who's trying to kid whom?"

Easy stirred; this was perilously close to feud material. Her husband, however, sensed the motion and touched her arm in a gesture she understood. He would take care of it. However, he let Aucoin make his own answer.

"Nobody's trying to kid anyone. I don't mean equipment maintenance, and I admit it was a poor choice of words. I should have said morale. The Mesklinites are a competent and highly self-reliant species, at least the representatives we've seen the most of. They sail over thousands of miles of ocean on these ridiculous groups of rafts, completely out of touch with home and help for months at a time, just as human beings did a few centuries ago. It was our opinion that making communication too easy would tend to undermine that self-confidence. I admit that this is not certain; Mesklinites are not human, though their minds resemble ours in many ways, and there's one major factor whose effect we can't evaluate and may never be able to. We don't know their normal life spans, though they are clearly a good deal longer than ours. Still, Barlennan agreed with us about the radio question—as you said, it was he who brought it up—and he has never complained about the communication difficulty."

"To us." Ib cut in at this point. Aucoin looked surprised, then puzzled.

"Yes, Alan, that's what I said. He hasn't complained to us. What he thinks about it privately none of us knows."

"But why shouldn't he complain, or even ask for radios, if he has come to feel that he should have them?" The planner was not completely sidetracked, but Easy noted with approval that the defensiveness was gone from his tone.

"I don't know why," Hoffman admitted. "I just remember what I've learned about our first dealings with Barlennan a few decades ago. He was a highly cooperative, practically worshipful agent for the mysterious aliens of Earth and Panesh and Dromm and these other mysterious places in the sky during most of the Gravity mission, doing our work for us just as we asked; then at the end he suddenly held us up for a blackmail jolt which five human beings, seven Paneshka, and nine Drommians out of every ten still think we should never have paid. You know as well as I do that teaching advanced technology, or even basic science, to a culture which isn't yet into its mechanical revolution makes the sociologists see red because they feel that every race should have the right to go through its own kind of growing pains; makes the xenophobes scream because we're arming the wicked aliens against us; gets the historians down on us because we're burying priceless data; and annoys the administrative types because they're afraid we're setting up problems they haven't learned to cope with yet."

"It's the xenophobes who are the big problem," Mersereau snapped. "The nuts who take it for granted that every non-human species would be an enemy if it had the technical capacity. That's why we give the Mesklinites only equipment they can't possibly duplicate themselves, like the fusion units: things which couldn't be taken apart and studied in detail without about five stages of intermediate equipment like gamma-ray diffraction cameras, which the Mesklinites don't have either. Alan's argument sounds good, but it's just an excuse. You know as well as I do that you could train a Mesklinite to fly a reasonably part-automated shuttle in two months if the controls were modified for his nippers, and that there isn't a scientist in this station who wouldn't give three quarts of his blood to have loads of physical specimens and instruments of his own improvising bouncing between here and Dhrawn's surface."

"That's not entirely right, though there are elements of truth in it," Hoffman returned calmly. "I agree with your personal feeling about xenophobes, but it is a fact that with energy so cheap that a decently designed interstellar freighter can pay off its construction cost in four or five years, an interstellar war isn't the flat impossibility it was once assumed to be. Also, you know why this station has such big rooms, uncomfortable as some of us find them and inefficient as they certainly are for some purposes. The average Drommian, if there were a room here he couldn't get into, would assume that it contained something being deliberately kept secret from him. They have no concept of privacy, and by our standards most of them are seriously paranoid. If we had failed to share technology with them when contact was first made, we'd have created a planetful of highly competent xenophobes much more dangerous than anything even Earth has produced. I don't know that Mesklinites would react the same way, but I still think that starting the College on Mesklin was the smartest piece of policy since they admitted the first Drommian student to M.I.T."

"And the Mesklinites had to blackmail us into doing *that.*"

"Embarrassingly true," admitted Hoffman. "But that's all side issue. The current point is that we just don't know what Barlennan really thinks or plans. We can, though, be perfectly sure that he didn't agree to take two thousand of his people including himself onto an almost completely unknown world, certain to be highly dangerous even for a species like his, without having a very good reason indeed."

"We gave him a good reason," pointed out Aucoin.

"Yes. We tried to imitate him in the art of blackmail. We agreed to keep the College going on Mesklin, over the objections of many of our own people, if he would do the Dhrawn job for us. There was no suggestion on either side of material payment, though the Mesklinites are perfectly aware of the relation between knowledge and material wealth. I'm quite willing to admit that Barlennan is an idealist, but I'm not sure how much chauvinism there is in his idealism or how far either one will carry him.

"All this is beside the point, too. We shouldn't be worrying about the choice of equipment provided for the Mesklinites. They agreed with the choice, whatever their private reservations may have been. We are still in a position to help them with information on physical facts they don't know and which their scientists can hardly be expected to work out for themselves. We have high-speed computation. Right now we have one extremely expensive exploring machine frozen in on a lake on Dhrawn, together with about a hundred living beings who may be personnel to some of us but are personalities to the rest. If we want to change policy and insist on Barlennan's accepting a shuttleful of new equipment, that's fine; but it's not the present problem, Boyd. I don't know what we could send down right now that would be the slightest help to Dondragmer."

"I suppose you're right, Ib, but I can't help thinking about Kervenser, and how much better it would have been if—"

"He could have carried one of the communicators, remember. Dondragmer had three besides the one on his bridge, all of them portable. The decision to take them or not was strictly on Kervenser himself and his captain. Let's leave out the if's for now and try to do some constructive planning."

Mersereau subsided, a little irritated at Ib for the latter's choice of words but with his resentment of Aucoin's attitude diverted for the moment. The planner took over the conversational lead again, looking down the table toward the end where the scientists had now fallen silent.

"All right, Dr. McDevitt. Has any agreement been reached as to what probably happened?"

"Not completely, but there is an idea worth checking further. As you know, the *Kwembly*'s observers had been reporting nearly constant temperature since the fog cleared; no radiational cooling; if anything, a very slight warming trend. Barometric readings have been rising very slowly at that place ever since the machine was stranded; readings before that time are meaningless because of the uncertain change in elevation. The temperatures have been well below the freezing points of either pure water or pure ammonia but rather above that of the ammonia monohydrate-water eutectic. We're wondering whether the initial thaw might not have been caused by the ammonia fog's reacting with the water snow on which the *Kwembly* was riding. Dondragmer was afraid of that possibility; and if so, the present freeze might be due to evaporation of ammonia from the eutectic. We'd need ammidity readings—"

"What?" Hoffman and Aucoin cut in almost together.

"Sorry. Office slang. Partial pressure of ammonia relative to the saturation value—equivalent of relative humidity for water. We'd need readings on that to confirm or kill the notion, and of course the Mesklinites haven't been taking them."

"Could they?"

"I'm sure we could work out a technique with them. I don't know how long it would take. Water vapor wouldn't interfere; its equilibrium pressure is four or five powers of ten smaller than ammonia's in that temperature range. The job shouldn't be too hard."

"I realize this is an hypothesis rather than a full-blown theory, but is it good enough to base action on?"

"That would depend on the action." Aucoin made a gesture of impatience, and the atmospheric physicist continued hastily.

"That is, I wouldn't risk an all-or-nothing breakout effort on it alone, but I'd be willing to try anything which didn't commit the *Kwembly* to exhausting some critical supply she carries, or put her in obvious danger."

The planner nodded. "All right," he said. "Would you rather stay here and supply us with more ideas, or would it be more effective to talk this one over with the Mesklinites?"

McDevitt pursed his lips and thought for a moment.

"We've been talking with them pretty frequently, but I suppose there's more good likely to come from that direction than—" he stopped, and Easy and her husband concealed smiles. Aucoin nodded, appearing not to notice the *faux pas.*

"All right. Go on back to Communications, and good luck. Let us know if either you or they come up with anything else that seems worth trying."

The four scientists assented and left together. The ten remaining conference members were silent for some minutes before Aucoin voiced what all but one were thinking.

"Let's face it," he said slowly. "The real argument is going to come when we relay this report to Barlennan."

Ib Hoffman jerked upright. "You haven't yet?" he snapped.

"Only the fact of the original stranding, which Easy told them, and occasional progress reports on the repair work. Nothing yet about the freeze-up."

"Why not?" Easy could read danger signals in her husband's voice, and wondered whether she wanted to smooth this one over or not. Aucoin looked surprised at the question.

"You know why as well as I do. Whether he learned about it now or ten hours from now or from Dondragmer when he gets back to the Settlement a year from now would make little difference. There is nothing Barlennan could do immediately to help, and the only thing he could do at all is something we'd rather he didn't."

"And that is?" interjected Easy sweetly. She had about made up her mind which line to take.

"That is, as you well know, sending one of the two land-cruisers still at the Settlement off to rescue the *Kwembly,* as he wanted to do for the *Esket.*"

"And you still object to that."

"Certainly, for exactly the same reasons as before—which Barlennan, I admit, accepted that time. It's not entirely that we have other specific plans for those two cruisers, but that's part of it. Whatever you may think, Easy, I don't dismiss life as unimportant merely because it isn't human life. I do object, though, to wasting time and resources. Changing policy in the middle of an operation generally does both."

"But if you claim that Mesklinite lives mean as much to you as human ones, how can you talk about waste?"

"You're not thinking, Easy. I understand and don't really blame you, but you're ignoring the fact that the *Kwembly* is something like ten thousand miles airline from the Settlement, and more like thirteen thousand by the route they took. A rescue vehicle could not possibly cover that track in less than two hundred or two hundred and fifty hours. The last part of it, which the *Kwembly* traversed by being washed down a river, might not be findable and the last four thousand miles across the snow field may no longer be passable."

"We could give them directions with satellite fixes."

"We could, no doubt. The fact remains that unless Dondragmer can get himself, his crew, and his vehicle out of their present trouble, nothing Barlennan can send out for him is likely to be of the slightest help *if* the *Kwembly* is in real and immediate danger. If she is not, if it's just a matter of being frozen in like a nineteenth-century whaler, they have indefinite supplies with their closed-cycle life system and fusion converters and we and Barlennan can plan a nice, leisurely rescue."

"Like Destigmet's *Esket,"* retorted the woman with some bitterness. "It's been over seven months, and you squelched all rescue talk then and ever since!"

"That was a very different situation. The *Esket* is still standing there, unchanged as far as her vision sets can tell us, but her crew has dropped out of sight. We haven't the faintest idea what has happened to them but since they're not on board and haven't been for all this time it's impossible to believe they're still alive. Even with all their abilities and physical toughness, Mesklinites couldn't live on Dhrawn for seven months without a good deal more equipment than their air suits."

Easy had no answer. On pure logic, Aucoin was perfectly right; but she could not accept the idea that the situation was purely logical. Ib knew how she felt and decided that the time had come to change course again. He shared the planner's opinion, up to a point, on basic policy; he also knew why his wife could not possibly accept it.

"The real, immediate problem, as I see it," Hoffman interjected, "is the one Don has with the men who are still outside. As I get it, two are under the ice, as far as anyone can tell; and no one seems to know whether that puddle is frozen to the bottom. In any case, judging by the work they were supposed to be doing, they're in among the *Kwembly*'s trucks somewhere. I suppose that means a straight icepick-and-search job. I can't guess what the chances are of an air suited Mesklinite's living through that sort of thing. The temperature won't bother them that far below melting water ice, but I don't know what other physiological limitations they may have.

"Don's first officer is also missing, overdue from a helicopter flight. We can't help directly, since he didn't take a communicator with him, but there is another flier available. Has Dondragmer asked us to assist while a search is made with the other machine and a vision set?"

"He hadn't up to half an hour ago," replied Mersereau.

"Then I strongly advise that we suggest it to him."

Aucoin nodded agreement, and glanced at the woman. "Your job, I'd say, Easy."

"If someone hasn't beaten me to it." She rose, pinched Ib's ear in passing, and left the room.

"Next point," Hoffman went on. "Granting that you may be right in opposing a rescue expedition from the Settlement, I think it's time Barlennan was brought up to date about the *Kwembly.*"

"Why ask for more troubles than we need?" retorted Aucoin. "I don't like to argue with anyone, especially when he doesn't really have to listen to me."

"I don't think you'll have to argue. Remember, he agreed with us the other time."

"You were saying a few minutes ago that you weren't sure how sincere his agreements have been."

"I'm not, but if he had been strongly against us that time he'd have done just what he wanted and sent a crew out to help the *Esket.* He did, remember, on a couple of other occasions when there was a cruiser in trouble."

"That was much closer to the settlement, and we finally approved the action," retorted Aucoin.

"And you know as well as I do that we approved it because we could see that he was going to do it anyway."

"We approved it, Ib, because your wife was on Barlennan's side both times and out-talked us. Your argument, incidentally, is a point against telling him about the present situation."

"Whose side was she on during the *Esket* argument? I still think we should tell Barlennan the present situation pronto. Plain honesty aside, the longer we wait the more certain he is to find out, sooner or later, that we've been censoring expedition reports on him."

"I wouldn't call it censoring. We've never changed a thing."

"But you have delayed the relay plenty of times while you decided what he ought to know, and as I've said before I don't think that's the game as we agreed to play it with him. Pardon my reactionary sentiments, but on purely selfish grounds we'd be well advised to keep his confidence as long as possible."

Several of the others, who had listened in silence up to this point, spoke up almost at once when Hoffman expressed this sentiment. It took Aucoin several seconds to untangle their words, but it eventually became clear that the feeling of the group was with Ib. The chairman yielded gracefully; his technique did not involve standing in front of the bull.

"All right, we pass on the complete report to Barlennan as soon as we adjourn." He glanced at the winner. "That is, if Mrs. Hoffman hasn't sent it already. What's the next point?"

One of the men who had done little but listen up to this point asked a question. "Forgive me if I didn't follow you too clearly a few minutes ago. Ib, you and Alan both claim that Barlennan agreed with Project policy in limiting to an absolute minimum the amount of sophisticated equipment his expedition was to use. That was my understanding also; but you, Ib, just mentioned having doubts about Barlennan's sincerity. Do any of those doubts stem from his accepting the helicopters?"

Hoffman shook his head. "No. The arguments we used for their necessity were good, and the only surprising thing to me was that Barlennan didn't anticipate them and take the equipment without argument."

"But Mesklinites are acrophobic by nature. The thought of flying, to anyone from a world like that, must be just unimaginable."

Ib smiled grimly. "True. But one of the first things Barlennan did after he made his deal with the Gravity people and started learning basic science was to design, build and fly, on Mesklin, in the polar zone where gravity is at its highest, a hot air balloon. Whatever is motivating Barlennan, it isn't acrophobia. I don't exactly doubt him; I'm just not sure of his thinking, if you'll forgive a rather crude quibble."

"I agree," Aucoin interjected. "And I think we're running dry. I suggest we break up for, say, six hours. We can think, or go down to Comm and listen to the Mesklinites or talk with them; anything that will keep your thoughts on Dhrawn questions. You know my ideas about that."

"That's where mine have been." It was the same speaker. "I keep wondering about the *Esket,* every time one of the cruisers runs into trouble, even when the trouble is obviously natural."

"So do we all, I imagine," rejoined Aucoin.

"The more I think of it, the more I feel that her crew must have run into intelligent opposition. After all, we know there is life on Dhrawn, more than the bushes and pseudo-algae the Mesklinites have found. They wouldn't account quantitatively for that atmosphere; there must be a complete ecological complex somewhere. I'd guess in the higher-temperature regions."

"Such as Low Alpha." Hoffman completed the thought. "Yes, you don't have ammonia and free oxygen in the same environment for very long, on the time scale of a planet. I can believe the possibility of an intelligent species here. We haven't found any sign of it from space and the Mesklinite ground parties haven't met it, unless the *Esket* did, but seventeen billion square miles of planet make a lot of good reasons for that. The idea is plausible and you're not the first to get it but I don't know where it leaves us. Barlennan thought of it too, according to Easy, and debated sending another cruiser to the area of the *Esket*'s loss specifically to seek and contact any intelligence that may be there; but even Barlennan was doubtful about undertaking a search. We certainly haven't pushed it."

"Why not?" cut in Mersereau. "If we could get in touch with natives as we did on Mesklin the project could really get going! We wouldn't have to depend so completely on—oh."

Aucoin smiled grimly.

"Precisely," he said. "Now you *have* found a good reason for wondering about Barlennan's frankness. I'm not saying that he's an ice-hearted politician who would give up the lives of his men just to keep a hammerlock on the Dhrawn operation, but the *Esket*'s crew was pretty certainly already beyond rescue when he finally agreed not to send the *Kalliff* in the same direction."

"There is another point, though," Hoffman said thoughtfully.

"What?"

"I'm not sure it's worth mentioning, since we can't evaluate it; but the *Kwembly* is commanded by Dondragmer, who is a long-time associate of Barlennan's and should by ordinary reasoning be an extremely close friend. Is there any chance that his being involved would influence Barl's judgment about a rescue trip or even make him order one against his better judgment? Like you, I don't think that caterpillar is just an administrative machine. His cold-bloodedness is purely physical."

"I've wondered about that, too," the chief planner admitted. "It surprised me greatly months ago when he let Dondragmer go out at all. I'd gotten the impression that he didn't want him to take major chances. I didn't worry too much about it—certainly no one knows enough about Mesklinite psychology in general or Barlennan's in particular to base any serious planning on. If anyone does, Ib, it's your wife, and she can't or won't put what she understands about them into words. As you say, we can't assign weight to the friendship-influence possibility. We just add it to the list of questions. Let me hear any ideas about those crewmen who are presumably frozen under the *Kwembly* and then we really must break up."

"A fusion converter would keep a good, large heating coil going, and resistors aren't very complex equipment," Mersereau pointed out. "Heaters aren't a very unreasonable piece of equipment on Dhrawn, either. If only—"

"But we didn't," interrupted Aucoin.

"But we did, if you'd let me finish. There are enough converters with the *Kwembly* to lift her off the planet if their energy could be applied to such a job. There must be some metal aboard which could be jury-rigged into resistors or arcs. Whether the Mesklinites could operate such gadgets I don't know. There must be a limit even to their temperature tolerance but we might at least ask if they've thought of such a thing."

"You're wrong on one point. I know there is very little metal either in their equipment or the supplies on those land-cruisers and I'd be startled if Mesklinite rope turned out to be a conductor. I'm no chemist, but anything bonded as firmly as that stuff must have its electrons pretty well latched in place. By all means check with Dondragmer, though. Easy is presumably still in Comm; she can help you if there are no linguistically broad Mesklinites on duty at the other end. We're adjourned."

Mersereau nodded, already heading toward the door, and the meeting broke up. Aucoin followed Mersereau through one door; most of the others went other ways. Only Hoffman remained seated at the table.

His eyes were focused nowhere in particular, and there was a frown on his face which made him look older than his forty years.

He liked Barlennan. He liked Dondragmer even better, as did his wife. He had no grounds for the slightest complaint about the progress of the Dhrawn research, considering the policies he himself had helped set up, nor did the rest of the planners. There was no concrete reason whatever, except a trick of half a century before, to distrust the Mesklinite commander. That he might want to keep hypothetical natives of Dhrawn out of the picture could hardly be given credence. No, certainly not. After all, the problems of transferring responsibility to such beings, even if they existed, for the Dhrawn research project, would cause even more delay, as Barlennan would surely realize.

The occasional case of disagreement between explorers and planners was minor. It was the sort of thing which happened ten times as often with, say, Drommians. No, there was no reason to suppose the Mesklinites were already going off on independent plans of their own.

Still, Barlennan had not wanted helicopters, though he had finally been persuaded to accept them. He was the same Barlennan who had built and flown in a hot air balloon as his first exercise in applied science.

He had not sent relief to the *Esket,* although all the giant land-cruisers were necessary for the Project and despite the fact that a hundred or so of his people were aboard.

He had refused local-range radios, useful as they would obviously be. The argument against them was the sort that a firm-minded teacher might use in a classroom situation, but this was real life and deadly earnest.

He had, fifty years before, not only jumped at the chance to acquire alien knowledge; he had maneuvered deliberately to force his non-Mesklinite sponsors to give it to him.

Ib Hoffman could not rid himself of the notion that Barlennan was up to something underhanded again.

He wondered what Easy thought about it.

7: Iced Wagon

Beetchermarlf and Takoorch, like the rest of the *Kwembly*'s crew, were taken by surprise when the lake froze. Neither had had any occasion for several hours to look around, since the maze of fine cords on which their attention was focused was considerably more complicated than, say, the rigging of a clipper ship. Both knew exactly what to do, and there was little need for conversation. Even had their eyes wandered from the job, there was little else to see. They were under the immense bulk of their vehicle, roofed by the pneumatic "mattress" which distributed its weight among the trucks, walled partly by the trucks themselves and partly by the blackness of Dhrawn's night which swallowed everything beyond the range of their little portable lights.

So they had not seen, any more than the sailors inside the *Kwembly*, the tiny crystals which began to form at the surface of the lake and settle to the bottom, glinting and sparkling in the *Kwembly*'s floods.

They had completed reconnecting on the port row, Number 1, all the way from bow to stern and were working their way forward on Row 2 when they discovered that they were trapped.

Takoorch's battery light was fading a trifle, and he took it over to the nearest fusion converter, which happened to be on a Row 1 truck, for recharging. He was quite startled to find that he couldn't get at or even see the converter; after a few seconds of fumbling and looking he called Beetchermarlf. It took nearly ten minutes for them to establish that they were completely enclosed by an opaque white wall, impenetrable even to their strength. It had welded all the outer trucks together and filled all the spaces between them from mattress above to cobbles below, nearly three feet of height, on the average. Inside the wall they were still free to move about.

Their tools were edged rather than pointed, and too small to make appreciable way against the ice, though it took fully an hour of scraping to convince them both of that. Neither was greatly concerned as yet; obviously the ice was immobilizing the *Kwembly,* and the rest of the crew would have to dig down to them in the interest of freeing the vehicle if not for the prime purpose of rescue. Of course their supply of life hydrogen was limited, but this meant less to them than a corresponding oxygen shortage would have to a human being. They had at least ten or twelve hours yet of full activity, and when the hydrogen partial pressure dropped below a certain value they would simply lose consciousness. Their body chemistry would slow down more and more, but fifty and perhaps a hundred hours would pass before anything irreversible occurred. One of the reasons for Mesklinite durability, though human biologists had had no chance to find it out, was the remarkable simplicity of their biochemistry.

The two were calm enough, in fact, to go back to their assigned work; and they were almost to the front of Row 2 before another discovery was made. This one did perturb them.

The ice was creeping inward. It was not coming rapidly, but it was coming. As it happened, neither of them knew any better than Ib Hoffman what being frozen into a block of the stuff was likely to do to them. Neither had the slightest desire to learn.

At least there was still light. Not all the power units were on outside trucks, and Takoorch had been able to recharge his battery. This made it possible to make another, very careful search of the boundaries of their prison. Beetchermarlf was hoping to find unfrozen space either near the bottom or, preferably, near the top of the walls around them. He did not know whether the freezing would have started from the top or the bottom of the pond. He was not familiar, as any human being would have been, with the fact that ice floats on liquid water. This was just as well, since it would have led him to an erroneous conclusion in this instance. The crystals had indeed formed at the top, but they had been denser than the surrounding liquid and had settled, only to redissolve as they reached levels richer in ammonia. This pseudo-convection effect had had the result of robbing the lake rather uniformly of ammonia until it had reached a composition able to freeze almost simultaneously throughout. As a result, the search turned up no open spaces.

For some time the two lay between two of the trucks, thinking and occasionally checking to see how far the freezing had progressed. They had no time measuring equipment, and therefore no basis for estimating the speed of the process. Takoorch guessed that it was slowing down; Beetchermarlf was less sure.

Occasionally an idea would strike one of them but the other usually managed to find a flaw in it.

"We can move some of these stones, the smaller ones," Takoorch remarked at one point. "Why can't we dig our way under the ice?"

"Where to?" countered his companion. "The nearest edge of the lake is forty or fifty cables away, or was the last I knew. We couldn't begin to dig that far in these rocks before our air gave out, even if there was any reason to suppose the freezing didn't include the water between the rocks underneath. Coming up before the edge wouldn't get us anywhere."

Takoorch admitted the justice of this with an acquiescent gesture and silence fell while the ice grew a fraction of an inch nearer.

Beetchermarlf had the next constructive thought.

"These lights must give off some heat, even if we can't feel it through the suits," he suddenly exclaimed. "Why shouldn't they keep the ice from forming near them, and even let us melt our way to the outside?"

"Worth trying," was Takoorch's laconic answer.

Together they approached the frosty barrier. Beetchermarlf built a small cairn of stones leaning against the ice, and set the light, adjusted for full brightness, at its top. Then both crowded close, their front ends part way up the heap of pebbles, and watched the space between the lamp and the ice.

"Come to think of it," Takoorch remarked as they waited, "our bodies give off some heat, don't they? Shouldn't our just being here help melt this stuff?"

"I suppose so." Beetchermarlf was dubious. "We'd better watch to make sure that it doesn't freeze at each side and around behind us while we're waiting here."

"What will that matter? If it does, it means that we and the light together are enough to fight the freezing and we should be able to melt our way out."

"That's true. Watch, though, so we'll know if that's happening." Takoorch gestured agreement. They fell silent again.

The older helmsman, however, was not one to endure silence indefinitely, and presently he gave utterance to another idea.

"I know our knives didn't make much impression on the ice, but shouldn't it help if we did some scraping right here where it's nearest the light?" He unclipped one of the blades they carried for general use and reached toward the ice.

"Wait a minute!" exclaimed Beetchermarlf. "If you start working there, how are we ever going to know whether the heat is having any effect?"

"If my knife gets us anywhere, who cares whether it's the heat or the work?" retorted Takoorch. Beetchermarlf found no good answer ready, so he subsided, muttering something about "controlled experiments" while the other Mesklinite went to work with his tiny blade.

As it happened, his interference did not spoil the experiment, though it may have delayed slightly the appearance of observable results. Body heat, lamp heat, and knife all together proved unequal to the job; the ice continued to gain. They had to remove the lamps from the cairn at last, and watch the latter slowly become enveloped in the crystalline wall.

"It won't be long now," Takoorch remarked as he swung the lights around them. "Only two of the power units are free, now. Should we charge up the lights again before they go, or isn't it worth the trouble?"

"We might as well," answered Beetchermarlf. "It seems a pity that that's the only use we can get out of all that power. Four of those things can push the *Kwembly* around on level ground and I once heard a human being say that one could do it if it could get traction. That certainly could chip ice for us if we could find a way to apply it."

"We can take the power box out easily enough, but what we'd do afterward beats me. The units put out electric current as one choice, but I don't see how we could shock the ice away. The mechanical torque you can get from them works only on the motor shafts."

"We'd be more likely to shock ourselves away if we used the current. I don't know very much about electricity, it was mostly plain mechanics I got in the little time I was at the College, but I know enough of it can kill. Think of something else."

Takoorch endeavored to comply. Like his young companion, he had had only a short period of exposure to alien knowledge; both had volunteered for the Dhrawn project in preference to further classwork. Their knowledge of general physics might have compared fairly well with that of Benj Hoffman when he was ten or twelve years old. Neither was really comfortable in thinking about matters for which no easily visualized model could be furnished.

They were not, however, lacking in the ability to think abstractly. Both had heard of heat as representing a lowest common denominator of energy, even if they didn't picture it as random particle motion.

It was Beetchermarlf who first thought of another effect of electricity.

"Tak! Remember the explanations we got about not putting too much power into the trucks until the cruiser got moving? The humans said it was possible to snap the treads or damage the motors if we tried to accelerate too fast."

"That's right. Quarter power is the limit below a hundred cables per hour."

"Well, we have the power controls here where we can get at them, and those motors certainly aren't going to turn. Why not just power this truck and let the motor get as hot as it wants to?"

“What makes you think it will get hot? You don’t know what makes those motors go any more than I do. They didn’t say it would make them hot, just that it was bad for them.”

“I know, but what else could it be? You know that any sort of energy that isn’t used up some other way turns into heat.”

“”That doesn’t sound quite right, somehow,” returned the older sailor. “Still, I guess anything is worth trying now. They didn’t say anything about the motor’s wrecking the rest of the ship too; if it ruins us, well, we won’t be much worse off.”

Beetchermarlf paused; the thought that he might be endangering the *Kwembly* hadn’t crossed his mind. The more he thought of it, the less he felt justified in taking the chance. He looked at the relatively tiny power unit nestling between the treads of the nearby truck, and wondered whether such a minute thing could really be a danger to the huge bulk above them. Then he remembered the vastly greater size of the machine which had brought him and his fellows to Dhrawn and realized that the sort of power which could hurl such immense masses through the sky was not to be handled casually. He would never be afraid to *use* such engines, since he had been given a chance to become familiar with their normal and proper handling; but deliberately *misusing* one of them was a different story.

“You’re right,” he admitted somewhat inaccurately. Takoorch had been, after all, willing to take the chance. “We’ll have to work it differently. Look, if the tracks are free to turn, then we can’t damage the motor or the power box and just stirring up water will warm it.”

“You think so? I remember hearing something like that, but if I can’t break up this ice with my own strength it’s hard to see how simply stirring water is going to do it. Besides, the trucks aren’t free; they’re on the bottom with the *Kwembly*’s weight on them.”

“Right. You wanted to dig. Start moving rocks; that ice is getting close.”

Beetchermarlf set the example and began prying the rounded cobbles from the edges of the treads. It was a hard job even for Mesklinite muscles. Smooth as they were, the stones were tightly packed; furthermore when one was moved, there was not too much room in which to put it. The stones under the treads, which were the ones which really had to be shifted, could not even be reached until those at the sides were out of the way. The two labored furiously to clear a ditch around the truck. They were frightened at the time it took.

When the ditch was deep enough, they tried to pry stones from under the treads and this was even more discouraging.

The *Kwembly* had a mass of about two hundred tons. On Dhrawn, this meant a weight of sixteen million pounds to distribute among the fifty-six remaining trucks: the mattress did a good job of distributing. Three hundred thousand pounds, even if it is a rather short three hundred thousand, is too much even for a Mesklinite, whose weight, even at Mesklin's pole, is little over three hundred. It is a great deal even for some eight square feet of caterpillar tread. If Dhrawn's gravity had not done an equally impressive job of packing its surface materials, the *Kwembly* and her sister vehicles would probably have sunk to their mattresses before travelling a yard.

In other words, the rocks under the tread were held quite firmly. Nothing the two sailors could do would move one of them at all. There was nothing to use as a lever; their ample supplies of spare rope were useless without pulleys; their unaided muscles were pitifully inadequate—a situation still less familiar to them than to races whose mechanical revolution lay a few centuries in the past.

The approaching ice, however, was a stimulus to thought. It could also have been a stimulus to panic but neither of the sailors was prone to that form of disintegration. Again, it was Beetchermarlf who led.

"Tak, get out from under. We can move those pebbles. Get forward; they're going to go the other way." The youngster was climbing the truck as he spoke, and Takoorch grasped the idea at once. He vanished beyond the next-forward truck without a word. Beetchermarlf stretched out along the main body of the drive unit, between the treads. In this foot-wide space, beneath and in front of him, was the recess which held the power converter. This was a rectangular object about the same size as the communicators, with ring-tipped control rods projecting from its surface and guide loops equipped with tiny pulleys at the edges. Lines for remote handling from the bridge were threaded through some of the guides and attached to the rings but the helmsman ignored them. He could see little, since the lights were still on the bottom several feet away and the top of the truck was in shadow; however, he did not need sight. Even clad in an air suit he could handle these levers by touch.

Carefully he eased the master reactor control to the "operate" position; then, even more gingerly, started the motors forward. They responded properly; the treads on either side of him moved forward, and a clattering of small, hard objects against each other became audible for a moment. Then this ceased, and the treads began to race. Beetchermarlf instantly cut off the power, and crawled off the truck to see what had happened.

The plan had worked, just as a computer program with a logic error works: there is an answer forthcoming but not the one desired. As the helmsman had planned, the treads had scuffed the rocks under them backward; but he had forgotten the effect of the pneumatic mattress above.

The truck had settled under its own weight and the downward thrust of the gas pressure until the chassis between the treads had met the bottom. Looking up, Beetchermarlf could see the bulge in the mattress where the entire drive unit had been let down some four inches.

Takoorch appeared from his shelter and looked the situation over, but said nothing. There was nothing useful to say.

Neither of them could guess how much more give there was to the mattress, and how much further the truck would have to be let down before it would really hang free, though they knew the details of the *Kwembly*'s construction. The mattress was not a single gas bag but was divided into thirty separate cells, having two trucks in tandem attached to each. The helmsmen knew the details of the attachment—both had just spent many hours repairing the assemblies—but even the recent display of the *Kwembly*'s underside with the weight off nearly all the trucks left them very doubtful about how far any one truck could extend by itself.

"Well, back to stone lugging," remarked Takoorch as he worked his nippers under a pebble. "Maybe these have been jarred loose now; otherwise it's going to be awkward, getting at them only from the ends."

"There isn't enough time for the job. The ice is still growing toward us. We might have to get the treads a whole body-length deeper before they'll run free. Leave the trucks alone, Tak. We'll have to try something else."

"All I want to know is what."

Beetchermarlf showed him. Taking a light with him this time, he climbed once more to the top of the truck. Takoorch followed, mystified. The younger sailor reared up against the shaft which formed the swiveling support of the truck, and attacked the mattress with his knife.

"But you can't hurt the ship!" Takoorch objected.

"We can fix it later. I don't like it any better than you do, and I'd gladly let the air out by the regular bleeder valve if we could only reach it; but we can't, and if we don't get the load off this truck very soon we won't do it at all." He continued slashing as he spoke.

It was little easier than moving the stones. The mattress fabric was extremely thick and tough; to support the *Kwembly* it had to hold in a pressure more than a hundred pounds per square inch above the ground. One of the nuisances of the long trips was the need to pump the cells up manually or to bleed off excess pressure, when the height of the ground they were traversing changed more than a few feet. At the moment the mattress was a little flat, since no pumping had been done after the run down the river, but the inner pressure was that much higher.

Again and again Beetchermarlf sliced at the same point on the taut-stretched surface. Each time the blade went just a little deeper. Takoorch, convinced at last of the necessity, joined him. The second blade's path crossed that of the first, the two flashing alternately in a rhythm almost too fast for a human eye to follow. A human witness, had one been possible, would have expected them to sever each other's nippers at any moment.

Even so, it took many minutes to get through. The first warning of success was a fine stream of bubbles which spread in all directions up the slope of the bulging gas cell. A few more slashes and the cross-shaped hole with its inch-long arms was gushing Dhrawnian air in a flood of bubbles that made the work invisible. The prisoners ceased their efforts.

Slowly but visibly the stretched fabric was collapsing. The bubbles fled more slowly across its surface, gathering at the high point near the wall of ice. For a few moments Beetchermarlf thought the fabric would go entirely flat, but the weight of the suspended truck prevented that. The center of the cell or the point at which the truck was attached (neither of them knew just where the cell boundaries were) was straining downward: it was now pull instead of push.

"I'll start the engine again and see what happens," said Beetchermarlf. "Get forward again for a minute." Takoorch obeyed. The younger helmsman deliberately wedged a number of pebbles under the front ends of the treads, climbed the truck once more and settled down. He had kept the light with him this time, not to help him with handling controls but to make it easier to tell how and whether the unit moved. He looked at the point of attachment a few inches above him as he started the engine once more.

The pebbles had provided some traction; the fabric wrinkled and the swivel tilted slightly as the truck strained forward. An upper socket, inaccessible inside the cell, into which the shaft telescoped, prevented the tilt from exceeding a few degrees. The trucks, of course, could not be allowed to touch each other but the strain could be seen. As the motion reached its limit the trucks continued moving, but this time they did not race free. Sound and tactile vibrations both indicated that they were slipping on the pebbles and after a few seconds the feel of swirling, eddying water became perceptible against Beetchermarlf's air suit. He started to climb down from the truck and was nearly swept under one of the treads as he shifted grips. He barely stopped the motor in time with a hasty snatch at the control. He needed several seconds to regain his composure after that; even his resilient physique could hardly have survived being worked through the space between treads and rocks. At the very least, his air suit would have been ruined.

Then he took time to trace very carefully the control cords leading from the reactor to the upper guides along the bottom of the mattress, following them by eye to the point above the next truck forward where he could reach them. A few seconds later he was on top of the other truck, starting the motor up again from a safe distance and mentally kicking himself for not having done it that way from the beginning.

Takoorch reappeared beside him and remarked, "Well, we'll soon know whether stirring water up does any warming."

"It will," replied Beetchermarlf. "Besides, the treads are rubbing against the stones on the bottom instead of kicking them out of the way this time. Whether or not you believe that stirring makes heat, you certainly know that friction does. Watch the ice, or tell me if the neighborhood is getting too hot. I'm at the lowest power setting, but that's still a lot of energy."

Takoorch rather pessimistically went over to a point where the cairn should be visible if it were ever freed of ice. He settled down to wait. The currents weren't too bad here, though he could feel them tugging at his not-too-well-ballasted body. He anchored himself to a couple of medium-sized rocks and stopped worrying about being washed under the treads.

He did not really see how merely stirring water could heat anything but Beetchermarlf's point about friction was comforting. Also, while he would not have admitted it in so many words, he tended to give more weight to the younger sailor's opinion than to his own and he fully expected to see the ice yielding very shortly.

He was not disappointed; within five minutes he thought that more of the stony bottom was becoming visible between him and the barrier. In ten he was sure, and a hoot of glee apprised Beetchermarlf of the fact. The latter took the risk of leaving the control lines untended to come to see for himself and agreed. The ice was retreating. Immediately he began to plan.

"All right, Tak. Let's get the other units going as fast as they melt free and we can get at their controls. We should be able to melt the *Kwembly* loose from this thing, besides getting ourselves out from under."

Takoorch asked a question.

"Are you going to puncture the cells under all the powered units? That will let the air out of a third of the mattress."

Beetchermarlf was taken slightly aback.

"I'd forgotten that. No, well, we could patch them all, but—no, that's not so good. Let's see. When we get another power unit clear we can mount it on the other truck that's on this cell we've drained already; that will give us twice as much heat. After that I don't know. We could see about digging under the others—no, that didn't work so well—I don't know. Well, we can set one more driver going, anyway. Maybe that will be enough."

"We can hope," said Takoorch dubiously. The youngster's uncertainty had rather disappointed him, and he wasn't too impressed with the toned-down substitute for a plan; but he had nothing better himself to offer. "What do I do first?" he asked.

"I'd better go back and stand by those ropes, though I suppose everything's safe enough," replied Beetchermarlf indirectly. "Why don't you keep checking around the edges of the ice, and get hold of another converter as soon as one is unfrozen? We can put it into that truck," he indicated the other one attached to the deflated cell, "and start it up as soon as possible. All right?"

Takoorch gestured agreement and started surveying of the ice barrier. Beetchermarlf returned to the control lines, waiting passively. Takoorch made several circuits of the boundary, watching happily as the ice retreated in all directions. He was a little bothered by the discovery that the process was slowing down as the cleared space increased but even he was not too surprised. He made up his mind eventually which of the frozen-in power boxes would be the first to be released and settled down near it to wait.

His attitude, like that of his companion waiting at the controls, cannot be described exactly to a human being. He was neither patient nor impatient in the human sense. He knew that waiting was unavoidable, and he was quite unaffected emotionally by the inconvenience. He was reasonably intelligent and even imaginative by both human and Mesklinite standards, but he felt no need of anything even remotely resembling daydreaming to occupy his mind during the delay. A half-conscious mental clock caused him to check the progress of the melting at reasonably frequent intervals; this is all a human being can grasp, much less describe, about what went on in his mind.

He was certainly neither asleep nor preoccupied, because he reacted promptly to a sudden loud thud and a scattering of pebbles around him. The spot where he was lying was almost directly aft of the truck which was running, so he knew instantly what must have happened.

So did Beetchermarlf, and the power unit was shut down by a tug on the control line before a man would have perceived any trouble. The two Mesklinites met a second or two later beside the truck which had been running.

It was in a predictable condition, Beetchermarlf had to admit to himself. Mesklinite organics are very, very tough materials and the tread would have lasted for many more months under ordinary travel wear: deliberate friction against unyielding rocks, even with very modest engine power, was a little too much for it.

Perhaps the word "unyielding" does not quite describe the rocks; those which had been under the moving band of fabric had been visibly flattened on top by the wear of the last hour or so. Some of them were more than half gone. The young helmsman decided, after careful examination, that the failure of the tread had been due less to simple wear than to a cut started by a formerly spherical pebble which had worn down to a thin slice with sharp edges. Takoorch agreed, when the evidence was pointed out to him.

There was no question about what to do, and they did it at once. In less than five minutes the power converter had been removed from the damaged truck and installed in the one aft of it, which had also been unloaded by puncturing the pressure cell. Without worrying about the certainty of destroying another set of treads, Beetchermarlf started this one up promptly.

Takoorch was uneasy now. The reasonable optimism of an hour before had had the foundation cut from under it; he was doubtful that the second set of treads would last long enough to melt a path all the way to freedom. It occurred to him, after some minutes of wrestling with the question, that concentrating the warmed water on one spot might be a good idea and he suggested this to his companion. Beetchermarlf was annoyed with himself for not having thought of the same thing earlier. For half an hour the two labored, heaping pebbles between and around the trucks surrounding their heat source. They eventually produced a fairly solid wall confining some of the water they were heating to a region between the truck and the nearest part of the ice wall. Takoorch had the satisfaction of seeing the ice along a two-yard front toward the starboard side of the *Kwembly* melting back almost visibly.

He was not completely happy, of course. It did not seem possible to him, any more than it did to Beetchermarlf, that the treads could last very long on the second truck either; and if they went before the way out was clear, it was hard to see what else they could do toward their own salvation. A man in such a situation can sometimes sit back and hope that his friends will rescue him in time; he can, in fact, carry that hope to the last moment of consciousness. Few Mesklinites are so constituted, and neither of the helmsmen was among the number. There was a Stennish word which Easy had translated as "hope" but this was one of her less successful inferences from context.

Takoorch, driven by this indefinable attitude, stationed himself between the humming truck and the melting ice, hugging the bottom to keep from deflecting the warmed current of water, trying to watch both simultaneously. Beetchermarlf remained at the control lines.

Since no digging had been done under the second truck, the friction was greater and the heating effect stronger.—The control was for speed rather than power, in spite of the words the helmsman had used. Naturally but unfortunately, the wear on the treads was also greater. The heavy thud which announced their failure came annoyingly soon after the completion of the rubble wall. As before, the two bands of fabric gave way almost simultaneously: the jerk imparted to the drive shaft as one let go was enough to take care of the other.

Again the Mesklinites acted instantly, in concert, and without consultation. Beetchermarlf cut the power as he plunged away from his station toward the melting surface; Takoorch got there before him only because he started from halfway there. Both had blades out when they reached the barrier, and both began scraping frantically at the frosty surface. They knew they were fairly close to the *Kwembly*'s side; less than a body length of ice remained to be penetrated, at least horizontally. Perhaps before freezing took over once more sheer muscle could get them through...

Takoorch's knife broke in the first minute. Several of the human beings above would have been interested in the sounds he made, though not even Easy Hoffman would have understood them. Beetchermarlf cut them off with a suggestion.

"Get behind me and move around as much as you can, so that the water cooled by the ice is moved away and mixed with the rest. I'll keep scraping, you keep stirring." The older sailor obeyed, and several more minutes passed with no sound except that of the knife.

Progress continued, but both could see that its rate was decreasing. The heat in the water around them was giving out. Though neither knew it, the only reason that their environment had stayed liquid for so long was that the freezing around them had cut of the escape of the ammonia. The theoreticians, both human and Mesklinite, had been perfectly correct, though they had been no help to Dondragmer. The freezing *under* the *Kwembly* had been more a matter of ammonia slowly diffusing into the ice through the still-liquid boundaries between the solid crystals.

The captain, even with this information, could have done no more about it than his two men now trapped under his ship. Of course, if the information had come as a prediction instead of an inspired afterthought, he might have driven the *Kwembly* onto dry land, if she had been able to move in time.

Even if Beetchermarlf had had all this information at the time, he would not have been considering it consciously. He was far too busy. His knife flashed in the lamp light as rapidly and as hard as he dared. His conscious mind was concerned solely with getting the most out of the tool with the least risk of breaking it.

But break it he did. He never cared to discuss the reason later. He knew that his progress was slowing, with the urge to scrape harder changing in inverse proportion; but being the person he was, he disliked the faintest suggestion that he might have been the victim of panic. Being what he was also prevented him, ever, from making any suggestion that the bone of the knife might have been defective. He himself could think of no explanations but those two. Whatever the reason, the knife gripped in his right-forward pair of chelae was suddenly without a blade, and the sliver of material lying in front of him was no more practical to handle for his nippers than it would have been for human fingers. He flung the handle down in annoyance and since he was under water didn't even have the satisfaction of hearing it strike the bottom violently.

Takoorch grasped the situation immediately. His comment would have been considered cynical if it had been heard six million miles above, but Beetchermarlf took it at face value.

"Do you think it would be better to stay here and freeze up near the side or get back toward the middle? The time won't make much difference, I'd say."

"I don't know. Near the side they *might* find us sooner; it would depend on where they come through first, if they manage to do it at all. If they don't, I can't see that it will make any difference at all. I wish I knew what being frozen into a block of ice would do to a person."

"Well, someone will know before long," said Takoorch.

"Maybe. Remember the *Esket.*"

"What has that to do with it? This is a genuine emergency."

"Just that there are a lot of people who don't know what happened there."

"Oh, I see. Well, personally I'm going back to the middle and think while I can."

Beetchermarlf was surprised. "What's there to think about? We're here to stay unless someone gets us out or the weather warms and we thaw out naturally. Settle down."

"Not here. Do you suppose that running the drivers, with no treads on them, would make enough friction with anything to keep the water nearby from—"

"Try it if you like. I wouldn't expect it, with no real load on them even at their fastest. Besides, I'd be afraid to get close to them if they're really turning up speed. Face it, Tak, we're under water, water, not regular ocean, and when it freezes we're going to be inside it. There's just nowhere else to—oh!"

"What?"

"You win. We should never stop thinking. I'm sorry. Come on."

Ninety seconds later the two Mesklinites, after some trouble in wriggling through the knife slits, were up inside the punctured air cell, safely out of the water.

8: Fingers in the Broth

Dondragmer, dismissing as negligible the chance that one of his missing helmsmen might be directly underneath, had ordered his scientists to set up the test drill near the main lock and get a sample of the ice. This established that the puddle in which the *Kwembly* was standing had frozen all the way to the bottom in at least one spot. It might be hoped that this would not apply directly under the hull, where neither heat nor ammonia could escape so rapidly; but the captain vetoed the suggestion of a slanting bore into this region. That did seem to be the most likely whereabouts of the missing helmsmen. They had been at work there and it was hard to imagine how they could have failed to see the freeze coming if they had been anywhere else.

There was no obvious way to get in touch with them, however. The *Kwembly's* plastic hull would transmit sound, of course; rapping would have solved the problem if it had not been for the mattress. On the off chance that hull sounds might be heard even through its bulk, Dondragmer ordered a crewman to go from bow to stern on the lowest deck, tapping with a pry bar every few feet. The results were negative, which meant inconclusive. There was no way to tell whether there was no one alive below to hear or no penetration of the sound or simply no way for those below to reply.

Another group was outside working at the ice but the captain had already learned that progress would be slow. Even with Mesklinite muscular strength little was being accomplished. Tools about the size of a human machinist's center punch, wielded by eighteen-inch, twenty-pound caterpillars, would take a long time to get around some two hundred and fifty feet of hull circumference to an unknown depth. They would take even longer if detailed chipping around drivers, trucks, and control lines were to be necessary, as seemed likely.

Besides all this, the second helicopter was aloft again with Reffel again at its controls. The communicator was still aboard and the human beings were examining as carefully as Reffel himself the landscape revealed by the little machine's lights. They were also cursing as heartily as the pilot the length of Dhrawn's nights; this one had well over six hundred hours yet to go and, until the sun rose, really quick and effective searching would be impossible.

To be helpful to either Mesklinite eyes or the video pick-up of the communicator, the lights had to be held to a rather narrow beam, covering a circle only a few hundred feet across. Reffel was flying a slow zigzag course which swept this circle back and forth across the valley as he moved slowly westward. At the station far above, the televised image on his screen was being recorded and reproduced for the benefit of topographers. These were already working happily on the structure of an intermittent stream valley under forty Earth gravities. Of the search for the missing Kervenser, little could be expected for some time; but pure information was coming in so no one was complaining, not even the Mesklinites.

Dondragmer was not exactly *worried* about his first officer and helmsman, since he couldn't really worry. It would be fair to say that he was concerned: but he had done all he could about the missing crewmen and having done it, his attention had turned elsewhere. He had two principal things on his mind. He would have liked information about how soon the ice was likely to melt, compared with how soon another flood might arrive. He would also have given even more for a workable suggestion on how to get rid of the ice quickly and safely. He had expressed both wishes to the human beings as well as to his own scientists, though he had made it clear to the latter that he was not demanding a crash program. The search for ideas could be combined with, or even subordinated to, the basic research they were carrying on. Dondragmer was not exactly cold-blooded, but his sense of values included the notion that even one's final act should be a useful one.

The human reaction to this remarkably objective and inhumanly calm behavior was mixed. The weather men and planetologists took it for granted. Most of them probably weren't even aware of the *Kwembly*'s predicament, much less of the missing Mesklinites. Easy Hoffman, who had stayed on watch after bringing Barlennan up to date as Aucoin had directed, was not surprised. If she had any emotional reaction so far, it was one of respect for the captain's ability to avoid panic in a personally dangerous situation.

Her son felt very differently about it. He had been released temporarily from duty in the aerology lab by McDevitt, who, as a tactful and sympathetic person, had been aware of the friendship developing between the boy and Beetchermarlf. Benj had become a fixture in the communication room as a result.

He had watched quietly while arrangements were being made by Dondragmer to dispatch the helicopter and the ice-chipping crews. He had even been somewhat interested in the exchange between the human and Mesklinite scientists. McDevitt had been a little reluctant to risk more weather predictions, feeling that his professional reputation had taken jolts enough recently, but he promised to do his best. When all these matters had been settled and Dondragmer seemed willing to do nothing but lie on his bridge and wait on events, the boy grew uneasy. Patience, the closest human equivalent to the Mesklinite reaction now being displayed, was not yet one of his strong points. For some minutes he shifted uneasily in his seat before the screens, waiting for something to happen. Finally, he could restrain himself no longer.

"If no one has any immediate material to send, is it all right for me to talk to Don and his scientists?" he asked.

Easy glanced at him, and then at the others. The men shrugged or otherwise gestured indifference, so she nodded. "Go ahead. I don't know whether any of them are in a mood for casual chatter, but the worst they'll do is tell you they aren't."

Benj didn't waste time explaining that he was not going to indulge in chatter, casual or otherwise. He switched his microphone to Dondragmer's bridge set and began to talk.

"Don, this is Benj Hoffman. You have nothing but a bunch of sailors chipping away the ice at the *Kwembly*'s bow. There is a lot of energy in your power units, more than a planetful of Mesklinites could put out by muscle in a year. Have your scientists thought of using converter output either to run that test drill for moving ice, or in some sort of heater?

"Second, are your sailors just removing ice, or are they specifically trying to get down underneath to find Beetchermarlf and Takoorch? I know it's important to get the *Kwembly* loose, but the same ice will have to be taken out sometime anyway. It seems to me there's a good chance that some of the water under the ship hasn't frozen yet, and that your two men are still alive in it. Are you tunneling, or just ditching?"

Some of the human listeners frowned slightly at the boy's choice of words, but no one saw fit to interrupt or even comment. Most of those who heard glanced at Easy and decided against saying anything which might be interpreted as criticism of her son. Some, as it happened, did not feel critical anyway; they had wanted to ask similar questions but had not quite wanted to be heard at it.

As usual in conversations between the station and Dhrawn, Benj had plenty of time while waiting for the answer to think of other things he might have asked or said, and of better ways in which he might have put the things he did say. Most of the adults knew from experience what was going on in his mind at this point; some were amused; all were to some degree sympathetic. Several bet that he would not be able to resist the temptation to send a reworded version of his message before the answer came back. When Dondragmer's response came from the speaker with Benj still silent no one actually cheered, but those who knew Easy best could read and understand the satisfaction in her expression. She had not dared to bet, even with herself.

"Hello, Benj. We're doing all we can, both for the helmsmen and my first officer. I'm afraid there is no way to apply ship's power to any of the tools. The converters produce electric current and also supply rotating torque fields to the truck motors, as I am sure you know, but none of our ordinary equipment can use this, just the helicopters, some of the research equipment in the laboratory, and the lights. Even if we could work out a way to apply the drive motors to digging, we can't get at them; they're all under the ice. You must remember, Benj, that we deliberately chose to remain as independent as possible of really complex equipment. Just about everything we have on the planet which we couldn't make ourselves is directly concerned with your research project." Ib Hoffman was not present to hear that sentence, which was unfortunate; later he spent a long time trying to make sure of its exact wording from his son's memory.

"I know that, but—" Benj fell silent; none of the words he wanted to say seemed to have ideas under them. The lights, he knew, could not be used as heaters; they were solid state electroluminescent devices, not arcs or resistance bulbs. They had, after all, been designed not only to last indefinitely but to operate in Dhrawn's atmosphere, with its free oxygen and enormous pressure range, without killing the Mesklinites. If Beetchermarlf had realized this he might have wasted less time, though he might not have accomplished any more. "Can't you, can't you just run the current from a converter through some heavy wires, and melt the ice with the heat? Or even run it straight through the water? There must be plenty of ammonia left—it would surely conduct."

Again there was a pause, while Benj hunted for flaws in his own suggestions and the message flashed its way across emptiness.

"I'm not sure I know enough about that sort of physics, though I suppose Borndender and his men would," Dondragmer replied doubtfully. "More to the point, I don't know what we'd use for wires and I don't know what current would flow. I know that when the power units are connected to regular equipment like lights or motors there is automatic safety control but I have no idea of how that works or whether it would work on a simple, direct, series circuit. If you'll find out from your engineers what sort of risk we'd be running, I'll be glad of the information but I still don't know what we'd use to carry the current. There just isn't much metal in the *Kwembly.* Most of our maintenance supplies are things like rope and fabric and lumber. Certainly there's nothing that's *meant* to carry heavy electrical current. You may be right about using the ice itself as a conductor, but do you think it would be a good idea with Beetchermarlf and Takoorch somewhere under it? Although I can see they wouldn't be right in the circuit, I'm still a little uncertain that they'd be safe. There again one of you people could probably help out. If you can, if we can get enough detailed information from you to plan something really promising, I'll be glad to try it. Until that happens, I can only say we're doing all we can. I'm as concerned about the *Kwembly,* and Kervenser, and Beetchermarlf, and Takoorch as you can possibly be."

The captain's closing sentence was not entirely true, though the error was not intentional. He did not really grasp how a friendship could become at all close in a short time and without direct contact between the parties; his cultural background included neither an efficient mail service nor amateur radio. The concept of a microphone relationship developing emotional weight may not have been completely strange to him: he had, after all, been with Barlennan years before when Charles Lackland had accompanied the *Bree* by radio across thousands of miles of Mesklin's oceans; still, real friendship was, to him, in a different category. He had been only conventionally regretful at the news of Lackland's death years later. Dondragmer knew that Benj and the younger helmsman had been talking to each other a great deal, but he had not overheard much of their conversation and would probably not have fully understood the feelings involved even if he had.

Fortunately Benj did not realize this, so he had no reason to doubt the captain's sincerity. However, he was not satisfied with either the answer or the situation. It seemed to him that far too little was being done specifically for Beetchermarlf; he had only been *told* about this. He could not participate in the help. He could not even see very much of it happening. He had to sit and wait for verbal reports. Many human beings both more mature and more sedate by nature than Benj Hoffman would have had trouble enduring that situation.

His feelings showed clearly enough in his next words, as far as the human hearers were concerned. Easy made a half-completed gesture of protest. Then she controlled herself; it was too late, and there was always the chance that the Mesklinite would not read as much into the words and tone as the speaker's mother had.

"But you can't just sprawl there and do nothing!" Benj exclaimed. "Your men could be drowning this very second. Do you know how much air they had in their suits?"

This time temptation won. Realization of what he had said caught up with him within seconds, and in less than half a minute he had what he hoped were better chosen words on their way to Dhrawn.

"I know you're not doing *nothing* but I just don't see how you can simply wait around for results. I'd have to go outside myself and chip ice or something, but I can't, up here."

"I have done all that can be done in the way of starting rescue action," Dondragmer's response to the first part of the message finally arrived. "There is no need to worry about the air for many hours yet. We don't respond to its lack as I understand you human beings do. Even if the hydrogen concentration goes too low for them to stay conscious, their body machinery will just slow down more and more for several eights of hours. No one knows just how long and it probably isn't the same for everyone. You needn't worry about their—drowning—I think was the word you used, if I have guessed its meaning correctly.

"All the tools we have are in use. There would be no way for me to help outside if I did go, and it would take me longer to get reports from Reffel through your people. Perhaps you can tell me how his search for Kervenser is coming on. I assume that nothing meaningful has turned up, since the light from his flier is still visible from here and his flight pattern has not changed. Perhaps there is description you could pass on to me. I'd like to know as much about this region as possible."

Easy once again stifled an exclamation before it could be noticed by Benj. As the boy shifted his attention to the screen carrying the helicopter's signal, she wondered whether Dondragmer were merely trying to keep her son out of his figurative hair or whether he had some real grasp of the human need to be busy and feel useful. The latter seemed unlikely but even Easy Hoffman, who probably knew Mesklinite nature better than any other human being then alive, was not sure.

Benj had not been watching the other screen at all and had to ask whether anything had been happening. One of the observers replied briefly that all anyone had seen had been a surface of pea-to-house-sized cobbles, interrupted by frozen pools similar to the one holding the *Kwembly.* There had been no sign of the other helicopter or its pilot. No one really expected any for some time. The search had to be slow to be complete. If Kervenser had actually crashed this close to his starting point the accident would probably have been seen from the cruiser. The little fliers did carry lights and Kervenser had certainly been using his.

Benj relayed this information to Dhrawn, then threw in an obvious question of his own.

"Why is Reffel making such a slow and careful search so close to you? Wasn't Kervenser at least watched out of sight?"

The delayed response provided a little relief for the boy's feeling of helplessness.

"He was, Benj. It seemed more reasonable to make a complete coverage centering here and starting outward, which would also have the advantage of providing more complete data for your scientists. If they can wait for the information, please tell Reffel I said to fly straight west along the valley until he can just see my bridge light, then resume the search pattern at that point."

"Sure thing, Captain." The conversation had been in Stennish, so none of the watching scientists had understood it. Benj did not bother to ask their approval before passing on the order in the same language. Reffel seemed to have no trouble understanding Benj's accent and in due course his little machine headed west.

"And what's happening to our map?" growled a topographer.

"You heard the captain," replied Benj.

"I heard something. If I'd understood it I'd have entered an objection but I suppose it's too late now. Do you suppose when they return they'll fill in the gap they're leaving now?"

"I'll ask Dondragmer," the boy replied obligingly, but with an uneasy glance toward his mother. She had put on the unreadable expression which he could read all too well. Fortunately, the scientist was already leaving the communication room growling under his breath; and fortunately Benj turned his attention back to Reffel's screen before Easy lost her gravity. Several other nearby adults who had gleaned the substance of the conversation with Dondragmer were also having trouble keeping their faces straight. For some reason they all enjoyed putting one over on the scientific group. But Benj failed to notice. He was still worried about Beetchermarlf.

Dondragmer's assurance that lack of hydrogen would not be an immediate problem had helped but the idea of the crewmen being frozen solidly into the ice was still bothersome. Even if this took longer to happen under the *Kwembly*'s hull, it would happen at last. It might even have happened already. It should be possible do *something.*

Heat melts ice. Heat is energy. The *Kwembly* carried enough energy to lift her out of Dhrawn's gravity well, though there was no way to apply it to that task. Didn't the huge vehicle have any sort of heaters in its life-support equipment which could be disassembled and used outside?

No. The Mesklinites were unlikely ever to need heat on Dhrawn. Even the parts of the planet where internal heat seemed to be lacking were kept close to fifty degrees absolute by the sun. The regions they would have most to do with for many years yet, such as Low Alpha's center, were too hot rather than too cold for them. The *Kwembly* did have refrigeration equipment powered from its fusion converters but as far as Benj knew, it had never been used since the original testing. It was expected to be useful during penetration of the central part of Low Alpha, not scheduled for at least an Earth year yet, possibly even later. The fate of the *Esket* had made some of the original plans rather shaky.

But a refrigerator is a heat pump. Even Benj knew that and at least in theory, most pumps are reversible. This one must have, somewhere *outside* the cruiser's hull, a high-temperature section for dumping heat. Where was it? Was it removable? At what temperature did it run? Dondragmer must know. But wouldn't he have thought of this already? Maybe not. He was far from stupid, but his background wasn't human. What physics he knew had been picked up from non-Mesklinites long after he was adult. It would not, presumably, be part of the basic stock of knowledge which most intelligent beings lump under the concept of "common sense." Benj nodded at this thought, spent another second or two reminding himself that even if he made himself look silly this might be worth it and reached for his microphone switch.

This time there was no amusement among the surrounding adults as the message pulsed toward Dhrawm. None of those present knew enough about the engineering details of the land-cruisers to answer the questions about the refrigerator heat-dump, but all knew enough physics to be annoyed with themselves for not having thought of the question earlier. They waited for Dondragmer's answer with as much impatience as Benj.

"The refrigerator is one of your solid-state electronic devices which I don't pretend to understand in detail," the captain's words finally reached the station. He was still using his own language, to the annoyance of some of the listeners. "We haven't had to use it since the acceptance tests; the weather here has sometimes been pretty warm, but not really unbearable. It's a simple thing to describe; there are metal plates in all the rooms which get cold when we turn the power on in the system. There is a metal bar, a sort of loop, running along each side of the hull up at the top. It starts near the stern, runs forward about half a body-length to the port side of the center-line, crosses over about four body-lengths back of the bridge and goes back along the other side to a point even with its start. It runs through the hull at start and finish, one of the few things that does. I assume that bar must be the heat radiator. I see, as you imply I should, that there must be such a part to the system and that it must be outside. Nothing else seems to qualify. Unfortunately, it couldn't be further from the ice than it is, even if it runs hot enough to melt it, which I don't know, offhand. I realize that it could be made as hot as you please by running enough electricity through it but I'm not sure I like the idea of trying to take if off the hull for such a purpose."

"I suppose it would wreck your refrigeration system, especially if you couldn't get it back," agreed Benj. "Still, maybe it's not that bad. Let me find an engineer who really knows that system. I have an idea. I'll call you back later." The boy slid out of his seat without waiting for Dondragmer's reply, and left the communication room on the run.

The moment he was gone, the observers who had not understood the language asked Easy for a summary of the conversation, which she gladly supplied. When Benj returned with an engineer in tow, those in hearing frankly abandoned their jobs to listen. Several heartfelt prayers of thanksgiving must have ascended when it was noted that the newcomer was not a linguist, and the boy was interpreting for him. The two settled into seats before the screens, and Benj made sure he knew what to say before energizing his microphone.

"I should tell the captain that most of the fastenings holding the radiator bar to the *Kwembly*'s skin are sort of nails; they only go a little way into the skin and can be pried out without damaging the hull. It might be necessary to use cement to fasten them back in afterward but the supplies are there. The connections at the rear will have to be cut, though. The alloy isn't very hard and saws will be able to handle it. Once detached, the bar can be used as a resistance heater simply by pushing its ends into the D.C. holes in a power box. I can tell the captain that there is no danger from a short circuit, since the converters have internal safeties. Is that right, Mr. Katini?"

"That's it," the small, grizzled engineer replied with a nod. He was one of those who had helped design and build the land-cruisers and one of the very few human beings actually to spend much time at Mesklin's three-gravity equator. "I don't think you'll have any trouble making it clear to Dondragmer, even without translation; I'll tell him directly if you wish. He and I always got along easily enough in my own language."

Benj nodded acknowledgment of this, but started speaking into his microphone in Stennish. Easy suspected that he was showing off and hoped that it wouldn't backfire on him too badly but saw no real need to interfere. She had to admit that he was doing a good job of the translation. He must have picked up a great deal from his friend Beetchermarlf. In some ways he was doing better than she would have herself; he was using analogies which should be meaningful to the captain but which would not have occurred to her.

When the captain's answer came back it was in the human tongue. Dondragmer had seen the most probable reason why Benj, rather than the engineer who had provided the information, should be doing the talking. The boy looked a little startled, and confirmed his mother's suspicions by glancing quickly at her. She carefully kept her eyes on Dondragmer's screen.

"I have the picture," the Mesklinite's slightly accented voice came through. He was not always perfectly successful in confining his voice to the human audibility range. "We can detach the refrigerator bar and use it, with a power box, as a heater to melt the ice around the ship. There will be plenty of power in the converter and no danger of blowing it up. Please clear up two points, however.

"First, how can we be sure that we can reconnect the bar electrically afterward? I know enough to doubt that cement is the right method. I don't want to lose the refrigerator system permanently, since Dhrawn is approaching its sun and the weather will be getting warmer.

"Second, with the metal carrying a current touching the ice, or dipping into the melted water, will there be any danger to people on, in, or under that water? Will the air suits be protection enough? I suppose they must be pretty good electrical insulators, since they are transparent."

The engineer began to answer at once, leaving Benj to wonder what connection there might be between transparency and electrical conductivity and how Dondragmer, with his background, happened to be acquainted with it.

"You can make the connection easily enough. Simply have the metal ends pressed tightly together and use the adhesive to fasten a wrapping of fabric around the joint. You're right about the glue's conductance; make sure it doesn't get between the metal surfaces.

"Also, you needn't worry about electrocuting anyone in an air suit. They'll be adequate protection. I suspect that it would take a lot of voltage to hurt you people anyway, since your body fluids are non-polar, but I have no experimental proof and I don't suppose you want any. It occurred to me that you might do better by striking an arc at the surface of the ice, which should have enough ammonia to be a fair conductor. If it works at all, it should work very well. Only it may be too hot for any of your men to stay in the neighborhood and it *would* have to be controlled carefully. Come to think of it, the procedure would destroy too much of the bar to let you get the system together again afterward. We'd better stick to simple resistance heating, and be satisfied with melting the ice rather than boiling it." Katini fell silent, and waited for Dondragmer's answer. Benj was still thinking, and all the others within hearing had their eyes fixed on the captain's screen. His shift of language had attracted even those who might otherwise have waited patiently for a translation.

This was unfortunate from the human viewpoint. Barlennan, later, wrote it off as a stroke of luck.

"All right," Dondragmer's answer finally came. "We will take off the metal bar and try to use it as a heater. I am now ordering men outside to start detaching the small brackets. I will have one of the communicators set up outside so that you can watch as we cut through the conductors, and check everything before we turn on power. We will work slowly, so that you can tell us if we are doing something wrong before it has gone too far. I don't like this situation—I don't like doing anything when I am so unsure of what is happening and what is likely to happen. I'm supposed to be in command here and I can only wish I had learned more of your science and technology. I may have an accurate picture as far as it goes and I'm sure I can trust your knowledge and judgment for the rest but it's the first time in years I've been so uncertain of myself."

It was Benj who answered, beating his mother by a fraction of a second.

"I heard you were the first Mesklinite to grasp the general idea of real science and that you were the one who did most to get the College going. What do you mean, you wish you had learned more?"

Easy cut in; like Benj, she used Dondragmer's own language.

"You know far more than I do, Don, and you *are* in command. If you hadn't been convinced by what Katini told you, you wouldn't have given those orders. You'll have to get used to that feeling you don't like; you've just collided with something new again. It's like that time fifty years ago, long before I was born, when you suddenly realized that the science we aliens were using was just knowledge carried on past the common-sense level. Now you have bumped into the fact that no one, not even a commander, can know everything, and that you sometimes have to take professional advice. Live with it, Don, and calm down!"

Easy leaned back and looked at her son, who was the only one in the room to have followed her speech completely. The boy looked startled, almost awe-struck. Whatever impression she had made on Dondragmer or would, when her words got to him, she had certainly gotten home to Benjamin Ibson Hoffman. It was an intoxicating sensation for a parent; she had to fight the urge to say more. She was assisted by an interruption in a human voice.

"Hey! What happened to the helicopter?"

All eyes went to Reffel's screen. There was a full second of silence. Then Easy snapped, "Benj, report to Dondragmer while I call Barlennan!"

9: Crossed Purposes

The weather had long since cleared at the Settlement, the ammonia fog had blown into the unknown central regions of Low Alpha and the wind had dropped to a gentle breeze from the northwest. Stars twinkled violently, catching the attention of occasional Mesklinites who were outside or in the corridors but going unnoticed by those in the better lighted rooms under the transparent roof.

Because Barlennan was in the laboratory area at the west side of the Settlement when Easy called, her message did not reach him at once. It arrived in written form, borne by one of Guzmeen's messengers who, in accordance with standing orders, paid no attention to the fact that Barlennan was in conference. He thrust the note in front of his commander, who broke off his own words in mid-sentence to read it. Bendivence and Deeslenver, the scientists with whom he was speaking, waited in silence for him to finish, though their body attitudes betrayed curiosity.

Barlennan read the message twice, seemed to be trying to recall something, and then turned to the messenger.

"All this just came in, I take it."

"Yes, sir."

"And how long has it been since the preceding report from Dondragmer?"

"Not long, sir, less than an hour, I'd say. The log would show; shall I check?"

"It's not that urgent, as long as you know. The last I heard was that the *Kwembly* had grounded after drifting down a river for a couple of hours and that was a long time ago. I assumed that everything was all right, since Guz didn't pass any more on to me about it. I assume now that he either heard interim reports at the usual intervals or asked the humans about it?"

"I don't know, sir. I haven't been on duty the whole time. Shall I check?"

"No. I'll be there in a little while myself. Tell Guz not to send anything out after me; just hold any calls." The runner vanished, and Barlennan turned back to the scientists.

"Sometimes I wonder whether we shouldn't have more electrical communication in this place. I'd like to know how long it's taken Don to get into this mess, but I want to learn some other things before I walk all the way to Guzmeen's place."

Bendivence gestured the equivalent of a shrug. "We can do it if you say the word. There are telephones here in the lab which work fairly well and we can wire the whole Settlement if you want the metal used that way."

"I don't yet. We'll keep to the original priorities. Here, read this. The *Kwembly* has gotten herself stuck in frozen water or something and both her helicopters have disappeared. One had a communicator to the human beings aboard and it was in use at the time."

Deeslenver indicated his emotion by a soft buzz, and reached for the message in turn. Bendivence passed it over silently. The former read it silently, twice, as Barlennan had done, before he spoke.

"You'd think the humans would have a little more information if they were watching at all carefully. All this says is that Kervenser failed to come back from a flight and that a flier searching for him with a communicator on board suddenly stopped sending; the screen just went blank all of a sudden."

"I can see one possible reason for that," remarked Bendivence.

"I thought you would," returned the commander. "The question is not what blanked the screen but why it should have happened there and then. We can assume that Reffel used the shutter on his set. It would have been nice if you'd thought of that trick before the *Esket* went out; it would have simplified that operation a lot. Something must have come into his field of view which wouldn't have fit in with the *Esket* story. But what could it have been? The *Kwembly* is five or six million cables from the *Esket*. I suppose one of the dirigibles *could* be down that way, but why *should* it be?"

"We won't know until another flight gets back from Destigmet's place," replied the scientist practically. "What interests me is why we didn't hear about Kervenser's disappearance earlier. Why was there time for Reffel's mission to be flown and for him to disappear too before we were told about it? Was Dondragmer late in reporting to the human observers?"

"I doubt that very much," replied Barlennan. "Actually, they may have told us about Kervenser when it happened. Remember, the runner said that other messages had been coming in. Guzmeen might not have thought the disappearance worth sending a runner for until Kerv had been gone for a while. We can check up on that in a few minutes but I imagine there's nothing funny this time.

"On the other hand, I have been wondering lately whether the people up there have always been relaying information completely and promptly. Once or twice I've had the impression that, well, things were being saved up and sent in one package. It may be just sloppiness, or it may not really be happening—"

"Or they may be deliberately organizing what we hear," said Bendivence. "Half our crew could be lost at this point without our knowing it, if the human beings chose to play it that way. I can see their being afraid we'd quit the job and demand to be taken home, according to contract, if risks proved too high."

"I suppose that's possible," admitted Barlennan. "It hadn't occurred to me just that way. I don't think that particular notion is very likely, but the more I consider the situation, the more I'd like to think of a way of checking things; at least, to make sure they're not taking time to hold conferences on just how much to tell us every time something does go wrong with an exploring cruiser."

"Do you really think there's much likelihood of that?" asked Deeslenver.

"It's hard to tell. Certainly we've been a bit less than completely frank with them and we have what we consider some very good reasons for it. I'm not really bothered either way. We know some of these people are good at business, and if we can't keep even with them it's our fault. All I really would like to be sure of is whether it's business or carelessness. I can think of one way to check up, but I'd rather not use it yet. If anyone can suggest an alternative, it will be very welcome."

"What's the one you have?" both scientists asked together, Deeslenver perhaps half a syllable ahead.

"The *Esket,* of course. It's the only place where we can get an independent check on what they tell us. At least, I haven't thought of any other so far. Of course, even that would take a long time; there won't be another flight from there until sunrise and that's twelve hundred hours or so away. Of course, we *could* send the *Deedee* even at night—"

"If we'd set up that light relay I suggested—" began Deeslenver.

"Too risky. It would have much too big a chance of being seen. We just don't know how good the human instruments are. I know most of them stay way up at that station overhead, but I don't know what they can see from it. The casual way they distribute these picture-senders for us to carry around here on this planet suggests that they don't regard them as very fancy equipment, as does the fact that they used them twelve years ago on Mesklin. There's just too much chance that they'd spot any light on the night side of this planet. That's why I overrode your idea, Dee; otherwise, I admit it was a very good one."

"Well, there's nothing like enough metal yet for electrical contact that far," added Bendivence. "I don't have any other ideas at the moment. Come to think of it, you might make a simple test on how well the humans can pick up lights."

"How?" the question came in body attitudes, not verbally.

"We could ask them innocently if there were any way of their hunting for the running lights or the floods of the missing fliers."

Barlennan pondered the suggestion briefly.

"Good. Excellent. Let's go. However, if they say they can't, we won't be sure that they aren't just keeping it from us. You might be thinking of a further check for *that.*" He led the way out of the map room where the discussion had been held, along the corridors of the Settlement toward the communication room. Most of the passageways were relatively dark. The sponsors of the expedition had not stinted on the supply of artificial lights but Barlennan himself had been rather close-nippered with their distribution. Rooms were adequately lit; hallways had a bare minimum of illumination.

This gave the Mesklinites the comforting feeling that there was nothing overhead, by letting them see the stars without too much trouble. No native of that planet was really happy to face the fact that there was anything in a position to fall on him. Even the scientists glanced up occasionally as they went, taking comfort from the sight of stars not even their own. Mesklin's sun, which men called 61 Cygni, was below the horizon at the moment.

Barlennan looked upward more than he looked ahead; he was trying to get a glimpse of the human station. This carried a beacon light visible from Dhrawn, bright as a fourth-magnitude star. Its barely visible crawl against the celestial background was the best long-term clock the Mesklinites had. They used it to reset the pendulum-type instruments which they had made, which seldom agreed with each other for more than a few score hours at a time.

Stars and station alike faded from view as the trio entered the brightly lighted communication room. Guzmeen saw Barlennan and instantly reported, "No further news of either flier."

"What reports have you had from Dondragmer between the time the *Kwembly* ran aground and now; the last hundred and thirty hours or so? Do you know how long ago Don's first officer disappeared?"

"Only roughly, sir. The incident was reported, but nothing specific was said about how recently it had happened. I took for granted it had just occurred, but didn't ask. The two disappearances were reported quite close together: less than an hour apart."

"And you didn't wonder when the second one came in why we heard about both disappearances so nearly simultaneously, even though they must have occurred some time apart?"

"Yes, Sir. I started wondering about a quarter of an hour before you did, when the last message came in. I don't have any explanation, but I thought I'd leave it to you to ask the humans if you think one is needed."

Bendivence cut in. "Do you suppose Don failed to report the first disappearance because it resulted from a mistake, and he hoped to be able to minimize it by reporting disappearance and recovery at the same time, as minor incidents?"

Barlennan looked at the speaker speculatively but lost no time in answering.

"No, I don't suppose that. Dondragmer and I don't always agree on everything but there are some things that neither of us would do."

"Even if an immediate report couldn't really make a difference? After all, neither we nor the human beings could really help even after we'd heard the news."

"Even then."

"I don't see why."

"I do. Take my word for it; I haven't time for a detailed explanation and I doubt that I could compose one anyway. If Dondragmer failed to make that initial report, he had a very good reason. Personally I doubt very much that the failure was his. Guz, which humans gave you the reports? Was it always the same one?"

"No, Sir. I didn't recognize all their voices, and they often didn't bother to identify themselves. About half the time nowadays the reports come in human language. Most of the rest come from the Hoffman humans. There are others who speak our language but those two seem the only ones who do it comfortably. With the young one particularly, I got the impression that he'd been talking a lot with the *Kwembly* and I assumed that if there were casual chatter going on, nothing much serious could be happening."

"All right. I'd probably have done the same. I'll use the set; I have a couple of questions to put to the humans." Barlennan took his place in front of the pickup, the speaker on watch making way for him without being ordered. The screen was blank. The captain squeezed the "attention" control and waited patiently for the minute to pass. He could have started talking at once, since it was a safe bet that whoever was at the other end would lose no time readying his receiver, but Barlennan wanted to see who was there. If the delay made anyone suspicious, he'd have to live with it.

The face which did appear was unfamiliar to him. Even fifty Earth years of acquaintance with human beings had not sufficed to educate him in such matters as family resemblance, though no human being would have failed to guess that Benj was Easy's son. Actually, the fifty years had not supplied many different people for comparison; fewer than two score men, and no women, had ever landed on Mesklin. Guzmeen recognized the boy but was spared the need to tell Barlennan by Benj himself.

"Benj Hoffman here," the image spoke. "Nothing has come from the *Kwembly* since Mother called you about twenty minutes ago and there are no engineers or scientists in this room at the moment. If you have questions which need technical answers, tell me so I can call the right one. If it's just a matter of detail as to what's been happening, I've been here in the comm room most of the last seven hours and can probably tell you. I'm waiting."

"I have two questions," Barlennan responded. "One of them you can probably answer, the other perhaps not. The first has to do with the second disappearance. I am wondering how far from the *Kwembly* the second helicopter was when it ceased communicating. If you don't know the distance, perhaps you can tell me how long its pilot had been searching."

"The second does depend on a bit of your technology which I don't know but you may. Is there any possibility of your seeing lights such as those on the helicopters from where you are? I suppose it couldn't be done by your unaided eyes any more than it could be done by mine but you have many optical devices which I know little about, probably some which I've never heard of. I'm standing by."

Benj's screened image held up one finger and nodded just as Barlennan finished speaking but the boy waited for the other question to reach him before he spoke.

"I can answer your first question, and Mr. Cavanaugh has gone to find someone who can take care of the second," were his opening words. "Kervenser started out on his scouting flight about eleven hours ago. It wasn't realized that he must be in trouble until about eight hours later, when everything popped at once: Kervenser and his flier gone, the *Kwembly* frozen in and Beetchermarlf and Takoorch somewhere under the ice; at least, no one knows that's where they are but they were working under the hull and there's no other place anyone can think of for them to be. One of the sailors, Reffel, took up the other flier with a vision set to look for Kervenser, and searched very close to the *Kwembly* for a while. Then we suggested that he move out to where an accident to Kervenser wouldn't have been seen or heard from the cruiser, which he did; of course Dondragmer lost sight of him from the bridge. Then we got into a discussion with the captain; everyone up here got interested and it turned out that no one was watching Reffel's screen for several minutes. Then someone noticed that the screen had gone completely blank: not no-signal-*blank* but no-light *black;* that was that."

Barlennan glanced at Guzmeen and the scientists. None of them spoke, but none of them needed to. No one had been watching the screen when Reffel used the shutter! It was not the sort of luck one counted on.

Benj was still speaking.

"The sound wasn't on, of course, since no one had been talking with Reffel, and no one has any idea what happened. This was just before my mother called you, less than half an hour ago. That would make something like two and a half hours between the two disappearances. We'll have to wait for your other answer, since Mr. Cavanaugh isn't back yet."

Barlennan was a little bewildered by the arithmetic, since the boy had used Mesklinite number-words with human number-background. He got it straight after a few seconds of thought.

"I'm not complaining," he returned, "but I gather from what you say that over two hours passed between the *Kwembly*'s freezing in and Kervenser's disappearance, and our being told about it. Do you know why that might have happened? I realize, of course, that there was nothing I could have done but there was some understanding about keeping me up to date with the land-cruisers. I don't know just what your job is at the station; you may not have that information; but I hear from my communications man that you have been talking a lot to the *Kwembly,* so you may be able to help. I'm waiting."

Barlennan had several motives behind his closing remark. One was obvious enough; he wanted to learn more about Benj Hoffman, especially since the latter was good with the Mesklinite language and if Guz were right, seemed to want to talk to Mesklinites. Maybe he would be like the other Hoffman, a second sympathy-center in the station. If so, it would be important to know just how much weight he could swing.

Also, the commander wanted to check unobtrusively on Guzmeen's notion that Ben had been chattering with *Kwembly* crew members. Finally, even Barlennan could tell that Benj was young for a human being doing serious work: his selection of words and general narrative style had been a give-away. That fact might well be put to good use *if* a reasonably close relationship could be established.

The boy's answer, when it finally came, was inconclusive in one way but promising in another.

"I don't know why you weren't told about Kervenser and the freeze-up right away," he said. "Personally, I thought you had been. I'd been talking a lot with Beetchermarlf; I guess you know him; one of Don's helmsmen; the one you can talk with and not just listen to. When I heard he'd disappeared I was concentrating on what could be done about it. I wasn't here in the comm room quite all the time; it's not my duty station. I just come when I can to talk with Beetch. I admit someone should have told you sooner. If you'd like I'll try to find out who should have and why he didn't. My mother ought to know, or Mr. Mersereau.

"I don't know how much explaining I'd better supply about the background to my job here. On Earth, when someone finishes basic education (the sort of thing everyone has to get, like reading and physics and sociology) he has to work at unskilled labor on some essential job for two to three of our years before he is eligible for either specialized or general higher education. Nobody says it right out, but everyone knows that the people you work for have the main say in what you can do afterward. Nominally I'm assigned to the aerology lab here as a sort of picker-upper and hey-you; actually anyone in the station who yells first and loudest gets me. I must admit they don't make my life very hard. I've been able to spend a lot of time talking to Beetch the last few days." Barlennan was able, with fifty years experience, to translate without effort the thought behind a human being's use of the word *day.* "Of course," the boy went on, "knowing your language helps. My mother's a language nut, and I picked it up from her. She started on yours ten years ago when Dad was first connected with the Dhrawn project. I'll probably be doing comm work semi-officially a good deal of the time from now on. Here comes Mr. Cavanaugh with one of the astronomers whose name I think is Tebbetts. They'll answer your question about seeing lights, and I'll try to find out about the other business."

Benj's face was replaced on the screen by that of the astronomer, a set of broad, dark features which rather surprised Barlennan. He had never seen a bearded human being, though he was used to wide variations in cranial hair. Tebbetts' was a small Van Dyke adornment quite compatible with a space helmet but it made a drastic difference to the Mesklinite's eye. Barlennan decided that asking the astronomer about it would be tactless. It might be better to get the information from Benj later. There was nothing to be gained by embarrassing anyone.

The facial extension, to the commander's relief, did not interfere with its owner's diction. Tebbetts had evidently been given the question already. He started to talk at once, using the human tongue.

"We can detect from here any of the artificial lights you have, including the portables, though we might have trouble with beamed ones not pointed our way. We'd use regular equipment: photomultiplier mosaics behind an appropriate objective; anything you're likely to need could be set up in a few minutes. What do you want us to do?"

This question caught Barlennan by surprise. He had, in the few minutes since discussing the matter with his scientists, been growing more and more certain that the men would deny being able to detect such lights. Certainly if the commander had been a little more foresighted he would not have answered as he had. In fact, he was regretting what he said well before the words reached the station.

"You should have no trouble spotting our land-cruiser *Kwembly;* you already know its location better than I do, and its bridge lights would be on. Its two helicopters have just disappeared, and they normally carry lights. I'd like to have you scan the area within, say, two hundred miles of the *Kwembly* as carefully as you can for other lights, then tell both me and Dondragmer the positions of any you find. Would that take long?"

The message lag was quite long enough to let Barlennan realize how he had slipped. There was nothing to be done about it now but to hope, though that word is a bad translation of the nearest possible Mesklinite attitude. The answer did cause him to brighten up a little; maybe the slip hadn't been too serious: as long as the human beings didn't find more than two other lights near the *Kwembly*!

"I'm afraid I was thinking merely of detecting lights," said Tebbetts. "Pinpointing the sources will be harder, especially from here. I'm pretty sure we can solve your problem if your missing helis are shining their lights. If you think they may have crashed, I shouldn't think there'd be much chance of light, but I'll get right to it."

"How about their power plants?" asked Barlennan, determined to learn the worst now that he had started. "Aren't there other radiations than light given off in nuclear reactions?"

By the time this question reached the station Tebbetts had left, according to his promise; fortunately Benj was able to supply the answer. The information happened to be basic to the Project, which had been carefully explained to him right after his arrival.

"The fusion converters give off neutrinos which we can detect, but we can't spot their source exactly," he told the commander. "That's what the shadow satellites are for. They detect neutrinos, which are practically all coming from the sun. The power plants on Dhrawn and up here don't count for much against that, even if it isn't much of a sun. The computers keep track of where the satellites are and especially whether the planet is between a given one and the sun, so there's a measure of the neutrino absorption through different parts of the planet. In a few years we hope to have a statistical x-ray of Dhrawn. Maybe that isn't a good analogy for you: I mean a good idea of the density and composition of the planet's insides. They're still arguing, you know, whether Dhrawn should be called a planet or a star or whether the extra heat is from hydrogen fusion in the middle or radioactivity near the surface.

"But I'm sure as can be that they couldn't find your missing fliers from their neutrino emission, even if their converters are still on."

Barlennan managed to conceal his glee at this news; he merely answered, "Thanks. We can't have everything. I take it you'll tell me when your astronomer finds anything, or when he is sure he'll find nothing; I'd like to know if I have to stop counting on that. I'm through talking for now, Benj, but call here if anything comes up on either the fliers or those friends of yours. After all, I'm concerned about them, though perhaps not the way you are about Beetchermarlf. Takoorch is the one I remember." Barlennan, having had more direct contact with human beings and more selfish reasons to develop such skills, had been able to read more accurately between the lines of Benj's talk and obtain a more nearly correct picture of the boy's feelings than Dondragmer had. It would, he was sure, be useful; but he put it from his mind as he turned away from the communicator.

"That could be both better and worse," he remarked to the two scientists. "It's certainly just as well we didn't set up that blinker system for night communication; they'd have seen us certainly."

"Not certainly," objected Deeslenver. "The human said they *could* spot such lights but there was no suggestion that they made a habit of looking for them. If it takes instruments, I'd bet the instruments are busy on more important things."

"So would I, if the stakes weren't so high," returned Barlennan. "Anyway, we wouldn't dare use it now because we know they'll be looking this way with the best machines they have. We just asked them to."

"But they won't be looking here. They'll be searching the neighborhood of the *Kwembly,* millions of cables from here."

"Think of yourself back home looking up at Toorey. If you were supposed to examine one part of it closely with a telescope, how much of a slip would it take to make you glance at another?"

Deeslenver conceded the point with a gesture.

"Then we either wait for sunrise, or fly a special if we want to use the *Esket* as you suggested. I admit I haven't thought of anything else. I haven't even thought of what we might do there which would make a good test."

"It shouldn't matter too much. The real question would be how soon, and how accurately and completely, the human beings do report whatever we set up for them to see. I'll think of something in the next couple of hours. Aren't you researchers setting up for a flight to leave soon, anyway?"

"Not that soon," said Bendivence. "Also, I don't agree with you that details don't matter. You don't want them to get the idea that *we* could possibly have anything to do with what they see happen at the *Esket.* They certainly aren't stupid."

"Of course. I didn't mean that they should. It will be something natural, making full allowance for the fact that the human beings know even less than we do about what's natural on this world. You get back to the labs and tell everyone who has equipment to get onto the *Deedee* that departure time has been moved ahead. I'll have a written message for Destigmet in two hours."

"All right." The scientists vanished through the door, and Barlennan followed them more slowly. He was just beginning to realize how valid Bendivence's point was. What could be made to happen, in range of one of the *Esket*'s vision transmitters, which would not suggest that there were Mesklinites in the neighborhood but which would attract human interest *and* tempt the big creatures to edit their reports? Could he think of such a thing without knowing why the reports were being held up? Or, for that matter, without being quite sure that they were? It was still possible that the delay on the *Kwembly* matter had been a genuine oversight; as the young human had suggested, each person might have thought that someone else had attended to the matter. To Barlennan's sailor's viewpoint this smacked of gross incompetence and inexcusable disorganization, but it would not be the first time he had suspected these qualities in human beings; not as a species, of course, but on an individual basis.

The test certainly had to be made, and the *Esket*'s transmitters might surely be tools for the purpose. As far as Barleunan knew, the transmitters were still active. Naturally, care had been taken that no one enter their field of view since the "loss" of the cruiser, and it had been long since any human being had made mention of them. They would have been shuttered rather than avoided, since this would obviously have left the Mesklinites at the place much greater freedom of action; but the idea of the shutters had not occurred until after Destigmet had departed with his instructions to set up a second Settlement unknown to the human beings.

As Barlennan remembered, one of the transmitters had been at the usual spot on the bridge, one in the laboratory, one in the hangar where the helicopters were kept. The helicopters had been carefully arranged to be out on routine flights when the "catastrophe" occurred; and the fourth was in the life-support section, though not covering the entrance. It had been necessary to take much of the equipment from this chamber, of course.

With all the planning, the situation was still inconvenient; having the lab and life rooms out of bounds or at best accessible only with the greatest care, had caused Destigmet and his first officer, Kabremm, much annoyance. They had more than once requested permission to shutter the sets, since the technique had been invented. Barlennan had refused, not wanting to call human attention back to the *Esket;* now, well, maybe the same net could take two fish. The sudden blanking of one or perhaps of all four of those screens would certainly be noticed from above. Whether the humans would feel any inclination to hide the event from the Settlement there was no way of telling; one could only try.

The more he thought it over the better the plan sounded. Barlennan felt the glow familiar to every intelligent being, regardless of species, who has solved a major problem unassisted. He enjoyed it for fully half a minute. At the end of that time, another of Guzmeen's runners caught up with him.

"Commander!" The messenger fell into step beside him in the nearly dark corridor. "Guzmeen says that you should come back to Communications at once. One of the human beings, the one called Mersereau, is on the screen. Guz says he ought to be excited, but isn't, because he's reporting something going on at the *Esket*—something is moving in the laboratory!"

10: Weighted Data

Keeping in phase with Barlennan as he switched directions took some doing but the messenger managed it. The commander took his continued presence for granted.

"Any further details? When, or what was moving?"

"None, sir. The man simply appeared on the screen without any warning. He said, 'Something is happening at the *Esket.* Tell the commander.' Guzmeen ordered me to bring you back on hurricane priority, so I didn't hear any more."

"Those were his exact words? He used our language?"

"No, it was the human speech. His words were—" the runner repeated the phrase, this time in the original tongue. Barlennan could read no more into the words than had been implicit in the translation.

"Then we don't know whether someone slipped up and was seen, or dropped something into the field of the lens, or—"

"I doubt the first, sir. The human could hardly have failed to recognize a person."

"I suppose not. Well, some sort of detail should be in by the time we get back there."

There wasn't, however. Boyd Mersereau was not even on the screen by the time Barlennan reached Communications. More surprising, neither was anyone else. The commander looked at Guzmeen suspiciously; the communication officer gave the equivalent of a shrug. "He just went, sir, after that one sentence about the lab."

Barlennan, mystified, squeezed the "attention" control.

But Boyd Mersereau had other concerns on his mind. Most, but not quite all, involved events on Dhrawn, not the *Esket.* There were a few matters much closer to home than the giant star-planet.

The chief of these was the cooling down of Aucoin. Aucoin was annoyed at not having been brought into the exchanges between Dondragmer and Katini, and the captain and Tebbetts. He was inclined to blame young Hoffman for going ahead with policy-disturbing matters without official approval. However, he did not want to say anything which would annoy Easy. He regarded her, with some justification, as the most nearly indispensable member of the communications group. In consequence, Mersereau and others suffered fallout from the administrator's deflected ire.

This was not too serious, as far as Boyd was concerned. He had years ago classified the pacifying of administrators along with shaving as something which took time but did not demand full attention; it was worth doing at all only because it was usually less trouble in the long run. The real attention-getter, the thing which kept even news from the *Esket* in the background, was the state of affairs at the *Kwembly.*

Left alone Boyd might have been moderately concerned, but only moderately. The missing Mesklinites weren't close personal friends of his. He was civilized enough to be bothered by their loss as much as if they had been human, though they were not his brothers or sons.

The *Kwembly* herself was a problem, but a fairly routine one. Land-cruisers had been in trouble before; so far they had always been extricated sooner or later. All in all, Mersereau would have been merely absorbed, not bothered, if left to himself.

He was not left to himself. Benj Hoffman felt strongly about the whole matter and had a way of making his feelings clear, not entirely by talking, though he was perfectly willing to talk. Even when silent he radiated sympathy. Boyd would find himself discussing with Dondragmer the progress of the melting-out plan or the chances of another flood in terms of their effect on the missing helmsmen, rather than with reasonable and proper professional detachment. It was annoying. Beetchermarlf and Takoorch, even Kervenser, just weren't that central to the work; the real question was the survival of the crew. Benj, whether sitting silently beside him or interjecting a few remarks, somehow managed to make objectivity seem callous. Mersereau had no defense against that particular effect; Easy knew perfectly well what was going on, but she did not interfere because she almost entirely shared her son's feelings. Partly because of her sex and partly because of her own background she felt a very intense sympathy for Beetchermarlf and his companion, and even for Takoorch. She had been caught in a rather similar situation some twenty-five years before, when a concatenation of errors had stranded her in an unmanned research vessel on a high-temperature, high-pressure planet.[1]

[1] This story is told in *Close to Critical,* which is contained in *The Essential Hal Clement, Volume 1: Trio for Slide Rule and Typewriter.*

In fact, she went further than Benj would have dared. Dondragmer might and probably would have sent a ground party to the site of Reffel's disappearance, since the location was fairly well known; it was unlikely that he would have risked sending one of his three remaining communicators along. Yet Easy, partly by straightforward arguments of her own and partly by using her son's techniques to swing Mersereau to her view, convinced the captain that the risk of *not* taking the communicator along would be even greater. This discussion, among many others, was conducted in Aucoin's absence; even as he argued with Dondragmer, Mersereau was wondering how he would justify the step to planner Aucoin. Nevertheless, he argued on Easy's side, as Benj suppressed a grin in the background.

With this claim on his attention, Boyd scarcely noticed the call from another observer that a couple of objects were moving across the screen which showed the *Esket*'s laboratory. He switched channels briefly and passed the word on to the Settlement, cutting back to the *Kwembly* without waiting for the end of the communication cycle. Later he claimed that he had never been really conscious of the *Esket*'s name in the report; he had thought of the message as a routine report from some observer or other; his principal feeling had been one of irritation at being distracted. Some people would have snapped at the observer; Boyd, being the person he was, had taken what seemed to him the quickest and simplest way of disposing of the interruption. He had then quite genuinely forgotten the incident.

Benj had paid even less attention. The stranding of the *Esket* had occurred long before his arrival at the station, and the name meant nothing in particular to him, although his mother had once mentioned her friends Destigmet and Kabremm to him.

It was Easy, of course, who had really reacted to the call. She scarcely noticed what Mersereau did or said, and never thought of telling Barlennan herself until more details came in. She moved immediately to a chair commanding a view of the "lost" cruiser's screens and relegated the rest of the universe to the background.

Barlennan's return call therefore brought him very little information. Easy, to whom it was passed, had seen nothing herself; by the time she had reached her station all motion had ceased. The original observer was only able to say that he had seen two objects, a reel of cable or rope and a short length of pipe, roll across the *Esket*'s laboratory floor. It was possible that something might have pushed them, though there had been no sign of life around the vehicle for several terrestrial months; it was equally possible, and perhaps more probable, that something had tilted the *Esket* to start them rolling. So said the observer, though he could not suggest what specifically might have tipped the monstrous machine.

This left Barlennan in a quandary. It was possible that one of Destigmet's crew had become careless. It was possible that natural causes might be operating, as the humans seemed to prefer to believe. It was also possible, considering what Barlennan himself had just been planning to do, that the whole thing was a piece of human fiction. The commander's conscience made him attach more weight to this possibility than he might have done otherwise.

It was hard to see just what they could expect to accomplish by such a fiction. It could hardly be a trap any sort; there could be no wrong reaction to the story. Complete mystification was the only possible response. If there were something deeper and more subtle involved, Barlennan had to admit to himself that he couldn't guess what it was.

He didn't like guessing anyway. It was much easier to take reports at face value, allowing only for the capabilities of the speaker without worrying about possible motives. At times, the commander reflected, Dondragmer's annoying directness which had made him disapprove of the whole *Esket* trick had something to be said for it.

Yes, he had to assume that the report was truthful. By so doing, he would turn any human trick against its planners. Well then, there was nothing to do except check with Destigmet. That was simply another message to send on the *Deedee.*

Come to think of it, that was another way to check the veracity of the human reports. This report, whatever else could be said for or against its truth, showed signs of having come through quickly. And Mrs. Hoffman must be involved.

The thought that Easy's involvement made the situation a special one was the only idea on the incident Barlennan and Aucoin would have had in common. Of course, the latter hadn't heard anything about the new *Esket* incident so far; even Mersereau hadn't really thought about it. He was still otherwise engaged.

"Easy!" Boyd turned from his microphone and called across to her new station. "We seem to have convinced Don. He's sending a vision set with his six-man search party. He wants to check his own estimate of the distance at which Reffel vanished. He thinks we can pinpoint where his transmitter was. We might have estimated it at the time, but I'm not sure it was recorded. Do you want to take over here while I check up with the mappers, or would you rather go yourself?"

"I want to watch here a little longer. Benj can go up, if he can stand leaving the screens for a minute." She looked half-questioningly at the boy; he nodded and disappeared at once. He was gone longer than she expected and returned somewhat crestfallen.

"They said they'd gladly give me the map recorded from the first part of Reffel's flight, before I had told him to go on until he could barely see the *Kwembly.* All they could say about where he disappeared was that it must be off that map; the map covers the valley for about a mile westward of the cruiser."

Mersereau grunted in annoyance. "I'd forgotten about that." He turned back to his microphone to relay this not very helpful information to Dondragmer.

The captain was neither particularly surprised nor greatly disturbed. He had already discussed his own estimate of the distance and direction involved with Stakendee, who was leading the search party.

"I suppose the human beings were right about having you take the set along," the captain had remarked. "It will be a nuisance to carry and I don't much like risking its loss, but having it will cut down the risk of losing you. I'm still concerned about a repetition of the flood that brought us here, and the people up above can't give us any definite prediction. They do agree that there should indeed be a flood season coming. With the set, they'll be able to warn you directly if they get any definite information, and you'll be able to reach me through them if you do find anything."

"I'm not sure in my own mind what's best to do if a flood does come," said Stakendee. "Of course if we're close to the *Kwembly* we'll do our best to get back aboard, and I suppose if we're really distant we'd make for the north side of the valley, which seems to be nearer. In a borderline case, though, I'm not sure which would be best; surviving the flood would do us little good if the ship got washed a year's walk further downstream."

"I've been thinking about that, too," replied the captain, "and I still don't have an answer. If we're washed away again there's a very large chance the ship will be ruined. I can't decide whether we should take time to get life-support equipment out and set up on the valley side before we get on with trying to melt her out. Your own point is a good one, and maybe I should have the set there for your sake as well as ours. Well, I'll solve it. Get on your way. The sooner the search is done, the less we'll have to worry about floods."

Stakendee gestured agreement, and five minutes later Dondragmer saw him and his group emerge from the main lock. The communicator gave the party a grotesque appearance; the block of plastic, four inches high and wide and twelve in length, was being carried litter fashion by two of the searchers. The three-foot poles were only two inches apart, supported on yokes at the mid-point of the eighteen-inch-long bodies of the bearers. The poles and yokes had been fashioned from ship's stores; the Mesklinite equivalent of lumber. There were tons of the stuff in the store compartments: another of the incongruities with which the nuclear-powered cruiser was loaded in such profusion.

The search party rounded the bow of the *Kwembly,* which was facing northwest, and proceeded straight west. Dondragmer watched its lights for a few minutes as they wound around and over the boulders but had to turn to other matters long before they were out of sight.

Elongated figures swarmed over the hull working the radiator bar loose. Dondragmer had not liked to give the order for such destructive activity; but he had weighed as best he could the relative risks of doing it or of leaving it undone; having reached a decision it was not in his nature to keep on worrying about its rightness. Just as most human beings thought of Drommians as typically paranoid, most Mesklinites who knew them at all thought of human beings as typically vacillating. Dondragmer, the decision made and the order given, simply watched to make sure that minimal damage was done to the hull. From the bridge he was unable to see over its curve to the point, far astern, where the conductors came through; he would have to go outside a little later to oversee that part of the work. Maybe it would be even better to take a vision set outside and let the human engineers supervise it. Of course, with the communication delay it would be difficult for them to stop a serious error in time.

For the moment the job could be left in Praffen's nippers. The problem the captain had mentioned to Stakendee needed more thought. The life-support equipment was easy to dismount and he could spare the men to transport it without cutting into the ice-removal project too badly; but if a flood came while it was ashore and carried the *Kwembly* a long distance, things might become awkward. The system was a closed-cycle one using Mesklinite plants, depending on the fusion converters for its prime energy. By its nature, it had just about the right amount of vegetation to take care of the crew; had there been much more, there would not have been enough Mesklinites to take care of the plants! It might be possible to carry part of the system away and leave the rest, then expand each part to take care of the whole crew should circumstances force a decision between ship and shore. It would be easy enough to make more tanks but making either culture large enough to supply hydrogen for the whole crew could take more time than they might have.

In a way, it was too bad that all the communication went through the human station. One of the major and primary tasks of the *Esket* crew was to modify the old life system or to produce a new one capable of supporting a larger population. For all Dondragmer knew, this might already have been accomplished months ago.

His musings were interrupted by the communicator.

"Captain! Benj Hoffman here. Would it be too much trouble to set up one of the viewers so that we could watch your men work on the melting project? Maybe the one on the bridge would do if you just slid it out to starboard and faced it aft."

"That will be easy enough," replied the captain. "I was thinking perhaps it would be well for some of you people to watch the work." Since the set weighed less than five hundred pounds in Dhrawn's gravity, it was only its rather awkward dimensions which gave him trouble; he went about the problem like a man trying to move an empty refrigerator carton. By pushing it along the deck rather than trying to pick it up, he worked it into a good position in a few seconds. In due course, the boy's acknowledgment came back.

"Thanks, Captain; that's good. I can see the ground to starboard and what I suppose is the main lock and some of your people working along the sides. It's a little hard to judge distances, but I know how big the *Kwembly* is and about how far back the main lock is and of course I know how big your people are, so I'd guess your lights let me see the ice for fifty or sixty yards on past the lock."

Dondragmer was surprised. "I can see fully three times that far—no, wait; you're using your twelve-based numbers so it's not that much: but I do see farther. Eyes must be better than the pickup cells in your set. I hope that you are not just watching what goes on here. Are the other screens for the *Kwembly* sets all where you can see them? Or are there other people watching them? I want to be kept in as close touch as I possibly can with the search party that has just left on foot. After what happened to Reffel, I'm uneasy about both them and their set."

Dondragmer was debating with his own conscience as he sent this message. On the one hand, he was pretty certain that Reffel had shuttered his set deliberately, though it was even less clear to him than to Barlennan why this should have been necessary. On the other hand he disapproved of the secrecy of the whole *Esket* maneuver. While he would not deliberately ruin Barlennan's plans by any act of his own, he would not be too disappointed if everything came out in the open. There certainly was a good chance that Reffel was in real trouble; if, as seemed likely, whatever had happened to him had happened only a few miles away, he would have had time to get back and explain, even on foot.

In short, Dondragmer had a good excuse, but disliked the thought that he needed one. After all, there was Kervenser, too.

"All four screens are right in front of me," Benj's assurance came back. "Just now I'm alone at this station, though there are other people in the room. Mother is about ten feet away, at the *Esket*'s screens. Did anyone tell you that something had moved on one of those? Mr. Mersereau has just gone off for another argument with Dr. Aucoin." (Barlennan would have given a great deal to hear that sentence.) "There are about ten other observers in the room watching the other sets, but I don't know any of them very well. Reffel's screen is still blank; five people are working in whatever room in the *Kwembly* your other set is in but I can't tell just what they're doing. Your foot party is just walking along. I can see only a few feet around them, and only in one direction, of course. The lights they're carrying aren't nearly as strong as the ones around the *Kwembly.* If anything does come after them or some trouble develops, I may not even get as much warning as they do; and of course there'd be a delay before I could tell them anyway."

"Will you remind them of that?" asked Dondragmer. "The leader is named Stakendee. He doesn't have enough of the human language to do any good. He may very well be depending too heavily on you and your equipment for warning. I'm afraid I took for granted, without saying much about it, that your set would help warn him when we were planning the search. Please tell him that it is strictly an indirect communicator between him and me."

The boy's response was considerably longer in coming than light-lag alone would explain. Presumably he was carrying out the request without bothering to acknowledge its receipt. The captain decided not to make a point of the matter; Hoffman was very young. There was plenty else to keep Dondragmer busy, and he occupied himself with this, filing the unfinished conversation until Benj's voice once more reached the bridge.

"I've been in touch with Stak and told him what you asked. He promised to take care, but he's not very far from the *Kwembly* yet, still among the stones; they give out a little way upstream, you remember. He's still on the map, I think, though I can't really tell one square yard of that rock garden from another. It's either smooth ice or ice with cobblestones sticking up through it, or occasionally cobblestones with no ice between them. I don't see how they're going to search it very effectively. Even if you climb on the highest rock in the neighborhood, there are a lot of others you can't see beyond. The helicopters aren't very big, and you Mesklinites are a lot smaller."

"We realized that when we sent out the party," Dondragmer answered. "A really effective search will be nearly impossible among the stones if the missing are dead or even helpless. However, as you said, the stones give way to bare rock a short distance from here; in any case, it is possible that Kerv or Reffel could answer calls, or call for help themselves. Certainly at night one can be heard much farther than he can be seen. Also, whatever is responsible for their disappearance may be bigger or easier to spot." The captain had a pretty good idea how Benj would answer the last sentence. He was right.

"Finding whatever is responsible by having another group disappear wouldn't put us much farther ahead."

"It would if we actually learned what had happened. Keep in close touch with Stakendee's party, please, Benj. My time is going to be taken up with other matters and you'll learn whatever happens half a minute before I could anyway. I don't know that those seconds will make much real difference but at least you're closer to Stak in time than I am."

"Also, I have to go outside now. We're getting to a ticklish point in taking this metal bar off the hull. I'd bring one of the sets outside to keep in closer touch with you but I wouldn't be able to hear you very well through a suit. The volume of these communicators of yours isn't very impressive. I'll give you a call when I'm back in touch; there's no one handy to leave on watch here. In the meantime please keep a running log, in any way you find convenient, on what happens to Stakendee."

The captain waited just long enough to receive Benj's acknowledgment, which did arrive this time, before making his way down to the lock and donning his air suit. Preferring an inside climb to an outside one, he took the ramps back to the bridge and made use of the small lock which gave onto the top of the hull: a U-shaped pipe of liquid ammonia just about large enough for a Mesklinite body. Dondragmer unsealed and lifted the inner lid and entered the three-gallon pool of liquid, the cover closing by its own weight above him. He followed the curve down and up again and emerged through a similar lid outside the bridge.

With the smooth plastic of the hull curving down on all sides of him except aft he felt a little tense but he had long ago learned to control himself even in high places. His nippers flashed from one holdfast to another as he made his way aft to the point where the few remaining refrigerator attachments were still intact. Two of these were the ones which extended entirely through the hull as electrical contacts, and were therefore the ones which caused Dondragmer the most concern. The others, as he had hoped, were coming out of the cruiser's skin like nails; but these last would have to be severed, but severed so that they could be reconnected later on. Welding and soldering were arts which Dondragmer knew only in theory; he did know whatever procedure was to be used, it would certainly need stubs projecting from the hull as a starting point. The captain wanted to make particularly sure that the cutting would allow for this.

The cutting itself, as he had been told, would be no trouble with Mesklinite saws. He carefully selected the points where the cuts were to be made and had two of his sailors get started on the task. He warned the rest to get out of the way when the bar was free. This meant not only down to the surface but well away from the hull. The idea was to lower the metal on the lock side, once it was detached, but Dondragmer was cautious about weights and knew that the bar might possibly not wait to be lowered. Even a Mesklinite would regret being underneath when it descended from the top of the hull, feeble as Dhrawn's gravity seemed to them.

All this had taken the best part of an hour. The captain was wondering about the progress of the foot party but there was another part of the melting project to check first. He reentered the ship and sought the laboratory, where Borndender was readying a power unit to fit the makeshift resistor. Actually there was little to be done; polarized sockets, one at one end of the block and one at the other, would provide direct current if the bar could be gotten into the holes and any changes needed to make a fit possible would have to be made on the bar rather than the power box. It took only a moment to make this clear to the captain, who looked for himself, decided the scientist was obviously right and made his way hastily back to the bridge. Only when he got there and tried to call Benj did he realize that he had never removed his air suit; talking to Borndender through his suit was one thing, talking to a human over the radio quite another. He stripped enough to get his speaking-siphon into the open and spoke again.

"I'm back, Benj. Has anything happened to Stakendee?" He finished removing the suit while waiting for the answer, smoothed it, and stowed it close to the center hatchway. It didn't belong there, but there wouldn't be time to get it down to the rack by the main lock and return before Benj's words.

"Nothing really important, as far as I can tell, Captain," came the boy's voice. "They've walked a long way, though I can't tell just how far; maybe three miles since you went, but that's a guess. There has been no sign of either flier, and the only thing they or I have seen which might possibly have affected either of them has been an occasional patch of cloud a few hundred feet up; at least that's what Stak guesses, I can't see well enough myself, drifting back toward the *Kwembly.* I suppose if you accidentally flew into a big cloud you might get disoriented and if it was low enough you'd crash before you could straighten out; there aren't any blind flying instruments on those things, are there? It's hard to believe they'd do such a thing. Of course, if they were keeping their eyes on the ground instead of their flying...but none of the clouds we've seen so far is anywhere near big enough to give them time to lose their way, Stak says."

Dondragmer was inclined to share this doubt about clouds being responsible; he would have doubted it even had he not had reason for another opinion. An upward glance showed that no clouds had yet reached the *Kwembly;* the stars twinkled everywhere. Since Benj had said clouds were coming toward the cruiser, the ones Stakendee had seen must have been at the edge of the pattern and much farther to the west when the fliers were up. This might mean nothing as far as Kervenser was concerned; he could have been a long, long way from the *Kwembly.* Also Reffel had probably encountered them. Dondragmer brought his attention back to Benj, who had not paused for a reply.

"Stak says the stream bed is going uphill noticeably, but he didn't tell me how he knew; just that they'd gone up several feet since leaving the *Kwembly.*" Pressure change, Dondragmer assumed; it was always more noticeable in the suits. Just climbing around on the hull made a difference in suit tightness which could be felt. Besides, the stream which had carried the cruiser here had been flowing fairly fast; even allowing for Dhrawn's gravity, its fall must be fairly great. "The only other real change is the nature of the bottom. They're well away from the cobbles. It's mostly bare rock, with patches of ice in the hollows."

"Good. Thank you, Benj. Have your weather men come up with anything at all about the likelihood of another flood?"

The boy chuckled, though the sound meant little to the Mesklinite. "Nothing, I'm afraid. Dr. McDevitt just can't be sure. Dr. Aucoin was complaining about it a little while ago, and my boss just cut loose. He said that it had taken men a couple of centuries before they could make reliable ten-day forecasts on Earth, with only one phase-varying component, water, and the whole planet accessible for measurement. Anyone who expects forecasting perfected in a couple of years for a world as big as Dhrawn, when we know an area the size of a large backyard and that with two phase-variables and a temperature range from fifty to over a thousand degrees Kelvin, must still believe in magic. He said we were lucky the weather hadn't produced ice fields that turned into swamps when the temperature dropped and rain storms six feet deep with clear air underneath but icing up the cruiser bridges and forty other things that his computer keeps coming up with every time he changes another variable. It was funny watching Dr. Aucoin try to calm him down. Usually it's the other way around."

"I'm sorry I wasn't there to hear it. You seem amused," replied the captain. "Did you tell your chief about the clouds which Stakendee has reported?"

"Oh, certainly. I told everyone. That was only a few minutes ago, though, and they haven't come back with anything yet. I really wouldn't expect them to, Captain; there just isn't enough detailed information from the surface for interpretation, let alone prognosis. There *was* one thing though; Dr. McDevitt was very interested in finding out how many feet Stak's group had climbed and he said that if the clouds they reported hadn't reached the *Kwembly* yet he wanted to know as exactly as possible the time they do. I'm sorry; I should have reported that earlier."

"It doesn't matter," replied Dondragmer. "The sky is still clear here. I'll let you know the moment I see any clouds. Does this mean that he thinks another fog is coming, like the one which preceded the last flood?" In spite of his innate defenses against worry, the captain waited out the next minute with some uneasiness.

"He didn't say, and he wouldn't. He's been caught too wrong too many times. He won't take the chance again, if I know him, unless it's a matter of warning you against some very probable danger. Wait! There's something on Stak's screen." Dondragmer's many legs tensed under him. "Let me check. Yes, all of Stak's men but one are in sight, and he must be carrying the back end of the set because it's still moving. There's another light ahead. It's brighter than the ones we're carrying, at least, I think so, but I can't really tell its distance. I'm not sure whether Stak's people have seen it yet, but they should have; you said your eyes are better than the pickups. Mother, do you want to get in on this? And should we call Barlennan? I'm keeping Don posted. Yes, Stak has seen it and his party has stopped moving. The light isn't moving either. Stak has the sound volume up, but I can't hear anything that means anything to me. They've put the transmitter down, and are fanning out in front of it; I can see all six of them now. The ground is nearly bare, only an occasional patch of ice. No rocks. Now Stak's men have put out their lights, and I can't see anything except the new one. It's getting brighter, but I guess it's just the pickup cells reacting to the darker field. I can't see anything around it; it looks a little foggy, if anything. Something has blocked it for a moment; no, it's on again. I could see enough of a silhouette to be pretty sure it was one of the search party; he must have reared up to get a better look ahead. Now I can hear some hooting, but it's not any words I know. I don't see why...wait. Now Stak's people are turning their lights back on. Two of them are coming back toward the set; they're picking it up and bringing it forward toward the rest of the group. All the lights are up in front with them, so I can see pretty well now. There's mist blowing past only a few feet, maybe a few inches up; the new light *is* up in it a little way. I can't judge its distance yet at all. The ground has no marks to help; just bare stone, with six Mesklinites flattened down against it and their lights and a dark line beyond them which might be different colored rock or maybe a narrow stream slanting toward them from the far left and going out of sight to my right. Now I get a vague impression of motion around the new light. Maybe it's the running light of a helicopter. I don't know how they're arranged or how high off the ground they are when the machine is parked or how bright they are.

"Now it's clearer, yes, there's something moving. It's coming toward us, just a dark blob in the mist. It's not carrying any light. If my guess at distance means anything, which it probably doesn't, it's about the same size as the Mesklinites. Maybe it's Kervenser or Reffel.

"Yes. I'm almost sure it's a Mesklinite, but still too far away for me to recognize. I'm not sure I'd know either of those two anyway. He's crossing that line; it must be a stream; some liquid splashed up for a split second into the path of the light; now he's only a few yards away, and the others are converging on him. They're talking, but not loudly enough for me to make any of it out. The group is milling around, and I can't recognize anyone. If they'd come a little closer I'd ask them who's there, but I suppose they'll report pretty soon anyway and I can't make them hear through the air suits unless they're right beside the set. Now they're all coming this way and the bunch is opening out; two of them are right in front of the set; I suppose it's Stakendee and the one who's just—"

He was interrupted by a voice which originated beside him. It reached not only his ear, but three open microphones, and through them three different receivers on Dhrawn, where it produced three very different results.

"Kabremm! Where have you been all these months?" cried Easy.

11: Playing with Wire

It really wasn't quite Kabremm's fault, though Barlennan was a long time forgiving him. The transmitter had been away from the lights. When the newcomer had first joined Stakendee's group he had not been able to see it; later he had failed to notice it; not until he was within a foot or two did he recognize it. Even then he wasn't worried greatly; human beings all looked alike to him, he assumed that his own people looked at least as indistinguishable to the humans, and while he would not have put himself deliberately in view, a sudden withdrawal or any attempt to hide would have been far more suspicious than staying calmly where he was.

When Easy's voice erupted from the speaker with his name, it was obviously sixty-four seconds too late to do anything. Stakendee, whose reflex response to the sound was to reach for the shutter on top of the vision set, realized in time that this would only make matters worse.

What they should do was far from obvious to either of them. Neither was an expert in intrigue, though Mesklin was no more innocent of political deceit than it was of the commercial variety. Neither was particularly quick-witted. Both, unlike Dondragmer, were enthusiastic proponents of the *Esket* deception.

And both realized that whatever they did, or failed to do, about this mistake was likely to conflict with whatever Barlennan or Dondragmer might do. Coordination was impossible. Stakendee thought, after some seconds, of trying to address Kabremm as though he were the missing Reffel or Kervenser, but he doubted that he could get away with it. Mrs. Hoffman's recognition must have been pretty firm to let her speak as emphatically as she had, and Kabremm's response was unlikely to be helpful. He didn't, presumably, know the status of either of the missing men.

The human being had said no more, after the one question; she must be waiting for an answer. What had she seen between speaking and that time delay?

Barlennan had also heard Easy's cry, and was in exactly the same spot. He could only guess why Kabremm might be anywhere near the *Kwembly*, though the incident of Reffel's communication cutoff had prepared him for something of the sort. Only one of the three dirigibles was employed on the regular shuttle run between the *Esket* site and the Settlement; the others were under Destigmet's control and were usually exploring. Still, Dhrawn was large enough to make the presence of one of them in the *Kwembly*'s neighborhood a distinct surprise.

However, it seemed to have happened. It was simply bad luck, Barlennan assumed, compounded by the fact that the only human being in the universe who could possibly have recognized Kabremm by sight had been in a position to see him when the slip occurred.

So the human beings now knew that the *Esket*'s crew had not been obliterated. No provision had been made for such a discovery; no planned, rehearsed story existed which Barlennan could count on Kabremm's using. Maybe Dondragmer would fill in; he could be counted on to do his best, no matter what he thought of the whole matter, but it was hard to see what he *could* do. The trouble was that Barlennan himself would have no idea what Dondragmer had said and would not know what to say himself when questions came, as they surely would, toward the Settlement. Probably the safest tactic was to claim utter ignorance, and ask honestly for as complete a report as possible from Dondragmer. The captain would at least keep Kabremm, who had obviously been playing the fool, from leaking the whole cask.

It was fortunate for Barlennan's peace of mind that he did not realize where Kabremm had been met. Easy, a few seconds before her cry of recognition, had told him that Benj was reporting something from a *Kwembly* screen, or he would have assumed that Kabremm had inadvertently stepped into the field of view of an *Esket* communicator. He knew no details about the search party of Stakendee and assumed the incident was occurring at the *Kwembly* and not five miles away. The five miles was just as bad as five thousand, under the circumstances; communication between Mesklinites not within hooting range of each other had to go through the human linkage, and Dondragmer was in no better position to cover the slip than was Barlennan himself. However, the *Kwembly*'s captain managed to do it, quite unintentionally.

He, too, had heard Easy's exclamation, much more loudly than Barlennan in view of the woman's position among the microphones. However, it had been little more than a distraction to him, for his mind was wholly taken up with some words Benj had uttered a few seconds before. In fact, he was so disturbed by them as to do something which everyone at all experienced in Dhrawn-satellite communication had long ago learned not to do. He had interrupted, sending an urgent call of his own pulsing upward to the station while Benj was still talking.

"Please! Before you do anything else, tell me more about that liquid. I get the impression from what you've said that there is a stream flowing in the river-bed in view of Stakendee's vision pickup. If that is the case, please send these orders immediately: Stak, with two men to carry the communicator, is to follow that stream upward immediately, keeping you and through you, me, informed of its nature; particularly, is it growing any larger? The other three are to follow it down to find how close it comes to the *Kwembly;* when they have ascertained this, they are to come in with the information at once. I'll worry about whom you've found later on; I'm glad one of them has turned up. If this trickle is the beginning of the next flood, we'll have to stop everything else and get life-support equipment out of the ship and out of the valley. Please check, and get those orders to Stakendee at once!"

This request began to come in just as Easy finished her sentence and long before either Kabremm or Barlennan could have gotten a reply back to it. Mersereau and Aucoin were still gone, so Benj had no hesitation about passing Dondragmer's orders along. Easy, after a second or two of thought, shelved the Kabremm question and reported the same information to Barlennan. If Don saw the situation as an emergency, she was willing to go along with his opinion; he was on the scene. She did not take her eyes from the screen which showed Kabremm's image, however; his presence still needed explanation. She, too, helped Barlennan unwittingly at this point.

After completing the relay of Dondragmer's orders, she added a report of her own which clarified much for the commander.

"I don't know how up to date you are, Barl; things have been happening rather suddenly. Don sent out a foot party with a communicator to look for Kervenser and Reffel. This was the group which found the running stream which is bothering Don so much, and at the same time ran into Kabremm. I don't know how he got there, thousands of miles from the *Esket,* but we'll get his story and relay it to you as soon as we can. I've sometimes wondered whether he and any of the others were alive, but I never really hoped for it. I know the life-support equipment in the cruisers is supposed to be removable in case the vehicles had to be abandoned; but there was never any sign of anything's being taken from the *Esket.* This will be useful news as well as pleasant; there must be some way for you people to live on at least some parts of Dhrawn without human equipment."

Barlennan's answer was a conventional acknowledgment-plus-thanks, given with very little of his attention. Easy's closing sentence had started a new train of thought in his mind.

Benj had paid little attention to his mother's words, having a conversation of his own to maintain. He relayed Dondragmer's command to the foot party, saw the group break up accordingly, though he failed to interpret the confusion caused by Kabremm's telling Stakendee how he had reached the spot, then reported the start of the new mission to the captain. He followed the report, however, with comments of his own.

"Captain, I hope this isn't going to take all your men. I know there's a lot of work in getting your life equipment to the bank but surely you can keep on with the job of melting the *Kwembly* loose. You're not just giving up on the ship, are you? You still have Beetch and his friend underneath; you can't just abandon them. It won't take many men to get the heater going, it seems to me."

Dondragmer had formed by now a pretty clear basic picture of Benj's personality, though some detailed aspects of it were fundamentally beyond his grasp. He answered as tactfully as he could.

"I'm certainly not giving up the *Kwembly* while there's any reasonable chance of saving her," he said, "but the presence of liquid only a few miles away forces me to assume that the risk of another flood is now very high. My crew, as a group, comes first. The metal bar we have cut from the hull will be lowered to the ground in a few more minutes. Once that is done, only Borndender and one other man will be left on the heater detail. Everyone else, except of course Stakendee's crew, will start immediately carrying plant tanks and lights to the side of the valley. I do not want to abandon my helmsmen, but if I get certain news that high water is on the way we are all going to head for higher ground whether or not any are still missing. I gather you don't like the idea, but I am sure you see why there is no other possible course." The captain fell silent, neither knowing nor greatly caring whether Benj had an answer for this; there was too much else to consider.

He stood watching as the heavy length of metal, which was to be a heater if everyone's ideas worked out, was eased toward the *Kwembly*'s starboard side. Lines were attached to it, snubbed around the climbing holdfasts, and held by men on the ice who were carefully giving length under the orders of Praffen. Perched on the helicopter lock panel with his front end reared four inches higher, Praffen watched and gestured commands as the starboard part of the long strip of metal slid slowly away from him and the other side approached. Dondragmer flinched slightly as the sailor seemed about to be brushed off the hull by the silvery length of alloy, but Praffen let it pass under him with plenty of legs still on the plastic and at least three pairs of pincers gripping the holdfasts. With this personal risk ended he let the rope-men work a little faster; it took less than five more minutes to get the bar down to the ice.

Dondragmer had redonned his air suit during the last part of the operation and gone out on the hull again, where he hooted a number of orders. Everyone else outside obediently headed for the main lock to start transferring the life-support equipment; the captain himself reentered the bridge to get back in radio contact with Benj and Stakendee.

The boy had said nothing during the lowering-away, which had been carried out in view of the bridge communicator. What he could see required no explanation. He was a little unhappy at the disappearance of the crew afterward, for Dondragmer had been right. Benj did not like the idea of the entire group's being diverted to the abandon-ship operation. The emergence of two Mesklinites with a power box gave him something to watch besides Stakendee's upstream crawl on the adjacent screen.

Benj did not know which of the two was Borndender. However, their actions were of more interest than their identity, especially their troubles with the radiator.

The wire was rigid enough to hold its shape fairly well as it was moved; it now lay flat on the ice in much the same shape it had had when attached to the hull, rather like a long, narrow hairpin with a set of right-angle bends near the center where it had outlined the helicopter lock, the cut ends being some two feet apart. The original vertical component of its curvature, formerly impressed by the shape of the hull, had now flattened out under gravity. The unit had been turned over during the lowering so that the prongs which had attached it to the plastic were now pointing upward; hence there was good contact with the ice for its entire length.

The Mesklinites spent a few minutes trying to straighten it out; Benj got the impression that they wanted to run it around the side of the hull as closely as possible. However, it finally dawned on them that the free ends would have to be close together anyway in order to go into the same power box, so they left the wire alone and dragged the power unit aft. One of them examined the holes in the box and the ends of the wire carefully, while the other stood by.

Benj could not see the box very well, since its image on the screen was very small, but he was familiar with similar machines. It was a standard piece of equipment which had needed very little modification to render it usable on Dhrawn. There were several kinds of power takeoff on it besides the rotating field used for mechanical drive. The direct electrical current which Borndender wanted could be drawn from any of several places; there were contact plates on opposite sides of the box which could be energized; several different sizes of jack-type bipolar sockets and simple unipolar sockets at opposite ends of the box. The plates would have been easiest to use, but the Mesklinites, as Benj learned later, had dismissed them as too dangerous; they chose to use the end sockets. This meant that one end of the "hairpin" had to go into one end of the unit, and the other into the other end. Borndender already knew that the wire was a little large for these holes and would have to be filed down, and had brought the appropriate tools out with him; this was no problem. Bending the ends, however, so that short lengths of them pointed toward each other, was a different matter. While he was still working on this problem, the rest of the crew emerged from the main lock with their burden of hydroponic tanks, pumps, lights, and power units, and headed northward toward the side of the valley. Borndender ignored them, except for a brief glance, wondering at the same time whether he could commandeer some assistance.

The two ninety-degree bends he had to make were not entirely a matter of strength. The metal was of semicircular cross section, about a quarter of an inch in radius; Benj thought of it as heavy wire, while to the Mesklinites it was bar stock. The alloy was reasonably tough even at a hundred and seventy degrees Kelvin, so there was no risk of breaking it. Mesklinite strength was certainly equal to the task. What the two scientists lacked, which made the bending an operation instead of a procedure, was traction. The ice under them was fairly pure water with a modest percentage of ammonia, not so far below its melting point or removed from the ideal ice crystal structure as to have lost its slipperiness. The small area of the Mesklinite extremities caused them to dig in in normal walking, which combined with their low structure and multiplicity of legs, prevented slipping during ordinary walking around the frozen-in *Kwembly*. Now, however, Borndender and his assistant were trying to apply a strong sidewise force, and their twenty pounds of weight simply did not give enough dig for their claws. The metal refused to bend, and the long bodies lashed about on the ice with Newton's Third Law in complete control of the situation. The sight was enough to make Benj chuckle in spite of his worry, a reaction which was shared by Seumas McDevitt, who had just come down from the weather lab.

Borndender finally solved his engineering problem by going back into the *Kwembly* and bringing out the drilling equipment. With this he sank half a dozen foot-deep holes in the ice. By standing lengths of drill-tower support rod in these he was able to provide anchorage for the Mesklinite muscles. The rod was finally changed from a hairpin to a caliper shape.

Fitting the ends into the appropriate holes was comparatively easy after the filing was finished. It involved a modest lifting job to get the wire up to the two-inch height of the socket holes but this was no problem of strength or traction and was done in half a minute. With some hesitation, visible even to the human watchers, Borndender approached the controls of the power unit. The watchers were at least as tense; Dondragmer was not entirely sure that the operation was safe for his ship, having only the words of the human beings about this particular situation. Benj and McDevitt also had doubts about the efficacy of the jury-rigged heater.

Their doubts were speedily settled. The safety devices built into the unit acted properly as far as the machine's own protection was concerned; they were not, however, capable of analyzing the exterior load in detail. They permitted the unit to deliver a current, not a voltage, up to a limit determined by the manual control setting. Borndender had of course set this at the lowest available value. The resistor lasted for several seconds, and might have held up indefinitely if the ends had not been off the ice.

For most of the length of the loop, all went well. A cloud of microscopic ice crystals began to rise the moment the power came on, as water boiled away from around the wire and froze again in the dense, frigid air. It hid the sight of the wire sinking into the surface ice, but no one doubted that this was happening.

The last foot or so at each end of the loop, however, was not protected by the high specific and latent heats of water. Those inches of metal showed no sign of the load they were carrying for perhaps three seconds; then they began to glow. The resistance of the wire naturally increased with its temperature, and in the effort to maintain constant current the power box applied more voltage. The additional heat developed was concentrated almost entirely in the already overheated sections. For a long moment a red, and then a white, glow illuminated the rising cloud, causing Dondragmer to retreat involuntarily to the other end of the bridge while Borndender and his companion flattened themselves against the ice.

The human watchers cried out, Benj wordlessly, McDevitt protestingly, "It can't blow!" Their reactions were of course far too late to be meaningful. By the time the picture reached the station, one end of the wire loop had melted through and the unit had shut down automatically. Borndender, rather surprised to find himself alive, supplemented the automatic control with the manual one, and without taking time to report to the captain set about figuring what had happened.

This did not take him long; he was an orderly thinker, and had absorbed a great deal more alien knowledge than had the helmsmen, still hoping for rescue a few yards away. He understood the theory and construction of the power units about as well as a high school student understands the theory and construction of a television set; he could not have built one himself, but he could make a reasonable deduction as to the cause of a gross malfunction. He was more of a chemist than a physicist, as far as specific training went.

While the human beings watched in surprise and Dondragmer in some uneasiness, the two scientists repeated the bending operation until what was left of the resistor was once again usable. With the drilling equipment they made a pit large enough to hold the power box at the end of the deep groove boiled in the ice by the first few seconds of power. They set the box in the hole, connected the ends once more, and covered everything with chips of ice removed in the digging, leaving only the controls exposed. Then Borndender switched on the power again, this time retreating much more hastily than before.

The white cloud reappeared at once, but this time grew and spread. It enveloped the near side of the *Kwembly*, including the bridge, blocking the view for Dondragmer and the communicator lens. Illuminated by the outside flood lamps, it caught the attention of the crew, now nearing the edge of the valley, and of Stakendee and his men miles to the west. This time the entire length of the wire was submerged in melted ice, which bubbled away from around it as hot vapor, condensed to liquid a fraction of a millimeter away, evaporated again much less violently from the surface of the widening pool, and again condensed, this time to ice, in the air above. The steaming pool, some three quarters of the *Kwembly*'s length and originally some six feet in width, began to sink below the surrounding ice, its contents borne away as ice dust by the gentle wind faster than they were replenished by melting.

One side of it reached the cruiser, and Dondragmer, catching a glimpse of it through a momentary break in the swirling fog, suddenly had a frightening thought. He donned his air suit hurriedly and rushed to the inner door of the main lock. Here he hesitated; with the suit's protection he could not tell by feel whether the ship was heating dangerously, and there were no internal thermometers except in the lab. For a moment he thought of getting one; then he decided that the time needed might be risky, and opened the upper safety valves in the outer lock, which were handled by pull-cords from inside reaching down through the liquid trap. He did not know whether the heat from outside would last long enough to boil ammonia in the lock itself—the *Kwembly*'s hull was well insulated, and leakage would be slow, but he had no desire to have boiling ammonia confined aboard his command. It was an example of a little knowledge causing superfluous worry; the temperature needed to bring ammonia's vapor pressure anywhere near the ambient values would have made an explosion the least of any Mesklinite's concerns. However, no real harm was done by opening the valves, and the captain felt better as a result of the action. He returned hastily to the bridge to see what was going on.

A gentle breeze from the west was providing occasional glimpses as it swept the ice fog aside and he could see that the level of the molten pool was lower. Its area had increased greatly, but as the minutes passed he decided that some limit had been reached His two men were visible at times, crawling here and there trying to find a good viewpoint. They finally settled down almost under the bridge, with the breeze behind them.

For some time the liquid level seemed to reach a steady state, though none of the watchers could understand why. Later they decided that the spreading pool had melted its way into the still-liquid reservoir under the *Kwembly,* which took fully fifteen minutes to evaporate. By the end of that time, cobbles from the river bottom began to show their tops above the simmering water, and the problem of turning the power unit off before another length of wire was destroyed suddenly occurred to Dondragmer.

He knew now that there was no danger of the power unit's blowing up; however, several inches of the wire had already melted away, and there was going to be trouble restoring the refrigerator to service. This situation should not be allowed to get any worse, which it would if more metal were lost. Now, as the water level reached the cobbles and the wire ceased to follow the melting ice downward, the captain suddenly wondered whether he could get out to the controls fast enough to prevent the sort of shut-off which had occurred before. He wasted no time mentally blasting the scientists for not attaching a cord to the appropriate controls; he hadn't thought of it in time either.

He donned his suit again and went out through the bridge lock. Here the curve of the hull hid the pool from view, and he began to make his way down the holdfasts as rapidly as he could in the poor visibility. As he went, he hooted urgently to Borndender, "Don't let the wire melt again! Turn off the power!"

An answering but wordless hoot told him that he had been heard, but no other information came through the white blankness. He continued to grope his way downward, finally reaching the bottom of the hull curve. Below him, separated from his level by the thickness of the mattress and two thirds the height of the trucks, was the gently steaming surface of the water. It was not, of course, actively boiling at this pressure; but it was hot even by human standards and the captain had no illusions about the ability of an air suit to protect him from it. It occurred to him, rather late, that there was an excellent chance that he had just cooked his two missing helmsmen to death. This was only a passing thought; there was work to be done.

The power box lay well aft of his present position, but the nearest surface on which he could walk had to be forward. Either way there was going to be trouble reaching the unit, now presumably surrounded by hot water; but if jumping were going to be necessary, the hull holdfasts were about the poorest possible takeoff point. Dondragmer went forward.

This brought him into clear air almost at once, and he saw that his two men were gone. Presumably they had started around the far side of the pool in the hope of carrying out his order. The captain continued forward, and in another yard or two found it possible to descend to solid ice. He did so, and hastened on what he hoped was the trail of his men.

He had to slow down almost at once, however, as his course brought him back into the ice fog. He was too close to the edge of the pool to take chances. As he went he called repeatedly, and was reassured to hear each hoot answered by another. His men had not yet fallen in.

He caught up with them almost under the cruiser's stern, having walked entirely around the part of the pool not bounded by the hull. None of them had accomplished anything; the power unit was not only out of reach but out of sight. Jumping would have been utter lunacy, even if Mesklinites normally tended to think of such a thing. Borndender and his assistant had not, and the idea had only occurred to Dondragmer because of his unusual experiences in Mesklin's low-gravity equatorial zone so long ago.

But there could not be much more time. Looking over the edge of the ice, the three could catch glimpses of the rounded tops of the rocks, separated by water surfaces which narrowed as they watched. The wire must be practically out of water by now; chance alone would not have let it settle between the stones to a point much lower than their average height, and the protecting water was already there. The captain had been weighing the various risks for minutes; without further hesitation, and without issuing any orders, he slipped over the edge and dropped two feet to the top of one of the boulders.

It was the energy equivalent of an eight-story fall on Earth, and even the Mesklinite was jolted. However, he retained his self-command. A single hoot told those above that he had survived without serious injury, and warned them against following in case pride might have furnished an impulse which intelligence certainly would not. The captain, with that order issued, relegated the scientists to the back of his mind and concentrated on the next step.

The nearest rock with enough exposed area to accommodate him was two feet, well over a body length, away, but it was at least visible. Better still, another one only slightly off the line to it exposed a square inch or so of its surface. Two seconds after analyzing this situation, Dondragmer was two feet closer to the power box and looking for another stopping point. The lone square inch of the stepping stone had been touched by perhaps a dozen feet as the red-and-black length of his body had ricocheted from it to the second rock.

The next stage was more difficult. It was harder to be sure which way to go, since the hull which had furnished orientation was now barely visible; also, there were no more large surfaces as close as the one from which he had come. He hesitated, looking and planning; before he reached a decision the question was resolved for him. The grumbling sound which had gone on for so many minutes as water exploded into steam against the hot wire and almost instantly collapsed again under Dhrawn's atmospheric pressure abruptly ceased, and Dondragmer knew that he was too late to save the metal. He relaxed immediately and waited where he was while the water cooled, the evaporation slowed, and the fog of ice crystals cleared away. He himself grew uncomfortably warm, and was more than once tempted to return the way he had come; but the two-foot climb up an ice overhang with hot water at its foot, which would form part of the journey, made the temptation easy to resist. He waited.

He was still alive when the air cleared and crystals of ice began to grow around the edges of the rocks. He was some six feet from the power unit, and was able to reach it by a rather zigzag course over the cobbles once the way could be seen. He shut off the power controls, and only when that was done did he look around.

His two men had already made their way along the ice cliff to a point about level with the original front bend of the wire; Dondragmer guessed that this must be where the metal had again melted through.

In the other direction, under the bulk of the hull, was a black cavern which the *Kwembly*'s lights did not illuminate. The captain had no real wish to enter it; it was very likely that he would find the bodies of his two helmsmen there. His hesitation was observed from above.

"What's he waiting there at the power box for?" muttered McDevitt. "Oh, I suppose the ice isn't thick enough for him yet."

"That's not all of it, I'd guess." Benj's tone made the meteorologist look sharply away from the screen.

"What's the matter?" he asked.

"You must know what's the matter. Beetch and his friend were under there. They must have been. How could they have gotten away from that hot water? I bet the captain only just thought of it; he'd never have let them use that way if he'd seen what would happen, any more than I would have. Can you imagine what happened to Beetch?"

McDevitt thought rapidly; the boy wouldn't be convinced, or even comforted, by anything but sound reasoning, and McDevitt's soundest reasoning suggested that Benj's conclusion was probably right. However, he tried.

"It looks bad, but don't give up. It doesn't look as though this thing melted its way all the way across under the ship, but it might have; and either way there's some hope. If it did, they could have gotten out the other side, which we can't see; if it didn't, they could have stayed right at the edge of the liquid zone, where the ice could have saved them. Also, they may not have been under there."

"Water ice save them? I thought you said that this stuff froze because it lost its ammonia, not because the temperature went down. Water ice at its melting point, zero centigrade, would give heat-stroke to a Mesklinite."

"That was my guess," admitted the meteorologist, "but I'm certainly not sure of it. I don't have enough measurements of any sort. I admit your little friend may have been killed; but we know so little of what has happened down there that it would be silly to give up hope. Just wait, there's nothing else to do at this distance anyway. Even Dondragmer is staying put. You can trust him to check as soon as it's possible."

Benj restrained himself, and did his best to look for bright possibilities; but the eye he was supposed to be keeping on Stakendee remained fixed on the captain's image.

Several times Dondragmer extended part of his length onto the ice, but each time he drew back again, to the boy's intense annoyance. At last, however, he seemed satisfied that the ice would hold his weight, and inch by inch extended himself entirely onto the newly frozen surface. Once off the power box he waited for a moment as though expecting something to happen; the ice held, and he resumed his way toward the side of the *Kwembly.* The human beings watched; Benj's fists were clenched tightly and even the man was more tense than usual.

They could hear nothing. Not even the hoot which suddenly echoed across the ice penetrated the bridge to affect their communicator. They could not even guess why Dondragmer suddenly turned back from the hull as he was about to disappear under it. They could only watch as he raced back across the ice to a point just below his two men and waved excitedly at them, apparently indifferent to whatever there was to be learned about the fate of his helmsman and Benj's friend.

12: Guided Extrapolation

Dondragmer was far from indifferent, but by his standards it was normal to focus attention on a new matter likely to require action rather than to clear up an old one where action was unlikely to help. He had not forgotten the fate of his men but when a distant hoot bore the words "Here's the end of the stream," his program changed abruptly and drastically.

He could not see where the voice was coming from, since he was two feet below the general surface, but Borndender reported glimpses of a light perhaps half a mile away. At the captain's order, the scientist climbed the hull part way to get a better view, while his assistant went in search of a rope to get the captain out of the ice pit. This took time. The sailors had, with proper professional care, returned the lines used in lowering the radiator bar to their proper places inside the cruiser; and when Skendra, Borndender's assistant, tried to get through the main lock he found it sealed by a layer of clear ice which had frozen a quarter of an inch thick on the starboard side of the hull, evidently from the vapor emitted by the hot pool. Fortunately most of the holdfasts were projecting far enough through this to be usable, so he was able to climb on up to the bridge lock.

Meanwhile, Borndender called down that there were two lights approaching across the river bed. At the captain's order, he howled questions across the thouand-yard gap, and the two listened carefully for answers: even Mesklinite voices had trouble carrying distinct words for such a distance and through two layers of air suit fabric. By the time Dondragmer was out of the hole, they knew that the approaching men were the part of Stakendee's command which had been ordered downstream: they had reached its end less than a mile from the ship, but until the group actually reached them, no further details could be obtained.

When they were, the officers could not entirely understand them; the description did not match anything familiar.

"The river stayed about the same size all the way down," the sailors reported. "It wasn't being fed from anywhere, and didn't seem to be evaporating. It wound among the stones a lot, when it got down to where they were. Then we began to run into the funniest obstructions. There would be a sort of dam of ice, with the stream running around one end or the other of it. Half a cable or so farther on there'd be another dam, with just the same thing happening. It was as though some of it froze when it met the ice among the stones, but only the lead part. The water that followed stayed liquid and went on around the dam until *it* found some ice. The dams would build up to maybe half a body length high before the following water would find its way around. We reached the last one, where it was still happening, just a few minutes ago. We'd seen the bright cloud rising over the ship before that, and wondered whether we ought to come back in case something was wrong, but we decided to carry out orders at least until the river started to lead us away from the *Kwembly* again."

"Good," said the captain. "You're sure the stream wasn't getting any bigger?"

"As nearly as we could judge, no."

"All right. Maybe we have more time than I thought, and what's happening isn't a prelude to what brought us here. I wish I understood why the liquid was freezing in that funny way, though."

"We'd better check with the human beings," suggested Borndender, who had no ideas on the matter either but preferred not to put the fact too bluntly.

"Right. And they'll want measurements and analyses. I suppose you didn't bring a sample of that river," he said, rather than asked, the newcomers.

"No, Sir. We had nothing to carry it in."

"All right. Born, get containers and bring some back; analyze it as well and as quickly as you can. One of these men will guide you. I'll go back to the bridge and bring the humans up to date. The rest of you get tools and start chipping ice so we can use the main lock." Dondragmer closed the conversation by starting to climb the ice-crusted hull. He waved toward the bridge as he went, assuming that he was being watched and perhaps even recognized.

Benj and McDevitt had managed to keep track of him, though neither found it easy to tell Mesklinites apart. They were waiting eagerly when he reached the bridge to hear what he had to say. Benj in particular had grown ever more tense since the search under the cruiser had been interrupted; perhaps the helmsmen had not been there after all; perhaps they had been among the newcomers who had arrived to interrupt the search, perhaps, perhaps.

Although McDevitt was a quiet man by nature, even he was getting impatient by the time Dondragmer's voice reached the station.

The report fascinated the meteorologist, though it was no consolation to his young companion. Benj wanted to interrupt with a question about Beetchermarlf, but knew that it would be futile; and when the captain's account ended, McDevitt immediately began to talk.

"This is not much more than a guess, Captain," he began, "though perhaps your scientist will be able to stiffen it when he analyzes those samples. It seems possible that the pool around you was originally an ammonia-water solution (we had evidence of that before) which froze, not because the temperature went down but because it lost much of its ammonia and its freezing point went up. The fog around you just before this whole trouble started, back on the snow field, was ammonia, your scientists reported. I'm guessing that it came from the colder areas far to the west. Its droplets began to react with the water ice, and melted it partly by forming a eutectic and partly by releasing heat; you were afraid of something of that sort even before it happened, as I remember. That started your first flood. When the ammonia cloud passed on into Low Alpha, the solution around you began to lose ammonia by evaporation, and finally the mixture which was left was below its freezing point. I'm guessing that the fog encountered by Stakendee is more ammonia, and has provided the material for the rivulet he has found. As the fog meets the water ice near you they mix until the mixture is too dilute in ammonia to be liquid any more (this forms the dam your men described) and the liquid ammonia still coming has to find a way around. I would suggest that if you can find a way to divert that stream over to your ship and if there proves to be enough of it, your melting-out problem would be solved." Benj, listening in spite of his mood, thought of wax flowing from a guttering candle and freezing first on one front and then another. He wondered whether the computers would handle the two situations alike, if ammonia and heat were handled the same way in the two problems.

"You mean I shouldn't worry about a possible flood?" Dondragmer's voice finally returned.

"I'm guessing not," replied McDevitt. "If I'm right about this picture, and we've been talking it over a lot up here, the fog that Stakendee met should have passed over the snow plain you came from, or what's left of it, and if it were going to cause another flood that should have reached you by now. I suspect the snow which was high enough to spill into the pass you were washed through was all used up on the first flood, and that's why you were finally left stranded where you are. If the new fog hasn't reached you yet, by the way, I think I know the reason. The place where Stakendee met it is a few feet higher than you are and air flowing from the west is coming downhill. With Dhrawn's gravity and that air composition there'd be a terrific foehn effect (adiabatic heating as the pressure rises) and the stuff is probably evaporating just as it gets to the place where Stakendee met it."

Dondragmer took a while to digest this. For a few seconds after the normal delay time, McDevitt wondered whether he had made himself clear; then another question came through.

"But if the ammonia fog were simply evaporating, the gas would still be there, and must be in the air around us now. Why isn't it melting the ice just as effectively as though it were in liquid drops? Is some physical law operating which I missed in the College?"

"I'm not sure whether state and concentration would make all that difference, just from memory," admitted the meteorologist. "When Borndender gets the new data up here I'll feed the whole works into the machine to see whether this guess of ours is ignoring too many facts. On the basis of what I have now, I still think it's a reasonable one, but I admit it has its fuzzy aspects. There are just too many variables; with only water they are practically infinite, if you'll forgive a loose use of the word; with water and ammonia together the number is infinity squared.

"To shift from abstract to concrete, I can see Stakendee's screen and he's still going along beside that streamlet in the fog; he hasn't reached the source but I haven't seen any other watercourses feeding in from either side. It's only a couple of your body lengths wide, and has stayed about the same all along."

"That's a relief," came the eventual response. "I suppose if a real flood were coming, that river would give some indication. Very well, I'll report again as soon as Borndender has his information. Please keep watching Stakendee. I'm going outside again to check under the hull; I was interrupted before." The meteorologist had wanted to say more, but was silenced by the realization that Dondragmer would not be there to hear his words by the time they arrived. He may also have been feeling some sympathy for Benj. They watched eagerly, the man almost as concerned as his companion, for the red-and-black inchworm to appear on the side of the hull within range of the pickup. It was not visible all the way to the ground, since Dondragmer had to go forward directly under the bridge and out of the field of view; but they saw him again near where the rope which had been used to get him out a few minutes earlier was still snubbed around one of Borndender's bending posts.

They watched him swarm down the line into the pit. A Mesklinite hanging on a rope about the thickness of a six-pound nylon fishline, and free to swing pendulum-style in forty Earth gravities, is quite a sight even when the distance he has to climb is not much greater than his own body length. Even Benj stopped thinking about Beetchermarlf for a moment.

The captain was no longer worried about the ice; it was presumably frozen all the way to the bottom by now, and he went straight toward the cruiser without bothering to stay on the stones. He slowed a trifle as he drew near, eyeing the cavity in front of him thoughtfully.

Practically, the *Kwembly* was still frozen in, of course. The melted area had reached her trucks some sixty feet fore and aft, but the ice was still above the mattress beyond those limits and on the port side. Even within that range, the lower part of the treads had still been an inch or two under water when the heater had given out. Beetchermarlf's control cables had been largely freed, but of the helmsman himself there was no sign whatever. Dondragmer had no hope of finding the two alive under the *Kwembly;* they would obviously have emerged long ago had this been the case. The captain would not have offered large odds on the chance of finding bodies, either. Like McDevitt, he knew that there was a possibility that the crewmen had not been under the hull at all when the freeze-up occurred. There had, after all, been two other unexplained disappearances; Dondragmer's educated guess at the whereabouts of Kervenser and Reffel was far from a certainty even in his own mind.

It was dark underneath, out of range of the floods. Dondragmer could still see (a response to abrupt changes of illumination was a normal adaptation to Mesklin's eighteen-minute rotation period) but some details escaped him. He saw the condition of the two trucks whose treads had been ruined by the helmsmen's escape efforts, and he saw the piles of stones they had made in the attempt to confine the hot water in a small area; but he missed the slash in the mattress where the two had taken final refuge.

What he saw made it obvious, however, that at least one of the missing men had been there for a while. Since the volume which had evidently not frozen at all was small, the most likely guess seemed to be that they had been caught in the encroaching ice after doing the work which could be seen; though it was certainly hard to see just how this could have happened. The captain made a rapid check the full length of the ice-walled cavern, examining every exposed truck fore and aft, top and sides. It never occurred to him to look higher. He had, after all, taken part in the building of the huge vehicle; he knew there was nowhere higher to go.

He emerged at last into the light and the field of view of the communicator. His appearance alone was something of a relief to Benj; the boy had concluded, just as the captain had, that the helmsmen could not be under the hull alive, and he had rather expected to see Dondragmer pulling bodies after him. The relief was short, and the burning question remained: where was Beetchermarlf? The captain was climbing out of the pit and leaving the field of view. Maybe he was coming back to the bridge to make a detailed report. Benj, now showing clearly the symptoms of sleeplessness, waited silently with his fists clenched.

But Dondragmer's voice did not come. The captain had planned to tell the human observers what he had found, but on the way up the side of the hull, visible but unrecognized, he paused to talk to one of the men who was chipping ice from the lock exit.

"I only know what the human, Hoffman, told me you found when your party reached that stream," he said. "Are there more details I should know? I know that you met someone at the point where the ground reached up into the fog, but I never heard from Hoffman whether it was Reffel or Kervenser. Which was it? And are the helicopters all right? There was an interruption just then; someone up above apparently caught sight of Kabremm back at the *Esket;* then I broke in myself because the stream you had found worried me. That's why I split your party. Who was it you found?"

"It was Kabremm."

Dondragmer almost lost his grip on the holdfasts.

"Kabremm? Destigmet's first officer? Here? And a human being recognized him; it was *your* screen he was seen on?"

"It sounded that way, sir. He didn't see our communicator until it was too late, and none of us thought for an instant that there was a chance of a human being telling one of us from another; at least, not between the time we recognized him ourselves and the time it was too late."

"But what is he doing here? This planet has three times the area of Mesklin; there are plenty of other places to be. I knew the commander was going to hit shoals sooner or later playing this *Esket* trick on the human beings, but I certainly never thought he'd ground on such silly bad luck as this."

"It's not entirely chance, sir. Kabremm didn't have time to tell us much. We took advantage of your order about exploring the stream to break up and get him out of sight of the communicator, but I understand this river has been giving trouble most of the night. There's a buildup of ice five million or so cables downstream, not very far from the *Esket,* and a sort of ice river is flowing slowly into the hot lands. The *Esket* and the mines and the farms are right in its way."

"Farms?"

"That's what Destigmet calls them. Actually a Settlement with hydroponic tanks; a sort of oversized life-support rig that doesn't have to balance as closely as the cruiser rigs do. Anyway, Destigmet sent out the *Gwelf* under Kabremm to explore upstream in the hope of finding out how bad the ice river was likely to get. They had grounded where we met them because of the fog; they could have flown over it easily enough, but they couldn't have seen the river bed through it."

"Then they must have arrived since the flood that brought us here; if they were examining the river bed they flew right over us. How could they possibly have missed our lights?"

"I don't know, sir. If Kabremm told Stakendee, I didn't hear him."

Dondragmer gave the rippling equivalent of a shrug. "Probably he did, and made it a point to stay out of reach of our human eyes. I suppose Kervenser and Reffel ran into the *Gwelf,* and Reffel used his vision shutter to keep the dirigible from human sight; but I still don't see why Kervenser, at least, didn't come back to report."

"I'm afraid I don't know about any of that, either," replied the sailor.

"Then the river we've washed into must bend north, if it leads to the *Esket* area." The other judged correctly that Dondragmer was merely thinking out loud, and made no comment. The captain pondered silently for another minute or two. "The big question is whether the commander heard it, too, when the human—I suppose it was Mrs. Hoffman; she is about the only one that familiar with us—called out Kabremm's name. If he did, he probably thought that someone had been careless back at the *Esket,* as I did. You heard her on your set and I heard her on mine, but that's reasonable. They're both *Kwembly* communicators, and probably all in one place up at the station. We don't know, though, about their links with the Settlement. I've heard that all their communication gear is in one room, but it must be a big room and the different sets may not be very close together. Barl may or may not have heard her.

"What it all shapes up to is that one human being has recognized an *Esket* crew member, not only alive long after they were supposed to be dead but five or six million cables from the place where they supposedly died. We don't know how certain this human being was of the identification; certain enough to call Kabremm's name aloud, perhaps not certain enough to spread the word among other humans without further checking. I gather they don't like looking silly any more than we do. We don't know whether Barlennan knows of the slip; worst of all, we can't tell what he's likely to answer when questions about it come his way. His safest and most probable line would be complete ignorance seasoned with shocked amazement, and I suppose he'll realize that, but I certainly wish I could talk to him without having human beings along the corridor."

"Wouldn't your best line be ignorance, too?" queried the sailor.

"It would be," the captain answered, "but I can't get away with it. I've already told the humans your party was back, and I couldn't convince them that nothing at all had happened on your trip. I'd like to make

Mrs. Hoffman believe she made a mistake in identity and that you had met Reffel or Kervenser; but until we find at least one of them even that would be hard to organize. How did she recognize Kabremm? How does she recognize any of us? Color pattern and habitual leg stance, as you'd expect? Or what?

"And furthermore, what did become of that pair? I suppose Reffel came on the *Gwelf* unexpectedly, and had to shutter his set to keep the humans from seeing it; in that case we should be back in touch before long. I wash he looked more like Kabremm. I might take a chance on claiming that it was Ref she'd seen. After all, the light was pretty bad, even for those seeing machines, as I picture the situation, only I don't know what Barl is going to do. I don't even know whether he heard her or not. That's the sort of thing that's been worrying me ever since this *Esket* trick was started; with all our long-distance communication going through the human station, coordination was bound to be difficult. If something like this happened, as it was always likely to, before we got our own communication systems developed and working, we wind up on a raft with no center-boards and breakers downwind." He paused and thought briefly. "Did Kabremm make any arrangements with your group about further communication when we got the talking-box out of the way?"

"Not that I know of, sir. Your orders to break up and go different ways came before much was said."

"All right. You carry on, and I'll think of something."

"All that ever worried me," replied the sailor as he resumed chipping at the ice, "was what would happen when they *did* learn about what we were doing. I keep telling myself they wouldn't really abandon us here; they don't seem to be quite that firm, even on business deals; but they *could* as long as we don't have space craft of our own."

"It was something like that fear which caused the commander to start the whole project, as you know," returned Dondragmer. "They seem to be well-intentioned beings, as dependable as their life-spans allow; personally I'd trust them as far as I would anyone. Still, they *are* different, and one is never quite sure what they will consider an adequate motive or excuse for some strange action. That's why Barlennan wanted to get us self-supporting on this world as soon as possible and without their knowledge; some of them might have preferred to keep us dependent on them."

"I know."

"The mines were a long step, and the dirigibles were a triumph, but we're a long, long way from being able to make do without the human energy-boxes; and I sometimes wonder if the commander realizes just how far beyond us those things really are.

"But this talk isn't solving problems. I have to talk to the humans again. I hope that not mentioning Kabremm at all won't make them suspicious; at least it would be consistent with the mistaken-identity line, if we have to use it. Carry on, and give me a wave on the bridge when the main lock is clear."

The sailor gestured understanding-and-compliance, and Dondragmer at last got to the bridge.

There was plenty to say to the human beings without mentioning Kabremm, and the captain began saying it as soon as he had doffed his air suit.

"At least one of the helmsmen was under the hull for a while, and probably they both were, but I couldn't find any trace of either one just now except work they had done trying to get out; at least, I can't see any other reason for the work; it certainly wasn't an assigned job. They wrecked, or nearly wrecked, two of the trucks in the process. Much of the space under there is still frozen up, and I'm afraid they're probably in the ice. We'll search more carefully, with lights, when the crew comes back and I can spare the men. The water, or whatever it was, that was boiled away by our heater coated an ice layer on the hull which has sealed the main lock; we must get that back into service as quickly as possible. There is much equipment which can't now be moved out if we have to abandon the *Kwembly,* and much which can't be moved back inside if we don't, because it won't go through any other lock.

"Also, the use of that heater caused the melting of about a body length of the radiator wire, and I don't see how we are going to restore the refrigerator to service if we do get the *Kwembly* free. This may not be of immediate importance, but if we do get back into service we'd have to think twice about going very far into Low Alpha without refrigeration. One of the few things you people seem really sure of is that the low-pressure area is caused by high temperature, presumably from internal heat, and I know you set a very high priority on finding out about it. There is virtually no metal in the ship, and one of the few things I understand about that refrigerator is that its outside radiator must be an electrical conductor. Right?"

The captain waited for his reply with some interest. He hoped that the technical problem would divert human interest from the whole question of Kabremm and the *Esket;* but he knew that this would not have worked if he himself were on the other end of the conversation. Of course, Benj Hoffman was young; but he was probably not the only person there.

Benj answered; he didn't seem much interested in technology.

"If you think they're in the ice, shouldn't people get down there right away and look? They might still be alive in those suits, mightn't they? You said a while ago that no one had ever found out, but that at least they wouldn't suffocate. It seems to me that the longer you put off finding them, the less chance they have of living. Isn't that the most important problem right now?"

Easy's voice broke in before Dondragmer could frame an answer; she seemed to be talking to her son as well as to the captain.

"It's not quite the most important. The *Kwembly* is synonymous with the lives of its entire crew, Benj. The captain is not being callous about his men. I know how you feel about your friend and it's perfectly proper; but a person with responsibility has to think as well as feel."

"I thought you were on my side."

"I feel with you very strongly; but that doesn't keep me from knowing the captain is right."

"I suppose Barlennan would react the same way. Have you asked him what Dondragmer should do?"

"I haven't asked him, but he knows the situation; if you don't think so, there's the microphone; give your side of it to him. Personally I don't think he'd dream of overriding Dondragmer or any other cruiser captain in such a matter, when he himself isn't on the scene." There was a pause while Benj hunted for words to refute this claim; he was still young enough to think that there was something fundamentally inhuman about thinking more than one step ahead at a time. After ten seconds or so of silence, Dondragmer assumed that the station transmission was over and a reply was in order.

"Mrs. Hoffman, I believe I recognized her voice, is quite right, Benj. I have not forgotten Beetchermarlf, any more than you have forgotten Takoorch, although it is obvious even to me that you are thinking less of him. It is simply that I have more lives to consider than theirs. I'm afraid I'll have to leave any more discussion of it to her, right now. Would you please get some of your engineers thinking about the problem of my refrigerator? And you probably see Borndender climbing the hull with his sample; the report about the stream should come up in a few minutes. If Mr. McDevitt is still there, please have him stand by; if he has left for any reason, will you please have him come back?"

The watchers had seen a climbing Mesklinite as the captain had said, though not even Easy had recognized Borndender. Before Benj could say anything, McDevitt answered, "I'm still here, Captain. We'll wait, and as soon as the analysis is here I'll take it to the computer. If Borndender has any temperature and pressure readings to send along with his chemical information, they will be useful."

Benj was still unhappy, but even he could see that this was not the time for further interruption. Besides, his father had just entered the communication room, accompanied by Aucoin and Mersereau. Benj tactfully slid out of the seat in front of the bridge screen to make room for the planner, though he was too angry and upset to hope that his badly chosen words of the last few minutes would go unmentioned. He was not even relieved when Easy, in bringing the newcomers up to date, left the question of the missing helmsmen unmentioned.

Her account was interrupted by Dondragmer's voice. "Borndender says that he has checked the density and boiling temperature of the liquid in the stream: it is about three eighths ammonia and five eighths water. He also says that the outside temperature is 71, the pressure 26.6 standard atmospheres, our standard, of course, and the wind a little north of west, 21 degrees to be more precise, at 120 cables per hour. A very light breeze. Will that suffice for your computer?"

"It will all help. I'm on my way," replied McDevitt as he slid from his seat and headed toward the door. As he reached the exit he looked back thoughtfully, paused, and called, "Benj, I hate to pull you from the screens right now, but I think you'd better come with me for a while. You can check me on the input, then you can bring the preliminary run back to report to Dondragmer while I do the recheck."

Easy kept her approval to herself as Benj silently followed his superior. The approval was divided between McDevitt, for turning the youngster's attention in a safer direction, and her son for showing more self-control than she had really expected.

Aucoin paid no attention to the exchange; he was still trying to clarify his picture of the current state of affairs.

"I take it that none of the missing personnel have turned up," he said. "All right, I've been thinking it over. I assume that Barlennan has been brought up to date, as we agreed a few hours ago. Is there anything else which has happened, which he has been told about but I haven't?" Easy looked up quickly, trying to catch evidence of resentment on the administrator's face, but he seemed unaware that his words could possibly be interpreted as criticism. She thought quickly before answering.

"Yes. Roughly three hours ago, Cavanaugh reported action on one of the *Esket* screens. He saw a couple of objects sliding or rolling across the floor of the laboratory from one side of the screen to the other. I started watching, but nothing has happened there since.

"Then an hour or so later, the search party Don had out for the missing helicopters met a Mesklinite which we of course assumed at first to be one of the pilots; when he got close to the transmitter I recognized Kabremm, the first officer of the *Esket.*"

"Six thousand miles from where the *Esket*'s crew is supposed to have died?"

"Yes."

"You told this to Barlennan?"

"Yes."

"What was his comment?"

"Nothing specific. He acknowledged the whole report, but didn't offer any theories."

"He didn't even ask you how sure you were of the identification? Or on what you based it?"

"No."

"Well, if you don't mind I'd like to. Just how did you know this Kabremm, and how certain are you that you were right?"

"I knew him, before the loss of the *Esket,* well enough to make it difficult to say what I went by; he's simply distinctive, in color pattern, stance and walk, just as you and Ib and Boyd are."

"The light was good enough for color pattern? It's night down there."

"There were lights near the set, though most of them were in front of it, in the field of view, and Kabremm was mostly back-lighted."

"Do you know the two missing men well enough to be certain it was neither of them; do you know that neither one looks much like Kabremm?"

Easy flushed. "It certainly wasn't Kervenser, Don's officer. I'm afraid I don't know Reffel well enough be sure; that possibility hadn't occurred to me. I just saw the man, and called out his name pretty much by reflex. After that I couldn't do much but make a report. The Settlement microphone was alive at the time, and Barlennan or whoever was on duty could hardly have helped hearing me."

"Then there is a reasonable chance that Barlennan's lack of comment was a polite attempt to avoid embarrassing you, to gloss over what may have seemed to him a silly mistake?"

"I suppose it's possible." Easy could not make herself sound anything but doubtful, but even she knew that her opinion was unlikely to be objective.

"Then I think," Aucoin said slowly and thoughtfully, "that I'd better talk to Barlennan myself. You say nothing more has happened at the *Esket* since Cavanaugh saw those objects rolling?"

"I haven't seen anything. The bridge set, of course, is looking out into darkness, but the other three are lighted perfectly well and have shown no change except that one."

"All right. Barlennan knows our language well enough, in my experience, so that I won't need you to translate."

"Oh, no; he'll understand you. You mean you'd rather I left?"

"No, no, certainly not. In fact, it would be better if you listened and warned me if you thought there might be any misunderstanding developing." Aucoin reached for the Settlement microphone switch, but glanced once more at Easy before closing it. "You don't mind, do you, if I make sure of Barlennan's opinion about your identification of Kabremm? I think our main problem is what to do about the *Kwembly,* but I'd like to settle that point too. After you have brought the matter up with him, I'd hate Barlennan to get the idea that we were trying to, well, censor anything, to phrase it the way Ib did at the meeting." He turned away and sent his call toward Dhrawn.

Barlennan was in the communicator chamber at the Settlement, so no time was lost reaching him. Aucoin identified himself, once he was sure the commander was at the other end, and began his speech.

Easy, Ib, and Boyd found it annoyingly repetitious, but they had to admire the skill with which the planner emphasized his own ideas. Essentially, he was trying to forestall any suggestion that another vehicle be sent to the rescue of the *Kwembly,* without his suggesting such a thing. It was a very difficult piece of language manipulation, even though the matter had been uppermost in Aucoin's mind ever since the conference, so that while it was anything but an impromptu speech, it certainly had merit as a work of art, as Ib remarked later. He did mention Easy's identification of Kabremm to the commander, but so fleetingly that she almost failed to recognize the item. He didn't actually say that she must have been mistaken, but he was obviously attaching no importance to the incident.

It was a pity, as Easy remarked later, that such polished eloquence was so completely wasted. Of course Aucoin had no more way of knowing than did the other human beings that the identification of Kabremm was Barlennan's main current worry, that for two hours he had been concerned with nothing else. Faced with the imminent collapse of his complex scheme and, as he suddenly realized with embarrassment, having no ready alternative, he had employed those hours in furious and cogent thought. By the time Aucoin had called, Barlennan had the first steps of another plan. He was waiting so eagerly for a chance to put it into operation that he paid little attention to the planner's beautifully selected words. When a pause came, Barlennan had his own speech ready, though it had remarkably little to do with what had just been said.

The pause had not actually been meant as time for an answer; Aucoin had taken a moment to review mentally what he had covered and what should come next. Mersereau, however, caught him as he was about to resume talking.

"That break was long enough to let Barlennan assume you had finished and wanted an answer," he said. "Better wait. He'll probably have started talking before whatever you were just going to say gets down there." The administrator obediently waited; a convention was, after all, a convention. He was prepared to be sarcastic if Mersereau were wrong, but the Mesklinite commander's voice came through on the scheduled second—closer to it than they would have been willing to bet, Ib and Easy thought later.

"I've been thinking deeply ever since Mrs. Hoffman told me about Kabremm," he said, "and I've been able to come up with only one theory. As you know, we've always had to carry in mind the possibility that there was an intelligent species here on Dhrawn. Your scientists were certain there was highly organized life even before the landing, because of the oxygen-rich air, they said. I know we haven't run into anything but simple plants and practically microscopic animals, but the *Esket* had ventured farther into Low Alpha than any of the other cruisers, and conditions are different there; certainly the temperature is higher, and we don't know how that may change other factors.

"Until now, the chance that the *Esket* had met intelligent opposition was only one possibility, with no more to support it than any other idea we could dream up. However, as your own people have pointed out repeatedly, none of her crew could have lived this long without the cruiser's support system or something like it. They certainly couldn't have travelled from where the *Esket* still is, as far as we can tell, to Dondraginer's neighborhood. It seems to me that Kabremm's presence there is convincing evidence that Destigmet's crew has encountered and been captured by natives of Dhrawn. I don't know why Kabremm was free enough to meet that search party; maybe he escaped, but it's hard to see how he would have dared to try under the circumstances. More likely they sent him deliberately to make contact. I wish very much that you'd pass this idea along to Dondragmer for his opinion, and have him find out what he can from Kabremm, if *he* is still available. You haven't told me whether he was still with the search party or not. Will you do that?"

Several pieces fell into place in Ib Hoffman's mental jigsaw puzzle. His silent applause went unnoticed, even by Easy.

13: Fact Is Strange, Fiction Convincing

Barlennan was quite pleased with his speech. He had not told a single falsehood; the worst he could be accused of was fuzzy thinking. Unless some humans were already actively suspicious, there would be no reason for them not to pass on the "theory" to the *Kwembly*'s captain, thus telling him the line that Barlennan proposed to follow. Dondragmer could be trusted to play up properly, especially if the hint that Kabremm might not be available for further questioning were transmitted to him. It was too bad, in a way, to spring the "native menace" so long before he had meant to; it would have been much nicer to let the human beings invent it for themselves, but any plan which couldn't be modified to suit new circumstances was a poor plan, Barlennan told himself.

Aucoin was taken very much aback. He had personally had no doubt whatever that Easy was mistaken, since he had long ago written the *Esket* completely off, in his own mind, and Barlennan's taking her opinion seriously had been a bad jolt. The administrator knew that Easy was by far the best qualified person in the station to make such a recognition; he had not, however, expected the Mesklinites themselves to be aware of this. He blamed himself for not paying much more attention to the casual conversation between human observers (especially Easy) and the Mesklinites over the past few months. He had let himself get out of touch, a cardinal administrative sin.

He could see no reason for denying Barlennan's request, however. He glanced at the others. Easy and Mersereau were looking expectantly at him; the woman had her hand on the microphone selector in her chair arm as though about to call Dondragmer. Her husband had a half-smile on his face which puzzled Aucoin slightly for a moment, but as their eyes met Hoffman nodded as though he had been analyzing the Mesklinite's theory and found it reasonable. The planner hesitated a moment longer, then spoke into his microphone.

"We'll do that right away, Commander." He nodded to Easy, who promptly changed her selector switch and began talking. Benj returned just as she started, obviously bursting with information, but he restrained himself when he saw that a conversation with the *Kwembly* was already in progress. His father watched the boy as Easy relayed the Barlennan theory, and had some difficulty in concealing his amusement. It was so obvious that Benj was swallowing the idea whole. Well, he was young, and several of his elders seemed a bit uncritical too.

"Barlennan wants your thoughts on this possibility, and especially any more information you may have obtained from Kabremm," concluded Easy. "That's all—no, wait." Benj had caught her attention. "My son has come back from the aerology lab, and seems to have something for you."

"Mr. McDevitt has made one run with the new measures added to the earlier data and is making a second now," Benj said without preamble. "According to the first, he was right about the reason for the melting and freezing of your lake, and the nature of the clouds which Stakendee has encountered. The chances are better than even that condensation from these will increase, and make the stream near you bigger. He suggests that you check very carefully, as he mentioned before, the time the clouds reach the *Kwembly*. As he guessed, they are evaporating from adiabatic heating as the air carrying them comes down the ground slope. He says that the later they are in getting to you, the worse the flood will be when *it* does. I don't see why myself, but that's what the computer implies. He said to be sure to remind you that this was just another tentative calculation, just as likely to be wrong as any of the earlier ones. He went into a long speech about all the reasons he couldn't be sure, but you've heard it already."

Dondragmer's answer commenced almost on the light-echo; he could not have spent more than a second or two after the end of Benj's report in deciding what to say.

"Very well, Benj. Please tell Barlennan that his idea sounds reasonable, and at least fits in with the disappearance of my two fliers. I have had no opportunity to get information from Kabremm, if it really was he; I haven't seen him. He hasn't come back to the *Kwembly*. You could tell better than I whether he's still with Stakendee and those who went upstream. I will take precautions on the assumption that the commander is right. If the idea had occurred to me earlier, I certainly would not have sent out practically my entire crew to set up the safety base at the side of the valley.

"However, it may be just as well I did. I see no possibility of freeing the cruiser in any reasonable time, and if Mr. McDevitt is even moderately sure that another flood is on the way we'll have to finish moving out shortly. If a current anything like the one that brought us here hits the

Kwembly while she's fastened down like this, there'll be pieces of hull scattered for a million cables downstream. When my men come back we'll take one more load of necessary equipment and abandon the ship for the time being. We'll set up on the valley rim, and as soon as life-support equipment is running adequately there I'll start sending crews back here to work on freeing the *Kwembly,* provided the flood isn't obviously on the way. That's a firm basic plan; I'll work out details for covering the work crews with your assistance, and if Barlennan's theory calls for special action I'll take it, but I haven't time to argue the basic decision. I can see moving lights to the north; I assume it's my crew on the way back. I'll turn the set so that you can see them."

The view on the screen wavered, then panned jerkily as the captain nudged the transmitter box through a third of a circle. The result was no improvement, from the human viewpoint; the lighted region around the *Kwembly* where details could not only be seen but compared and interpreted, was replaced by almost total darkness relieved by a few specks of light. It took close, careful watching to confirm Dondragmer's claim that they were moving. Easy was about to ask that the lens be returned to its former position when Benj began talking.

"You mean you've given up all hope of finding Beetchermarlf and Takoorch and the others, and are just going off and leaving them there? I know you have nearly a hundred other people to worry about, but there are times when that seems a pretty thin excuse for not even trying to rescue someone!"

Easy was startled and rather dismayed at her son's choice of words, and almost cut in with a combined rebuke to the boy and apology to Dondragmer. She hesitated, however, in the effort to find words which would do this without doing violence to her own feelings; these bore a strong resemblance to Benj's. Aucoin and Mersereau had not followed the exchange at all closely, since both were concentrating on Barlennan on the other screen and Benj had uttered his tirade in Stennish. Ib Hoffman showed no expression which the casual observer could have translated, though Easy might have detected traces of amusement if she had been looking at him. McDevitt had just come in, but was too late to catch anything except Easy's facial expression.

The pause went overtime, so they waited for Dondragmer's answer. This revealed no annoyance in tone or choice of words; Easy wished she could see him to judge his body attitude.

"I haven't given them up, Benj. The equipment we plan to take includes as many power units as possible, which means that men will have to go under the hull with lights to get as many of them as they can from the unfrozen trucks. Those men will also have orders to search the ice walls carefully for traces of the helmsmen. If they are found, men will be assigned to chip them out, and I will leave those men on the job until the last possible instant. However, I can't justify putting the entire crew to work breaking ice until there is nothing else to be done to get the cruiser free. After all, it is perfectly possible that they discovered what was going on before the pond froze to the bottom, and were trapped while looking for a hole in the ice somewhere else in the pond."

Benj nodded, his face somewhat red; Easy spared him the need of composing a verbal apology.

"Thanks, Captain," she said. "We understand. We weren't seriously accusing you of desertion; it was an unfortunate choice of words. Do you suppose you could aim the communicator back at the lighted space? We really can't see anything recognizable the way it's pointed now."

"Also," McDevitt cut in without allowing a pause to develop at the end of Easy's request, "even though you are planning to leave the *Kwembly,* do you suppose you could leave a power unit on board to run the lights, and lash the bridge communicator about where it is so we can see the hull? That would not only let us observe the flood if it comes, which I'm almost certain it will in the next three to fifteen hours, but would also give us a chance to tell you whether there was any use looking for the cruiser afterward, and possibly even *where* to look for it. I know that will leave you with only two communicators, but it seems to me that this would be worth it."

Again, Dondragmer appeared to make up his mind on the spot; his answer emerged from the speaker almost with the sixty-four-second bell.

"Yes, we'll do it that way. I would have had to leave light power anyway, since I wanted crews to come back for work; and as I said, I wanted some sort of safety communication with them. Your suggestion fits that perfectly. I've turned the set back to cover the starboard side, as you no doubt see. I must leave the bridge now; the crew will be back in a minute or two, and I want to assign duties to them as they arrive."

Again, Benj began talking without checking with anyone else.

"Captain, if you're still in hearing when this gets to you, will you wave or signal some way, or have Beetch do it, if you find him alive? I won't ask you to make a special trip back to the bridge to give details."

There was no answer. Presumably Dondragmer had suited up and gone outside the moment he finished speaking. There was nothing for the human beings to do but wait.

Aucoin, with Easy's assistance, had relayed Dondragmer's answer to the Settlement, and received Barlennan's acknowledgment. The commander asked that he be kept up to date as completely as possible on *Kwembly* matters, and especially on any ideas which Dondragmer might have. Aucoin agreed, asked Easy to relay the request to the captain, and was told that this would be done as soon as the latter reestablished contact.

"All right," nodded the planner. "At least, there's been no mention so far of sending a rescue vehicle. We'll leave well enough alone."

"Personally," retorted Easy, "I'd have dispatched the *Kalliff* or the *Hoorsh* hours ago, when they first froze in."

"I know you would. I'm very thankful that your particular brand of ethics won't let you suggest it to Barlennan over my objections. My only hope is that he won't decide to suggest it himself, because every time I've had both of you really against me I've been talked down." Easy looked at Aucoin, and then at the microphone, speculatively. Her husband decided that distraction was in order, and cut into the thickening silence with a question.

"Alan, what do you think of that theory of Barlennan's?"

Aucoin frowned. He and Easy both knew perfectly well why Ib had interrupted, but the question itself was hard to ignore; and Easy, at least, recognized that the interruption itself was a good idea.

"It's a fascinating idea," the planner said slowly, "but I can't say that I think it very probable. Dhrawn is a huge planet, if it can be called a planet, and it seems funny, well, I don't know whether it seems funnier that we'd have met intelligence so quickly or that only one of the cruisers has done so. There certainly isn't a culture using electromagnetic energy; we'd have detected it when we first approached the place. A much lower one, well, how could they have done what seems to have been done to the *Esket*'s crew?"

"Not knowing their physical and mental capabilities, quite aside from their cultural level, I couldn't even guess," replied Hoffman. "Didn't some of the first Indians Columbus met wind up in Spain?"

"I think you're stretching resemblances, to put it mildly. There's a practical infinity of things which could have happened to the *Esket* without her running into intelligent opposition. You know that as well as I do; you helped make up some of the lists, until you decided it was pointless speculation. I grant that Barlennan's theory is a little bit more believable than it was, but only a very little."

"You still think I was wrong in my identification of Kabremm, don't you?" said Easy.

"Yes, I'm afraid I do. Furthermore, I just don't believe that we've run into another intelligent species. Don't compare me with the people who refused to believe that dePerthe's rocks were man-made tools. Some things are just intrinsically improbable."

Hoffman chuckled. "Human ability to judge likelihood, you might call it statistical insight, has always been pretty shaky," he pointed out, "even if you skip purely classical examples like Lois Lane. Actually, the chances don't seem to be that low. You know as well as I do that in the very small volume of space within five parsecs of Sol, with only seventy-four known stars and about two hundred sunless planets, what we have found in the way of intelligence: twenty races at about our own stage of development, safely past their Energy Crisis; eight, including Tenebra and Mesklin, which haven't met it yet; eight which failed to pass it and are extinct; three which failed but have some hope of recovery; every one of them, remember, within a hundred thousand years of that key point in their history, one way or the other! That's in spite of the fact that the planets range in age from Panesh's nine billion years or so to Tenebra's maybe a tenth of that. There's more than coincidence there, Alan."

"Maybe Panesh and Earth and the older planets have had other cultures in the past; maybe it happens to any world every few tens of millions of years."

"It hasn't happened before unless the earlier intelligent races were so intelligent from the beginning that they never tapped their planet's fossil fuels. Do you think man's presence on Earth won't be geologically obvious a billion years from now, with looted coal seams and the beer bottle as an index fossil? I can't buy that one, Alan."

"Maybe not, but I'm not mystical enough to believe that some super-species is herding the races of this part of space toward one big climax."

"Whether you like that Demon Hypothesis or prefer the ESFA Theory doesn't matter. There's certainly more than chance involved, and therefore you can't use the laws of chance alone to criticize what Barlennan has suggested. You don't have to assume he's right, but I strongly urge you to take him seriously. I do."

Dondragmer would have been interested in hearing this discussion, just as he would have appreciated attending the staff meeting of some hours before. However, he would have been too busy for either, even if attendance had been physically possible. With the return of most of his crew (some, of course, had stayed behind to continue setting up the life-support equipment) there was much to oversee and quite a lot to do himself. Twenty of his men were set to helping the trio already chipping ice from the main lock. As many more went under the hull with lights and tools to find and secure any power units not too solidly frozen in. The captain kept his promise to Benj, ordering this group to check most carefully for signs of Beetchermarlf and Takoorch. However, he emphasized the importance of examining the ice walls closely, and as a result the group found nothing. Its members emerged in a few minutes with the two power boxes from the trucks which the helmsmen had used, and two more which had been freed by the action of the heat. The rest, which according to

Dondragmer's recollection and the laws of arithmetic must number six, were unapproachable, even though the sailors could make a reasonably well-founded guess as to which trucks they were on.

Meanwhile, the rest of the crew had been entering the cruiser by the available locks: the small one at the bridge, the larger ones through which the fliers were launched and the pairs of one-man-at-a-time emergency traps at the sides near bow and stern. Once inside, each crewman set about an assigned job. Dondragmer had been thinking as well as talking to human beings during their absence. Some packed food to last until the life-support equipment resumed cycling normally; others readied coils of rope, lights, power units and other equipment for transportation.

Many were at work improvising carrying devices; one awkward result of the *Kwembly*'s being fusion-powered was a great shortage of wheels aboard. There were tiny pulleys carrying the control cables around corners. These were too small for wheelbarrows or similar devices and Dondragmer had firmly forbidden any dismantling of the vehicle. There was nothing like a fork-lift or even a dolly aboard. Such devices, the former muscle-powered, of course, were known and used on Mesklin for medium-to-long-distance carrying; but there was nothing on the *Kwembly* which could be moved at all which a Mesklinite could not easily carry to any part of the vehicle without mechanical assistance. Now, with miles to go and the necessity of moving many items complete rather than in pieces, improvisation was in order. Litters and travois were making their appearance. The corridors leading to the main lock were rapidly being stacked with supplies and equipment awaiting the freeing of the exit.

None of the bustle and thumping, however, penetrated the mattress where Beetchermarlf and Takoorch still lay concealed. As nearly as could be judged later, they must have sought this shelter within a very few minutes of the time the resistance heater went into action. The thick, rubbery material of the mattress itself, which had been so difficult for even a Mesklinite-wielded knife to penetrate, blocked the sounds made by the crackling steam-bubbles around the hot metal and the calls of the workers who entered later. Had these last been forced to communicate with anyone at a distance, their resonant hooting might well have made its way even through that tough material; but there was little for them to say even to each other; they all knew their jobs perfectly well. The slit through which the helmsmen had found their entrance was held tightly enough closed by the elasticity of the fabric so that no light reached them. Finally, the Mesklinite personality trait most nearly described as a combination of patience and fatalism assured that neither Beetchermarlf nor his companion was likely to check outside their refuge until the breathing hydrogen in their suits became a serious problem.

As a result, even if Dondragmer had heard Benj's appeal, there would have been nothing for him to signal. The helmsmen, some three feet above some of their companions and a like distance below many others, were not found.

Not quite all the *Kwembly*'s crew were engaged in preparation for the move. When the most necessary aspects of that operation had been arranged, Dondragmer called two of his sailors for a special detail.

"Go to the stream, head northwest and you can't miss it, and go upstream until you find Kabremm and the *Gwelf*," he ordered. "Tell him what we are doing. We will set up a livable site as quickly as we can, you tell him where; you've been there and I haven't. We will set up the human machines so they are looking into the lighted, active portion of that area. That will make it safe for him to bring the *Gwelf* down and land her anywhere outside that area, with no risk of being seen by the human beings. Tell him that the commander seems to be starting the native-life part of the play early, apparently to account for Kabremm's being seen in this neighborhood. He's suggested no details, and will probably stick to the original idea of letting the human beings invent their own.

"When you have seen Kabremm, go on upstream until you find Stakendee, and give him the same information. Be careful about getting into the view field of his communicator; when you think you may be getting near him, shut off your lights every little while and look for his. I'll be in touch with him through the human beings, of course, but not with *that* message. You understand."

"Yes, Sir," the two replied in unison, and were gone.

The hours passed. The main lock was freed and opened, and nearly all the material to be taken was outside when a call came from above. The communicator which had been in the laboratory was now outside, so Dondragmer could be reached directly. Benj was still the speaker.

"Captain, Stakendee reports that the stream he is following is getting noticeably broader and swifter, and that the clouds are becoming rain. I've told him to start back, on my own responsibility." The captain looked up at the still cloudless sky, then westward toward the place where Stakendee's fog might have shown if it had been daylight.

"Thanks, Benj. That's what I would have ordered. We're leaving the *Kwembly* right now before the stream gets too big to cross with the equipment. I have lashed the communicator down to the bridge and will leave the lights on as Mr. McDevitt requested. We'll hope you can tell us that it's safe to come back, before too long. Please report this to Barlennan, and tell him that we will watch as carefully as possible for the natives; if, as he seems to be suggesting, they are using Kabremm as a means of getting in touch with us, I will do my best to set up cooperative relations with them. Remember, I haven't seen Kabremm myself yet, and you haven't mentioned him since the first time, so I'm entirely in the dark about his status so far.

"Be sure to keep me informed of Barlennan's thoughts and plans, as far as you can; I'll do the same from here, but things may happen too quickly for any possible advance warning. Watch your screens. That's all for now; we're starting."

The captain uttered a resonant hoot which, fortunately for human ears, was not faithfully amplified by the set. The Mesklinites fell into rough line, and within two minutes were gone from the field of view of the bridge communicator.

The other set was being borne near the tail of the line, so the screen far above showed the string of lights bobbing in front of it. Little else could be seen. The nearest sailors, those within two or three yards of the lens, could be made out in reasonable detail as they wound among the boulders with their burdens, but that was all. The line could have been flanked on both sides twenty feet away by a legion of natives, without any human being the wiser. Aucoin was neither the first nor the last to curse Dhrawn's 1500-hour rotation period; there were still over six hundred hours to go before the feeble daylight from Lalande 21185 would return.

The stream was still small when the group splashed through it, though Stakendee's set a few miles west had confirmed the report that it was growing. Benj, noticing this, suggested that the small party also cross so that its members could meet the main body on the other side of the valley. Fortunately he made this suggestion to Dondragmer before acting on his own; the captain, remembering the two messengers he had sent upstream, hastily advised that the crossing be postponed as long as possible so that Stakendee and his men could compare more accurately the size of the stream with what it had been when they had passed the same area earlier. Benj and Easy accepted this excuse. Ib Hoffman, quite aware that the foot party was carrying no time measuring devices and could give no meaningful report on the rate of change, was startled for a few seconds. Then he smiled, privately.

For minutes, which stretched into one hour and then another, there was little to watch. The crew reached and climbed the bare rock sides of the valley at the spot where the first load of equipment had been left, and set about constructing something which might have been called either a camp or a town. Life-support equipment had first priority, of course. It would be many hours yet before any air-suits would need recharging, but the time would come. For organisms as profligate of energy as the Mesklinites, food was also a matter of immediate concern. They set about it quickly and efficiently; Dondragmer, like the rest of the cruiser captains, had given plenty of advance thought to the problem of abandoning ship.

Stakendee's group finally crossed the river and, somewhat later, reached the encampment. The crossing had been approved by Dondragmer after he had received through Benj a message which contained, quite incidentally, the name of one of the messengers the captain had sent from the *Kwembly*.

Consequently no one, either member of the *Kwembly* crew or human being, was able to watch the growth of the ammonia-water stream. It would have been an interesting sight. At first, as the witnesses had reported, it was little more than a trickle running from hollow to hollow on the bare rock in the higher reaches of the river bed, men winding among the boulders lower down. As the drops of liquid in the fog coalesced and settled out more rapidly, tiny new tributaries began to feed into the main stream from the sides, and the stream itself grew deeper and faster. On the bare rock it meandered more violently, overflowing the basins which had originally contained it. Here and there it froze temporarily, as water, supplied by the frozen puddles upstream, and ammonia from the fog, shifted about the eutectic, which was liquid at the local temperature: about 174 degrees on the human Kelvin scale, roughly 71 on that used by the Mesklinite scientists.

Among the boulders, as it neared the *Kwembly*, it accumulated more and more water ice, and the progress grew more complicated. The ammonia dissolved water for a time, the mixture flowing away as the composition entered the liquid range. Then the stream would stop and build up, as Benj had pictured it, like hot wax on a candle, solidifying temporarily from addition of ammonia. Then it would slump away again as underlying ice reacted with the mixture.

It finally reached the hole which had been melted along the *Kwembly*'s starboard side, where the human beings could watch once more. By this time the "stream" was a complex network of alternate liquid, solid, and slush perhaps two miles across. The solid, however, was losing out. While there were still no clouds this far downstream, the air was nearly saturated with ammonia: saturated, that is, with respect to a pure liquid-ammonia surface. The ammonia vapor pressure needed for equilibrium over an ammonia-water mixture is lower; so condensation was taking place on the mostly-water and low-ammonia ice. As it reached the appropriate composition for liquefaction its surface flowed away and exposed more solid to the vapor. The liquid tended to solidify again as it absorbed still more ammonia vapor, but its motion also gave it access to more water ice.

The situation was a little different in the space under the *Kwembly*'s hull, but not greatly so. Where liquid touched ice the latter dissolved and slush appeared; but more ammonia diffusing from the free surface at the side melted it again. Slowly, slowly, minute after minute, the grip of the ice on the huge vehicle relaxed so gently that neither the human beings watching with fascination from above nor the two Mesklinites waiting in their dark refuge could detect the change, and the hull floated free.

By now the entire river bed was liquid, with a few surviving patches of slush. Gently, very unlike the flood of a hundred hours or so before when three million square miles of water-snow had been touched by the first ammonia fog of the advancing season, a current began to develop. Imperceptibly to all concerned, the *Kwembly* moved with that current: imperceptibly because there was no relative motion to catch the eyes of the human beings, and no rocking or pitching to be felt by the hidden Mesklinites.

The seasonal river, which drains the great plateau where the *Kwembly* had been caught, slices through a range of hills, for Dhrawn respectable mountains; the range extends some four thousand miles northwest-southeast. The *Kwembly* had gone parallel to this range for most of its length before the flood. Dondragmer, his helmsmen, his air scouts, and indeed most of the crew had been quite aware of the gentle elevation to their left, sometimes near enough to be seen from the bridge and sometimes only a pilot's report.

The flood had carried the cruiser through a pass near the southeastern end of this range to the somewhat lower and rougher regions close to the edge of Low Alpha before she had grounded. This first flood was a rough, rather hesitant beginning of the new season as Dhrawn approached its feeble sun and the latitude of the sub-stellar belt shifted. The second was the real thing, which would only end when the whole snow plain was drained, more than an Earth year later. The *Kwembly*'s first motions were smooth and gentle because she was melted free so slowly; then they were smooth and gentle because the liquid supporting her was syrupy with suspended crystals; finally, with the stream fully liquid and up to speed, it was smooth because it was broad and deep. Beetchermarlf and Takoorch may have been slightly dazed by decreasing hydrogen pressure, but even if they had been fully alert the slight motions of the *Kwembly*'s hull would have been masked by their own shifting on the flexible surface that supported them.

Low Alpha is not the hottest region on Dhrawn, but the zone-melting effects which tend to concentrate any planet's radioactive elements have warmed it to around the melting point of water ice in many spots, over two hundred Kelvin degrees hotter than Lalande 21185 could manage unassisted. A human being could live with only modest artificial protection in the area, if it were not for the gravity and pressure. The really hot area, Low Beta, is forty thousand miles to the north; it is Dhrawn's major climate-control feature.

The *Kwembly*'s drift was carrying it into regions of rising temperature, which kept the river fluid even though it was now losing ammonia to the air. The course of the stream was almost entirely controlled by the topography, rather than the other way around; the river was geologically too young to have altered the landscape greatly by its own action. Also, much of the exposed surface of the planet in this area was bed rock, igneous and hard, rather than a covering of loose sediment in which a stream could have its own way.

About three hundred miles from the point at which she had been abandoned, the *Kwembly* was borne into a broad, shallow lake. She promptly but gently ran aground on the soft mud delta where the river fed into it. The great hull naturally deflected the currents around it, and set them to digging a new channel alongside. After about half an hour she tilted sideways and slid off into the new channel, righting herself as she floated free. It was the rocking associated with this last liberation which caught the attention of the helmsmen and induced them to come out for a look around.

14: Salvage Crew

It would be untrue to say that Benj recognized Beetchermarlf at first glance. As a matter of fact, the first of the caterpillar like figures to emerge from the river and clamber up the hull was Takoorch. However, it was the younger helmsman's name which echoed from four speakers on Dhrawn.

One of these was on the *Kwembly*'s bridge and went unheard. Two were in Dondragmer's encampment a few hundred yards from the edge of the broad, swift river which now filled the valley. The fourth was in Reffel's helicopter, parked close beside the bulk of the *Gwelf.*

The flying machines were about a mile west of Dondragmer's camp; Kabremm would go no closer, not wanting to take the slightest chance of repeating his earlier slip. He would probably not have moved at all from the site where Stakendee had found him if the river had not risen. For one thing, he had been fog-bound and had no wish to fly at all. Reffel had been even less eager to move. However, there had been no choice, so Kabremm had allowed his craft to float upward on its own lift until it was in clear air. Reffel hovered as close to the other machine's running lights as he dared. Once above the few yards of ammonia droplets, they could navigate, and had flown toward Dondragmer's lights until the dirigible's commander had decided they were close enough. Letting the *Gwelf* come to the attention of the men in orbit above would have been an even more serious mistake than the one he had made already; Kabremm was still trying to decide what he was going to say to Barlennan about that the next time they met.

Both he and Reffel had also spent some uncomfortable hours before concluding, from the lack of appropriate comment, that Reffel had shuttered his vision set quickly enough after coming within sight of the *Gwelf.*

In any event, Dondragmer and Kabremm had at last achieved almost direct communication, and had been able to coordinate what they would say and do if there were any further repercussions from Easy's recognition. One load was off the captain's mind. However, he was still taking steps connected with that mistake.

The cry of "Beetch!" in Benj's unmistakable voice distracted him from one of these steps. He had been checking over his crew for people who looked as much as possible like Kabremm. The job was complicated by the fact that he had not seen the other officer for several months. Dondragmer had not yet had time to visit the *Gwelf*, Kabremm would come no closer to the camp for any reason, and Dondragmer had never known him particularly well anyway. His plan was to have all crewmen who might reasonably be mistaken for the *Esket*'s first officer appear unobtrusively and casually but frequently in the field of view of the vision sets. Anything likely to undermine the certainty of Easy Hoffman that she had seen Kabremm was probably worth trying.

However, the fate of the *Kwembly* and his helmsmen had never been very far from the captain's mind in the twelve hours since his cruiser's lights had vanished, and at the sound from the speaker he snapped to full attention.

"Captain!" the boy's voice continued. "Two Mesklinites have just appeared and are climbing up the hull of the *Kwembly*. They came out of the water; they must have been somewhere underneath all the time, even if you couldn't find them. It couldn't be anyone but Beetch and Tak. I can't talk to them until they get to the bridge, of course, but it looks as though we might get your ship back after all. Two men can drive it, can't they?"

Dondragmer's mind raced. He had not blamed himself for abandoning the cruiser, even though the flood had been such an anticlimax. It had been the most reasonable decision at the time and with the available knowledge. By the time the actual nature of the new flood had been clear, and it was obvious that they could have remained in the cruiser with perfect safety, it had been impossible to get back. Being a Mesklinite, the captain had wasted no time on thoughts of the "if only" variety. He had known when he left his vehicle that the chances of getting back were rather small, and when she had drifted downstream intact instead of a shattered ruin they had grown smaller. Not quite to zero, perhaps, but not large enough to take seriously any more.

Now suddenly they had expanded again. The *Kwembly* was not only usable, but his helmsmen were alive and aboard her. Something might be done, if...

"Benj!" Dondragmer spoke as his thoughts reached this point. "Will you please get your technical men to determine as closely as they can just how far from us the *Kwembly* is now? It is perfectly possible for Beetchermarlf to drive her alone, though there are other problems in the way of general maintenance which will keep him and Takoorch busy. However, they should be able to manage. In any case, we must find out whether the distance involved is fifty miles or a thousand. I doubt the latter, since I don't think this river could have carried them so far in twelve hours, but we'll have to know. Get your people at it, and please tell Barlennan what is happening."

Benj obeyed quickly and efficiently. He was no longer overtired, worried, and resentful. With the abandonment of the *Kwembly* twelve hours before he had given up hope for his friend's life and had left the communication room to get some long overdue sleep. He had not expected to be able to accomplish this, but his own body chemistry had fooled him. Nine hours later he had returned to his regular duties in the aerology laboratory. It had been chance alone which had brought him back to the screens within a few minutes of the helmsmen's emergence. He had been sent by McDevitt to collect general data from the other cruisers, but had lingered for a few minutes to watch at the *Kwembly* station. The weather man had come to depend heavily on Benj's knowledge of the Mesklinite language.

The sleep, and the sudden discovery that Beetchermarlf was alive after all, combined to dispose of Benj's lingering resentment of Dondragmer's policy. He acknowledged the captain's request, called his mother to take his place, and headed for the laboratory decks as rapidly as his muscles would take him up the ladders.

Easy, who had also had some sleep, reported Benj's departure and her own presence to Dondragmer, briefed Barlennan as requested, and switched back to the captain with a question of her own.

"That's two of your missing men. Do you think there is still any chance of finding your helicopter pilots?"

Dondragmer almost slipped on his answer, carefully as he picked his words. He knew, of course, where Reffel was, since messengers had been passing steadily between the camp and the *Gwelf;* but Kervenser, to his disappointment, had not been seen by the crew of the dirigible or anyone else. His disappearance was perfectly genuine, and the captain now regarded his chances for survival as even lower than those of the *Kwembly* pair an hour before. It was safe, of course, to talk about this; his slip consisted of failing to mention Reffel at all. The Stennish forms equivalent to "him" and "them" were as distinct as the human ones, and several times Dondragmer caught himself using the former when talking about his lost pilots. Easy seemed not to notice, but he wondered afterward.

"It is hard to judge. I have not seen either one. If he went down in the area now flooded it is hard to see how they could be alive now. It is very unfortunate, not only because of the men themselves but because with even one of the helicopters we might be able to transfer more men to the *Kwembly* and get her back here more easily. Of course most of the equipment could not be carried that way; on the other hand, if it turns out that the two men cannot bring the cruiser back here for any reason, having one of the fliers could make a great difference to *them*. It is a pity that your scientists cannot locate the transmitter which Reffel was carrying, as they can the one on the *Kwembly.*"

"You're not the first to feel that way," agreed Easy. The matter had been brought up shortly after Reffel's disappearance. "I don't know enough about the machines to tell why the signal strength depends on the picture brightness; I always thought a carrier wave was a carrier wave; but that seems to be it. Either Reffel's set is in total darkness or it has been destroyed.

"I see your life-support equipment is set up and working."

The last sentence was not entirely an effort of Easy's to change the subject; it was her first good look at the equipment in question, and she was genuinely curious about it. It consisted of scores, perhaps over a hundred, of square transparent tanks covering altogether a dozen square yards, each about a third full of liquid, with the nearly pure hydrogen which constituted Mesklinite air bubbling through it. A power unit operated the lights which shone on the tanks, but the pumps which kept the gas circulating were muscle-driven. The vegetation which actually oxidized the saturated hydrocarbons of Mesklinite biological waste and gave off free hydrogen was represented by a variety of unicellular species corresponding as nearly as might be expected to terrestrial algae. They had been selected for edibility, though not, as Easy had been given to understand, for taste. The sections of the support equipment which used higher plants and produced the equivalent of fruit and vegetables were too bulky to move from the cruiser.

Easy did not know how the non-gaseous items in the biological cycle were gotten into and out of the tanks, but she could see the charging of air suit cartridges. This was a matter of muscle-driven pumping again, squeezing hydrogen into tanks which contained slugs of porous solid. This material was another strictly non-Mesklinite product, a piece of molecular architecture vaguely analogous to zeolite in structure, which adsorbed hydrogen on the inner walls of its structural channels and, within a wide temperature range, maintained an equilibrium partial pressure with the gas which was compatible with Mesklinite metabolic needs.

Dondragmer answered Easy's remark. "Yes, we have just about enough food and air. The real problem is what to do. We have saved very little of your planetological equipment; we can't carry on your work. Conceivably we might make our way back to the Settlement on foot, but we'd have to carry the life-support material by stages. That would mean setting up a camp only a few miles from here, transferring the equipment, recharging the air cartridges after cycling has resumed, and then repeating the process indefinitely. Since the distance to the settlement is about thirty thousand, excuse me, in your numbers about twelve thousand, of your miles, it would take us years to get there: that's no metaphor, nor do I mean your short years. If we're to be any further use to your project, we really must get the *Kwembly* back here."

Easy could only agree, though she could see an alternative which the captain had not mentioned. Of course, Aucoin would disapprove, or would he, under the circumstances? A trained and efficient exploring crew represented quite an investment, too. That might be a useful line to follow.

It was several more minutes before Benj returned with his information, and incidentally with a following of interested scientists.

"Captain," he called, "the *Kwembly* is still moving, though not very fast, something like twenty cables an hour. She is located, or was six minutes ago, 310.71 miles from your transmitter, in our figures. In your numbers and units that's 233,750 cables. There's a small error if there's much difference in elevation. That's great circle distance; we don't have too good an idea of the length of the river, though they have about twenty position readings taken along it since your ship started drifting, so there's a rough river map up in the lab."

"Thank you," came the captain's answer in due course. "Are you in verbal contact with the helmsmen yet?"

"Not yet, but they've gone inside. I'm sure they'll find the communicator on the bridge pretty soon, though I suppose there are other places they'd want to check first. The air must be pretty low in their suits."

This was perfectly correct. It took the helmsmen only a few minutes to ascertain that the cruiser was deserted, and to note that much of the life-support equipment was gone; but this left them with the need to check the air now aboard for contamination with oxygen from outside. Neither of them knew enough basic chemistry to invent a test, and neither was familiar with the routine ones used by Borndender and his colleagues. They were considering the rather drastic procedure of testing by smell when it occurred to Beetchermarlf that a communicator might have been left aboard for scientific reasons, and that the human beings might be of help. There was none in the laboratory, but the bridge was the next most likely spot, and Beetchermarlf's voice was on its way up to the station some ten minutes after the helmsmen had come aboard.

Benj postponed greetings when he heard Beetchermarlf's question, and relayed it at once to Dondragmer. The captain called his scientists and outlined the situation, and for over half an hour the relay was very busy: Borndender explained things, and Beetchermarlf repeated the explanations, then went to the lab to examine material and equipment, then came back to the bridge to make sure of some minor point...

Eventually both parties in the conversation felt sure that the instructions had been understood. Benj, at its pivot point, was nearly sure. He knew enough physics and chemistry himself to judge that nothing was likely to blow up if Beetch made a mistake; his only worry was that his friend might perform the tests sloppily and so miss a dangerous amount of oxygen. Was the risk simply one of poisoning, or did hydrogen-oxygen mixtures present other dangers? He wasn't quite sure; hydrogen-oxygen mixtures have other qualities. He remained rather tense until Beetchermarlf returned to the bridge with the report that both tests were complete. The catalyst which disposed of free oxygen by accelerating its reaction with ammonia was still active, and the ammonia-vapor concentration in the ship's air was high enough to give it something to work on. The helmsmen had already removed their air-suits and neither could smell any oxygen, though, as with human beings and hydrogen sulfide, smell is not always a reliable test.

At least, the two could live on board for a time. One of their first acts had been to "hand"-pump the feed tank which kept air bubbling through the life-support medium, and to satisfy themselves that most of the plants were still alive. The next problem was navigation.

Benj told his friend as much as possible about his location, that of the rest of the crew, and the *Kwembly*'s present rate and direction of travel. There was no problem about using the information. Beetchermarlf could determine direction easily enough. The stars were visible and he had a perfectly good magnetic compass. Dhrawn's magnetic field was a good deal stronger than Earth's, to the consternation of the scientists who had long since taken for granted a correlation between magnetic field and rotation rate for ordinary planets.

The discussion which produced a detailed operation plan was shorter than the one preceding the oxygen test, though it still involved the long relay. Neither Dondragmer nor the helmsmen had any serious doubts about what to do or how to do it.

Beetchermarlf was far younger than Takoorch, but there seemed no question as to who was in charge aboard. The fact that Benj always signalled Beetch by name, rather than signaling the *Kwembly* formally, may have contributed to the young one's authority. Easy and several of the other human beings suspected that Takoorch, in spite of his willingness to discuss his own past accomplishments, was in no great hurry to take on too much responsibility. He tended to agree with Beetchermarlf's suggestions either at once or after only token arguments.

"We're still adrift, and unless this river has some very funny loops farther down we'll never get any closer to the others with its help," the younger Mesklinite summarized at last. "The first job will be to get paddles on some of the powered trucks. Trying to do it with all of them will take forever; a couple of outboard-row ones aft, and maybe a central one forward should give control. With power available on other drivers we can either pull off or get safely ashore if we run aground. Tak and I will go outside and start work right now. You keep an eye on us as much as you can, Benj; we'll leave the set where it is."

Beetchermarlf did not wait for an answer. He and his companion suited up once more and broke out the paddles which were designed to be pinned onto the treads of the drivers. These had been tested on Mesklin but had never yet been used on Dhrawn; no one really knew how well they would work. Their area was small, since there was little clearance for them above the trucks, and some of that small area was taken up by a plastic shield designed to fold them flat as they were riding forward on the top side of the trucks. However, it had been proved that they would supply some thrust. What this would accomplish remained to be seen; the *Kwembly* was floating higher in the ammonia-water solution of Dhrawn, of course, than she had in the liquid hydrocarbon ocean of the world where she had been made.

Installation of the fins and shields was a long and awkward job for two workers. The pieces could be taken out only one at a time, since there was nowhere to put them down with the cruiser afloat. Safety lines persistently got in the way. Mesklinite pincers are rather less effective handling organs than are human fingers, though this is somewhat offset by the fact that their owner can use all four pairs of them simultaneously and in coordination—he has no asymmetry corresponding to human right- or left-handedness.

The need for artificial lights was still another bother. As it turned out, getting twelve paddles and one shield on each of three drivers took a total of almost fifteen hours. It could, Beetchermarlf assured Benj, have been accomplished in two with four workers on each truck.

By this time the trackers had learned that the *Kwembly* was not getting any farther from the camp, though she was still moving. Apparently she had been caught in an eddy some four miles in diameter. Beetchermarlf took advantage of this when he was finally ready to apply power; he waited until the human analysts could tell him that he was being carried south before he set the three finned trucks running. For some seconds it was not apparent that the power was doing any good; then, very slowly, helmsmen and humans alike saw that the great hull was moving gently forward. The Mesklinites could see from the bridge a feeble excuse for a bow wave; the human beings, looking aft, were able to detect small ripples spreading back from the sides. Beetchermarlf swung his helm hard over to bring the bow in line with Sol and Fomalhaut. For nearly half a minute he was left wondering whether there would be any response; then the stars began to swing overhead as the long hull swerved majestically. Once started it was hard to stop; he overcontrolled many times and for a period of many minutes, sometimes by as much as a full right angle, before getting the feel of the vessel. Then for nearly an hour he managed to hold a southerly heading, though he had no idea of his actual course at first. He could guess from the earlier information that the eddy would be bearing him in the same direction at the start, but then it would presumably carry him eastward.

It was some time, however, before the directional antennae on the shadow satellites and the computers in the station could confirm this guess. About the time they did, the *Kwembly* ran gently aground.

Beetchermarlf instantly shifted drive power to the two trucks farthest forward which had power boxes, letting the paddle-equipped ones idle, and pulled his cruiser out on the shore.

"I'm out of the lake," he reported. "Minor problem. If I travel for any distance on land with the paddles in place I'll wear them out. If it turns out that I'm on an island, or have to go back to the water for any other reason, an awful lot of time will have been wasted taking them off and putting them on again. My first thought is to do some exploring on foot, leaving the ship right here, to get some idea of what the chances of staying ashore may be. It will take a long time, but not nearly as long as waiting for daylight. I'll be glad of advice from you humans or orders from the captain; we'll wait."

Dondragmer, when this was relayed to him, was prompt with his answer.

"Don't go out. Wait until the map-makers up above can decide whether you are on the same side of the river as we are, or not. As I picture the map they've described, there's a good chance that the eddy carried you to the east side, which would be the right bank; we're on the left. If they are even moderately sure of this, get back into the water and head west until they think you're past it, no, second thought. Go until they think you're opposite its mouth, then head south once more. I'd like to find out whether you can travel upstream with any speed at all. I know it will be slow; it may turn out that you can't travel at all in some places along the bank."

"I'll tell Beetch and the map people, Captain," answered Benj. "I'll try to get a copy of their map and keep it up to date down here; that may save some time in the future."

The directional data was not, as it happened, definitive. The location of the *Kwembly* could be established well enough, but the course of the river down which she had come was much less certain. The checks were many miles apart, but sufficient in number to show that the river was decidedly crooked. After some further discussion, it was decided that Beetchermarlf should get back afloat and head westward as close to shore as he could; preferably within sight of it, if the range of his lights and the slope of the lake bottom would permit it. If he could find the river mouth by sight, he was to head up it as Dondragmer had wished; if not, he was to continue along the shore until the men above were reasonably certain that he had passed the rivermouth, then turn south.

It did prove possible to keep the shore within range of the *Kwembly*'s lights, but it took over two hours to reach the river. This had made a wide westward bend which had been missed in the checks of the cruiser's position during the downstream drift; then it turned again and entered the lake on an eastward slant which presumably caused the counterclockwise eddy. One of the planetographers remarked that you couldn't blame the eddy on Coriolis force because the lake was only seven degrees from the equator and on the south side, at that, of a planet which took two months to rotate.

The delta, which caused the shoreline to turn north briefly, was a warning. Beetchermarlf at the helm and Takoorch at the port wing of the bridge sent the *Kwembly* groping around the rather irregular peninsula, slowing noticeably several times as the trucks dragged in soft bottom silt, and finally found their way into a clear channel and headed into its current.

This was not swift, but the *Kwembly* still wasn't afloat. The Mesklinites were in no hurry; Dondragmer gave six hours and more to the experiment of fighting the stream. They made about ten miles progress in that time. If that rate could be maintained, the cruiser would be back at the camp by a day or two after midnight, that is, in a week or so by human reckoning.

It was impatience which changed the travel plans. This could not, of course, be blamed on any Mesklinite; it was Aucoin, of all people, who decided that a mile and a half an hour was not satisfactory. Dondragmer did not feel strongly about the matter; he agreed that research might as well be worked into the trip if possible. At the planner's suggestion he sent Beetchermarlf angling westward toward what was presumably the near bank of the river. The land seemed traversable. With some misgiving he had the helmsmen remove the paddles.

Removal proved much easier than installation, since the vehicle was now on dry land. Things could be laid down and life lines were not needed.

Benj, on his next visit to the communication room, found the *Kwembly* cruising smoothly south at about ten miles an hour over flat country, interrupted by an occasional outcropping of rock and studded here and there with scrubby brush, the highest life form so far encountered on Dhrawn. The surface was firm sediment; the planetologists judged the area to be a flood plain, which seemed reasonable even to Benj.

Beetchermarlf was willing to talk as usual, but it could be seen that his attention was not entirely on conversation. Both he and Takoorch were looking ahead as sharply as their eyesight and the *Kwembly*'s lights would permit. There was no assurance that the going was safe; without air-scouting, the ten-mile speed was all they dared use. Anything faster would have been overrunning their lights. Whenever other duties, such as airplant maintenance, had to be performed, they stopped the cruiser and did the work together. One set of eyes, they felt, was not enough for safe travel.

Every now and then, as the hours wore on, whoever was at the helm would begin to feel the treacherous assurance that there could be no danger; that they had, after all, come scores of miles now without having to change heading except to keep the river in sight. A human being would have increased the running speed bit by bit. The Mesklinite reaction was to stop and rest. Even Takoorch knew that when he was feeling tempted to act against the dictates of elementary common sense, it was time to do something about his own condition. Discovering the vehicle halted when he came to the screens on one occasion, Aucoin assumed it was a regular air-maintenance stop; but then he saw one of the Mesklinites sprawled idly on the bridge. The set had been put back in its old location, giving a view forward over the helm. Asking why the cruiser was not traveling, Takoorch simply replied that he had found himself getting casual. The administrator left in a very thoughtful mood.

Eventually, this care paid off, or seemed to.

For some miles the outcroppings of bed rock had been more and more frequent, though generally smaller, closer together, and more angular. The planetologists had been making guesses, futile ones with so little information, about the underlying stratigraphy. The basic surface was still hard-packed sediment, but the watchers suspected that it might be getting shallower, and that some time soon the *Kwembly* might find herself on the same sort of bare rock that formed the substrate at Dondragmer's camp.

The helmsmen occasionally found it necessary now to weave slightly left or right to avoid the rock outcroppings; they even had to slow down a little from time to time. Several times in the past few hours the planetologists had rather plaintively suggested that the cruiser stop before it was too late, and pick up samples of the sediment she was running over even if the rocks were too big to collect. Aucoin simply pointed out that it would be a year or two before the sample could get up to the station anyway, and refused; the scientists retorted that a year was much better than the time which would be needed if the specimens weren't collected.

But when the *Kwembly* stopped, it was on Beetchermarlf's initiative. It was a minor thing, or seemed to be; the soil ahead seemed a little darker, with a very sharp boundary between it and the surface under the cruiser. The line was not noticeable on the vision screen, but the Mesklinites spotted it simultaneously and, without words, agreed that close examination was in order. Beetchermarlf called the station to inform the human beings and his captain that he and Takoorch would be going outside for a time, and described the situation. Easy, translating the message, was promptly begged by two planetologists to persuade the Mesklinites to bring samples aboard. She assumed that even Aucoin would hardly object under the circumstances, and agreed to ask them when she called back with Dondragmer's clearance.

The captain, this time, approved the sortie, suggesting only that it be preceded by a careful look around from the bridge with the aid of the spotlights. This proved useful. A hundred yards ahead, not too far out of the range of the running lights, a small stream ran across their path and emptied into the river. Sweeping the light to starboard, this tributary could be seen arcing around parallel to the cruiser's path from the north, then reversing its curve somewhat astern of the big vehicle and disappearing to the northwest. The *Kwembly* was on a peninsula some two hundred yards wide and not quite as long, bounded on the east—left—by the main river she had been following and on the other sides by the small tributary. It seemed likely to Mesklinites and human beings alike that the change in soil color which had caught the helmsmen's attention was caused by wetting from the smaller stream, but no one was sure enough of it to cancel the proposed trip outside. Aucoin was not present.

Outside, even with the aid of extra lights, the line of demarcation between the two kinds of soil was much less visible than before. Eye distance, Beetchermarlf judged, was the main cause. The crew scraped up and packaged samples of material from both sides of the line; then they went on to the stream itself. This proved to be a swift-running but shallow brook three or four body-lengths in width, its level an inch or two below the soil through which it was cutting its way. After a brief consultation, the two Mesklinites began to follow it away from the river. They had no way of telling its composition, but a bottle of its contents was secured for later testing.

By the time they reached the spot where it was curving away, even the Mesklinites could see that the stream had not been in existence very long. It was eating with visible speed into its banks, washing the sediment on toward the main river. Now that they were on the outside of its curve, the undercutting of the near bank could be seen and even felt; Beetchermarlf, standing at the edge, felt it crumble suddenly away under him and found himself in the stream.

It was only an inch or so deep, so he took advantage of the occasion to take another sample from its bottom before climbing out. They decided to continue upstream for another ten minutes or so, with Beetchermarlf wading and Takoorch on the bank. Before the time was up they had actually found the source of the watercourse. It was a spring, not half a mile from the *Kwembly,* roiling violently in the center of its basin where an underground source fed it. Beetchermarlf, investigating the middle, was knocked from his feet and carried half a body length by the upward current.

There was nothing in particular to do; they had no camera equipment, no one had seriously suggested that they bring the vision set with them, and there was nothing obvious to be gained by collecting more samples. They returned to the *Kwembly* to give a verbal description of what they had found.

Even the scientists agreed that the best step now was to get the samples back to the camp where Borndender and his fellows could do something useful with them. The helmsmen eased their cruiser into motion once more.

It approached the stream and nosed through it; the mattress took up the slight dip as the trucks crossed the bottom of the widening valley, and nothing could be felt on the bridge.

Not for another eight seconds.

The hull was rather more than half way across the little brook when the distinction between solid and liquid began to blur. A slight lurch could be felt on the bridge; it showed on the screen far above as a tiny upward jerk of the few outside features visible.

Forward motion stopped almost instantly, though the drivers kept churning. They could accomplish nothing when completely immersed in slimy mud, which the surface had so suddenly become. There was neither support nor traction. The *Kwembly* settled until the trucks were buried; settled until the mattress was nearly out of sight; settled almost, but not quite, to the level where she would have been literally floating in the semiliquid muck. She was stopped by two of the rock outcrops, one of which caught her under the stern just aft of the mattress, and the other on the starboard side some ten feet forward of the main lock. There was an ugly scraping sound as the cruiser's hull canted forward and to port, and then came to rest.

And this time, as Beetchermarif's sense of smell warned him only too clearly, the hull had failed somewhere. Oxygen was leaking in.

15: Essence

"It boils down to this," Aucoin said from the head of the table. "We have the choice of sending down the barge, or not. If we don't, the *Kwembly* and the two Mesklinites aboard her are lost, and Dondragmer and the rest of her crew are out of action until a rescue cruiser such as the *Kalliff* can reach them from the Settlement. Unfortunately, if we do try to land the barge there's a good chance that it won't help. We don't know why the ground gave under the *Kwembly*, and have no assurance that the same thing won't happen anywhere else in the vicinity. Losing the barge would be awkward. Even if we first landed near Dondragmer's camp and transferred him and his crew to the cruiser, we might lose the barge and there is no assurance that the crew could repair the *Kwembly*. Beetchermarlf's report makes me doubt it. He says he has found and sealed the major leaks, but he's still getting oxygen inside the hull from time to time. Several of his life-support tanks have been poisoned by it. So far he has been able to clean them out each time and restock them from the others, but he can't keep going forever unless he stops the last of these leaks. Also, neither he nor anyone else has made any concrete suggestion for getting that cruiser loose from the muck or whatever it's stuck in.

"There is another good argument against landing the barge. If we use remote, live control, there is the sixty-second reaction lag, which would make handling anywhere near the ground really impossible. It would be possible to program its computer to handle a landing, but the risks of that were proved the hard way the first time anyone landed away from Earth. You might as well give the Mesklinites a quick lesson in flying the thing for themselves!"

"Don't try to make that last sound too silly, Alan," Easy pointed out gently. "The *Kwembly* is merely the first of the cruisers to get into what looks like final trouble. Dhrawn is a very big world, with very little known about it, and I suspect we're going to run out of land-cruisers for rescue or any other purpose sooner or later. Also, even I know that the barge controls are computer-coupled, with push-the-way-you-want-to-go operators. I admit that even so, the chances are ten to one or worse that anyone trying a ground-to-ground flight with that machine on Dhrawn without previous experience would kill himself, but do Beetchermarlf and Takoorch have even that much chance of survival on any other basis?"

"I think they do," replied Aucoin quietly.

"How, in the name of all that's sensible?" snapped Mersereau. "Here all along we've—" Easy held up her hand, and either the gesture or the expression on her face caused Boyd to fall silent.

"What other procedure *which you could conscientiously recommend* would stand any real chance of saving either the *Kwembly* herself, or her two helmsmen, or the rest of Dondragmer's crew?" she asked.

Aucoin had the grace to flush deeply, but he answered steadily enough.

"I mentioned it earlier, as Boyd remembers," he said. "Sending the *Kalliff* from the Settlement to pick them up."

The words were followed by some seconds of silence, while expressions of amusement flitted across the faces around the table. Eventually Ib Hoffman spoke.

"Do you suppose Barlennan will approve?" he asked innocently.

"It boils down to this," Dondragmer said to Kabremm. "We can stay here and do nothing while Barlennan sends a rescue cruiser from the Settlement. I assume he can think of some reason for sending one which won't sound too queer, after he failed to do it for the *Esket.*"

"That would be easy enough," returned the *Esket*'s first officer. "One of the human beings was against sending it, and the commander simply let him win the argument. This time he could be firmer."

"As though the first time wouldn't have made some of the other humans suspicious enough. But never mind that. If we wait, we don't know how long it will be, since we don't even know whether there's a possible ground route from the Settlement to here. You came from the mines by air, and we floated part of the way.

"If we decide not to wait, we can do either of two things. One is to move by stages toward the *Kwembly,* carrying the life equipment as far as the suits will let us and then setting it up again to recharge them. We'd get there some time, I suppose. The other is to move the same way toward the Settlement to meet the rescue cruiser if one comes or get there on foot if it doesn't. I suppose we'd even get *there,* eventually. Even if we reach the *Kwembly,* there is no certainty that we can repair her; if the human beings have relayed Beetchermarlf's feelings at all adequately, it seems rather doubtful. I don't like either choice because of the wasted time they both involve. There are better things to do than crawl over the surface of this world on foot.

"A better idea, to my way of thinking, is to use your dirigible either to rescue my helmsmen if it is decided to give up on the *Kwembly,* or to start ferrying my crew and equipment over to where she is."

"But that—"

"That, of course, sinks the raft as far as the *Esket* act is concerned. Even using Reffel's helicopter would do that; we couldn't explain what happened to the vision set he was carrying without their seeing through it, no matter what lie you think up. I'm simply not sure that the trick is worth the deliberate sacrifice of those lives, though I admit it's worth the *risk,* of course; I wouldn't have gone along with it otherwise."

"So I heard," returned Kabremm. "No one has been able to make you see the risk of being completely dependent on beings who can't possibly regard us as real people."

"Quite right. Remember that some of them are as different from *each other,* as they are from us. I made up my mind about the aliens the time one of them answered my question about a differential hoist clearly and in detail, and threw in my first lesson in the use of mathematics in science, gratis. I realize the humans differ among themselves as we do; certainly the one who talked Barl out of sending help to the *Esket* must be as different as possible from Mrs. Hoffman or Charles Lackland—but I don't and never will distrust them as a species the way you seem to. I don't think Barlennan really does, either; he's changed the subject more than once rather than argue the point with me, and that's not Barlennan when he's sure he's right. I still think it would be a good idea to lower the sails on this act and ask directly for human help with the *Kwembly,* or at least take a chance on their finding out by using all three dirigibles there."

"There aren't three, any more." Kabremm knew the point was irrelevant, but was rather glad of a chance to change the subject. "Karfrengin and four men have been missing in the *Elsh* for two of this world's days."

"That news hadn't reached me, of course," said Dondragmer. "How did the commander react to it? I should think that even he would be feeling the temptation to ask for human help, if we're starting to lose personnel all over the map."

"He hasn't heard about it, either. We've had ground parties out searching, using trucks we salvaged from the *Esket,* and we didn't want to make a report until it could be a complete one."

"How much more complete could it be? Karfrengin and his men must be dead by now. The dirigibles don't carry life-support gear for two days."

Kabremm gave the rippling equivalent of a shrug. "Take it up with Destigmet. I have troubles enough."

"Why wasn't your flyer used for the search?"

"It was, until this evening. There are other troubles at the mine, though. A sort of ice river is coming, very slowly, but it will soon cover the whole second settlement if it doesn't stop. It's already reached the *Esket* and started to tip it over; that's why we were able to salvage the trucks so easily. Destigmet sent me to follow back up the glacier and try to find out whether it is likely to keep coming indefinitely, or was just a brief event. I really shouldn't have come this far, but I couldn't make myself stop. It's this same river for the whole distance, sometimes solid and sometimes liquid along the way; it's the weirdest thing I've seen yet on this weird world. There isn't a chance of the ice's stopping, and the *Esket* settlement is as good as done for."

"And of course Barlennan hasn't heard about this either."

"There's been no way to tell him. We only discovered the ice was moving just before dark. It was just a cliff a few dozen cables from the mine up to then."

"In other words, we've lost not only my first officer and a helicopter but a dirigible with five men, and as an afterthought the whole *Esket* project, with my *Kwembly* probably on the same list. And you still think we shouldn't end this trickery, tell the human beings the whole story, and get their help?"

"More than ever. If they learn we're having this much trouble, they'll probably decide we're no more use to them and abandon us here."

"Nonsense. No one just abandons an investment like this project; but never mind arguing; it's a futile point anyway. I wish—"

"What you really wish is that you had an excuse for leaking the whole barrel to your oxygen-breathing friends."

"You know I wouldn't do that. I'm quite ready to use my own judgment in the field, but I know enough history to be afraid of making spot-changes in basic policy."

"Thank goodness. It's all right to like some humans, but they're not all like the Hoffman one. You admitted that yourself."

"What it boils down to," Barlennan said to Bendivence, "is that we were much too hasty in sending Deeslenver to the *Esket* with orders to shutter its vision sets. The whole *Esket* question seems to have quieted down, and that will bring it to life again. We're not ready for the main act yet, and won't be for a year or more. I wasn't sorry for the chance to start the human beings thinking along the lines of a native-menace idea, but Destigmet's crew won't be able to play the part until they have a lot more home-made mechanical and electrical equipment, things that the humans know we don't have. Certainly, unless the native menace seems real, the human beings aren't very likely to take the steps we want.

"If there were any way to go after Dee now and cancel his orders, I'd do it. I wish I'd dared let you go ahead with radio experiments, and had a set on the *Deedee* right now."

"It shouldn't be too risky, and I'd be more than glad to work on it," answered Bendivence. "The waves could be detected by the human beings, of course, but if we confined ourselves to brief and rare transmissions and used a simple off-on code they probably wouldn't realize what the source was. However, it's too late to get Deeslenver, anyway."

"True. I wish I knew why no one up there has said another word about Kabremm. The last time I talked to Mrs. Hoffman, I got the impression that she wasn't quite as sure as before that she'd really seen him. Do you suppose she really made a mistake? Or are the human beings trying to test *us,* the way I wanted to do with them? Or has Dondragmer done something to get us off that reef? If she were really wrong, we'll have to start thinking all over again..."

"And what about that other report we've heard no more of, something sliding across the *Esket*'s floor?" countered the scientist. "Was that still another test? Or is something really happening there? Remember, we haven't had any contact with that base for over a hundred and fifty hours. If the *Esket* is really being moved by something, we're much too badly out of date to do anything sensible. You know, without saying anything against the *Esket* act, it's an awful nuisance not to be able to trust your data."

"If there's real trouble at the *Esket* we'll just have to trust Dee's judgment," said the commander, ignoring Bendivence's closing sentence. "Actually, even that isn't the chief problem. The real question is what to do about Dondragmer and the *Kwembly.* I suppose he had good reason to leave his ship and let her drift away, but the results have been very awkward. The fact that a couple of his men got left aboard makes it almost more so; if they hadn't been, we could just forget about the cruiser and send out the *Kalliff* to pick up the people."

"Why can't we do that anyway? Didn't the human Aucoin suggest it?"

"He did. I said I'd have to think it over."

"Why?"

"Because there is less than one chance in ten, and probably less than one in a hundred, that the *Kalliff* could get there in time to do those two men any good. The chances are small enough that she could get there at all. Remember that snow field the *Kwembly* crossed before her first flood? What do you suppose that area is like now? And how long do you think two men, competent men, but with no real technical or scientific training, are going to keep that leaking hull habitable?

"Of course, we could confess the whole act, tell the humans to get in touch with Destigmet through the watch he keeps at the *Esket*'s communicators; then they could tell him to send a rescue dirigible."

"That would be wasting a tremendous amount of work, and ruining what still seems a promising operation," Bendivence replied thoughtfully. "You don't want to do that any more than I do; but of course we can't abandon those two helmsmen."

"We can't," Barlennan agreed slowly, "but I just wonder whether we'd be taking too much of a chance on them if we waited out one other possibility."

"What's that?"

"If the human beings were convinced that we could not possibly carry out the rescue, it's just possible, especially with *two* Hoffmans to do the arguing, that they'd decide to do something about it themselves."

"But what could they do? The ship they call the 'barge' will only land here at the Settlement by its automatic controls, as I understand Rescue Plan One. They certainly can't fly it around on this world from out at the orbiting station; if it took them a whole minute to correct any mistake, they'd crash it right away. They certainly can't fly it down personally. It's set up to rescue *us,* with our air and temperature control, and besides Dhrawn's gravity would paint a human being over the deck."

"Don't underestimate those aliens, Ben. They may not be exactly ingenious, but there's been time for their ancestors to think up a lot of ready-made ideas we don't know about yet. I wouldn't do it if I felt there was a real chance of our getting there ourselves, but this way we're not putting the helmsmen in any worse danger than they are already; I think that we'll let the human beings get the idea of making the rescue themselves. It would be much better than giving up the plan."

"What it boils down to," said Beetchermarlf to Takoorch, "is that we somehow have to find time between plugging leaks and cleaning poison out of the air units to convince people that the *Kwembly* is worth salvaging.

"The best way would be to get her going ourselves, though I doubt very much that we can do it. It's the cruiser that's going to set the policy. Your life and mine don't mean very much to the humans, except maybe to Benj, who isn't running things up there. If the ship stays alive, if we can keep these tanks going to supply us with food and air, and incidentally keep from being poisoned by oxygen ourselves, and make real, reportable progress in repairing and freeing the cruiser, *then* maybe they'll be convinced that a rescue trip is worth while. Even if they don't, we'll have to do all those things for our own sakes anyway; but if we can have the humans tell Barlennan that we have the *Kwembly* out and running, and will get her back to Dondragmer by ourselves, it should make quite a few people happy, especially the commander."

"Do you think we can do it?" asked Takoorch.

"You and I are the first ones to convince," replied the younger helmsman. "The rest of the world will be easier after that."

"What it boils down to," said Benj to his father, "is that we won't risk the barge for two lives, even though that's what it's here for."

"Not quite right on either count," Ib Hoffman answered. "It's a piece of emergency equipment, but it was planned for use if the whole project collapsed and we had to evacuate the Settlement. This was always a possibility; there was a lot that just couldn't be properly tested in advance. For example, the trick of matching outside pressure in the cruisers and air-suits by using extra argon was perfectly reasonable, but we could not be sure there would be no side effects on the Mesklinites themselves; argon is inert by the usual standards, but so is xenon, which is an effective anaesthetic for human beings. Living systems are just too complicated for extrapolation ever to be safe, though the Mesklinites seem a lot simpler physiologically than we are. That may be one reason they can stand such a broad temperature range.

"But the point is, the barge is preset to home in on a beam transmitter near the Settlement; it won't land itself anywhere else on Dhrawn. It can be handled by remote control, of course, but not at this range.

"We could, I suppose, alter its on-board computer program to make it set itself down in other places, at least, on any reasonably flat surface; but would you want to set it down anywhere near your friend either by a built-in, unchangeable program or by long-delayed remote control? Remember the barge uses proton jets, has a mass of twenty-seven thousand pounds, and must put up quite a splash soft-landing in forty gravities, especially since its jets are splayed to reduce cratering." Benj frowned thoughtfully.

"But why can't we get closer to Dhrawn, and cut down the remote-control lag?" he asked, after some moments' thought. Ib looked at his son in surprise.

"You know why, or should. Dhrawn has a mass of 3,471 Earths, and a rotation period of just over fifteen hundred hours. A synchronous orbit to hold us above a constant longitude at the equator is therefore just over six million miles out. If you use an orbit a hundred miles above the surface you'd be traveling at better than ninety miles a second, and go around Dhrawn in something like forty minutes. You'd remain in sight of one spot on the surface for two or three minutes out of the forty. Since the planet has about eighty-seven times Earth's surface area, how many control stations do you think would be needed to manage one landing or lift-off?"

Benj made a gesture of impatience.

"I know all that, but there is already a swarm of stations down there, the shadow satellites. Even I know that they all have relay equipment, since they're all reporting constantly to the computers up here and at any given moment nearly half of them must be behind Dhrawn. Why can't a controller riding one of these, or a ship at about the same height, tie into their relays and handle landing and lift-off from there? Delay shouldn't be more than a second or so even from the opposite side of the world."

"Because," Ib started to answer, and then fell silent. He remained so for a full two minutes. Benj did not interrupt his thinking; the boy usually had a good idea of when he was ahead.

"There would have to be several minutes of interruption of neutrino data while the relays were being preempted," Ib said finally.

"Out of the how many years that they've been integrating that material?" Benj was not usually sarcastic with either of his parents, but his feelings were once more growing warm. His father nodded silently, conceding the point, and continued to think.

It must have been five minutes later, though Benj would have sworn to a greater number, that the senior Hoffman got suddenly to his feet.

"Come on, son. You're perfectly right. It will work for an initial space-to-surface landing, and for a surface-to-orbit lift-off, and that's enough. For surface-to-surface flight even one second is too much control delay, but we can do without that."

"Sure!" enthused Benj. "Lift off into orbit, get your breath, change the orbit to suit your landing spot. and go back down."

"That would work, but don't mention it. For one thing, if we made a habit of it there *would* be a significant interruption of neutrino data transmission. Besides, I've wanted an excuse for this almost ever since I joined this project. Now I have one, and I'm going to use it."

"An excuse for what?"

"For doing exactly what I think Barlennan has been trying to maneuver us into doing all along: put Mesklinite pilots on the barge. I suppose he wants his own interstellar ship, some time, so that he can start leading the same life among the stars that he used to do on Mesklin's oceans, but he'll have to make do with one quantum jump at a time."

"Is *that* what you think he's been up to? Why should he care about having his own space pilots so much? And come to think of it, why wasn't that a good idea in the first place, if the Mesklinites can learn how?"

"It was, and there's no reason to doubt that they can."

"Then why wasn't it done that way all along?"

"I'd rather not lecture on that subject just now. I like to feel as much pride in my species as circumstances allow, and the explanation doesn't reflect much credit either on man's rationality or his emotional control."

"I can guess, then," replied Benj. "But in that case, what makes you think we can change it now?"

"Because now, at the trifling cost of descending to the same general level of emotional reasoning, we have a handle on some of man's less generous drives. I'm going down to the planetology lab and filibuster. I'm going to ask those chemists why they don't know what trapped the *Kwembly,* and when they say it's because they don't have any samples of the mud, I'm going to ask them why they don't. I'm going to ask them why they've been making do with seismic and neutrino-shadow data when they might as well be analyzing mineral samples carted up here from every spot where a Mesklinite cruiser has stopped for ten minutes. If you prefer not to descend to that level, and would rather work with mankind's nobler emotions, you be thinking of all the heart-rending remarks you could make about the horror and cruelty of leaving your friend Beetchermarlf to suffocate slowly on an alien world parsecs from his home. We could use that if we have to take this argument to a higher authority, like the general public. I don't think we'll really need to, but right now I'm in no mood to restrict myself to clean fighting and logical argument.

"If Alan Aucoin growls about the cost of operating the barge (I think he has too much sense), I'm going to jump on him with both feet. Energy has been practically free ever since we've had fusion devices; what costs is personal skill. He'll have to use Mesklinite crews anyway, so that investment is already made; and by letting the barge drift out here unused he's wasting *its* cost. I know there's a small hole in that logic, but if you point it out in Dr. Aucoin's hearing I'll paddle you for the first time since you were seven, and I don't think the last decade has done too much to my arm. You let Aucoin do his own thinking."

"You needn't get annoyed with *me,* Dad."

"I'm not. In fact, I'm not as much annoyed as I am scared."

"Scared? Of what?"

"Of what may happen to Barlennan and his people on what your mother calls 'that horrible planet.' "

"But why? Why now, more than before?"

"Because I'm coming gradually to realize that Barlennan is an intelligent, forceful, thoughtful, ambitious, and reasonably well-educated being, just as my only son was six years ago; and I remember your homemade diving outfit much too well. Come on. We have an astronautics school to get organized, and a student body to collect."

Epilogue: Lessons

At two hundred miles, the barge was just visible as a starlike object reflecting Lalande 21185's feeble light. Benj had watched the vessel as it pulled up to that distance and moved into what its pilot considered a decent station-keeping orbit, but neither he nor the pilot had discussed technical details. It was so handy to be able to hold a conversation without waiting a full minute for the other fellow's answer that Benj and Beetchermarlf had simply chattered.

These conversations were becoming less and less frequent. Benj was really back at work now and, he suspected, making up for lost time. Beetchermarlf was often too far away on practice flights to talk at all, and even more frequently too occupied to converse with anyone but his instructor.

"Time to turn it over, Beetch," the boy ended the present exchange as he heard Tebbetts' whistling from down the shaft. "The taskmaster is on the way."

"I'm ready when he is," came the reply. "Does he want to use your language or mine this time?"

"He'll let you know; he didn't tell me. Here he is," replied Benj.

The bearded astronomer, however, spoke first to Benj after looking quickly around. The two were drifting weightless in the direct-observation section at the center of the station's connecting bar, and Tebbetts had taken for granted that the barge and his student would be drifting alongside. All his quick glance caught was the dull ember of a sun in one direction and the dimly lit disc of Dhrawn, little larger than Luna seen from Earth, in the other.

"Where is he, Benj? I thought I heard you talking to him, so I assumed he was close. I hope he isn't late. He should be solving intercept orbits, even with nomographs instead of high-speed computers, better than that by now."

"He's here, sir." The boy pointed. "Just over two hundred miles away, in a 17.8-minute orbit around the station."

Tebbetts blinked. "That's ridiculous. I don't think this heap of hardware would whip anything around in that time at a distance of two hundred feet, let alone that many miles. He'd have to use power, accelerating straight toward us—"

"He is, sir. About two hundred G's acceleration. The time is the rotation period of Mesklin, and the acceleration is the gravity value at his home port. He says he hasn't been so comfortable since he signed up with Barlennan, and wishes there were some way to turn up the sunlight."

The astronomer smiled slowly.

"Yes. I see. That does make sense. I should have thought of it myself. I have some more practice exercises for him here, but that's about as good as any of them. I should do more of that sort of thing. Well, let's get at it. Can you stay to check my language? I think I have the Stennish words for everything in today's work, and space is empty enough so that his mistakes and mine should both be relatively harmless, but there's no need to take chances."

"It's too bad the *Kwembly* couldn't be salvaged after all," remarked Aucoin, "but Dondragmer's crew is doing a very good and effective study of the area while they're waiting for relief. I think it was a very good idea to send the *Kalliff* after them with a skeleton crew and let them work while they waited, instead of taking them back to the Settlement in the barge. That would have been pretty dangerous anyway, until there are practiced Mesklinite pilots. The single landing near the *Kwembly* to get the two helmsmen, and a direct return to space while they were trained, was probably the safest way to do it.

"But now we have this trouble with the *Smof*. At this rate we'll be out of cruisers before we're half way around Low Alpha. Does anyone know the *Smof*'s commander the way Easy knows Dondragmer? You don't, I suppose, Easy? Can anyone give a guess at his ability to get himself out of trouble? Or are we going to have to risk sending the barge down before those two Mesklinites are fully trained?"

"Tebbetts thinks Beetchermarlf could handle a surface landing now, as long as it wasn't complicated by mechanical emergencies," pointed out an engineer. "Personally I wouldn't hesitate to let him go."

"You may be right. The trouble is, though, that we certainly can't land the barge on an ice pack, and not even the barge can lift one of those land-cruisers, even if there were a way of fastening them together without an actual landing. Beetchermarlf and Takoorch may as well continue their training for the moment. What I want as soon as possible, Planetology, is the best direction and distance for the *Smof*'s crew to trek if they do have to abandon the cruiser, that is, the closest spot where the barge *could* land to pick them up. If it's close to their present location, don't tell them, of course; I want them to do their best to save the cruiser, and there's no point in tempting them with an easy escape." Ib Hoffman stirred slightly, but refrained from comment. Aucoin, from one point of view, was probably justified. The administrator went on, "Also, is there definite word on the phenomenon that trapped the *Kwembly?* You've had specimens of the mud, or whatever it is, that Beetchermarlf brought up, for weeks now."

"Yes," replied a chemist. "It's a fascinating example of surface action. It's sensitive to the nature and particle size of the minerals present, the proportions of water and ammonia in the lubricating fluid, the temperature, and the pressure. The *Kwembly*'s weight, of course, was the main cause of trouble; the Mesklinites could walk around on it, in fact, they did, safely enough. Once triggered by a pressure peak, the strength went out of the stuff in a wave—"

"All right, the rest can serve for a paper," Aucoin nodded. "Is there any way to identify such a surface without putting a ship onto it?"

"Hmm. I'd say yes. Radiation temperature should be information enough, or at least, it would warn that further tests should be made. For that matter, I wouldn't worry about its ever getting the barge; the jets would boil the water and ammonia out of such a surface safely before touchdown."

Aucoin nodded, and passed on to other matters. Cruiser reports, publication reports, supply reports, planning prospectuses.

He was still a little embarrassed. He had known his own failing, but like most people had excused it, and felt sure it wasn't noticeable. But the Hoffmans had noticed it, maybe others had. He'd have to be careful, if he wanted to keep a responsible and respected job. Alter all, he repeated firmly to himself, Mesklinites *were* People, even if they looked like bugs.

Ib Hoffman's attention wandered, important though he knew the work to be. His mind kept going back to the *Kwembly,* and the *Smof,* and to a well-designed, well-built piece of diving gear which had almost killed an eleven-year-old boy. The reports, punctuated by Aucoin's sometimes acid comments, droned on; slowly Ib made up his mind.

"We're getting ahead," remarked Barlennan. "There was good excuse for taking the vision sets out of the *Kwembly,* since she was being abandoned, so we've been able to work on her with no restrictions. We could use Reffel's helicopter, since the humans think it's lost. too. Jemblakee and Deeslenver seem to feel that the cruiser can be back in running state in another day." He glanced at the feeble sun, almost exactly overhead.

"The human chemists were certainly helpful about that mud she was in. It was funny how the one who talked to Dee about the stuff kept insisting that he was only guessing, while he made suggestion after suggestion. It's too bad we couldn't tell him how successful most of his ideas were."

"Self-doubt seems to be a human trait, if it's safe to make such a sweeping remark," replied Guzmeen. "When did this news get in?"

"The *Deedee* came in an hour ago, and is gone again. There's too much for that machine to do. It was bad enough when we lost the *Elsh,* and with Kabremm and his *Gwelf* overdue things are piling up. I hope we find him. Maybe the *Kalliff* will turn up something; he was supposed to be scouting a route to get her to Don's camp, so maybe one of Kenanken's scouts will spot him. He's less than a day overdue, so there's still a chance..."

"And with all this, you say we're ahead?" cut in Guzmeen.

"Sure. Remember, the whole aim of the *Esket* act was to persuade the human beings to let us use space ships. The self-support business was incidental, though useful. We expected to work the local-life myth up to a major menace before we could persuade Aucoin to let us fly, and spend months building up to it. We're far ahead on time, and haven't lost very much, the base at the *Esket* site, of course, and the *Elsh* and its crew, and just possibly Kabremm and his."

"But even Kabremm and Karfrengin aren't exactly expendable. There aren't very many of us. If Dondragmer and his crew don't keep alive until the *Kalliff* reaches them, we'll have taken a really serious loss; at least our dirigible crews weren't our scientists and engineers."

"Don's in no real danger. They can always be picked up by Beetchermarlf in the human space ship—I mean our space ship."

"And if anything goes wrong with *that* operation we're out not only our only space ship but our only space pilots."

"Which suggests to me," Barlennan said thoughtfully, "that we should try to regain some lost ground. As soon as the *Kwembly* is ready she should start hunting a suitable place and start replacing the *Esket* settlement. Don's scientists should have little trouble finding a good location; Dhrawn seems to be rich in metal ores. Maybe we should have him search closer to here so that communication will be quicker, though.

"We'll have to build more dirigibles; the one we have left isn't nearly enough for the work. Maybe we ought to design bigger ones."

"I've been wondering about that," a technician who had been listening silently up to this point spoke up. "Do you suppose that it would be smart to find out more, tactfully, of course, from the humans about dirigibles? We've never discussed the subject with them; they taught you about balloons years ago, and some of our own people got the idea of using the human power sources with them. We don't know if *they* ever used them at all. Maybe it isn't just bad luck that we've lost two out of our three in such a short time. Maybe there's something fundamentally wrong with the whole idea."

The commander gave a gesture of impatience.

"That's silly. I didn't try to pick up a complete scientific education from the aliens, since it was obviously going to take too long; but one thing I did gather was that the underlying rules are essentially simple. Once the humans started concentrating on basic rules, they went from sailing ships to space ships in a couple of hundred years. Balloons, powered or not, are simple devices; I understand them perfectly myself. Putting an engine aboard doesn't change that; the same rules have to be working."

The technician eyed his commander thoughtfully, and thought briefly of electron tubes and television circuits before replying.

"I suppose," he said thoughtfully, "that a piece of a tent being blown away by the gale, and a ship being tacked into the wind, are also examples of the same rules at work."

Barlennan didn't want to give an affirmative answer, but he could find nothing better.

He was still trying to shrug off the technician's remark, but only succeeding in growing more and more doubtful of his situation, some twenty hours later when a messenger called him to the communication room. As soon as he entered, Guzmeen spoke briefly into a microphone; a minute later, a human face which neither of them recognized appeared on the screen.

"I am Ib Hoffman, Easy's husband and Benj's father," the stranger began without preamble. "I'm speaking to you two, Barlennan and Dondragmer, alone. The rest of the observing crew here are concentrating on a new emergency involving one of the cruisers. I'm using your language as best I can, with my wife standing by; she knows what I want to say, and will correct me if I slip too badly. I have decided that it is time to clear up some misunderstandings, but I don't plan to tell everyone here about them; you'll see why before I finish, if you don't already. I'm bothered mostly because I hate to call anyone a liar in any language.

"First, Barlennan, my hearty congratulations. I am just about certain that when we turned the barge over to a Mesklinite pilot we fulfilled one of your chief plans, probably well before you meant or expected it to mature. That's fine. I wanted that to happen. Probably you want to make interstellar flights on your own later on, too; that's also fine with me. I'll help.

"You seem to feel that many or most human beings would try to thwart you in this, and I have to admit that some would, though I think we have the most effective one under control now. You can't be sure that I'm being sincere now, for that matter; you're tricky enough yourself to expect it of other people. Too bad. How much you believe of what I say is beyond my control; I still have to say it.

"I don't know how much of the basic situation you set up, but I can guess. I'm nearly sure the *Esket* disappearance was not genuine. I'm uncertain of the real status of the *Kwembly.* You probably know more of Dhrawn than you've reported. I won't say I don't care, because I do; we're here to learn as much as possible about Dhrawn, and what you don't tell us is a loss to the project. I can't threaten you with penalties for breach of contract, since I'm not completely certain you've broken it and am in no position to carry out threats. And in any case have less than no desire to even make threats. I do want to persuade you, though, that it will be better for both of us if we do without secrets. We're at a point where anything less than complete frankness is likely to cost us a lot and cost you everything. To make that point, I'm going to tell you a story.

"You know that human beings breathe oxygen much as you do hydrogen, though being so much larger we need a more complicated pumping system to get it through our bodies. Because of the details of that system, we suffocate if deprived of gaseous, free oxygen within a certain rather narrow range of pressures.

"About three quarters of Earth is covered by water. We cannot breathe under water without artificial equipment, but the use of such equipment is a common human sport. It consists essentially of a tank of compressed air and a valve system which releases the air to our breathing system as needed; simple and obvious.

"Six of our years ago, when Benj was eleven years old, he made such a device, designing it himself with my assistance. He made the pressure tank and regulator, using ordinary fabricating equipment such as may be found in most home workshops, just as he had made more complex things such as small gas turbines. He tested the parts with my help; they worked perfectly. He calculated how long the air in the tank would last him, and then tested the whole assembly under water. I went along as a matter of common-sense safety, using a commercial diving device.

"I am sure you know the principles of hydrostatics and the gas laws; at least, Easy has given me words for them in your language. You can see that at a certain depth, a lungful of air would have only half its volume at the surface. Benj knew this too, but reasoned that it would still be a lungful as far as oxygen content was concerned, so that a one-hour tank would be a one-hour tank regardless of depth, as long as tank pressure was above that of the water.

"To make a long story short, it didn't. He ran out of air in less than a third of the calculated time, and I had to make an emergency rescue. Because of the quick pressure change and some human peculiarities which you don't seem to share, he was very nearly killed. The trouble turned out to be that the human breathing rate is controlled, not by the oxygen in our blood, but by the carbon dioxide, one of the waste products. To maintain a normal equilibrium of that, we have to run normal *volumes* of air through our lungs, regardless of oxygen content or total pressure; hence, an hour's air supply at normal pressure is only half an hour thirty-three feet under water, a third of an hour at sixty-six, and so on.

"I don't want to insult anyone's intelligence by asking if he understands my point, but I'd like some comment from both of you on that story."

The answers were interesting, both in nature and arrival time. Barlennan's popped from the speaker with very little more than light-travel delay; Dondragmer's came much, much later, and did not overlap with his commander's.

"It is obvious that incomplete knowledge can lead to mistakes," said Barlennan, "but I don't see why that is especially applicable to the present case. We know that our knowledge can't be complete, and that our work here is dangerous for that reason. We have always known it. Why emphasize the point now? I'd much rather hear your report on the cruiser you say is in trouble. You make me suspect that you are leading up gently to the information that I have lost another cruiser because of something its designing engineers didn't know. Don't worry, I won't blame you for that. None of us could foresee everything."

Ib smiled sourly at the revelation of yet another human characteristic.

"That's not just what I had in mind, Commander, though there are valid aspects to what you have just said. I'd like to wait for Dondragmer's answer before I say any more, though."

It was another full minute, a slightly strained one, before the voice of the *Kwembly*'s captain arrived.

"Your account is plain enough and you would probably have been briefer had you not meant to imply more. I suspect that your key point is not so much that your son got into trouble through ignorance, but that he did so even under your experienced adult supervision. I would take the implication to be that even though you aliens do not claim omniscience or omnipotence, we are in a certain amount of danger here no matter how closely you supervise and assist us, and we are adding unnecessarily to our danger any time we act on our own, like the student chemist who experiments on his own." Dondragmer had spent much more time at the College than had his commander.

"Right. Just what I meant," said Ib. "I can't..."

"Just a moment," interrupted Easy. "Hadn't you better relay Don's remark to Barlennan first?"

"Right." Her husband gave a one-sentence summary of the captain's speech, and went on, "I can't force any policy on you, and would prefer not to even if I could. I don't expect you to make a complete revelation of everything that's gone on on Dhrawn since you first built the Settlement. In fact, I'd advise strongly against it; I have enough complications up here with the administration as it is. However, if Easy just happened to get an occasional talk with her old friends Destigmet and Kabremm, just as an example, I would have a better idea of what has gone on and be in a better position to keep things running smoothly at this end. I don't expect a spot decision on any matter of major policy change, Commander, but please think it over."

Barlennan, being a sea captain by training and trade, was accustomed to the need for quick decisions. Furthermore, circumstances had already compelled thoughts on similar lines to circulate in his tiny head. Finally, his only really basic policy was to ensure his own survival and that of his crew. He answered Ib promptly.

"Easy may get her talk with Destigmet, but not right away; the *Esket* is a long distance from here. I will also have to wait to tell you all that I'd like to, because I must first hear from you the details of the trouble you mentioned when you first called. You said that another of my cruisers was in trouble.

"Please tell me just what has happened, so I can plan what help to request from you."

Ib and Easy Hoffman looked at each other and grinned in mingled relief and triumph.

But it was Benj who made the key remark. This was later on, in the aerology lab, when they were recounting to him and McDevitt all that had been said. The boy looked up at the huge globes of Dhrawn, and the tiny area where the lights indicated partial knowledge.

"I suppose you think he's a lot safer now, down there."

It was a sobering thought.

Whirligig World[1]

Writing a science fiction story is fun, not work. If it were work I wouldn't be writing this article, which would then constitute a chapter for a textbook. I don't plan to write such a text, since if the subject is teachable I'd be creating competition and if it isn't I'd be wasting time.

The fun, and the material for this article, lies in treating the whole thing as a game. I've been playing the game since I was a child, so the rules must be quite simple. They are; for the reader of a science-fiction story, they consist of finding as many as possible of the author's statements or implications which conflict with the facts as science currently understands them. For the author, the rule is to make as few such slips as he possibly can.

Certain exceptions are made by both sides, of course. For example, it is commonly considered fair to ignore certain of Dr. Einstein's theories, if the story background requires interstellar travel. Sometimes a passing reference is made to travel through a "hyperspace" in which light can travel faster or distances are shorter, but in essence we ignore the speed-of-light rule since we can—so far—see no way around it. The author assumes that problem, or perhaps others equally beyond our present ability to solve, to be answered, and goes ahead from there. In such a case, of course, fair play depends that all such matters be mentioned as early as possible in the story, so that the reader has a chance to let his imagination grow into the new background.

I always feel cheated when the problem which has been developed in a story is solved by the discovery in the last chapter of antigravity, time travel, or a method of reviving the dead; such things *must* be at least near full development and known to the reader long enough in advance to

[1] This article originally appeared in *Astounding Science Fiction*, June 1953.

give him a chance to foresee the ending. I have always assumed, perhaps wrongly, that others felt as I do; I try to write accordingly.

In *Mission of Gravity* I've been playing this game as fairly as I could.

The author has one disadvantage, of course; all his moves must be completed first. Once the story is in print, the other side can take all the time in the world to search out the mistakes; they can check with reference libraries or write letters to universities, if they play the game that seriously. Sooner or later the mistakes will come out; there is no further chance to correct them. If *Mission of Gravity* contains such errors, they're out of my hands now. I did my best to avoid them, but you still have a good chance to win. As I said, my moves were fun, not work.

The basic idea for the story came nearly ten years ago. In 1943 Dr. K. Aa. Strand published the results of some incredibly—to anyone but an astronomer—painstaking work on the orbit of the binary star 61 Cygni, a star otherwise moderately famous for being the first to have its parallax, and hence its distance, measured. In solving such a problem, the data normally consist of long series of measurements of the apparent direction and distance of one star from the other; if the stars are actually moving around each other, and the observations cover a sufficient fraction of a revolution, it is ordinarily possible if not easy to compute the actual relative orbit of the system—that is, the path of one assuming that the other is stationary. Dr. Strand's work differed from the more usual exercises of this type in that his measures were made from photographs. This eliminated some of the difficulties usually encountered in visual observation, and supplied a number of others; but there was a net gain in overall accuracy, to the extent that he was not only able to publish a more accurate set of orbital elements than had previously been available, but to show that the orbital motion was not regular.

The fainter star, it seemed, did *not* move around the brighter in a smooth ellipse at a rate predictable by the straightforward application of Kepler's laws. It did, however, move in a Keplerian path about an invisible point which was in turn traveling in normal fashion about the other sun.

There was nothing intrinsically surprising about this discovery; the implication was plain. One of the two stars—it was not possible to tell which, since measures had been made *assuming* the brighter to be stationary—was actually accompanied by another, invisible object; the invisible point which obeys the normal planetary and stellar laws was the center of gravity of the star-unknown object system. Such cases are by no means unusual.

To learn which of the two suns is actually attended by this dark body, we would have to have more observations of the system, made in relation

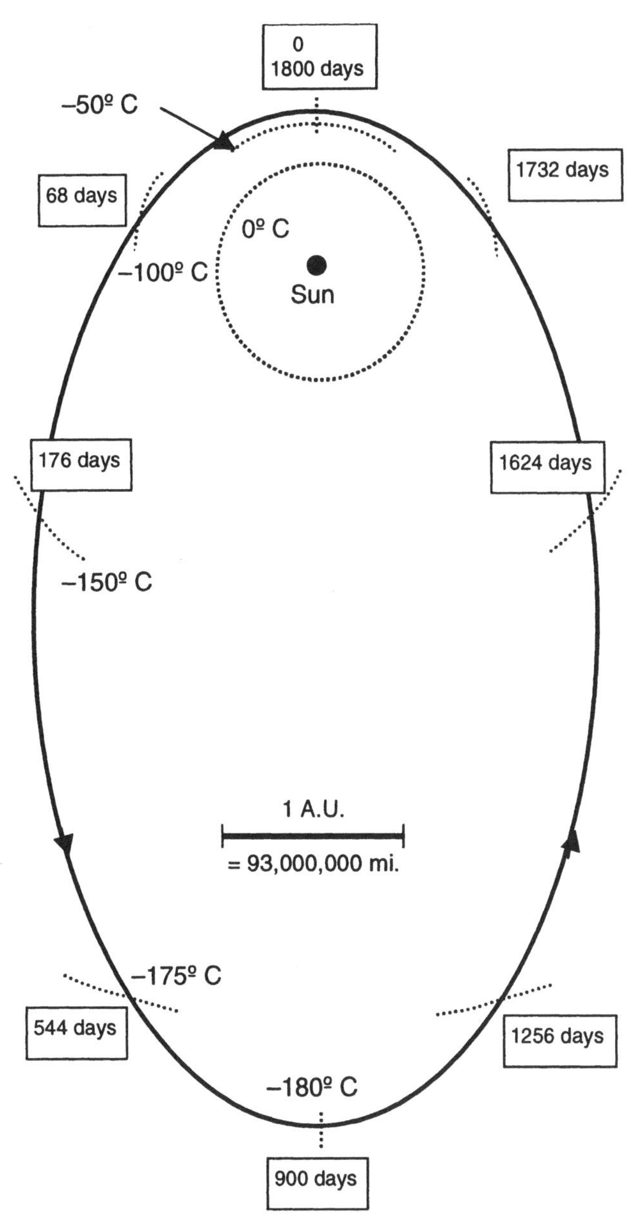

ORBIT of MESKLIN
The positions of the isotherms and time of isotherm crossing are approximate and assume that the sun is 61 Cygni A

to one or more stars not actually part thereof. Some stars exist near enough to the line of sight for such observations to be made, but if they have been reduced and published the fact has not come to my attention. I chose to assume that the object actually circles the brighter star. That may cost me a point in the game when the facts come out, but I won't be too disheartened if it does.

There was still the question of just what this object was. In other such cases where an invisible object betrayed its presence by gravity or eclipse, as in the system of Algol, we had little difficulty in showing that the companion was a star of some more or less normal type—in the case of Algol, for example, the "dark" body causing the principal eclipse is a sun larger, hotter, and brighter than our own; we can tell its size, mass, luminosity, and temperature with very considerable precision and reliability.

In the case of the 61 Cygni system, the normal methods were put to work; and they came up immediately with a disconcerting fact. The period and size of the orbit, coupled with the fairly well-known mass of the visible stars, indicated that the dark body has a mass only about sixteen thousandths that of the sun—many times smaller than any star previously known. It was still about sixteen times the mass of Jupiter, largest planet we knew. Which was it—star or planet? Before deciding on the classification of an object plainly very close to the borderline, we must obviously decide just where the borderline lies.

For general purposes, our old grade-school distinction will serve: a star shines by its own light, while a planet is not hot enough for that and can be seen only by reflected light from some other source. If we restrict the word "light" to mean radiation we can see, there should be little argument, at least about definitions. (If anyone brings up nontypical stars of the VV_2 Cephei or $Epsilon_2$ Aurigae class I shall be annoyed.) The trouble still remaining is that we may have some trouble deciding whether this Cygnus object shines by intrinsic or reflected light, when we can't see it shine at all. Some educated guessing seems in order.

There is an empirical relation between the mass of a star, at least a main-sequence star, and its actual brightness. Whether we would be justified in extending this relation to cover an object like 61 Cygni C—that is, third brightest body in the 61 Cygni system—is more than doubtful, but may be at least suggestive. If we do, we find that its magnitude as a star should be about twenty or a little brighter. That is within the range of modern equipment, *provided* that the object is not too close to the glare of another, brighter star and *provided* it is sought photographically with a long enough exposure. Unfortunately, 61C will never be more than about one and a half seconds of arc away from its primary, and an exposure sufficient to reveal the twentieth magnitude would burn the image of 61A or B over considerably more than one and a half seconds' worth of photographic plate. A rotating sector or similar device to cut down selectively on the light of the brighter star might do the trick, but a job of extraordinary delicacy would be demanded. If anyone has attempted such a task, I have not seen his published results.

If we assume the thing to be a planet, we find that a disk of the same reflecting power as Jupiter and three times his diameter would have an apparent magnitude of twenty-five or twenty-six in 61C's location; there would be no point looking for it with present equipment. It seems, then, that there is no way to be sure whether it is a star or a planet; and I can call it whichever I like without too much fear of losing points in the game.

I am supposing it to be a planet, not only for story convenience but because I seriously doubt that an object so small could maintain at its center the temperatures and pressures necessary for sustained nuclear reactions; and without such reactions no object could maintain a significant radiation rate for more than a few million years. Even as a planet, though, our object has characteristics which will call for thought on any author's part.

Although sixteen times as massive as Jupiter, it is *not* sixteen times as bulky. We know enough about the structure of matter now to be sure that Jupiter has about the largest volume of any possible "cold" body. When mass increases beyond this point, the central pressure becomes great enough to force some of the core matter into the extremely dense state which we first knew in white dwarf stars, where the outer electronic shells of the atoms can no longer hold up and the nuclei crowd together far more closely than is possible under ordinary—to us, that is—conditions. From the Jupiter point on up, as mass increases the radius of a body decreases—and mean density rises enormously. Without this effect—that is, if it maintained Jupiter's density with its own mass—61C would have a diameter of about two hundred fifteen thousand miles. Its surface gravity would be about seven times that of the Earth. However, the actual state of affairs seems to involve a diameter about equal to that of Uranus or Neptune, and a surface gravity over three hundred times what we're used to.

Any science fiction author can get around that, of course. Simply invent a gravity screen. No one will mind little details like violation of the law of conservation of energy, or the difference of potential across the screen which will prevent the exchange of anything more concrete than visual signals; no one at all. No one but *Astounding* readers, that is; and there is my own conscience, too. I might use gravity screens if a good story demanded them and I could see no legitimate way out; but in the present case there is a perfectly sound and correct means of reducing the effective gravity, at least for a part of a planet's surface. As Einstein says, gravitational effects cannot be distinguished from inertial ones. The so-called centrifugal force is an inertial effect, and for a rotating planet happens to be directed outward—in effect—in the equatorial plane. I can, therefore, set my planet spinning rapidly enough to make the characters feel as light as I please, at least at the equator.

If that is done, of course, my nice new world will flatten in a way that would put Saturn to shame; and there will undoubtedly be at least one astronomer reading the story who will give me the raised eyebrow if I have it squashed too little or too much. Surely there is some relation between mass, and rate of spin, and polar flattening—

I was hung up on that problem for quite a while. Since I had other things to do, I didn't really concentrate on it; but whenever a friend whose math had not collapsed with the years crossed my path, I put it up to him. My own calculus dissolved in a cloud of rust long, long ago. I finally found the answer—or *an* answer—in my old freshman astronomy text, which is still in my possession. I was forcibly reminded that I must also take into account the internal distribution of the planet's mass; that is, whether it was of homogeneous density or, say, almost all packed into a central core. I chose the latter alternative, in view of the enormous density almost certainly possessed by the core of this world and the fact that the outer layers where the pressure is less are presumably of normal matter.

I decided to leave an effective gravity of three times our own at the equator, which fixed one value in the formula. I had the fairly well known value for the mass, and a rough estimate of the volume. That was enough. A little slide rule work gave me a set of characteristics which will furnish story material for years to come. I probably won't use it again myself—though that's no promise[2]—and I hereby give official permission to anyone who so desires to lay scenes there. I ask only that he maintain reasonable scientific standards, and that's certainly an elastic requirement in the field of science fiction.

The world itself is rather surprising in several ways. Its equatorial diameter is forty-eight thousand miles. From pole to pole along the axis

[2] Indeed, he used it three more times—*Star Light* written at the request of John W. Campbell, "Lecture Demonstation" written at the request of Harry Harrison for *Astounding: The John W. Campbell Memorial Anthology*, and "Under" written at the request of NESFA Press for this book but first published in *Analog*, January 2000 as the cover story of its 70th Anniversary issue. —Editors

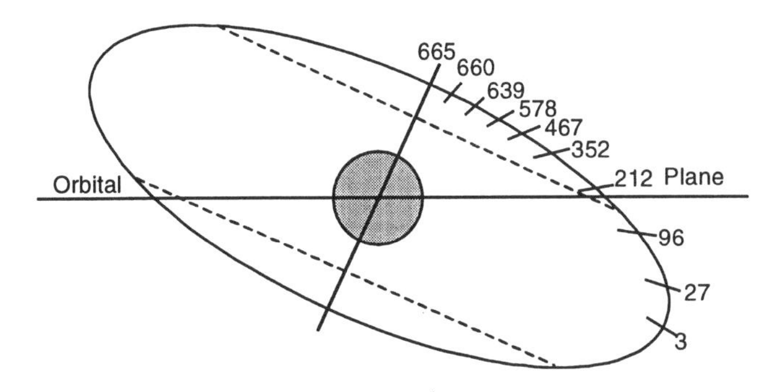

CROSS SECTION of MESKLIN
Shaded portion represents Earth on the same scale. Dotted lines are arctic and antarctic circles. Listed values of gravity (effective), represented by numbers at appropriate latitudes, are very *approximate.*

it measures nineteen thousand seven hundred and forty, carried to more significant figures than I have any right to. It rotates on its axis at a trifle better than twenty degrees a minute, making the day some seventeen and three quarter minutes long. At the equator I would weigh about four hundred eighty pounds, since I hand-picked the net gravity there; at the poles, I'd be carrying something like sixty tons. To be perfectly frank, I don't know the exact value of the polar gravity; the planet is so oblate that the usual rule for spheres, to the effect that one may consider all the mass concentrated at the center for purposes of computing surface gravity, would not even be a good approximation if this world were of uniform density. Having it so greatly concentrated helps a great deal, and I don't think the rough figure of a little under seven hundred Earth gravities that I used in the story is too far out; but anyone who objects is welcome if he can back it up. (Some formulae brought to my attention rather too late to be useful suggest that I'm too high by a factor of two; but whose formulae are the rougher approximations I couldn't guess—as I have said, my math has long since gone to a place where I can't use it for such things. In any case, I'd still stagger a bit under a mere thirty tons.)

I can even justify such a planet, after a fashion, by the current(?) theories of planetary system formation. Using these, I assume that the nucleus forming the original protoplanet had an orbit of cometary eccentricity, which was not completely rounded out by collisions during the process of sweeping up nearly all the raw material in the vicinity of its sun. During the stage when its "atmosphere" extended across perhaps several million miles of space, the capture of material from orbits which were in general more circular than its own would tend to give a spin to the forming world, since objects from outside its position at any instant would have a lower velocity than those from farther in. The rotation thus produced, and increased by conservation of angular momentum as the mass shrank, would be in the opposite direction to the world's orbital motion. That does not bother me, though; I didn't even mention it in the story, as nearly as I can now recall.

The rate of spin might be expected to increase to the point where matter was actually shed from the equator, so I gave the planet a set of rings and a couple of fairly massive moons. I checked the sizes of the rings against the satellite orbits, and found that the inner moon I had invented would produce two gaps in the ring similar to those in Saturn's decoration. The point never became important in the story, but it was valuable to me as atmosphere; I had to have the picture clearly in mind to make all possible events and conversations consistent. The inner moon was ninety thousand miles from the planet's center, giving it a period of two hours and a trifle under eight minutes. The quarter-period and third-period ring gaps come about twelve and nineteen thousand miles respectively from the world's surface. The half-period gap would fall about thirty-three

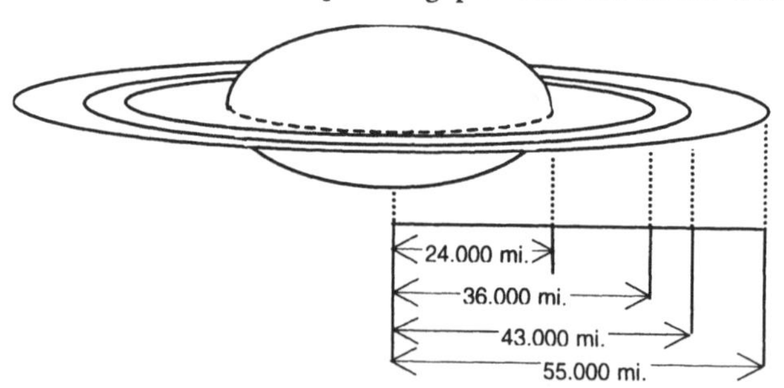

SCALE DRAWING of MESKLIN and RING SYSTEM

Inner ring reaches to less than 1,000 miles of planet's surface; gaps are of corresponding width.

thousand miles out, which is roughly where Roché's Limit would put the edge of the ring anyway. (I say roughly, because that limit depends on density distribution, too.)

On the whole, I have a rather weird-looking object. The model I have of it is six inches in diameter and not quite two and a half thick; if I added the ring, it would consist of a paper disk about fourteen inches in diameter cut to fit rather closely around the plastic wood spheroid. (The model was made to furnish something to draw a map on; I like to be consistent. The map was drawn at random before the story was written; then I bound myself to stick to the geographic limitations it showed.) I was tempted, after looking at it for a while, to call the book *Pancake in the Sky,* but Isaac Asimov threatened violence.[3] Anyway, it looks rather more like a fried egg.

There are a lot of characteristics other than size, though, which must be settled before a story can be written. Since I want a native life form, I must figure out just what conditions that form must be able to stand. Some of these conditions, like the temperature and gravity, are forced on me; others, perhaps, I can juggle to suit myself. Let's see.

Temperature depends, almost entirely, on how much heat a planet receives and retains from its sun. 61 Cygni is a binary system, but the two stars are so far apart that I needn't consider the other one as an influence on this planet's temperature; and the one which it actually circles is quite easy to allow for. Several years ago I computed, partly for fun and partly for cases like this, a table containing some interesting information for all the stars within five parsecs for which I could secure data. The information consists of items such as the distance at which an Earth-type planet would have to revolve from the star in question to have the present temperatures of Earth, Venus, and Mars, and how long it would take a planet to circle the sun in question in each such orbit. For 61 Cygni A, the three distances are about twenty-eight, thirty-nine, and sixty-nine million miles, respectively. As we have seen, 61C's orbit is reasonably well known; and it is well outside any of those three distances. At its closest—and assuming that the primary star is 61A—it gets almost near enough to be warmed to about fifty below zero, Centigrade.[4] At the other end of its rather eccentric orbit Earth at least would cool to about minus one hundred eighty, and it's rather unlikely that this world we are discussing gets too much

[3] This refers to Isaac Asimov's novel *Pebble in the Sky.* —Editors
[4] Hello 1953, from 2000—we now know that the superjovian planet in the 61 Cygni system is in orbit around 61 Cygni B. —Editors

more out of the incoming radiation. That is a rather wide temperature fluctuation.

The eccentricity of the orbit is slightly helpful, though. As Kepler's laws demand, the world spends relatively little time close to its sun; about four fifths of its year it is outside the minus one hundred fifty degree isotherm, and it is close enough to be heated above minus one hundred for only about one hundred thirty days of its eighteen-hundred-day year—Earth days, of course. Its year uses up around one hundred forty-five thousand of its own days, the way we've set it spinning. For practical purposes, then, the temperature will be around minus one hundred seventy Centigrade most of the time. We'll dispose of the rest of the year a little later.

Presumably any life form at all analogous to our own will have to consist largely of some substance which will remain liquid in its home planet's temperature range. In all probability, the substance in question would be common enough on the planet to form its major liquid phase. If that is granted, what substance will meet our requirements?

Isaac Asimov and I spent a pleasant evening trying to find something that would qualify. We wanted it not only liquid within our temperature limits, but a good solvent and reasonably capable of causing ionic dissociation of polar molecules dissolved in it. Water, of course, was out; on this world it is strictly a mineral. Ammonia is almost as bad, melting only on the very hottest days. We played with ammonia's analogues from further along the periodic table—phosphine, arsine, and stibine—with carbon disulfide and phosgene, with carbon suboxide and hydrogen fluoride, with saturated and unsaturated hydrocarbons both straight and with varying degrees of chorine and fluorine substitution, and even with a silicone or two. A few of these met the requirements as to melting and boiling points; some may even have caused dissociation of their solutes, though we had no data on that point for most. However, we finally fell back on a very simple compound.

It boils, unfortunately, at an inconveniently low temperature, even though we assume a most unlikely atmospheric pressure. It cannot be expected to be fruitful in ions, though as a hydrocarbon it will probably dissolve a good many organic substances. It has one great advantage, though, from my viewpoint; it would almost certainly be present on the planet in vast quantities. The substance is methane—CH_4.

Like Jupiter, this world must have started formation with practically the "cosmic" composition, involving from our viewpoint a vast excess of hydrogen. The oxygen present would have combined with it to form water; the nitrogen, to form ammonia; the carbon to form methane and perhaps higher hydrocarbons. There would be enough hydrogen for all, and plenty to spare—light as it is, even hydrogen would have a hard time escaping from a body having five thousand times the mass of Earth once it had cooled below red heat—at first, that is. Later, when the rotational velocity increased almost to the point of real instability, it would be a different story; but we'll consider that in a moment. However, we have what seems to be a good reason to expect oceans of methane on this world; and with such oceans, it would be reasonable to expect the appearance and evolution of life forms using that liquid in their tissues.

But just a moment. I admitted a little while ago that methane boils at a rather lower temperature than I wanted for this story. Is it *too* low? Can I raise it sufficiently by increasing the atmospheric pressure, perhaps? Let's see. The handbook lists methane's critical temperature as about minus eighty-two degrees Centigrade. Above that temperature it will always be a gas, regardless of pressure; and to bring its boiling point up nearly to that value, a pressure about forty-six times that of our own atmosphere at sea level will be needed. Well, we have a big planet, which should have held on to a lot of its original gases; it ought to have a pressure of hundreds or even thousands of atmospheres—whoops! we forgot something.

At the equator, *effective* gravity—gravity minus centrifugal effect—is three times Earth normal. That, plus our specification of temperature and composition of the atmosphere, lets us compute the rate at which atmospheric density will decrease with altitude. It turns out that with nearly pure hydrogen, three g's, and a temperature of minus one hundred fifty for convenience, there is still a significant amount of atmosphere at six-hundred-miles altitude if we start at forty-odd bars for surface pressure—*and at six hundred miles above the equator of this planet the centrifugal force due to its rotation balances the gravity!* If there had ever been a significant amount of atmosphere at that height, it would long since have been slung away into space; evidently we cannot possibly have a surface pressure anywhere near forty-six atmospheres. Some rough slide-rule work suggests eight atmospheres as an upper limit—I used summer temperatures rather than the annual mean.

At that pressure methane boils at about minus one hundred forty-three degrees, and for some three hundred Earth days, or one-sixth of each year, the planet will be in a position where its sun could reasonably be expected to boil its oceans. What to do?

Well, Earth's mean temperature is above the melting point of water, but considerable areas of our planet are permanently frozen. There is no reason why I can't use the same effects for 61C; it is an observed fact that the axis of rotation of a planet can be oriented so that the equatorial and orbital planes do not coincide. I chose for story purposes to incline them at an angle of twenty-eight degrees, in such a direction that the northern hemisphere's midsummer occurs when the world is closest to its sun. This means that a large part of the northern hemisphere will receive no sunlight for fully three quarters of the year, and should in consequence develop a very respectable cap of frozen methane at the expense of the oceans in the other hemisphere. As the world approaches its sun the livable southern hemisphere is protected by the bulk of the planet from its deadly heat output; the star's energy is expended in boiling off the north polar "ice" cap. Tremendous storms rage across the equator carrying air and methane vapor at a temperature little if any above the boiling point of the latter; and while the southern regions will warm up during their winter, they should not become unendurable for creatures with liquid methane in their tissues.

Precession should be quite rapid, of course, because of the tremendous equatorial bulge, which will give the sun's gravity a respectable grip even though most of the world's mass is near its center. I have not attempted to compute the precessional period, but if anyone likes to assume that a switch in habitable hemispheres occurring every few thousand years has kept the natives from building a high civilization I won't argue. Of course, I will also refrain from disagreement with anyone who wants to credit the periodic climate change with responsibility for the development of intelligence on the planet, as our own ice ages have sometimes been given credit for the present mental stature of the human race. Take your pick. For story purposes, I'm satisfied with the fact that either possibility can be defended.

The conditions of the planet, basically, are pretty well defined. There is still a lot of detail work. I must design a life form able to stand those conditions—more accurately, to regard them as ideal—which is not too difficult since I don't have to describe the life processes in rigorous detail. Anyone who wants me to will have to wait until someone can do the same with our own life form. Vegetation using solar energy to build up higher, unsaturated hydrocarbons and animal life getting its energy by reducing those compounds back to the saturated form with atmospheric hydrogen seemed logical enough to me. In the story, I hinted indirectly at the existence of enzymes aiding the reduction, by mentioning that plant tissues would burn in the hydrogen atmosphere if a scrap or two of meat were tossed onto the fuel.

The rest of the detail work consists of all my remaining moves in the game—finding things that are taken for granted on our own world and would not be true on this one. Such things as the impossibility of throwing, jumping, or flying, at least in the higher latitudes; the tremendously rapid decrease of air density with height in the same regions, producing a mirage effect that makes the horizon seem *above* an observer all around; the terrific Coriolis force that splits any developing storm into a series of relatively tiny cells—and would make artillery an interesting science if we could have any artillery; the fact that methane vapor is denser than hydrogen, removing a prime Terrestrial cause of thunderstorm and hurricane formation; the rate of pressure increase below the ocean surface, and what that does to the art of navigation; the fact that icebergs won't float, so that much of the ocean bottoms may be covered with frozen methane; the natural preference of methane for dissolving organic materials such as fats rather than mineral salts, and what that will do to ocean composition—maybe icebergs *would* float after all. You get the idea.

The trouble was, I couldn't possibly think of all these things in advance; time and again a section of the story had to be rewritten because I suddenly realized things couldn't happen that way. I must have missed details, of course; that's where your chance to win the game comes in. I *had* an advantage; the months during which, in my spare hours, my imagination roamed over Mesklin's vast areas in search of inconsistencies. Now the advantage is yours; I can make no more moves in the game, and you have all the time you want to look for the things I've said which reveal slips on the part of my imagination.

Well, good luck—and a good time, whether you beat me or not.

ADDENDUM TO "WHIRLIGIG WORLD"[5]

When *Mission of Gravity* was finished in late 1952, I had a perfectly honest degree in astronomy. I nevertheless made a few mistakes, including one in basic physics; I said, somewhere in the story, that the *Bree* would sail faster with the wind behind her. Predictably, a sailor caught that one.

More seriously, I erroneously took for granted that the figure of rotation which was Mesklin would be an oblate spheroid, and did all the gravity calculation (on a slide rule) assuming that most of its mass was degenerate matter very close to the center. John Campbell told me when he accepted the story that a mathematician had told him that Euler must be spinning in his grave, but I still don't know what theorem I violated.

More usefully, a few years after the story was published, members of the M.I.T. Science Fiction Society (MITSFS) managed to get enough computer time to figure out more nearly what the planet's shape would be. They were presumably right; all I could console myself with was the realization that I had written the story to give pleasure to people even if that wasn't quite the specific pleasure I'd had in mind.

I eventually did get a computer, wrote a relevant program in BASIC[6], and came up with an object looking more like the discus used in field and track sports—an object fairly sharply curved at the poles, much flatter in the mid-latitudes, and coming almost to a real edge at the equator. With arbitrarily chosen three g's at the equator, the polar gravity came out to only about 275, as I recall.

I assume that readers with appropriate background knowledge and computer hardware will want to check this. Maybe someone will want to write a book on the things that minor differences in the basic assumptions will do to Mesklin's shape.

Personally, I wound up doing forty years of high school teaching instead of being an astronomer essentially because of my mathematical weaknesses.

[5] This addendum, written in March 1999, first appeared in print in *Analog Science Fiction and Fact,* January 2000.

[6] The author can no longer find this program, or we would have included it as an appendix. —Editors

I Discover Hal Clement
by Anthony R. Lewis

My introduction to Hal Clement was in 1950, when I was nine years old. My father handed me a copy of *Needle*. It had been recommended to him by his old radio club buddy, Hugo Gernsback, who thought that Hal Clement was one of the few real science fiction writers. I liked the book. Very much. Upon finishing it, I immediately turned back to the beginning and read it again. I was hooked. I still have that 1950 Doubleday Young Moderns edition sitting in my library with its high-acid pages happily digesting themselves—it's autographed now.

In late 1953 I joined the Science Fiction Book Club[1], and one of my first purchases was *Mission of Gravity* (the June 1954 selection). It had not occurred to me that one could buy back issues of the magazines, so I had never read his shorter works until I went to college.

In September 1957 I entered M.I.T. and immediately joined the Science Fiction Society (MITSFS). MITSFS, along with other student activities, had "smokers"[2] where entering freshmen could learn about the activities of the organization and pony up dues. At this meeting MITSFS had both Hal Clement and Isaac Asimov as guests. They were apparently real people. One project MITSFS had undertaken was the microfilming of back issues of *Astounding*. This meant I could look up Harry's stories in the Day index, find them, and read them.

Over the years, as I got to know Harry, I learned of his military career, of the consequences of learning to fly before learning to drive[3], and why he used a pseudonym. Harry was working on his Master's degree in astronomy at Harvard when he began writing and selling to John W. Campbell at *Astounding*. He was worried that his advisor, Professor Donald

[1] I have been a member continuously for 47 years.
[2] Well, the protagonists in *Iceworld* are selling "tofacco."
[3] When the car in front of you stops, you step on the accelerator, pull back on the wheel and try to fly over it—it doesn't work.

H. Menzel, would look askance at such frivolity. So, Harry Clement Stubbs became Hal Clement to the science fiction readership. He later found out that Professor Menzel consulted for Gernsback and later wrote non-fiction articles for Gernsback's magazine *Science Fiction Plus.*

Harry always considered himself a fan, showing up at conventions and the annual MITSFS picnic at Blue Hills Reservation in Massachusetts. He was a member of The Stranger Club in Wartime Boston and much later, when Boston convention fandom revived in the 1960s, he was a founding member of the Boston Science Fiction Society and a member of the committee that bid for the 1967 Worldcon for Boston.[4] When BoSFS metamorphosed into the New England Science Fiction Association, Harry was a charter member.

Harry donated the manuscript of *Star Light* to the auction at St. Louiscon (1969 Worldcon), so I had the pleasure of reading it on the plane flight to the convention. At this 1969 convention, Boston was awarded the 1971 Worldcon. Harry was the convention treasurer. The next year his novel *Star Light* was nominated for a Hugo. When it was pointed out to him that the rules did not permit a committee member to be nominated, his immediate response was to say he would withdraw the novel from contention. The rest of the committee would not allow this and fired him as Treasurer. Harry still helped with the convention and worked registration at the convention, to the amazement of fans and the amusement of pros. Unfortunately for Harry, *Star Light* did not win.

In 1987, CactusCon, the North American Science Fiction Convention (NASFiC), invited Harry to be their Guest of Honor. The convention committee requested that NESFA Press produce a small book with Harry's writings in it. After some discussion, Harry said he would prefer to see the Laird Cunningham stories in print and would write a new one to make the book a proper size. This book, *Intuit,* was popular at the convention and afterward; it is now out of print, as were so many of Harry's best works.[5]

It is astounding to those who know him and his stories that he was not chosen to be a Worldcon Guest of Honor until 1991 at Chicon V in Chicago. This was a well-deserved and long overdue recognition.

As the 1990s rolled on, Mark Olson and I became appalled to realize that almost nothing of Harry's was in print. He and I both felt that NESFA Press ought to do something about it. In NESFA this is identical to volunteering to do the project. So, at Readercon in July 1997, Mark and I

[4] It lost to New York City—NYCon III.
[5] The Laird Cunningham stories were reprinted in *The Essential Hal Clement, Volume 2: Music of Many Spheres.*

negotiated with Harry for a three-volume set of his works. I felt odd at this negotiation, thinking back almost fifty years to my first enjoyment of Harry's writing.

As soon as some other projects were finished, we turned to volume 1—a collection of three novels. This was scheduled to be introduced at Boskone 36, February 1999. By the usual weird synchronicity, SFWA had decided to make Harry their latest Grand Master. This would normally have been announced at the April Nebula Awards banquet, but Michael A. Burstein, Secretary of SFWA[6], arranged for an earlier announcement to coincide with the release of volume 1. The initial printing of 1500 sold out and we had a second printing.

Our main problem for volume 2 was selecting which of the shorter works we wanted to print. After we picked the stories we agonized over the order—publication date, length, distance of the setting from Earth. Finally, we decided to put them in an order that was pleasing to us. Volume 2 was introduced at Boskone 37, February 2000.

Both volumes had covers by George Richard, who in real life is Hal Clement, who in real life is Harry Stubbs. Harry has been interested in painting for many years. When he first started exhibiting his astronomicals in science fiction art shows, he did so under a pseudonym to be sure that anyone buying the painting was doing so for the art and not just because it had been painted by Hal Clement.

We knew the final volume must contain the Mesklin stories—the two novels *Mission of Gravity* and *Star Light,* the article "Whirligig World," and the novella "Lecture Demonstration"—written for *Astounding: The John W. Campbell Memorial Anthology*. We wanted another story to make volume 3 something special, and Harry agreed. At the end of 1998 he finished "Under" and turned it over to us. We avidly read the story, knowing that we were the first to have done so. At the 1998 Worldcon in Baltimore I was eating lunch with Stanley Schmidt and telling him of NESFA Press's plans. The interchange went something like this:

Lewis: ...and we have a new Mesklin story.

Schmidt: (stopping his fork) Am I going to see it?

Lewis: Possibly not. Harry thinks you wouldn't be interested; it's too old-fashioned.

Schmidt: Who's paying him to edit *Analog?*

And so, "Under" was the cover[7] story for the 70th anniversary issue, dated January 2000.

[6] ...and Vice-President of NESFA.

[7] Cover by Kelly Freas, of course.

This volume is scheduled for the September 2000 Worldcon, Chicon 2000. We intend to keep all three volumes—as well as all NESFA's Choice books—in print so that everyone can read and enjoy classic SF.

As we move into the next millennium[8], I look forward to reading many more of Harry's books.

[8] Being careful not to specify whether it starts in 2000 or 2001.

A Perfect Hard SF Novel

by Mark L. Olson

I first encountered *Mission of Gravity* when I was in my teens and I thought it was one of the best SF novels I'd read. Now, many years and many, many books later I'm sure of it: *Mission of Gravity* is a perfect hard SF novel, perhaps the best ever written.

Back in the dawn of time, Hugo Gernsback saw SF as a teaching tool; he wanted stories to illustrate a scientific point and didn't care greatly if they were well-plotted, or well-written, or had interesting characters—those were only the lures which enticed readers to accept the science. While (fortunately!) SF soon grew beyond that pedagogical model, it still lurks there in the deepest corners of the field: *SF should be about science.* The science doesn't have to be real, perfectly accurate science, but it has to *feel* like real science and show the same respect for the real world that good science displays. SF needn't—shouldn't—be a scientific text, but in some significant fashion, science should be central to the story.

Hard SF is the form truest to SF's roots, a hard SF story is based on science—the story derives its strength from that science.

If Gernsback officiated at the birth of SF, its childhood and adolescence were in the pulps—and in the pulps, adventure and sense of wonder were the valued commodities. Whether fighting monsters on an impossible Venus or blowing up suns somewhere out in the Galaxy, adventure in an exotic place marked the adolescence of SF—See strange places and even stranger creatures! SF has matured beyond the pulps, also, but thrilling a reader's sense of wonder remains essential to great SF.

Mission of Gravity is a story of the scientific exploration of a most exotic place.

It's a straight-forward book; it tells the story of a sea captain who encounters wonderful aliens, bargains with them, takes a long and difficult journey on their behalf, learns from them, and finally bests them. The characters in *Mission of Gravity* are *not* the center of the story. None of the characters are particularly nasty—perhaps the least sympathetic person in the book suffers mainly from an unconscious sense of superiority. They are hard-working, basically honest, decent people who are intensely interested in the world around them and in living their lives. They take adventure when it is thrust upon them, but don't seek it out. They never trust in The Force, instead they think their way through their problems.

While Clement's characters are complicated enough to make a good story, these characters are not the center of the story—the center of the story is the planet Mesklin and the natural history of a really strange world. And Mesklin has *sturm und drang* enough to carry the story.

The world Mesklin is one of the earliest successful attempts to imagine and describe a truly alien world which actually might *be*. (That fifty years later we realize that isn't completely accurate isn't important. The errors are minor; Mesklin might well be a real world.) And what a world! A giant world with an 18-minute day whose rapid spinning so distorts its shape that gravity at the equator is a mere 3 Gs while the polar gravity is 800 Gs! A world with methane seas and ammonia snow! A planet where water ice is a building material! A place whose inhabitants are small, tough and intelligent, look something like giant centipedes—but think like better-than-average humans!

Each step of the way, science and a scientific worldview permeates the story. Right at the start we learn that Barlennan isn't human, but little more. Slowly the evidence builds up—the nature of the liquids on the planet, the ferocity of the storms, the high gravity at the starting site—and the fact that the natives think themselves to be dangerously *light*. Even the length of the days is presented so that the reader has a chance to figure out that they are unusually short before anyone says so outright.

Once the expedition is underway, the odd nature of the planet is the direct cause of many of the adventures, from the hurricane which strands the *Bree* on an island (low pressure at the eye) to the winds near the pole. Other events are caused by people, but solved by the use of science or the scientific method—the removal of the spears on the island, for example. The mystery of why the canoe sank gets as much attention as an attack by a giant beast.

Mission of Gravity has no waste in its prose. It tells a great story of the scientific exploration of a very strange place, tells it well and tells it all—and tells nothing extra.

Two postscripts on Hal Clement the person:

Hal Clement as seen in his characters: If you'd like to know what Hal Clement is like as a person you need only look at the characters in his books. He's like Dondragmer, Charles Lackland, Easy Rich, Barlennan, Laird Cunningham, and Sallman Ken. He's a natural teacher and a man who loves reason and civility and science and displays these qualities in the sorts of people he writes about. His humans and his aliens are all people you'd like to meet and have as a friend.

Priscilla & Hal: My wife, Priscilla, tells of meeting Hal Clement at her first convention. It was the 1969 Philcon and she, for two months now a freshman in college, had swiped a weekend's worth of sandwiches from the cafeteria and headed down to Philadelphia in a car full of fans. It was overwhelming and on Saturday morning she found herself sitting in a corridor outside the Huckster's Room with a huge pile of books and a big smile on her face. A middle-aged man wandered by and greeted her with "This is your first convention, isn't it?" They talked and she realized that this was *Hal Clement* the writer who'd stopped to chat with her and make her welcome.

It's thirty years later and Hugo-winner and Grand Master Hal Clement still comes to conventions and still makes everyone around him feel welcome.

Acknowledgments

Rick Katze for enormous help in scanning.

George Flynn for his usual able and quick job of proofreading under pressure.

This book was typeset in Adobe Garamond using Adobe Pagemaker and printed by Sheridan Books of Ann Arbor, Michigan, on acid-free paper.

— Mark Olson and Tony Lewis
July 2000

The New England Science Fiction Association (NESFA) and NESFA Press

Recent books from NESFA Press:

- *The Essential Hal Clement, Volume I* $25.00
- *The Essential Hal Clement, Volume II* $25.00
- *Shards of Honor* by Lois McMaster Bujold $22.00
- *Moon Dogs* by Michael Swanwick... $22.00
- *Rings* by Charles L. Harness $25.00
- *The Compleat Boucher: The Complete SF of Anthony Boucher* .. $25.00
- *Frankensteins and Foreign Devils* by Walter Jon Williams $23.00
- *First Contacts: The Essential Murray Leinster*........................... $27.00
- *An Ornament to His Profession* by Charles L. Harness $25.00
- *His Share of Glory: The Complete Short SF of C. M. Kornbluth* $27.00
- *Ingathering: The Complete People Stories of Zenna Henderson* $25.00

Find details and many more books on our web page: www.nesfa.org/press

Books may be ordered by writing to:

NESFA Press
PO Box 809
Framingham, MA 01701

We accept checks, Visa, or MasterCard. Please add $2 postage and handling per order.

The New England Science Fiction Association:

NESFA is an all-volunteer, non-profit organization of science fiction and fantasy fans. Besides publishing, our activities include running Boskone (New England's oldest SF convention) in February each year, producing a semi-monthly newsletter, holding discussion groups relating to the field, and hosting a variety of social events. If you are interested in learning more about us, we'd like to hear from you. Write to our address above!